YOUNG HITLER

YOUNG HITLER

CLAUS HANT

with

JAMES TRIVERS AND ALAN ROCHE

with a Foreword by

DR KLAUS LANKHEIT

QUARTET

First published in 2010 by
Quartet Books Limited
A member of the Namara Group
27 Goodge Street, London W1T 2LD

A catalogue record for this book
is available from the British Library

ISBN 978 0 7043 7182 8

Typeset by Antony Gray
Printed and bound in Great Britain by
T J International Ltd, Padstow, Cornwall

Contents

Foreword

Historical novels serve to convey the atmosphere and the feelings of the past to a broader readership. The closer the historical events of the story are to our time and the more the story concerns an acting historical personality, the harder historical novels are to write. The rise and fall of Adolf Hitler is one of the most disturbing yet simultaneously fascinating developments of the last century and is the subject of intense popular interest. Facts and figures of Hitler's active political career are well known. But what happened before he stepped into the spotlight of the German and later the international political scene?

In his semi-autobiographical pamphlet 'Mein Kampf' Hitler painted a picture in which he arranged the facts in a manner which diverged from the truth in preparation for his own canonisation. On the occasion of the 'Party Rally of Honour' 1936, Hitler, by then the 'Führer', announced to the cheering audience: 'This is the miracle of our time, that you have found me, that you have found me amongst so many millions! And that I have found you, that is Germany's fortune!' Hitler's adolescence and early manhood apparently gave not the slightest indication, that his actions would ever have any effect on the course of history. By the time he committed suicide he was responsible for the death and eradication of millions of human beings and left behind a ruined continent, including the nation whose saviour he pretended to be. It is really a 'miracle' how this at first lazy and untalented, as well as demanding and megalomanic character inspired millions of Germans a few years later. The attentive reader of this book will be able to follow this evolution and its turning points. The things we know about his youth and adolescence we know from his companions. Although these companions did not know one another, their evidence contains a lot of corresponding elements. Combined with the facts from reliable sources, their evidence is the material this novel is founded on. The first person narrator is not the leading character, which is of course Hitler; rather, the narrator accompanies Hitler through the traceable phases of his life.

Based on thorough reading and extensive research, this novel minimises the prophylactic scepticism of the professional historian about fiction dealing with the protagonists of the Third Reich. The story fits the acknowledged historical facts as known to date, while at the same time leaving space for individual interpretation: plenty of matter, with plenty of art.

DR KLAUS A. LANKHEIT

Dr Klaus A. Lankheit is deputy chief of the world's most extensive archive of documents relating to the Nazi dictatorship in the Institute for Contemporary History (*Institut für Zeitgeschichte)* in Munich. He is author, editor and co-editor of several publications on Hitler and the Third Reich, among them several editions of the series of books entitled *Hitler: Reden, Schriften, Anordnungen* (Hitler: Speeches, Scripts, Orders), Munich, 1994–2003. Dr Lankheit regularly reviews books on Hitler and the Third Reich for the *Frankfurter Allgemeine* newspaper.

Author's Note

'Tis strange – but true; for truth is always strange; stranger than fiction: if it could be told, how much would novels gain by the exchange!

Byron, *Don Juan*,
Canto 14, Stanza ci, 801–3

In October 1906, seventeen-year-old Adolf Hitler began taking piano lessons. On 31 January 1907, after only four months, the young student abandoned them. A plethora of information is available about this abortive endeavour, even though it has no bearing on Hitler's later life: we know how much these lessons cost; we know how he paid for them; we know the make of the piano he played; we know what the teacher thought of his student; we know the teacher's professional and personal background – we even know his family history. The volume of documentation on this rather inconsequential footnote gives us an idea of how much information has been accumulated about the life of Adolf Hitler.

Countless historians, psychologists, psycho-historians, medical doctors, and sociologists have dissected Adolf Hitler's life like no one else's who lived in the twentieth century. And yet, 'Adolf Hitler [. . .] is an existential research problem for historians and psychologists alike',[1] as the psycho-historian and Hitler researcher T. Kronbichler states. Despite decades of research, historians and psychologists are still perplexed by his rise to power. To these, Hitler is still 'a riddle wrapped in a mystery inside an enigma' (Churchill). Sir Allan Bullock, the eminent author of an early biography of Hitler, admits: 'For my part, the more I learn about Adolf Hitler, the harder I find it to explain and accept what followed. Somehow the causes are inadequate to account for the size of the effects. It is offensive to our reason and to our experience to be asked to believe that

1 'Ein zusammenfassender Überblick ergibt, dass Adolf Hitler [. . .] für Historiker wie für Tiefenpsychologen gleichermaßen ein existenzielles Forschungsproblem ist.' T. Kornbichler, Adolf-Hitler Psychogramme, Frankfurt 1994, p. 139

the youthful Hitler was the stuff of which [. . .] the Caesars and Bonapartes were made. Yet the record is there to prove us wrong.'[2]

So – who was Adolf Hitler?

How did a lowly World War One veteran, with neither substantial education nor wealth, rise to become the most powerful leader in Europe in the space of just fifteen years? What turned the mediocre artist and eccentric of pre-1919 into the conqueror of Europe, and one of the shaping hands of today's world? What planted the seed in Hitler's early life that made him what he became: the very personification of evil?

Young Hitler attempts to shed light on the riddle that has puzzled historians and psychologists for decades in a novel way – literally, in the form of a 'non-fiction novel'. Unlike a scientific biography, this book does not portray the events from a distanced perspective. The 'non-fiction novel' enables the reader to experience young Hitler's development first-hand while adhering to the researched facts. All of the major events the Hitler character experiences, as well as the depiction of the social and political conditions of the time, are based in fact. In order to substantiate the factual details, appendices have been included, complete with researched data and its sources.

Young Hitler is told from the perspective of someone who knew Hitler extremely well: his best friend. This unique viewpoint allows readers to observe the unfolding events and developments in Hitler's life as if present. In reality, the young Hitler had not one best friend, but four: August Kubizek, who shared a room with him in Vienna; Joseph Neumann, who sold his paintings when Hitler lived in a men's hostel; Rudolf Häusler, with whom he shared a room in Munich; and Ernst Schmidt, his comrade during and after World War One. In this account, the four friends associated with Hitler during this tumultuous period have been consolidated into one character.

The young Hitler's dialogue is taken partly from his own writings and speeches. I have also drawn from books he often quoted, with psychological analysis of Hitler's emotional and mental constitution shedding additional light. These conversations illustrate Hitler's way of thinking and give the reader an insight into the development of his character, a

2 Franz Jetzinger, *Hitler's Youth*, foreword to the English translation, London 1958, p. 10 quoted from: R. G. L. Waite, *The Psychopathic: God Adolf Hitler*, New York 1977, preface

development which is particularly important because the nature of Hitler's rule was so personal.

To really understand how the young Adolf Hitler became a tyrant and mass murderer, we must separate what we know of the dictator from the young man whose development we aim to observe. Any anticipation of his future actions would obscure our vision and distort our understanding. I have therefore intentionally abstained from any comments relating to Hitler's subsequent crimes.

Claus Hant

PART ONE

ART

The Prince of Linz

He was a stranger, yet familiar.

March 1905, Linz

Monocled men and women wrapped in muslin sat in velvet chairs around marble-topped tables as they met for a late Sunday afternoon rendezvous. They sipped their coffee, chattering bon mots in each other's ears. Laughter circulated softly in the smoke-hazed room. This is how Vienna must feel, I thought; the place I longed to be.

I could have ordered the house specialty, the Linzer Torte, but no, I had chosen the Viennese Sacher Torte instead, as today was my birthday. My sixteenth birthday. When the stars had aligned sixteen years ago, I wondered, had they predestined my life? My life, and my fate? Had the stars created the 'me' within me? Had the heavens decided I would be a musician? I didn't know. But what I did know was that music came effortlessly to me; any time I heard a melody, I could sit down at a piano and pick out the tune much as some people could naturally sing and stay in key. I yearned to be a trained, working musician. If only . . . if only I could attend the music conservatory in Vienna! I sipped my demitasse contemplatively and gazed out of the arched windows that framed the promenade leading to the Landhaus. As I did, a farmer and his wife lumbered down the street like a pair of packhorses hauling a cart. My Viennese fantasy shrivelled instantly, and I was reminded of where I was: Linz. Everything outside this café was just so unspeakably unsophisticated. I glanced around the room, and at that moment, I made a vow to myself: I swore to be as urbane as this café's clientele. After all, I was a sixteen-year-old gentleman now. I was old enough to have my own Viennese style. From now on I would remain impervious to the barrage of insults my brutish, unenlightened father launched at me. As I thought about it now, it almost seemed a compliment when he sneered and called me a pompous fool.

A young man entered the room. He was no older than I but was dressed as though twice my age. He wore an expensive charcoal business suit and a blue and black striped tie framed by a high starched collar. A slate-grey derby perched deliberately askew shaded his features. For a moment he was faceless, a shadow of the life I longed to lead. His wiry build was strangely familiar. A curious aura surrounded him, making my heart quicken. But no one else in the café paid him any notice. No heads turned, no eyes followed. To them, he was one of their own. Laughter flitted across both rooms of the café. A woman concealed by her fan was hitting a high C; even the chess players looked up. She must have been privy to something deliciously depraved. For a moment, she had been transported from the backwaters of Linz. For a moment, she too had been in Vienna. The stranger moved among the tables and waiters with the graceful elegance of a matador. His brown hair was perfectly trimmed and slicked back. I was irresistibly drawn to him, yet intimidated by him.

Who was he?

He ambled towards the periodicals, hanging like slack sails from their wooden holders. Each reader who picked them up sailed away to exotic shores, where outrageous ideas thrived and taboos were broken. Every radical thought from evolution to feminism to anticlericalism was displayed here like available but forbidden fruit. The afternoon light silhouetted the young man's profile as he plucked a paper from the rack with an air of arrogance, and I glimpsed the masthead of *Der Hammer*. He leaned over to see what else was there for the taking, and then grabbed a *Neues Wiener Tagblatt* and *Unverfälschte Deutsche Worte*. A Communist, a German Nationalist and a Liberal Jewish paper. A truly eclectic choice. He came to sit at a window-side table no more than twenty feet from me, and began to read. The waiter's back was towards me as he approached the young gentleman, who had just lowered his paper. His eyes squinted as the waiter recited the array of pastries and cakes on offer. His eyebrows rose and he ordered with measured nonchalance. The waiter seemed to recognise him. Probably the young gentleman spent his days here, not slaving away at a job he loathed as I did. I wondered who he might be: the son of a wildly successful industrialist? The cousin of a prince? I imagined him living in a luxurious mansion with spacious hallways full of exquisite portraits.

The young man raised his newspaper again. He flicked it open and folded the pages over with his manicured fingers. They were long and white. They could easily span a full octave on a piano. He had the immaculately groomed hands I coveted. I looked down at my grubby labourer's hands. How could they ever do justice to Chopin? It was a concern for which my father had no sympathy whatsoever. He was adamantly opposed to me studying music in Vienna. My hands were stained from horse-hoof glue, and my fingernails were discoloured from emptying and re-stuffing sagging mattresses. My father constantly harangued me with his plans for me to take over his upholstery business so he could retire. I looked across at the stranger behind the newspaper. He was perfect; I was not. Maybe he was a musician. A professional. An artiste. But if so, what was he doing here in Linz, in this pitiful backwater? I tried to make out his face but it was concealed, nose-deep in one of the papers. He was a stranger, yet familiar. Did I know him from somewhere? His fingers gripped the edges of the newspaper with what seemed to me a menacing force. There was something about those hands; I could easily envision them strangling someone. This is absurd, I thought: the caffeine has gone to my head.

As I sat there, sneaking furtive glances at him, he read all three papers. He ate his pastry, drank his Kleiner Brauner and stood up, carefully positioning his hat on his head, and then cutting a path between the tables. At the entrance, he caught the front doors as they swung open out on to the street and was gone. My chest heaved with relief: just watching him read the papers had exhausted me. Through the window, I saw him stop amid the pedestrian traffic and turn west down the Promenade. His walking stick pushed him along the pavement and he disappeared into the grey shadows of late afternoon. I felt compelled to record the whole disconcerting incident, of which I had evidently been the sole observer, so I took out my leather-bound diary and began to write.

I had spent an agonising afternoon in my father's workshop repairing and stuffing a cheap rococo-style sofa, and I reeked of glue and sweat. I hurried home to wash, eat and dress for that night's performance of *Tristan and Isolde*. It was imperative that I arrive at the Landestheater early to secure my favourite spot in the Standing Room Only section. My preferred position was in front of either of the two wooden columns that supported the Royal Box above; that way I had the luxury of leaning back during the performance. Having procured my favoured place, I rested against the pillar to watch Linz's coifed, erudite set file down the aisles and into their seats. In their midst, a raven-haired lady glided down the aisle with a fan in her hand. The fingertips of her escort, a gentleman in a black velvet jacket with tails, guided her by the elbow to her seat. I gazed down at my mustard-coloured wool suit and loathed the person I was. Would I ever amount to more than a petty manual worker?

My eyes shifted to the pillar across the section, and there he was again, whoever he was: the Sunday afternoon phantom of Café Traxlmayr. Right across from me, leaning against the other column with a cape draped around his shoulders. His gloved hands held his top hat and cane. He spotted me studying him and we acknowledged one another: one opera lover to another. Suddenly my collar seemed to choke me. The uneasiness I had felt that afternoon crept up my spine; my heart pounded and my palms perspired. I could feel the sweat start to bead on my forehead just as the lights mercifully dimmed, quieting the audience. The first lingering notes of the overture soothed my flustered nerves. Gently and invisibly the notes wandered through the hall, and the stalls rang with the death throes of love. I wondered whether I would ever fall in love, and if I did . . . Would it end tragically like Tristan and Isolde? The music stands in the orchestra pit were illuminated, the light catching the brass and reflecting golden rays across the rows of heads. The music ebbed and flowed with my thoughts. Who is he? I thought, as my eyes wandered back to the figure leaning against the other column. Why does he make me feel so uncomfortable? Where do I know him from? I closed my eyes and racked my mind.

Who was he?

The violins and woodwinds complemented each other like male and female. It was Tristan's and Isolde's last night, and the music struggled to cling to the darkness and resist the inevitable dawn. Tristan and Isolde peered deep into each other's soul like refugees seeking to escape their impending doom. Why was it all so tragic – life, love? I looked across and saw him engrossed by the music and the drama. His eyes glistened with rapture. His hands hovered, keeping time; dancing to the music that swirled around them. The tips of his right index finger and thumb lightly touched as if catching the musical notes in the air. His hands were playful, yet exuded strength: a strength that could kill. God, there was that thought again. Where was it coming from?

At the end, Tristan and Isolde were separated forever. The curtain fell and the lights went up. The audience blinked its way back from orchestrated fantasy to spectators' reality. People rose and stretched their backs. Some checked their watches, some yawned. A number of the ladies flicked open their fans to revive themselves. The stranger across from me stepped away from his column, his eyes still glazed by the spectacle. I was about to head past him towards the exit when he took a step in my direction. My throat squeezed tight, then tighter still with each step as I approached him; with the crowd at my back there was nowhere for me to escape. We brushed shoulders and regarded each other face to face.

'Excuse me,' he mumbled, still captivated by the music.

My eyes glanced down to his cane, where his hands were squeezing the ivory handle. Then I looked him in the eye, and I knew I had looked into those eyes before. I had stared into those eyes as those hands had gripped my throat. Suddenly I realised who he was: I remembered him from primary school: we had played at Boer War and he had made me a Brit; an evil, imperialistic Brit. He had been as tough as a real fighting Dutchman defending his South African territory. 'You British scum!' he had screamed in my face. His eyes had flashed and his teeth had been clenched as his thumbs pushed down hard on my throat. I felt my hands begin to sweat as I recalled it.

'Martl!' he exclaimed merrily, remembering me too.

We laughed. As children we had both lived in Lambach.

'Dolferl,' I said, 'You must forgive me. I can't quite remember your surname.'

'Hitler,' he said. 'Adolf Hitler.'

Belle Époque on the Danube

> Standing on the shoulders of giant thinkers he would find the key to explain the world in a revolutionary way. All by himself. Alone in the world.

Two years later, we found ourselves again at the Café Traxlmayr, but this time at the same table.

'Vienna!' I sighed. 'You're going to Vienna! I do envy you, Dolferl.' As his childhood friend, I was the only person allowed to call him by his nickname.

'After my father's death,' Dolferl said solemnly, 'I finally started to lead the life I wanted to live. No more schooling as I had known it. I learn from life, from experience only. But I understand that society has to validate you. Which is why I agreed to go to Vienna and attend the Academy of the Arts.' He sipped. 'My dear, wonderful mother understands.'

'I wish my mother were still alive,' I said.

'Dear God!' Dolferl looked up. 'I would be devastated if my mother died. She's just recovered from an operation. I hope that . . . ' His voice choked. He shook his head, not wanting to contemplate her death. 'When I am in Vienna,' he said, 'I'll miss my mother terribly. But I certainly won't miss that tiny little apartment on Humboldstraße.'

Humboldstraße was a nice enough street, but not the street where I had imagined he would have resided when I first saw him at the Traxlmayr two years before. The illusion of spacious hallways with sumptuous portraits had soon been shattered.

'My mother is a saint, she truly is,' said Dolferl pensively.

She certainly seems to dote on him, I thought. He had the luxury of his own room while his aunt, his younger sister, Paula, and his mother shared the parlour and kitchen. "I'm the "man of the family"!' Dolferl had boasted with an air of self-entitlement when I questioned him about it.

'I'd love to go to Vienna as well.'

'Well, come with me!' he said.

'Come with you? How?'

'All we have to do is convince your father.'

Dolferl sat at my father's table with respectful aplomb. 'This food is fit for a king,' he flattered.

Roast pork and cabbage steamed on the platter. It was Saturday lunch and my father was exhausted from the week's work. His stubby fingers picked up the knife and he began to carve. My two sisters giggled.

'Girls, stop!' barked my father.

I shook my head, annoyed at my younger siblings. I smiled nervously. My leg was bobbing up and down beneath the table. Hilda, my stepmother, eyed Dolferl warily.

'Well,' began Dolferl, 'you must agree with me, kind sir' – my father's eyebrow rose – 'that Martin has a remarkable talent. He plays the piano so naturally and beautifully. And I should know, I'm an opera and music aficionado.'

'Oh, you are, are you?' replied Father.

'Yes, I've studied music all my life,' answered Dolferl in a quiet but firm tone. 'And when I heard Martin play . . . '

'Where?'

'Oh . . . At a friend's house. The way Martin plays Bruckner is transcendent, it really is.'

Dolferl had never heard me play. He was lying: I prayed that I wouldn't go red.

Father said nothing as he continued to cut the meat. 'I'll tell you what transcendent is,' he then said. 'My son making a living! Making a living . . . working.' Father passed a plate to Dolferl and looked at him. 'And he will make a living. I've set it all up for him to follow me into my trade.' He smiled.

'I agree with you totally,' said Dolferl. 'Martin must make a living. I understand and respect that. But certainly, you must understand that as a concert pianist, Martin will earn a handsome salary.'

'The upholstery business is real life, whereas playing the piano is' – Father paused – 'at best, a dream.'

Dolferl sat back in his chair. 'I couldn't agree with you more! But how can we know unless he gives it a try? Just give him the three months. That's all I ask.'

'What do you mean, three months?' asked my father.

'Three months with me in Vienna,' Dolferl replied, as if it were already a fait accompli. 'You see, I'll be attending the Academy in autumn. Martin could stay with me at my residence.'

'To do what?'

'To attend the Conservatory.'

'But he hasn't even applied, let alone been accepted there.'

'Well, then allow him to try. If Martin is accepted at the Conservatory, then let him join me for the winter season in Vienna.'

Father grimassed and shook his head, irritated.

'Let his talent decide,' continued Dolferl undeterred. 'When Martl plays the piano, I can see in him his mother's gift for music.'

Taken aback, my father set down his knife and fork. He was visibly moved by Dolferl's ploy. Dolferl hadn't even known my mother.

'You know how much your wife loved music,' added Dolferl.

A stunned silence descended upon the table; the glint of a tear was visible in my father's eye. Hilda stared down at her lap as she allowed her husband to silently mourn his previous spouse.

'Well,' said my father eventually, 'when is the entrance exam?'

I leaned back and gazed over at Dolferl, gaining a better perspective on my friend. I didn't know how I could ever repay him for what he had just done for me. The manipulative little genius had successfully negotiated for me the one thing I wanted most dearly in my life: the one thing I felt destined for. If ever there were such a thing as fate, then meeting Dolferl had surely been it.

April 1908, Vienna, Stumpergasse 31
Nine women wearing pelts chant forlorn words in a lost tongue. They sit in a circle and their words emanate from their guttural, Icelandic souls. A shaman stands in front of the women, next to a chained bull. He swings a granite axe upward with both arms. The singers' voices escalate to a feverous pitch. Just as the shaman prepares to smash the bull's neck, King Nidur, the Great King of Iceland, crosses the nearby field astride a galloping horse. Dozens of warriors carrying spears and swords follow behind him. King Nidur is brandishing a silver sword. He rides up behind the shaman and roars, 'Blasphemer!' The shaman spins around quickly and sees the King rearing up on his stallion. Then the King's blade swiftly lops off the shaman's head.

Dolferl looked up from his manuscript. 'Do you like it?' he asked.

I was stunned.

'When this is staged well,' he announced, 'it will have an impact on all future opera productions. Can't you just see it?'

'A horse and a bull on a stage . . . ' I stammered. 'Isn't that a bit . . . elaborate?'

'Well, what are operas if not elaborate?' he snapped. 'And besides, circuses do it all the time! Here . . . ' he said, reaching for a stack of sketches on his cot. 'That will be the set. There's the horse, the bull, the men and the women. It all fits.' He handed me the designs. 'See for yourself.'

'What stage can support all that?' I asked.

Dolferl shook his head: details, details, details. 'If you will it,' he said, 'anything can be done.'

I knew why this opera had to be performed. Dolferl had often preached about it. 'Art,' he would say, 'is a unique form of perception. When we perceive art, we lose ourselves in the object. We forget about our individuality, and we become the clear mirror of the object. Through aesthetic perception of the manacled bull, we perceive the eternal notion of all bulls. It's the Platonic Idea'. I endured these pedantic lectures nightly. Once his mind was going, his thoughts poured out of him relentlessly. Often these long-winded discourses lulled me to sleep, in which case Dolferl would rouse me back to consciousness so that I might savour some more of his wisdom.

'This opera is too important not to be produced! It's the story of our Nordic forefathers; how we almost lost our heritage. And it is our duty to bring that to the attention of our people!'

The book, *Legends of Gods and Heroes: the Treasures of Icelandic Mythology*, lay open beside him. He stared at me as if willing me to understand that bringing this opera to the nation was our destiny. 'Art is the only way out; the only escape from our cultural mess. By creating art, we can elevate the spirit of each individual in the audience. It is only from here that something new can emerge: a cultural revolution! And we artists have been called to pave the way.' He swept his hair away from his forehead and turned to me. 'Your job is to score this scene. I want the music to be so vivid and precise that even a blind man can see what I've envisioned!'

'Precise? With crude wind instruments, primitive harps and bone flutes?'

'That's all they had in Iceland at the time. Look it up for yourself in the Hof Library.'

The kerosene lamp cast a dim light over the grand piano in the middle of our room. It seemed stolen, taken from the parlour where it belonged. The piano was the most cherished hostage of our poverty; it was our altar. Its raised black lid was like the outstretched wing of a black swan, fighting for the limited space. It was a constant reminder of why we were both here in Vienna: we were here for our art. Dolferl's class schedule at the art academy was curiously unstructured. It allowed him plenty of time to stroll through the city and spend entire days in the coffee houses, art exhibits, libraries and city parks. He was free to sleep until noon and let his mind wander wherever his shifting whims would take him. Painter, definitely. Architect, probably. Writer, perhaps. Composer and librettist – why not? For Dolferl, even the role of city planner was a possibility: 'Whatever my passions demand of me, I become for the moment,' he once told me. I, for my part, had passed the entrance exam and was now a proud student at the Vienna Conservatory of Music.

'Now, I do have some ideas for the bull's theme,' said Dolferl. 'I want all the notes on the scales, all at once. I want the sound of chaos and death from the orchestra, like this.' He pounded on the keys with both arms bent at the elbows, fist to fist. He hammered on the ivories and stamped his feet on the floor. Down he slammed, again and again, screaming, 'This, this, *this* is what I want!'

The socks and underwear that hung over our beds trembled. He hit the piano keys for a third time, blasting out another dissonant bombardment.

'Dolferl,' I warned, 'the neighbours.'

Dolferl was beyond hearing me. He pulled away from the piano. 'I can feel this,' he said, 'I see it. The prelude to our opera!'

He stopped suddenly and stared at me. Nothing was said, but a thought was conveyed: he who attains his ideal thereby transcends it. I was in no doubt: I was in the presence of greatness. Dolferl stood up and began pacing the narrow space between the piano, the table and our beds. Back and forth, back and forth he went, narrating. His elongated shadow was cast on the wall and up on to the ceiling. Back and forth it paced. 'When King Nidur falls to his knees at the end, the audience will linger there, spellbound for a long moment, and then I can hear scattered claps that swell slowly to waves of applause. Followed by standing ovations and cheers! It's clear that our music has touched them deeply: they've experienced a catharsis, they've reconnected with their true selves. We will have transformed them!'

'I don't know . . . ' I said.

His eyes widened. How dare you! How can it be more obvious? Then his expression softened. He grinned. 'What do you want, then? Shall we write a nice little drawing-room comedy instead?'

Dolferl never doubted that he was a great artist, an artist of many faces and moods – ranging from bright and confident to dark and doubting. More often than not, however, he saw in himself an unacknowledged genius. A genius spurned and neglected; a genius so great that no one, not even other acknowledged geniuses, would have the brilliance to comprehend and accept his intimidating and revolutionary ideas.

'We live in despicable times,' he said. 'We are resigned to the fact that art, in most cases, is nothing but cheap entertainment. But this is not what art was meant to be! Art was born as religion! And it must be reborn as religion! We must go back to a time before history. To the timelessness of mythology! As Wagner made clear, we need to delve beneath the superficial sentiment of these rotten times. This shallow society betrays the true, vivid nature of man! Our aim must be to uncover man's lost vitality through art, and radically transform him!'

'I know, I know!' I managed to interject. 'But our piece isn't even written yet, and it's already too daunting to produce.'

'Who's designing the stage settings?' he retorted. 'You or me? Who designs all the costumes? I do! All you have to do is to put my ideas to music.'[3]

'I need to learn more about music if I'm to – '

'Oh, you and your Conservatory! It makes you trivial. Insignificant,' he said with a growl. 'The true artist can't be bound by lessons in school. The true artist must free himself of all rules and restraints.' He stared at me. His pale blue eyes seethed. There was an understanding, tacit but palpable: we share this squalid little room, but this is the conservatory for our complementary talents. Our joint effort will bring our vision into the world.

This is our fate. This is the story of our lives.

This is. *Is*.

'Music is our religion!' To emphasise his statement, Dolferl's fists crashed down on the keys again. Uproarious discordant notes sounded from the piano's reverberating body. 'I'll build an opera house worthy of our music,' he declared and smashed his arms down again on the piano. An angry, haunting chord issued, like a dying gasp from the mythological bull. 'I will build a temple!' he proclaimed.

Muted thumping could be heard against the ceiling beneath, which only made Dolferl raise his voice and stamp his feet in response. 'A sacred temple of music!' he cried, slamming each foot down to a word.

Four booms resounded from the floor in answer. Oh Christ, now Schrobner was awake! Enraged bellowing could be heard through the floorboards.

3 See: Appendix 1, Hitler's Opera

'Hear that, my dear Martin?' Dolferl noted in his most inimitable gentlemanly manner. 'Proletarian gibberish! What an ugly, guttural sound!'

Another cry rose from below.

'Listen!' he said. 'Those subhuman howls are just like the music we want to compose! Don't you think?'

The muffled sound of wild curses filtered up through the floor boards.

'My my!' Dolferl goaded. 'Whatever would make someone lose his composure so?' He turned to me with a sneer. Tsk tsk tsk. 'You cyclops!' he screamed at the floor, kneeling down. 'You tower of stupidity! The Stone Age is over, idiot!'

Dolferl picked up my leather toolbag and climbed on to the piano bench. He swung the heavy bag over his shoulder; the metal tools inside the bag clinked against one another.

'What are you doing?' I cried.

'I was thinking,' declared Dolferl, 'our scene needs a little more action. Perhaps just as King Nidur slices off the shaman's head, the clouds should part and a volcano could erupt with a bolt of lightning.' Dolferl reached into my leather pouch and pulled out my heavy upholsterer's mallet.

'Dolferl!'

'The scene needs a stronger ending!' he said with a mischievous grin. 'So what I want from you is the musical equivalent of this . . . ' He hurled the hammer at the floor.

Bang!

Now everyone else in the house had been woken as well. Dolferl jumped down from the chair.

Boom!

I gripped him by the shoulders and shouted, 'Dolferl, must you? Must you behave like this?' I shook him.

He was staring at me, but miles away.

There was a knock on our door.

'Now you've done it,' I said, shaking my head in dismay. More knocking.

'I'm coming,' I said in a hoarse, apologetic voice. I unhooked the latch, turned the knob and opened the door.

Leaning against the doorframe was Frau Zakreys, who sublet our room to us. Even at eleven o'clock at night she reeked of cheap magnolia perfume. She was fortyish and fashioned herself after Klimt's gold-lamé ladies. Dolferl had nothing but contempt for painters like Klimt. Degenerated international artists', he called them.

'What's going on here?' Frau Zakreys asked angrily, tugging at the butterfly collar of her dressing gown. 'This is the third time in two weeks!' she erupted, her face purple with rage. 'You're putting my position with the landlord in jeopardy! If the tenants complain that I don't keep a peaceful house, I'll be put out on the street with you! 'You leave me no choice. You're . . . ' Her lips were pursed so tight, she couldn't even say that inevitable word: evicted.

Dolferl stepped towards the door. 'My good and fair lady, we understand completely. We were composing music. We just got caught up in a creative frenzy.'

Her blue eyelids dropped. Not again, she sighed; decadence and freedom are wonderful, but there are limits. 'This can't go on! I told you three days ago this has to stop!'

Dolferl lowered his eyes. 'I admit that things got a little out of hand, but you know us. It wasn't done with any malicious intent.'

Dolferl could be such a beguiling fop – so easily did he assume an air of most earnest gentry, in fact, that his ludicrous but ostensibly sincere pleading transformed her mood. Frau Zakreys was so taken that she blushed involuntarily.

'You young boys have all this energy; you should put it to better use.' She winked, and her lips formed a smile. She behaved like one of Klimt's women, too, even though she was too old and too fat to be one of his sirens.

As I turned away from Frau Zakreys the door flew open and my shoulder was gripped from behind by a calloused hand. I swung around and was suddenly confronted with the crimson face of our downstairs neighbour.

'Let me at that little fool –' Schrobner snarled. I stood slightly taller, but Schrobner was broader: a hundred kilos broader. Schrobner's left 'eye' was just a fleshy socket, barely covered by a black leather patch. His seeing eye was bloodshot, a precursor to his morning hangover. A dense, inebriated fog swirled around him.

'Lazy, decadent degenerate!' Schrobner yelled. 'Robbing decent workers of sleep!' He had horses to shoe in the morning. He took one step forward but I stood my ground. Dolferl was a frail china doll compared to Schrobner's robust bulk. Blood pumped through my veins at a dizzying pace: I straightened my back, stuck out my chest and looked Schrobner straight in the eye. I had the advantage: two eyes to one eye and one patch.

'Please,' I said firmly. 'Let me explain!'

'Get that *Dummkopf* out of here!' screamed Dolferl.

As much as Dolferl wanted 'the working masses' to admire his art, he succumbed to arrogant petit-bourgeoisie when physically confronted by one of them. I stepped away from Schrobner towards Dolferl and pushed him hard in the chest. Dolferl flew backwards on to his bed.

I quickly turned back to Schrobner. 'As you can see, I've taken care of this. Please accept my deepest apologies,' I said, and as I advanced, Schrobner retreated. 'Again, I'm very, very sorry to have disrupted your evening,' I finished, closing the door on him and Frau Zakreys. I leaned back on the door and glowered at Dolferl, sprawled across his scattered sketches on the bed.

'Why do you have to make everything more difficult than it already is?' I chided.

'*Me?* How dare you push me!' he snapped, massaging his chest.

'Dolferl! Didn't you hear Frau Zakreys?'

'I don't care about her. It's that moron's fault. Interrupting our creative process!'

Astonishingly, Dolferl was serious. In his eyes, a man like Schrobner had no right to anything.

The eruption of a class war in the middle of our bedroom had drained us of our artistic energies. Without a word, we retreated to our separate corners of the room to sleep. My corner was clean and neat; my white top sheet was folded over my black woollen blanket, and reminded me a little of a piano. I closed my eyes and turned over on my side, retreating inwards, digging my way into the grey mist of sleep, far, far away from this cramped little room. I burrowed deep into my sheets to escape my obsessive roommate. Away I drifted. Away . . . Dear sweet sleep, take me away. Away. Away . . .

Bump!

'Dolferl . . . ' I groaned. 'I need to sleep . . . '

I rolled over and peered between the legs of the grand piano. There was Dolferl, leaning over the edge of his bed to retrieve a book that had fallen on the floor.

He looked over at me. 'Blame Livy,' he said. 'If his *History of Rome from its Foundations* weren't so bulky you'd still be asleep.'

There were stacks of books by his bedside with titles that ranged from Immanuel Kant's *Critique of Pure Reason* to *A Treatise on Electricity and Magnetism*.

'I can't sleep,' he said, as he reached for the tome on the floor. 'There are too many questions I need answered.'

Dolferl's head was propped up against a pillow and his knees were bent under the cotton sheet and satin bedspread. With the light of the kerosene lamp behind him, Dolferl used a magnifying lens to read the works of the geniuses of our time word by word, line by line, paragraph by paragraph, page by page: Ludwig Feuerbach, Ernst Haeckel, Samuel Smiles, Gustave Le Bon, Jacob Burckhard, Otto Weininger, Ludwig Büchner and Friedrich Hebbel. And, of course, the geniuses of all time: Epiktet, Plato, Augustus, Caesar, Homer, Plutarch, Shakespeare, Luther, Dante, Goethe, Schiller, Augustinus and Cicero. And then there were innumerable volumes written by those not considered geniuses of their own or any other time; but Dolferl read them anyway. The bookstand beside his bed was his altar. It had been the first thing he bought after moving in, finished oak with two supports that could be adjusted to fit the dimensions of any book. He put the leather-bound volume of Livy open on the bookstand. Dolferl would be reading until dawn.

'There's an answer to all this! One unified *Weltanschauung!* It is there! I can feel it!'

Dolferl was positive that standing on the shoulders of giant thinkers he would find the key to explain the world in a revolutionary way. All by himself. Alone in the world.[4]

Dolferl was sitting in the waning light of day when I returned from the Conservatory. I walked over to the kerosene lamp, struck a match and was about to light it when he said: 'Don't.' His voice was exhausted. His lifeless eyes gazed at me, devoid of emotion. Periodically, after a phase of frenzied cerebral excitement, a depleted Dolferl would sink into this maudlin mood.

'Why can't I light the lamp?'

'Because it won't make any difference.'

'Well, that's a stupid thing to say.'

'The lamp only sheds light on how pitiful the world is,' he lamented.

'Did you have a dumpy model posing for you in life drawing class today?' I quipped, trying to lighten his frame of mind.

'I didn't even bother to go to the Academy today.'

'Maybe if you had, it might have lifted you out of this mood,' I said.

'Nothing can lift me out of this. The world is doomed.'

4 See: Appendix 2, Hitler and Books

I chose my next words carefully, to avoid triggering a verbal attack. 'Something must have prompted this.'

'Nothing prompted it,' he said, 'because there is nothing.' He gripped his collar with both hands. 'Schopenhauer is right. The world is ruled by some utterly senseless and ruthless entity. There is no higher purpose.'[5]

'Schopenhauer's is just one idea,' I said. 'But there are other ideas too. Take Goethe, for example – '

'Stop it!' he shouted. 'Stop it!' His hands clenched into fists. 'This life is nothing but agony,' he cried. 'Long, lonely agony.'

'But what about art, and invention, and – '

'You numb yourself with distractions. You're blind to the truth. This is a world founded on senseless chaos.'

'But, Dolferl – '

'We live on a frozen lake, all aware that, little by little, the ice is melting. And one day we'll all drown.'

'Okay Dolferl: where is this coming from?'

'Nothing!' he snapped. 'I just realised how futile it all is. I'm sick of living this dog's life. Do you hear me?' he erupted. 'Dog's life!' His words collapsed into anguished sobs. 'Dog's life,' he repeated, wearily. He raised his head and glared at me. 'If you ever tell anyone you've seen me like this, I'll . . . I'll . . . '

'I would never tell anyone,' I said.

'Lucie must never know. I must be the ideal to her that she is to me.'

Lucie Weidt was a famous soprano who was currently very popular in Vienna. Dolferl worshipped her from afar; though ten years older than him, she had aroused his interest in the role of Elsa in *Lohengrin*.

'Dolferl,' I said, 'I'm your friend. I would never tell anyone.'

'You'd better not,' he said, wiping his nose.

'And besides,' I said flippantly, 'who would I tell?'

There was a lot of truth in that. I didn't speak to anyone else on a daily basis. 'The only person I could tell would be me,' I added, in an attempt to lighten his mood.

'You could tell people back in Linz,' he said.

'Like who?' I said. I wanted to say 'Who would care?', but I didn't.

A door slammed below us. Schrobner was home after a gruelling day shoeing horses. I could hear him stamp around, then open the cupboard where he kept his vodka. There was a lull as he took his first long mouthful

5 See: Appendix 3, Arthur Schopenhauer

from the bottle, then the springs of his mattress groaned, followed by two thuds as he kicked off his shoes.

'Now may I turn on the lamp?' I asked.

'Sometimes,' Dolferl said, oblivious to me, 'sometimes, I ask myself, who do I think I am? And when I see myself for who I really am, I see clearly how hopeless everything is.' The grim truth of his words sank in. His pained mood was tangible. 'This is truly the way things are,' he went on. 'Even if the sun comes up tomorrow – who cares? What difference does it actually make?'

'Every artist experiences what you're feeling. Even the Master of Bayreuth contemplated suicide.'

'I know! I know! But he was Richard Wagner. I'm nothing!'

'Look,' I said, picking up a pile of his notes and drawings that were lying on top of the piano. 'Look how much you create . . . '

There were countless sketches of a revolutionary layout for the city of Linz, with wider streets and a flamboyant bridge. River nymphs, fish and a rider on his steed graced the grand marble bridge that was to span the Danube. This particular pile of illustrations bore testimony to his photographic memory, with every little detail of our hometown reproduced.

I unrolled the blueprint for a submarine inspired by an article he had read in a scientific journal. 'Look how meticulous this drawing is, Dolferl,' I said, marvelling at his draughtsmanship. On the floor were details of a reform of the landlord system, as well as his ideas about a more efficient public health service. Under his bookstand, there were notes on a travelling orchestra: he had felt it unfair that only the elite in major cities should be able to attend first-rate performances; his premiere mobile orchestra would travel to small towns all over the countryside. He had worked out every intricate detail, including the composition of the orchestra, the works they would perform, their meals, dress, direction and rehearsal time.

'You're so *vital*,' I said.

'So? What does this get me?'

There was a knock on the door. 'Martl?' Frau Zakreys. She had asked me to repair her love seat. I grabbed my toolbag and left.

Frau Zakreys' room was decorated similarly to ours: the contents overwhelmed the space. She had furnished it like a grand salon. Red velvet curtains with gold fringes framed a window that looked out onto the dismal backyard. There was an overpowering queen-sized bed, covered with a colourful chintz spread so it could also serve as a makeshift couch.

There were china tea services on embroidered doilies. Fancy half-empty perfume bottles and dolls lay scattered on side tables. Cleopatra, her lazy, dour Persian cat, oozed between the sofa, the bed and the table. My eyes were itching already just from looking at her.

'Please take a look at my love seat,' said Frau Zakreys in her thick Czech accent. She had dressed up for me, donning a harsh red silk Chinese bathrobe. It clashed magnificently with the green chintz bedspread.

'Is there anything you can do?' she asked, pointing at the sofa. Cleopatra had clawed at the legs and the fabric; the padding was protruding between the velvet seat and the wooden frame.

'To think it was once the pride of my mother's lounge!'

I put down my toolbag. 'I can re-stuff the seat and tack down the fabric,' I said. 'Though you'll have to keep Cleopatra away from it while the glue is drying.'

'Oh, I will!' she replied enthusiastically. 'I can't thank you enough! You are just adorable to do this . . . '

'It's no problem,' I said. I knelt down and took out a canister of upholsterer's glue, brass tacks and my hammer.

'You're such a dear!' she said, 'but your friend . . . As charming as he is . . . I've been thinking it over again, and I'm afraid . . . Enough is enough.' I froze and looked up at her.

'He'll have to move out.'

Cleopatra skimmed my ankles and rolled up against my calf. My nose began to run. I shooed the cat away.

'I can't tell you how difficult a decision it was for me,' she said. 'You know how accommodating I was when he asked if you two could have the bigger room for the piano – I would have done anything! But that last episode was a step too far.'

'But – ' I started.

'But nothing! The other evening not only Schrobner complained, but also the Grubers from next door. If the landlord finds out he'll stop me subletting my rooms.' She raised her arms. 'Do you want me to put my livelihood at risk?'

'Of course not, but – ' The cat brushed up against me again; I shooed it away. My skin tingled, the precursor to a rash.

'I'm sorry,' she said, 'but that's how it is.'

I could feel a small tear leak from the corner of my eye, but it only made it as far as my lashes.

'Please reconsider!' I pleaded.

I took out a needle and thread and carefully stitched a rip in the seat.

'I wish I could, but I just can't.' Frau Zakreys sighed.

I craned my neck to face her. 'I promise I'll keep an eye on him,' I said.

Frau Zakreys checked herself in her full-length mirror; she fluffed up her hair. 'It just can't go on,' she said. 'This is a humble residence, but a respectable one.'

I coughed, because it would have been rude to laugh.

'Believe me,' she said, 'I understand the artistic temperament. I've lived many years here in Vienna and have known many a great artist.'

'I'm not surprised.'

'You know, when I was young, I used to dance.'

'I'm sure you did,' I said, focusing on the chair.

'Well, I do feel for him,' she said. 'But I just can't tolerate that kind of behaviour any longer.'

I pulled the fabric over the glued edge of the chair, pressed it down and smoothed it out.

She looked at her fixed love seat. 'My Lord, you would never know Cleopatra had almost destroyed my precious heirloom!'

'You must understand that Dolferl is going through a hard time. His mother died only four months ago . . . '

Cleopatra slinked by me again, settling around my knees and bringing more tears to my eyes.

'A mother's death is always hard,' she sympathised. 'But his behaviour is unacceptable.'

'He and his mother were very close. She lost three children before he was born, so she was very attached to him.' I explained. I stopped for a moment and wondered if there were any succinct words that could convey Dolferl's despair at the time of her death. 'Dr Bloch, the family doctor, told me that he had never in his career seen anyone so overcome with grief as Dolferl,' I said then. 'Dolferl hasn't been the same since.'

There was a pause.

'You like my necklace?' Frau Zakreys asked suddenly. She bent down to show me a jade pendant above her breasts. Like everything else in the room, they were on display. She smiled and stared into my eyes.

'Yes,' I said, remembering that, ironically, 'Zakreys' came from the Czech '*zakryt se*' – 'to cover oneself'. I looked at her swelling bosom. 'Did you know Dolferl's mother died of breast cancer?'

'Oh, my!' said Frau Zakreys, recoiling.

'He left Vienna and nursed her at home for weeks. All the money left from his father's inheritance was spent on looking after her. He moved her bed to the kitchen because it was the only warm room in the flat. He put a sofa there for himself as well. He had to watch her decline as she suffered through iodoform treatment. Liquid acid on an open wound – imagine having to see your mother suffer like that. And three days before Christmas, she died, right there in front of the tree.'

'Please,' Frau Zakreys gasped, putting her hands to her ears.

'My own mother died in childbirth,' I continued. 'My brother died, too.'

'You poor thing!' exclaimed Frau Zakreys. 'You're crying!'

I turned my head away as I struggled to hold back my tears – caused by Cleopatra.

'In my case,' I wept, 'it all happened years ago, but it's only been four months for Dolferl . . .'

'You poor darlings, I'm so sorry,' Frau Zakreys yielded. And I knew that Dolferl could stay.

'Without this book, I'd be lost,' announced Dolferl. 'We'd all be lost!'

We were sitting high on a set of stands overlooking the Ring Boulevard. The book Dolferl held in his hand was his latest obsession: Darwin's *On the Origin of Species*.

'Finally, someone makes sense of the bloody mess that is life,' Dolferl said. 'Darwin tells us what we have to do: accept the eternal struggle. Accept that we are destined to fight. We humans are part of life, and as such, it is our mission to fight. Because fighting leads to the higher development of our species.'

The June sun shone down on us, as we waited with the crowds of spectators for the parade to begin, a parade celebrating the magnificent march of the Dual Monarchy into the illustrious pages of history.

'I feel sorry for Schopenhauer,' said Dolferl. 'Had he lived to know Darwin's work, his philosophy would have been different. Thanks to Darwin, we now know the driving force behind everything: evolution.'[6]

This was going to be a morning of great pomp and circumstance commemorating Franz Josef's sixty-year reign, and I was excited.

Dolferl turned to me. 'I hate those Habsburgs!' he spat. 'I hate their empire! It only serves them! They marry Czechs, Slovaks, Poles, Ruthenians, Slovenians, Serbo-Croats, Magyars and Romanians. And then we Germans have to put up with these inferior species! Species!' he snarled

6 See: Appendix 5, Darwin-Schopenhauer

and made a sweeping gesture with his hand, taking in all of the people in the stands. 'Here you can study all stages of human development. Just as Darwin taught us!'

Dolferl's political opinions had not changed since Linz. Like Dr Pötsch, his esteemed history teacher, Dolferl was an ardent German nationalist. He looked around. The stands were abuzz with a medley of Slavic languages.

'Can you hear that?' Dolferl sneered in disgust. 'It's the Habsburgs' fault! They're plotting against us Germans,' he said, more to himself than to me. 'Can you believe we're sitting among so-called "fellow citizens"? That these brainless scumbags have equal rights?'

'Dolferl,' I warned as I noticed heads turn.

'They can't even speak their own languages properly, much less understand ours. And anyway, I don't care what these cretins think!' He was getting louder. At secondary school, Dolferl had already aligned himself with the German Nationalists, proudly using a pencil displaying the German colours: black, red and gold.

The *Alldeutsches Tagblatt* was the paper of the Pan-German movement, which campaigned for the unification of Austria with the German Reich of Kaiser Wilhelm II. It was printed around the corner on Stumpergasse and displayed its editorials proudly in a glass case outside, allowing Dolferl to feed his xenophobia every time he walked past their building.

A ruddy-faced Czech dressed in his Sunday best, sat down in front of us.

'We have to move,' ordered Dolferl, 'My nose is too sensitive for this filth!'

'Try breathing to the side,' I whispered. I wasn't going to surrender these seats so easily; we were in a prime location. In fact, when the seats had first been made available, they were too expensive for anyone to afford and it had appeared that these stands would be left empty. The situation was compounded when a rumour circulated that the carpenters who had built the seats were angry about not getting paid and were planning on collapsing the stands during the procession. In the end, the tickets had been given away for free.

'This spectacle was supposed to demonstrate our unity,' Dolferl began again. 'But what does it actually show? The mess we're in. The Hungarians refuse to participate in the parade; the Czechs bow out and the Italians don't even bother to show up.' Dolferl guffawed. 'Just like in parliament, where they constantly stab each other in the back. You should come with me someday. I told you – it's truly entertaining.'

'I can't spend my days in parliament like you, I have to attend school. I don't understand how you have so much spare time.'

'School!' he said scornfully. 'All I want to know is, how much longer will this farce of an "empire" last? Two years? Three?' He pinched his nose. 'This stench is too much.' He gripped my arm. 'Let's go!'

With his petulant behaviour, it would clearly have been easier to just leave. But as we were about to stand up a trumpet heralded the approach of the parade. A drum pounded in rhythm to the hooves of the first white stallions trotting down the boulevard. Soon the noble families of various nations and kingdoms rolled past us in the most ornate carriages, complete with oxen, horses and cannons. In real life, the Royals were not as impressive as in their luxuriant oil portraits. Their historic costumes glinted and shone, but their faces were ashen.

Dolferl turned to me in wonder. 'My God, these people really do exist!'

The crowd clamoured to catch a glimpse of the elite, usually cloistered in their castles, the privileged few who lived a real-life fairy tale while we, 'the people', eked out an existence in our meagre personal realities. Knights and soldiers marched by, resplendent in their uniforms. 'Magnificent!' gasped Dolferl, transfixed.

Like the masses, we no longer felt hungry; we felt less dirty; we had transcended such banality. Everyone had been elevated by the mere presence of these people in their costumes and finery.

Dolferl turned to me, mesmerised by the scene. 'There is a certain power to this kind of thing,' he said. 'I'm glad I persuaded you to stay.'

What is music but the sound of emotion? As one emotion tapers off, another begins, and one surge leads to another. Dolferl was in awe of music; I even think there was a part of him that envied my musical abilities. He would often lecture me, late in the evening and into the early morning, about how music was the highest of arts. 'Music,' he said, 'is the immediate objectification of "the will". It is a reflection of the law that moves everything.' He would never have admitted to it, but I knew that these were not his own words. With his exceptional memory, he could recite Schopenhauer's words by heart.[7] 'Music is a reflection of the will itself. Music allows us to perceive the quintessence of emotional life, without the contents that would typically cause suffering. By expressing or experiencing emotion in this detached way, music allows us to comprehend

7 See: Appendix 4, Photographic Memory

the nature of the world without the frustration involved in daily life. Music is a mode of aesthetic awareness that is akin to the tranquil philosophical contemplation of the world.' I didn't know if Schopenhauer ever composed music. Composition is a blend of emotion and logic. The logic is in the mathematics of the measures, numbers and beats that seek a balance. A fugue is a balancing act as the right-hand notes reply to the left-hand notes. And what is it that these hands and notes seek? *A resolution*. A climax. A fade-out.

My classmates were seated along both sides of the aisle leading to the piano. The morning sun tumbled in through the arched windows and my growing sense of dread made the room unbearably warm. The professor adjusted his glasses and tugged on his goatee.

I sat down on the bench. 'The composition . . . ' I cleared my throat and started again. 'The composition I will play for you today is entitled *Rage to Joy*.'

My composition was inspired by Dolferl's turmoil. I flexed my hands; my fingers stretched and hovered above the ivory. I raised my shoulders and let my hands slowly drift down to the keys. My fingers created a whirlwind of notes and chords, whipping across a landscape of sound. It was easy to portray Dolferl's fury, a raging storm of ideals compromised by realities. I let the music stutter for a moment, lingering softly much as his mood could abate for a moment; and then in an instant he would launch into a raging tirade on the banality of our existence. Triumphantly I flung my hands hard on to the keys. The bang; the explosion; the eternal inferno all around us; the downfall as resolution. It was over.

Silence.

I turned on the bench and faced my class.

'*That's* supposed to be an ending?' exclaimed the professor. 'That's a disaster. Abysmal! You can't leave the listener in the middle of all that chaos and call that an ending! In music, even chaos has a structure .'

'I . . . ' I started to speak but he raised his hand, palm out. Halt.

'If you expect to pass your examinations, you'll have to do much, much better than that!'

I was speechless. My arms hung lifeless by my sides. How could he not understand my composition? Couldn't the professor see that it was about a real person? *Much better than that. You'll have to do much better than that*, echoed through my mind.

Trembling with shame I walked out of the classroom and down the hall, hearing others play their music: the sounds of violin and brass. I barely managed to open the front doors of the Conservatory and left the building. Outside the air stank of horse dung and exhaust fumes. My head hung low as I watched my feet tumble down the Conservatory's steps to the street. Women in broad-rimmed hats glided along the sidewalk, their long skirts making it appear as though they were floating. I heard men talking business. I heard horses whinny as they plodded by. I heard engines spluttering. I saw the granite office buildings whose windows concealed lives and careers. Where do I fit in? I wondered.

Maybe I was destined to be an upholsterer after all.

I lay on my bed staring at the kerosene smear on the ceiling. My mind echoed it over and over again: *you will have to do much better than that*. I had to rework *Rage to Joy*. I had to rethink the ending. I had only emphasised the rage in my arrangement, not the joy. What was needed was a structure within the battling elements that would culminate in a resolution. Not only did I need it in my music, I realised, but in my life as well. I had so many conflicting feelings about Dolferl. He was domineering yet needy. And there were times when I questioned who needed whom more. He truly was the 'philosopher king', idealistic and pigheaded; but at the same time he was vulnerable and helpless, especially when it came to day-to-day living. I was sick of these swirling thoughts that always seemed to come back to Dolferl. I jumped up from my bed and sat down at the baby grand, nervous, though I had no audience. My fingers crept along the keys, and notes drifted from the piano, fluid and sad. From depression comes rage, as Dolferl had shown me many times. My fingers hammered down on the keys as if to shatter my listlessness when the door burst open in an explosion of energy as Dolferl rushed into the room. 'We have to get going!' he called.

'Get going where?'

'To queue for the opera.'

'I can't, I have to stay home and work on my piece. "Abysmal", the professor called it.'

'What does he know?'

'My father was right!' I snapped back. 'Maybe I am no musician! If I had listened to him I'd have a profession by now.' Insecurity whirled around me and sucked me down in a merciless vortex. I could doubt myself as much as Dolferl.

'Some irrelevant old man expresses an opinion and you doubt your vocation?'

'If my teacher doesn't know, who does?'

'How many times do I have to tell you about teachers!' fumed Dolferl. 'What do you think you can learn from them? Conventional ideas and techniques. Platitudes! But what does the true artist want with platitudes?'

'If I can't even get through the composition class and perform this simple task, how will I ever be a composer?'

'You don't *train* to become an artist! True artists are *born*. A true artist will always clash with those petty, small-minded school teachers.' Dolferl's hand chopped the air around him. 'There is something very special that differentiates us artists from those ordinary people. Something unique.' His hair was flopping back and forth with every syllable. 'We have a voice within us telling us we are destined to be artists. Can you hear it? That clear voice urging you on? That speaks to you constantly?'

'At times, yes, I do hear it,' I said quietly.

'Well then,' he replied, 'that's all you need.'

'But if I don't pass – '

'Get dressed,' ordered Dolferl, as he lifted up his mattress and pulled out a neatly folded tailcoat and perfectly creased trousers.

'We've seen *Lohengrin* eight times,' I objected.

'And every time is a revelation! But more importantly, my Lucie is singing *Lohengrin* tonight.' 'His' Lucie was the soprano Lucie Weidt. Dolferl said her voice sounded like a 'heavenly sigh'. 'To think, I'll be in the same opera house as her!'

'Please,' I said, 'I have to study, I have so much to learn . . . '

'Every time you see *Lohengrin*, you learn something.'

'You only go to the opera to escape to some mythical past, to some ideal world where – '

'Escape? Me? Don't be ridiculous! *Lohengrin* only reaffirms what is absolutely real and true.'

I got up and walked towards the washbasin. I looked in the mirror and saw Dolferl gazing at his reflection from a distance. He pushed on his top hat, slipped on his grey gloves, and picked up his ivory-topped ebony cane. He looked dapper: a pure bourgeois illusion, considering the squalor he lived in. He turned and checked himself out from the other side. 'You know,' he said, 'we artists need inspiration. And Wagner is always the best inspiration.'[8]

8 See: Appendix 6, Richard Wagner

Unrequited Obsession

> What if everyday life becomes art? If everything happens as if it were on a stage?

'Behold the Duke of Brabant. He shall be your leader,' sang Lohengrin, as he leapt on to the boat. Elsa was overjoyed at the sight of Gottfried, but then she caught sight of Lohengrin withdrawing into the blue-green glen. He was leaving her because he was keeping his promise and she hadn't kept hers.

'My husband,' she sang mournfully, my husband!' And the chorus wailed, 'Weh!' The music built into a discord that suddenly exploded with distinct and prominent harmonies within all the noise. Subtly but clearly, they took over and drowned out the disharmony, emerging as a sweet diminish that ended softly.

That was it! That was how to end my composition! Now *Rage To Joy* had a working finale! As the singers came out on the stage to take a bow, I took out my pad and scribbled some notes. I looked over at Dolferl. He was miles away from me there on the third-tier promenade, in the men-only standing area of the Vienna Court Opera. Dolferl was back in the year 900 watching Lohengrin depart. I nudged him. He looked over at me with a confused expression, then turned back to watch the curtain calls. Lucy Weidt had just been presented with a huge bouquet of flowers. Her jet-black curls shone under the lights. She cradled the flowers and bowed. Dolferl watched her silently, in stupefaction.

'She is remarkable,' he whispered, 'perfect beyond perfection. She is purity.'

'I have my ending,' I grinned.

He looked back at me, not understanding. 'What ending?' he said, still in a dream.

'For my composition!' I replied excitedly.

'Good,' he said, smiling. 'What did I tell you? The answers to everything can be found in Wagner's operas.'

The audience began filing out of their stalls and seats to the foyer's marble staircase. People moved slowly down the steps, forming a clogged river that stopped and started. Dolferl was impatient, as usual. 'This is exasperating, Martl. It's ruining my evening.'

'I'm so happy!' I exclaimed, thrilled that I had an ending. 'I could hug the world.'

'Well, go ahead and hug it,' retorted Dolferl, 'but leave me out.'

I looked ahead at the bobbing heads moving towards the main entrance. A woman's red hair caught my eye. The man next to her said something, causing her to turn so that I could see her profile: a delicate nose and cherry lips. She smiled, her skin like white cream. Then a man on the opposite side of her said something. She turned and shook her head, her curls moving. She laughed and, even from that distance, she was radiant.

'They'll be playing your music in here one day,' predicted Dolferl. 'I can already picture the night when all these people will be here to watch our opera.' He suddenly stopped and grabbed my elbow. He looked up at the statues of the goddesses that graced the balustrade up above, revelling in the imagined event. 'It will happen,' he said. 'I promise!'

But I didn't hear him as I watched this redheaded goddess drift away into the street. I quickened my pace and zigzagged through the crowd to get a little closer to her. Dolferl kept up with me as we snaked through the throng of people outside on the path. I focused on the woman's shoulders, her porcelain neck below the abundance of red curls. Finally I was close enough to eavesdrop on their conversation.

'Why did they keep to Mahler's version?' said one of her companions. 'Our new director knows how to interpret Wagner so much better.'

'Nonsense,' she said, 'you just don't like Mahler because he's a Jew.' Her voice was melodic, musical.

'Well,' said the other man, 'that's exactly the point. As a Jew, Mahler shouldn't have tried to mess with Wagner.' His tone was snide, arrogant.

Dolferl and I stood just behind them.

'No one has ever interpreted Wagner more perfectly than Mahler,' interrupted Dolferl.

The elegantly dressed threesome turned simultaneously and stared, dumbstruck, at Dolferl and me.

'Do excuse me, I couldn't help but interrupt,' said Dolferl. 'Mahler is certainly more a German than a Jew. It's clear in the way he allows Wagner's works to be performed in their entirety the way Wagner intended. Mahler respects the Master's work, while Weingartner butchers it to get the audience home early.'[9]

'Well, those are considerations in the business of art that Weingartner has handled masterfully.' The gentleman winked as he said 'masterfully', alluding to Dolferl's description of Wagner as 'the Master'.

Dolferl glared furiously at the young man as if he had been personally insulted.

'My good man,' continued the gentleman, 'I happen to be friends with the orchestra's second violin player. He constantly criticised Mahler as a loathsome Jewish swindler!'

'It would seem your friend is blinded by jealousy and envy.' Dolferl adjusted the carnation in his lapel. 'What does Mahler's religion have to do with his achievement as an artist?' Dolferl leaned towards the trio. 'Nothing. Absolutely nothing.'[10]

'Well said!' applauded my alabaster vision. She smiled fondly at Dolferl.

Why were women all drawn to Dolferl before they even noticed me? I glanced over at Dolferl as he noticed her looking at him. He tilted his head to hide his blushing face behind the rim of his top hat.

'Well said,' she repeated, spinning around to the gentleman to nod: take that. 'I feel exactly the same way about Mahler.'

'Whatever you say,' said the other gentleman, 'I'm all for the new production.'

'Just as I'm for the new Vienna!'

'Absolutely, with all those ugly Otto Wagner buildings!' said Dolferl. 'The project he proposed for Karlsplatz is an outrage!'

'That, my friend,' said the man, 'is called progress.'

'Well, if that is progress, I don't want any part of it!' snapped Dolferl. 'This "modern architecture" is destroying our cities!'

We were all standing on a street corner waiting for the traffic to calm so we could cross. I looked over to the woman, this heavenly apparition. She nodded to me and smiled. She had noticed me! I didn't mean to stare but couldn't help myself. Her physique was flawless, like her skin. She moved with frivolity, vibrant and alive.

'Would anybody like a demitasse?' I interjected.

'Capital idea,' said the man on her right.

9 See: Appendix 7, Gustav Mahler

10 See: Appendix 9, Hitler and Jews in Vienna

'Marvellous,' said Dolferl, who had plenty more to say. 'And allow me, kind people, to make this my treat!'

The Heinrichshof Café was a stylish establishment with high vaulted rooms, filled with caffeinated chatter. At this hour, opera-lovers were debating what they had just seen and heard. We took a seat at a small round table.

'All I am saying, dear boy . . . ' said Herbert – at least, I think it was Herbert, although it could have been Leopold – the two well-groomed escorts of the red-haired lady were indistinguishable to me. They were actors. And as they spoke, I realised that they were also – how can I put it? 'Sodomites' would be the rather indelicate Biblical term. Dolferl had said that 'these people' were an abomination. Had he realised that he was not only sitting with two Sodomites, but buying them cups of coffee and possibly a pastry, he would have bolted. I for one was entirely indifferent. Actually, I was rather relieved, as this meant they weren't competing for the affections of my new-found figure of adoration.

When we introduced ourselves, Dolferl announced himself as 'Adolf'. 'Adolf as in Adalwolf, the noble wolf,' he said, with a slight bow, holding the lady's hand.

She presented herself as Francisca. We hadn't yet ordered when the subject of our conversation returned again to the Jews.[11]

'Our mayor,' said Leopold, 'stated that, had it been his decision, he would never have handed our opera house to a Jew, be it Mahler or anyone else.'

'Let me put it this way,' said Dolferl, 'I'd prefer to have Mahler handle my *Wieland the Smith* rather than the current artistic director, that fool Weingartner!'

'Adolf,' I said, taking care not to refer to him as 'Dolferl', 'don't you think we should write it first before you – '

'That's not the point,' retorted Dolferl.

'Think of it this way,' said Herbert, 'who do you think Wagner would prefer to have a demitasse with after a performance of *Lohengrin*: Mahler or Weingartner?'

'Mahler,' said Dolferl, 'definitely.'

'But he's a *Jew*!' said Herbert.

'Do you think I don't know what Wagner said about the Jews? I've read his every word. Of course he hated the Jews, because he was

11 See: Appendix 8, anti-Semitism in Vienna

persecuted by Jewish bankers. But he always revered genius. And Mahler is certainly that!'

'Jews are the killers of Christ, Mahler or not.'

Dolferl sat up slowly and authoritatively in his chair. 'I beg your pardon, sir,' he said gruffly, 'I would assume that as a thinking man you would know by now that Christianity is the problem, not the Jews! Our priests preach of a man who was killed because he tried to challenge the Jewish religion. But they also preach that same Jewish religion – or what else do you call the Old Testament?'

There was a stunned silence around the table. Dolferl took out his handkerchief and dabbed his mouth with it. Intrigued as he was by racial theories, he saw the Jews as a religious group, not a race. 'Religions are a thing of the past,' pronounced Dolferl. 'Science is the religion of the future. Science is the über-reality to which artists should aspire, as the pioneers of this new century.'

'Über-reality,' repeated Francisca slowly, as if sampling a new recipe for the first time. 'I like that.'

Dolferl gestured to her with a nod. 'You're too kind, my lady.' He was barely audible.

'My dear Adolf, I find you absolutely captivating!' she exclaimed.

Dolferl blushed shyly. 'Thank you,' he replied, in his most delicate tone. He fumbled with his handkerchief. 'I'm only speaking my mind. And when I speak my mind, I speak my heart.'

Around the table, we exhaled softly as we allowed the moment to pass.

Leopold rapped on the tabletop, abruptly changing the mood of the conversation. 'Now tell me, sir,' he said, 'whatever do you mean by this über-reality?' He sipped from his coffee with practised urban ease and Dolferl had never appeared more provincial than now as he strove to achieve the same effect.

'If art is the way to overcome suffering,' Dolferl said, 'what if everyday life becomes art? If everything happens as if it were on a stage? If we can see through the individual appearances and see the whole, connected reality?' Dolferl's voice trembled with sincerity. 'This is what I want to achieve. I *live* art to be an artist.'

'He sounds like another Rodin, doesn't he?' said Leopold.

'Oh, thank you!' responded Dolferl. 'Rodin may be a Frog, but he's a great artist.'

'And what, may I ask, makes Rodin a great artist – in your humble opinion?' Leopold asked, sniggering.

'The fact that he reveres the human figure so. He sees the greatness within us all,' said Dolferl, becoming emotional. 'Take *The Kiss*. If only all kisses were as transcendent.'

I ran my finger along the rim of my cup and as I did, its delicate porcelain hummed. Suddenly I felt self-conscious, and clumsily placed cup and saucer back on the table.

'So you're a musician?' Francisca asked me. She smiled. 'A performer!'

'He is a great composer,' boomed Dolferl, 'and soon we will all attend his masterpiece at the Vienna Court Opera!'

'That would be wonderful,' cooed our new acquaintances.

'Please,' I said, then asking 'and what do you do?' although I could barely hear myself.

'I'm an actress,' she said. 'I'm appearing at the National Theatre, but on the minor stage.'

'That's wonderful,' I said, awestruck.

'We're both artists. No wonder there's this thing between us. This . . . ' – I longed for Francisca to say 'magnetism' but she stopped short – '*simpatia*?' She smiled.

I felt a tug at my trouser leg and looked down to see her hand holding a folded note. I took the note, touching her fingers as I did. A charge passed between us: I looked up at her, she at me. Our little secret.

'Hey! What are you two whispering about over there?' asked Leopold. 'Oh! Look, they're blushing!'

It was a little embarrassing, but I didn't mind.

'Are you passing notes again?' continued Leopold.

'Why, yes I am,' said Francisca, rising to the moment. 'It is the twentieth century after all, and it's a woman's prerogative to invite two gentlemen to come and see her perform on stage.'

On the way home, I asked Dolferl, 'why do you think she invited me – I mean, *us* – to see her play?'

'She's an actress,' said Dolferl, 'part of her art is to gain as many admirers as possible, to make sure her dressing room is filled with bouquet after bouquet every night.'

'Oh, come on, she's not that superficial,' I said.

'She told you, she's an actress,' said Dolferl. 'She might as well just say she needs attention and flattery like a plant needs sunlight and water. What play is it, anyway?'

I unfolded the tickets. 'Molière,' I said, feeling a burst of pride.

'Oh, Moliere,' sniffed Dolferl. 'Molière and his so-called "comedies"!'

I was dreaming. I was in love. I was in Vienna. I was young. I was young and idealistic enough to believe that my life would have a happy ending. I believed my life was a series of events that would lead me to my higher purpose: I was born to be an artist and born to love Francisca. She was by far the most enchanting feature of *The Misanthrope*. When we spoke after the show, I couldn't stop raving about her presence on stage. All light seemed to be drawn to her. We kissed, softly at first, then her mouth opened slightly like a rose bud, and the tip of her tongue tempted me in. We kissed again and were a duet in every sense, on every level. She had slipped off her brassiere, revealing her breasts. My God, they were just as Rubens painted them! I was about to touch them when I was torn from my fantasy by an anguished scream.

I lit the lamp and peered under the piano across to Dolferl's bed. A nightmare had twisted his face into a startling, rigid expression. He was shivering. 'I . . . I . . . ' Dolferl gasped. 'I . . . ' His voice trembled in his disoriented state. Having escaped from his mental hell, he was coming to terms with his reality: his shabby purgatory. 'Oh my God!'

'Are you all right?'

'My father,' he said. 'My father . . . he was alive!'

I got out of bed to cross over to him, stepping over the drawings scattered on the floor.

'He was staying at a small lodge on the road outside Leonding. We used to pass it all the time. He didn't know he was dead, and he didn't know why he was staying at that dreary lodge. He wanted to go home and didn't know why he couldn't.'

I sat on the edge of the bed. In his distress, Dolferl had ripped a tear in his nightshirt from collar to navel. In the murky light, I could make out white scars on his pale chest.

'He had his horsewhip,' Dolferl said.

I looked at the floor where his father's horsewhip lay,and began to realise why Dolferl treasured it.

He swept his hand over his eyes, wiping tears away. I was engrossed in the cross-hatching of his scars: the more I looked at them, the more I realised what a hellish childhood he must have endured. Dolferl grabbed the twisted bed sheet and brought it up to his chin.

'I'm the reason he drank,' he whispered. 'I'm the reason he beat my mother.' Dolferl covered his face with his hands. 'He hated me because I didn't want to be like him!' Dolferl choked. 'He hated me for being me – for being born different to him!'

I was speechless. It was very unlike Dolferl to bare his innermost feelings like this.

'I'm a failure! My struggle is wasted!' he cried. 'I can never make up for what I've done to him.' Dolferl sat up in his bed, burying his head in his hands. 'I'm worthless. I'm shit!' He wept. 'Shit! Shit! Shit!'

'You're going to be a success. Look at all the good work you've done,' I said, gesturing to the drawings and notes spread over the piano, table, chairs and floor. I picked up one of his designs for housing for the homeless. This had been a breakthrough for Dolferl; he was addressing a social problem.

'You know how important this is,' I said. I didn't know if he heard me.

He had once taken me to a small plot of land where a landlord had stacked three homes, one on top of the other. The basement apartment had no windows; the first- and the second-floor apartments had only one window each. This had utterly appalled Dolferl. 'How can a child live like this?' he had said, shaking his head sadly at the sight of children running in and out of the place. Immediately after our trip Dolferl had set out to design affordable housing for all. The plans he had drawn up were remarkably practical: rooms, wardrobes and shelves were arranged so they could accommodate any possible situation. This rush of social responsibility had lasted for a considerable period, during which he had worked from dusk to dawn. He insisted that these designs should benefit those in society who were always overlooked.

'You have a wonderful mind,' I said, 'and you have the talent. It's just a matter of time before your ideas become reality.'

'Do you really think so?' he asked, with a new vulnerability. His eyes were still wide and scared, but now there was a tiny glimmer of hope. A hint of promise. He tucked his legs up to his chest and wrapped his arms around his knees, hugging himself. I knew then that I was his only friend, his only friend in the world. It was sad. Dolferl gulped. He was soothed by my reassuring words. 'Remember the bridge I want to build? In Linz?' he asked.

'Yes.'

'It will be glorious! You must come to the opening ceremony. I'll get them to hire an orchestra.'

'An orchestra?'

Dolferl's lower lip stiffened resolutely. 'Yes. I will demand it!'

I heard someone burst into our room. I sat up in my bed and stared at the alarm clock. It was 8 a.m. Dolferl slammed the door behind him. 'Frau Zakreys is a harlot!' he cried in his most urgent voice. His face flushed furiously. 'She's a Czech whore!'

'What are you doing up so early?' I asked, rubbing my drowsy eyes.

'I've been violated!' Dolferl screamed. 'I'm serious. We have to leave!'

'What exactly happened?' I asked, restraining a smirk.

'I was over in the kitchen eating one of her apple strudels.'

'And?'

'It was warm and delicious. It made me think of my mother. She made the best strudel.' Dolferl knew exactly how to get older women to indulge him. Frau Zakreys treated him just like his own mother had. She spoiled him. 'So I was lost in my thoughts,' Dolferl continued, 'when that tart noticed I had dribbled some apple on my shirt. She took a damp cloth and wiped it clean, talking the whole time.'

I shrugged. 'So what's the problem?'

'Well, you know how she's always harping on about how a "real woman" knows what a man craves?'

'That's just how she is.'

'Well, it's absolutely disgusting.'

'Look, at worst, it's provocative . . . '

'I'm not finished yet. The next thing I know, the Czech whore touches my cheek!'

'So what?'

'*So?* My best friend – in fact, my only friend in the world – dares to question me? I need methylated spirits to clean my cheek! I have to go to the doctor!'

'Dolferl, you're giving me a headache.'

'Headache? Not now! We have to leave!'

'Leave? Why?'

'We have to get away from that slut. Immediately!'

'Calm down,' I groaned 'There's no reason to go anywhere!'

'Let's take a trip,' he said. 'I've been thinking about going away for a while! It will help our work.'

'What work?'

'*Wieland the Smith*, of course. Our opera! Getting out of here will revive our creative energy.'

'But – Dolferl, I have real work I have to complete, or else – '

'Or else what?'

'I'll be kicked out of the Conservatory.'

'So what? Wagner left college without finishing. I left secondary school! So can you.'

'Two return tickets to Linz,' said Dolferl to the man behind the window. 'First class,' he added, with a fake sigh and took out his wallet.

I tapped his shoulder. 'Dolferl, we should go second class,' I said.

'I beg your pardon, kind sir, but we are travelling first class because I am dressed first class.'

Dolferl tipped his top hat with his cane. He was wearing a grey striped jacket and waistcoat, a starched white shirt and black-and-grey striped trousers. Even though he readily sympathised with the 'simple, decent but underprivileged people', the 'common man' and the 'poor betrayed masses', he did all he could not to resemble them. Dolferl counted out the gold coins and pushed them through the opening in the window to the ticket agent.

'But the money . . .' I cautioned.

'To hell with money! Money is to be spent, not hoarded! It's my prerogative to spend my inheritance as I see fit.'

It seemed that I was the only one who was watching Dolferl's finances.

'I hate money,' he continued. 'It's the cold heart of this despicable capitalist world, a world where art and culture are considered waste.'

Dolferl had grown up with a reckless attitude towards money. Back in Linz, his mother had paid for his opera tickets, his extravagant clothes and his books. Now his mother's inheritance was paying for everything. Within just a few months, Dolferl had attended countless performances at the opera house and by the Vienna Philharmonic Orchestra. He had seen *Tristan and Isolde* eight times in a row, spending a small fortune on concert and opera tickets alone – and he often paid for my tickets, too. In February, Dolferl had come to Vienna with several hundred kronen inheritance, a huge sum of money considering that we paid only ten kronen each per month for our room. Now it was April, and I was curious to know how much of his former wealth remained.

'A penny for your thoughts,' said Dolferl, as if reading mine, 'is nothing but a petty little saying for petty little people.'

'I just don't want you to waste your – '

'All credibility, all good conscience, all evidence of truth comes from the senses,' said Dolferl, handing me my ticket. 'Quote one hundred and thirty-four from "Maxims and Interludes" in *Beyond Good and Evil*.'

'But what will you do once the money is gone?'

'As Schopenhauer so eloquently pointed out, an ascetic lifestyle elevates one's spirituality. The sooner I spend my money, the sooner that will be.'

'Very well then,' I said. If that's the way you want it, I thought, there's nothing I can do about it.

We walked across the marble floor of the station and Dolferl gazed up at the pillars and domed ceiling. 'What a noble building! It's a monument to itself. It reminds me of a mausoleum; it commemorates people's departures.'

'But,' I interjected, 'aren't train stations also about arrivals?'

'Train stations are much more about departures than arrivals,' Dolferl stated in that absolute manner of his. 'Look,' he said, pointing towards the impressive steel and glass dome. 'Who in his right mind could doubt that we northern Europeans are the cradle of civilisation?'

I looked at my friend. 'But didn't our civilisation develop from the Romans and the Greeks?'

Dolferl shook his head. 'Only the birth of the Germanic culture enabled the achievements of the Roman and Greek cultures to be reborn. Without the emergence of the Northern Europeans in 1200 BC there would have never been any culture, anywhere in the world.' His face lit up as he spoke. 'First the Northern Europeans had to resist the chaos of the downfall of the Roman Empire, and then gradually all the other races of the world.'

We strolled in the direction of our platform.

'Houston Stewart Chamberlain put it perfectly,' he said. 'He proved repeatedly in *Foundations of the Nineteenth Century* that our race is superior to all others. It's biology. Pure science. Everybody who's read his book knows that. Including his most devoted convert, our Kaiser Wilhelm the Second.'

'What about the Arabs?' I asked.

'The Muslim culture?' Dolferl said, shaking his head. 'What the Arabs create doesn't last. The Mongolians can destroy but they can't build anything new. The Egyptian, Chinese, Indian and all other earlier cultures are long gone.'

'And the Renaissance?'

'Renaissance? What Renaissance? It impeded our progress as much as it encouraged it.' Dolferl smiled smugly. 'Besides, Shakespeare, the greatest innovator of that entire era, could speak neither Greek nor Latin. And Michelangelo and all of the other great Italians of the Rinascimento all came from northern Italy where Gothic, Lombardic and Frankish bloods all intermingle.' He shook his head in disapproval. 'The instant the Northern Europeans emerged, a new world came into existence, and everything in our modern world can be traced to them. This isn't the "progress of mankind" that we're witnessing; it's the progress of one particular type of man, one specific race. Just as the Chinese or Egyptian races were the sources of progress in the past, the Aryan race is the source of all progress today.'

Dolferl looked down at the polished white marble floor and I caught him gazing at his dark reflection. We walked on to the platform, boarded the train, settled into the fine suede seats of our first-class compartment and ordered two demitasses.

Dolferl pointed contemptuously to a flyer on our table advertising a cabaret show. 'Diversion and escapism – that's what people seem to do best these days. No wonder, because they only live to exist. Life has lost all sense and meaning, and the only solution they can see is escapism through distraction.'

'But didn't you say a minute ago you that our civilisation is the only salvation for mankind?'

'That's true.' He sipped his demitasse. 'But if we're not careful, our civilisation will drown in mediocrity, corruption and decadence. We must be vigilant! We cannot let the blood of our race be diluted any further.'

Dolferl leaned back in his seat in preparation for the jolt of the train as it began to move off.

'I prefer dogs to men. Wagner said the same. And I also agree with him that only the most horrific and destructive revolution could make these so-called civilised people "human" again.' The train's lumbering movement seemed to spur Dolferl on. 'That's why our opera is so important. I see *Wieland* as the opera Wagner had wanted it to be,' he declared, as if introducing the performance. 'It will be an act of artistic terrorism. Just as Wagner had dreamed.'

Grey foundries, battered brick walls and green weeds protruding through cracked concrete blurred past the window of the swaying train.

'And what form does artistic terrorism take, exactly?'

'Just as the Master said: it will be a "*Gesamtkunstwerk*", with space, sound, light and words arranged so that the audience becomes part of one great, stimulating emotion. By becoming part of the *Gesamtkunstwerk* as an audience, people will experience a blissful moment of significance, and the memory of that moment will revolutionise the way they live. Society as we know it will implode, and disappear into oblivion. *That* is artistic terrorism!'

I set down my cup. 'That all remains to be seen.'

'It has been seen! I've already imagined and visualised it. In my mind, the opera has already opened to rave reviews at La Scala.'

'And Milan is awaiting our call?'

'Yes!' he cried. 'As will Vienna, and New York, and Paris, and Berlin, and London. Even Tokyo!'

The carriage rattled along the tracks.

'The main drama of the opera will take place in Nidur's court,' Dolferl said. 'Wieland will forge the strong, sturdy armour that the King will use to expand his empire.'

'But the irony is that Wieland is creating the tools that will be used to imprison him?'

'Exactly. Isn't that what our society does? The more fanatical a Christian, the more he's a prisoner of his beliefs,' said Dolferl, with a laugh.

He had adopted this view from Nietzsche, who believed that far from healing the troubles of modern man, Christianity was the source of them. Dolferl both loved and hated Nietzsche: he loved the Nietzsche who wrote that the will to power was the most basic impulse of all living things and that the God of religion was dead; but he hated the Nietzsche who admired the French and Russian cultures and considered himself a European, rather than a German. He hated the Nietzsche who said that the 'vigour' of any population could only be increased by merging with other races. And he particularly hated the Nietzsche who said that liberation was only possible for the individual, never for an entire nation. Dolferl quoted the Nietzsche he admired on a regular basis, never mentioning the Nietzsche he despised.[12] He did the same with Schopenhauer and Schiller – everyone, in fact. He dismembered the ideas of others to incorporate the elements he liked into his own *Weltanschauung*.

Dolferl's eyes glazed over in pensive contemplation. 'It's only when society oversteps itself and demands too much of its people that we realise how trapped we really are. That's when the worker realises that all of his good intentions and hard work have merely imprisoned him more.' Dolferl snapped his fingers. 'I can't wait to write the scene where Wieland realises this!' He was silent for a moment and then continued: 'It happens after the King has severed the tendons in Wieland's foot and he's unable to walk.'

Row after row of dilapidated houses sailed past the window. The

12 See: Appendix 10, Friedrich Nietzsche

morning sun beamed down, bathing the dismal sight in a defiant light. Dolferl stared out of the window. His head bobbed gently with the motion of the train.

'The light must win out in the end,' he said. 'Despite all of Wieland's tragedies.' He looked up at the roof of the compartment. 'The light must triumph' he repeated. 'That which opposes the laws of nature must be defeated. The creators must triumph over the destroyers; the children of light must triumph over the children of darkness. The dark and evil forces must be defeated in the end. Absolutely.' Dolferl smoothed out the fabric of his trousers.

'But how can Wieland defeat the evil forces?' I asked. 'He's totally trapped at the end. Nidur's court is burning, it's surrounded by enemies and Wieland can't even walk.'

'I can picture it,' he said. 'Wieland forges wings that allow him to fly away from the court that imprisoned him. And he will fly into the light.'

'Like Daedalus!'

'No, not like Daedalus: Wieland's wings won't melt. These wings are Nordic. They're made of iron, they resist the heat of the sun. Wieland's wings will triumph.'

The sun caught the golden spikes atop the twisted stone pillar of the *Dreifaltigkeitssäule* in the centre of Linz's main square. Cherubic angels adorned the Baroque monument. Dolferl glared at it and erupted in a patronising laugh. 'That's some cake decoration, not a monument! A monument should inspire one to higher ideals. A monument should exalt!' he said, emphatically. 'This will have to go. I can already see the gleaming bronze statue of Frederick the Great. He shall be brandishing his sword like so' – Dolferl raised his arm over his head, his elbow bent, his hand gripping an invisible weapon – 'and the main square lacks a suitable finishing touch near the bridge. Two buildings are needed there, one on the left and one on the right. Then, when you stand where we are now, you can just see the bridge. I will build all of this, as well as a new concert hall and a much grander theatre. And Linz needs an observatory, to educate people and elevate their minds beyond Christian superstition.' Dolferl straightened his tie, thought for a moment, and continued: 'Once the new "Reich" is in place, all this will be built. Then Europe will be brought to its knees before this jewel on the Danube.'

Dolferl was fixated on this 'Reich' the fantasy Reich instilled in his mind by his favourite history teacher in school; an empire that would unite Germanic Austria with Germany. This new 'Reich' was also a constant feature in the mountain of pan-Germanic pamphlets he read. I let a laugh escape, but instantly regretted it.

'What's so funny?' he snarled.

'Nothing,' I replied, quietly. Mocking Dolferl was strictly *verboten*; although he took great pleasure in ridiculing everyone else, he took himself very seriously.

'Dilettante!' he screamed. 'Charlatan! Pseudo-intellectual!' He roared so loudly that the cabmen atop the waiting carriages turned to see what the commotion was. 'I want nothing more to do with you!' he shouted, as he stormed away.

'Dolferl, I'm sorry!' I called, running after him.

'I've had enough of this so-called friendship!'

'I made a mistake, I apologise! Please, Dolferl.'

He stopped. 'What were you laughing at?' he demanded.

'Well, it was just because . . .' My mind raced to work out the least offensive reply.

'Why?' he insisted.

'It's just that your elaborate designs are . . . Well, they seem a little implausible, for Linz.'

He stood there silently, staring me down like a school-yard bully. I averted my gaze, and he started to speak. 'You don't understand how the universe works.'

Thankfully, he had calmed down. 'Explain it to me then.'

'How was it possible for us to travel the distance so quickly between Vienna and Linz?' he asked.

'I . . . I don't know . . . '

'The wheel!' he cried. 'Someone invented the wheel! Don't you see? Everything starts up here!' he said, tapping his temple. 'There was a time when the wheel seemed a far-fetched idea, but not any more. Why?' He tapped his temple again. 'Because someone conceived it! Intuition! Nothing is ever impossible. *Nothing!* One brilliant idea is of far greater value than an entire life spent behind some office desk!'

It occurred to me again how irresponsible it was for me to be here with Conservatory deadlines looming, but I didn't dare to ask why he had taken us to Linz, or what we were doing here, in the main square.

'You need to read Goldzier!' he exclaimed. Hans Goldzier was a private scholar Dolferl held in high regard and who claimed rather fantastically that Newton's theories were wrong; that the moon was made of iron and that electricity moved everything – people were mere puppets, manipulated on invisible electric strings.[13]

Dolferl jumped. 'There . . . I knew it!'

The shimmering mirage of a girl with a parasol floated over the bridge towards the main square. 'There she is.'

For the first time that day, Dolferl fell silent. His eyes sparkled and he watched enraptured as the girl glided along the far end of the square in the company of an older woman. I knew immediately who they were: Stefanie Isak and her mother. Dolferl had admired Stefanie from afar three years previously, often standing in this spot to watch as she escorted her mother on their afternoon walk. He had designed a house for them to live in together, but had never spoken a single word to her, which had only allowed the fantasy to flourish.

A few months after Dolferl had first told me about Stefanie, I met a cellist who by chance turned out to be Stefanie's brother, and so I gleaned some information about her. Her father had been a senior government official who had died a few years earlier, leaving her mother to live comfortably on a pension with which she funded the best possible education for her children. Stefanie was fond of dancing and had a great many admirers but was not engaged at that time, much to Dolferl's relief. He had been too shy to ever approach her, and the strict etiquette of petit-bourgeois Linz was also an obstacle: if a gentleman wished to make a lady's acquaintance, it was necessary and fitting that he be gainfully employed. Dolferl would never be financially situated to court his chosen girl. Ultimately, however, I felt sure that he was greatly relieved that he had never had to prove his virility. And so, Stefanie had remained a distant object of adoration, like a Madonna in a grotto.

'I'm surprised,' I said, 'doesn't your heart belong to Lucie Weidt now?'

'I love Lucie Weidt as an artist, not a woman,' he snapped back.

'You've never loved Stefanie as a woman, either.'

'What would you know?' he hissed. 'You have no idea what real love is!'

Stefanie had a unique air about her. She was blonde with soft peach skin, petite with excellent posture. She wore subdued pastels, and was always beautiful, especially when listening to her mother, when her head would gesture thoughtfully.

'So what do we do now?' I asked.

13 See: Appendix 11, Hans Goldzier

But Dolferl didn't hear me. He was transfixed by Stefanie's every step.

She strolled down the square towards us with her mother, stopping every so often to peer into a shop window.

'Look, you've come all this way – won't you at least go and talk to her?' I said.

'Are you crazy?' he exploded. 'I've come here to *see* her. And as you may have noticed, she's come here too. She knows I'm here. Anyway, we don't need to "talk"; our love is sacred, it transcends such trivialities. To talk to her right now would only sully it.'

'Dolferl,' I said guardedly, 'how could talking to her sully anything?'

'When a love is as pure as ours, talking is base and lascivious.'

'How do you know that she loves you?'

'Because this is real love! And it's real for her, too, as real as her beating heart.' His face was a picture of self-righteous conviction. 'As real as your asinine face,' he added quickly, to pre-empt any mockery.

I pretended not to hear, and pursued the real matter at hand. 'How real can her love be when she doesn't even know you exist?'

'It's more real than anything else. It's *a priori*. It's a given. Do I have to tell you to read Kant for the thousandth time? Maybe then you'll understand.'

His beloved Stefanie crossed the street, turned the corner and was out of sight, but not of mind. Dolferl closed his eyes. A moment passed. I nudged him. His eyes opened.

'We came here for that?' I asked incredulously.

He said nothing. For him, the moment had been so wondrous it needed no justification. Then I reminded myself that he had paid for my ticket, first class.

'Why don't we visit my parents?' I suggested. 'My stepmother will make us a nice meal. Father always liked you.'

I nodded my head, willing him to say 'yes', because after the meal I wanted to take the train back to Vienna. We had to be back in time to attend that night's performance of *The Misanthrope* so I could be with *my* beloved! Then I would talk to her and sense if she had any feelings for me, because so far the only thing I knew was that I loved Francisca.

I nodded my head enthusiastically: say yes, Dolferl, *please* say yes.

'No,' he replied.

'Why not?

'Because I said so,' he declared brusquely. 'We're going to go visit *my* parents.'

To get to the cemetery in neighbouring Leonding, we took a short-cut through some coniferous woodland. Shafts of light crisscrossed the spiky canopy overhead and Dolferl slipped through the woods with instinctive ease. 'I feel like one of Karl May's Indians,' he said. 'May says that Indians only began to lie and steal after the arrival of the Christian white man. Before that they were pure, as pure as nature.' Dolferl bounced through the sun-dappled forest like an exuberant child. 'In nature I feel free: free from Christianity, free from commandments and laws.' He jumped. 'Isn't this what life is about?' he asked aloud. 'All of the basic questions of life are answered here amid nature.' He spun around with his arms outstretched, his polished shoes screwing into the pine needles on the forest floor. The ivory handle of his ebony cane flitted between light and shadow. Dolferl laughed, covering his teeth with his hand. 'I feel wonderful!'

Then suddenly his legs braced to a stop and he fell to his knees. His top hat flew from his head, and his gloved hands braked against the ground as he hunched over and then was still. A breeze whistled through the trees. The branches groaned above. Green needles fell around him. Beside him there was a sapling protruding from the earth, no more than a foot tall with five spindly limbs. Dolferl stared at the skinny fir tree. His hands encircled the plant in a reverent gesture of wonder: he was evidently quite taken by this fragile sapling. He took his gloves off and started to dig around its roots.

'I must take this to my mother,' he said, tears welling in his eyes.

The steeple of the church in Leonding jutted up against the bright afternoon sky. Dolferl shook his head. 'Eighty years ago Charles Lyell showed that the earth is much older than the Bible claims. The Bible is a scam! But that doesn't stop people from going to church.' He paused. 'A moment ago I felt like an Indian in the woods.' He stopped and turned to me. 'Indians have respect for nature; Christianity conflicts with it.' Dolferl looked up at the church tower. 'Man thinks he can dominate nature. He's forgotten that he's utterly dependent on it. Ancient culture understood and abided by nature; Christianity systematically destroys it. Don't you agree?' he asked, as if he would ever actually permit me to answer, much less oppose, his rhetoric. Dolferl only repeated what most progressive intellectuals were saying. They all rejected faith and religion but in my mind, the redeeming virtues of Christianity outweighed its shortcomings. Of course I knew not to mention this to Dolferl. You were never really allowed to discuss anything with him, only to listen.

'God does not live in the twilight of confessionals,' he continued. 'He lives in the murmur of the trees and the springs, in the twinkle of the stars and in the radiance of the cornfield. God is not Christianity.' Dolferl clasped his hands around the pine tree in mock prayer. 'Christianity is the systematic cultivation of human failure. Turning the other cheek is the triumph of defeatism. It contradicts Darwin. When will people finally overcome this slave morality that's been drummed into them? Someday, somehow, something new will emerge. It must!'

Dolferl stood and gazed up beyond the steeple's cross into the infinite blue. With the pine tree in his hand, we walked towards the cemetery. 'Do you remember when we were altar boys in Lambach?' he asked me. 'How we had to wake up extra early on Sunday to prepare for seven o'clock Mass? And Father Bernhard, that pompous, God-fearing idiot! What a sanctimonious old fool. The rubbish he used to spout!'

'Didn't you get anything positive from that whole experience?' I asked.

'I've learned the entire litany of the Mass: all the responses, all the movements; and what did it teach me? Not to go to church, except for funerals or weddings.'

Dolferl led the way through the gate and into the graveyard. 'I can see the temples of the future,' he said. 'Tens of thousands of men will gather, awestruck by the grandeur of the shrine built to reflect the grandeur of the universe. The sheer scale of the temple will teach them humility, a humility that will instantly wipe out the superstitions of the church.'

The consecutive granite tombstones formed irregular rows across the well-tended yard. We proceeded to the east wall, where his parents lay in rest.

'Isn't it strange,' he murmured, 'I've accepted the death of my parents, yet I feel a sense of disbelief that they're actually dead.' Dolferl shook his head.

'Maybe,' I said, 'there's still a child inside you longing for your parents to return and protect you. Maybe you're craving that security.'

'Nonsense. The strong man recognises the transient, indeterminate nature of all things. Others in my place may experience some disconcerting sensation that consumes their every conviction and courage, but not I. The boundaries between what is and what should be have dissipated for me.'

We arrived in front of his parents' headstone. A photo of his father graced the oval-shaped metal plate set into the granite. His father's full, bushy moustache fanned out over his lip along the bottom of his cheekbone to his jaw, where the hair joined with his sparse sideburns. It was his official civil servant portrait. Beneath the name, Alois Hitler, white letters on the black marble proclaimed the respect and admiration held for him as a customs officer. Alois had been a staunch German nationalist, but unlike Dolferl, he hadn't opposed Habsburg rule. After all the Kaiser was paying his pension. I remembered his father treating Dolferl like a dog: he would put two fingers into his mouth and whistle to summon Dolferl from wherever he might be. When Dolferl was six, his fourteen-year-old half-brother, Alois, had run away from home, never to return, leaving Dolferl to endure his choleric father's temper as the only other male in the household.

Dolferl's eyes trailed down to the bottom of the plate, to the words 'Klara Hitler'. Beneath the name, her dates of birth and death and 'RIP' were engraved, and there was a small oval portrait of Dolferl's mother below the rim. Dolferl's hands dropped to his side and he sank to his knees there amidst the patch of yellow and purple pansies in front of the stone.

'Do you know what man is?' he asked me suddenly. 'Nature itself,' he continued, before I could respond. 'But nature is only the objectified will to live, so he who understands this will not suffer when contemplating death for himself or his loved ones. He will focus on the immortality of nature, which he himself is, and see that birth and death are really both part of life.'

Dolferl stared silently at the grave, playing the part of the 'strong man' who has come to see things as they truly are. I could see him acting out Schopenhauer's 'Mystic', for whom everything that comes to pass is complete and beautiful in itself and who is beyond suffering. He gazed down at the fir tree. 'I have to plant this,' he said. With his bare hands, he started to dig, scooping clumps of dirt from the grave. Then he lowered the sapling into the hole, refilled the soil and softly patted it down around the base of the sapling. 'Our little tree must be thirsty.' He smiled down on the plant. 'See if you can find a watering can, Martl.'

I had noticed a hoe and a rake by the cemetery gate, so I ran alongside the squat gravestones, where I found a half-filled watering can.

When I returned, Dolferl was standing, facing the grave.

'Oh, Mother!' he whispered, his slumped torso weighed down in despair. 'I can never repay you for what you gave me. Oh God, I am but a worm!' Dolferl stumbled backwards in shock, realising that I had overheard him. I looked at him. His eyes were piercing: you can never tell anybody what I just said. 'Please,' he said, holding his hands near the spout of the watering can. 'Rinse them off.'

I did as he asked, and then he took the can and poured water around the small tree. 'Dolferl?' I said enquiringly.

'Yes?' he replied, looking down at the fir.

'May we go and see my mother's grave? She's just on the other side of the graveyard.'

'No,' he said, brushing off his trousers. 'Today belongs to my parents, not yours.'

On the way back to town, all I could think about was how incredibly selfish and callous Dolferl could be. It was clear that in Dolferl's mind, my mother's death didn't matter. I glared over at Dolferl as we walked along, straining to resist punching him in the face for refusing to let me visit my mother's grave. His gall wouldn't even allow us to discuss it, and yet here I was, abiding by his decision. I should have walked across the cemetery and tended my mother's plot despite his insistence and despite any ensuing tantrum. But I was such a weak fool. Why did I tolerate such behaviour? What was it that made me allow this egomaniacal tyrant to continually insult me? Was it the Christian in me, the Christian Dolferl scorned so much? I turned the other cheek so often my head practically rotated. I glanced across at Dolferl: his satin top hat; his suit tails flowing in the wake of his stride; his ivory-topped cane tapping the ground, preceding each step along the path. The sunlight fell on his shoulders and cast his shadow ahead of him, which I felt sure he was admiring.

He sensed my gaze and smiled at me. 'Isn't it a delightful afternoon?' he said gaily. The bastard was completely oblivious to my feelings: his selfishness was so absolute it was almost admirable.

We returned along the bank of the Danube. The dark, churning river imbued the air with its scent, making its presence smelt and felt. I looked ahead to the bridge that led to Urfahr on the other side, where yellow neo-classical buildings flanked both sides of the distant boulevard.

'I have great plans for that bridge,' said Dolferl.

'Do tell,' I said caustically.

'I'm going to rebuild it as one sweeping arch,' he said, gathering pace. 'It will rise to about three hundred feet; the entire span will be fifteen hundred feet.'.

Reconstruction again! 'What's the point? The bridge is fine as it is.'

'I want the bridge to inspire! When people cross the Danube here, I want them to remember the legend associated with this place.'

Dolferl was referring to the story of a daring horseman who, pursued by his enemies, was said to have jumped from a soaring height to swim across the Danube and reach the other side.

'Think how splendid Linz will be then! People will cross this magnificent span to get to the concert hall named after you.'

'After me?' I said.

'Of course! The concert hall should be named after Linz's most famous and revered musician. Doesn't that make sense?'

'About as much sense as renaming the opera house after you . . . '

'No, no, no!' admonished Dolferl. 'The Centre for the Performing Arts will be named after me! It will be a complex that will include an opera house named after Wagner, the concert hall named after you, and a theatre named after Schiller.'

'Really?'

'Absolutely. It's only a matter of time,' Dolferl answered, seemingly unaware of the pomposity of it all.

'I am greatly humbled,' I replied, 'to be ranked not only with masters such as Wagner and Schiller, but with you.'

'You shouldn't be,' he said, oblivious to my tone. 'It's well deserved.'

We had reached the foot of the bridge. Dolferl bowed to me and said, 'today is a great day, for it is particularly momentous that the bridge should be completed as I have just described, so if you will permit me' – he formed the shape of scissors with his forefinger and middle finger – 'to cut the ribbon! I dedicate this bridge to all the unsung geniuses of Linz!' Dolferl then officiously cut an imaginary red ribbon in pantomime. I applauded, and we crossed the bridge together singing the triumphant aria from *Parsifal*. We stopped in the middle of the bridge and peered down at the slowly rolling current of the Danube as it flowed beneath us. Suddenly Dolferl turned and said, 'If it were just a little warmer, I would dive in.' He stared at me intently, defiantly: dare me.

I remembered I had seen the same stare before, under a bridge by the Lambach canal. We were ten years old, and six of us had gathered one day in March to watch the slippery ice floes drift by. Hannes Dangl, a cocky local boy, had challenged Dolferl to hop across the 20-feet-wide canal. Dolferl had studied the floating slabs of ice and glared at him: you dare to dare me! Watch me, shithead! He'd looked at the moving ice and water, and then, without a second's hesitation, he leapt on to the nearest floe.

The impact as he landed caused the chunk of ice to dip down into the freezing water, soaking his shoes and socks. We screeched as the floe quickly rose up and supported Dolferl's weight. It occurred to me then just how dangerous a prank this was: if Dolferl jumped short of the next piece of ice, he would surely drown. But he was unfazed by this. He glared at us all on the canal's edge: danger is my passion. It moves me. Intoxicates me! Now or never! *Now or never!* He jumped on to the edge of the next floe. The ice dipped, and Dolferl quickly jumped again and landed right in the centre. Then, with three more bounds from floe to floe, he was across the canal. At the time, our peers had cheered at his bravery; but now that I had known him for so long, I wasn't so sure it had been bravery after all, but an uncontrollable need to prove himself.

The Clutches of Decadence

Masks allow for a greater exchange of ideas and . . . everything.

When we returned to the apartment, I immediately started to browse through my wardrobe.

'And where do you think you're going?' asked Dolferl.

'We're going to see Francisca tonight!' I said, taking off my trousers.

'Oh. . .' he sighed. 'I'm not interested in going there.'

'But I am.'

'Why waste your time with a bunch of fools mouthing clichés?' he said, 'You'd do better to stay at home and work on *Wieland*.'

'Well, I'm going to see *The Misanthrope* tonight.' I looked at the clothesline: my clean, white, pressed shirt awaited me. I could feel his eyes pierce me, burrowing into me: I had betrayed him.

'You're going to sit through five acts of that tripe? Just for some girl?'

'If it was Stefanie,' I replied, 'you would go.'

'Stefanie is no mere actress – and an actress who doesn't mind lowering herself to play Molière at that!' spat Dolferl.

I stopped buttoning my shirt. I could have taken offence at that, but chose not to. 'Me attending Francisca's performance is like you observing Stefanie from a distance, with the crucial difference that Francisca knows I exist! We actually talk to one another. In fact, that's exactly what I plan to do after the show!'

Dolferl remained silent for a moment, and then retorted, 'How dare you even mention your harlot of an actress, who dyes her hair the colour of cheap rouge, in the same breath as Stefanie!'

I fastened the collar button and searched for my trousers as I struggled not to punch him. 'She doesn't colour her hair,' I hissed, through gritted teeth. 'It's as natural as Stefanie's!'

'Stefanie?' exclaimed Dolferl. 'She wouldn't even waste her time *watching* Molière. She knows *true* art!'

I put my foot through the leg of my trousers, clenching my jaw.

'And you, my dear friend,' said Dolferl, patronisingly, 'you are clueless about love.'

Not again! 'How can you deny that you're just – ' I stopped short, and tucked in my shirt.

'I'm just *what*?'

'I have to get ready,' I said, not wanting to tell him the pitiful truth. I buttoned up my trousers.

'*What?*' screeched Dolferl.

'You know what.'

'If you go, I never want to see you again! I mean it!'

I squinted at my best friend. Unbelievable. I slid an arm into my dress coat and was ready to go. I opened the door. 'See you tomorrow.'

After the final curtain, I came upon a uniformed usher as I walked down a side aisle and asked him how I could get the rose I was holding to Francisca. When he rolled his eyes, I told him I was a friend of hers, so he asked me to prove it. I wanted to show him my complimentary ticket, but couldn't find it.

'Fine,' he said, gruffly. 'Follow me.'

He led me out to the lobby and then out on to the street. I turned just as he slammed the door on me. Silly fool.

I ran to the side of the theatre and down the alleyway to the stage door. Eventually a man in a business suit came out, swinging the door wide open. I straightened up to look like I knew where I was going and entered the building. People, costumes and props swirled around me as I moved through the shadowy corridors to where I imagined the dressing rooms would be. I glanced at the darkened set behind the fallen curtain, bumped into a hanging sandbag and skirted up a winding hallway, which led to an open door. A soft butterscotch glow pushed into the corridor. Slowly I approached the door.

Then I saw her. She was wearing a white bathrobe and was sitting in a chair talking to her wardrobe mistress. Some musicians were rehearsing next door, so I couldn't hear what was being said. Francsica tilted her head backwards as she was laughing. Her face was powdered white with a round black beauty mark, like a semibreve in musical notation. Her satin skirt hung on a rack behind her, and her ivory hand moved from her throat to her chest as she talked. She was shaking her head as if to say 'What was I to do?', before her expression transformed to a gentle smile. The mistress took the wig off her head, revealing a cap that covered her hair. Francisca continued with her story and as she smoothed cold cream across her face, she shook her head repeatedly and giggled. She applied more cream to her face as she continued talking. Then she took a towel and wiped it all off. Once the make-up had been removed, the unhealthy, anaemic look so fashionable in the 1600s was thankfully gone. She took the rubber cap from her head, shook out her hair, and finally all traces of Célimène had disappeared. Francisca was back.

I decided to present her with the rose and then leave. I had just taken one step towards her dressing room when suddenly Herbert and Leopold came around the corner. They were chattering so animatedly that they didn't see me. As they scurried into the dressing room, I watched from the doorway, peering in. When Francisca turned to them, they all raised their hands in mock surprise. *That must be how actors greet one another*, I thought. Then I heard one of them say, 'Everyone's going to the Ballhaus.'

They clapped their hands in delighted unison.

The wardrobe mistress closed the door.

I left.

I left, even though I had a wealth of glorious compliments to pay her: how she was a revelation, and how I would now always think of *The Misanthrope* as the story of Célimène, not Alceste; how she had brought light, realism and insight to the role; how she had projected the most subtle of emotions on stage. Secretly, the most intriguing part of the evening for me had been her dressing-room transformation from courtly coquette to twentieth-century artiste. But when her friends had entered the room and I had beheld that elite trio, radiating success, I knew I was out of my league. Who was I to think that I could ever possibly . . . what? Steal a kiss? Hold her in my arms? Connect with her on a spiritual level? Maybe, I thought, I'm more like Dolferl than I want to admit. As I wandered away in my numbed state, I dropped the rose in the gutter by the stage door.

Outside the sky unleashed a torrent of rain. All around me it crashed down on the ground. I looked up between the two walls of the alley, up at the endless, sorry night. Raindrops pelted my upturned face. Why hadn't I even had the courage to say 'thank you' to her? I thought, as I ran for cover under the theatre's awning.

'There you are!' I heard Dolferl exclaim. He was standing by the theatre poster, dressed in his top hat, as if he had attended tonight's performance as well.

'The very man!' I said.

'See?' he answered, with a laugh. 'I came to save you from the clutches of decadence!'

'Hardly,' I said. 'I didn't even get a chance to thank her.'

I could see a smile emerge on Dolferl's face, and with that the sky erupted with an even heavier downpour, mirroring the misery in my heart. The driving rain struck hard against the city's stone, glass and metal; its rhythms were relentless daggers, piercing me to my core.

'I'll get us a cab,' announced Dolferl, apparently relieved and enlivened by my sadness. 'My treat!'

Dolferl waved his cane out into the street whenever a cab trotted by. I couldn't believe what I'd done, or rather, what I hadn't done: there I was, right outside her door; why hadn't I given her the rose?

'I've got one,' panted Dolferl, as he signalled frantically. The sound of hooves came closer. The carriage stopped. Dolferl opened the door and turned to me; I was too stricken with remorse to think about what I should do. It was clear to me that I would never have her; why get in the carriage? I'd rather have been washed away by the rain. 'Come on,' shouted Dolferl, 'get in!'

Suddenly a well-dressed man ran up to us. 'I've been trying for an eternity to wrangle one of these! Could I possibly share this cab with you? I would be pleased, not to say honoured, to pay your fare.'

'But of course,' said Dolferl. 'I'm just waiting for my friend.'

'Well, get in!' They both beckoned to me.

As the coach pulled away from the theatre, Herr Maurer offered his hand as he introduced himself. 'You never know whose acquaintance you might make when you travel,' he said, 'but in cabs like this you can be sure to be travelling with those of your own intellect, at least,' he said, smiling.

'I couldn't agree with you more,' answered Dolferl. 'What's that scientific expression . . . ?' he wondered aloud, squinting up at the mahogany-panelled roof as if he might find the answer there. 'Yes, yes! "Water seeking its own level", and all that!' he said, as the rain battered the cab's roof relentlessly.

Both Dolferl and Herr Maurer were sporting similar walking canes: ivory handle, ebony base with a white band at the tip. They were both dressed as if on their way to the races, but there were also differences between the two. Herr Maurer had gold and ruby cufflinks, while Dolferl's were silver and topaz. Herr Maurer wore spats; Dolferl did not. And Herr Maurer did not wear a top hat. He was also older, but probably only by a few years.

'You know, they have a wonderful, efficient system in the United States for separating the classes – specifically the Negroids,' continued Herr Maurer.

'I've never been,' Dolferl confessed.

'Well, I have,' responded Herr Maurer. 'When I visited the capital, Washington, I was impressed with how they dealt with those dark-skinned people.'

'Do tell,' said Dolferl.

'Well, they segregate them as much as possible. On public transport, they sit in the back. There are separate entrances and separate water fountains in public places for Whites and Negroes. And they house them far, far away from decent neighbourhoods. In fact, a whole separate set of laws applies to them.'

'That is utterly inspiring. We need to do the same with the Slavs in Vienna!'

Herr Maurer sat up in his seat. 'Absolutely, my good man!' he said. 'How can Habsburg give *their* votes the same weight as ours? They pay no taxes and have no education. How can they be equal to us?'

I could hear the two talk, but I wasn't listening. I was gazing out of the window, through the sheets of rain, to the soaked cobblestoned street. The shops were closed and the open coffee houses with their amber lights appeared to glow even more warmly and invitingly than usual.

'Exactly!' said Dolferl. 'When it comes to understanding race problems, the US is streets ahead of us! White Americans know what it means for a civilisation to mix with low races.'

'Interbreeding destroys character,' philosophised Maurer.

'I've studied the caste system in the Hindu scriptures,' said Dolferl.

'Did you read them in Sanskrit?'

Dolferl raised an eyebrow: doesn't everybody? But he didn't reply, as that would have required an overt lie.

'The caste system was created to keep the races apart,' began Dolferl. 'As long as that worked, the Aryan-Hindu culture was the leading culture of the world. But when some idiots destroyed the caste system, Hindu culture deteriorated.'

'That certainly won't happen in America,' said Herr Maurer.

'How can you be so sure?'

'Not only do the Yanks separate the Blacks, they do the same with their red-skinned savages. They isolate them in desolate, restricted areas, where they lose their natural resistance to illness. The Indians die at a much higher rate than if they lived in their own villages. The American

Government has studied it all scientifically: it's all geared towards a final solution to the Indian situation.'[14]

'You know, Martin, I think we should visit America sometime soon!'

I still wasn't listening; no matter how I tried, my thoughts returned to Francisca, recurring like the motif in a tragic overture. I groaned to myself quietly. What could I have done differently? How could I have walked in on their merriment without feeling like an interloper? I would have felt painfully awkward. Those theatrical types would be rambling on about people I didn't know and I would have had to nod my head knowingly just to conceal my ignorance. Clearly, my only option had been to walk away from a potentially humiliating situation.

'Are pedigree hunting dogs reared by chance? The result of promiscuity and equal rights?' Dolferl asked. 'No: they're a product of natural selection and strict adherence to purity of race. Why should human beings be any different?'

'Well said,' applauded Herr Maurer.

'All this talk of equality is insane!' said Dolferl. 'There are higher and lower races! It is scientific fact and people simply have to accept it.'

'I agree entirely.'

'Dolferl,' I said. 'I think . . .'

Dolferl glared at me, his mouth contorted in disgust: how dare I interrupt his conversation with another gentleman!

'I think . . .' I repeated. 'Improvement of ethnic purity' was a popular topic of conversation. I found this kind of 'civilised' talk barbaric. After all, whatever the hues of our skin, we were all pink inside.

'What, exactly, do you think?' snarled Dolferl.

'Forget it,' I retreated. Who was I to tell anyone else what they should or shouldn't think? After all, we were living in the greatest 'free-thinking' era in cultural history. So what if my dear friend, like so many others in Vienna, didn't like Czechs, or Negroes? Wasn't that his right? 'Nothing,' I said.

'Good,' Dolferl replied and turned to Herr Maurer. 'So tell me, kind sir, how did you find the transatlantic voyage?'

'When you travel first class, extravagant though it may be, it's like staying in a grand hotel,' Maurer answered.

'Money is there to be spent,' commented Dolferl.

'That's why I like to make a lot of it,' said Herr Maurer, with a burst of laughter.

14 See: Appendix 12, Racism in 1900

'If I may be so bold, how is it that a young man like yourself can afford to indulge himself in the luxury of first-class travel?'

Herr Maurer pondered for a moment, as if choosing a card to set down in poker. Perhaps he realised then that he had really begged the impertinent question himself. He sighed. 'Pork bellies and futures,' he answered, finally.

'Excuse me?' enquired Dolferl.

'I'm a stockbroker,' said Herr Maurer. 'You?'

'Well,' said Dolferl with a laugh, 'I do what I like.'

Dolferl handed Herr Maurer a card. Embossed gold letters stood out regally from the white background. It read: A. Hitler, Painter, Vienna.

'And you?' said Herr Maurer, turning towards me.

'I attend the Conservatory. I hope to be a composer.'

'He *is* a composer,' Dolferl corrected.

Herr Maurer looked around; it appeared that water had indeed found its own level in that little hansom cab, making its way through a rain-swept Vienna.

'If you're interested in a good investment,' announced Dolferl, 'have you ever considered financing an opera? Many colleagues of mine have said it's very rewarding, not just spiritually but financially.'

'Entertainment is quite a risky business,' said Herr Maurer.

'But some risks are worth taking,' replied Dolferl. 'I happen to know of a very promising work in its initial stages of development; now is the time to get in on it, before a bidding war breaks out.'

'And who is writing this magnificent opus?' asked Maurer.

'Why, we are!' proclaimed Dolferl triumphantly.

'Oh, really?'

'Yes!'

I was astounded: Dolferl was negotiating with the tenacity of a con artist: he, of all people, who had railed against the 'privileged position of the upper classes', and stockbrokers in particular, for nights on end! He had condemned their 'unrestrained accumulation of wealth', their self-indulgence and wasteful extravagance in vulgar contrast to the simultaneous poverty, need and hunger on Vienna's streets. And now, having met an actual broker for the first time, he couldn't stop himself attempting to negotiate a deal.

'A renowned industrialist has already expressed interest,' As always, Dolferl lied without any trace of guilt. As a genius he was not bound by moral concepts.

Herr Maurer's eyebrows rose. 'I'm planning a little soiree in nine days,' he said. 'Perhaps you could prepare a proposal about this opera so that I can take a look at what you gentlemen have in mind?'

'It would be our pleasure,' said Dolferl.

The pavement was packed with people dressed for the blustery winds that would herald the death of autumn, the passing into winter. I was already dead: my heart was dead. I had lost Francisca forever because I had been scared to death. And now I was dying of shame. I felt a consummate failure. I couldn't even muster the courage to . . . what, give her a rose? Talk to her? I looked over at Dolferl, and shuddered to think I could be his emotional double.

Dolferl had a ten-page proposal for the *Wieland* opera tucked securely under his arm. We had worked on it for days. When I had asked him how he felt about accepting money from a despised stockbroker he had, as always, come up with a revised set of ethics. He had convinced himself that he was working for the greatest of all possible goals: having our opera produced.

'How decadent,' he said, 'to have a party on a Wednesday evening, right in the middle of the working week. What is society coming to?'

Straightening his back, he walked taller as we turned north on Börsengasse. A November chill pervaded the bustling street. A man and a woman clearly enamoured with one another walked ahead of us, using the cold as an excuse to huddle together to keep each other warm. With every step, they held each other closer and closer. Every so often the man's hand would make a light sweeping pass over the small of her back. They were so in love that they walked in step. I had never experienced love like that; in fact, I had never experienced love at all. I began to imagine what it must be like to walk the street like that with Francisca. My God, I thought, that would be so wonderful, so wonderful. But I will never know.

'Why do we feel?' mused Dolferl, watching the couple.

'We're human; as humans, we feel,' I replied.

'Wrong! We feel not because we're humans and because all humans feel the same; that's just sentimental rubbish. We feel because we have been fooled by society. We feel what we're supposed to feel in our culture.'

'What about love songs?' I said, tipping my head in the couple's direction. 'All the love songs we hear tell us what love is like.'

'Exactly, it's pure indoctrination. Now, if we were cannibals, our greatest pleasure would be eating our enemies,' said Dolferl. 'So that culture would abound with songs about the joys of eating people.'

We laughed.

'The cannibal can only see things as they really are by liberating himself from his cultural brainwashing. In that respect, we're no different to him,' Dolferl concluded. 'To be free, we must overcome these culturally imposed sentiments. Only then can we connect with the infinite potential within us!'

We were walking at a brisk pace now. Dolferl's eyes were on the path under his feet. 'Thinking patterns have been drummed into us from childhood,' he continued, without looking where he was going. Suddenly, he bumped into a prostitute reeking of cheap perfume.

'Oh, excuse me, madam! I do beg your pardon,' he said. The girl was wearing a silk coat with a fur collar. Her thick hair was an aubergine-tinted swirl wound around a parrot-green feather. She had powdered her face so much that white drifts had lodged in her laughter lines. When Dolferl looked up at her, I was sure I saw a glimmer of recognition. She registered his face and her eyes popped open. Did they know each other? Dolferl stepped back. Her ruby lips parted to say something.

'Again,' Dolferl stammered, as he bowed, 'a thousand apologies!' He grabbed me by the elbow and picked up speed.

'You know her?' I enquired.

He said nothing.

'She looked at you like she knew you,' I insisted.

'How dare you!' Dolferl growled. 'I am a gentleman!'

Yes, a *Viennese* gentleman! I thought. Even though he strove to behave differently to the decadent, insincere members of the Viennese elite, he still conducted himself like an upper-class gentleman of Vienna – notorious precisely for their duplicity. It was a Viennese gentleman's prerogative to say one thing and do another – how else could his needs be met? An attractive whore traded immorality with the cool manner of a merchant. It was an unspoken rule that all gentlemen feigned shock and outrage at the impiety of others when they themselves had very likely solicited similar company the night before. Dolferl had supposedly willed himself beyond good and evil, but had he risen above sexual desire as well? I thought back to those nights when Dolferl hadn't come home – once he was gone for three days, and when he finally returned, he was exhausted. When I asked him where he had been, he had replied tersely, 'Exploring the city.' I never broached the subject again. Dolferl was certainly not uninterested in women; on the contrary, after he'd seen a pretty girl, he could talk about her for hours. But when he talked about girls he spoke like an art critic: it was all theory; dry, with no passion. And even though Dolferl christened these women 'goddesses of beauty', he never seemed to have any desire to be intimate with them.[15]

Herr Maurer had given us his address as 28 Thurngasse, but had not included an apartment number, much to my dismay. I imagined we would have to wait outside the building, introduce ourselves to other party-goers and follow them to the correct apartment. However, much to our surprise, we found on our arrival that 28 Thurngasse was all the information we needed: Herr Maurer owned an entire, newly built, neo-classical six-storey town house. On the ground floor, his butler took our coats and asked us where our costumes were.

'Herr Maurer didn't mention that it was a costume ball,' replied Dolferl.

'Sometimes he tells his guests what kind of party it is, and sometimes he doesn't,' said the man, with a smile. 'No matter,' he continued, 'we have a selection of masks for you to choose from. Follow me,' he said, as he led us to a small pantry off the kitchen.

'The master of the house calls this little alcove our "Fat Tuesday Room",' announced the servant.

A myriad of lavishly coloured papier-maché masks were on offer, some on the counter and some in the open cabinets; profile after profile, ranging from pirates to princesses; heroes to hedonists; noble Greek Gods to devious ghouls; all kinds of birds to all species of beasts; ambiguous harlequins to avaricious harlots. I was amazed that a gentleman such as Herr Maurer, so pragmatic about profit, would invest in such frivolity.

'Ah, the painter and his loyal cohort!' called out Herr Maurer from behind us.

I swung around and beheld our host – though I recognised him only by his voice. Herr Maurer was wearing an oversized Greek tragedy mask: the furrowed brow, the downward-curving eyes, the drooping mouth, all fixed in a permanent expression of sorrow. To complete the illusion, he sported a brightly patterned toga with thick-soled sandals.

'Masks are mandatory,' explained Herr Maurer, through the mask's gaping mouth.

'Masks are for children! For make-believe!' grumbled Dolferl.

'As if you don't live in a world of make-believe,' replied Herr Maurer.

15 See: Appendix 13, Hitler and Sex

'No, sir! I live in a world of ideas!' retorted Dolferl.

'A mask is an idea,' countered Herr Maurer. 'Think of it as an idea that allows you to say and do anything you want amongst strangers who are also posing as ideas. Therefore, everyone and everything is on an equal footing. I find masks allow for a greater exchange of ideas and . . . everything.'

'I don't need any mask to hide behind,' declared Dolferl.

'Then find a mask instead that allows you to become more of who you are,' replied Herr Maurer.

'I have that already,' said Dolferl, pointing to his face. 'I say whatever I want to whomever I want. And I allow that person the privilege of looking me directly in the eye. And sometimes that, my gracious host, is the most effective mask of all.'

At that, Herr Maurer applauded. 'That's why I invited you, my dear friend – such wonderful repartee! Come, come inside! Wear what you want, or don't, as you prefer.'

Herr Maurer turned and walked away.

'Oh, my! I nearly forgot!' called Dolferl. 'Herr Maurer!'

Herr Maurer stopped and looked at us in his mask of sorrow. He propped his hands on his hips as if to ask: 'What now?'

'I brought the proposal with me!' said Dolferl, hurrying after him. 'Let me show you!'

Herr Maurer opened his hands, at a loss for words: this is what I get for inviting an acquaintance made in a hansom cab!

'Everything is outlined perfectly,' pressed Dolferl. 'If you have any questions, this document will certainly answer them.'

Dolferl accompanied the prospective investor up the stairs to the party in the second-floor parlour.

I chose an innocuous harlequin mask with a pink and grey diamond design. I climbed to the top of the stairs, where a white-gloved butler handed me a glass of champagne as I entered the living room, which was filled with laughter and animated conversation.

'Evidently Otto Wagner is obsessed with dominoes, because his buildings look exactly like them!' I heard a female voice say from behind a camel mask.

'Nothing compared to Adolf Loos', answered a Henry VIII mask.

'Tattooing a number on the forearms of gypsies,' said an elephant, 'would make it far easier for the police to identify them, as with automobiles.'

I passed a butler in a gazelle mask, set my empty champagne glass down on his tray and took another.

'Investing in the US? I wouldn't! I hear they're on the verge of another civil war!'

Words, snatches of conversations and fatuities drifted towards me – some carried on waves of opium smoke.

'The women's movement is a sign of progressive decay,' said a rotund man in a buccaneer mask.

A hysterical laugh pealed forth from the face of a guffawing hyena. 'I've never heard it put like that before!'

In the midst of the masks, Dolferl's bare face stood out, even though he was in the corner. As I made my way over to him, I relished the delightful nectar that was good champagne. How could a drink be so subtle? Maybe if I'd had a few glasses of champagne, I wouldn't have been too frightened to approach Francisca that night after the show. Why can't I stop thinking about her? I wondered. There must be something there, even though nothing had happened. But maybe there could be something – that was, if I made it happen.

How could I do that?

I looked around, taking in the bizarre carnival of carpetbaggers, artistes and sophisticates around me. I was mixing with the most scandalous and most envied of Viennese socialites. My goodness, I realised: I was a world away from stuffing sofas in Linz! I was a musician studying in the most vibrant city on earth! The world was opening before me like a flower on the cusp of full bloom! Life would be wonderful – if only Francisca could be mine.

'And what about that melodramatic nonsense you saw in Paris?' asked someone in a mask of sequins and silk.

'Do tell,' urged another, in a ball gown and devil mask.

'It was embarrassing. It's so lightweight, to call it "superficial" would credit it with too much depth.'

The person in the silk and sequined mask recoiled. 'It shows the world just how provincial Paris really is!'

'Don't miss Sergei Diaghilev as long as he's in town!' said a chicken mask.

'I heard it was outrageous!' said a pirate.

'That's certainly not my idea of theatre!' exclaimed ball gown and devil mask, clutching her pearl necklace.

'But at least it's not mere bourgeois trash!' replied a gorilla, emptying his glass.

So many interesting people with so many varied opinions! Battling through the maze of social interaction I gradually made my way over to Dolferl. He was holding the proposal close to his chest.

'Are you all right?' I asked him.

Dolferl shook his head in disgust. 'I feel dirty,' he said, grabbing me by the arm and dragging me after him.

Outside the room, I stopped. 'Where are you going?' I asked.

'Home! Where do you think?'

'I thought you wanted to try and find backers?'

'Don't be ridiculous!' he spat. 'These decadent fools aren't worthy to invest in our masterpiece.' He glared at me. 'Come on. I don't want to tarnish my work or myself by staying here another moment.'

I didn't move.

'Well, are you coming?'

A waiter happened by, so I picked up another glass of champagne.

'I think I'll stay. I'm learning more here than I ever could studying a book,' I said. 'I'm sounding a bit like you, aren't I?'

'I don't slur my words,' retorted Dolferl. And with that, he turned and left.

I returned to the party and merged with the crowd once again. See, all of these people accept me, I thought. Here I am, one of them. If I have the right to fit in with this menagerie, who are Leopold and Herbert to intimidate me? I'm a composer! I'm as much an artist as any of these fools. I laughed, sipped again from my glass and the bouquet wafted up my nose. I was having the most wonderful time here; why couldn't it be the same with Francisca?

I looked at my watch.

Her show had just ended. And now, no doubt, she would be waltzing the night away at the Ballhaus. Why not go there and show her just how cosmopolitan and cultivated I could be?

The paths of Ringstraße were teeming with theatre- and opera-goers, savouring the aftermath of their catharsis. I hummed Beethoven's string quartet. Opus 131, first movement, *adagio ma non troppo e molto espressivo* while my gaze travelled up the Corinthian columns running alongside the façade of the imperial palace. It was Dolferl who had taught me to see these magnificent buildings as music in stone. We often came here to be amongst these great works of art, so that we could transcend our mundane existences. Beethoven's string quartet chimed perfectly with the buildings, especially with the grand entrance of the Burgtheatre. Gottfried Semper – what an architect! What a genius! The opulence all around me eased the yearning in my heart and quieted me.

I was observing how the granite slabs of the pavement were laid out like a chess board when a drunk in a tuxedo barged into me. His monocle popped out. 'Watch where you're going!' he barked at me, before lurching on into the evening. The door through which he had appeared swung closed. It was the main entrance to the Ballhaus.

The music spilled out on to the street, and it suddenly struck me that perhaps it wasn't such a great idea to show up at the Ballhaus and surprise Francisca. Maybe I needed to reconsider. I peered through a window and saw waltzing couples swirl as they rotated around the dance floor. And there, in a corner, I saw her. Leopold was leaning over kissing her hand as she stood with an exaggerated rigidity; then they collapsed into laughter. What heinous torture to be there, where Francisca was dancing the night away! How excruciating; how stupid I felt being here. I was sober and sombre. The champagne had worn off. I turned and made my way home. I looked up at the night sky, willing the hand of God to seize me and carry me off above this Renaissance pile of bricks and stone.

I had expected Dolferl to be sitting on his bed, working feverishly on his latest obsession. I pictured him composing lyrics or designing the set for our opera, blaming me for having wasted my time with champagne and prattle. My feet clattered up the stairs to the third floor. I opened the door of our flat and hurried down the hall to our room.

'Dolferl!' I exclaimed, bursting into the room. 'I owe you an apol – ' The room was dark. He wasn't there. I lit a match, walked over to the lamp and lit the wick. As I turned the dial, the flame grew brighter. I looked around and was stunned: not only was he not there, but his clothes, artwork and books had all disappeared too. I looked at my watch; was it too late to ask Frau Zakreys about this? Just as I turned to go to her room, she appeared in the doorway.

What's going on? my eyes asked.

She shrugged: I don't understand either. She leaned against the door-frame, smoking a black cigarette, wearing a bathrobe with wide-flowing arms and a train, like a bride's on her wedding night.

'He paid his rent for the whole month,' she said, 'and then he left.'

'Where did he go?'

'He didn't say. He just wanted out of here. What did you say to him?'

'Nothing.'

'I worry about him,' she said, flicking her ash on the floor. 'You know how unpredictable he is.'

How very strange, I thought, looking over at Dolferl's stripped bed.[16]

16 See: Appendix 14, Hitler's Disappearance

Dolferl's Disappearance

How was he surviving? Where did he live?

Dolferl had disappeared. He and all his belongings were gone, vanished into thin air as if he had never lived there. I looked out of the window into the night. Why, why, why? Why did he always have to overreact? An innocent word from me, a slip of the tongue could suddenly mushroom into an acrimonious dispute, even a blazing row.

What had I done that was so terrible? Stay at a party when he chose to leave? Did something so trivial warrant such an extreme response? Surely he would come to his senses – he would have to come to his senses! Even he would see how silly he'd been. I imagined him returning, dishevelled, starving and hypersensitive. I would beg him to forgive me, and after much pleading, he would concede. Then all would be right with the world again. But he didn't return.

After a week, I decided to track him down at the Arts Academy. The students' work graced the walls of the hallway leading to the admissions office, impressive still lifes of particularly difficult objects to paint: a thimble, a sculpture of a foot and a goblet of water. There were life studies and landscapes reminiscent of Böcklin, Spitzweg and Makart, the painters Dolferl adored. But there were also attempts at the 'new style' of painting which Dolferl scorned as 'international' and 'perverted'.

'His last name is Hitler, you say?' asked the secretary, as she searched the file cards of students under 'H'. 'Nothing there,' she said, shaking her head. Her bifocals magnified her eyes.

'But he's a student here!' I insisted. 'I was with him when he applied!'

'When was that?'

'Last summer,' I said. 'He applied for the autumn.'

'Well then,' she said, 'perhaps we'll find him there.' She stood up and went to another filing cabinet, pulled out a drawer and started fingering through the files, whispering every surname she passed. 'Ah, here he is!' she exclaimed, with relief. Then: 'Oh – *him!*'

Oh, no! I thought.

'How could I forget? He's quite an angry young man! I've never seen such a hostile response to a rejection.'

'He was *rejected*?'

'Twice,' she confirmed, nodding. 'The first time was last autumn. And two weeks ago he tried again but he wasn't even admitted to the test. He stormed in here, demanding to see the director. She laughed. 'Thankfully our director was able to calm him. He praised his talent for architecture and advised him to become an architect rather than a painter.'

'Do you mean to say he was never a student here?' I asked.

'Never.'

Dolferl had dumbfounded me twice now. He had moved out suddenly without warning, and he had been lying to me for almost a year about being a student of the Academy. In fact, not only had he lied, he had lived his lie daily to give it credibility. How often had he complained about his teachers, and shown me artwork that was supposedly an assignment for class? He had claimed he'd handed in the work and it had been examined by his teachers. But now that I thought of it – something had always seemed amiss. His 'homework' was always in the exact same place. I'd never seen him leave with any completed assignments. At the time, it had seemed as though the work had never left the room: now I knew this was true.

No wonder he could do whatever he wanted, whenever he wanted! No wonder he had accumulated all that random knowledge! Instead of going to the Academy he must have spent all his time in the public libraries, sifting through and researching every facet of his various obsessions. No wonder Dolferl could stay up as late as he wanted to, reading, painting and preaching to me. Now I knew why he could sleep late all those times. He didn't have any morning classes – in fact he didn't have any classes at all. He had fooled me completely.

He was a better actor than Francisca.

But I was not to be deterred: I had to find out where he'd gone. A few days later, I went to the train station and bought a return ticket to Linz.

A green velvet peaked cap with a curved ostrich feather stood on display atop the glass counter. The glower of the woman behind the glass case reminded me of Dolferl's; after all, they had the same father. Angela was his half-sister.

'It's all so strange,' I said. 'I've never known him to run off like this. It's been more than a week!'

'He was here just two-and-a-half weeks ago,' said Angela, matter-of-factly. 'He came to visit his little sister, Paula, and gave her a book, *Don Quixote*. It's very fitting, don't you think? Chasing windmills and all that.' She laughed to herself sadly. 'Chasing windmills, that's exactly what he's doing!' Angela stared directly at me. 'When he visited, he told me he was going to be moving.'

'Moving? He said that? Really?' I was relieved: obviously he had been planning his disappearance for some time, and the costume party had not been the reason for it. 'What else did he tell you?'

'We got into an argument. I told him to come to his senses and get a real job, as our father had wanted.'

'I can imagine his reply.'

'He's still trying to escape reality. I asked him how he was going to make a living as an artist, and tried to pin him down with specifics, but he just grew more and more vague. Then he became moody and quiet, as he does. He just glared at me, like I was the one who was crazy.'

Angela picked up a duster. 'And that just made me more angry. I told him exactly what I thought of his "plans" in no uncertain terms. And then he came over all grand and told me he would contact me once his opera was produced.' She shook her head. 'Paula is eleven years old. Next year she'll go to the lyceum; she needs his part of the orphan's allowance as well. I told him that. But he refused to sign it over to her.'

'His allowance is only twenty-five kronen. You can't exist on that kind of money in Vienna.'

'Is he a pensioner? Who does he think he is?' Angela threw the duster on the counter.

'He must have spent all of his inheritance by now,' I said. 'What's he going to do?'

'Come, now! He's a man, isn't he? What do other men do? They work!'

A bell over the door jingled and a woman in a white coat entered. The hem of her skirt dragged on the floor as she approached the counter. The parakeet-green hat drew her attention and Angela gestured with her hands: please, try it on. She slipped the hat on to her head. It was designed to be worn at a forty-five degree angle, tilted on the head; she smiled as she admired herself in the mirror. Then she slipped the hat off her head and rested it back on the stand.

'I shall consult my husband,' she said, then left and the bells over the door jangled once more.

Again I was alone with Angela. She had the stern bearing of Dolferl's late father, as well as his robust physique. She turned to me. 'Quite frankly, if I hear from Adolf again it will be too soon. He has no feelings, he just fakes them and manipulates others into feeling sorry for him. And once they do, he uses the emotional tie to manipulate them even more. He always tries to control people. But then, if something goes wrong, even if he is clearly responsible, he will deny it. He will always find someone else to blame!' She paused and rearranged a stand with a blue felt hat with black netting, then she turned back at me, her face conveying the unhappiness of her day-to-day life. 'Let me tell you, I didn't expect to be raising my half-sister as well as my own three children, plus working part-time in this shop, while my dear half-brother has nothing better to do than evade his responsibilities.' She sighed. 'If his mother were still around, at least there would be someone else to deal with the situation. She was only forty-seven! Why did she have to die so young . . . '

'Dolferl hasn't been the same since his mother died,' I said. 'He's grown so serious. His humour is full of the darkest sarcasm now.'

'Why didn't you tell him to grow up and get a civil service job?' She threw the duster down hard on the counter. 'It was good enough for his father, but obviously people like you convinced him it wasn't good enough for him!'

'What?' Why was I being attacked? I had come here out of genuine concern. I was taken aback.

'If he had taken a job with the municipal administration here in Linz, he'd have an address and not be destitute!'

'He wants to be an artist! And I honestly think he has it in him. He has the ideas, the inspiration and the talent!'

Angela nodded her head. 'See! There it is! That's exactly what I'm talking about. That kind of talk destroyed him.'

'You know your brother! Do you think I could ever convince him of anything that he would not want for himself?'

'You allowed him to fantasise, but about what? The cities he would redesign? The operas he'll never write? Idle, self-indulgent dreams! The two of you living in one small room, calling each other great artists day and night. What did it get him? Now he's out there somewhere. Adrift!' She gestured out of the store window to the street. 'Out there doing God knows what! All because of you!' Her arms swung widely. 'Real friends watch out for each other.' Her arms knocked over the felt hat and its stand. 'Now look what you've made me do!' She quickly retrieved the hat and put it back in its place.

Clearly she had inherited her father's bitterness. I had already had to endure this kind of abuse from one Hitler; I certainly wasn't going to endure it from another.

'I must be off,' I said. 'If you do hear from your brother, please tell him to contact me. Thank you.' I tipped my head and started retreating. 'Good day.' I turned on my heel and walked away.

'People don't leave the place where they live for no reason at all!' Angela shouted after me.

She was right, but at the time, it had certainly appeared that way.[17]

For weeks I was immersed in confusion. I wandered the streets aimlessly, imagining that Dolferl would be doing the same. I hoped we would encounter each other, that the magnetism of our friendship would draw us back together. But there was no such reunion. Then I decided to be more specific in my approach: where was I most likely to come across my dear friend? Perhaps I might run into him leaving the opera, I thought. So, for many nights during the performance of *Parsifal*, I waited by the entrance. Streams of elegant attendees flowed from the Vienna Court Opera, but, alas, there was no sign of Dolferl. Vienna seemed to have swallowed him up. One night after waiting outside the opera, I was walking home through the rain. The streets had become slick, occasionally making the automobiles lose their grip. And when the drops caught their headlights they twinkled in a glimmering veil. I felt lonely and I was in no mood to go home. If I can't find Dolferl, I thought, I might as well find Francisca. I bit my lip, and without another thought I headed straight for the Ballhaus.

I could hear the walz from outside, strolled through the doors and into the cyclone of jewels, feathers, red lips, white carnations, silk gowns, cigars, tuxedos, clinking glasses and sophisticated laughter. Everyone glittered, laughed, moved, talked, smoked and drank in three-four time. I edged through the intoxicated exuberance, and then caught a glimpse of shimmering red hair. Francisca! Her porcelain shoulders twirled in the middle of the dance floor with a colonel whose rosy complexion gave away his inebriated bliss. The waltz ended and the uniformed man bowed to Francisca's curtsey. She floated over to what looked like her usual assortment of friends. As I headed towards her, she took a seat but then she noticed me and rose again in surprise, emptying her champagne.

17 See: Appendix 15, The Hitler Family

'So there you are!' she exclaimed.

'You remember me?'

'Don't be silly! I've missed you. Didn't you want to come and see our play?'

'I did see it.'

'Well,' she said, with a little colour arising in her cheeks. 'Didn't you like it?'

'Oh, you were magnificent.'

Her face relaxed and glowed.

'You outshone – what's his name?'

'Alceste,' she said.

'Yes, that's it. You carried the play!'

'Let me tell you,' she said, 'you're not the only one of my friends to tell me that.'

My heart quickened. I was one of 'her friends'.

She tilted her head and then, in a sudden flash of insecurity, asked, 'are you just saying that? Or do you really mean it?'

'I mean it. I mean it! You were wonderful.'

A smile appeared briefly on her face, then her lips pursed, her head tilted again and she regarded me with questioning eyes. 'So why did I have to wait so long to hear this? Why didn't you tell me on the night?'

'I wanted to, but I didn't want to call on you unannounced.'

'Please,' she groaned. 'Why are you Austrians so complicated? Or is it just the Viennese?'

I shrugged bashfully.

She saw my blushing face. 'I'm from Munich,' she said. 'We Bavarians aren't so proper. We're much more at ease.'

Then she laughed, and everything about her relaxed.

'You laugh beautifully.'

'Perhaps you should try smiling at least.'

'I can't,' I said. 'It takes too many muscles.'

'No, it doesn't,' she said. 'Silly,' she added, like a teasing friend. Or a lover.

As the music launched into a waltz Francisca took my hand.

I shook my head. 'I'm not good at . . . '

'Come on! You're from Vienna!'

'Actually, I'm from Linz.'

'OK, OK!' She tugged at my hand.

'But I can't!'

'You're a musician. You can keep time.'

'Well, of course.'

'That's all that matters.'

'But – '

'I'll lead,' she said, swinging me around. 'Just follow me.'

'But – '

'Look like you're the one in control,' she said. 'No one need ever know.' I straightened my back and held her hand. 'I'm so clumsy at this,' I insisted.

'Just relax,' she replied, with a sly twinkle in her eye.

Her hand guided my back, and together we launched into a series of rotations, around and around the other dancers: *Oom-pah-pah, oom-pah-pah.*

'You're doing fine,' she encouraged me. 'Now let's weave through the crowd and remember, nobody else knows what they're doing either. It doesn't matter, just waltz!'

I smiled.

'Having fun?' she queried.

Dolferl had once compared the waltz to horses on a merry-go-round, rotating, rising and dipping. He had said it was for children, not grown men. Satin skirts swished by me and perfume and music wafted around us and the other rotating couples.

'Are you having fun now?' she asked again.

'Yes,' I said, this time with more conviction.

'I thought you were an artist!'

'Yes, so?'

'Artists create cheerful moments like these.'

'I think artists have a more important duty. I believe that the artist's role is to create an über-reality. And what I mean by über-reality is . . .' I could see recognition in her face, so I stopped short.

'I remember what your friend meant by that,' she said, with a sly little smile.

'Well, that spares me a lot of explaining,' I said, feeling like an exposed fraud. 'But none of that matters. I have to return to Linz anyway.'

'To Linz? Why?'

'Well . . .' I sighed. I looked around at the ballroom of spinning dancers and chandeliers. 'I have to go back there and fix armrests.'

'My God,' she said, as if it meant eternal damnation; which, in a sense, it did.

'My father is an upholsterer.'

'But you're an artist! You said you were studying at the Conservatory!'

'I still am. But my family wants me to come home.'

'I understand. I'm in a similar situation.'

'You are?'

'My father owns a hotel back home in Munich, and I can't tell you how many times he's begged me to "come to my senses" and work for him.'

'So what do you say to him?'

'I tell him that performing my art is the only way I can exist; the only way I *will* exist.'

'I don't think I'm as lucky as you,' I said. 'I just can't afford Vienna. Dolferl, my roommate, has left, and the rent is just – '

'You're going to throw your art away because of – that?'

'Maybe it's just not meant to be. Fate has worked against me.'

'Nonsense. You have to believe in yourself, that's the only thing that matters.'

'That's what Dolferl says.'

We smiled.

'Fate can work for you,' she said, 'just as easily. This is Vienna. Anything can happen!'

We were still in the middle of the dance floor.

'Let me think . . .' she said.

'About what?'

'Can you play the organ?'

'Well, a little Bach.'

'Do you know the "Ave Maria"?'

'I could learn it in a morning.'

'Then we've solved your problem.'

We moved out of the inner circle and drifted towards the periphery of the dancers. Francisca looked around the room. 'I know she's here somewhere.'

'Who?'

'Erica.'

Her eyebrows rose. 'There she is!' Francisca clasped my hand as our dance came to a halt and we walked around the dance floor to an elegant elderly woman. A red feathery hat rested in Erica's grey hair. She had the friendly face of a camel and was drinking a *Fledermaus*, the latest Viennese cocktail.

'Erica,' called Francisca, leaning over so the woman could hear her better. 'Erica, I think we've found the church an organist.'

'Oh! Is he good?' she asked.

'He's a student at the Conservatory.'

Erica smiled. 'That's good enough for me. I'm friends with the director of the Conservatory, Igor Stringbrod.' Erica took a sip of her *Fledermaus*. 'Igor runs a very tight ship,' she continued, 'he turns out one great musician after another. So am I right to assume that your young friend . . .'

'Martin,' said Francisca.

'Martin,' Erica said, looking at me, 'am I correct in presuming you are also a great musician?'

I was about to say, 'I hope to be . . .' but Francisca cut in again. 'Oh, he is! I've heard him! He's wonderful.'

I was touched she was willing to lie so readily for me. Vienna is wonderful, I thought. I love Vienna!

Every Sunday I now played the organ and on numerous Sundays after the mass I would visit Francisca at Villa Erica. We would sit in the parlour having tea, and sometimes sherry, with Lady Erica, discussing our art and our ideals. Lady Erica would often talk about her deceased husband, for whom she would pine for the rest of her days. Every widow's anecdote felt to me like a prompt to propose to Francisca, but as much as I wanted to, it simply wasn't feasible: after all, I was only a music student. Lady Erica had just finished talking yet again about the day her husband had died, and was awash with emotion. Reliving the trauma had left her torn between reaching for her handkerchief or her sherry.

Here I was, my attention forcibly drawn to Lady Erica, when all I wanted was to be alone with Francisca. Why couldn't we find our own private sanctuary, even for just a moment? I had to get Francisca alone, so we could talk without anyone else around. Just the two of us. I had to tell her how I felt without anyone else interrupting. I settled on my humble quarters. It wasn't quite as luxurious as Lady Erica's parlour, but it provided the tranquillity I needed to tell her what I had to say. Yes, I wanted to be with Francisca for the rest of my life. I needed to tell her that I would propose to her eventually, even if I couldn't officially propose to her that day – it would be months before I could save up for a ring . . .

Frau Zakreys strictly enforced a third-floor house rule at Stumpergasse 31, forbidding young ladies from visiting a male tenant's room. However, a rare opportunity presented itself when I learned that Frau Zakreys would be attending a Sunday afternoon christening: I could finally invite

Francisca to my room. Francisca provided some supportive assistance as well, lying to Lady Erica that she had to attend an emergency Sunday rehearsal, to 'break in' a replacement for another cast member leaving the play. Such duplicity was a tawdry but necessary device to enable us to meet in private, so we could be honest with one another, away from the prying eyes of the world. Finally, I could get down on one knee and pose the question my heart had been longing to ask for months.

While playing the organ helped me to survive, with Dolferl gone, I could no longer afford both the room and the piano rental, so with a heavy heart, I had bid farewell to the baby grand. Consequently, the small room now seemed spacious to me. On Sunday morning, I washed the window sills and panes, scrubbed the floor, and swept the cobwebs from the ceiling corners. After hearing Frau Zakreys leave the building, I waited for five minutes and then went to a flower shop where I bought a bunch of lilacs, hoping their fragrance would mask the odour of kerosene that permeated the room. I didn't have any vases, so I had to improvise with some of Schrobner's empty vodka bottles from the rubbish bin.

'It smells like a garden in here!' remarked Francisca as she stepped in to the room. Precisely the effect I wanted. She doffed her blue bonnet and set it down on the table by a vodka bottle with a bunch of purple buds. She smiled at the flowers and their impromptu vase, taking her overcoat off her shoulders. She then turned around slowly, taking in my abode.

'But how in the Lord's name did you fit a piano in here?'

'And it was a grand piano!'

'My goodness, a grand piano in such a small place?' she asked, turning around again.

'It was cramped, but we had to make do.'

'I forgot there were two of you in here!' She shook her head. 'How did you do it?' She walked to the window and looked out on the squalid courtyard.

'When you live for your art, you can put up with anything,' I said.

'I couldn't live here, not at my – ' Francisca was about to say 'age', but she caught herself in time. She was older than me by at least five years. Maybe even ten. 'Not in my *situation*,' she corrected, smiling quickly. One day I'll have to ask her how old she is, I thought. But now was not the time.

'Please have a seat,' I said, pointing to the bed. I had covered it with one of Frau Zakreys' spreads so it looked more like a sofa.

'It's a shame that the piano is gone,' she said, sitting down. 'I would have loved to hear you play something non-religious for me.'

Francisca had only heard me play at the High Mass, which she attended regularly with Lady Erica.

'Well, there are other things to do,' I said, as I opened the window and retrieved a bottle of wine that had been cooling on the outside ledge.

'Oh, marvellous!' said Francisca, opening her handbag. 'I happened to bring a little treat that goes wonderfully with a Veltliner.' She fished around for a few seconds and brought out a wrapped handkerchief, unfolding it to reveal some brown paste. I sat next to her and uncorked the bottle as she put some of the tar into a tiny brass pipe. She struck a match and placed the pipe to her lips, inhaled and closed her eyes. The sweet, incense-like aroma of the opium mingled with the perfume of the lilacs. Her closed eyelids fluttered, then flicked open.

I passed her a glass of wine. She giggled as she passed me the pipe.

'I've never . . .' I started to say.

'Just inhale and hold it in. Almost swallow the smoke,' she said.

I put the pipe in my mouth and did as being told.

I coughed.

Francisca smiled: that's to be expected. 'Try again,' she said. She lit the match for me and I inhaled again. I looked at her hand as she held the match over the pipe and was captivated by her slender ivory fingers. As the paste began to glow again, she removed the lit match.

This time I held the smoke in longer. It was sweet and delicious.

Never before had my little hovel seemed so luxurious. Everything seemed to be in its place. Everything radiated. Our movements were like a masterfully choreographed dance.

'Well, this is our little rebellion, isn't it?' she said. 'I don't know if Lady Erica would approve.'

'Dolferl definitely wouldn't,' I said.

'But he's such a free-thinker,' said Francisca, in a syrupy voice.

'Only if you agree with him,' I replied.

We laughed.

I mocked Dolferl's stern face. ' "Rodin is a great artist," ' I mimicked in Dolferl's sternest voice. ' "Almost as great as me!" '

'You're fantastic!' she exclaimed, clapping her hands enthused. 'How about this?' She got up, raised her brows and pointed to the ceiling. ' "All kisses must be transcendent!" '

' "And monumental!" I added with Dolferl's voice.

We laughed and she let herself fall on to the bed. Life is wonderful, I thought: here she was, next to me, my dream and my reality having merged. I turned to her and was drawn into the whirlpool of her red lips, and suddenly I was kissing her; tasting her.

I kissed her because I was so much in love with her. I kissed her because it was my way of expressing my intention, an overture of my marriage proposal. I kissed her because she was the woman of my life. I forgot, and she forgot. We wrapped around one another, two exquisite beasts ravishing each other with lips and tongues, yearning to merge. She undid the top of my shirt as I opened the buttons that ran down the back of her blouse. Suddenly my fingers stopped: this is wrong! This is so wrong, whispered my conscience. Marriage is sacred. Only after our wedding could I bed her. I looked at her. Could this be right?

She pressed a finger to my mouth. 'Come on . . .' she urged gently and as if by itself my hand went to her back and inside her blouse.

I heard a slamming door.

Frau Zakreys!

I froze. I looked Francisca in the eye: she's back!

Our lips and our bodies so close; yet we couldn't go any further.

Frau Zakreys stamped down the hall.

I understand, Francisca's green eyes said.

I was frustrated, yet relieved: fate had elevated me beyond my animal spirits. No mortal sin would tarnish my soul today.

We spoke in whispers.

'I'll go to Frau Zakreys' room and distract her,' I said, 'while you slip out.'

It was logical and simple.

I walked up the hall as Francisca waited to make her escape.

November 1909, Vienna, Brigittenau

There was something wrong with the church organ, it was emitting hoarse gasps rather than notes. The pastor knew of an instrument repair shop which might be able to help. It was in the Brigittenau district: warehouses, foundries and factories peppered with residential pockets: a gloomy consequence of the Industrial Age. It was raining, so I stayed close against the walls of the houses on Wallensteinstraße as I walked. The air stank of lard and tanned leather. People with sullen faces trudged down the street, past dimly-lit shops and half-empty taverns. The brick houses along the street leaned into each other, barely standing after another hard day of existence. Behind their walls, six to eight people would be cooking, washing and sleeping in one room. Some people rented out space on their bed to complete strangers; others lived in the sewage system. People whose eyes reflected the day-to-day torment of poverty had wrapped themselves in rags to protect against the wind and the sleet. These were the people who had fled the poverty in the rural regions of the Empire and had come to Vienna for a better life, labourers with nothing to show for their hard work but their callused hands; and yet, their children were playing with delight in the time before dinner. They threw frozen horse dung as they chased each other, squealing in some Slavic tongue.

The organ shop was in a nondescript three-storey building. On the first floor there was a printworks. To get to the stairwell that led to the repair shop, I had to walk across a warehouse which was imbued with the odour of ink.

De-chugga, de-chugga, groaned the printing press. I covered my ears to protect against the deafening noise. *De-chugga, de-chugga.*

On the other side of the hulking black iron monster I noticed a skinny figure with a full beard picking up paper scraps by a cutting machine. As the man moved between the machine and a rubbish bin, it struck me that there was something familiar about him – was it his walk? A nimble gait that could easily navigate the narrow space between our grand piano and his bed . . .

Could it be him?

'*Dolferl!*' I shouted.

De-chugga, de-chugga.

He didn't hear me and disappeared behind the printing press.

De-chugga, de-chugga.

I couldn't run over to him. The printing machinery was between us.

Dechugga, de-chugga.

I saw the man go to a locker and take out a coat, and then an umbrella, which I instantly recognised. It was an extravagant purchase bought with his mother's inheritance, made of blue and black silk with a bronze handle. It was definitely him. Dolferl with a full beard!

De-chugga, de-chugga.

'*Dolferl!*' I yelled, as loud as I could.

But he couldn't hear me. He was speaking to a man wearing a leather apron.

De-chugga, de-chugga.

I decided to time my calls to coincide with the lulls in the machine noise. '*Dolferl!*

Neither the man with the apron nor Dolferl heard me. Their ears were probably deafened by the constant noise.

De-chugga, de-chugga.

Dolferl walked away from the man and disappeared behind another iron monster.

De-chugga, de-chugga.

I wanted to run over and catch him. But to get to him, I had to work my way through a labyrinth of printing stock and machines.

Dechugga, de-chugga.

I saw him head towards the side entrance, oblivious to my shouts.

He opened the door to the street, and was gone.

De-chugga, de-chugga.

I ran around another colossal machine and past the man with the apron until I finally reached the door through which Dolferl had left. I opened it and saw him shielding himself against the sleet with his broken umbrella.

I had come far from the centre of town to this desolate area and I wasn't going to give up so readily. I ran as fast as I could, my clothes soaked with rain. I looked ahead at my friend as he hurried on down the dimly lit street with his tattered umbrella; my lungs ached and I felt piercing stitches in the sides. Clearly I was no long-distance runner.

'*Dolferl,*' I called out through the rain and the sleet. But he didn't hear me.

I paused, panting heavily, and glimpsed him catching the first of two horsedrawn trams. With my last ounce of strength, I managed to make it on to the second tram.

The coach rocked from side to side. People sat or stood, stupefied in their exhaustion. All they did was work, sleep and eat. They were too resigned and too apathetic to dream. I fought my way through their midst battling against the stench of perspiration and camphor. The rain had soaked people's overcoats and rugs, releasing the pungent odour of mothballs. When I reached the front end of the carriage, I saw the other tram stop. Should I jump out? Would I make it in time to get to the other tram before it moved on? I decided that I was still too exhausted, so I waited for the next stop. The rain pounded against the trolley's roof. Through the window, I could see Dolferl in the tram in front. How was he surviving? Where did he live? Unskilled labourers had to work ten hours a day, including weekends to afford a room. Did Dolferl go to the shelters, where hundreds waited in rows for hours to get a roof over their heads for the night?

Our horses halted. The people standing in the aisle leaned forwards and then teetered back. Now would be the chance to jump out, but the instant I decided to jump, Dolferl's tram moved off. Better wait; conserve my energy. For endless minutes, our tram stubbornly refused to move on. People were getting on and off, and I was asking myself whether I should have at least tried to get on to the other tram. Finally we began to move again. I was praying that we would catch up when I saw the other tram stop in the distance, and watched Dolferl jump out.

'*Dolferl!*' I screamed, knowing full well that he couldn't hear me.

He jumped into another horse-drawn tram, which promptly took off.

'*Dolferl!*' I screamed again.

He was gone.

I returned to the printing press and spoke to the foreman. He told me that Dolferl had been a 'day labourer' hired for that one day only. He was too feeble a worker to ever be hired again. He didn't know where Dolferl lived.

That was it.

That was it for Dolferl.

That was it for me.

Playing music was, for me, what praying must be like for most people. Dolferl would call it 'making contact with the will'. To me it was all the same. Music was my true spirit, my *raison d'être*. It was the only way I knew to exist. Music was what Dolferl and I had in common. He had said that music allowed him to experience emotional peaks without the elements of normal life that caused suffering. He had never admitted it, but I knew that this notion was a concept he had adopted from Schopenhauer. The difference between Dolferl and me was that he strove to isolate himself from that 'everyday emotional life'. He had set out to find a way to attain what his beloved Schopenhauer had said was impossible: a state of mind where all suffering had ceased. While he acted as if he willingly accepted pain and suffering, I knew this was not the case; I had been there when he descended into his depressions.

I sat down at the organ, which had been repaired since I had seen Dolferl five months ago in the printworks. It was a masterpiece of musical instrumentation: it suited the Rococo church with its curving red marble pillars supporting the gilt canopy over the altar. Legions of angels were painted on the ceiling, flying like a flock of birds upward to the heavens that awaited those who still believed in a God, despite what Kant, Marx, Schopenhauer, Nietzsche and all the others were saying. I played the processional, with all of my fingers pressing down on the keys, my feet on the pedals, the horn pegs extended, the resonating pipes emulating a celestial brass, and as always, it was other-worldly. But once the priest entered the chancel and turned to the congregation, my music had to stop, It was 20 April 1910, Dolferl's twenty-first birthday, and once again I sat wondering what I was doing here in this church. I hadn't set out to be an organist. Granted, it was better than stuffing couches, but this wasn't who I really wanted to be, who I really was.

The priest droned on and on. As a child, I would always daydream during the sermon, and now I found myself doing the same thing as an adult. When Dolferl and I were altar boys at Lambach, our eyes would drift between the images on display in the church. The spear puncturing Christ's side, Jesus whipped and nailed, Jesus suffering wounds and bruises, his hands and feet bleeding. All of it so mysterious. And then the Easter procession; with masses of people, with flags, with fanfares, with holy blessings and sacred prayers. All of it so powerful – larger than anything in the world to us then. The reading was followed, as ever, by the Ave Maria, the paean to women everywhere. I finished with a triumphant flourish.

What's it like to be with a woman? I wondered.

I thought of that Sunday afternoon with Francisca in my room. So many Sundays had passed since then, and there had not been a chance for a second encounter; Frau Zackreys had never left the flat for more than a few hours. And even if she had, I wasn't sure if I had the nerve to ask Francisca again. Did she love me, or was it more pity? Was I making her happy or unhappy? Why did she like me at all? She was a beautiful woman with a career and all those friends. What did I have to offer? I was nothing in comparison. And then my thoughts turned to the troubling enigma that was Dolferl.

Where was he?

Would I ever see him again?

I peered over my shoulder and saw that the last old lady had left. I closed the organ cover and walked down the steps to the main floor; and there, in the back pew, was Francisca. A black lace veil was draped over her hair. I walked down the aisle and slid into the pew. Gingerly, I stroked the back of her neck: relax. She stared at me coolly. Something was wrong.

'What's the matter?' I whispered.

I put my arm around her shoulders; she tilted her head away from me and frowned: take your arm off me. Maybe her 'monthlies', I thought.

'What is it?' I asked.

'You . . .' she said. 'You make me sad.'

'What do you mean?'

'I never feel as though you're really with me. You say you love me . . .'

'I do love you!'

'Why don't I believe you, then?' she said. 'There's something missing. And I wish you'd tell me what it is.'

'You know what's missing,' I mumbled, more to myself than to her. I was convinced that we wouldn't be having this discussion if Frau Zakreys hadn't come home earlier than expected that day.

'There's something going on inside you,' she said, 'I can sense it,'

'Everything's great,' I said, in my most natural voice.

'It doesn't sound "great".' She groaned. Her eyes said: I know anyway. Just be a man and tell me.

'I miss my friend.' I had finally said it aloud.

'Why?'

'A big part of me left when he left,' I tried to explain. 'I haven't written a note in months. There hasn't been a hint of a melody; I don't even hum to myself.'

I could see from her face that she didn't understand.

'He inspired me.'

Her eyebrows arched: and I don't?

'When I'm with him every moment is meaningful and exciting.'

'And I dull your senses?' she snapped. 'Is that it?'

'No! Not at all!' I replied quickly. 'I'm not talking about you, I'm talking about him: our project, our opera! He had so many ideas, and such energy. It inspired me.'

Francisca sat hunched over in the pew. She shook her head sadly: Why can't he let *me* be his muse?

'It's not your fault,' I said. 'It's me! The artist in me. Maybe that person is gone.'

'Just because your friend is no longer around?'

I covered my eyes with my hands. I didn't know what to say.

'Well,' she said, 'I have some news that will cheer you up,'

I took my hands off my eyes: Tell me!

'Erica and I have been talking . . . And we've arranged something on your behalf.'

I instantly thought of another church scenario: a parish wants someone to play the organ during Vespers.

'What is it?' I asked, in a dour voice.

'We want you to give a little recital at her villa. You know, her drawing room is quite famous.'

'Yes, I remember you telling me that.'

'Well, Erich Mahler is attending in a fortnight.'

I shook my head in disbelief. 'Erich Mahler? The cousin of Gustav . . .?'

'That's right,' she said, with a smile. 'The music critic.'

I jumped up from the pew. 'This is just too marvellous!' I exclaimed. I was already thinking that I'd play my own composition, *Rage to Joy*, and for variety, perhaps, Beethoven's Sonata No.23 in F Minor.

Her eyes sparkled: this is your chance of a lifetime, and only I can offer it to you – not him.

I had to make amends to Francisca. Tonight was the recital, and I wanted to give her a small token of my appreciation; a book perhaps, something that reflected the depth of my feelings for her.

I knew of an antiquarian bookshop on Liebgasse which I thought might have the ideal gift: a symbol of my sincerity and my passion at an affordable price.

Entering the 'Hermetic Chest' was like entering a wizard's study – a wizard who didn't bother ordering his broom to clean. Fine particles of dust covered the books in the cramped shop. The place smelled of mildew and the low ceiling was oppressive, but it was the one place to find books you couldn't chance upon anywhere else in town. When I had opened the door, the bells had jingled but the clerk didn't look up. He sat at the counter reading a book. Behind the clerk, on the wall, hung an intricately embroidered green silk cloth. Geometric forms were woven into one another and formed two red swastikas, one facing to the left and the other to the right.

'What can I do for you?' asked the clerk, slowly as if his mind were still in another dimension. He was bald and bespectacled.

'I'm looking for a book for a young lady.' I said.

'How nice,' he said, closing his eyes. 'Is this gift a token of apology or appreciation?'

'Both,' I said. 'Like the two spinning symbols behind you.'

'Ah yes, the swastikas. The right and the left. Yin and Yang. It's the balance we all seek,' he said with a little laugh. 'So you want to show this girl that you're really a caring and thoughtful young man?' His eyes had remained closed for the entire conversation so far.

'Yes,' I said.

'I suggest you look over on the left side of the shop, the stacks next to the periodicals.'

I glanced over the pile of books next to the astrology, health, and spiritual magazines. Many of them related to '*Lebensreform*', a protest and decampment movement promoting a healthier and more natural lifestyle.

I noticed a stack of Hans Goldzier publications, the bizarre philosopher Dolferl had often mentioned. Dolferl's affinity for academic renegades made all the more sense now that I knew he had failed his entrance exams to the academy. *Ostara* was one of the many Pan-German periodicals Dolferl read. Few newsstands carried it, and the ones that did usually stacked it with the children's magazines. Dolferl had once shoved a copy into my hand, proclaiming that 'This magazine will open your eyes.' Its headline read: 'Are you blond? Then you are a creator and guardian of culture. Are you blond? Then you are in danger.' The article was illustrated with drawings comparing the noses and ears of different races. It also included a rabid editorial about the link between race and morality. Another column preached that Negroes and Mongolians would rob Germanic women of their virtue. I had been stunned that Dolferl, an ardent rationalist who read Auguste Compte and Ernst Haeckel, would give any credence to such irrational, simplistic drivel. 'Once you relate *Ostara*'s ideas to giants like Darwin and Schopenhauer, it all fits,' he had replied.

As I browsed through the books, something familiar caught my eye: *Legends of Gods and Heroes: the Treasures of Icelandic Mythology*. What a coincidence! I thought: the third publication that reminded me of my lost friend. I picked it up, and opened it; there was a bookplate pasted on the end page which read '*Ex Libris*' in print between oak branches and an eagle, and there, scrawled in pencil beneath, was 'A. Hitler', the last three letters trailing downward like an un-spooling ribbon.

'Where did you get this?' I asked the old man, pointing to the book.

'It's from a collection,' he said. 'There's what's still left of it.' He pointed towards a stack of books to my right.

I opened one book, then another, and then another. They all had Dolferl's bookplate. This was his library, from Hans Hörbiger to David Hume to Seneca to Gobineau to Herbert Spencer!

His books! The most sacred of all his belongings. To think he would ever sell his most prized possessions for money! Money, of all things – something he always scorned.

'How . . . ? Who . . . ?' I stammered.

'You want to know who sold them to me?' asked the clerk.

'Yes.'

'Why do you ask?'

'These books belonged to a friend of mine. We used to live together, and one day he just disappeared. Without leaving an address, without saying anything, and without any reason.'

'When was that?'

'Seven months ago.'

'I understand.'

'But how? I certainly don't.'

'I can see why he took such a drastic step.'

'How could you possibly know?'

'From the kind of books he was reading at the time.'

'You mean, these books told him to abandon his home and his friend from one day to the next?'

'It's an old practice.'

'What kind of practice is that, exactly?'

'Leaving your past behind.'

I didn't know what to say.

'Your personal history,' the clerk continued. 'Your friends, your surroundings, your job, the social class you belong to . . . Everything.'

'Why would anyone do such a thing?'

'It's a very important step on the way to – '

'To what?'

'Enlightenment.' The old man smiled. 'Once you've shed your past, you can seize the present moment. Every shaman goes through that practice.'

'Dolferl a *shaman*? That's ridiculous! There isn't anyone I know who considers himself rational like Dolferl. A scientist, yes; but a shaman? That's ludicrous!'

'People change. Shamans especially. They're sometimes called shape-shifters.'

I shook my head in disagreement. 'He was rejected by the Academy of the Arts, and he knew I'd find out. That's why he left.'

'If that's what you believe . . . '

'Can you tell me where I can find him?'

'Normally I wouldn't tell you. When someone makes the decision to cut their ties to a world they no longer belong to, that is solely that person's business and nobody else's.'

'Could you please make an exception?' I begged.

'I might. I can see that you care about your friend. And to tell you the truth, I fear for him.'

'Why?'

''You may not know this' – the old man gestured towards the books around us – 'but I specialise in books about the occult sciences. There is a time when these books are extremely helpful to the disciple. But there are also times when they do more harm than good. They may actually become a danger – to your spiritual wellbeing.'

'What's happening to him?'

'He's alone. And that isn't doing him any good.'

'Can you tell me where to find him?'

The Sorcerer's Apprentice

Many are called. Few are chosen

Meldemannstraße 27 had recently been whitewashed. It was one of the few better-maintained buildings in a district where run-down factories and warehouses with broken windows dominated the neighbourhood. There was an air of resignation throughout the entire district, making the six-storey men's hostel all the more noticeable. In the afternoon sun, it appeared as if the building was striving to set an example for its inhabitants. It was modest but clean and functional, with no frills; austere, yet with an unspoken dignity. I was about to enter when a skeletal man in a bathrobe stopped me. 'Too late, we're already full up for the night.'

'I . . . I'm looking . . .' I stuttered.

'The shelter is full for the night,' he repeated.

'I'm looking for a friend,' I said. He jerked open the door, and a gust of disinfectant wafted out. 'Go and find him yourself.'

The hall was a once-pristine white that had turned a sickly yellow over the years. The air was enriched with an assortment of odours that ranged from garlic to disinfectant to talcum powder. At the empty reception a sign read: '30 kreuzer per night'. Not expensive; but still, an unskilled worker had to work hard every day to be able to afford this and groceries as well. On the main floor there were two reading rooms, one for smokers and one for non-smokers. Daily newspapers hung on the wall and books were stacked in racks: popular novels and writings on popular science, that gave this clean, meagre room a certain bourgeois feel. Run-down aristocrats, failed tradesmen and casual workers were writing letters or engaging in games of chess, draughts and dominoes. I passed four men who were seated around a table and overheard their conversation as I passed.

'I don't know why Franz Joseph didn't kill the Empress sooner!'

'Who said he killed her?'

'If your wife adored Heinrich Heine, you'd kill her too!' They laughed and someone playing solitaire at another table shushed them.

I climbed the main staircase to the second floor which was sectioned off into cubicles by wooden partitions. There were no doors, just curtains. Each space had a bed, a table and a small closet. Some of the cubicles at the perimeter had a window, the others were windowless. But they all had an electric light bulb in the ceiling: state-of-the-art. I poked my head through a curtain and caught a glimpse of a swarthy, muscled man sleeping on his cot. The creases in his face and hands were lined with soot, and the air reeked of a full day's work. It was early in the evening and already his snores indicated that he was in a deep, deep sleep. In another cubicle, there was a man pasting matchsticks to make model ships, to be put into glass bottles.

'Full house,' said a man with blotchy skin to his tatooed opponent as they sat in their underwear playing cards on a bed.

I peeked into another room and caught my breath. Was that him? It was! I could only see his profile as he was bent over beside his bed. He looked like a biblical figure: his full-grown beard was bushy, and his lank hair extended down to his shoulders. It was as if I was seeing him in a dream, where the mind alters well-known people in obscure, incongruous ways. I was taken aback by his dishevelled state but so relieved that I had finally found my friend. He was in his underwear, bringing out a pair of blue chequered trousers from under the mattress and checking them: they were pressed and clean but bleached. Then, with one hand, he changed his underpants while pulling his undershirt down past his knees with his other hand, rigorously concealing his privates, even from himself – a manoeuvre I knew well from Stumpergasse 31. Once his trousers were buttoned, I knocked on the wall. He jumped.

'Dolferl . . .' I said.

He turned, and his face blushed with mortification that he had been seen changing.

'It's rude to spy on people!' he exclaimed. 'Turn around!'

I did as I was told.

'What do you want?' he said. 'I put the past behind me. Completely.'

'I saw you some time ago,' I said. 'You were working at that print shop.'

He didn't respond. I turned around to face him. My eyes scanned him from top to bottom as he stood there, resolute and barefoot, changing into a shirt. By Dolferl's ankle I spotted the horsewhip: his father's tool of punishment and power. If the clerk at the bookstore had been right, and Dolferl had shed his old skin, as it were, what was he doing with this keepsake that had so tortured his past?

'What's this?' I asked, quickly picking up the horsewhip. 'Isn't this a memento from Linz?'

His eyes narrowed and he tore the whip from me. 'That belongs to me!'

'My apologies,' I said, as I noticed paintings on his bed. 'My God! They're beautiful!' There were drawings of the Court Opera, Ringstraße, Vienna City Hall and Auersburg Palace. They were executed with skilled accuracy, every brick and every crevice radiating conviction and precision. This new work was definitely a departure from his earlier, clumsier drawings. 'Honestly,' I said, 'this is your best work.'

My praise immediately defused the tension. 'Thank you,' said Dolferl. 'I've also been working on my plans for the concert hall and the observatory for Linz,' he said, kneeling down and pulling more artwork out from under the bed. He shoved the drawings of Linz's new Centre For The Arts in front of me: sweeping white buildings with columns.

'I was inspired by the Acropolis.'

'No doubt,' I answered.

'Have you noticed how I refined the lines?'

'Absolutely,' I said, as I marvelled at his greatly improved draughtsmanship.

'I do the watercolours purely for money. But these drawings are clearly where my genius lies,' he said. He smiled. 'I'm an architect as well as a painter.'

His new beard. His new hairstyle. His new work.

'You have changed,' I said. 'It's revolutionary. I'll have to get to know you all over again.'

'You can't. You'll always be stuck in the past. But I've taken a critical step.'

'How so?'

'I know I'm on the right path now.'

'You've certainly become a better artist!'

'I no longer have to become anything. I am who I am. Therefore I am.'

On his bedside table, I spotted a book with the title *The All-Seeing Eye*. Next to me on the floor there were more books. I picked up some of them, glancing through the titles. *Agartha – The Hollow Earth*, *Amulet and Superstition*, *Sexual Magic*, *Isis Unveiled*, *Ancient Wisdom*, *The Secret of the Runes* – I felt like I was back in the Hermetic Chest. I was baffled. Here I was sitting with someone who had preached that all meaning came from reason and intellect alone. And now this most fervent of rational thinkers was studying *alchemy*! My shock must have been evident.

'In almost any book,' said Dolferl, as if reading my mind, 'there is something worth retaining. A man who possesses the skill of correct reading can immediately and instinctively filter that out.' I wondered what he was searching for in this array of books.

Dolferl lit a candle. He then lifted up one of his drawings and held it over the flame, rotating it slowly: yellowing it; ageing it. 'The tourists like it better that way,' he said.

On his night desk, there was a stack of papers with handwritten notes. I picked up a paper and started to read.

'Hands off!' he yelled.

I was surprised; I had always been allowed to study his writings before – in fact, he had been insulted if I didn't show any interest. But now he quickly snatched the paper from my hands.

'What is it?' I asked, perplexed.

'It's a book I'm writing.'

'You're writing another manuscript?' I asked. This wasn't his first: in Stumpergasse he had started to work on a short story, a play about Christian monks colonising Bavaria and a drama about the Spanish painter Bartolome Murillo. After a while he had abandoned all of these projects.

Dolferl remained silent as he put the paper back on the stack.

'What's it about?' I enquired.

'Religion.' Dolferl sat down on the bed.

I was about to ask Dolferl why he had left our apartment in Stumpergasse so suddenly, and why he had lied to me about attending the academy, when the stench of a sweating absinthe-drinker pervaded the air. I turned and saw a man with a red tartan shirt and green striped trousers.

'Oh, sorry,' said the man, with exaggerated politeness. 'I didn't know you had a visitor.' I was instantly suspicious of him. 'My name is Walter Fritz,' he continued, turning towards me.

I shook the man's hand and immediately wanted to wash mine. Dolferl stood up, his legs braced, as if anchoring himself to the floor. He stared at the man combatively.

'Where's my money?' snarled Dolferl.

'Look at that,' the man said, turning to me, 'this is how he speaks to an old pal. I'm his best and only friend in here, and all he's interested in is money.'

'I demand that you pay what you owe me!' barked Dolferl.

'What?' the man said, in mock surprise. His jaw dropped exposing gaps between his yellow teeth. 'I'm the one who brought him here,' he said to me. 'I taught him how to make a living from his art. Without me he'd still be on the streets.' He turned to Dolferl. 'This is your way of saying thanks! Thanks for showing you how to milk the Sisters of Mercy. Thanks for getting you into the Warming House on Erdberg Straße. Thanks for introducing you to the Rubin family, where you ate a free three-course dinner.' Fritz turned to me. 'Really, it was such a delightful evening.'

'Enough!' yelled Dolferl. 'You've cheated me out of my share!'

'Without me you'd still be at the mass quarters in Meidling!'

'I trusted you with my paintings!' Dolferl cried. 'But you've cheated me! You sold them for more!'

'Here we go,' Fritz said, turning to me again, 'he thinks he's Rembrandt. But you never get more than one krone for his postcards, at most. And for the bigger ones, you're lucky if you get five!'

I was surprised that Dolferl had trusted this ratbag; usually he didn't trust anyone but himself. He was always expecting to be the victim of a con.

'Morgenstern told me how much he paid you!' yelled Dolferl.

Fritz opened his mouth. But before he could say anything, Dolferl went on. 'Give me a complete list of your customers. Now!'

This was something Walter Fritz had obviously not expected. 'I don't have to give you anything,' he mumbled, visibly disturbed. 'Excuse me,' he added, and when I looked up he had already left.

'I'll file a complaint with the police!' Dolferl screamed, following Fritz out into the hallway.

He came back, fell on to the bed and hid his face in his hands. 'Bastard!' he said. 'I need what he owes me so I can pay my rent, otherwise' – Dolferl looked up at the ceiling – 'tomorrow morning I'll have to pack up and move out.'

'But – to where?'

'I've lived on the street before.'

How ironic that on the day that I found him he was on the verge of being lost to the world again!

'I don't have much,' I said. 'But . . .' I reached into my pocket and took out my last few kreuzer.

Dolferl shook his head. 'What I need is someone selling my art.'

'Maybe I can be your seller.' The moment I said it, I had an idea.

'You?'

'Give me some of your paintings . . .'[18]

18 See: Appendix 16, Hitler in the men's hostel

I had just been to a place where delousing was mandatory, and now here I was in a grand residence where congeniality was *de rigueur*. Vienna was the blessed and the bleak, the decadent and the deprived, the opulent and the oppressed. A duality separated by a mere thirty-minute walk. The parlour at Villa Erica was like a waltz: a constant swirl of people and poses. Guests were sipping after-dinner drinks.

'People have been waiting for you,' said Francisca in a tense voice when I arrived. 'What's that?' she said, looking at the portfolio with Dolferl's artwork under my arm.

'I've changed the programme,' I said so quietly that she couldn't hear me. I wasn't sure if I really wanted to change the programme.

'Come on,' she said, and took my hand, 'let me introduce you to some people... This is Erich Mahler!' Erich was sitting cross-legged on Erica's ruby-red chaise lounge wearing a three-piece worsted-wool suit.

I shook his hand. 'Pleasure, sir,' I said, noticing a resemblance to his famous cousin in his eyes and mouth.

'So good of you to come . . . *finally*,' Erich said, with a slightly accusatory laugh.

'And Erica,' said Francisca, 'you already know.' Erica waved her hand back and forth distantly, as if she were on a departing ocean liner.

'So sorry that you missed dinner, darling,' she said.

'It was exquisite, as expected,' said Mahler, laughing at his own little joke.

'And over here, dear, is *Graf* Schönborn,' said Francisca, continuing to usher me around the room.

Schönborn was wearing a tuxedo and spats. Dyed reddish-brown hair framed his sallow face. There was something so manifestly dreary about him, I wondered what he had to tell himself to be able to face the mirror every morning. 'Pleasure, sir,' I lied.

'And this,' continued Francisca, 'is Hildegard von Ferenczy.' She presented a bejewelled matron in elbow-length leather gloves. She held out her hand: 'Charmed.'

'I've heard so much about you,' I said. She was a great patron of the arts and was not only was rich but royalty, a second cousin of Kaiser Franz Joseph's sister-in-law. In fact, it was her six white horses that had pulled the Emperor's cousin's carriage at the sixtieth anniversary parade.

Francisca then spun me around to more handshakes. My head was spinning from all of the polite salutations. Someone in an officer's uniform asked what I was doing with the cardboard portfolio; was it the sheet music? Would people have to hear all of that? There was an awkward pause where I didn't know what to say, until Francisca would haul me off to the next patron I was supposed to impress. And I did: after all, I was there to perform.

It was now or never, now or never. What I really wanted to do was help my friend Dolferl, not play my over-rehearsed composition.

My plan unsettled me as I pretended to listen as people babbled about the uppity Czechs; the plight of the labourers; the irksome Jews; mismanagement of the city's funds; the horse excrement on the streets; the decline of quality in, and escalating price of, everything. All I could think of was Dolferl's predicament. Then I stopped myself: why was I thinking more about Dolferl than myself? Tonight was my night, my opportunity of a lifetime. But for some reason, I couldn't put Dolferl out of my mind. I believed in my heart that by helping my friend I would be serving a much higher purpose than just my career. I came to just as I was nodding in agreement to a woman's moving lips. 'I just adore what's going on in the arts today. The twentieth century is already very different to the last.'

'Why, yes,' I said. 'I would say that.' *I must help Dolferl. I must help Dolferl.*

'I think dissonance is the new "harmony",' she continued.

'I couldn't agree with you more,' I said.

'Now, we've been waiting long enough,' commanded Erica. 'Our dear, sweet Francisca can't stop talking about your composition *Rage to Joy*. We are all keen to hear it!'

'Perhaps, it will be "all the rage",' chortled Erich, already thinking of a headline he might use.

Now or never! Now or never!

Francisca led me to the piano. I set the drawings down on the bench. She turned to the guests in the parlour, straightened up and her stage presence suddenly emerged. 'Esteemed guests!' Her voice articulated each syllable precisely. 'It is my great privilege and honour to introduce to you an extraordinarily gifted young composer. Martin Bichler!'

There was a polite sprinkling of applause.

I took a bow and laid the portfolio of paintings on the floor. Then I sat down on the bench. I turned towards the ivories. My fingers hovered over the piano keys. *Now or never!* I inhaled, and exhaled. Sweat was already dripping down my brow, before I had even struck a note. Oh, God, God, direct me. I suddenly took my hands away from the keyboard. I cleared my throat, got up again, picked up the portfolio of paintings and flipped up the cardboard lid. I had been going over and over my reason for doing this for the past ten minutes, but I didn't know how I had the nerve to do what I was doing, even as I did it.

'Tonight, I would like to do something a little different,' I began. 'I would like to present some scintillating watercolours by a very gifted young artist . . .' Francisca's face crumbled, but I continued as if I hadn't noticed. 'This is his depiction of our City Hall,' I said, unfurling a 6- by 12-inch painting and waving it as if it was a banner. I paused. 'I also have this subject in postcard size so it can fit on any wall.'

Mahler guffawed. 'My, God. If we want to see City Hall, all we have to do is walk down the street! We live here. We're not tourists!'

'Just look at this painting!' I continued. 'It has a life of its own.'

'When I see a painting, I want to see some bulging breasts,' said Lady Erica in her woozy alcoholic rasp. She pointed to the painting on the wall where a half-clothed Teutonic Samson and a naked Delilah were languishing on a Sphinx-motifed *chaise longue*. 'Just look at my Makart,' Erica name-dropped. Delilah's arm reached across the canvas as Samson was being dragged away by Titans. Painting was the only colour pornography at the time.

'Just look at the extreme precision and attention to detail!' I started again. 'It never ceases to amaze me.'

'Makart is a name,' said Mahler. 'Now if your little artist was a name too, perhaps these trinkets would be easier to sell.'

Francisca shook her head, turned and hurried from the room, mortified.

Graf Schönborn approached me and looked over the paintings. 'I have a doddering aunt whose birthday is coming up,' he said. 'And she just loves this kind of quaint little thing.' As I watched him studying the watercolours, I heard a slight commotion from the seats: people whispering to the person next to them, some behind opened fans and others with cupped hands. I could hear sniggers and giggles and muffled exclamations.

'The concert will start momentarily,' I assured them, which was greeted by a few scornful laughs. I smiled and focused on Graf Schönborn.

'I do like the one of the Opera House,' praised the gentleman.

'Well,' I said, 'the artist is a Wagner devotee.'

'Oh, it shows! It really does,' he said.

By the time Graf Schönborn and two older ladies had rummaged through all of the paintings and drawings and finally had purchased four of them, I was ready to begin. But when I looked out at the audience I was dismayed to see that almost all of the red velvet chairs were empty. Only two enamoured couples remained, totally preoccupied with themselves and each other: everyone else had left, and, more importantly, so had Erich Mahler.

Francisca came up to me.

'You . . .' she stammered.

'I found him again! He . . . He's struggling. I had to – '

'Dolferl, Dolferl, Dolferl!' she snapped. 'You're beyond help!'

She stormed out of the parlour and I followed her with the portfolio into the vestibule, where the last guests were about to take their leave and where Lady Erica was sleeping off the evening's drinks on a sofa.

'Please understand!' I said, running after Francisca.

'I understand perfectly,' retorted Francisca, turning and raising her eyebrows. 'I'm very happy for you both! Now you have your friend back at last. It's all just a little troubling. It would be one thing if he really were a genius; that I could understand! But all I see is a conceited little postcard painter!'

I looked down at the floor. 'Francisca,' I said, 'please listen – '

'*You* listen! You're running after a self-absorbed loudmouth and you're either too blind or too dumb to see it!'

'He's in trouble. I had to help him!'

She walked towards the entrance and opened the door.

'Whatever we had was not just a waltz to me. I loved you from the bottom of my heart. I tried earnestly to help you and this is my reward!'

'You don't understand! I love you too!'

'I think it's time you left,' she said. 'For good . . . '

'Not for good. Please . . . '

'I know now why this' – she gestured with her hands: whatever we had – 'wasn't real.' She stared into my eyes: understand. Try understanding yourself.

The door was opened before me.

Outside on the street, the balmy evening air was filled with the sounds of carriages and puttering cars.

'Please,' I repeated, 'we need to talk about this!'

She exhaled exhaustedly. 'There's nothing more to say. Good luck in your new career as an art pedlar.'

I walked out and the door slammed shut behind me. I turned and yelled her name, but the door remained shut. I stumbled down the steps. Once more I called her name, and all of a sudden the door flew open again. She stormed out on to the porch. 'Here! Have them back!' she shouted, holding my love letters in her fist. Then she ripped them into pieces and threw the fragments into the air. With that, she slammed the door and was gone.

Gone forever.

The shreds of my letters fluttered on to the pavement. Part of me wanted to collect them, but what was the sense of that? I shrugged sadly with a deep sense of remorse and, not wanting to return to the empty apartment, went back to the men's hostel, but the doors were already closed: visitors were not admitted after 9 p.m.

The next day, I got up early and caught Dolferl before he had to leave the hostel at 7 a.m.

'Be glad she's gone,' he said, sitting in a chair by the little table in his cubicle. He had positioned himself so that his bent arm rested on the table and his fist was lodged beneath his cheek: the pose of a great thinker, like Beethoven or the Master of Bayreuth. A heap of coins was stacked at his elbow, the money I had made for him. Dolferl threw a coin over to the bed, where I was sitting. 'Here's your commission,' he said, laughing.

On his table, there was a framed photograph of his mother. Her pose was pensive, but the picture did actually resemble her; her eyes were open, and they stared fearlessly into the camera lens. His father's riding crop lay dutifully at Dolferl's feet. I wished I had a camera at the ready: Dolferl with long hair and beard posing like Beethoven, with a photo of his mother and his father's whip.

'This actress,' Dolferl said, 'she would have buried the artist in you, Turned you into an ordinary person forever. Eventually, you'd marry her, you'd have children, and then you'd have to work day in and day out, just to feed the gluttonous mouths of your brood. And there would have been nothing left for the artist.' He clapped his hands, jumped to his feet, and started pacing. Thinking and speaking, thinking and lecturing. 'Family is for mundane people, not for the likes of us.' He stopped and eyeballed me. 'Or do you believe art can arise from that? Do you really believe timeless works of art are born from worries about the milkman, carpet-sweepers and home-grown vegetables?'

'All I know is that I miss her,' I said. 'And that she's on my mind all the time.' There. I'd said it aloud. I'd said it to Dolferl.

He tittered like the guests in Erica's parlour. 'Your instinct to mate is driving you to distraction. Why don't you go to Siebensterngasse instead?'

I looked at him. That's not my way, I thought – though it very possibly could have been his. Should I mention the whore we met on the way to Herr Maurer's? I decided against it.

Dolferl returned to his chair. Spine erect; lungs, diaphragm, and vocal cords all aligned, in place for a lecture. 'The true artist is free of all that. He has learned to transform that primitive urge into something higher.'

I remembered the book with the scarlet binding. 'With sexual magic?'

'How do you think the Yogis in India can allow themselves to be buried alive?' he asked. 'Or stop their hearts beating? Or walk through fire without getting burned?'

'I don't know.'

'Because they will it! It's that simple. All it comes down to is the will.' Dolferl got up. 'Look . . .'

He lit a candle, held his hand above the flame, slowly lowered the palm of his hand to the tip of the flame and held it there.

'Dolferl!' I cried.

'The pain is outside my body,' he said. The smell of singeing flesh drifted up between his extended fingers. 'I don't feel it. It is a glowing dot and I am reducing it in my mind until . . .' He yanked his hand back from the flame, no trace of any struggle to hide the pain betrayed on his face.

'See?' he said.

His indifference to pain was remarkable. But I didn't believe for a moment that reading those books had turned him into a Yogi. I could still remember the time he had been badly beaten in the schoolyard, and how he had reacted in the same stoic way. Then, as now, I had witnessed his ability to disassociate himself from his body to the point that he did not feel much pain, if any. I wondered if his detached relationship with his own body had seeped into his relationships with people as well.

Dolferl was studying his opened hand. 'Mind over matter,' he said to his hand, which was turning red. Unfazed by worldly affairs he was now Schopenhauer's 'mystic'. A sly smile curved his bottom lip. His eyes narrowed to two slits and he asked: 'Are you truly, absolutely, completely committed to your art?'

'Of course I am. You know that.'

'Then prove it!' he exploded.

'How?'

He looked at me and smiled.

'It's really quite simple,' he said, extending his fingers and shaking his hand to cool it.

'What do I have to do?'

'Follow me,' he said, simply.

'To where? To this hostel?'

'It's the cleanest in the city – and, believe me, I know them all,'

He was simply unbelievable.

'Live here? This is miles away from the church where I play the organ!'

'You don't need that *Krampf* any more. Give up your past! The church, the Conservatory . . . '

'And then?'

'Then you'll be entering the realm of the extraordinary. You'll develop beyond the mediocre. You'll create eternity.' Dolferl's eyes glazed over as he witnessed things that most people could never envision, much less sense. I wished that I could sense it too, but I was obviously one of those who couldn't. 'Rubens grew up in extreme poverty,' he said, 'as did Makart.'

'You want me to leave everything behind? Then what?'

'More will be revealed then,' said Dolferl teasingly.

'I can't do that,' I said. Even I had to eat.

'Many are called, few are chosen,' said Dolferl, in the same cadence as the bookshop clerk had spoken. 'Come back when you're ready.'

My boots crunched the icy snow as I trudged through the city park on a dreary December day. The sun had set; the blue snow had turned to grey; the sky to black. Francisca had stopped coming to Mass and it had been half a year since I last saw her. Villa Erica had become a distant dream. Where was the sense in all this? Had I come to Vienna to perform for a throng of rosary-clutching hens? Was this all my life had amounted to? Or did I need to accept who I really was, go back to Linz and become an apprentice, stuffing sofas for the same god-fearing crowd? I couldn't bear the thought. I was sick of myself. And I was alone. Francisca wanted nothing to do with me, and I wanted nothing to do with Dolferl.

Ahead of me, three schoolboys scurried about, pelting one another with snowballs. One of them was struck on the forehead. The boy's face transformed from an initial look of shock to an expression of pain. The boy swore, calling his friend a bastard, and they all laughed at the wicked thrill of it all. Then they scampered off, past a monument to the Kaiser that was a mottled reddish colour. I thought it was rust, but as I came closer, I realised that it was paint. A red star was clearly visible on the base. A sharp gust blew, cutting and cold, across my face. I had reached the steps of 'my' church, the Church of the Annunciation. A crowd of Jews in mourning-wear passed, solemnly marching along in triangular formation, going to a funeral. The sound of their footsteps marked out their own rhythm against a slogan that a group of protesters were chanting: 'Jews inherit, Germans perish. Jews inherit, Germans perish.' Some were carrying placards with the portrait of Karl Lueger, the Viennese mayor.

I entered the church: it was early evening and the priest was still hearing confession. Ascending the steps to the balcony, I took a seat in front of the organ and removed my gloves and overcoat. I opened the lid and regarded the span of keys stretching out before me. I wondered if Dolferl was right; if life was just a struggle, if we were nothing but playthings in the iron grip of the eternal law of evolution. At times there was venom in his words, which rang cruel yet true; but when he spoke of love, his words were mawkish and melodramatic – to the point of nausea. He was certainly right about one thing, though: love transcends words. Music transcends words.

My fingers ran across the keyboard, saying things I could only convey musically. The five-lined staff. The minim, crotchet and quaver. The sharp; the flat. The notes would at times be hopeful, only to retreat into dark turmoil. My hands surging across the keys, allowed me to cry in public without humiliation. My darkest moments were there, abstracted in sound. There was no need for anyone to console me; the dirge swathed me in a shroud of music and laid me to rest. My loneliness flowed through my fingers into the organ. I was purging my sorrow. I was in despair.

I had said it.

I stopped.

All was quiet again in the church.

I felt a tap on my shoulder. I turned to find Francisca standing behind me.

'That was beautiful,' she said. I looked up at her and into those eyes. We lingered, gazing into each other.

'It was just how I felt,' I answered.

She sat down beside me on the bench.

'I was kneeling, praying,' she said. 'And when I heard the organ, I knew my prayers had been answered.'

'I just want to say I – ' I began.

She pressed her finger to my lips, stopping me short. 'You've already said it.'

Tailcoated waiters scurried around Francisca and me. Every so often they would summon guests to their waiting coaches outside: Herr Councillor, Herr Professor, Herr Engineer, Herr Consul. It was distracting, but we 'had to talk', and Café Central's restrained commotion was just the right amount of background activity for our purposes. Sparkling chandeliers hung from the arched ceiling; the paladin windows were framed by embroidered curtains. A marble fountain burbled at the entrance. At the centre there were three newspaper stands: one for Austrian papers, one for German papers and one for the rest of the world. A pianist played Chopin softly, allowing people to murmur to one another in low voices. The ambience made it seem almost like a library, which in a sense it was, with so many people reading quietly.

'We have to be honest with each other,' said Francisca, stirring her coffee. With each motion of the spoon, she seemed to ponder the intricacies of our relationship.

'Yes,' I said, a note of restrained urgency in my voice. 'Let's talk.'

'Otherwise,' she continued, 'I don't know how our love' – she accentuated 'love' with an ominous sharpness – 'will survive.'

I had to look away at the sugar cubes in the silver bowl, allowing myself to remain calm despite the significance of the moment.

'Fine,' I replied.

She sighed as she did on stage when she wanted to convey impatience. 'Now tell me honestly, what is your relationship with Dolferl?'

I set down my spoon, exhaling in response to her sigh. 'He's an old friend.'

'And . . . ?'

'I've known him since childhood. In fact, apart from you, he's the only real friend I have here in Vienna. And . . .' I paused, taking care to phrase my next words correctly.

'And what?'

'He's . . .' Perhaps it was the combination of the caffeine and the spirit of the moment that led me to say: 'Remarkable.'

'Remarkable?' she repeated in disbelief. 'How?'

The tails of a coated waiter flapped as he floated by. I turned my glance back to Francisca. 'His ideas . . . '

'From what you've told me, he simply takes other people's ideas and combines them.'

'His genius is his ability to condense complex issues down to their simplest terms. It makes everything he says sound definite and true.'

'I asked you about your relationship.'

I hesitated for emphasis, and she gasped. 'What?'

'He's my pal, my *Kumpel*. That's all. But as it happens . . .'

'As it happens what?'

'As it happens we've parted ways.'

'Why?'

'He wanted me to give up everything,' I began to explain. Our table was by a large window; outside, red-nosed pedestrians with winter coats leaned into the whipping wind.

'What do you mean?'

'He wanted me to give up school, the organ, the room in Stumper gasse . . .'

'And then what?'

'I don't know.' My eyes traced the geometrical patterns in the carpet. 'He wanted me to join him.'

'Join him in what?'

'His destiny, I suppose. I don't know. He was vague.'

'What did you say to him?'

'I said I couldn't do that. I said no.'

'When was that?'

'The day after you tore up my letters.'

'And you haven't seen him since?'

'No.'

'Has anything ever happened between you two?'

'Happened? What do you mean?'

'Darling,' she said, 'I work in the theatre. I'm quite open-minded and accepting . . .'

'I'm no Sodomite!' I cried.

She fell silent.

'Have you ever, say, massaged his back?'

'God, no! Dolferl hates people touching him.'

She leaned back and stared at me in silence. 'All right,' she conceded. 'I believe you.'

It was the moment I had been waiting for, the moment when everything would be all right. Everything would go back to where it belonged: I belonged to her; our lives belonged together. That much was clear. I extended my hand across the table and peered into her green eyes: the eyes of my future. My fingers intertwined with hers. We held our future together.

'Good,' I said, releasing her hand. 'Now you have to be honest with me.'

'Fair's fair,' she said. She averted her gaze to her cup, then looked back to me. She tensed.

I was uneasy too. I cleared my throat, steeled myself, and asked, 'Do you love me?'

Her eyebrows rose incredulously. 'What's got into you, Martin?'

'We've never talked about it, but I've thought about it. There's a big difference between us, and I don't just mean our ages.'

'What do you mean?'

'You're everything any man would want in a woman. You're beautiful, you're generous and kind. You're a wonderful actress. You're twenty-seven,' I said, knowing full well that she was older. Even so, on hearing twenty-seven, she smiled. 'You're the perfect age for a woman. You can have any desirable, well-off gentleman in this town. You don't need a first-year music student in your life.'

She stared at her plate and said nothing.

A wave of insecurity swept over me. That's it, I thought. That's exactly it. She can't answer because what I've just said is the truth. 'I have nothing to offer,' I went on. 'I'm reasonably talented but I'm far from a genius. I'm not wealthy. I'm just an average guy. Maybe not even an artist. A petit bourgeois. Absolutely average, boring, conventional. I can't even waltz properly. The Ballhaus, the parties . . . It all just makes me feel awkward . . . '

'Martl!' she interrupted, grabbing my arm and squeezing it.

I looked into her eyes.

She smiled. 'You want to know why I want to be with you?'

I nodded.

'Because you make me happy. That's why. And when I'm not with you, I miss you and think about you.' She gulped. 'I just can't help myself.' She looked up at me, at a loss for words.

'Really?'

'Yes. Really.'

'But there are so many other men out there who could make you happy. Happier than I can, I'm sure.'

'Oh, Martin . . .' she stroked my arm. 'Don't think that I haven't tried. I have. Many times. But these other men, they're just not right for me. Yes, I love the theatre, and yes, I love dancing and I love the nights at the Ballhaus. But there is something else too, something that's much more important to me.'

'And what is that?'

'Respect. You may think you're average but I admire you. I trust you,' she said. 'I'd trust you to be the father of my child.'

A silence settled over the table. I wanted to say something but didn't know what. When I looked at her, she lowered her gaze and patted her face with a handkerchief.

'See,' she finally said, looking at me. 'It seems you're not the only one at this table with artistic pretensions and bourgeois conventions!'

I laughed.

We laughed.

Finally.

Francisca and I walked arm in arm after dinner one night, a few weeks after our reconciliation. The light of the gas lamps and the cool, clear air accentuated the details on the buildings' facades. Everything now seemed crisper and cleaner. I had a clear perspective on my life. I paused in my thoughts and changed 'my life' to 'our lives'. I pulled her closer.

'I'm willing to do whatever I have to do to make you happy,' I said suddenly, with a dry throat.

'And what sort of thing does that entail?'

'You tell me,' I offered.

Francisca fell silent. We walked for a while without saying a word. Then she stopped, so I stopped, and looked at her.

'Your little friend,' said Francisca. 'Will you promise never to see him again?'

I listened and said nothing.

'Well?' she asked.

'I will,' I replied. 'I question what Dolferl and I were searching for. It certainly wasn't each other. He lives in a world of ideals that are beyond reach.' I paused and lowered my voice. 'But you're real.' I took her hand. 'I'll . . . ' I had to cough. 'I'll devote myself to making our lives work together. My love for you will support me, and my musical talent will provide for us. I don't care if I have to play in some rowdy wine cellar for a drunken crowd, or in church for deaf parishioners. I'll persevere.'

Her eyes filled with relief. "I believe you, Martl! I know things will be different this time!'

Joy surged through me. My love! I thought to myself, it's finally here. She loves me. She loves me! Over and over my mind chanted the words to my disbelieving ears.

I smiled. She smiled.

Over her shoulder, across the street, I saw a man staggering in the midst of the bustling hordes. The colour must have drained from my face.

'What is it?' enquired Francisca.

I didn't reply. My tongue swelled with the shock. I wasn't even capable of pointing. She turned to see where I was looking. On the other side of the street was Dolferl, limping along like a wounded animal.

'Oh my God . . . ' said Francisca.

Dolferl's body was trembling. He spun on his heel and collapsed on to a bench. I ran over and sat down beside my friend from Linz. His complexion was ashen. He was smiling, yet not, drifting in and out of consciousness. Under his battered bicycle coat he wore a frayed singlet.

'We've got to get him warm,' said Francisca, who had followed me.

I said nothing, noticing his lips turning blue.

'I know a doctor,' she said.

'Your friend doesn't have a strong constitution,' said doctor Udrzal, wiping his hands. 'He's lucky you found him.'

Dolferl lay on the bed dressed in the clinic's linen shirt.

'Thank you for treating him,' I said, then added, 'at this time of night,' after checking my watch.

'It's my job,' the doctor said, with a shrug.

Dolferl stirred in his bed. He groaned.

'I think he's coming around,' said the doctor, with a smile. We all breathed a sigh of relief.

Slowly Dolferl came to. His eyes opened and then focused slowly: the electric light overhead. The three people close by.

'Where am I?'

'At a doctor's,' I said. 'Francisca and I brought you here.'

'Dr Udrzal works for the theatre company,' added Francisca.

'Doctor who?' said Dolferl.

'Dr Udrzal.'

The doctor got up and stepped over to the bed.

Dolferl focused on the doctor's features: his protruding forehead, his reddish-blond hair, his brown eyes.

'Another Czech idiot stealing our jobs!' Dolferl barked at me. 'You of all people should know I'd rather have a veterinarian tend to me than a corrupt crook from Prague.'

I got up from his bed and turned to the doctor. 'He doesn't know what he's saying.'

The doctor stared directly at me. 'Yes he does.' His brown eyes penetrating, he heaved a sigh. 'You have to be thick-skinned to be a Czech in Vienna. Believe me, I stopped caring years ago. First and foremost, he's a patient.'

'What's wrong?' called Dolferl. 'Why am I here?'

I turned towards him. 'You collapsed.'

He smiled.

'How long have you been feeling ill?' I asked. 'You're emaciated! You have to eat!'

'There are more important things to do than eat.' A distant look swept over his face. 'People should fast,' he declared, with a sudden newfound defiance and directed his glare at the doctor. 'Especially you, parasite!'

'Shut up!' called Francisca. 'This gentleman was kind enough to treat you.'

'Treat me for what? For money! We pay them so they can pollute our country. How many children does the good doctor have? Enough to fill an orphanage! Did you know a Czech pregnancy lasts only three weeks? Funny that, isn't it?'

Francisca stormed over to Dolferl. 'You'd be dead if it weren't for Dr Udrzal!'

Dolferl laughed with a slight knowing sneer. 'You don't like me, do you?' he asked. 'Don't deny it.'

'Dr Urdzal is a dear friend of mine, and – '

'Oh, is he? Really?' Dolferl stopped and silently looked first at me and then back at Francisca. And then he took me by surprise: he apologised. 'I'm sorry,' Dolferl said to Francisca. 'Please accept my apologies,' he added in his most remorseful tone. 'I didn't mean to offend you, Francisca.' His last words were swallowed up by a coughing fit.

Francisca was at a loss: which Dolferl should she believe? The victim, or the viper?

'Please! My deepest apologies to you too, Martl,' Dolferl uttered between coughs. 'I want to make this up to you. I promise. I will. Truly. I truly will,' he said.

Francisca looked over to me, but I was just as perplexed. Could there really be an ounce of decency in him? her eyes asked. Francisca, Dolferl and I were so enmeshed; perhaps she was thinking that someone I called an old friend couldn't be all bad. All right, she smiled, I'll give him the benefit of the doubt. 'OK, Dolferl,' she conceded.

'Adolf,' Dolferl corrected.

'OK, Adolf.'

'Truce!' He offered his hand, and she took it.

'Good!' Dolferl announced. 'We Germans have to stick together.'

The carriage moved along a road that ran next to a railway track. Francisca had left the carriage at Villa Erica, and was now alone with Dolferl in the back seat; A train whistle blew in the night and startled the hansom's horse, causing it to rear up. The carriage wheels rolled backwards as the coachman pulled on the reins and we were jostled about in the back. The wail of the train whistle was soon followed by the chugging of an engine and clattering wheels. The hansom driver pulled the carriage brake, jumped out of his seat and ran to the horse, gripping the bridle and whispering soothingly into the horse's ear to calm the panicking animal as the train thundered past. From our seats, both Dolferl and I could see the mighty engine as it hurtled into the night, pulling a succession of open cars. Each bore two grey cannons with their barrels pointing eastwards, towards the Balkans: car after car, cannon after menacing cannon.

'I've never seen so much artillery in my life,' I said, turning to Dolferl.

He smiled smugly. 'You'll be seeing a lot more of that, believe me,' he said, with a knowing laugh. 'Don't you know what's going on?'

I shook my head. It was a disturbing sight; not just the weaponry, but the volume of it.

'What kind of world are we living in?' I mumbled, more to myself than to him.

Dolferl's eyes lit up. 'You mean, what kind of *war will* we be living in.'

PART TWO

WAR

To Munich

In politics you must always focus on one enemy.

It was Sunday afternoon. Erica had dozed off on her ruby-red chaise lounge. 'Why don't we take a walk down to the *Eislaufplatz*?' I whispered. 'It'll take our minds off – ' I didn't want to say 'Dolferl'. I didn't have to.

Francisca's eyes narrowed at my pause. After the two had made peace the other night, I had assumed it would be acceptable for me to see him at the shelter. But when I had told her about my plan to visit him, she had erupted with anger.

'Why do you waste your time with that talentless egomaniac?'

'Please, Francisca, have you forgotten? He asked for your forgiveness.'

'Pah!' She shook her head. 'A "truce", he called it! Life is nothing but a series of rivalries to him. All he wants to do is stage and orchestrate his little battles. And he'll stop at nothing to win.'

'He loves to pick fights, I know. But what does it matter?'

'You're blind to the simple fact that there are people in this world who are loathsome and unscrupulous. And your friend is one of them.'

'Look, why don't we just go and watch people skating on the pond?' I said, changing the subject. 'You never know, Princess Sölleszy may be out this afternoon.'

'All right,' she consented, resolving to break out of her foul mood. She jumped to her feet, and wrapped herself in her coat. Then she hooked her arm in mine and we left Villa Erica.

The air was heavy with the impending snowfall and we strolled along the slush-covered footpath. As we passed by other couples, we nodded and acknowledged each other.

'Feeling better?' I enquired.

Her expression softened as she tried to muster a smile. A couple with a pram mounted on sleigh runners waited next to us at a crossroads. Francisca leaned down to admire the sleeping infant and was instantly transformed, her scowl replaced with a broad grin. There and then I resolved not to believe that the world would be annihilated in war, as Dolferl asserted. I could envision happier beginnings and endings. All of a sudden, snow began to drift down from the clouds: light, white, pure.

'See,' I said to Francisca, 'magic does exist, even on a brooding Sunday afternoon like this.'

Francisca's eyes smiled. 'I love you,' she said.

'I love you too,' I replied. I loved her when she sulked, but I loved her even more when she didn't.

We embraced and kissed, passionately, honestly and fervently, there amidst the falling snow.

Dolferl's hair hung down to his shoulders, and a full unruly beard covered his chin and cheeks. His health and finances had improved markedly in the six months since his collapse in the street; Löffner and Neumann, two Jewish fellow lodgers, sold Dolferl's paintings to Jewish art dealers who appreciated his work by paying him well. Neumann had also become something of a friend.[19]

Dolferl sat at 'his' place in the non-smoking section of the reading room. The other boarders were sufficiently fearful of his explosive temper to keep his seat free even when he wasn't there. There was no immediate evidence of his temper today. Dolferl sat painting peacefully in the afternoon light, quietly humming a serene passage from *The Ring* in blissful awareness of who he was: a painter, doing what he was born to do. A true artist amongst artisans, valiant and industrious. Inevitably, the tune he hummed would become more vehement, as did the drama it expressed. Operatic retribution always suited Dolferl; he enjoyed the beauty of vengeance. Walter Fritz had got his comeuppance. The homeless man, whose real name was Hanisch, had conned him out of a few kronen, and for that Dolferl demanded retribution. How dare anyone cheat him! It was irrelevant that Hansich had taught him how to turn his art into money and that in reality, Dolferl was indebted to Hanisch. He felt utterly entitled to ask his friend Löffner to report Hanisch to the police, giving him a criminal record in one fell swoop. Ha! Take that, you crook! His humming reached a crescendo as Dolferl imagined himself vindicated.

Dolferl was deep in concentration, darting back and forth from the drawing he was producing. He had just finished sketching the stairs next to the Ratzenstadel, rendering the architectural elements so precisely it

19 See: Appendix 18, Hitler's Jewish Friends

was almost photographic. How he could reproduce something so accurate from memory alone always intrigued me. However, the people in his paintings were poorly drawn, ruining the illusion. Even in his artwork, it was other people that caused the problems.

Dolferl squinted and tilted his head back. Then he looked at me, satisfied. 'It looks impressive,' he said, lifting up his pen and ink sketch. 'It looks real, but it isn't. A bit like Schopenhauer. The will and its representation, you know.'

'I've no doubt it will sell,' I said, studying his new piece.

'No!' he cried.

'What do you mean, no?' I asked, before realising that his 'no' hadn't been directed at me. Evidently he had been eavesdropping on the conversation among a group of lodgers at the back of the room.

He turned towards them. 'How often do I have to tell you that socialism isn't the answer?'

'I didn't say socialism,' said a lanky young man in a shabby suit. 'I said communism.'

Dolferl's eyes glowered. 'It's all the same!' he shouted. 'It's all the same poison.' He stood up. 'Can't you see this will kill us all one day?'

'What I see is starving masses,' said the young man. His eyes looked distant behind his bifocals. 'I see homeless people barely managing to survive. I see millions of workers out of work. What is responsible for that, if not capitalism?'

'You're right!' said Dolferl. 'Something must be done! Something must be done about the stock companies, the large industries, all those greedy people and their unearned wealth. We must fight!' he said. 'We must fight against a world dominated by finance. That world will annihilate our culture, our traditions, and our moral values. But Marxism isn't the way!'

'Why not?'

'Because there's no international brotherhood between workers. Marxism destroys the nation state with that delusion. But the nation state is the only force that can counter capitalism!'

'If the working class doesn't fight for its rights, no one else will!' With that, the young man stood up, followed swiftly by his four companions.

'We are not born into classes!' yelled Dolferl. 'We are born into races!'

The men retreated to the door.

'If we want to overcome capitalism,' Dolferl shouted after them, 'we must do so as a race!'

The room was now empty, but Dolferl continued: 'There are no classes in nature, only species and races!' He turned towards me but I barely registered a word. My mind drifted back to Stumpergasse, where he would lecture into the night and through to the morning.

'We humans are vessels of life, as much as panthers, pythons or piranhas,' he declared to the vacant chairs. 'History is an endless fight and the strongest wins, thus earning the right to live while the others must perish. But fighting within our race is against nature. What we must do is fight the others! That is what nature demands! It's purely scientific, purely Darwin . . . '

'What are you doing with those insipid drawings?' Francisca asked me, pointing to the portfolio under my arm. I didn't reply. Music students were mingling in front of the Conservatory. Francisca and I were planning on attending a string quartet performing Schubert. I had brought the portfolio because I was hoping to sell some of Dolferl's works to one of my professors after the concert.

'We should go in and get seated,' I said.

'I thought we'd come to an agreement about your friend.'

'We have.'

'Not from what I can see.'

'Please. Let's go in.'

'No,' she said. 'No.'

'Look, I know you don't like him, but you still found it in yourself to forgive him.'

'That doesn't mean we have to hawk this rubbish on his behalf. Remember how he insulted my friend, the doctor?'

'He wasn't in his right mind that night,' I said. 'You saw that.'

'Oh, come now! He's a petty, prejudiced little man, like thousands of others in this town. He wants to be an artist but he's nothing more than a small-minded bigot with small-minded fears and small-minded preconceptions. He's utterly mediocre, yet supremely arrogant.'

My first instinct was to respond with indignation, but I stopped myself: I didn't want us to argue again. 'You're right,' I conceded, 'he can be a pompous fool. But he does have some redeeming qualities.'

'Really? Such as?'

'He has so much creative energy, an energy you rarely encounter in other people.'

'What else?'

'He's not afraid to speak his mind. Actually, sometimes I think he's not afraid of anything.' I stopped. 'And . . . '

'What?'

'He's quick-witted and . . . he can be quite funny . . . '

'Sarcastic maybe.'

'And charming . . . '

'Only when it serves his purpose.'

'Francisca, please understand. He's my oldest friend.'

'You're so wrong! You mean nothing to him. You're like a pawn to him, to be manipulated and dominated. He orders you around, he uses you, he imposes his will on you; and at some point, he'll get rid of you. I really don't understand why you're always so willing to look for good in him.'

'There are times when I can't stand him too, believe me. But those aren't my finest moments. If I hate him, how am I any different to any other hatemonger?'

There was a silence.

'Oh, very well then,' Francisca finally yielded, letting me take her hand and the portfolio so we could enter the building together.

Dolferl bit a piece off the brown bread and chewed it contemplatively. 'The taste is acceptable,' he said, 'but this bread will destroy the middle class.' He shoved the rest of the roll into his mouth. 'How will a small bakery compete with that bread factory?' Dolferl was sitting at 'his' table, speaking to a small circle of lodgers sitting within earshot. 'If Mayor Lueger were still alive,' said Dolferl, 'that factory wouldn't be allowed to operate!'

'What's wrong with affordable bread?' asked one of the lodgers.

'The bread factory is a first step in the destruction of small business,' answered Dolferl. 'I'm all in favour of closing it down.'

The pros and cons of the 'Hammer' bread factory were a hotly debated topic, and Dolferl, devouring the various reading-room periodicals daily, knew more about it than anyone else present. He was increasingly obsessed with reading the press, the 'select tool of the Antichrist', as Bismarck had called it. It didn't matter to Dolferl how radically left- or right-wing a publication was: he had to read them all.

'Lueger's association with the Catholic Church was a huge mistake,' said one of the lodgers.

'I disagree!' Dolferl shouted. 'I totally disagree.'

'Yesterday you said that we'd be better off without the Catholic Church.'

'Of course! But the church exists, and it wields enormous power over the masses. A clever politician will never defy it. Look what happened to Schoenerer!'

'But you agree with him, don't you?'

'I agree entirely with Schoenerer's stance: he fights for the Germans in Austria like no other. He reintroduced the role of "Führer". He did away with the weak Viennese "Servus" and replaced it with "Heil". All of this was excellent work. But look at what happened to him: he lost the elections. Why? Because he amassed too many enemies! You cannot fight against the Habsburgs, the Czechs, the Catholics and the Jews all at the same time. In politics, you must always focus on one enemy.'

'So who do you think that enemy is?'

'Well, Habsburg of course!' said Dolferl. 'Karl-Hermann Wolf is saying exactly what I have been saying all along. We Germans in Austria must never forget that we are living in a threatened land. We must all stick together, whether Catholic, Protestant, Jew, or whatever.'

'But Lueger was an outspoken critic of the Jews!'

'Of course he was, because anti-Semitism is popular. Lueger was a great politician. But he fought for the wrong cause. He fought to save the doomed empire of the Habsburgs.'[20]

Dolferl was looking better. His hair was still shoulder-length, but it was well trimmed, as was his beard. He wore clean clothes and new shoes, thanks to the paintings that I and his Jewish friends Löffner and Neumann had been able to sell for him.

'Right now, our most pressing problem is the infiltration from the East,' Dolferl said. 'Once that problem is solved, we can think about how to deal with the churches . . . '

Dolferl paused, and just as he was about to continue, I interjected.

'I have to speak to you. Now!'

Dolferl glowered: not when I'm lecturing!

But I had to talk to him, so I proceeded. 'As you know, I've done well selling your paintings.' Dolferl nodded impatiently. 'But my professor's wife has been waiting for you to finish her painting for two weeks now.' My tone was urgent, as was the situation. 'If we can't deliver as assured, she may lose interest.'

20 See: Appendix 19, Political Role Models

'Can't you see I'm explaining how our present political situation must be dealt with? And that, my good friend, is much more important than pleasing some conceited housewife.'

'But Dolferl, you have to eat and – '

'I don't *have* to do anything!' he retorted. Evidently he had been reading Schopenhauer again.

'But – ' I said.

'You have my answer. Now leave me alone,' he said, turning back to his audience.

And with no other choice, I did.

I lay beside Francisca in the tall grass of a pasture near the mountain top. Dolferl was within sight as he continued his climb towards the peak. The sky directly above was an inky blue, lightening gradually as it extended to the horizon.

'The air is divine here,' said Francisca.

'You're divine,' I said dreamily.

It was September, and with much cajoling I had convinced Francisca to accompany Dolferl and me to Semmering on a day trip out of Vienna. Francisca and Dolferl hadn't seen one another since the incident with Dr Udrzal.

'You go with your friend,' she had said. 'I'll stay in town.'

'But I really want you two to become friends,' I pleaded. 'I love you, and I owe Dolferl so much.'

'So you want to prove your loyalty to him? Because he says "the greatest Germanic virtue is loyalty"? Isn't that it?' snapped Francsica.

'He talks a lot about loyalty, yes; loyalty to his race and his nation. But to me loyalty is a personal thing. I want to be loyal to Dolferl because if it were not for him, I'd still be in Linz and would never have met you.' There was an earnestness to my voice and I could see in Francisca's eyes that I had convinced her: Dolferl had brought us together.

She said nothing for a moment and then replied, 'What if he bursts into one of his tirades again?'

'He won't.'

Francisca looked at me sceptically.

'You'll see: as soon as Dolferl lays his eyes on his blue Danube he'll be transformed.'

And he was: out here in nature, he became a sweet, docile person and scampered off up the mountainside playfully like a dog off its leash.

'It would be lovely to take some sun,' Francisca announced as she unbuttoned her blouse. 'Don't you think?' She smiled. 'My breasts need some fresh air.'

'You are a true maenad,' I said.

She grinned. 'I would *love* to play in *The Bacchae*! There are so many wonderful parts for women in that tragedy.'

In fact, Francisca would have loved a part in any play; it had been months since she had last worked. But she didn't want to think about such things now, as she slipped off her blouse. 'I shall commune with the chorus of wood nymphs.' She smiled.

My eyes trailed up the mountain. Dolferl's back was to us. 'Francisca...' I cautioned.

'What?' she said, undoing her bra and squatting on my legs.

She basked semi-naked in the sunlight before me: I had never seen a real woman's chest before. Dear Lord, I thought: you can see me now! This is worse than the capricious decadence in that painting by Watteau. Is this a venial or a mortal sin? But those breasts, those beautiful breasts!

'I offer up my bosom to Dionysus,' she said, laughing and jiggling her breasts. 'Take them, Bacchus, and make them yours! Breathe in my dear little twins, revel in the wonder of God's green earth.'

'Francisca!'

'What?'

'Francisca, the thin air is going to your head!'

'What do you mean?'

'What if he sees?'

'He's too far away to see anything. At most I'm a pink blur from that distance.'

'You're acting like you're drunk!'

'No wonder! The gods come here to mate. The goddesses don't need alcohol to feel high-spirited.'

'Francisca, we can't go on like this,' I said.

'Whatever do you mean?'

'I need clarity. Get off for a minute, I want to show you something.' She rolled off me, and I was able to fish into my trouser pocket and pull out a box. I had been struggling to decide on the best time to do this; as it happened, the opportunity had presented itself here on this pristine mountain top.

She clicked open the red velvet box. Two rings lay within, side by side.

'Let's get married.'

'This is very sweet of you,' she said hesitantly, studying the rings. 'But . . . '

'You said you loved me!'

'It's too fast. We need time. We . . . '

'It's been almost three years!' I said.

'I know, but . . . I've been thinking,' she continued.

'Thinking what?'

'What if I have to go back to Munich?'

'Why?' I asked, incredulous: here I was, offering to commit, and she was being as evasive as the stereotypical man.

'My father's written to me: he needs me at the hotel.'

'But you always said that your art was the only way you could be happy. You're the one who told me never to falter.'

'I was scared to give up my career. But now I've had a career. No one can take away the parts from me that I've already played. I know now that I'll always be an actress. No matter what.'

I took back the box.

Francisca caressed my face.

'Just give me some time,' I said earnestly. 'Once I'm finished at the Conservatory we can make plans together; go where we want together.'

Francisca inhaled deeply and sighed. She thought for a moment, and then turned towards the mountain, putting her underwear and blouse back on.

'What about him?' she said. 'Your source of inspiration?'

'I don't need him to compose any more. I can do it on my own. But I need you to live!'

'Oh,' she said quietly. 'Really?'

Just then Dolferl's voice came echoing down from the mountain. 'Come up here, quickly! Come up here! I have something to show you!'

Francisca and I walked silently through a meadow towards Dolferl. He was holding a flower. 'Look,' he said. 'It's burdock! It's incredibly rare. But just look around, it's everywhere!' We were standing in a green and purple carpet of it. 'Here,' he said, offering the flower to Francisca. 'You can wear it in your hair, and then afterwards you can brew a tea from it. It's good for your kidneys.' With that, he ran to the far end of the meadow. 'Come over here!' he called again. 'Look at this one!' There on the mountain top, the lighter side of my friend emerged. 'Isn't it beautiful,' he said, giving a tiny red mountain rose to Francisca, 'a beautiful little flower for another beautiful little flower.'

Francisca bowed and laughed as she did with Leopold and Herbert.

'True beauty is unspoiled nature,' proclaimed Dolferl.

I couldn't argue with that in these surroundings.

'We artists are always on the lookout for beauty!' Dolferl exclaimed. 'Right, Martl?'

I put my arm around Francisca and nodded.

Then Dolferl pointed up to the summit. 'The bluest gentian in the world grows up there.'

Francisca turned to me, pointing to the sky: menacing, black-bellied storm clouds were gathering around the neighbouring peaks.

'Look,' she said anxiously, 'the weather's about to turn.'

'This is his mountain,' I said, 'he knows his way up here like a chamois.'

Francisca looked down at her feet, and shook her head. 'I'm not wearing the right shoes.' She looked back to me: please, no.

Dolferl was scrambling up the mountain with an infectious eagerness: it seemed as if, with every twist in the path, he came across another revelation of the mountain's natural beauty and grandeur.

'Don't worry!' I reached out my hand. 'We've come this far, and it isn't much further to the top.' Reluctantly, Francisca took my hand.

The shrubs were becoming increasingly sparse the higher we climbed. Grey granite rock began to protrude and cover the ground as the incline steepened. The wind picked up as we continued climbing the slope and I was watching Dolferl as he scaled closer to the top when all of a sudden I heard Francisca scream. I turned to see her gripping a dead bush as she lost her footing and landed flat on her stomach.

She looked up at me, visibly distressed. 'Why are we following him? Let's go back, please!'

I peered back up at Dolferl. He had almost reached the cross at the summit.

'It's really not that much further,' I said.

'But look, I'm bleeding!' she said, getting up.

'It's just a scratch. We have to – '

'No, we *don't*!' she snapped angrily. 'Only *he* has to get to the top.'

'But what kind of people would we be if – '

'Sensible people!' she screamed. 'Just because your little friend cajoles you into these childish antics, you feel you have to do whatever he wants. Even when the woman you want to marry asks you not to.'

'But . . . ' I said. 'There's nothing to be afraid of . . . '

'No wonder I have my doubts!' she retorted.

Dolferl was within reach of the cross.

'Look, he's – ' I said, just as a bolt of lightning shot across the sky.

Dolferl, amazed, spun around with his arms outstretched. Wonderful! I am part of all this! I am nature!

Suddenly the heavens opened in an enormous torrent of rain. Francisca pulled her coat over her head and turned, took one step down, slipped, fell on her behind with a damp thud and slid down the mucky trail.

Dolferl and I burst out laughing at the impromptu slapstick.

She skidded to a stop and turned on her stomach, piercing us with a searing glare. She bristled: puerile, spiteful bastards! She slipped again and began to slide over a grassy ledge. It was like an exercise in divine comedic justice. I doubled over with laughter, tears in my eyes when I realised that she couldn't stop herself. Her fingers were clawing and scrambling to find anything on the slope that she could grip. Her face was panic-stricken as she slowly continued to slide towards the brink on her stomach.

Jesus Christ, I thought, she could be seriously hurt! I skidded down the hillside after her as Francisca dug her fingers ferociously into the earth, but to no avail. She managed to grab hold of a scrawny bush and bring herself to a stop for a moment, but then the bush gave way and her descent resumed. Within moments, her legs were hanging over the lip of the ravine. As I edged closer, I realised she was dangling over a sixty feet drop. God, no! I scrambled down towards her. She threw her arm out, and with a lunge I grabbed it. I dug my heels into the granite ledge and pulled her back from the abyss.

Back on solid ground, she pushed me away from her. 'You bastard! You disgust me!' she sobbed. 'You let him lead us on this treacherous path and when I end up in trouble – you laugh! You callous bastard!' She stepped back. 'Don't touch me!'

On our descent from the mountain, she said nothing to either of us.

Francisca had tipped the porter and boarded the train, which had a red and white Vienna–Munich sign bolted to its side. I ran alongside the carriage, looking through the windows. My eyes tailed her red hair as she moved down the passageway to a compartment where Herbert and Leopold were loading their bags on to a luggage rack. Having all come to

Vienna together, they had decided to leave together. Francisca sat down and pretended not to see me. I tapped on the window. She looked at me: what do you want?

I motioned for her to open the window: please.

She shook her head: more aggravation. But then she sighed: at least this will be the last of it. She coerced Herbert and Leopold to help pull down the window. The train whistle blew and steam rushed out from the undercarriage. The two strained and finally managed to crack the window enough for Francisca and me to speak.

'Please,' I said, 'don't go.'

She looked at me: I went through all that trouble with the window to hear that? She leaned down. 'I almost died because of you and that fool.' Her eyes hardened to a stony glare. 'You were supposed to protect me,' she snarled. 'Some husband you'd make. Goodbye, Martin.'

'Give me another chance!' I pleaded.

She was incensed. 'You're a soft touch to that delusional dreamer! You're incapable of mature behaviour.'

'Francisca, please understand – '

'I understand only too well! It's obvious that you choose him over me, and I've accepted that now.'

The train shuddered. Its wheels rocked back and forth, and then slowly began to roll forward.

'I can't help you any more,' she said, struggling to project her voice over the engine's noise. 'You have to break away from him yourself.'

'I'll write,' I shouted, running alongside the train.

She shook her head: don't bother.

'No letters?'

She shook her head again: no. Behind her, Leopold and Herbert waved goodbye with sarcastic exaggeration. I was out of breath and stopped. I watched as the window with Leopold's and Herbert's waving hands departed. The train disappeared down the track and into the distance.

'I've never felt such heartache,' I said to Dolferl as he sat at his writing desk. It had been three months since Francisca had left for Munich. Dolferl was busy with his 'reading' and his 'discussions', and didn't want to take the time to see me; I was sure he found my company excruciating as he deemed any talk of my broken heart 'silly nonsense'.

'She doesn't matter now,' he said, 'she's away in Munich. Not waltzing the night away as they do here; most likely in the arms of another, doing what they do in Munich.'

'Don't, Dolferl,' I said. 'It would kill me to think of her even talking to other men, let alone . . . being with them.'

Evidently Dolferl's words hadn't evoked the desired response. 'If you can't overcome your emotions you will never be able to achieve greatness! My emotions died with my mother, and I'm thankful for that.'

'I see this as a loss, not an advantage.'

'Nonsense! It is emotions that make us weak. Read Schopenhauer! If I want to feel something I can always go and listen to Wagner.'

'I'm not like that. Francisca is in my heart. Forever.'

'You have such a small mind. You pine after that worthless whore. There are so many more pressing matters to consider!' he said. 'If we're not vigilant, what predicament will our race be in a thousand years from now?' He stopped to let the thought sink in. 'If we don't keep our blood pure, the blacks will have taken over, or the Asians. Races come and go like the Ice Ages.'

'What does that have to do with me?'

'Nothing. You don't matter: no individual matters. We create all that drama, but it's only in our heads. We individuals don't matter to nature. We're just vessels, carrying the traits of our race in our blood.'

I wasn't listening; my mind had wandered back to the smell of wet metal at the Central Station. I recalled watching my feet tumble along the platform, away from the end of my love affair. 'All that matters to me is Francisca,' I said glumly. 'Nothing else.'

'How dare she consume you like this! How dare you fall under her spell!' he blurted out, and then laughed. 'My God, I'm doing battle with a witch! And while I'm at it' – he looked around his room at his books – 'I'm getting rid of this rubbish, once and for all. 'I'll trade in these books and get some money. Then we can go and get tickets for the opera tonight!'

'But – ' I started to say.

'But nothing. Come with me!'

We took the tram to Adlerstraße, entered the Hermetic Chest bookstore and wove our way through the musty labyrinth of mystical knowledge formed by the columns of books. The clerk was reading behind the counter. Dolferl slammed the box of books down in front of him.

'Take these back!' he boomed.

'Now then, what's with all the commotion?' asked the clerk, unfazed. A black cat came and curled up on his lap, regarding us both with unblinking eyes.

'I've read these books on the so-called "occult sciences" thoroughly and found that they are remiss in what they promise. I want to sell them back to you.'

'Fine,' said the old man. He raised his eyes fleetingly to the peeling, discoloured ceiling and then looked back to Dolferl. 'However,' he said, 'I think you should understand that the books are not remiss; the reader is.'

'These are felonious works and frivolities, written by charlatans!' exclaimed Dolferl. 'I spent my hard-earned money on these books and I expect a good price for them.'

'Well,' said the book dealer, picking up a book and running his finger along the edges, 'I'll have to see if they're damaged in any way.' Then he stared back at Dolferl. 'And my cat and I would appreciate it if you would lower your voice.'

'I do not take orders!' Dolferl erupted.

'And that is precisely why these books don't work for you. You don't follow instruction, as a result of which you can never grasp the essence of the matter.'

'Swindler! Enough of this fraud! Chicanery!' Dolferl screamed, pushing over a pile of books. The volumes scattered across the floor and a cloud of dust billowed up.

'Anger is a major obstacle on the path to higher consciousness,' muttered the man. 'I can see,' he continued, looking at me, 'that you were unable to help your friend out of the darkness that surrounds him.'

'You two know each other?' Dolferl asked, surprised.

'Well . . . ' I mumbled. I was on the floor, picking up the books.

'How do you think your friend found you?' the shop clerk interjected.

'All I want is my money, and I'll leave.'

The clerk carefully opened *The Secret of the Runes* and studied the binding.

'You won't achieve any spiritual growth that way,' he said. 'It's obvious that you're groping in the dark, my son. As I told you before: you need someone to lead you.'

'I am my own leader!' snapped Dolferl.

'You know neither the way nor the destination. How will you get anywhere?'[21]

21 See: Appendix 17, Hitler and the Occult

'Come on,' said Dolferl, gesturing towards a coffee house.

'Sorry,' I said, 'I can't afford it.'

'I'll treat you.'

'You can't afford it either.'

The sale of his books had covered the price of theatre tickets and concerts, but that had been three months ago; now all of the money was gone and it had been a while since Dolferl had last completed a painting.

'Tomorrow's my birthday,' he said.

'That doesn't change the fact that we're penniless.'

'Ah, but it does!'

We entered the coffee house. Dolferl ordered a Sacher Torte, and a hot chocolate; I ordered the smallest coffee there was.

'You won't have enough money for the hostel,' I said.

'I'll be twenty-four tomorrow,' he replied.

I had no idea what he meant.

'On my twenty-fourth birthday, the court will release my father's inheritance: I'm rich!'

I pictured Dolferl resuming his previous lifestyle: coffee houses, extravagant clothing, concert visits, first class train rides and opera tickets.

'I won't stay here,' he said. 'I've had my fill of Vienna. People have marzipan for brains in this city. It's gone to the dogs.'

'What are you planning to do?'

'I'm emigrating. I'm going to Germany.'

'To Germany? What about the Draft Board?'

'The military? Do you really think I'm going to risk spilling my blood for this multiracial cesspool?'

Men our age had been called for medical examination by the army two years previously. I had attended in Linz, but had been rejected on account of my 'frail health'. Dolferl had refused to go; as much as he upheld the ideals of wars and battles, he hated the idea of serving in the Austrian army and being stationed somewhere in Herzegovina or Galicia.

'Come with me,' he said. 'Let's start a new life in Munich!'

Munich, I thought. Francisca. 'Count me in.'

'I'm home! I've come home at last!' proclaimed Dolferl. 'Munich is the home I've been searching for!' Dolferl was full of life as he skipped along Kaufingerstraße. It was May 1913 – one month after he'd come in to his inheritance. Shoppers and students conversed about current affairs, discussing the many divisive issues affecting life in this great twentieth century: the new railroad under construction to link the Bavarian lakes with the city; the steadily rising property prices (which increased their affluence) and the rising hems that dared to reveal women's ankles.

'Finally! Finally people who know how to speak German!' rejoiced Dolferl. 'Not one mispronounced syllable by some Slavic slob!'

There were immigrants in Munich, but nothing compared to the ethnic mix of Vienna. Munich felt more like an immense Bavarian village than a European hub, a placid town with all the opportunities of a metropolis.

'Munich is friendlier than that detestable Vienna,' said Dolferl. 'Munich is "grand". It's a city that adores itself.'

He was right: Munich was proudly ostentatious. Its people were generous, hedonistic – and corrupt, but easy-going with it. Corruption was just part of their way of life, considered a 'venial sin'. At first, the locals seemed rather brusque (especially the waitresses in the beer halls), but behind that façade they were courteous and warm-hearted. This was in stark contrast to the insincere Viennese, who tended to be spiteful and arrogant. Munich had the air of an amicable beer garden with an even mix of townsfolk and artists. And not only were artists plentiful here, they were also quite influential: some, such as the painters Franz von Lenbach or Franz von Stuck, became so successful that they could afford grandiose villas. Naturally, this inspired Dolferl to assume that finally, in this city, his genius would be acknowledged. Before leaving Vienna, he had bought himself an expensive new wardrobe and had his shoulder-length hair trimmed. He had scrutinised the barber's work as he sat in the chair, instructing the poor man on exactly how his hair should be cut at each step. Now the beard was gone, leaving only a moustache which Dolferl planned to groom and point upwards at the tips like Kaiser Wilhelm's.

'Everything has worked out well, hasn't it?' His tone craved reassurance and encouragement.

I grimaced: sort of.

I hadn't told my family that I had failed to complete studies at the Conservatory, abandoning my degree and with it any chance of obtaining a chair at the Vienna Philharmonic. This had pleased Dolferl, because without my degree I had less chance of becoming another of the 'musical bureaucrats' he so despised. Now we were more alike: fugitives from accepted schools of art, two outcasts bound together by similar circumstance. In his eyes, this elevated me to the arty superiority of his own existence.

'What would have become of Wagner had he not come to Munich?' said Dolferl. 'The world had worn him down for decades. Only in Munich did he find the peace he needed to complete his life's work!' Dolferl looked up the facade of a building. 'The architecture in Munich is actually better than Vienna's.'

'They do have fine buildings here,' I conceded, 'but I wouldn't go that far.'

'Think of Munich's inner city. And you can't deny the grandeur of Ludwigstraße. My paintings of these buildings are my best work.'

'Yes, they are,' I agreed, wearily.

'When I paint the buildings here, the subject matter inspires me more than anything in Vienna.'

'That's because you're happier here.'

'I am happier because the buildings are better, the people are better, everything is better. Even the way they talk!'

Despite his negative world view, Dolferl was ever the optimist: he believed not only in the evolution of the human race, but also of his own life. He was absolutely convinced that now, finally, his big breakthrough would come. Time and again he talked about Makart and Feuerbach as two geniuses who, like him, had supposedly been rejected by the academy in Vienna and who had made their breakthrough in Munich. There was no doubt that Dolferl had improved as an artist, but it was much more difficult to find proper outlets to sell his work here. The competition among artists was just too great: a quarter of all German painters lived here.

Dolferl's hope to study architecture and my aspiration to continue my music studies had dissipated within the first weeks. Rent in Munich was much higher than in Vienna; travellers reported that rents were more expensive than even in Paris, Rome or London. Dolferl's inheritance was dwindling rapidly. I tried to sell his paintings, while he painted (and read), mostly during the night. We accepted any job, even to paint signs that read 'Fresh Milk' or 'Come Back Soon' for local shops.

Our daily fight for survival distracted me from thoughts of Francisca. After nearly two months, I still hadn't mustered up the courage to seek her out and attempt a reconciliation. When Dolferl wanted to be alone to paint, I would sneak off to the centre of town, where Francisca's father's hotel was. But every time I arrived at the corner of Maximilianstraße, I froze: I was too petrified to turn the final corner. I yearned for Francisca and knew that I would never get over her. I needed her so much, yet I was incapable of approaching her. My heart was timid and my apprehension overwhelming, rendering me paralysed. For now.

'You have to admit that things have improved for us now,' Dolferl said. 'Take our flat and our landlord.'

'It's still a little cramped.'

We lived in a small room: a bed, a sofa, a chair, a table and two oleographs. Dolferl slept on the bed, I on the sofa.

'Yes, but unlike our last place, this room faces west, so we get the afternoon light.'

'But we still have kerosene lamps, no electric light!'

'That we do,' he conceded. 'But Frau Popp isn't a meddling old bat: she's a true German lady, not some Czech slut. She minds her own business and is always friendly, like the rest of the people in this town. Think of the art exhibits! The galleries! The new Pinakothek! The first museum to exhibit contemporary German art only!' Dolferl's eyes glistened. 'Isn't it magnificent?'

One afternoon as I was leaving our room with a stack of his paintings to sell on the streets, Dolferl put his hand on my shoulder. This was unusual: he rarely touched anybody. In fact, I doubted he even touched himself.

'I had a dream,' he said. 'I was back in Austria. But I know this is not going to happen. Nothing or nobody could draw me back to that Habsburg hell.' He paused. 'Not even Stefanie.'

'Stefanie?'

'I still love her,' he said, slowly and firmly, as if acknowledging it for the first time.

I was stunned. How could he still be infatuated with Stefanie? I thought back to our visit to Linz when he had 'seen' goodbye to her.

'But . . . you said your emotions were a thing of the past.'

'Of course they are,' he replied. 'When I speak of love, I'm not referring to the sentimentalities or animal instincts that you and most people mean when they misuse the word "love". I'm speaking of eternal love, that holy love that Wagner depicts in his works.'

'So, do you think you'll see Stefanie again sometime?'

'It doesn't matter. True love doesn't exist on this earth anyway. The

Master from Bayreuth said it perfectly. True love can only be found in renunciation or death.'

The mention of Stefanie's name triggered a sequence of thoughts with one inescapable conclusion: I had to talk to Francisca, not just pine for her. I didn't want to end up like Dolferl, alone and trapped in a Wagnerian fantasy world. I had to go to her father's hotel. I had to talk to her and try to win her back.

September 1913, Munich

Francisca's father's hotel was the most magnificent in all of Munich. The Four Seasons was on Maximilianstraße, near the opera house and a range of theatres and museums, as well as the most expensive shops in town. You had to be – or appear to be – a duke, a thriving industrialist or a successful opportunist just to get past the hotel's discerning doorman. In my opera wear, a black satin tuxedo, I was sure to gain entrance to the lobby.

I approached the front doors with the tails of my tux fluttering behind me, affecting the demeanour of a man with too much to do and too many places to be to acknowledge anyone but himself. I strode directly past the doorman, looking straight ahead and not making eye contact. The lobby of the Four Seasons was imposing yet dignified, with the unmistakeable undercurrent of affluence. People spoke in hushed tones, and the hotel employees walked with their heads down in deference.

I hadn't contacted Francisca to tell her I was coming: I wanted to surprise her; to ambush her and catch her unprepared so that she might listen to me even for a moment before her defences were raised. With a single red rose in my hand, I walked over to the reception desk. What am I doing here? I thought suddenly: Francisca came to Munich to get away from me. She hadn't left Vienna because of her father, or her stagnant career: it was because she wanted to get away from me.

'Yes?' said the woman behind the desk. 'May I help you?'

'Ah . . . ' I said, resisting the urge to turn and leave. I had come this far.

Then out of the corner of my eye, I glimpsed Francisca emerge through a swinging door marked 'Employees Only'. She was arm in arm with a redheaded man. My thumb pressed against the thorns on the stem of the rose and was pierced. Ouch! I squeezed my index finger against my thumb to stop the bleeding.

They were laughing.

She was laughing the way she had once laughed only with me, I was sure. I broke into a cold sweat: she was so happy, she was almost floating. It was too much. Just as I had decided to cut and run, however, she spotted me.

'Martl!' she exclaimed, cheerfully.

There was no turning back: I had to walk over to her.

'You're in Munich? What are you doing here?'

I didn't know what to say. I just stood there staring at her, wondering whether to give her the rose.

'I'd like you to meet my brother,' she said. 'Frederick. The photographer.'

'Sorry,' I said, not taking Frederick's hand. I showed them my bleeding finger and waved instead.

'And this is the composer I told you about.'

She had talked about me! She had told her brother about me!

'I've heard so much about you!' Frederick said. 'Great to meet you.'

I gave her the rose and she smiled.

We secluded ourselves at a table at the back of a small café near her hotel, and both ordered absinthe. Her thumb and index finger almost touching, she winked to the waiter. 'Just a small one. I may have to do some paperwork later.' She laughed. I laughed with her. Finally, we were laughing together once more. My hand crept slowly across the round marble tabletop, desperate to touch hers.

'So here we are, in the same city again. Is it fate?' she mused.

'No!' I blurted out. 'No, it's not fate. I wanted to be here with you.' The words spilled out of me, uncontrollably. I had waited months to tell her. 'You're the reason I'm here. I can't live without you.'

'My!' she exclaimed. Was she trembling?

'I missed you. Though "missed" is much too inadequate a word to describe the loss I've felt since you left,' I said, struggling to curb my surging emotions, wishing the absinthe would arrive.

'I just can't believe you came all this way for me,' she said. 'What about your graduation?'

'It would mean nothing without you.' My forefinger was a hair's breadth from her hand.

'You left before finishing?'

'Yes.'

'Oh, Martin,' she cried, and turned her hand over to accept mine.

'Your drinks,' announced the waiter, setting the small-stemmed glasses on the table. We each took a sip of the aniseed-flavoured spirit. It soothed and coated our throats.

'I love you, Francisca,' I said. 'I love you so much.'

'I love you too,' she replied, as we looked into each other's eyes. 'I'm so glad you've come,' she said, tears welling. 'I've been so lonely without you.' The warm, cosy sensation of the absinthe complemented her words perfectly. 'So tell me,' she asked, caressing my hand, 'where are you staying?'

'I would have come here sooner except . . . I can't tell you how often I tried. Well, you know how demanding Dolferl can be . . . '

'Who?' she said, snatching her hand back from mine.

'I've been representing him, selling – '

Her hands pressed against her ears. 'Please,' she groaned, struggling to speak. 'I don't want to hear any more.' After a moment she lowered her hands, and looked around for her handbag so she could leave quickly. 'You live with him?' she asked.

'Yes.'

'Oh, really?' she said, rising.

'Please, hear me out! Listen! Don't break my heart again. Please.'

She froze. 'Break *your* heart?'

'You've only half-finished your absinthe. Hear me out,' I pleaded.

She sat down again and looked at her glass. 'I'll need this to listen to you.'

'Dolferl wanted to come here to be among Germans. Only Germans.'

'Of course!' she snapped, with venom.

'He wants to make a new start here. But I only came to make a new start with you.'

She brought her glass to her lips, tilted her head back and let the greenish liquid flow into her mouth. She put the glass down in front of her and pointed to it: I want another.

I motioned to the waiter: two more glasses.

She sighed to herself. 'I can't believe you're still involved with him.'

'Believe me, it's purely for financial reasons, I – '

'I don't want to hear it.' She emptied her glass.

'I can't tell you how tired I am of his endless midnight sermons. I'd love to move out. But I can't. You know what the rents are like. And selling his paintings at least covers . . . '

The waiter set the glasses down in front of us and she emptied her glass in one swoop.

'Would you work at the hotel?'

'Of course!' I said overjoyed.

'Even low-level management?'

'Anything!'

'OK,' said Francisca. 'I'll see what I can do.'

She smiled at me, but now there was a distance between us.

'All of this can be ea–ea–easily explained,' stammered Dolferl. He was dressed in his 'poor artist' costume: scruffy trousers and an unironed shirt missing an occasional button. He was talking to an Austrian consular officer sitting with folded arms. The man's lips thinned: so explain.

It was January 1914 and Dolferl had been arrested for not attending his mandatory appointment with the Austrian Draft Board. I was sitting next to a police officer at the back wall of the office. Dolferl straightened his gaunt frame. His fingers extended like the teeth of a comb as he swept his hair back. He inhaled with an audible groan and began to speak.

'There is nothing I would rather do than serve my beloved Austria,' he said, in his most sincere tone.

'Mein Gott!' I muttered to myself, remembering Dolferl's diatribes vowing never to defend anything Habsburg. And now here he was, the duplicitous prodigal son begging for forgiveness.

'I had filed a request to have myself physically examined in Vienna instead of Linz. You see, sir, I was pursuing a career in the arts there in my dear Vienna. I have no idea what might have happened to the letter I sent to the Board.' His voice pleaded for clemency. 'And as it was, I was striving desperately to make ends meet. Being a working artist is my greatest joy, but also an extremely difficult path to follow. I never know where my next meal will come from. My companions in life are sorrow and need.'

The official's elbows rested on the table, as he listened intently. At the words 'sorrow and need', he smiled sympathetically.

'I do the work I do because it is my calling,' Dolferl continued. 'I live as honestly as I can. I am not a rich man, but I am a hard worker. I beg you, sir, please have mercy. I am an orphan and have no one else on this earth to beg for compassion but you.'

The official scribbled on a piece of paper. 'You will report to Salzburg for your physical exam in ten days' time.'

Dolferl's art of persuasion had worked: he had evaded arrest, and Salzburg was much closer than Linz. Again, Dolferl had proved himself a master of manipulation: whether an uncompromising parent, an agitated landlady or a gullible civil servant, Dolferl had a gift for garnering sympathy with his words and theatrics to serve his own ends.

At Salzburg, Dolferl became a walking collection of progressively deteriorating nervous tics, and the Draft Board deemed him unfit to perform his military service.

When I told Dolferl of my decision to move he was surprisingly calm. 'I don't mind living alone,' he said. 'On the contrary: greatness can only be achieved by the lonesome individual in self-determined solitude.'

As a hotel employee, I could now afford my own room and had arranged with Frau Popp to relocate down the hall from Dolferl. A few days after I had moved, Dolferl knocked on the door to 'my' room.

'I've been in the library all day,' he complained from the doorway. 'And I spend my nights reading and painting. All I do is work! And for what?'

I knew that was my cue to console him in his self-pity. But I was in no mood.

'Well, I've been dealing with the public all day,' I said, undoing my cufflinks.

'I need a hot chocolate,' he whined.

'I've no desire to go out. I don't want to see another human face or hear another human voice for the next sixteen hours.' I was now one of those people behind a hotel desk. I had often wondered how anyone could do such a tedious job. Being constantly courteous required vast amounts of energy. And if I wasn't dealing with annoying customers, it was the irascible cleaning ladies whose work I oversaw; they were demanding in a different way. Those grey-haired varicose-veined crones had given up smiling long ago. I had to check and sometimes recheck their work. At that moment, I'd had enough of everyone, including Dolferl.

'Today in the library, I had a revelation,' Dolferl continued undeterred.

'Let me rest, Dolferl, I'm tired.' My braces dangled by my thighs. My back ached for my bed. But he ignored me and swept into the room, gravitating towards the window to peer down to the street.

'It came to me when I read that Plato has Thrasymachus say that the ruling class decides what's good and what's evil.'

I kicked off my shoes as he continued speaking.

'So ultimately – what are good and evil?' he said. 'Certainly not anything that can be judged objectively. Yet we all think in these terms. We're convinced that we know, but ultimately history decides what's good and what's evil. Those who win gain legitimacy simply by winning.' He looked at me, expecting rhapsodic approval.

But I just said with an exhausted voice, 'That was your revelation?'

'Can't you see the genius of it?' he exploded. 'Success alone determines right or wrong, good or evil! It's not a question of morals! It's about success! Success is the only yardstick by which history measures our actions. And as Darwin has shown, nature does exactly the same.'

'Is that so?' I said, as I continued to undress and change into more comfortable attire.

'Right is what the mighty declare to be right,' he asserted solemnly. 'That's the whole truth. It's that simple.'

'I'm sorry,' I interrupted, 'but I'm exhausted.'

'How can you be tired?' he whined. 'I need to talk! Since you moved out I haven't spoken to anyone. And I need to talk now; I need it to organise my thoughts.'

'Why don't you write it down?' I suggested.

'If only that would work!' He shook his head sadly. 'My thoughts come to me faster than my fingers can move. When I try to write something, the struggle between thought and fingers obscures the original clarity of the thought. Even my tongue gets in the way,' he said, with a laugh. 'If only I could communicate by thought alone.'

I yawned, communicating without words how I felt. Sometimes living down the hall is not far enough away, I realised. I lay down on my bed. I felt I should be allowed to feel comfortable in my own home.

'It's been days since I've gone to the beer halls to sell paintings,' he said. 'I just don't have the inclination lately.'

'Why don't you go to Café Stefanie?' I asked. 'You said yourself that Café Stefanie stimulates you.'

It wasn't only the name that Dolferl liked: at Café Stefanie in Schwabing, he was surrounded by people much like himself; failed students and struggling artists hammering out grand plans on how to solve the problems of the world. However, all of the ideas given vent there just gathered in the air with the cloud of cigarette smoke that permeated the café. Nothing expressed there ever came to fruition: it was a world of pure ideas. Some called Café Stefanie *Café Größenwahn*: Café Megalomania. Remarkably for such a thinker and talker, Dolferl never participated in any of the discussions there, but merely sipped his chocolate and listened. He was too shy; even though his extensive reading had taught him more than most of them, he was intimidated by their academic vocabulary.

'I don't feel like listening to that haughty language tonight,' he said. 'Those people bore me, even the Pan-Germans amongst them. I can't listen to them for more than a minute. They fixate on one subject, whereas I'm interested in everything, in finding connections.'

'Yes I know, you think you're quite remarkable,' I said.

'If I read a book, I can take out the one sentence that is original and new and skip the rest. But I can't do that with people. I have to listen to them for the entire evening. And that makes me sick!'

'So then you understand why I don't want to go,' I said.

'Perfectly.'

'Good,' I said, as I got up, walked him out of the room and closed the door.

'Hilda, darling!' exclaimed the dashing scoundrel, theatrically summoning his lover, an immaculately dressed girl.

'Yes, Rudolf?' she said, with drunken indifference. She held her six-month-old toddler on her lap. 'What is it you want?'

There was another question in the air at the Café Luitpold: were Rudolf and Hilda really having a private conversation, or were they having a private conversation for all to hear? The volume of their voices suggested they were both hoping to gain legendary status in Munich's bar culture.

'Darling, did you walk the streets today?' Rudolf asked. His words were delivered with the timing and swagger of well-rehearsed cabaret.

'Of course I did.' Hilda smirked. 'How do you think I made my way here?'

I looked across at Francisca. Her elbow rested on the bar as she observed the couple. Hilda sat in self-styled splendour. She was a countess, writer and painter, firm in the belief that she was the reigning queen of Munich's bohemia.

'What I want to know is,' said Rudolf, bending down on one knee in front of Hilda as if proposing, 'did you sell your body today?'

'Darling!' she cried out, 'you know me better than that. I don't whore when I'm nursing!'

'And why is that, my dear?'

'Baby doesn't like to share!'

Laughter enveloped them. Café Luitpold was different to Café Stefanie –

very different. Café Luitpold was the place to see and be seen. Here, Munich was playing itself. Everyone was acting, not only for his or her own entertainment but also for the amusement of others, including provincial types like me.

'Hilda,' announced the gaunt Rudolf, 'you are my blessed harlot. You are the whore and the Madonna. You fire my imagination.'

Hilda picked up the baby and switched him to her other leg with a grace that was both tender and efficient. Then she looked away from the baby, up at her tall lover.

'I want you to be the mother of my children!' pleaded Rudolf.

'Please!' answered Hilda. 'As far as I'm concerned it's always an immaculate conception!'

Rudolf looked around. As well as Francisca and myself, everyone else at the bar was eavesdropping. 'See how women have all the power!' he said to his audience.

He's not wrong there, I thought. Women do have all the power. I was exhausted, and had it not been for Francisca I certainly wouldn't have been here; but Francisca was barely aware of my presence. She revelled in the last exchange of the couple and gently bounced up in her bar stool. Then she twisted her hair up and tucked it under her blue velvet beret.

'I disagree,' said a gentleman with a deep voice. But the two actor-lovers weren't listening. They were ravishing one another, Hilda bent over the bar and Rudolf about to undress her, right then and there. The baby scuttled along the counter towards the glass of the gentleman who was speaking.

'I don't believe that the women have all the power,' continued the man, dressed in an expensive three-piece suit. 'Nor do I believe that women should have any more power than they already have. On the contrary!' He raised his glass from the bar. 'The women must be put back where they belong: in the family. That's their place. That's where they should have all the power. But not in public and, please – not in politics.'

'What a disgusting attitude!' retorted Francisca, theatrically.

I hovered my opened hands over the bar in an attempt to quiet her, but this only riled her more, and she turned towards the gentleman. 'Pigs like you will not stop the progress of our society!' she snarled, with such hostility that it drew even Rudolf's and Hilda's attention.

The gentleman looked at Francisca. 'Allow me to introduce myself,' he said, addressing the audience. 'My name is Lehmann. The publisher.'

'So you're the man who writes the rubbish my father reads!' Francisca exclaimed in outrage. She laughed to herself. 'What's the latest?' she questioned. 'A Germanic Christianity, right?'

Herr Lehmann nodded affirmatively. The publisher's name rang a bell: Dolferl had spoken highly of him and his books.

'And what the hell is that supposed to be?' asked Francisca.

Herr Lehmann answered with a composed smile. 'Read the book and find out for yourself.'

'Buy that conceited drivel? Never!' shouted Francisca. 'That interview with you in the *Neueste Nachrichten* was more than enough. Your talk of the "new Luther" made me sick! I had to take an aspirin after I read it.'

I tensed, ready to intervene. Or was I overreacting? Surely he wouldn't attack her physically, would he? This was Munich, where everyone was allowed to say whatever they liked, however disagreeable. Anyone could say anything and everything. Unless it was insulting to the Emperor, of course.

'You may not like it, my dear' – Lehmann stepped closer to Francisca – 'but the "new Luther" will come!' Lehmann, turned towards his audience, as the entire coffee shop was now listening. 'There will be a man who will lead Germany out of its current morass. The new Luther will allow us to adapt to the greater importance of Germany in the world. And here at home, he will deal with all of the vermin that pollute our society, especially the greedy, contemptible Jews!'

Francisca closed her eyes and gently massaged her eyelids with her fingertips. 'He's giving me a headache again,' she said to me. 'Let's go.'

I got up.

'And let me assure you,' Lehmann continued, glaring at Francisca as she rose, 'this Luther will be a man. Not a woman!'

'Martin,' said Francisca, firmly, demanding my attention.

I saw her collecting her things. 'Yes!' I said, as I slid my arm into the sleeve of my overcoat. My eyes were still glued to this pompous creature before me.

'The new Luther must have the courage to fight.' Lehmann continued. 'Because ultimately he will be fighting against the entire world!'

Francisca pressed her hand into mine. She looked at the floor and dragged me out of the place.

'The new Luther will fight, just like his predecessor. The course of this conflict is not known, yet its outcome is certain . . . '

A light rain fell and the scent of foliage permeated the city. We were walking along quietly together, arm in arm.

'Feeling better?' I asked Francisca.

'A little,' she said, and then shook her head: why, why, why?

'What's wrong?' I asked.

'I don't know. I'm confused, I guess.'

'Confused? About what?'

'Why do I love you?' she asked.

'Well,' I said, 'why? Why *do* you love me?'

She looked into my eyes. 'In all honesty,' she said then, 'I don't know if what I feel for you is destructive or not. But on some level, it doesn't matter. All I know is that I have to act on it.'

I shrugged and smiled. 'I know why I love you,' I said.

'Why, then?'

'You're my missing half.'

She grinned. 'How can you be so sure?'

'It's something I never question. It just is. As sure as the beating of my heart.'

'That doesn't answer my question.'

'Well, then,' I said, 'here's your answer.' I took her in my arms as the rain fell harder and we kissed, as if nothing mattered except our love.

'Come,' she said, as we scurried up the path and ducked into the service entrance of the hotel. She climbed up the back staircase, trailing me behind her: she was taking me up to her room. What was she doing? What was I doing? Was this right?

Could I live with myself if I did this?

Could I live with myself if I didn't?

Those breasts, those perfect breasts I had beheld in the sunlight, that unforgettable moment on the mountain! I longed to have them all to myself. Now, in her room at the top of the stairs, they could finally be mine! But we had promised each other that we would marry . . . We had to get married now.

How would our love be consummated? All those years, imagining how it would be – and now I was about to find out. I hurried up the stairs, as images of the reproductive organs of flowers from school biology flashed through my mind. She laughed as she ran up the steps before me and threw off her beret, shaking her head to let her curls tumble down. I imagined her peeling her dress from her body. I remembered staring at statues of nudes in the museums, and wondered how different it would be to experience a real naked woman. Francisca turned and smiled at me with a mischievous look in her eyes: just you wait! She took my hand and squeezed it reassuringly: she would teach me everything I needed to know. We ran up the next flight of stairs. I was breathless now. We stopped on the landing. The stairs and the walls were spinning. I opened my mouth and spoke as I tried to catch my breath.

'What floor?'

'We're on the' – she looked around – 'third.' She exhaled. 'Only two more.'

Two more. How many steps? I wondered. I calculated about thirty more steps. One, two, three, I started counting. What was I going to do once I got there? Would I have the strength to take her? Would I have the strength to say 'no' and save my soul?

She turned, glanced at me and said, 'Nonsense!' before running further up the stairs. Had she read my mind? Could she sense the thoughts racing through my head as I followed her up these infernal steps?

Fifth floor.

'Hurry, darling,' she said, as she raced ahead to the door of her room.

She snapped open her handbag and searched for her keys. The key circled erratically in her quivering hand as it made its way to the keyhole. The tip of the key missed the hole, clinking against the door's brass plate. She was as nervous as I was, clearly. She giggled and shook her curls, scattering raindrops everywhere. She tried again, and with a focused effort guided the key to the key hole. She thrust it in, turned the key and I heard the clicking of the lock. I readied myself for heaven . . . and the hell that would undoubtedly follow. She pulled me inside. I was in her room: there was her bed, in the corner.

She turned to me. 'You will marry me?' she asked.

I was just about to answer when the name 'Francisca!' echoed down the hall. It was Edgar, her father.

I turned and saw him peering into the room. 'I've been waiting for you,' he said gruffly, He looked at her, then me. 'What do you two think you're doing?'

Francisca smiled. 'I wanted to show Martin next week's schedule.'

'Oh, really?' replied Edgar sarcastically.

'Of course.'

'I don't need to repeat the rules of the house, do I?'

'Not really,' she said.

'Well, I will anyway,' he said, speaking slowly and clearly. 'You live here under the same roof and the same rules as every other employee.

There will be nothing resembling cohabitation or coitus. We will not set a bad example,' he said. 'Do I make myself clear?'

We nodded, and I breathed a sigh of relief.

Fate had saved me from hell.

Again.

The First Great Battle for Civilisation

We would bring our ideals to our oppressed neighbours, liberate them and inaugurate a new age in European civilisation.

A tap sparkled golden in the sun as it was hammered triumphantly into a beer keg. A brass band played the *Bavarian Defile March*, and beer began to squirt from the tap. The sun's rays were reflected in the stream of golden liquid flowing into *Steins* held firmly in the hands of a sturdy waitress. In Munich in the summer, the beer gardens are the only places to be. And there we were at the Hofgarten, opposite the Cuvellier Theatre: Francisca, Dolferl, Frederick and I. Needless to say, it had taken various forms of enticement and coercion to get Francisca and Dolferl to the same table. I pleaded with both of them to do just this 'one thing' for me. I wondered how the two most important people in my life could despise one another. Why couldn't they just grow up and get along, as I did with them?

'The kind of photographer I am,' said Frederick, 'captures the moment.' Francisca's brother Frederick had made quite a name for himself. For his most famous collection, he had travelled to the Greek Islands, hired local male peasants to dress up in togas, and shot them as they posed among the ruins. 'The genius of that,' he said, 'is that there were no photographers in the Age of Pericles, so I was recreating the photos that would have been taken then.'

'Painters have been recreating subjects like that for centuries,' countered Dolferl, 'and they do it better, believe me.'

'I beg to differ, Adolf!' Frederick wagged his index finger, stained a dirty brown from the camera's silver-nitrate-coated plate. 'A photograph is the convergence of science and creativity. It's the moment caught in the aperture of light.'

Dolferl laughed politely. 'Surely you must be joking! A great painting unveils the essence of the subject it portrays. It's the expression of the Platonic idea behind the appearance. How can photography ever do that?'

Frederick shook his head vigorously. 'Photography is the way of the future; painting is dead.'

Dolferl drank from his *Apfelschorle*, a mixture of mineral water and apple juice. 'I wonder if anything will have a future,' he murmured ominously.

'You're right,' said Frederick. 'War is more than a possibility,'

'I'm terrified at the very thought,' said Francisca, 'But why is war inevitable?'

'May I?' interjected Dolferl, his eyes on Frederick, who shrugged. Dolferl turned to address Francisca. 'People have grown complacent and superficial in these prosperous, peaceful times. We've turned a blind eye to Serbia, and now the Russians have used it to gain a foothold in the Balkans. We must neutralise Serbia and disarm it. We must teach those warmongering Slavs respect.'

'I can't believe my ears!' said Francisca. 'This from someone who came to Munich to avoid military service in Austria . . . '

Dolferl glared at her, infuriated. 'Indeed, dear lady! I refuse to give my life for a senile Kaiser who has allowed my Austrian capital to become a breeding ground for sub-humans. The Habsburgs are the cause of the rising influence of the Slavs! It was poetic justice that the Kaiser's successor to the throne should be killed in Serbia by Slavic bullets that he himself had helped to make.'

'They were staying in our hotel,' said Francisca, 'Archduke Franz Ferdinand and his wife! It's only two weeks. And now they're dead.'

Dolferl clenched his fists and placed them on the table. 'I am a student of history,' he said, 'and let me tell you: we are surrounded by enemies. The French have been awaiting an opportunity for revenge since 1871. Why else would they ally themselves with Russia? Why does any state join a confederacy? That pact is a preparation for war!' He pointed a finger towards the sky and concluded: 'The price of our freedom is eternal vigilance! If we don't act now, they will!'

'But why start a war?' called Francisca. 'Because some Bosnian nationalist struck it lucky killing Franz Ferdinand and Sophie? Let the police deal with this!'

'The Serbian Government is known to have close ties to these terrorists,' boomed Dolferl. 'They harbour them. They breed them.'

'Why do people want to inflict such horror on us?' said Francisca.

'My dear,' said Dolferl, 'you know nothing about wars. I have studied them in detail, as I have many other things.'

'So what's your answer then? Why can't we all live together peacefully?'

'Have you ever bothered to read Darwin? Or John Fiske?' asked Dolferl, clutching his table napkin. 'All higher forms of life have come into being through a process of natural selection in which only the strongest survive. And what constitutes the strongest?' Dolferl paused. 'It's all in the blood! War is just an accelerated process of natural selection: it's the nature of nature. Every war is just another step on the evolutionary ladder.' Dolferl stopped. He put the napkin down and cleared his throat to make way for more of his rhetoric. 'The only question is: who will win? And the answer is: we will.' Dolferl turned to Frederick. 'We must seize the moment. Germany is producing more steel than Britain. Our electrical and chemical industries have left them in the dust.'

'I read in the paper that we can drop shells from airships now,' I remarked.

'Yes!' shouted Dolferl euphorically. 'All of the glorious fruits of the Industrial Revolution are at our disposal: trains, iron-clad warships, airships, and all the rest. Look at Big Bertha! It has more firepower than any other cannon ever built. It will blast the way for us, right to the top of the world. Because one day, the twentieth century will be remembered as "the German century".'

'Who cares!' Francisca shouted. 'Who cares! Live and let live, that's what it should all be about!'

'And that is exactly what Germany stands for!' said Dolferl, smiling. 'That's our principle. *Freedom*. Freedom from the imperialists of the West, and the barbarians of the East. Freedom for the world!'

'Adolf,' chimed in Frederick, 'I couldn't agree with you more. If war breaks out, I'm going to take my camera. Imagine having soldiers pose with their bayonets as a real battle rages behind them! Reality and fantasy will merge into a new art form!'

'At last, my good Frederick, we agree on something,' said Dolferl.

'Adolf,' said Francisca, 'care for a cigarette?'

Dolferl shook his head. 'Thank you, dear, but smoking kills everyone, not just the racially inferior.'

'Is that so?' replied Francisca as she lit up.

Then she gave me a look: do it now.

'Dearest friends and brothers,' I began, 'Francisca and I . . . ' I fumbled to remove the red velvet box from the hip pocket of my jacket. 'Francisca and I, we . . . ' I snapped open the box, revealing the two gleaming rings inside. 'We're getting engaged. Today. Now!'

Frederick applauded. 'Bravo! Bravo! *Hoch soll'n Sie leben!* Bravo!'

Dolferl's eyes froze. 'Engaged?'

'A toast, perhaps?' suggested Francisca.

Frederick raised his *Stein*. 'Here's to two wonderful artists! May their honeymoon last a hundred years!'

Everyone had raised their *Stein* except Dolferl. All eyes were on him.

'A true Viennese,' offered Francisca, as a reason for Dolferl's reluctance. 'He only drinks wine.'

'Alcohol poisons the spirit,' he pronounced.

Francisca eyed the glass of *Apfelschorle* by Dolferl's plate. 'Well, then I imagine that will have to do,' she said.

'Oh, no! No!' I interrupted, as I pushed my beer in front of Dolferl. 'I'm going to drink from Francisca's and we'll all have a proper toast!'

Dolferl glared at me. 'And to think, I had such big plans for you!'

'My Lord!' Francisca guffawed. 'How you deceive yourself! Such grandiose plans from such a nobody!' Francisca bent over and stared Dolferl right in the face. 'Ha!' she shouted. 'Ha to you!'

Dolferl pushed back his chair from the table and rose. Below his right eye, a nerve began to twitch. He crossed his arms. 'How dare you speak to me like that!' he began, but before he could continue, a voice cried out.

'*Krieg!*'

And then dozens of voices could be heard shouting: '*Es ist Krieg!*'

Roaring students in straw boaters swarmed into the garden, waving black, white and red flags. They grabbed any unattended *Stein*, sending foam flying everywhere as they began to drink wildly. We were caught up in the flow and dragged out into the street on to Odeonsplatz, into a raucous whirlpool of people.

I grabbed Francisca's hand as the current of the frenzied crowd carried us along around the tables and trees. I looked up at the garden lanterns overhead as we were dragged into the midst of the heaving crowd. Dolferl was torn between elation at the cause for celebration, and abhorrence at his immersion in this sweaty tide of men. Frederick wished he had his camera in place, his eyes calculating the exposure and the lens that would best capture this moment, this urge to fight, this shared patriotic ecstasy.

Some people began to sing, '*Es braust ein Ruf wie Donnerhall.*'

'It's war!' yelled others.

The brass band from the beer garden had followed and played along with the roar of the masses.

'*Wie Schwertgeklirr und Wogenprall!*'

The delirium of war. Bombs were exploding in our minds, out of our mouths, all around us. We were united, inhaling and absorbing the irresistible power of raw camaraderie, which would make us all real men. We clamoured for sweet revenge, a nation's unrequited love and generosity exploding into hate: burning, immediate and bloodthirsty.

'Lieb' Vaterland magst ruhig sein . . . ' they chanted, and I chanted too. War is great! War is the best excuse for destroying things, and killing people! War means I don't have to think! War is fun! War means I'll get married later! War will make me brave! War will make me a man!

Someone shouted: 'If we enlist now, we'll be the first at the front!'

Frederick grabbed my hand.

'Am Rhein, am Rhein, am deutschen Rhein . . . ' roared the crowd.

'Come on,' shouted Frederick, squeezing my hand harder. 'They're not going to win this war without us!'

Francisca took hold of me. 'Have you gone totally insane?'

'This doesn't concern you, Francisca,' I replied. 'This is something that I, that we' – I motioned to Frederick and Dolferl – 'all share! This is a matter for men.'

A look of helpless anger came over Francisca's face. The brass band of the King's Regiment had lined up at the Field Marshal's Hall opposite us, and started to play. Everyone joined in: *'Fest steht und treu die Wacht, die Wacht am Rhein!'*

Dolferl had fallen to his knees, praying: 'Dear God! The joy is almost too much for me to bear!'

More and more people fell to their knees around him, as did Frederick and I. 'Thank you for granting us all the good fortune to live in this time,' Dolferl cried.

Arms around each other, Dolferl, Frederick and I then got up and bellowed with the crowd: *'Wir alle wollen Hüter sein!'*

I had never seen Dolferl so happy. He was experiencing what he had never experienced in his life before: belonging.

'How do I look?' I asked Francisca. My newly-issued uniform jacket was neatly pressed and hung immaculately from my shoulders.

'Move a bit to the right,' said Frederick, looking through the aperture of the camera mounted on its tripod.

Francisca and I shifted as instructed.

'That's fine,' he said. 'Stay there.'

The peak of my cadet's hat concealed my eyes, leaving just my nose, mouth and jaw visible.

'Well, do I look brave?' I asked Francisca.

She gave me a look that was both sad and fearful. 'The colour does suit you, I suppose,' she said. It was an overcast grey. 'At least it's not red. You won't be as much of a target.' She sighed.

'It'll be all right,' I comforted her.

'Would you two stop talking and look at me?' complained Frederick.

'I'll never understand why you joined up,' she mumbled, trying not to move her mouth. 'It's not as though we've been attacked . . . '

'If we don't act now – ' I began to reply.

'I'm trying to take a photograph here!' griped Frederick from beneath the black velvet hood of the camera. His right arm held the flash, which was shaped like a metal 'T' and contained magnesium powder along its horizontal edge. The line of powder would be ignited in a flash, creating enough light for the silver-nitrate photographic plate to record an image.

'Francisca,' I persisted, 'we don't have a choice. If we don't attack them, sooner or later they'll attack us. You heard what Dolferl said.'

'Dolferl, Dolferl, always Dolferl! And what about what *I* say?' Francisca snapped, furiously. '*I'm* the one you plan to marry!'

'Please,' Frederick interrupted, clearly frustrated, 'at least postpone your argument until after I've taken the picture.'

Francisca and I resumed our positions, feigning harmony where there was none.

'Don't be so stiff, you two! Relax and be your loving selves! Make this a keepsake worth keeping . . . ' he said. 'Don't move!' he warned.

Puff! The 'T' exploded, flashing like lightning and causing our eyes to snap shut. A cloud of powder rose and an acrid smell permeated the room.

We coughed and dusted ourselves off.

'I think we should take another,' said Frederick, taking out the black glass plate from the camera and putting it into its protective black sleeve. 'Just to be on the safe side, in case something goes wrong in the darkroom.'

'Fine,' said Francisca. She turned back to me. 'I think what you're involved in is' – her eyes scanned me from my military hat to my brass buttons and down to my black army boots – 'jingoism at its worst. It's foolhardy, perilous and utterly unnecessary.' She fixed my collar. 'I think it very selfish on your part. And I can't help but think you're running away from something.'

'And what do you suppose that might be?'

'Me,' she said.

'You? But I'm crazy about you!' I exclaimed.

'You don't want to grow up and be the man you ought to be. Maybe you're just too young for me.'

'How can you say that? I'm fighting this battle to secure us the freedom to be together!'

'But Martl, we have that already.'

'Not really, my love.'

'You have no idea what you're getting yourself into.' She sighed.

'Come now, is this really the way to talk to your fiancé just hours before he leaves for war?'

'Yes! This is the only way! I have to try and talk some sense into you!' she sobbed.

'Darling, you've read the papers. Our military is vastly superior, there's nothing to fear.'

She looked down at the floor and shook her head.

I took out the red velvet box and handed it to her.

'And what am I supposed to do with these?' she responded, angrily.

'Keep them safe for us. Please,' I said, softly. 'You have to believe that everything will be all right. You have to have faith.'

'I wish I could,' she replied, her voice cracking.

'Just try,' I said, still holding the box.

She thought for a moment. 'I'll look after them,' she said then, taking the box. 'Until you come back.'

Frederick had slotted a new plate into the camera and refilled the flash's groove with powder. He took up position again to take the picture. There I stood, imagining the glory I hoped the war would lead me to. I was a valiant knight in the renascent age of chivalry, a gentleman warrior who would defeat our reviled enemy at the pull of a trigger. As I stared into the lens of the camera, doubts were beginning to circle in my mind. What if Francisca was right? What if what I was doing was foolhardy and dangerous? A nervous tremor rumbled through my belly as it dawned on me that I was entering the uncharted. I might be about to step into a man-made hell: the coupling of man's most vicious nature with his latest technological advances.

'Okay you two,' said Frederick, 'let's try this again.'

The train hurtled into the night. The windows had been whitewashed to subdue any light from within the carriages and conceal the train in darkness: a forty-ton secret snaking towards the dawn. A celebratory mood reigned in the cars, replete with scenes of festivity and feasting. The recruits chatted excitedly like youngsters on the way to a holiday camp as the train rocked us gently from side to side. We had been chosen to take part in the Great Fight for Civilisation. We would bring our ideals to our oppressed neighbours, liberate them and inaugurate a new age in European civilisation. It was German culture and wisdom versus French superficiality and frivolity; Germany's idealistic heroes against England's avaricious materialists.[22]

For six weeks we had practised saluting and marching, followed by three weeks of instruction in bayonet and rifle practice. Along with the other recruits of the 16th Bavarian Reserve Infantry Regiment, known as the List Regiment, we had sworn allegiance to Ludwig III, King of Bavaria, and to Kaiser Wilhelm II of Germany. We were itching for our great and glorious adventure to begin. According to reports, our army had overrun Belgium and penetrated over one hundred miles into France. The French government had fled Paris. Our advance was unstoppable. It was now October, and the consensus was that we would be home by Christmas, decorated as heroes, perhaps sporting a battle scar or two that would merely enhance our sexual appeal. My comrades talked excitedly about the passion that the sight of a uniform and a scar aroused in women, confident that it would prove a man's willingness to defend his woman against any threat from a hostile world. There was only one fear we all shared: we worried that the war might end before we saw action.

We had been on the train for hours and rumours began to circulate about where we were; some said we had passed the Rhine long ago, while others believed we were heading to Ypres. Eventually the chatter in our coach peaked and then slowly wound down and dissipated as our anticipation exhausted us. The singing had died down, and most men were now dozing or sitting silently in the dark. Light from the lamps along the railway line shone intermittently through the whitewashed windows and flickers illuminated the faces of zombie-eyed men who couldn't sleep.

'I wish there was some way I could shoot this,' commented Frederick. 'This is quite unique, don't you think?'

'Yes,' agreed Dolferl. 'I was just wondering how to recreate this kind of atmosphere on stage.'

22 See: Appendix 20, German Superiority

'The dramatist has an advantage there. All he needs is a pen.'

The folded tripod, the camera and his suitcase filled with heavy plates and chemicals penned Frederick in.

'One must take what one needs,' said Dolferl, philosophically, patting his backpack. 'I have my books.' He closed his eyes. 'They keep my body and mind together; especially Schopenhauer. His words help me withstand any pain, physical or spiritual.' He exhaled, deep in thought.

Men snored and the train rattled on in three / four time. It was curiously calming, this graceful mechanical waltz. Then a bell rang. Its peal was octaves higher than the clanking steel wheels, adding a counterpoint to the percussive sound of the train. Our corporal came walking down the aisle, shouting: 'Everyone get ready!'

The train whistle blew, signalling the approach to the station and calling to mind the squeal of the train the night I had taken Dolferl back from Dr Udrzal. My mind wandered to the flat cars transporting the ominous grey artillery.

Now it was happening. Our destiny was unfolding.

'Prepare to disembark!' shouted the corporal as he rang the bell.

We looked at each other. Was this it? The front line?

'We may have to change trains,' said Frederick.

'Maybe we can travel through as far as Paris,' said Dolferl, as if en route to the Louvre rather than the battlefield that lay in wait for him. For us.

'Perhaps we'll end up in Bordeaux,' said Frederick, always the gastronome, thinking of the region's exquisite wines.

The train's whistle wailed again. As the brakes were applied, the carriages rattled and Frederick threw one arm around his photographic equipment while his other hand gripped the seat. My feet pressed against the floor as the train shuddered to a halt, finally snapping us all backwards with one immense jolt. Rucksacks skidded under the seats, and boxes fell from the overhead rack.

'Everyone out on the double. Forward march!' ordered the corporal. He swung the bell, ringing it loudly. The men gathered their belongings and filed groggily into the centre aisle of the carriage. The door flew open and night air seeped into the train, moist and with the coolness of morning. The soldiers stretched their arms, arched their backs and yawned. Frederick's tripod rested on his shoulder alongside his rifle. His suitcase bumped against the seats as he made a staggering, erratic exit from the carriage.

'I'm so sorry,' he said to those behind, who were forced to stop and start continually as he struggled along. Eventually he navigated his way down the steps.

The soldiers piled out on to the platform, which was dimly lit by gas lanterns placed every few metres on its far side. In the midst of the soldiers hauling their belongings, Frederick remained oblivious to the commotion that surrounded him as corporals barked orders for the men to form orderly lines. Frederick heard none of that; instead, he stepped to the middle of the platform and positioned his tripod before quickly setting up his camera, pulling its front accordion section out. He was consumed with his mission: this was a moment not to be missed, creating a record of the soldiers' first step into the war zone. Frederick poured powder into the flash's horizontal groove. Then he stooped down under the black hood and looked through the lens. *Shoot before you think. Camera verité.* Soldiers shuffled back and forth in front of the door of the carriage. Dolferl and I had left the train and were standing in line further down the track. We turned and watched with incredulity at the gall of our friend. An unsuspecting private climbed down the steps and was greeted by the blinding explosion of light as the flash went off, casting a shadow from the girders above like the legs of an enormous spider. The disoriented man stumbled sideways, blinking as he tried desperately to regain his sight and overcome the shock.

'Great! Great!' shouted Frederick, congratulating himself on his first shot of the war. 'The face of victory!'

October 1914, Ypres

We had marched twenty-five miles and then spent the night in a schoolhouse in a little village behind the front line. Early the next morning, our regiment had linked up with others; all of the soldiers' spirits were higher than ever before. With *Deutschland über alles* on our lips, we proceeded westwards, all longing for the ardent intoxication of battle, that wildest, most masculine of acts.

As we rested at a barn, Frederick asked Dolferl if he could take his photo.

'I haven't had my picture taken since I was a child,' replied Dolferl.

'Well, all the more reason that I should . . . '

'No!' snarled Dolferl. 'Now is not the time!'

'Of course it is!' shot back Frederick. 'You can't go marching off to your first battle without having the moment captured for posterity!'

Dolferl finished tying his bootlace. 'I'm just a common foot soldier,' he replied. 'It is my cause, my country that will have its place in posterity.'

'Oh, don't be so modest,' said Frederick. 'Frankly, it's not convincing.'

'Please,' said Dolferl, 'I want these moments before I go off to the battle to be mine alone.'

'All the more reason for you to have your picture taken. You don't have to do anything, just stay where you are. I'll set everything up around you.'

Dolferl rolled his eyes, resigning himself to the situation.

'Don't sulk, Dolferl!' said Frederick. 'It'll be over before you know it.'

Within moments Frederick had set up the tripod. The men around Dolferl stood up and were preparing to march out to the front line. Frederick looked over at his subject as he sprinkled the black powder into the flash. 'Perfect! Hold that expression!' Frederick scrambled under the camera's cloak. 'You look very dashing with that Kaiser moustache!'

'It's an homage to Germany,' replied Dolferl.

'No talking,' called Frederick, 'I'm focusing.'

'The moustache symbolises the spirit of Germany, the ideals we're all fighting for,' said Dolferl, through clenched teeth.

'No talking!' repeated Frederick.

There was a moment of silence.

'Think of the battle that lies ahead!' said Frederick. 'Think of the glory!'

Suddenly Dolferl was consumed by the magnitude of the moment. The flash powder exploded in a puff of smoke.

'That will be incredible, Dolferl,' said Frederick, popping out from under the camera.

'Should we try another from my right side?' asked Dolferl.

It was a lovely scene for a massacre.

The fields of Flanders were green and endless and the wispy clouds and blue skies above only served to enhance the spectacular panorama. We had taken up our positions near a forest. As we waited for the order to attack, we all felt the pull of something mysterious and wonderful lying in wait out there in the distance. The bold gamble of life or death seemed superior to anything civilian life had to offer. The look and feel of our brand new weapons – the bayonet, the trench knife and the ammunition pouches on our belts – were testament to our invincibility: impassive instruments of fate. We were about to leave the narcissistic nineteenth century behind and enter the audacious twentieth.

At 6.45 a.m., our artillery began to fire. We could hear our heavy guns discharge behind us as wave after wave of shells zoomed over our heads towards the enemy. A storm of steel and flames raged in the air. We were all ready to scourge the green earth, to flatten any obstacles and force our way into the wide and untouched land before us. Every day we would reach new frontiers, new villages and new towns where we would preside over life and death.

Our objective was to attack across an open field and eliminate any British soldiers who remained after the bombardment. The Brits had dug in on the other side and we were still waiting. Frederick was one of the lucky ones allowed to witness the action directly. He was sent to the first line while Dolferl and I were relegated to the third. I glanced over at Dolferl. His moustache was waxed, its tips pointed, curved and contoured into two mirror-image 'c' shapes. For someone who was usually so prickly and irritable, he now appeared composed and relaxed. His gaze was calm, focussed and self-assured.

All of a sudden, the enemy's artillery located us and our entire area was under heavy fire. Shells splintered trees as if they were straws. But we were not afraid: everyone waited impatiently for the command: 'Forward!' And finally, it came. Out we ran into the gunfire-riddled field. The sight and sound of ammunition piercing the pastoral landscape created a jarring contrast. War was a new state of consciousness for me: instinct prevailed, only the present moment existed. Gunshots came from all directions. Shells exploded. Bullets whistled above and between us as we ran helter skelter over the clumpy grass and cowpats. The row of men ahead of us fell in a spray of bullets, crashing to the ground like a human wave breaking. I hit the ground and with my legs and arms grasping at whatever was around me, I crawled onward. There was a lull in the artillery barrage but the machine guns continued to fire. Smoke lingered overhead. With my head to the ground, my eyes scanned for Dolferl. He was nowhere to be seen on my right so, with my body pressed to the ground, I turned my head and looked to the left. As I shifted my line of sight, I glimpsed him: he was running towards the enemy lines and moved as if somehow directed towards the most strategically advanced position. His moustache glistened as it caught the sun; strangely, his gangly figure seemed made for war.

But where was Frederick? I hadn't seen him since the attack had begun. I looked ahead: in the grass, there were lines of bodies all wearing our grey uniform. Some were screaming in agony, others silent in death. When the gunfire ceased, the air was pungent with the sickly sweet scent of warm blood. Beyond the sprawled corpses lay the glen where the enemy was entrenched. We had no choice but to inch forward. The smell of scorched flesh and hair invaded my nostrils. And there was another smell; the release of bowels as life departed. Insects had already begun feasting on the corpses and I realised how lucky I had been not to be part of this first wave. Some dead looked familiar from the train; others were unrecognisable. Directly in front of the bodies I could make out an irrigation ditch: safety. If the men had been able to make it just a few more feet, they might have lived.

Gingerly I slid down the muddy incline to where a stream of water was gently flowing, like the mythical Styx, the river between life and death: the dead behind me, the living ahead. Kill or be killed.

'*Martl!*'

The voice came from behind me. I turned: someone was lying in the shrubbery. I moved closer and there he was.

'Frederick!'

A huge pool of blood had collected around his crotch. I knelt down beside him. 'You're going to be okay,' I lied. 'It's not as bad as it looks.'

'Really?' he groaned, gritting his teeth from the agonising pain.

'I'll get you a medic!' I scrambled back up the bank to look out over the field. But there were no medics, just freshly dead bodies.

'*Dolferl!*' I screamed, and waved. He was further ahead in the ditch.

'*Help!*' I screamed.

He turned and with his head cocked inquisitively, he ran back.

'Just be calm,' Dolferl told Frederick, crouching down. 'Have you ever read Schopenhauer?'

'Only a little,' Frederick admitted.

'In *The World as Will and Representation*, Schopenhauer talks of a leaf that is afraid to fall off the tree in autumn,' said Dolferl, calmingly. ' "Foolish leaf!" says Schopenhauer, "where do you think you're going? And where do you think the new leaves will come from? Where is the oblivion you so dread? It is part of you!" '

'Where's the medic?' Frederick asked.

'He's on his way,' I lied. Frederick's breathing was becoming erratic. The meal we had feasted on in celebration of this great war was climbing back up his throat.

'Do you . . . think I took . . . good pictures?' he asked, gasping for breath.

'Incredible pictures,' I assured him.

'My sister spoke of you often, you know,' he said to me. 'And fondly. She loves you very much. Take good care of her.'

My fingers interlaced with his. I squeezed his hand.

'I will, Frederick, you have my word. I promise.'

'Good,' he said, weakly. 'When did you say he was coming?' he mumbled.

'Soon.'

'I hope so. I feel faint.' His face turned ashen. 'Like I'm already a ghost,' he whispered. And he was gone. There was no pulse in his fingers. Saliva pooled in his mouth. Slowly, I pulled my hand from Frederick's and closed his eyes. His eyelids were blue.

I felt a tap on my shoulder. Dolferl stood over me and nodded in the direction we were to go. With our heads stooped, we ran along the ditch to where the others had disappeared. Looking out, we saw that three hundred feet across lay the promise of temporary salvation: a forest and a pond. We had no option but to run across the open field, trying to dodge the hail of bullets that would be waiting for us. My gut clenched and my heart cried out to God to protect me. Now or never! Life or death! Dolferl jumped out and I followed, machine-gunfire and bullets hitting the ground around us. All I could see were my sprinting legs and in one frantic leap I was there, under the protective cover of the trees.

Within the woodland, we regrouped. Dolferl and I looked around and I realised how much of our squad had been lost. Two-thirds of our platoon were missing. A wan sergeant major was the only one with rank enough to lead us.

'We have to proceed,' he panted, exhausted. His wide eyes were fearful, betraying his feigned valour. 'It's our duty,' he said half-heartedly.

'On to the West!' Dolferl interjected resolutely.

The sergeant major, and everyone else, looked askance at Dolferl. We fell in and broodingly made our way through the wood until we came to its limits, where we began to crawl on our stomachs. Pine needles snapped beneath me as I elbowed my way through the forest's undergrowth. I peered through the arching limbs and spiky sprigs and saw that we had come up behind the yellow-jacketed British who had been shooting at us. Dolferl crawled next to me, his stomach rumbling in anticipation. 'Those bastards took Frederick's life. Now we will take theirs,' he whispered. We lined up along the shadowy forest edge, and stealthily loaded and aimed our rifles. 'Lovely, lovely,' Dolfer sniggered, as we waited for the sergeant major to give the signal to shoot the Brits in the back. Lovely. Lovely.

I peered to the right and waited for our leader to wave his arm forward, unleashing the burst of gunfire. A bird chirped and insects chattered. A moment passed. A balmy breeze swept across my face, briefly reminding me of kinder afternoons. I looked towards our leader. His hand rose up slowly above the bush. I placed my finger on the trigger and aimed down the barrel, keeping his raised hand in my peripheral vision. The hand lingered and then fell in an arc. Our sudden volley of gunfire hit the British from behind. Their bodies slumped forward as blood sprayed out from their backs. Droplets of blood caught the dust that was stirred and created an ephemeral, sanguine mist. Bodies bounced into the air only to flop back to the ground, lifeless. We couldn't see their eyes as we slaughtered them, only the backs of their capped heads. A few months before this would have been considered murder. Now murder was a good thing, heroic even. I remembered Dolferl saying that 'good' and 'evil' had nothing to do with 'humanity', and everything with the whims of those in power.

When our sergeant major gave the order to move forward, Dolferl was the first to charge at the enemy soldiers, shooting at the bodies on the ground making sure they were dead. Then he turned towards the open field where a few survivors were fleeing and looked back at me, beaming triumphantly. Spreading his arms, he screamed, 'For Frederick!' and set off after the English.

At a deserted enemy barricade, I found Dolferl standing triumphantly with fellow infantrymen. 'Today,' he crowed, 'we have made history.' I wondered how many times I would have to congratulate him on 'making history' in the days and weeks that lay ahead. Just then, I noticed something move in the shadows behind Dolferl. I blinked again and saw a wounded British soldier stagger forward with a gun aimed at Dolferl's back. Dolferl heard him cock his weapon and turned, crying out, '*Nein!*' and diving to the ground as the gun fired. Instantly, the soldier was peppered with a spray of bullets. Dolferl pulled himself up and looked down at the dead man's body: a bronze medal glinted on his bloodstained jacket. Dolferl bent down and, with almost tender carefulness, removed the medal from his would-be assassin.

'The Brits know how to fight,' declared Dolferl, holding the medal up to show us its embossed lion's head.

At dusk, we looked out on the field we had taken. The death rattles of countless men echoed eerily across the land. Dead eyes open, mouths closed. Dead eyes closed, mouths open. A lone horse lay on the ground, then rolled back and forth twice, and with a third roll managed to get back up on all fours. He was a chestnut-coloured stallion, his well-developed hind legs indicating that he was probably a jumper. Even in his present disorientated state, the horse was still majestic. He stood by his dead British rider, waiting in vain for him to arise.

I grabbed Frederick's legs and Dolferl hooked his hands under his shoulders. Gunfire flared and boomed in the distance as together we carried Frederick down the field to the enemy dugout, which was now ours. An officer checked Frederick's pulse, and then told us to take him to the burial area, where we stood in line with fellow soldiers carrying other dead. Eventually we moved up to an officer who took Frederick's nametag and wrote an entry in a book. Dolferl and I were told to carry Frederick's corpse to a crater which was being used as a mass grave. Inside were about thirty bodies in a row, as well as severed limbs and body parts. They were all sprinkled with lime, then covered with a bed of straw, followed by another layer of bodies, more lime, another topping of straw, more bodies, and so on.

We queued up again and waited for our turn at the edge of the pit, where a priest stood with a crystal decanter of holy water. He looked too young to be a priest, but maybe he had a gift for languages; maybe Latin came easily to him. I wondered how he felt about war: had he blessed our artillery and assured himself and the battalions that God was walking with us? Had he questioned why God let so many of us die, as I had? As the priest sprinkled holy water over Frederick, I noticed his hand was shaking.

'In the name of the Father, the Son and the Holy Ghost.' The priest nodded for us to throw Frederick on to the pile. We swung Frederick once, then twice, and on the count of three we released him; he sailed through the air and down on to the pile of bodies with a dull thud. His legs and arms rose up slightly on impact and then dropped. Frederick was gone forever.

'Next!' shouted the priest, as Dolferl and I walked away.

'Sooner or later, we all have to die,' said Dolferl.

'I know,' I replied. 'But if we have to die anyway, where's the sense in all this?'

'The sense is the nation; the race. That's why we are here. We're all serving a higher purpose.'

'Do you believe in God?' I asked him.

'I believe in evolution,' he replied, and then raised himself up on the balls of his feet, straightening his back, adding an inch or two to his height. 'If you read history as I have,' he said, 'you would know that things like this are all part of the greater scheme. You must look ahead and envision our victory.'

As I looked at him, I noticed that his moustache had grown thicker and longer. In a few days, he would have to wax it again. Soon he really would look like the Kaiser.

November 1914, Wyschaete

The low-lying terrain, meadows and fields had become endless, murky pits. Out of these, we had created a web of trenches, shelters, sandbag parapets, concrete pillboxes, barbed-wire barricades, lairs and pitfalls. We had planted land mines and had dug communication trenches leading back to second-line trenches, artillery stations, third-line trenches, supplies, company kitchens, field hospitals, arms depots, machinery repair shops and yet more trenches. Days on end were spent knee-deep in water under heavy artillery fire.

Dolferl strolled through our underground quarters with the carefree exuberance of a child. The dire conditions didn't seem to faze him, while I was in a state of permanent disgust. I did what I was told to do apathetically, while Dolferl was always ready to volunteer, which surprised me: back on Stumpergasse, he had been a half-hearted defeatist when he encountered even a hint of resistance.

'Why are you so enthusiastic?' I asked him one night after he returned from fortifying another battalion's trench. I couldn't comprehend his eagerness. So much at Ypres had gone so terribly wrong: of the 3,600 men in our regiment, 2,722 had been either killed or injured in just one month. Even Colonel Von List, after whom our regiment was named, was among the dead. We had been confronted with the disheartening reality of our failure to break the enemy lines, yet Dolferl was whistling *Ode to Joy* as he prepared his *Strohsack* to sleep on. At that moment it dawned on me that maybe I knew the reason for his cheerfulness: every day there were new and unforeseen circumstances, new dangers, new missions, new attacks and counter-attacks. Out here on the battlefield, his craving for stimulation was finally satiated. His rapturous state reminded me of our evenings at the opera, when he had been equally blissful, captivated by every moment of the production. The experience of true emotion was apparently exclusive to Wagner. And war.

I asked him again. 'How can you be so happy?'

'If we want to survive, we have to fight. It's Darwinian. It's simple,' he answered.

Darwin's principles certainly seemed borne out by life in the trenches. Only the most adaptable among us 'human animals' survived amidst the unceasing din of artillery blasts and shortages of food and medical supplies. Our filthy clothes were lice-ridden and our open wounds were cleansed using the polluted water that seeped into our trench. Disease killed as many of us as enemy fire. Those who survived lived like rats. Our storm troopers scavenged among the dead Brits for their weapons, maps and communiqués, returning back to camp to feast on British rations, which were better than the Kaiser's supplies. Through the wooden planks and holes in the walls, a multitude of rodents would look on as their human counterparts devoured tins of shepherd's pie and drank flasks of sherry. Rats were ever present in our subterranean quarters. They were fearless, and paddled around with little or no concern for our presence. They put up with us the way an older tenant tolerates a new neighbour. We made their lives easier as we had brought food to their home: not a single loaf of bread or corpse had escaped their gnawing teeth. Periodically we would rebel and start shooting or knifing the little bastards, but soon we would tire of it and the rats would return with indefatigable persistence.

Dolferl was sitting alone by a kerosene lantern, staring into the void. Out of the corner of my eye I noticed that his chest no longer rose and fell as he breathed. He was immersed in a serene trance. His face bore no expression, just a wondrous vacancy. *Caesar as Military Strategist*, a history book, lay by his knee. I thought about the letter I needed to write to Francisca. By now she would certainly have heard about Frederick. I imagined she would be anxious to find out what had really happened, rather than what the army had told her. I planned to write and tell her that he had died as an artist and that she should be proud. But I doubted she would be. Her words to me when we had enlisted still rang in my ears, louder than ever before: '*Jingoism at its worst . . . Foolhardy, perilous, utterly unnecessary . . .* ' It was clear now that she had been right. But what did that change? Frederick was dead and I knew she would suffer. I'd lie and tell her that it had happened quickly, with no prolonged pain. I opened my knapsack, rifled through it and took out my pen and paper. I was just about to begin when I noticed that Dolferl had come out of his trance.

'Writing a symphony?' he asked.

'No,' I said, 'a letter.'

'Ah! To Francisca?'

'Sure.'

'A soldier must not be bound,' he declared.

'I couldn't endure all of this without the thought of Francisca waiting for me.'

'Sentimentalities! I have no need for such distractions.'

The amber light from the lantern cast a shadow of the moustache that curved upward on his face.

'I've renounced worldly love. I find my serenity in this war. You hear that?' he asked.

Somewhere in the distance heavy shells were exploding. I had become so used to it that I didn't always notice it any more.

'Yes,' I said.

Another cannon boomed. The noise made the chestnut horse, which was tied up nearby, stir in his sleep.

'That's the symphony you should be writing,' he said. 'That's our music.'

'It's ugly,' I retorted.

'Ugly? It's glorious! Can't you hear that?' He was thrilled: this was his opera. 'Can't you see the beauty in all this? This enticing game, on the edge of existence? A world filled with all possibilities and every tension! This war is perfection to me! Every emotion is here, from the most excruciating pain of loss to the greatest joy of victory. And it all blends into one instant image of life. Sing, pray, fight, curse, cry – what more could you want? Here, everyone can give their all, and show who they really are.'

I lay sleepless on my *Strohsack* that night. What a fool I had been! When I enlisted, I had believed myself invincible, that neither I nor my friends would die or be maimed. I had believed my deep faith in God and my conscientious, honourable intentions would protect me. I was wiser now. I knew now that I knew nothing. The only thing I was sure of was immense uncertainty.

November 1914, Messines

Perhaps it was our proximity to the ocean that made the November rain so pervasive, saturating everybody and everything. The rain was our winter. But winter brought no end to the artillery fire. Indeed, it seemed to become even heavier with the rain.

'Two volunteers!' the corporal's voice boomed through our underground quarters. We pretended not to hear. A rat skirted the corporal's boots. He ignored it.

'Two volunteers!' barked the beefy Bavarian again, just as a missile could be heard closing in on our bunker. The sinister rumble overhead made our bunker shake and the corporal looked up at the low wooden ceiling. This was one of their larger warheads. On impact it would create a 75-foot crater, maybe even bigger. We covered our heads and waited to hear how far away – or near – the shell would strike. It climaxed in a deafening explosion somewhere beyond us; the fools had overshot. The walls rumbled and sand spilled from between the stacked bags.

The corporal kicked at the rat, in a vain effort to hide his relief. 'I need two runners,' he continued. 'The bombing has taken out all of our communication lines.'

'Send the dogs,' called out an insubordinate from the back.

'We've sent dogs; they haven't returned,' replied the corporal, in a disgruntled tone. 'And as you may or may not know, our runners haven't returned either. But there's a message that must be delivered.'

He stood and waited. Perhaps another blast would interrupt and we could avoid responding for another minute, maybe two: but nothing came, except the distant rattle of machine-gunfire.

'This message will save lives!' the corporal shouted, 'maybe even our own. So I need two runners!'

All ten of us remained silent, feigning distraction in books or card games, or sleep. Runners were the least likely to see the end of this war. Runners had to maintain communications between the front line and the command post. They had to leave the protection of the trench, often during heavy artillery volleys and raging firestorms. They were always sent out in twos, and sometimes in fours, to increase the chances of at least one of them making it back with the message. At times, runners accompanied the attacking storm troops, crossing battlefields where they were vulnerable to both friendly and enemy fire.

'I'll do it,' said a voice behind me. I turned and looked over at Dolferl aghast: what are you saying?

'Very good,' said the corporal, giving Dolferl a thumbs-up. 'Who else?'

Again there was a tense silence.

'Well then, I suppose I'll have to choose the second volunteer.' The corporal walked down the dugout slowly, scrutinising every soldier. When he came to me, he stopped.

'You two are friends, correct?' he asked.

Oh God, I thought, please, let this poisoned chalice pass me by.

'Well?' the corporal insisted. 'Are you his friend or aren't you?'

'Y–Yes,' I stammered.

'Okay then. You go with him.' And with that, the corporal handed me my death sentence, turned and left.

'Thank you,' I said to Dolferl, still not fully grasping what had just happened to me.

'Food's great as well as everything else,' Dolferl replied, referring to certain privileges enjoyed by the messengers. They lived in the trenches, but also at the command post, where food and living conditions were better, and they were free to do whatever they wanted during their spare time. For Dolferl, this guaranteed more hours of reading and painting. It also meant being away from the crowd, retreating to the solitude in which he was most comfortable.

'I can see you're overjoyed,' I said. 'But unlike you, I want to live. I have someone to live for.'

'You and your bourgeois worries,' he grumbled, as he closed his backpack. 'We have far more important things to live for!' He turned and addressed me like a commanding officer. 'Don't just stand there. Get ready!'

'Why?' I asked. 'Why did you do this?'

Dolferl stopped and looked straight into my eyes. 'The highest purpose we can achieve in this life is the pursuit of a heroic journey: striving for a purpose that benefits all, and struggling against enormous difficulties for little reward, or no reward at all.'

I knew he was just rehashing words he'd read somewhere, but it made me wonder if the writers or philosophers behind such concepts had any idea of the damage they would cause when people like Dolferl appropriated them.

Human Smoke

Were God and evolution one and the same?

December 1914, Messines

We were on our way back from the command post. The uneven ground made me stumble as I ran, but Dolferl bounded through the abused landscape like some beast in its natural habitat. A shrieking shell approached, making my eardrums vibrate as I hit the ground. The explosion blasted earth into the air and made the ground ripple in waves like a stone cast into calm water. The impact threw me against the ground. I lay there looking up at the battle-filled night sky gasping for breath, when I realised I had to move if I was to stay alive. Instantly I rolled over, got to my feet and ran in the same direction as Dolferl. Between intermittent flashes, I spied a line of sandbags just beyond Dolferl's head: we were almost there, almost safe, when I heard the wail of a colossal rocket approaching from behind. The piercing sound grew louder and louder, and then I felt something punch my shoulder and throw me to the ground.

When I came to, I saw that the bomb had burrowed into the ground, carving a trail right through to the trench: miraculously, it hadn't detonated. The soldiers in the dugout were staring dumbfounded at the gargantuan three-thousand pound missile. Had it detonated, no one would have survived. Momentarily the enemy fire had ceased. There were no shells raining down on us, and we were dumbstruck at our extraordinary luck. The bomb had hit its target, but no one had died. I staggered to my feet, and climbed into the trench struggling to comprehend what had just happened. A cork was popped and cognac was poured. Suddenly the trench was awash with celebration. My shoulder was slapped continuously as I staggered around, tin cup in hand, filled with precious cognac to toast to our precious lives.

I walked down the passageway looking for Dolferl and poked my head into our quarters. There was no celebrating or drinking for him: he just sat there in his solitude. I recognised these moments from Vienna.

Around Christmas time he sat alone for hours, silent and brooding. His mother had died at Christmas, and he had lost his faith in the God of his childhood.

The rain pounded our trenches relentlessly. We had both been given afternoon leave, and I asked Dolferl to come with me to the village and offered to buy him a chocolate pastry. After all, it was Christmas, as well as the anniversary of his mother's death.

'I've nothing to give you in return,' he replied in a low monotone.

'It doesn't matter,' I replied. 'Come on, the fresh air will do you good.'

The downpour on the way to the village had loosened the stiffly waxed curlicues of Dolferl's moustache and they were drooping now. But the chocolate croissant lifted his spirits, and he smiled for the first time in days. He chewed methodically, slowly savouring the croissant's rich flavour. The warm glow of the hearth and the inviting aromas made the bakery a haven from our hellish existence. When we had first arrived at the pâtisserie, our guns, uniforms and language had terrified the woman tending the shop. She had flapped around in a frenzy and only when I muddled through some schoolboy French did she begin to relax. I was as polite as I could possibly be, and as I struggled with French pronunciation, she was disarmed and charmed, and finally served us our pastries with visible relief. Dolferl gazed over at me, thanking me silently for his Christmas treat.

'Belgian pastries are unparalleled,' raved Dolferl. 'The French are said to be equally good. What I don't understand is, how can a country that creates such delicious delicacies breed such disgusting politicians?'

'Pastries are one thing; politics are entirely a different matter,' I replied.

His eyes narrowed. 'After we win the war, justice will be meted out to the French leaders, and they'll get the punishment they deserve. The war will be seen as a blessing by both the French and German peoples. The French will acknowledge their Germanic roots. Our two great nations will unite, and create a harmonious new Europe.' He bit into his croissant. 'I can taste it.'

The bells over the door chimed as a mother and her young son hurried into the shop. '*Joyeux Nöel*,' greeted the mother. She put down her parcels and rummaged through her purse as the baker placed a log-shaped cake into a box. The young boy then spotted Dolferl and approached him tentatively, fascinated. The untainted innocence of the child engendered an unfamiliar kindness and warmth in Dolferl, and the two were transfixed with each other, not a word passing between them. Dolferl beamed. The child beamed.

'Jacques,' called the mother as she grouped all the parcels together. '*Allons-y tout de suite!*'

'*Non, Maman*,' pleaded the little boy, his eyes still on Dolferl.

The mother smiled nervously. '*On y va, maintenant*!' she insisted, taking his hand and leading the reluctant boy out of the door.

After enjoying our cosy respite for half an hour, we wrapped the rest of our pastries up for later. Our coats and rifles were still dripping wet as we prepared to leave. My teeth chattered as I wrapped myself up in my saturated winter gear. Dusk was approaching, and the village was now under curfew. Outside, the rain pummelled us again, each drop quickly eroding my physical and mental state. The village disappeared into the distance behind us as we trudged along the road to the woods, back to our home in the trenches.

'*Merde!*'

The shout rang out between the drumming of the rain. We stood silently and listened: by now no one was allowed out except us. We strained to distinguish any sound from the incessant rainfall. Muffled words emerged from the dripping woods, then stopped. Someone was nearby, risking his life just by being in this dark, damp forest. Dolferl slipped behind a tree. I followed quietly behind him. Just then a dark figure staggered out into the path. Water poured from his drenched blue jacket, away from his red trousers. A soldier! A French soldier! All at once, he burst into song: '*Contre nous de la tyrannie, victime du tyrannie du diplomacie!*'

He was drunk. He had probably been drafted into the army against his will, dragged to this forgotten pit to uphold the pride of his nation in a war he didn't give a shit about. '*Allons enfants de la Patrie! La jour de gloire est arrivé*,' he sang sarcastically. There had been Christmas encounters between our men and the French, scenes of fraternisation, much to the dismay of our superiors. Soldiers from both sides had laid down their arms and shared Christmas cake and cognac. What was I to do now? Offer him my pastry?

The Frenchman was getting closer. The peak of his hat jutting out over his head barely managed to keep the lit end of his cigarette dry. He stopped and inhaled intently.

'Filthy habit,' seethed Dolferl, as he took out his pistol.

'Leave him alone,' I whispered. 'It's Christmas!'

Dolferl glared at me. 'Christmas has nothing to do with this. We're at war.'

The Frenchman laughed to himself and fell to his knees, arms outstretched.

'He's drunk. He's not on patrol,' I continued. 'He's like us, doing what we're doing. We're all wandering around in the dark.'

Dolferl shook his head. 'No wonder you never get anywhere in life.'

He stepped out from behind the tree with his weapon drawn. 'Prepare to die, frog!'

Startled, the Frenchman rolled back on to his feet and grasped for his rifle. Dolferl pulled the trigger but instead of a gunshot, there was a dull thud, and nothing happened. The rain had made his pistol useless.

'Martl!' cried Dolferl, begging for help.

I raised my pistol. I didn't want to kill anyone on Christmas Eve, but I pulled the trigger. Nothing. The rain had foiled me as well.

The Frenchman pulled up his gun and was about to shoot.

'Charge him! Martl, charge him!'

My feet slipped on the mud as I ran at him. My shoulder knocked his rifle and a bullet exploded, shooting up into the night sky. My bayonet plunged through his coat and he fell backward. I tumbled on top of him, pulling the bayonet from his coat, yanking out only white insulation. He clutched my throat and started squeezing, his thumb pressing into my larynx with all of his strength. My hands freed the bayonet from my rifle while the Frenchman cried out, focusing all of his strength on his tightening grip, exerting even more pressure. I began to feel faint. He shook me violently and with one last desperate burst of energy I sank the blade right into his eye. He gave a bone-chilling shriek as I stabbed the bayonet repeatedly into his face. Then I slid the blade across his throat. A surge of blood rushed out of his jugular. Blood and rain. Blood and rain. It was over.

I staggered up and looked at Dolferl, standing next to us.

'Check his pockets,' I said.

He hesitated.

'Now!' I shouted. 'Christ!'

Dolferl bent down and rifled through the soldier's jacket. He found a bottle of cognac and held it up in the rain.

Back in our trench I stared at the potato soup before me, asking myself why I was sitting down to eat when I wasn't hungry. I looked around the table at the men I called my 'comrades'. I was there in body but not in spirit. I had stabbed the Frenchman in the *face*. Blood had spurted from his throat like a red fountain. For the first time in this war, I had seen the face of a man I had killed. I had taken a life. Brutally. Yet everything just continued as normal. Business as usual.

'So,' said a stubby corporal to Dolferl, 'what kind of girl are you going for when we finally get to Paris?' He took a long swig from the Frenchman's cognac.

Dolferl stared into his soup and said nothing. He brought the spoon to his lips, tipped it and drank the broth.

'I know what I want,' said the corporal, with a lascivious grin. 'A redhead.'

'They have African *Mädels* in Paris,' said another. 'They're the best.'

I shuddered to myself as I recalled the cries of the man I had murdered. Some lost soul who longed to be home with his wife, his parents on Christmas Eve. I had felt his life ebb away as I extinguished it. Perhaps he had been a father.

'Black girls are as hot as fire, and I want a hot – '

Dolferl threw down his spoon and exploded. 'You degenerate fool! Longing to corrupt your body! You're a disgrace to your ancestry! I'd die of shame, lusting after some negress!'

Laughter erupted around the table.

'Have you lost all sense of your true nature?' Dolferl continued, unflustered. 'If you don't follow your purest thoughts – '

'My thoughts *are* pure,' guffawed the man. 'Pure sex!'

'Those are the decadent thoughts of the enemy!' Dolferl was trembling with rage. I grabbed his shoulder. 'Calm down!'

'Go back to your knitting, Grandma!' shouted someone. Dolferl's lip quivered as he glared at me: I will not be censored.

I looked at him: please. I've already killed for you today.

After dinner, Dolferl worked on *The Sunken Lane at Wyschaete*. The dark drawing depicted a path through a scorched forest of stumps. A bleak light lingered over the site of the slaughter of one hundred and ninety-two of our comrades and friends. The memory didn't depress Dolferl: on the contrary, he seemed uplifted; his Christmas melancholia had dissipated. While Dolferl painted, everyone else celebrated Christmas by getting drunk. This time I was the one sitting on my bed and staring into the night, thinking about the man I had just murdered. Thinking about God. Thinking about taking a life God had created. Should I have acted differently? If I hadn't killed the French soldier, he would have killed me. I was only alive because I had killed. Did God favour me? Did God love the perpetrator? Was it God's will that the fittest survive? Was Dolferl right? Were God and evolution one and the same?

For some reason, the rats who shared our accommodation were elsewhere that night. Perhaps the rain had drowned them, or they had found their way into one of our mass graves, but either way it was a reprieve to spend Christmas Eve without vermin. Some of the men sang *Oh Tannenbaum* in a feeble effort to bolster our sagging spirits. Outside, the chestnut horse stood sleeping in the rain.

Drip . . . drip . . . drip . . .

I couldn't sleep, so I composed an imaginary letter to Francisca.

Dear Francisca, it would begin; *it's Christmas Eve and I miss you terribly. Today I butchered a man. I witnessed his life slip away as I took it. I don't know what I feel. I feel nothing; it's almost as if someone else killed that Frenchman today. I wish I were back in Vienna with you two years ago, at midnight Mass. I'd be playing Stille Nacht on the organ in the balcony, and you'd be sitting in the pew below. I'd even pay attention to the priest's sermon. I wish we both could be happy again. I . . .*

I looked across the dugout.

Dolferl lay on his *Strohsack* reading a book by the light of a lantern. His eyesight was weak but he was too vain to wear glasses. He used a magnifying glass instead, as he had done so many nights in Vienna. I envied him: he was so completely at ease. Was it because of his belief in evolution? How could that faith provide so much comfort? Perhaps he really had 'conquered' his emotions. But how? Because of what Schopenhauer had written? Maybe he had never experienced emotions at all. I remembered reading a book once in which a doctor described a mental disorder that caused sufferers to feel no emotion: they feigned their feelings from an early age to respond as was expected of them, but never truly felt love or experienced fear. The doctor had referred to the condition as 'blindness of the heart'.

I struck a match and lit the lantern by my bed, then turned the knob slightly to brighten the flame so I could read too. I opened one of Dolferl's Karl May books in the hope that it would lull me to sleep. The story was set on a parched desert mesa in Arizona, home to the Apache Indians. Old

Shatterhand, the hero of German descent persistently fought off grasping Yankees and punished their misdeeds and crimes with vigilante justice.

Drip . . . drip . . drip . . .

Water was a scarcity there in Arizona, a commodity for which people killed. The relentless sun made the desert a furnace, causing people's skin to blister and bleed. It all sounded heavenly as I lay there reading in a cold Belgian puddle.

Splash . . . splash . . . splash . . .

Just then came the sound of paws paddling through pools of water in the dark: it was the biggest rat I had ever heard. I peered into the blackness and saw two reflective onyx eyes staring back at me. I grabbed one of my boots.

Splash . . . splash . . . splash . . .

The rat scrambled towards me. The light caught its nose, pink and black, followed by its snout. I bellowed at the top of my lungs as I hurled the boot at it, striking it in the head: it yelped like a dog and began to whine, attracting Dolferl's attention. Three other men poked their heads out. 'Quiet, you bastard,' mumbled one of them.

'What the – ?' shouted Dolferl.

I lifted the lantern and saw a mangy white terrier. Where the hell had he come from? Maybe he belonged to a British officer.

'How could you!' Dolferl chided me. 'You've hurt him!' He glared at me like I was some callous ogre. 'Have you no heart?'

So said the man who had caused me to kill another man earlier that day.

'You should be ashamed of yourself!' snarled Dolferl, as he got up from his *Strohsack* and hurried across the room, fell to his knees and started to coax the dog out of the shadows. The terrier crept towards him slowly and tentatively. It had brown eyes and a red button nose. Its shaggy white hair was tangled with muck. The terrier's tail wagged frenetically as Dolferl called out to it. Then the dog pounced forward, ready to play, and Dolferl was instantly enamoured, sharing the rest of his chocolate croissant with it.

'Foxl!' he called out to it. 'Foxl!' *I'll teach you tricks. Don't understand German? Don't worry, I'll teach you that too. I'll look after you. I'll love you.*

Silently, he thanked the war for his new friend.

March 1915, Battle of Neuve Chapelle

The rain had eventually subsided, but the booming Howitzers had not. We were just one division, defending ourselves against four attacking British divisions. Our losses were appalling. In the command post, I overheard an officer saying that over twenty thousand of our soldiers had been killed or wounded. The unrelenting horror of war had made me a fragile husk of my former self. I hadn't showered for days, or had a moment's respite from the hell without or within. When the bombing stopped, I was so relieved; I could leave our cramped hole and go outside, draw a breath of air, maybe even see the horizon, no matter how mangled it might be. I could look out and see where the sky met the earth. I was not so deluded to think the air would be 'fresh', but it would at least be fresher than the underground air I had been breathing for days on end.

I emerged from the shelter and walked along the wooden pathway that linked the ravines of sand bags that were now my home. When I came to a ladder, I mounted it in the hope of catching a glimpse of the sun's corona beyond the swirling clouds of sulphur. My hands grabbed the rungs as I climbed up to the edge of the trench and looked out upon the burnt earth. It was a landscape of twisted metal. Was this what the Masters of War envisioned as they shuffled their pawns around their board? I imagined the white-coated engineers extrapolating flight paths and predicting explosive effects. To them it was all just a matter of arithmetic; a scientific experiment. If they could only see the charred wasteland they had created! I scanned the sky for the sun behind the shifting clouds of lead and dust. But all I could see, was a faint circle, like a lunar eclipse. Our magnificent, life-giving star had been relegated to a feeble white shadow.

A whistle was blown and a siren screeched like a startled crow. The Tommies were launching a new type of shell at us: gas bombs. So much for breathing the air! I hurried down the ladder and ran to my bedding to grab my mask. The gas masks were heavy and unwieldy, and the goggled eyepieces and the hanging muzzle made us all look like huge rubber insects. I had no choice but to pull it over my face and pray it would safeguard me against the disorientation, spasms, blisters, blindness and death caused by the nerve agent. Sometimes these things had to be worn for days, even in the hottest weather. They made eating and drinking impossible. To add to our discomfort, beneath our helmet we were forced to wear a woollen cap pulled over the ears and tied beneath the chin. This was not quite the war I had expected to fight: I had assumed it would be a battle between men, where traits like fortitude, vigour and endurance would determine the outcome. I had naively expected it to be a chivalrous struggle. What a fool I'd been. Even with the gas mask on, I could hear the inbound shells as they whistled through the air. The eyepieces in my mask kept clouding over from my breath and I felt detached from the explosions around me. We're destined to be victims of the 'civilisation' of our time, I thought; and then I fainted.

Visions of coal mines, furnaces, steam engines and flywheels floated through my mind, illuminated by gleaming white artificial light. Countless faceless, nameless workers were manufacturing weapons on a production line. My slumber was simultaneously interrupted and fuelled by voices around me. 'Look at this mass-produced brutality!' I heard a deep, baritone voice saying. 'Where's the conscience of a society that finances and orchestrates such awful things? ' said another voice. 'Doesn't that industrialised mass murder clearly show that our Western civilization deserves to go down? 'Hypocrites!' said the baritone voice. 'They're just too dishonest to admit the truth! It is our Judaeo-Christian culture that upholds the myth of a "conscience", and most people have learned to pretend that it really exists. But as soon as some legitimate authority comes along and orders them to act against that same "conscience", they're happy to do so . . . '

When I awoke, it was curiously quiet. The bombardment had stopped, someone had removed my mask and I lay on the ground. I turned and looked around. At the other end of the room I saw a circle of men, with Dolferl standing in the centre. He had one arm hooked behind his back and was walking with a limp. One eye was closed while the other was open, as if gripping a monocle.

'Gentlemen,' he said, affecting a strong Berlin accent, 'I am appalled at the mess this barracks is in!'

Dolferl was mocking an officer we called Colonel Cyclops.

'I cannot impress upon you enough how cleanliness in the most bleak of circumstances can win a war!' Dolferl wiggled his buttocks as he hobbled around in little circles.

The men guffawed.

'What's so funny?' exploded Dolferl comically. 'Will someone please tell me what's so funny?'

The group laughed even harder.

There was some irony to these histrionics: Dolferl normally preferred to be alone rather than associate with his comrades, but when the mood took him, he would occasionally go to extreme lengths to put on a show for them, imitating not only our superiors, but the sounds of geese, ducks, cows, horses, sheep and goats as well. Foxl started yapping at his master.

Dolferl wagged his finger at the dog. 'You're very close to a court-martial, soldier!'

Foxl only barked more.

'You're on very thin ice, young man,' reprimanded Dolferl. 'I want to see an improvement in your behaviour! Heel!' he ordered.

The dog instantly moved to stand by Dolferl's boot. At that, the men applauded and cheered. Dolferl was much more successful with these little shows than with his moralistic sermons on the evils of drinking, smoking and fornication. Foxl wagged his tail eagerly, expecting a treat.

'Roll over!'

The dog obeyed.

'Now this is a good example for all of you,' said Dolferl, addressing the crowd. 'Why can't I have more soldiers like Foxl? We'd all be home by now!'

April 1915, Fournes

Dear Francisca – We've just eaten, and I've never had such inedible food in my life. The bombing has stopped momentarily. The Tommies must be having their dinner, too. I look around and wonder how I got here. I'm a fool. I miss you! You're my reason to live, the only thing I believe in. My belief in our 'mission' fades with every passing day. Does it make sense to wage a barbaric war just to force the world to comply with our way of thinking? I consider myself a spiritual and moral person, and that I should be forced to behave in this ruthless, bloodthirsty way clashes with who I am. I constantly ask myself where God fits into all of this. I had always believed that God loved me; I had always been grateful to Him for the world He provided as my home. I remember the philosophical novels I would read in my youth, all with plenty to say about young men and women facing 'the problem of life'. I had no idea what that problem was: now I know. I'm confused: I'm horrified that God could allow this relentless suffering. I have nothing but doubts and unanswered questions.

I wish my faith were as strong as Dolferl's. I've never seen him happier, more adjusted and more alive. He believes himself to be a conscious part of the evolutionary process, and therefore somehow protected. And it almost seems to be true: he has returned unscathed from every one of his deadly missions. We're all aware of it. What can I call it – a miracle? Luck? Divine intervention? Dolferl is convinced he's protected by Providence. And he's not alone. Lately some in our unit are saying it's safest to be where he is when there's an attack –

I stopped: I had sworn to myself I would never mention Dolferl in my letters to Francisca, yet here I was, compulsively writing about him. I stared angrily at what I had just written, then ripped it up. Dolferl, Dolferl, Dolferl! That human obstacle between Francisca and me. In Vienna, he'd been the reason that we had found one another, but my friendship with him and Frederick had led me to be in this carnage! Why had I listened to them and not to Francisca? How could I have been so stupid? It had been three weeks now since Francisca's last letter. Had she found someone else? Her past letters had constantly assured me otherwise, but maybe she was just being kind because I was at war. Maybe she didn't want to tell me the truth. Why shouldn't she become involved with someone else? Why should she be loyal to a man who had hardly been loyal to her?

'*Maikäfer flieg, dein Vater ist im Krieg . . .*' – a child's lullaby accompanied me day and night. Herbert, my neighbour, constantly sang the song to himself. '*Die Mutter ist im Pommernland. . .*' Herbert never slept, just played solitaire and sang. '*Und Pommernland ist abgebrannt . . .*' I looked over to him just as he turned over another card. Survival had come at a price: our minds had nowhere to retreat but deeper and deeper inside.

'*Maikäfer flieg . . .*'

We had all become a bit odd; some more, some less. Rudi and Albert played the card game 'Watten' incessantly; Walter from Regensburg muttered senselessly as he paced up and down in our underground shelter; a recruit who had come from another unit huddled in a corner, rocking in the foetal position. And even Dolferl was not immune. His craving for sweets had developed into an insatiable obsession: when he stood guard, he 'requisitioned' tins of jam which he would then secretly devour.

Although we had all developed curious behaviours, there was an understanding, a feeling, an intangible connection that bound us together. In the face of death, we were all equal, and this equality was real, not some imaginary construct. It permeated every fibre of our bodies – bodies that had become different parts of a single entity, a single being. Aiding and protecting our comrades was the same as aiding and protecting ourselves. We were experiencing real fraternal love in the most unlikely of places:

the hellish reality of war. I turned over on my side, and saw that Dolferl was still awake, reading. At that moment I realised what the army meant for him: it was his emotional awakening. The bond we felt was as nurturing to him as only the connection to his mother had been. Now this yearning, this longing, this tie had been transferred to a company of men, soldiers who were ruthlessly butchering their fellow men. It was a curious and disturbing thought.

'Here comes one,' Dolferl said, looking up from his book.

Foxl suddenly jerked awake, his ears erect. He started whining and buried into Dolferl's underarm for cover and comfort.

At first it was faint, barely audible. Then it grew steadily louder: a rocket whistling through the wind. As it became a shrill wail, it woke the slumbering soldiers one by one, their eyes popping open with glassy fear. There was a collective exclamation: *oh shit!* Some jumped up and ran outside. On the bed next to me, Josef from Garmisch sprang up, half-awake and half-asleep. He was bathed in sweat as he came around from his nightmare into an even more horrific reality. His wide eyes darted around like a panicked animal's and landed on Dolferl, questioning. What was he to do? Run outside like the others? But Dolferl just sat on his bed with the dog and listened as the incoming shell approached. More men left the room. The shell was nearing; its desperate scream resonated through our subterranean barracks and I knew it was too late to leave now. There was nowhere to hide. All I could do was cower down and think of Francisca. Suddenly, there was an enormous explosion. The impact forced us down into our bedding, and the canvas that hung over the exit flapped towards us. Debris from outside poured into our underground quarters, an arm flew into the centre of the room, its fingers still wriggling. Some of us screamed. I did too. I turned to Dolferl in shock; he stared back at us all coolly: he said nothing, but his eyes told us that if we followed his lead, Providence would protect us too.

April 1916, Fromelles

We spent endless days in mind-numbing boredom, which sometimes manifested itself as a practical joke. Wilhelm, from Würzburg, a guy with the physique of a Greek statue, was unsettled by how Michael was constantly staring at him. Michael was intrigued by Wilhelm, but Wilhelm simply didn't want to be stared at. These were things that couldn't be helped, but were magnified because of our close quarters.

One afternoon while Michael was away from our cave, Wilhelm defecated in Michael's palliasse to the amusement of those of us in the pit at that time. From that moment on, we waited with bated breath for Michael to crawl into his bedding and when he finally did, smelt something rank and felt something squishy, he almost vomited, causing the rest of us to explode in roaring laughter. It was very funny, but then again, you had to be there. Such tales of war never make the history books; nor does the unending limbo, the waiting within a multitude of tiny eternities for something horrific or ridiculous to happen. Mired in the bleakness of our subterranean purgatory, I sifted through my life with the crystal clarity of hindsight. Repetitive memories, regrets and 'what if's were scrutinised with obsessive precision. Boredom is subtle torture for the mind, your only escape mealtimes – or the arrival of post from home.

My hands shook as I pushed my way out of the group of men who were swarming around the mail carrier. I held an envelope that was postmarked Munich. My fingers fumbled around the edges of the envelope, my nervous anticipation rendering me incompetent at opening the letter. What was she going to tell me? That it was over? That she hoped I would understand? After what seemed a lifetime, I finally managed to rip it open, and unfolded the letter.

Munich, 18 March 1916

Dearest Martin – Every moment of the day, I feel the gravity of loss. I have lost Frederick forever. And it seems it will be forever before this war is over. The pain of the war is everywhere; it is etched on Father's face permanently now. People have lost their loved ones and they are weighed down simply by surviving from day to day. The war affects everyone. It is personal, and malicious, and evil. And for what? But let us not get into that argument again: instead, let us gather our thoughts, and look forward to a time when all of this will be behind us. When love, not hate, will prevail. When there will be hope. When we will recreate a world without war. We must learn from these painful lessons, and forge a sane, benevolent future. I long for the day when I will walk hand in hand with you again. When I am saddest, I often imagine what our future will be: I picture the child we will have together, and wonder which features of yours he will have, and which of mine. How pure and tender his heart and mind will be! He will be the flower of our love. I . . . I have been crying again, thinking of you. Thinking of us. Thinking of our child. And hoping it will all still come to be.

All my love,

Francisca

A tear ran off my nose to land on the last 'a' in Francisca, which expanded to become a blue blot. I was overcome with sadness, yet I had never been happier in the knowledge that she still loved me.

June 1916, Fromelles

Dear Francisca –

I stopped. What should I write? That hundreds of shells have been pummelling us for days? Or would she rather read about the vile, ever-present stench of war? How our sense of smell is assaulted by the stench of earth mixed with old faeces and the sulphurous odour of decomposing flesh? Should I describe how the heat from an exploding missile burns first your lips and then your throat? How the blast peels the skin off your face? Should I tell her about Peter, my friend from Augsburg, dragging his disembowelled intestines behind him? Or Wilhelm, who used to compose music like me, screaming in pain and hobbling for cover on the bloody stumps that remained of his legs? Or the piles of flesh no longer resembling any human form, yet still managing to breathe and suffer? Perhaps she'd be interested in reading about the crates behind the hospital tents, crammed with layer upon layer of amputated limbs. Or the bodies that haven't made it into a mass grave, which lie rotting in the open for all of us to see, their open eyes staring at us, framed by swollen purple faces. Or those corpses that liquefy iridescently into a saturated pulp and that are feasted upon by a squirming mêlée of worms?

What should I write about?

July 1916, Fromelles

Across the room Dolferl was painting a wall. He and I had been instructed to 'brighten up' the officers' mess. Painting the canteen wall powder blue was a welcome respite from the savagery of the battlefield. Dolferl had been chosen because the officers liked his savvy choice of colours. The blue he had selected set a relaxed and easy tone for the eye, mind and belly. I had been chosen because my recruitment papers listed me as an upholsterer, even if I really considered myself a composer. In wartime, however, 'composing' is considered a dilettante's self-indulgent hobby. Even painting a room was incongruous with our current life. I glanced over at Dolferl. He was so immersed in his work that he hadn't noticed I had stopped painting.

'Maybe we aren't the strongest nation in Europe,' I said, to provoke him.

'Are you insane?' he snapped. 'Of course we are! Who else could be? If the decadent French didn't have the Brits – '

'Well, maybe it's the Brits then,' I said.

Dolferl glowered at me in silence. I knew that he saw the British as the only force to be reckoned with. The bronze metal badge he had torn from that dead British officer's chest in our first battle was still pinned to his knapsack. 'The British?' he said. 'May I remind you that their royal family has German roots?'

A fly buzzed about Foxl. The dog was hypnotised by the insect as it flitted around his moist nose.

'Even "their" Shakespeare had German blood in his veins,' Dolferl continued. 'Otherwise how could he have conceived his plays? The Brits lack any sense of creativity. Genius is obsession, demonic nature! Do you think any Anglo-Saxon could ever give birth to a Bach or a Beethoven?'

The dog leapt up, snapping and chasing after the fly.

'Music is universal,' I objected. 'Music transcends national barriers.'

'Our barriers, yes! Why do you think all those American and British composers and performers come to study in Germany? You're so superficial! You never try to get to the heart of things, just like the Brits. Look at their philosophy: completely unsystematic, grandiose and empirical. They haven't the slightest understanding of metaphysical truth. To them, fact and essence are the same.'

'Maybe we have better musicians and better philosophers, and they have the better army. Maybe it's as simple as that.'

'What do you think this war is? Just some event on the political calendar?'

'What else could it be?'

'War is always a fight between different bloods. And different bloods produce different ideas, different values. Our values are metaphysical; the Brits' values are purely empirical. British blood isn't capable of comprehending absolutes.'

'Well then,' I said, taking up my brush again, 'if we have the superior blood and the superior spiritual system, why didn't we win the war long ago?'

October 1916, Iwuy

The train jolted forward and rebounded back, knocking me awake.

I blinked myself awake. Dolferl was beside me.

'We're here,' he said.

Everyone in the car started to gather his equipment. Dolferl slipped his book into his backpack.

'Hurry up!' ordered the commanding officer.

'Yeah, yeah, yeah,' I muttered.

I followed behind Dolferl as he walked down the aisle and stepped off the train on to the platform. His backpack opened, and I was about to warn him when books spilled from his bag and fell under a boxcar. In a matter of seconds, we were both on our knees retrieving the precious books from beneath the carriage. As we did, I looked up through the throng of soldiers' legs and noticed the sergeant overseeing the disembarkation running along the platform. Even before he had time to shout his warning, the wail of an artillery shell was heard tearing through the sky, growing louder and louder as it neared. The warhead crashed through the frosted glass skylight, sending thousands of shards flying through the station, exploding on the adjacent track with the merciless impact of a meteorite. A ferocious white fiery ball shot upwards to the shattered glass ceiling, and a shower of burning metal fragments fell on to the men on the platform below. We heard a chorus of screams as we retreated further underneath the carriage.

A solitary siren wailed, followed soon by several more. I was about to crawl out from under the carriage when Dolferl grabbed my shoulder.

'Stay here!' he said, firmly.

'Why?'

Dolferl said nothing, he just sat there motionless.

'Let's get out of here,' I said.

'Stay!' He commanded.

I didn't see any reason to stay and was about to climb up to the platform when I heard another shell penetrating the air. I turned and hastily ducked under the boxcar. There was another crash of smashing glass – and an enormous detonation on our other side. The carriage above us rocked violently and an explosion blasted the other side of the train. More sirens, more screams.

I looked at the soot-blackened Dolferl, his cheekbones outlined by the tangerine glare of the flames: how were you able to warn me? my eyes asked. How did you know? He looked back at me. His eyes were steely and calm: Providence.

October 1916, The Battle of the Somme, Le Barque

The ground erupted with a searing blast of white fire, as if a passage had been cleared right through to Hades. The earth shook, my knees buckled and as I fell backwards into a crater. I could feel the glowing heat of the explosion. Dolferl and I had been given parallel routes: I was to run along the east side of the bombardment, and he was to run along the western perimeter. Our mission was to bring back information from our storm-troops to the front line. In my backpack, I held details of the exact locations where the British had mounted their attack, specifying the longitude and latitude of their big guns. I carried the information that could put an end to this very real hell.

But first I had to make it through this deadly hail of friendly and enemy fire. We were at the River Somme. For two weeks the battle had raged; for two weeks we had been almost without food and medicine. At Verdun, our troops advanced about five miles, while at the Somme the enemy advanced about the same; for that stalemate, our officers reckoned, over one-and-a-half million men had been added to our list of casualties. When the battle began we had exchanged our spiked helmets for rounded steel helmets, leaving the nineteenth century behind and entering a new age, even more savage than all the bloody centuries before. Was it evolution in reverse? Above me, the sky blazed red, with flashes of blinding white. Barrages of missiles, machine gunfire and hand grenades wove an impenetrable web of death. I rolled on to my side, clambered to all fours and looked around at the death surrounding me: the exposed flesh of the dead stormtroopers was the same colour as our grey uniforms. Distended faces projected from collars like over-inflated balloons, distorted in terror and suffering. Death was overtaking life here: harrowing yelps of pain from those who hadn't died intermingled with the crackling yellow-orange flames that consumed corpses piled up on an impromptu funeral pyre. Mustering all of the strength I had within me, I stood up and checked my compass. As the light flickered, I squinted to make out its quivering arrow and braced myself to run through the pillars of fire. I took a deep breath and was about to start when I was suddenly struck by a tepid downpour of fluid: a headless torso had landed on top of me and blood from the severed neck squirted into my aghast, open mouth and down my throat. His larynx flapped before my eyes and I swallowed in shock. The stink of his last bowel movement filled my nostrils as I pushed the corpse away. I dropped on to my belly, burying my face into the earth and retching as I tried to expel the vile mouthful I'd ingested. What lower levels of savagery could I descend to? What new depth of pain would I have to suffer? God, where are you?

'Where are you?' I cried aloud and slowly raised myself up to a kneeling position, pooling my concentration as I deliberately inhaled long and slow before standing. My hands pushed off just as a muddy boot struck me in the ribs. I hit the ground again, my head ringing, and gazed up at whom or what had floored me. Dolferl!

What was he doing over here? The hyena-like shriek of a missile barrelled overhead. He dived to the ground, covering his ears and closing his eyes while we waited for the missile to strike. An ear-spliting blast exploded sixty feet from where we lay. The earth rolled, throwing up clumps of dirt like the crest of a wave, only to be followed by a rain of body parts cast into the air by the explosion. The bombshell had hit a nearby crater where bodies had been dumped. The rotting heads and limbs were accompanied by chunks of the vermin that had been feasting on them.

'God isn't dead,' I said to myself.

'What?' Dolferl asked.

'God isn't dead,' I cried. 'It's worse. He's alive, and he's insane. And who is there to stop him?'

'Look at you!' smiled Dolferl. 'Shedding your Catholic baggage! Finally!'

It was always night in our bunker. There was never any sunlight, and barely any ventilation in our sandbagged dungeon. Any escaping bodily gases lingered in the air for eternal minutes. It was a foul, cramped hovel. Often we not only had to sleep there but eat there as well, so we did everything possible to get away from it whenever we could.

As we all sat by a fire outside the trench at night, we heard another of those piercing screams from somewhere in the dark distance. We scrambled to get back into the trench, tumbling down a small stairway into the shelter. The air was close, almost suffocating. We heard the shell gather momentum and hitting its apex before diving earthwards. Our hands covered our ears; our eyes squinted shut, and our jaws clenched. Some men crouched and hugged their legs to themselves as they awaited the inevitable impact. The sandbags started to vibrate. Sand streamed out of the burlap pores.

Boom!

The earth shook, and the blast launched me into the air, only to slam me down hard on the bunker floor. A string of aftershocks lifted me off the ground again and again. Part of the ceiling collapsed, the soil and gravel raining down on all of us. After the haze cleared, I saw that Dolferl was bleeding: a blossom of blood was expanding across his trouser leg. A terrified Foxl was yelping by his side. Some shrapnel had caught Dolferl's left thigh.

'It's not serious,' he said, trying to stem the bleeding with his hands. Then he turned to Foxl and made a shushing sound to quieten his pet.

Those of us who could still walk hoisted Dolferl out of the collapsed dugout. Foxl barked as he followed us outside, where the bursts of light from the battle alternated with the black night sky. I looked up and down the trench; 'Medic!' I cried, raising my head beyond the edge of the sandbags.

A red glow ran along the night skyline from one end to the other. It fluctuated continually, punctuated with erupting white blasts. A flare zoomed up high overhead, and exploded into a silver globe that floated gently down to the ground. For a moment everything was illuminated as bright as noon. The soldiers beside me cast sharply outlined shadows along the trench's sandbags and wooden planks. My eyes darted to Dolferl's bloodied leg, which I could see now with disturbing clarity. The open wound was deep enough to expose the white surface of his femur.

'Nothing to worry about,' said Dolferl.

How could he not feel the pain? Was he in shock?

'I will stay with the regiment,' he said, calmly. I looked more closely at him: he wasn't sweating or disoriented, he had none of the symptoms of shellshock – except that he wasn't in much pain.

Dolferl sat up, tore some cloth from his trousers and wound it around his thigh indifferently, as if bandaging somebody else's leg. I remembered his yogi stunt with the candle in the shelter and the indifference he'd shown when he'd been injured as a boy.

Boom! Another earth-shattering eruption spewed debris at us. Foxl burrowed under Dolferl's arm for cover.

Damned Brits!

Even though Dolferl had tried hard to convince us otherwise, we all knew that his injury was bad and he would be sent away. And he was.

December 1916, Linz

I didn't know what I dreaded more: the enemy advancing or facing the truth; the truth about Francisca. The wretched truth that our love – her love for me – had died. It was inevitable, and tragic, like everything else in this war-torn world. At first, I had received a letter from her almost every week; then the intervals had become longer; and now, her last letter was seven weeks old. In it, she had written about the hard times she was experiencing at the hotel. The word 'love' had appeared only to conclude the letter. When I was eventually given home leave, it petrified me, because I knew that if I went home, I would have to learn the truth about Francisca and me.

All eyes were upon me as I served myself half of what would satisfy my appetite. I put the ladle down and pushed the bowl into the centre of the table. I looked across at my father, my stepmother and my two sisters, then down at my bowl, and brought the spoon to my lips. The watery taste of the soup merely hinted at turnips. I smiled tentatively: I was back home on leave. Sleeping on clean white sheets and a mattress was like floating on air. It was a luxury to sleep somewhere I didn't have to keep one eye open. I was safe in my own home, free to sleep without explosions or rats scrambling across my face.

'This roll looks delicious,' I said.

Something as mundane as a roll was an extravagance now. There were two. Father was given the honour of cutting them up into five equal portions. Only the rich could eat real food like meat and potatoes. The rest of us couldn't afford the scandalous black market prices. Infants, the sick and the elderly were dying: in the past year alone, the British naval blockade has caused a multitude of civilian deaths. The blockade was a clear violation of international law, but, 'in war', I remembered Dolferl saying, 'all that matters is who wins'. If the Brits lost the war the history books of the future would brand them as barbaric war criminals; if they won, their atrocities against the civilians would soon be forgotten.

The two rolls my elder sister had managed to scavenge were old and hard, but we had developed the eating of stale bread into an art form: hold a bite in your mouth until your saliva slowly softens it; then chew very, very slowly. An additional benefit of this newly acquired skill was that the longer I chewed, the longer I could avoid making conversation. I had nothing to talk about: the carnage of war wasn't a suitable topic for the dinner table. Neither could I talk about my prospective plans because the war had put paid to any immediate hope for a future. It had condemned us to silence, except for the sound of chewing. I pushed back from the table. 'I have to leave,' I announced. 'I need to make a phone call.'

In the post office I asked the operator to put me through to Francisca.

'Five minutes to Munich will be half a krone, sir,' she replied.

Half a krone, I thought, that's half a week's pay for almost getting killed because some bastard Kaiser's nephew I never gave a damn about had been assassinated. But half a krone was nothing for the precious sound of Francisca's voice, even if only for a moment. What would I say? I would admit that I had been wrong and plead for her forgiveness. I would tell her that I now saw things as she had seen them so long ago. I would praise her for taking me to task about my idiotic decision to enlist. How could I have chosen the romance of war over my romance with her? I'd get down on my knees and beg her to give me another chance. I handed my last half-krone to the operator. What does money matter, I thought, when nothing matters?

Even if I pleaded for forgiveness, maybe it was already too late. Perhaps she had found someone else. Someone wiser than me, no doubt; someone less foolish than me, who hadn't allowed himself to be dragged into this nightmare. I wished now that I'd been a real man; a mature adult, not the silly boy Francisca had known; the boy who had skipped off to war thinking it would be a picnic with guns. I turned and looked out to the main square. The Christmas decorations promised a very meagre Christmas, a Christmas with no sugar, a Christmas with strikes and demonstrations against the war.

'Sir,' the operator turned to me, 'I'm afraid there appear to be technical problems today.'

'As there are every day,' I said, frustratedly, keeping my tongue as civil as I could; she had been trying to connect me for an hour and twenty minutes, after all.

'Well,' she said, 'that's the way things are now.'

'That's the way things are now,' I repeated. The way things are now. Have a very meagre Christmas. Christ – what had he died for? To take away the sins of the world? What a joke! His death had been as wasted and as cruel as all of the deaths I'd witnessed on the battlefield.

'Have a listen yourself,' said the operator.

I grabbed the receiver, and could hear mechanical tinkering on the line; then it went dead. Nothing.

'Hello?' I said, into the mouthpiece.

Nothing.

That was the way things were now. Nothing. Dead phone lines. No sugar at Christmas.

When the train finally arrived in Munich, it was two-and-a-half hours late. It was filthy too, by previous standards; presumably the people who used to clean trains were now in the trenches, filthy and bloodstained, if they were still alive. And as different as the train and Linz had been compared to before, so too was Munich. The town was anaemic. Pale. Neglected. Morose. Instead of the usual hustle and bustle in the streets, there was an air of helplessness and stagnation. On the corner of Maximilianstraße, where students had previously sold chocolates and flowers to passing lovers, shady characters now sold flour, soap, and day-old bread at extortionate prices. Francisca's hotel was run-down and grubby, it too a ghost of its former self. I braced myself for the worst as I stepped into the lobby. By now I had come to the conclusion that our relationship had ended: I just had to hear it from her; to have her look me in the eye and tell me that she had found someone else, someone better than me. I wanted her to see my emotional breakdown.

'Excuse me, sir,' I said to the concierge at the desk. 'I'm looking for Miss Francisca.'

A sly smile appeared on the emaciated face of the clerk. Did he know something I didn't?

'I'm so sorry, sir,' he said, 'Miss Francisca is out.'

'Well then, I'll wait,' I replied.

'Well then, you'll be waiting for a week!' he said.

'What do you mean?' I asked, feeling my eyes water.

'She's gone to Hanover.'

'Why Hanover?'

'I don't know, sir. That's really none of my business.'

Disappointment overwhelmed me. Could she be on a trip with another man? My head began to ache. Even if I'd had the money to go to Hanover, I didn't have the time: I was due to go back, and probably get killed, in two days.

'Can I speak to Edgar, her father?' I asked. Surely her father would know why Francisca was gone.

'Her father is travelling with her,' said the clerk.

What were they both doing in Hanover? Had they gone there to meet Francisca's new in-laws?

'Did they know you were coming?' the clerk asked.

'No.'

'You should have called first.'

'I did. The phones weren't working.'

'I see. Well, that's the way things are now.'

I wanted to ask him if he knew her fiancé. But the moment I opened my mouth I changed my mind. I was handed two sheets of hotel stationery and an envelope, sat down and wrote her a pathetic, self-pitying note. Because that was who I was then.

What We Learned in Hell Today

Numerically, we were all dead.

April 1917, Ypres

I sat in a house near the front line. A shell had hit the front of the residence, leaving a gaping hole in what would have been the entrance to the front parlour. A comfortable burnt velvet couch and other partly ruined furniture was strewn around the room. The singed armrests of the reading chair I was sitting on were more or less intact, but if you looked up to where the lamp had once hung, you could see the cloud-laden Belgian sky. Thoughts of Francisca were torturing me since my return to the front. If she had found someone else, why hadn't she had the decency to write and tell me? Was Dolferl right? Was Francisca just a deceitful, spineless whore? After five months in Germany, Dolferl had also returned to the front line, and to the endless affection of Foxl. Dolferl limped, but was healthy and had styled his moustache into two meticulous tight-curled tips. After being treated in a hospital near Berlin, he had been transferred to our battalion in Munich. He could have sat out the war there, but had written to our commander and requested his urgent transfer to the front.

'I can't tell you how disgusted I was in the Munich barracks.' Dolferl paced back and forth, limping. 'The scum they've drafted! They sneer at us for fighting in the trenches!'

Two lance-corporals sat on the charred couch playing cards, trying to ignore Dolferl.

'They're always skiving off! They're a bunch of spineless cowards and work-shy opportunists, lazing around in their clean, well-kept barracks.' He paused, taking in the half-demolished parlour. 'I'm so relieved to be back home!'

I listened incredulously: how could he feel at home in this insanity? How could he find comfort in this destruction? How could he ever request to be sent back to this?

Dolferl straightened himself up and smoothed out his clean, new uniform. 'Now that the enemy has rejected our peace proposal, we must show them who they're dealing with!'

The enormous combat losses coupled with the mounting civilian unrest had convinced the government that peace was now a better option than war, but Dolferl was of the same mind as the battle-hungry French and British politicians: he didn't want peace. He wanted war. Still.

'By iron and blood will the great questions of our times be decided,' he said, fondly quoting Bismarck, 'not through speeches and majority decisions.' His eyes glistened. 'Our army is unbeatable,' he said.

'That was before the war started,' countered Sepp, a lance-corporal from Mühldorf.

'Do you mean to tell me that there is any match for our army? Who?' taunted Dolferl. 'The French? The Russians? The Italians, maybe?'

'True,' said Sepp, 'each of them doesn't pose much of a threat, but – '

'That's exactly what I was saying! Germany has the power to rule over Europe and over Russia as well. Easily!'

'Maybe. Probably. But England has intervened. And that's simply one army too many.'

We had paid for the miscalculation of the Allies' strength with too much of our blood. That's what everyone felt. Everyone, except Dolferl.

April 1917, The Battle of Arras

The stormtroopers were tallying up their day's bounty and some were trading their newly pilfered spoils. A sergeant-major swapped a jar of jam from Harrods Food Hall with a corporal for a pack of King Albert cigarettes. Overhead, eight Fokker E1s flew from behind us in V formation. It was the squadron of Baron Manfred von Richthofen, a revered war hero. The sun shone down over the planes, casting eight shadows that glided smoothly over the trench's winding aisles. We took off our helmets and waved as the pilots returned our salute by dipping the wings of their planes – the wonders of the modern age. Foxl jumped and yapped at the cheers and commotion. Captain Amsfeld emerged from his quarters, forgot his rank for a moment, and waved wildly to the airmen.

The planes zoomed on ahead to the battle's smouldering horizon. I sat on the bank of sandbags and peered out to where the planes were heading, now small crosses in the blue sky amongst the wispy clouds. Then the planes began dropping bombs. Orange flames followed by black plumes of smoke dotted the horizon. We cheered with each explosion. Foxl grew so excited he chased his tail in frantic circles.

Suddenly there was an enormous blast, an eruption from hellish depths that rained lumps of earth down on us. A shell had exploded less than fifty feet from us and no one had been prepared. I was knocked to the ground as I heard the whistle of another bomb. It exploded beside me, bathing me in a cloud of dirt.

'Foxl!' shouted Dolferl. '*Foxl!*' His helmet had been blown off and his forehead cut by a piece of flying debris. Clumps of soil stuck to his waxed moustache. The yelping dog ran towards the captain who had been knocked to the ground beside the embankment, and was now slowly rising to his feet. There was a cackle of gunfire nearby. A string of bullets flew over the edge of the trench, whipping sand up from the bags. The trail of gunfire was heading towards the captain. Foxl scooted across the sandbags, and would have been right in the line of fire along with Amsfeld in two swift leaps.

'No!' screamed Dolferl, jumping on to his beloved terrier, and landing on the captain. Just then the gunfire struck right where the captain had been trying to regain his footing. *Pew! Pew! Pew!* Sand spilled out on to the captain's forehead from the bullet holes in the bags. For demonstrating remarkable courage and valour by saving the life of his dog and consequently that of his commanding officer, Dolferl received the Bavarian Military Merit Cross, third class with swords. He was a hero, not only to himself, but to the nation. And now he had a medal to prove it.

June 1917, Ypres

As we marched towards the forest I couldn't help but remember the first time I had stormed these once green and perfect plains. We were back at Ypres, where we had fought our first battle. I remembered my first scent of war: back then it had seemed the smell of valour, not of disgust and senseless waste. Back then, the battle fires had forged a new and righteous world order. I had been a sword-wielding crusader, saving the world from itself by defeating barbarism for all time. I had been intoxicated by the glamour of war, pledging fervent allegiance to my ideals. Now it was the morning after, and I was living the bleak purgatory of a three-year hangover. I didn't know how it all changed. Had I seen one too many decapitated heads? Had it been killing the Frenchman on Christmas Eve? Or had the hangover kicked in earlier, perhaps the day Frederick had been slaughtered? The ditch where Frederick had died had been so pummelled during the war I almost didn't recognise it. But here I was, revisiting my first charge across this field, feeling like an old man: the war had aged me, as it had the handful of comrades of my regiment who were still alive.

What remained of the romantic notions of my youth?

I had become something between a grave-digger, a butcher and a surgeon specialising in swift death. There were days when I didn't even notice the stench any more, or give a second glance to the sight of a bullet-ridden corpse or severed limb. The war had deadened me: in our blood-drenched reality, nothing mattered; whatever they had told us we were fighting for – decency, humanity, freedom – none of it counted. This war would be won by the more vicious opponent.

We were preparing for another attack by the enemy. The trenches were reinforced with planks and fringed on top with barbed wire as the occasional distant boom reminded us that the French were redirecting their cannons. The threat of gas attacks meant that we wore rubber coats and woollen caps underneath our helmets, making every moment even more nightmarish.

Back when mail was still being delivered, I had always hoped for the mail sergeant to call out my name, even though I had accepted that it was over between Francisca and me. But now even that hope had vanished as we had gone weeks without mail. For one week we even went without food. Water was scarce and we were all starving: we would make balls of wheat, water and sawdust and chew on them – hardly satisfying, but better than nothing.

The war hadn't been kind to the once proud chestnut stallion we had confiscated in this very place at my first battle. The Bavarian Infantry had put the steed to work; back when it still had a majestic presence, the horse had carried our commanders. Then, when its hindquarters had been struck by shrapnel, it had been relegated to hauling supplies on wooden wagons with crooked wheels. Now its once lustrous coat was discoloured and the pathetic creature struggled to move with a limp. At times, its hind legs would slip, and then stiffen in a desperate attempt to steady its rear end.

'The horse will make us a nice lunch,' someone said one day. Others chorused in agreement, and a bonfire was built from spare planks of lumber and sawdust. Large, glowing flames flickered in the heat of the day. Thirty or so men in their coats drew close, sweating even more.

'Bring me the horse,' commanded a sullen-faced corporal. The horse stepped backwards instinctively. Hungry eyes turned towards the animal: it neighed.

'There's enough there to feed us for a week!' someone shouted from the shadows.

Then a voice dissented: 'There's no need to kill this noble creature!' It was Dolferl. He strode up to the front of the crowd.

'You keep eating sawdust, then,' said the sullen-faced thug, brandishing his pistol. 'I'm a butcher. I need meat in my belly.'

Dolferl stepped in front of the horse. 'Why don't you shoot me instead?' he shouted.

'Shut up, you fool!' shouted another. 'The horse will taste better.'

'How vile you all are!' howled Dolferl. 'For three years this horse has been our loyal comrade, and now you want to cannibalise him, just because you haven't stuffed your face for a few days?'

'Look,' yelled another, 'you're not going to stop us.'

'Don't you have any sense of honour?' countered Dolferl, 'And besides we may still need the horse to provide essential services for us.'

'Hey, *Mensch*, in case you haven't been listening, that's exactly what it'll be doing!'

They all laughed.

Dolferl glared at the heckler: how dare he ridicule him! But he managed to compose himself and proclaimed: 'We live in this fire of war. The fire burns us!' His face was stoic and severe. 'The fire wears us down. But it keeps us true to our core. We know who we are from the fire of war. And we are not like the enemy! We will never be!'

'I don't care, I'm hungry!' shouted the butcher, and with that he pulled the trigger and shot the horse just below the ear. It collapsed with a resounding thud, urinated and defecated, and was dead. Dolferl walked away, and sat on the ground with his back towards us. As the scorching sun beat down on him, in his helmet and coat, he sat there staring into the void.[23]

July 1917, The Third Battle of Ypres

After the blazing sun came fiery rain, all day and all night. It was Britain's latest ingenuity: shells containing what we called 'liquid fire'. The shells ravaged the land, robbing it of any remaining verdure and finally reducing it to scorched earth. Real rainfall had turned the soil into a slimy, stinking morass. In the middle of all this we had become twentieth-century cavemen; eating, sleeping and dying in our makeshift caves. Dolferl and I had left the command post and hiked through the rain towards the front line, sweating in our rubber coats. We headed straight for a sky-high wall

23 See: Appendix 21, Hitler and Animals

of fire, and heard the billowing blasts of shells fanning the flames. Somewhere within this hellhole was our destination – the front line. I had overheard our officers talk in disturbed voices about the order we were delivering to the frontline, which prompted me to do something I had never done before: I opened the dispatch.

Dolferl was appalled. His eyes narrowed: it was *verboten*. 'What do you think you're doing?' he snapped.

'What do you think?' I replied, reading the communiqué.

I could hear the inferno crackle ahead of us as I unfolded the message. My eyes and mouth were startled at the barbaric lunacy of the order: as soon as the fire abated, our troops were instructed to leave the protection of the trenches – and attack the British.

'This is suicide!' I exclaimed. Our commanders were hoping for the element of surprise but all I could see was a senseless sacrifice.

'Dolferl,' I said, 'do you realise – '

'I do,' he said, coolly. 'Many will die.'

'That's all you have to say?'

'What's so bad about dying?' He shrugged.

'It's barbaric! They're just sending them out to be slaughtered! It doesn't make any sense. We shouldn't deliver this order. Let's say – '

'You're not only insubordinate, you're insane!' fumed Dolferl. 'We will not defy orders. That's treason!' He glared at me: consider yourself lucky I'm not reporting you!

Dolferl secured the message under his arm and darted right into the erupting volcano as if in a race. I remembered him jumping from one ice floe to the next as a kid and recalled Francisca's words: 'His only thrill is to live on the edge and gamble his life.' Dejected I resigned myself to my fate.

I folded the message and put it back into its envelope. And I waited. If we both made it through that blaze to the front line, Dolferl should get there first: let him deliver that death sentence. I put on my gas mask and stood in the rain, waiting and trembling, staring into the blaze, overwhelmed by my fear. But then, all of a sudden, the bombardment stopped. I couldn't believe my luck as I stepped on to the smouldering black terrain.

When I arrived at the front line our soldiers had left the trench: Dolferl had obviously delivered the order. The rain hadn't abated and I slipped down on to the water-soaked planks of the trench.

'Dolferl!' I shouted, as I ran down the wooden-planked ditch. All along, there were niches where we would sit and relax during battle. In one alcove I came across a recruit encrusted in mud, hiding.

'Come out,' I said, gently. 'I'm not going to report you.'

The poor bastard wouldn't budge. He was too petrified to even look at me. I moved in on to what appeared to be a boy, no older than seventeen, crouching. I crept up closer and touched his shoulder. Nothing. No response. I touched him again and he fell over. Dead.

As I moved further along, I passed one corpse after another, hunched bodies trying to dig their way into the earth like worms. An incendiary shell had hit this part of the trench. This could have been my grave.

'Oh, you're here,' shouted Dolferl, running up from the other side of the trench. 'Finally!' His arms were spread. 'What took you so long?' I said nothing and Dolferl kept talking. 'Well, our men are all gone. Attacking the enemy.'

'Attacking? They'll sink into the mud before they can even think of attacking. They'll all be slaughtered!'

'They don't have much of a chance, that's true.'

'That order was criminal!'

'Shut up!' he fumed. 'The command knows more than we do. They know why they sent them out there.'

I looked at Dolferl. He was unshakeable, blindly obeying his orders. What a self-righteous fool!

'Don't you get it?' I shouted.

'And what, pray tell, am I supposed to get?'

'The generals see us as tin soldiers, pawns that are nothing more than shifting lines on their board game. You've heard them talk about "necessary sacrifices". They don't see us as people with families and loved ones, people who have the right to live!'

'That's exactly how it must be,' he said. 'An army commander must never be distracted by such thoughts; he must live solely in the realm of abstraction. War means that you must see people as tools; anyone who develops emotional attachments is just not up to the job.'

August 1917, Colmar

'There's no question who is superior!' said Dolferl, as he began winding up the afternoon's lecture.

Dolferl was now joining in general discussions frequently, although discussion with him was impossible: he insisted on talking, but refused to listen. He anticipated his opponents' arguments, challenging their viewpoints before they had voiced them and as a result, every discussion became a monologue from Dolferl, which was mainly a boring, long-winded discourse on Germanic loyalty, obedience and sacrifice. This created a tense atmosphere in our part of the trench, especially so because there were many of those new recruits, 'divisive minds', Dolferl called them, who not only questioned the wisdom of the commanding generals but of the war as a whole. They came as replacements for the dead and the injured in our regiment, and their numbers rose daily.

'We are a nation of heroes!' Dolferl exclaimed. 'And what are they? Tea-drinkers and gastronomes!'

'You've seen their trenches,' interrupted one such 'divisive mind'. 'Are their trenches any different from ours? I've heard they use different-sized planks, but I imagine that's the only difference!'

Dolferl didn't say a word. He just stared at his younger challenger.

'Well,' the recruit said, 'that's about it! Other than that, they're just like us. They are people. They want to live. Why should we keep killing them? Because they use different sized wooden planks to us?'

The men laughed as a fuming Dolferl turned red.

'You're a coward!' howled Dolferl. 'A new race is being bred here! Bred by struggle and victory! Let those who want to live, fight. Those who do not want to fight in this world of perpetual struggle do not deserve to live!'

In a huff, Dolferl got up and stormed off.

The next day Dolferl's belongings were ransacked, his paintings ripped to shreds.

'Traitors!' bellowed Dolferl. 'There are traitors among us!'

More shells struck our trench. Clumps of dirt spewed out between the planks of wood. Men were running towards the underground bunkers.

'I think Foxl is gone,' Dolferl said, oblivious to the chaos around us. 'Foxl!' he screamed. '*Foxl!*' Then he grabbed me. 'Come with me!' he cried, pulling me along with him down the wooden walkway fogged by metallic dust.

'Foxl!' Dolferl whimpered, between fits of coughing. We ran further down the trench and turned in to a crowded alcove. 'This is where I last saw him,' shouted Dolferl to the men huddling for safety there. 'My Foxl is gone!' he howled, trying to make himself heard over the racket of the bombardment. Dolferl paced around and around the centre of the recess repeating his pet's name over and over. 'Foxl!' he called out again, hoarsely. The name hung in the dead air momentarily only to be absorbed by the next volley of missiles. 'Where could he be? I love that little dog!'

To hear that he actually 'loved' someone was a shock to me: the last time he had said that was more than four years ago, when he had waxed lyrical about Stefanie.

He turned to me. 'He's gone, isn't he?' he said, his voice quivering.

'I'm afraid so,' I conceded.

Dolferl gaped at me in shock at his loss. 'He was all I had in this world,' he sobbed.

I sighed: there was nothing I could do. I felt pity for him, but then I remembered his sister Angela's words: 'He has no feelings, he just fakes them.'

After four hours there was still no sign of Foxl; he seemed to have dissolved into the dense, smoky air, but Dolferl continued to search anyway after the blasts subsided. 'Where is he?' he asked each of us for the thousandth time. 'Have you seen him?' The men didn't react any more. They were tired of being asked the same question over and over again. Dolferl turned to me. 'See the indifference that breeds among us?' Then he turned on the men and screamed: '*There are traitors among us! Traitors!*' There was paranoia in Dolferl's grief; it was as if the disappearance of his dog had exposed a conspiracy against Germany. 'We're confronted with two enemies,' Dolferl exclaimed, 'not just one!'

The commotion came to the attention of Lieutenant Colonel Spatny, who warned Dolferl to be reasonable and calm himself. However, with every passing hour, Dolferl's accusations gathered momentum and became wilder and more inflammatory. '*Murderers!*' screamed Dolferl. '*Thugs! Criminals! Pigs! They must be exterminated!*'

He was ordered to report to the colonel, but nothing changed; in fact, Dolferl worked himself up into an even more rabid fury. 'This is not the enemy beyond the trench; this is an even more dangerous enemy! Much more dangerous! Because we trust him! We think that he's one of ours, but while we're fighting the Brits and the French, this enemy is stabbing us in the back!'

'Quiet, Private!' ordered Colonel Spatny. 'Stop!' The officer studied his trembling subordinate. 'Anyone else would have been severely punished by now. But your service is exemplary. You fulfil your orders admirably. Your loyalty to "our great cause" is unsurpassed.'

'I'm only doing my duty, sir.'

'Did I ask you to speak?' rebuffed the officer.

'No, sir,' replied Dolferl, meekly.

'I thought not,' said Colonel Spatny, adjusting his belt. 'As you know, this is the second of these little talks we've had to have.'

'Sir, if you only knew – '

'I do know. You've told me twice. I have no other recourse but to order you to . . . ' Spatny paused.

'To what?' Dolferl's eyes widened.

'To take eighteen days' leave,' said Spatny, gently.

'No,' Dolferl whimpered. 'Under no circumstances could I leave. This is my home!'

'That's an order, Private!' retorted Spatny, raising his voice.

'But – '

'But nothing,' Spatny growled. 'Pack and leave here immediately.'

It was Dolferl's first leave in three years of war.

The gentle rocking of the train lulled the passengers as they gazed out of the window at the passing countryside. My forehead rested against the plate glass. Spatny had deemed Dolferl too unstable to travel alone, so I had been ordered to accompany him on leave to Berlin. This gave me a hiatus from the war and granted me the luxury of reflecting on my life and my loss. The note I had left for Francisca in Munich had never been answered; of course, the postal service over the past few months had been virtually non-existent; but then, why would she want to write to me anyway? I was sure that she'd done what was best for her. I had to be pragmatic and mature about my situation. If she had moved on, all I could do was wish her well. If I hadn't been ordered to accompany Dolferl to Berlin, would I have wanted to try and find Francisca in Munich? The terrible irony of it all was that I could face a barrage of bullets and shells on a daily basis, but not seeing her with someone else. It would be the end of me. Christ, I thought, what a life I lead! I massaged my closed eyelids, then slowly opened my eyes. The landscape outside the window was reassuring: here was a world untouched by the war. Brown, harvested fields sailed by, orange and red leaves fluttered on the tips of branches; nature was blissfully unaware of world events. It was like going back in time, to a time before the war.

I glanced over at Dolferl, who was in another world entirely. It was his first visit to Berlin, the capital of the second Reich. Bismarck's Reich. The Reich he had dreamt about in Vienna; the Reich he now risked his life for.

'Do you know what I think?' said Dolferl, out of the blue.

'What?'

'I think that one day I'll have a mountain-top retreat. In the Alps, in those blue mountains. Topped with snow through most of June. Mountains so blue they're almost purple. I'll have my retreat, you mark my words. I've already designed it.' He tapped his head. 'Up here.'

He shifted on his bench.

'My living quarters will be carved out of the mountain granite. There'll be guest accommodation. It will be glorious! I'll invite you there. We'll have wonderful times there. I promise you.'

'So this is Berlin?'

The city stank of rotten eggs. Maybe some factory was belching sulphur nearby and we were caught downwind, I didn't know, but the stench sank straight to the pit of my stomach. We were on Friedrichstraße, once a busy shopping area; now the store fronts were boarded up. It was raining, but the street was packed with drifting crowds. Some were clad in rags, and some were barefoot. With every step I took, another famished hand emerged from the faceless crowd. The naval blockade had left its mark: Berlin was a teetering Goliath ready to keel over and perish from a sickness within. I wondered if it would be long before Berlin's newspapers started publishing recipes for dog stew – for those fortunate enough to find a dog. Dog owners were hiding their pets, afraid they could end up on their neighbour's plate. Soon cat meat would probably be a luxury too.

Dolferl chatted to me as we walked. 'I wonder if the Berlin Opera is hosting one of Wagner's major works.'

'I doubt it,' I said, as a man approached me, bulging eyes, sunken cheeks, emaciated. 'Soldier, could you possibly help . . .?'

I averted my gaze and quickened my step.

'Why do you doubt they'd be showing Wagner?' asked Dolferl.

I looked at my friend: here the city writhed in a gruesome struggle with death, yet he seemed to view it as a haven of fine art and culture.

'I'm sure Berliners love Richard Wagner just not as much as you, but – '

'I'm sure they do! They must! This is the capital of the Reich! Wouldn't it be great to see a decent production of *Lohengrin*?'

'Look around you!' I called, as I passed by another outstretched hand.

'Yes,' said Dolferl, 'times are hard, but this is precisely when we need Wagner most!'

We walked along silently through the rain when he suddenly cried: 'Look!' directing my attention to a poster. It was a picture of a red clenched fist holding a bolt of lightning. Below it were the words: *General Strike! Protest Against the War! A Moratorium on the Production of Weapons! Attend the Rally! Our Babies are Starving to Feed the War Machine! Join Spartakusbund Today!*

Dolferl stepped back, his face displaying disgust and dismay. 'Can you believe this? We're expected to fight in the trenches, and our homeland goes on strike against us! How can they allow this kind of demonstration? This is enemy propaganda! This war must be fought from within as well!' Dolferl stormed off, gesturing angrily. 'Have we become so lax that we allow Marxists to infiltrate our society? They demoralise it to destroy it!' He swung around. 'I'm appalled, but we will strike back! Believe me, we will!'

A black limousine rounded the corner, causing pedestrians to stop and stare resentfully at the occupant in the back seat. Fringed curtains bordered both sides of the passenger window. A darkened profile was reading a paper.

'AEG shares are up five hundred per cent this year alone!' Dolferl screamed. 'Those bastards are making their money from weapons, but not because they want us to win the war: they only care about their profits!' He leaned towards the car. 'How are your British investments doing, you worthless, two-faced crook! Look up from your paper, you bastard! Look out of the window and see what you're doing to us!' he bellowed. 'You want our economy to collapse! You want international capital to rule and ruin our country!'

He had that crazed look in his eyes again, the same glazed, piercing stare as when he had ranted about Foxl's disappearance. Now it was the Trotskyites and the rich conspiring against all things good and German. I was desperately hoping that there was still a Berlin opera season. I unfolded the city map. 'You know, Dolferl, we're just around the corner from the Berliner Dom,' I said, trying to divert his attention away from the limousine. 'Haven't you always wanted to see the cathedral?'

'I'm no longer an architect,'he replied. 'I'm a soldier now.'

It was a cold, drizzling September afternoon. The nineteenth-century buildings that formed the perimeter of Alexanderplatz were dilapidated and grim, their windows staring emptily out on to the square, where fifty or so people had congregated. In the centre, a platform had been erected, at the back of which a banner hung between two poles. The rain had caused the banner to sag in the middle like a wet nappy. Yellow letters sewn on a red background proclaimed: *Workers of the World Unite.* The podium was empty but for a slight frizzy-haired woman sitting on a chair to the side of the stage. She was chewing tobacco and reading a pamphlet.

'Filthy traitor,' spat Dolferl. 'Do you know what I'd do if I were in power?'

'No,' I said, 'but I can imagine.'

'Communist vermin,' he sneered. 'I'd round up all those conniving bastards, and those stockbrokers too, and force them to work in the factories and make weapons. Ha!' Dolferl jumped at the idea. 'What delicious irony that would be! Forcing that scum to make the very bullets that will wipe them out.' Dolferl spun around to face me: wouldn't it be wonderful?

Clump . . . clump . . . clump . . .

It was coming from Rathausstraße. Marching echoed off the brick canyon of buildings in two-four time. Clump . . . clump . . . clump . . . Like a sleeping giant, rudely awoken and furious. Clump . . . clump . . . clump . . . Beating in time to the march of history. From the sound of things, something or someone was in real trouble. A crowd riotous with disillusionment, spilled into the square, led by three wet red flags flapping in the wind and rain. The yellow hammers and sickles swayed angrily and in a flash the square was awash with hundreds of people, their slogans and chants filling the air.

'No more war!'

'We want to eat!'

'Bring home the fleet!'

Dolferl staggered at the sight of the whirlpool of red flags circling the square, round and round. 'We want to eat! We want meat! We want flour! We want power!' they chanted in unison.

'My God,' Dolferl cried in despair, 'there are so many of them!' He shook his head, bewildered at the incomprehensible spectacle. 'We've been defending these cowards!' he wailed. 'These losers!'

His fist clenched, forming a line of white knuckles; the worst had happened, and was getting worse. Behind him, the drenched flags flapped around in circles as the people cheered and jeered and the rain continued to fall.

Suddenly Dolferl covered his face with his trembling hands, groaned loudly and then lowered his hands again.'This feud between the German tribes must end!' he declared. 'This is clearly a conspiracy. But the German people will not be undone. They will see through this ploy. They will not be deceived by this scum!'

November 1917, South of Ailette River

'Dolferl, for God's sake, move!'

Everyone was fleeing our cave into the darkening day but Dolferl stood his ground, defiantly ignoring the evacuation orders issued fifteen minutes before. I had packed up all my belongings in less than five: part of the fine art of soldiering.

I tugged on Dolferl's arm.

He glowered: what's wrong with you?

'Let's get out of this hell!'

We had been holed up in the caves above the Ailette River, where unprecedented amounts of gas had been fired at us. An unbroken cloud of noxious fumes had settled over the entire Ailette valley, and for days we had been unable to remove our masks.

'Dolferl,' I screamed as loudly as I could within the mask. 'We have to move!'

Even through his goggles, I could see that condescending stare: what's with all the panic? Everything will be fine.

The deep maze of tunnels and caves in the Ailette hills had given us a sense of security, but once the French had unleashed their heaviest artillery, that feeling of safety had quickly evaporated. The relentless pounding had pulverised the bedrock: one more strike and our cave would surely collapse. Like everyone else, Dolferl was aware of the imminent danger; but he didn't care. This wasn't courage: it was suicide.

'Fine,' I said, exasperated, 'but I'm going!' My body tensed as I briskly walked five steps away from him; five steps out of there. But then, I stopped. I couldn't abandon my friend.

So I turned back.

Dolferl was still right where he had been, standing amid the torrent of fleeing soldiers. He had thrown off his helmet and mask and was just wearing his woollen cap. I came up in front of him and shouted: 'Dolferl! Come on!'

He refused to move. A flood of men rushed by us, pulling out and escaping.

'Look!' I screamed.

Through the mouth of the cave, we saw a distant white ball exploding from one of the French cannons. The bombshell hurtled across the plain, grating the air with its sinister whistle. Instinctively I seized Dolferl and we hit the ground. There was a rumbling crash above us, and the left side of our underground room began to give way.

I grabbed Dolferl and dragged him out of the mountain's filthy hole.

Dolferl was incensed. 'We're not going to win this war if we retreat!'

He seemed completely oblivious to our plight. 'We must fight!' he screamed. 'The stain of cowardly retreat can never be erased! Clausewitz says as much in his *Three Confessions*!'

I shook Dolferl: not now!

'Why are you all the same?' he screamed. 'Where's your courage? Your loyalty?'

Another wailing shell approached and the earth jolted as I dived to the ground, praying. The cave behind us collapsed.

Silence.

'Now!' I shouted, wrenching Dolferl up.

We ran.

'We must fight!' panted Dolferl, as we sprinted eastwards. 'To the last man, we must fight!'

December 1917, North of Ailette River

Last New Year's Eve, everyone had believed that the year to come would bring us victory. This year there was almost no one among us with such optimism. We had come to the sombre realisation that, after our initial successes in the first months of the war, we had failed to make any substantial advances. Three years had passed: the front line had barely moved, and now even holding our ground was becoming increasingly difficult. With the Americans arriving in ever-greater numbers, the consensus was that the situation would only worsen – an opinion not shared by Dolferl.

'Wake up!' Dolferl bellowed. 'Wake up, you defeatists! If we ride out this storm, it's just a matter of harvesting the fruits of our efforts! And then you'll see that we have already won!'

Our casualties had been staggering. When the war began, our regiment consisted of 3,600 men; now more than that number had been replaced by new recruits. Numerically, we were all dead.

Twilight of the Gods

'It's all in there,' he whispered, pointing to the book.
'What is?' I asked. 'What's in there?'
'Everything,' he said.

June 1918, Reims

The tide of the war turned for me when I read the words 'Love, Francisca'. I read the letter again and again just to reach those closing words. My heart and my hands trembled as I realised that she hadn't abandoned me. With great relief, I learned that she had written to me many times. She wrote that when she prayed at night, she asked that her dreams and mine would meet and then, in the world of dreams, we would join and be together. She told me that she had dreamt of me often, and that, in a sense, this had helped her endure the wait. Had it helped me? Had I met her in my dreams?

'Oh, yes,' I whispered to myself. Yes, she had visited me there on that subconscious plane. Yes, my love, we are not now, nor ever will we be, apart. Never. Never! I wept. Tonight I would dream of her purposefully. And in our dream, we would be together. I couldn't wait to fall asleep in my bedroll that night.

Everything was wonderful.

Even the war!

On the 3rd of March, Russia had signed a peace treaty with Germany: we had won the war on the Eastern front! Germany now had access to huge supplies of natural resources and industries in the territories that Russia had conceded. And most importantly, more than a million German soldiers were relocating from Russia to reinforce us here on the Western front. For the first time in the war, we had as many soldiers as the British and the French. Finally, victory was at hand! The Eiffel Tower was already within the view of our advancing forces. We were about to take Paris, and I was in love. Suddenly it was all so intoxicating.

Everyone around me was exhilarated as well, elated by the will to fight – even the socialists and 'divisive minds'. Any talk of 'doing the sensible thing', 'laying down our arms' and 'reaching out for peace' had vanished in no time. I had to concede that Dolferl had been right all along: evidently his prediction of triumph and victory hadn't been as preposterous as I had originally thought. Maybe he wasn't such an *Arschloch* after all; less an ass, more an oracle.

Our instructions now were to carry our attack forward until total victory was declared. I was under no illusion: it would be a gruesome, arduous path littered with victims. We would be facing battle-hardened British and French troops; the bastards would not give up easily, so we were in for a fight to the death. Yet I had been through worse; much worse. I had sat in those grim holes for years, and the thought of finally marching into that green, promised land had an undeniable, overpowering charm. We were leaving these damned trenches and their damned rats behind for good.

Now we could show our enemies who we really were. Now the world was finally going to see who had the better army. Our leaders' determination had been instilled in the steel-clad heart of their troops. Who would have expected anything from those famished and apathetic men in their tattered uniforms? But since the twenty-first of March, the first day of our advance, we had overrun the enemy's positions in an onslaught of fire and steel. The desire to fight had unleashed previously unimaginable strengths, and we had merged into one ferocious creature: a powerful giant, seething with rage and the desire for vengeance. Dolferl told us that the experience of war had shaped us into a new species of fearsome warriors. And who could doubt him?

'This experience was given to us by destiny,' he proclaimed, intoxicated by the thought of victory. 'It will always be with us. Now we know how it feels to have a strong will guiding a community of equals. We know now that we must never be deterred by thoughts of defeat. And this is not knowledge born of intellectual contemplation. No! This is the experience of our flesh and our blood . . . '

We were stationed near Reims. Every stable and house in the little village was crammed to the rafters with soldiers, guns and ammunition. New supplies had arrived, and hundreds of crates with brand new cartridges and grenades were stockpiled in the farmers' living rooms. Machine guns were stashed in their hay lofts and barns. And at the end of the village, our menacing arsenal of cannons lay waiting. Wheel after wheel, barrel after barrel pointing towards the West. There were small howitzers that fired with fearful accuracy. There were bigger calibres whose shells filled the air with their deadly howl. And there were chubby mortars and huge naval guns, and artillery mammoths that annihilated entire battalions with one strike. Our firepower had yet to be unleashed. Its full force remained mere menacing potential, still unrealised for now. But its time would come soon.

'Tomorrow we'll see who owns this land,' pronounced Dolferl. 'It will welcome the victor on to its smoking fields. But it will accept only the strongest, and dash the weak to damnation.'

Just a few weeks before, he would have been ridiculed for this kind of rhetoric, but now his energised words seemed apt. We were about to write history with our blood.

I lay in a barn and looked up at the roof: it was after midnight and I couldn't sleep. War made you realise how precious and ephemeral every moment is, and how crucial it is to cherish every second. It reminded you constantly that, sooner or later, life comes to an end. I turned over in my bedroll, closing my eyes tighter and straining to conjure up Francisca: her radiance, her fiery hair, her taste, the beat of her heart beneath her ivory breasts . . . I must have drifted off, because suddenly I was woken by the grunts of metallic movement. I got up and stepped out into the cool air of the night. Artillerymen were helping the gunners to roll the cannons out of the barns; some with tractors, others manually. There would be no sleep tonight, tonight of all nights. The war might be decided tomorrow.

Some of the soldiers rolling the cannons were inexperienced new recruits. They were wearing new, over-large boots and over-sized coats that draped comically from their shoulders. Their naïve enthusiasm reminded me of my own initial experiences in this war. For the first time in a long time, marching songs were sung. The new recruits started them, and the veteran soldiers, feeling sentimental, joined in. But even with the singing, we veterans knew this was not going to be one of those rhapsodic attacks, as in our first days. We kept our mouths shut about the high number of recruits that would die on the first day of attack. We had told them all of our survival strategies, fully aware that they would still do exactly the wrong thing. The 'meat wagons' were already waiting to haul their bodies to the burial dumps.

The slaughter of an adversary is an unemotional, pragmatic task: ideally there should be no consideration for the enemy's suffering, nor should the suffering of your own comrades matter. A callous heart is the key. A merciless heart is the most valued asset a front-line soldier can cultivate. Dolferl's character certainly provided the most fertile ground for attaining such an unperturbed state. Now, after thirty battles, he was equipped with a psyche impervious to emotional distractions. He had become an exceptional predator; the disregard he had developed for his own life as well as the lives of others inspired awe in even the most decorated of combatants.

A whistle signalled the artillery to prepare the bombardment. In twenty minutes everyone had to be with his unit. Finally, our great day had come.

Again.

Soon the land was teeming with soldiers, and the village was transformed into a crowded metropolis. Cannoneers lined up behind hundreds of guns. The barrels were angled precisely to aim the missiles at their targets. Behind me a flashing blast shot from a cannon, followed by a deafening roar. The recoil forced the cannon backwards half a revolution, only to lunge forward again. Howitzers, mortars, Big Berthas and navy guns joined in like a dissonant orchestra. The noise of individual guns melded into one sprawling din. My body reverberated with the ground as I watched the missiles fly in steep arcs beyond the blanket of smoke on the horizon. Ahead of us, more and more targets lit up, forming a flickering, burning corona which became increasingly animated before finally blending into one glowing curtain of fire.

Soon our stormtroopers would charge into battle and attack the enemy's advanced positions. Dolferl and I were taking up our positions in the middle of the pack. Together with four other runners we would tail the stormtroopers, ready to run back and report the latest developments to the front line. Lieutenant Gutmann, who had ordered us to line up, was a delicate man; an artist maybe, or a scientist. He informed the captain that we were ready and then gave us the sign to advance. We began marching towards the West, eyes fixed straight ahead as our weaponry's devastating torrent cleared our way. The firestorm was so ferocious that nothing could withstand it: we were hypnotised by its magnificence.

The young recruits began to sing and we all joined in. The earth quaked and pounded with our every step. We had surrendered to the imperative iron will that led us. Nothing was going to stop us as we stormed on to the open field. All of the battles we had fought before paled in comparison with what lay ahead. Finally the time had come to settle all of the old scores. Who was I to think about my own safety now? All of my plans for caution had vanished. I was now part of this living force. And even if I was to die: everyone dies, but few die valiantly.

We had advanced to a position from where we could see streams of light rising from behind the flaming wall of fire: the enemy artillery was responding. Because of the boom of our cannons, we barely heard the noise from their incoming shells. But when I hit the ground and rolled with the thundering rumble just feet away, I knew that the enemy gunners had guessed our position. Another rocket flew its apex, then tipped earthward to make a whistling descent.

Gutmann and his troops were further ahead. Shells exploded around me and as I tried to catch up I glimpsed Gutmann raising his hand; his men advanced and disappeared into a trench: we had reached the enemy's first line of defence. The fortification had been deserted: smoke hovered over what remained of the wooden-planked ditch, grates and tunnels. I jumped down into the sandbagged ravine and saw about thirty corpses, blackened and partially dismembered. Helmets, guns and knapsacks were scattered about. I ran further down and saw more bodies in burnt yellow uniforms. Our guns had done an impressive job. Some of our men were bent over the dead and had begun systematically rifling through the knapsacks, pockets and wallets. Gutman ordered us to line up and found that eighteen of us were missing. I hadn't even noticed. Only eighteen out of 180: not bad.

After a few minutes we continued westward, over barbed wire, empty ditches, scarred and scorched ground. The second, third and fourth trench lines revealed the same: charred death. In some trenches there were survivors: all were shot, whether they were trying to defend themselves or surrender. Those who escaped could give themselves up further behind where the Geneva Convention was in effect.

We ran towards a hill where we came under fire ourselves. A machine-gunner holed up in a cave fired a tight spray of bullets. We flung ourselves to the ground and crawled forward. The men at the front of our group grabbed their hand grenades, pulled the pins and hurled them towards the enemy. Meanwhile, our gunners speedily set up our machine gun in a nearby crater. Endless streams of shining cartridge belts were fed into the belly of our machine gun, which spat out a barrage of bullets that annihilated everything in its path. From behind the rocks the enemy's machine gun fell silent. Yellow figures escaped from the cave to be instantly mowed down. Behind me new recruits and veterans alike jumped for joy. I leapt from my position and ran towards the enemy hideout: all were dead, their lone machine gun buried beneath a mound of cartridges. The air rippled above the glowing hot barrel. Sweet, wonderful victory!

Faster and faster we ran across the charcoal black land. How many of us might have been killed by now? How many might be lying somewhere, slowly bleeding to death? A hail of enemy bullets sliced through the air like hornets, but it didn't stop our advance. No one could stop us now; we were confident of our superiority. We would bring death to the enemy, wherever they were. I was jumping between craters and zigzagging like a gazelle. Boundless rapture superseded all reason: courage and fear were one. I was transported to a new, ethereal sense of security. Another spatter of machine-gunfire was directed at us against the roar of our artillery. I was on the ground, pointing my gun. I pulled the trigger and I picked off one fleeing Brit after another. *Ping! Ping! Ping!* The bullets found their mark and blood spurted like pus from a lanced boil. I heard comrades shouting but couldn't grasp what they were saying. I got up and ran forward, and saw the others doing the same. There were no orders and no communication, but we were all perfectly synchronised. We all shared the same consciousness. *Kill. Kill. Kill.* All coordinated by the same instinct. All animals of war.

Suddenly our advance came to a jarring halt. Two squealing hums from artillery shells crisscrossed above me, and I threw myself on the ground, eyes and ears covered. I could taste the wet soil and feel the pebbly loam against my skin. The earth quaked from the impacts behind and in front, as scorched debris flew up and around me. I had just picked myself up when another shell came howling towards me. Again I threw myself on the ground and pressed my face into the dirt. The impact numbed me: this must be how death feels, I thought. The shell hammered down and I heard screams. Konrad was crawling up next to me. I saw the tattered flesh of his leg with its burst blood vessels and his wide, petrified eyes. Is this it? his eyes asked me. Is this how I die? I lifted myself up, amazed that I had escaped unscathed. I wanted to help but I didn't know how. Dolferl and two others came running towards us. They pulled me with them as I heard another shell approach. A piercing whistle seared across the sky, and we all dived to the ground. The earth convulsed, jumbling us around. Debris flew through the air. I raised my head and looked back to see where the shell had hit. Konrad was gone.

Between explosions and bullets, we crawled forward to where the land gave way to a flickering horizon of flames. The terrain ahead of us raged orange and yellow. I tasted blood in my mouth, and had an overwhelming feeling that this time I wouldn't escape death.

'Diverge!' I heard Gutmann call out. Further ahead I saw our platoon run in different directions; then there was an eye-searing blast, flinging bodies and rocks into the air. I heard screams and with my belly to the ground I skimmed towards a thick black cloud belching forth from a crater and peered over the edge. Through layers of smoke I made out limbs twitching in the mud; arms and legs squirming like worms. The screams were more audible now, and then in the middle of the crater I saw a red flash. Someone pulled me away; I heard an explosion, then another, and another. The screaming grew louder and more and more despairing; in the crater, the heat was igniting more and more hand grenades, flares and cartridges. Slowly the screaming died down to a few sporadic wails.

Gutmann signalled ahead towards a line of sandbags. We stumbled forward exhausted, and fell into the ditch. Knapsacks, cans, mugs, plates and British newspapers covered the ground. Above us, yellow, black, white and red blasts filled the sky. We were cloaked in black smoke, staring in silence at the blaze. Intermittent flashes lit up the ditch and we could see each other's faces: deadened soldiers' eyes in faces caked with grey ash. Someone found some cognac and it was passed around. I gulped it down as if it was water, and then passed the bottle to Dolferl, who declined, as expected.

Lieutenant Gutmann knelt down, trying to light a cigarette. But the changing air pressure of the exploding shells extinguished his match again and again. When he finally managed to light up, he bent over a map. I had no idea where we were. Gutmann didn't know either. We just weren't accustomed to 'wars of movement', as the strategists called it. Suddenly Gutmann leaned back. 'Oh my God!' he cried.

'What?' we asked.

'We're under attack from our own side!'

Rocks, splintered wood and earth were showering us. We weren't behind that wall of fire any more: we were in the middle of it. Our artillery, the embodiment of our power, had unwittingly turned against us. We had all seen what this wall did to those who hoped to sit out the storm underground.

'Someone has to go back and tell them our position!' said Gutmann. 'Fast!'

But who? Who would venture into that all-consuming conflagration?

Our eyes fell on Dolferl. He nodded. He would do it. He got up from the group and ambled into the underground barracks.

I followed.

He sat down alone in the dark, lacing his boots and quietly watching a rat gnawing on the belly of a British corpse.

'I wonder if it can taste anything of the bastard's last meal.' Dolferl laughed. 'Perhaps a hint of those dreadful beans and sausages. Maybe some Earl Grey tea – who knows?'

Dolferl's tone was distant. I wasn't sure if he was addressing his comments to himself or to me.

'Are you OK?' I asked.

There was a thundering explosion above us. Streams of soil flowed between the wooden boards into the cavern.

'You're not afraid?' I persisted.

'No.'

'I would be.'

'I'm not afraid of death,' Dolferl said, staring me straight in the eye.

'No?'

' "If death seems so cruel because we dread the thought of not existing, then we would have to dread the time before we were born as well. Our non-existence after death can't be any different to our non-existence before we were born. An eternity passed before we were born but that doesn't sadden us at all . . . " '

I sighed.

'That's the beauty of Schopenhauer,' he said, took the gun out of his holster, pointed the barrel at his temple and cocked it.

'Dolferl!' I screamed. 'What are you doing?'

Slowly, he lowered the gun, un-cocked it and put it back.

'As long as you have an exit strategy,' he said, 'you will always be okay.'

He got up, waved goodbye to the platoon, jumped over the sandbags and was gone. Heading into that hell was like crawling along a railway track with a train barrelling overhead. If I'd been thinking about it rationally, I wouldn't have given him the slightest odds of survival: no one would have. But then, none of us were thinking rationally. The bottle of cognac circled the group again. Just as Gutmann raised the trembling bottle to his lips, the ditch quaked from a blast. His fingers froze, and the bottle dropped to the ground, leaving the liquid to soak into the earth. Gutmann looked around at us, mortified. If it hadn't been for his rank, we would have battered him with insults; but we didn't. We shrugged, and said it could have happened to any of us. We watched the orange and black sky as we waited, all hoping for a miracle, all hoping for Dolferl to get through. Then, after what seemed an infinity, the bombardment suddenly ceased. The miracle had happened! Dolferl had evidently made it to the base camp. Providence had safeguarded him again.

August 1918, Le Cateau

Being awarded the Iron Cross First Class was Dolferl's greatest joy since that day in Munich when war had been declared. Maybe even greater. He had waited all his life for this. He had waited all his life to be recognised.

The ceremony was held in the ballroom of a castle where the command post was sited. The glass doors were opened out to the terrace that overlooked the scorched farmland. Gentle sunlight and country air infused the room from the west. The officers lounged in their seats, the medals pinned to their uniforms gleaming proudly. Major von Tubeuf, an imposing man with brilliant blue eyes and a sombre voice, stood on the stage where the orchestra would usually play. His silver hair was slicked back and he was standing as upright as the Major General pictured in the army handbook. In his right hand, he held the Iron Cross.

'Private Adolf Hitler,' he called.

Dolferl walked down the aisle, proud and embarrassed. The medal's importance far exceeded the five medals he had already received: the Iron Cross First Class was usually reserved for high-ranking officers. Out of 11 million soldiers, Dolferl was one of just a handful of lance-corporals ever to be honoured in this way.

The French windows on the east wall looked out over the courtyard where the injured lay. They were closed to muffle the wounded men's cries. 'Morphine!' we heard someone scream. The officers looked at one another with displeasure. Everyone silently wished for the semblance of a peaceful afternoon, even if just for a moment.

Dolferl blushed deep red as he ascended the steps to the stage and saluted the officer.

Major von Tubeuf began to read: 'As a runner, his coolness and speed have been exemplary and unwavering. He has shown himself ready to volunteer for tasks in the most difficult situations and at the greatest danger to himself.'

Dolferl's moustache was combed out to pristine thin curls. His eyes focused on the splayed concave arms of the Iron Cross.

'It has been thanks to Hitler's tenacious and devoted efforts that important messages continued to get through despite the greatest of difficulties.'

The major paused.

'*Morphine!*' begged the voice from the courtyard.

As the major pinned the medal on Dolferl's tunic, we all applauded, drowning out the agonised cries outside. For the first time in his life, Dolferl was not fantasising alone about his personal brilliance. Now he had proof that others could see it, too. After the ceremony, custard-filled pastries and coffee were served. Dolferl was unusually talkative, chatting with officers and lance corporals alike about the pastries, Providence and, of course, Wagner.[24]

September 1918, Bapaume

We followed the railroad tracks heading towards the east. The Eiffel Tower was no longer in the sights of our vanguard: the joy we had felt on learning of Russia's surrender had been replaced by despair. American soldiers were arriving by the shipload, and with the Yank Army came their endless reserves of bullets and butter. Damn that tyrant Wilson, how dare he wage a war of aggression against us! We had done nothing to them!

Slowly but surely, all of the advances we had made over the past months had to be surrendered. Our lines hadn't been breached, but our retreat continued. As we marched eastward, Dolferl held his Iron Cross in his hands, staring at it intently. It was his life's crowning achievement. It was who he believed himself to be: valour and duty uniting to create a destiny, a future, a just world to come.

Max from Garmisch hobbled beside us. His makeshift crutch had been bound together from random pieces of wood. Bundled rags cushioned his underarm. He stopped and swung a step, stopped and swung, on and on. He nodded to us and continued.

Dolferl grimaced at Max and turned to me. 'We need more men like that,' he said. 'Have you noticed that he never complains?' Dolferl gazed heavenward. 'With men like him and with our courage and loyalty, we'll be victorious in the end.' He pressed the Iron Cross into his palm.

Max stopped and rested, turning to see if there was a horse-drawn cart following behind. Surely they'd take pity on him and make room. Surely anyone would.

24 See: Appendix 22, Hitler's War Record

'What we have to ask ourselves is why this war is dragging on,' Dolferl continued. 'What went wrong?'

'According to your theory, nothing,' I said. 'The events just prove that we're not who we thought we were. We don't have the better blood.'

'But we do!' shouted Dolferl.

'Well then, why are we retreating?'

Dolferl thought silently for a moment. Then he said, 'I don't know.' This was an unusual admission for someone who always claimed to know everything.

'You don't know why we're retreating?'

'Well, it somehow must have to do with mixed bloods. That always results in a decline of racial quality. That must be the reason.'

The sound of horse hooves could be heard from behind. As the wagon creaked closer, Max's face relaxed with a glimmer of hope.

Dolferl stopped. He looked me intently in the eye, as he always did when making a point. 'We're lacking the force of resistance,' ha said. 'Only pure blood possesses that.'

Over my shoulder, Max was standing in the path of the horse and cart. The wagon was filled with wounded men, all cramped and all uncomfortable. The driver pulled on the reins, the horse stepped back, the wagon shuddered to a stop with a jolt, and the wounded toppled over one another, emitting agonised wails.

With his back turned, Dolferl was unaware of the commotion. He continued: 'Pure blood is lacking in those capitalists, those pacifists, those internationalists, communists, socialists, those shirkers. They're the scum of our race. We should have locked them away when the the war started. We should have put them in camps, and let them die there! Like the Brits let the Boers die in their camps during the Boer War!'

Again, Dolferl and his assumptions about the war weren't at fault: it was 'them', 'the traitors'. They were guilty. As obsessed as Dolferl had been with our victory, he was now obsessed with blaming our impending defeat on the traitors who had robbed him of Foxl.

'Is there any room for another man?' asked Max.

'Fuck, no!' screamed the wounded, in furious unison.

'But – '

'But nothing, you bastard, at least you can walk!'

'I can't any more!' pleaded Max.

'Well, then, wait for the next wagon to come.'

'Is another one coming?'

'Sure,' said the driver, sarcastically, 'there's one every fifteen minutes.' He laughed, releasing the brake and snapping his whip.

The wagon took off again, leaving Max behind. I turned, and we walked on, leaving Max behind too. It was every man for himself, even if he was only half a man.

October 1918, Ypres

Dear Francisca – I've thought long and hard about whether I should write what I am about to write to you. I am lonely. All my old comrades are dead, severely wounded or psychologically damaged. Every one of them is irretrievably changed. One way or another, they are all gone.

They still haven't granted me leave. We're short of men. The Allies have started a new offensive. Many are dying and our ranks are filled with new recruits. Our battalion has a strike leader from Worms. He was sent to the front as a punishment. Now he incites the troops. We veteran soldiers are called fools. We're considered insane for risking our lives for four years in a war we can't win. The new recruits refuse to take orders that put them in danger. Yesterday some of them even cursed the Kaiser.

I stopped – I ripped the letter up and started again.

Dear Francisca – You are the only light in this desolation! I want to be home with you. I wish I were home with you now, in that quiet, safe place. I wish I were back with you, looking into your eyes. So we could say things to each other that we say to no one else. Be with each other to make up for the rest of humanity. Hold on to each other as we both hold on to this life.

I wish . . . well, you know what I wish.

Love always,

Martin

I had gone to the train station, or rather what remained of it: there was no station house or platform, only rubble and tracks. And a sign that read: Halt. Dolferl was late. I had been sitting on the rails for over an hour when I felt a slight tingling vibration, followed by the faint shriek of a whistle, still far away. Dolferl's leave had been an additional bonus for being awarded the Iron Cross. This time it was a matter of honour, so he willingly took the time off and visited Berlin again. Witnessing the desecration of his most treasured of Germanic virtues – loyalty – on Alexanderplatz during his last trip there had radicalised him. Since then, his anger had had only one focus: the enemy within. How might this trip have affected him? I wondered. I stood up and looked in the direction the train was coming from. I could see a cloud at first; then, slowly, the locomotive emerged from the distance. The whistle blew again and I heard the sound of distant chugging. The noise grew louder, and the train grew steadily bigger until, finally, the gasping black locomotive came to a stop at the Halt sign. Soldiers tumbled out of the train, looking bleak, dishevelled and tired. Then Dolferl emerged, his uniform neatly ironed and his shirt starched. He looked like he was on his way to a banquet rather than the front line. He must have found another mother figure, another Frau Zakreys or Frau Popp, in Berlin, I surmised.

Dolferl walked towards me.

'Martl, my man!' he said, as a greeting, and then shook his head. 'Berlin!'

'What do you mean?' I asked.

'Let's go,' he said, gesturing with his head.

We strolled towards the demolished village. I could see from his face that something had changed; he carried himself differently, too; he seemed somehow more determined and more focused than before.

'How was it?' I asked.

'Oh, well,' he said, rubbing his hands.

'What?'

'Berlin!'

'Yes? What about Berlin?'

He didn't answer, just accompanied me silently to our trench.

What was he hiding from me?

At the trench, he reported to the Staff Sergeant and then immediately went to our sleeping quarters.

He took off his clothes and slid into his bedroll. 'I'm tired.'

'Dolferl,' I said, 'something's happened, I can tell. What is it?'

'Not now.'

'Come on,' I said. 'Tell me, Dolferl.'

He raised his head, checking if anyone was listening. Then he whispered into my ear. 'I know now.'

'What?'

'I've been on the wrong track. We've all been on the wrong track.'

'I don't understand. What do you mean?'

'Do you remember that I was trying to figure out why this war is going the way it is?'

'Sure.'

'Think how an astronomer would handle a similar situation. Suppose he's observing the motion of a celestial body. According to his calculations, this body is located somewhere else, not where he sees it through his telescope. But why is that?' He stopped.

I shrugged: I don't know.

He chose his words carefully. 'There must be a hidden force somewhere which is responsible for the deviation. And now, using his observations, the astronomer performs calculations and determines the location of a planet, which no eye has yet seen, but which is there nevertheless.'

'And . . . ?'

'History is exactly the same.'

He paused at the sight of my confused expression, and then continued.

'It never occurred to us that there's a hidden force. But it's there! It's been there since the beginning of time!' He looked at me. 'Do you know what that force is?'

I shook my head.

He grabbed his knapsack and took out a breviary, about the size of a schoolbook. It had a black cover with no title on it.

'It's all in there,' he whispered, pointing at the book.

'What is?' I asked. 'What's in there?'

'Everything,' he said.

'I don't understand,' I said.

'Don't worry,' he answered. 'You will.'

I opened the book. The title read *The Rabbi's Speech*.[25]

Dolferl was standing heel to heel in a half-obliterated farmhouse. He was admiring his Iron Cross in the mirror; it was pinned on his chest, over his heart. His moustache was perfectly waxed into its Kaiser Wilhelm curlicues, his jaw was clenched, making his already gaunt features sterner. He would have liked a photograph of himself right then, at his most majestic. How stunning that photograph would be, over the fireplace in the alpine manor of his dreams.

I chuckled.

25 See: Appendix 23, The Jewish Conspiracy

He turned, without a trace of embarrassment that I had caught him in a moment of vanity.

'I've heard it said all my life,' he exclaimed, 'but I never realised its full meaning until now!'

'What do you mean?' I asked.

'The Jews!' he snarled. 'It's them! They're the ones behind it all! They make our nations fight one another. There's no reason for us to fight, but the Jew makes us. The Jew!'

That again! Since his return from Berlin, he had talked of nothing else. Like most other German nationalists, Dolferl didn't want to admit that the war had been a mistake: instead he had found a scapegoat. *The Rabbi's Speech* claimed that Europe had been plunged into the war because of a Jewish conspiracy.

'The Jews control not just the international stock markets but the communist movement too!' he whispered, secretively. His right hand curled into a fist and he bellowed: 'Their aim is to dominate the world!'

He knew every word of the pamphlet by heart. Its content had become the cornerstone of his unified *Weltanschauung*. The Jews alone were responsible for everything that had gone wrong: it was obvious now that the Jews were even behind the disappearance of his beloved Foxl.

'They're not a religion! The Jews are a race! Their religion is the biggest scam ever invented! It only serves them to keep their race pure!'

Jewish Dr Bloch, who had kindly treated his mother and of whom Dolferl had been very fond, was forgotten. His veneration of Mahler was forgotten. His Jewish friends at the shelter were forgotten. Our Jewish comrades who had died in the battlefield – all forgotten. Had Dolferl even forgotten Gutmann, his Jewish superior who had recommended him for the Iron Cross?

'Why didn't I listen to Wagner!' he lamented. 'He knew better than anyone! He always said that the Jew was the curse of this world. But now I will fight them! I promise! Not with emotion, but with ice-cold reason! Emotion only leads to pogroms, and nothing is really gained. We must use reason to cut this cancer from the body of our nation. Once and for all.'[26]

His eyes scanned me from boot to helmet and then settled on my chest.

He raised an eyebrow inquisitively. 'Where is it?'

He was referring to my Third Class Bavarian Bravery Medal, which I had received the day he was awarded his Iron Cross.

26 See: Appendix 24, The Beginning of Hitler's anti-Semitism

'My medal?' I asked.

'Yes. Where is it?'

'In the shit box,' I said. A shit box was a wooden commode with side handgrips that made it portable.

'What?' Dolferl cried. 'You didn't throw your medal in there!'

'I certainly did.'

'Are you out of your mind?'

'No,' I said. 'I'm very much in my mind! Why should I cherish a piece of metal on a strip of ribbon? Why should I celebrate that fact that I have relentlessly butchered men who are no better or worse than me? It's insane!'

'You disgusting pig!' he shrieked, flying into a ferocious rage. 'You're just like them!' Then all of a sudden, he spat at me.

I wiped the saliva from my face.

Dolferl continued: 'That medal is an honour that our army – '

'I haven't finished yet!' I screamed, so loudly that it rendered even Dolferl momentarily silent. 'So many people have died for worthless, convoluted reasons based on grandiose logic and noble talk. I threw my medal in the shit box because I see it for what it is: a disgrace to me and to humanity.' I trembled with such revulsion that Dolferl took a step back.

'M . . . Martl . . . ' he stuttered.

'My name is Martin!' I barked, and marched out of the farmhouse through where the front door had once been.

14 October 1918, La Montagne, Werwick

There had been no sleeping at any time that night. Our underground quarters quaked continuously with blast after blast, and every blast created new cracks in the wooden rafters above.

I was lying on my side, staring tiredly across the cave, where Dolferl was sitting in a cross-legged position next to his kerosene lamp, reading. He noticed me looking at him and smiled over at me. I smiled back. We were friends, it seemed, no matter what.

The room quaked again. Then the siren sounded.

Gas!

The men jolted up from their beds. Was I imagining it or were my eyes already beginning to tear? And was my throat really itching? No, it wasn't my imagination – that acrid smell was real! It smelled of garlic, mustard, bitter almond, horseradish and fire. We were already in the middle of a gas cloud! Now everyone was up. We all scrambled to put on our gas masks. I had to suppress the impulse to cough: breath slowly, I told myself. If I breathed too fast my mask's glass goggles would condense and impede my vision.

Dolferl sat there calmly. His eyes still, his voice steady, he said, 'we've been attacked like this before. The only sensible response is to confront them and defeat them.'

'Dolferl!' I shouted. 'Put your mask on!'

He glared over at me and I thought I heard him mumble something as he unfolded from his position.

Richard, one of the new recruits, burst into the room, running to grab his mask from its hook on the wall. He pulled his mask on quickly, but evidently not quickly enough, as he fell to the floor contorting with violent spasms. Reluctantly Dolferl reached for his own mask, seemingly undeterred by what was going on all around him.

Outside, the putrid fog swallowed up the sun and any illusion of hope we may have harboured. Günther, Dolferl and I were standing above the trench surveying the desolation around us. The British bombardment had been relentless. There was no earth left for them to destroy, and now they were bombing the craters they had already created. Dolferl was on my left; on my right I suddenly heard muffled screams. I looked across and saw Günther heave his insides out, the vomit filling his mask. He collapsed, twitched a few times and was dead.

Within my mask, my breathing resounded and I could hear my respiring lungs echo. If I listened intently, I could hear my thumping heart. In different circumstances, my breathing and heartbeat could have been soothing, but now their panicked rhythms only reinforced the horror surrounding me. I turned to Dolferl and, even through the condensed lenses, I could see his eyes widen with worry. His legs began to falter, and he fell forwards on to a sandbag. He pushed himself off the bag again, trying to stand on his own. Then Dolferl tore his mask off. 'Damn thing doesn't work!' he screamed, before vomiting on himself. Then he collapsed.

October 1918, Qudenaarde Hospital

The first thing I saw when I woke up was the white ceiling. I knew instantly where I was. I turned my head and looked up, down, and around the crisscrossing aisles of the ward. All around there were soldiers just like me, laid out on beds one after another.

'Dear God!' I said aloud, when I noticed a rubber tube sprouting out from my arm and leading to the hanging glass bottle on the stand by the bed. 'Dear God!' I rejoiced. My throat was dry: I wanted a drink of water, and then I wanted to sleep some more. I was relieved to know that I could sleep safe and sound and that I was lying in crisp clean sheets, safely wrapped in this white medical cocoon.

I woke up again.

It was a month later and I was still there.

I sucked diluted lentil soup through a straw. I sat up and assessed my situation. My battalion was no longer in the filthy trenches; we were now in the sanitised setting of a hospital. Most of us had their eyes bandaged, sucking liquids through straws. I was lucky: I could still see. I could still walk. I knew I was in a hospital, but I didn't know where the hospital was. They told me the hospital was in Qudenaarde, wherever that was . . .

As the train snaked towards Hamburg, my mind was slowly coming back to me. I remembered my life before the trenches; I remembered my father, mother and sisters; I remembered Francisca. I remembered that I was in love with Francisca. I remembered what love was. I was starting to remember what some longer words meant. I knew where Hamburg was. I knew where Hamburg was in relation to where I was coming from, and in relation to where I wanted to go: Stettin. I knew what things I had packed in my bag. I remembered when I hadn't always felt this nauseous. I remembered when the ground I walked on had been firmer than it was now. I remembered asking the nurse in Qudenaarde why they had shipped Dolferl to Stettin. I remembered her telling me that he'd been blinded. But so had most of my comrades, who were all still in Qudenaarde with me. Why would they separate a blind man from his platoon and send him on a five-day train journey to the north? I'd asked. The nurse hadn't been able to tell me.

I picked up the day-old newspaper in front of me. It looked foreign to me: it was written in German, but current affairs in Germany made it seem like another country. On the front page, there was a photograph of a crowd of German sailors and shipyard workers waving flags with hammers and sickles in front of Kiel's city hall. The caption read: *Thousands of navy personnel take over Kiel.* The article detailed a situation in which officers and policemen had been killed, armouries looted, and the city's food supply confiscated. Most of the troops sent to suppress the uprising had deserted or joined it. There had been no news of this at the front; our infantry had been completely isolated from such events. I stared at the paper. The printed words began to swim before my eyes as the train leaned to the side, making me dizzy. I had been discharged because they needed my bed for the more seriously wounded, and had been instructed to take two weeks' leave. They knew I would only be a burden if they returned me to the front.

'Are you okay, sir?' asked a man sitting opposite me in a three-piece suit. He was my father's age.

'What's going on in Kiel?' I asked.

The man looked around. There was no one else. He shrugged. 'Here' – he pointed to his newspaper – 'this is today's paper.'

Naval revolt spreads to Hamburg, Lübeck, Bremen and Wilhelmshafen, the headline read. A photo showed rioters fighting the police. This was exactly what had happened one year ago in October in Russia. Would the German Revolution become known as the 'November Revolution'? What would happen if this news made its way to the battlefields?

'Any news from the front?' I asked.

The man shrugged. 'The war seems to be over for Austria.'

'Did the Austrian Kaiser surrender?'

'There is no Austrian Kaiser any more. The Austrian royalty fled Vienna a week ago. The Habsburg Empire has collapsed.'

'There's a revolution in Austria as well?'

The man nodded.

I wondered to myself whether our future would be communist.

'Six hundred and thirty-five years of Habsburg rule in Austria have come to an inglorious end,' said the man. 'You look hungry. Would you care for a cup of borscht?'

I nodded yes.

'My name's Herman,' he said. 'I run a shoe shop in Hamburg. My wife packed me a lunch.' He whispered the last word as if borscht were contraband.

I said nothing.

'It's still hot and still good.' Herman smiled. 'My wife has her own garden. She grew the beets herself. We tried wheat because bread was so scarce.' He shook his head. 'You know how many grains you have to grind just to get enough flour to make a decent-sized piece of toast?' He leaned back in his seat. 'Forget about it!'

I smiled for want of something to say.

He leaned to the side, unlatched his valise and pulled out a silver canister. I had never seen such a smooth, shiny flask before. He unscrewed the cap and poured the vermilion soup into it.

'Here,' he said, offering it to me. 'Go on, drink, it's hot.'

He noticed me staring at the flask.

'Great, isn't it? It keeps the soup hot, and beer, if you drink it, cold.' He smiled. His bow tie rose and fell as he spoke. 'I may be a shopkeeper by trade, but I'm an inventor at heart.'

I sipped the soup. It was thick and filling, as soup had been before the war. My cheeks glowed. I smiled: delicious.

He held the container, scrutinising it. 'It only took me a few weekends to design it, but four months to actually make this prototype. My cousin helped me. He's a silversmith, with a small jewellery shop in Bremen. The soup is hot, isn't it?'

I nodded.

'I have a patent; now I need a manufacturer. But these dreadful times have made it impossible to find one.'

'Out in the field, this would be – ' I began.

'Exactly,' he said. 'You'd think the army would be interested. But they weren't.' His eyes welled up, and he sighed, resignedly. He looked out of the window and bit his lip, deep in thought, as the landscape glided by. Windswept trees. Harvested fields. Houses huddled around the centre of a small village. And then again fields and trees and another village, almost identical to the one we had just passed.

I finished my soup. 'Thank you,' I said.

'It was an honour.' Herman lowered his eyes to the paper, and pointed to the photograph of the rebels fighting the police in Hamburg. 'Can you believe that?' He gazed up at me and answered his own question. 'After what you've been through, I suppose you can probably believe anything.'

I smiled wanly: you said it.

'Our progress was extraordinary under Hohenzollern rule! We now have health, accident and disability insurance. We established old-age pensions and the most advanced welfare system in the world.' He coughed. 'We were a model of social progress. Even the English adopted some of our ideas! And now the Allies won't even negotiate with us. They call the Kaiser "an obstacle to peace". They forced him to resign. They're responsible for this turmoil!' He folded his arms. 'They're responsible for obliterating the most humane society in Europe. And who knows what will follow?' He looked at his shoes. 'I wonder what will happen to my shop,' Herman mused. 'I wonder what will happen to people like me.

There's no place for people like me in a communist utopia. But I doubt very much that I'll be better off if those capitalist Anglo-American bastards get their way.'

The train was rumbling through the outskirts of Hamburg. Dead factories. Strewn rubbish intermingling with clumps of weeds. Three children shmashing warehouse windows with rocks.

'If the capitalists win,' he continued, 'the corporations will take over. They'll force us small shopkeepers out of business. They call it "free enterprise".' He paused. 'But how free is that? Free to become an employee in their stores! And if the communists win – I'll be an employee as well. Employed by the state in my own shop!' His eyes filled with despair. 'I'm caught in the middle. We're all caught in the middle. This country's entire middle class is caught in the middle.'

How full of remarkable promise the country had been just a few years ago, I thought, and how fraught with misery it is now. What was the way forward?

'What we need is a strong leader,' Herman said, as if he had just read my thoughts. 'What we need is someone with the guts to fight the capitalists as well as the Bolshevists.'

The train turned and crossed a trestle. Our view overlooked a major boulevard in central Hamburg, where a churning grey mass of people was waving red flags.

'My God!' exclaimed Herman.

The train screeched and came to a stop, allowing us to peer down at the commotion. The crowd was surging down the street angrily, some holding rifles over their heads. In the distance we could see the blue-and-brass mounted police on horses. The protesters rushed towards the police, giving them no option but to charge. Rifles were fired. An almond coloured horse reared up, teetering on its hind legs. Another shot rang out and spouts of blood spurted from its belly. The steed stepped back and then toppled backwards on to the police. The people cheered as the train pulled away.

I looked at Herman. He was sweating.

'Four long years we've been living through this nightmare,' he said. 'I'd like to believe that this is the end of it. But something tells me that it's only the beginning.'

People snarled at me because of the uniform I was wearing, and the sour lady in the ticket booth told me that it would be days before there was a train for Stettin. I didn't care – nothing really mattered. But what was I to do until then? I exited the station.

I was avoiding the streets where people were singing *The Internationale* arm in arm. A few corners before, I had made a wrong turn and had been confronted with a crowd of labourers with axes and monkey wrenches. They had hoisted their weapons and had brandished them at me, ready for attack. Soldiers like me who didn't march with them were considered traitors.

'Arise ye workers from your slumbers, arise ye prisoners of want. For reason in revolt now thunders . . . '

They were giving me a headache. I'd been released from the hospital too early: I was feeling sick.

'. . . and the last fight let us face. The Internationale unites the human race!'

I keeled over and the borscht Herman had so kindly given me erupted out of my mouth and on to the street. It was red, like everything else. I stood up and leaned against a wall.

A dumpy prostitute in an ill-fitting dress strutted up to me. 'Looking for some fun, soldier boy?' She jiggled her breasts.

'I don't need a whore,' I groaned, as everything around me began to swim. 'I need a nurse.'

I came to in a room with fringed curtains. I was lying on satin sheets in a four-poster bed with a canopy overhead. The prostitute was making herself up at her vanity table. She was no older than twenty. Instinctively, I checked to make sure I was all zipped and buttoned up. I patted my trouser pocket to be sure my wallet was still there. It was.

She looked at me in the mirror. 'Don't be like that! I didn't take anything. Promise.'

'How did I get here?'

'We walked up here. You took one look at the bed, climbed on to it and fell asleep right away.'

I looked around. 'How long was I asleep for?'

She counted her fingers. 'Sixteen hours.'

'Oh, God,' I said, wondering if the effect of the gas would ever leave me.

'I know you wanted a nurse, but this is the best I could do. All the hospitals are full,' she said. 'You know, the riots.' She ran her lipstick along her bottom lip. 'I always wanted to be a nurse,' she said. 'Well, in a way, I suppose that's what I am.' She turned on her stool and stuck out her dainty hand. 'My name's Kitty,' she said. 'And just between you and me, dear boy, Kitty is my honest to God, baptised name. My mum had a thing for it.'

I said nothing.

'I tell most guys my name's Catherine,' she smiled, revealing ochre teeth between her ruby-red lips. 'It's funny, isn't it? I was given a whore's name, but my whore name is a patron saint.'

'It was very nice of you to help me,' I said, sitting up. 'I can't believe I slept that long.'

'A lot has happened,' she said.

I was bewildered. Had I had sex and couldn't remember?

'Not between us, silly!' She laughed. 'You slept and I just watched. I like taking care of people. You have a sweet sleeping face.'

'What happened?'

'The Kaiser is gone.'

'What?' I cried, jumping up. 'Where?'

'No one knows,' she answered, pointing to a paper. *Germany Declared Republic*, read the headline.

'There's a revolution going on . . . ' She turned and looked at me. 'Now the Kaiser's been put out on the street like everyone else.'

I rolled over on the bed and wondered how much longer the war could continue.

'So you're with us?' said the foreman, one eye closed the other open. He banged down his glass on the bar, and beer splashed up and over the rim.

'Yes, absolutely,' I said. 'Who doesn't want that bloodbath to be over?'

'This war will end now,' the foreman said. 'Fucking royalty. Look what they've done to us! Fucking militarists! It was their war. It always has been. It was the industrialists' war, not ours. They get the profits, not us. To us workers it doesn't matter who wins the war!'

I drank to his words as I repressed thoughts of Dolferl. I never thought in a million years that I would live to see a government intending to establish a utopia in Germany.

The foreman had worked the docks all his life. He had a hearty laugh. His tattooed forearm was bandaged. 'Our time has finally come,' he said, and smiled, half his teeth missing. 'And that means that this war will be the last war. Ever. We won't fight any more wars for them!' He laughed. 'We won't need soldiers like you in the future!' He guffawed and slapped my back.

I shot forward and almost dived head first into my beer.

'You get it, don't you?' he said. 'Wars only fatten accountants and shareholders. But not with us, never again! Ever!'

I drank the beer he'd bought me and thought of Dolferl, and what he would scream at this drunk.

'Did you know there is a people's government now in Hanover and in Cologne? And in Frankfurt and Stuttgart as well?'

I shook my head.

'The Russians are already our brothers,' the foreman continued. 'In no time at all there'll be nothing but brothers on this entire continent. I promise. You'll see. Those who were our enemies yesterday will be our brothers tomorrow. Now that Germany has woken up, all of Western Europe will wake up!' He lit a cigarette. 'And what reason could a German worker then have to fight a war against workers from France? Or England?' He inhaled, and smoke escaped from his nostrils. 'We'll only fight the accountants, shareholders and industrialists in our own countries.'

His right hand held the glass; his left curled into a tight fist. I was afraid he would burst into the *Internationale*. Instead he banged on the bar. 'We will fight those who made us fight wars for their profit!' he bellowed. 'We will all finally live in a civilised world!'

The word 'civilised' emerging from his gap-toothed mouth was jarring. Even with my mustard-gas hangover, I knew something wasn't right.

'Everyone's a fucking loser in war, *Mensch*,' he said, gripping me by the shoulder. His fingers pressed into me firmly; his breath reeked of beer. 'I mean that!' he said, earnestly

And then, thankfully, he let go.

The train pulled into Stettin at dusk. My stay in Hamburg had been aimless and drunken. I had heard lots of talk; too much talk. Kitty did offer some solace. She would dab herself with a concoction from a little pink glass vial, thinking it was the scent of Parisian glamour when in fact she smelled like cold cream. It made me miss Francisca, because she had used cold cream to remove her stage make-up. When I told Kitty this, she understood; she was happy I had a girl I loved. I'd had enough of Hamburg and I was glad to be leaving it, but from the raucous look of things, Stettin was no better. Yellow hammers and sickles could be seen wherever you could hang a flag. It seemed the Northern provinces of Germany were preparing to model themselves on their new soviet stepmother, Russia, or even annex themselves to her. The town square was draped in red banners. Bonfires burned in the streets. The taverns were filled with rhetoric and rebellion.

I walked to the hospital. Like the rest of the city, it was in turmoil.

The nurse behind the desk was bewildered by the constant chaos. She looked weary. Her hazel eyes studied me coldly, having heard similar stories before. She opened her register and looked down the column of patients' names.

She sighed. 'I'll see what I can do, but it's bedlam in here.' Her pale lips tensed. 'Eureka! There he is,' she exclaimed.

'Fantastic!' I replied 'Which ward?'

She paused. 'He's not here.'

'What?'

'Sorry.' She shrugged.

'What do you mean, he's not here?'

'He's been transferred,' she explained, curtly.

'Again? They just transferred him here from Belgium, nearly six hundred miles! Why would they do that to an injured, blinded man? Why didn't they just leave him in Belgium? The army hospital was well equipped! And why are they still transferring him?'

'Even if you were a relative, I wouldn't be allowed to reveal any further information,' she said guardedly, implying that there was more to it.

'So where is he now?'

'In Pasewalk. It's only an hour away.'

What was another hour after five days on a train?

The bus rolled into the town square. It was packed with soldiers and civilians, celebrating. The windows overlooking the town centre were full of dangling legs and swinging arms. People here were singing with joy, not with the anger I had become accustomed to when labourers sang *The Internationale*. That was an improvement, at least. But I didn't discover the cause for celebration until I got off the bus.

'An armistice has been signed. It's over!' cried a matronly woman, wearing a crucifix that bobbed up and down over her bouncing breasts.

Shouts of the latest news erupted from the ebullient crowd like fireworks. There were rumours that the newly established republican government had signed the armistice but our military leaders had refused to go along. If that were the case, that armistice didn't hold great promise for a lasting peace.

'It's over. It is finally over!' yelled a spindly old man.

The throng leapt up and down in the cobble-stoned square, everyone toasting each other. Four years ago, this same crowd had celebrated the war. Now the war had been lost and they were celebrating that too. What lessons had been learned? They didn't know. They would never know.

I observed the crowd, feeling something shift internally: I had become so enmeshed in the war that now, with the return of peace, I felt strangely displaced. The war had chewed me up, and now that it was finished with me it had spat me out.

PART THREE

PEACE

Pasewalk

I've been given an order. By the Lord who created our people.

I found Dolferl's name in a list of patients in Ward VI of Pasewalk Hospital. At the ward, I was surprised to be welcomed by a professor. He introduced himself as 'consultant neurologist' Dr Edmund Forster from the Royal Charité Hospital in Berlin, an extremely reputable institution. He was a surgeon-lieutenant with the navy. I wondered why Dolferl, a humble lance corporal, was receiving such expert medical attention. I imagined a permanently blind Dolferl, and how devastating that would be for someone who had once dreamed of becoming a world-renowned architect and painter. Before I went to see Dolferl, the professor asked me to come to his office.

I hadn't even taken my seat when the question escaped my lips. 'How is his sight?'

'His vision? Oh, that,' said the professor. 'Well, we hope it will correct itself.'

I was so relieved. 'That's great news!'

'It isn't all that unusual for patients who've been exposed to mustard gas to regain their sight fully.' Dr Forster smiled slightly and adjusted his round-rimmed glasses. His face was drawn with exhaustion and he stank of sweat. 'It isn't his initial blindness that we're concerned about,' he said. 'It's the . . . other thing.'

'What "other thing"?' I asked. Was it a euphemism for something so terrible it was unmentionable – or even worse, something that they, the professionals, didn't have a name for?

A white-veiled nun entered with her head bowed. She set a file down on the doctor's desk and walked briskly back out of the office.

'What do you mean, "other thing"?' I asked again.

'You're aware he's in a separate part of the hospital?'

I had no idea what the doctor meant. 'All I know is that this is Ward Six,' I said.

'Around here, it's called the "*Schützenhaus*". It's for patients who exhibit erratic behaviour.'

'What's wrong with him?' I asked, with growing apprehension.

The doctor gave a shrug of his shoulders. 'Maybe it's the result of shellshock; maybe it's the gas poisoning; maybe it's something to do with the hypnosis treatment; maybe it's a combination. A conclusive diagnosis is impossible at this point. I'm working on a scientific paper about war psychosis, and all I can say is that his case is, shall we say . . . highly unusual.'

'So he's suffering from war psychosis?'

The doctor nodded.

'Is that why he was moved from Belgium to here?'

Again the doctor nodded. 'Conditions of mental disturbance must be treated separately from the physically injured soldiers.'

So that was why they'd transferred him all the way from Belgium! I knew that the army treated hysteria like an infectious disease that could undermine the fighting spirit of other patients if it spread. They had established special sick wards for mental disorders, mostly in remote, rural areas like Pasewalk.

'Tell me,' the doctor interrupted my thoughts, 'has your friend shown any particular symptoms in the past?'

'Well – Dolferl has always been a little "unusual".'

'In what sense?'

'Well, he . . . ' I paused. I had to think. Of course I'd always had that feeling that my friend was somehow 'special'. But hearing the question from a psychiatrist cast Dolferl's eccentricities in a very different light.

'He has a very short fuse,' I said.

The doctor pushed his glasses up to his forehead and opened the file the nun had brought in. 'Please continue,' he said, beginning to make notes.

'I have to think.' My mind raced, recalling behaviour that might be of interest to the doctor. But the more I thought about it, the less noteworthy his traits seemed to be. There was nothing truly 'abnormal' or 'severe' about Dolferl that I could think of; at least, nothing of interest to a psychiatrist.

'His memory is impressive,' I said, finally. 'And he's very moody. And there are times when he's extremely depressed. But is that so unusual?'

'Go on,' said the doctor. 'Just tell me what he's like. Anything that comes to mind.'

'He wants to be a painter and an architect. His desire for self-glorification is uncontainable. He has an extreme need to prove himself.' I thought for a moment. 'He loves to bear a grudge. He's vindictive – ' I stopped.

'What else?' asked the doctor

'He's arrogant. He's listless when there's nothing "grand" for him to do. But – ' I stopped again. 'Isn't that all part of being an artist?'

The doctor was scribbling notes into the file. His other hand directed me to continue.

'He's a dreamer, more than anything else. He lacks the focus to bring any idea to fruition. In all the years I've known him, he hasn't developed a single idea beyond its initial conception. As soon as he encounters any obstacle, he gives up – ' I stopped again: I felt guilty dissecting my friend's character like this.

'Please, carry on.'

I paused, wondering what else might be of interest to the psychiatrist. Then I thought of something that might in fact be of great interest. 'Well,' I went on, 'now that I think about it . . . there is something about him that's rather unusual: he seems to find it difficult to experience anything – any feeling or emotion. And if he does, like when he lost his dog, it feels artificial, as if he's acting. He also doesn't seem to have any fear. None at all. And he doesn't seem to feel much pain either. In fact, – '

'Well,' Dr Forster interrupted, 'that's not what concerns me. It's not about how well he functions. The question is: will he ever function again in our society?'

'Is it that bad?'

The doctor shrugged. 'His diagnosis reads' – the doctor read from the file – ' "psychopath with symptoms of hysteria".'

'What does that mean?'

'Not much. He doesn't fall into any clear category. As I said earlier: his case is unique.'

'What's so unique about it?'

'Usually after shellshock, the victim feels fearful and disoriented. Combined with his partial blindness, one would think that Lance-Corporal Hitler would fall into that category.'

'He doesn't?'

'Quite the opposite. He's grounded, self-assured, and insane.'[27]

27 See: Appendix 25, Hitler at Pasewalk

The stinging smell of disinfectant saturated the hallway that led to Dolferl's ward. I was walking behind a nun, passing patient after patient; all soldiers. They had gauze wrapped around different parts of their bodies, some on their heads, others over their eyes. Some were walking on crutches, and some had lost arms or legs. They were all mutilated, physically and mentally. Every face mirrored the horror they had experienced. When I looked at them, they leered back with contempt: they saw my uniform and knew that I had been through the same ordeal, but despised me because I appeared unscathed. They hated me for being able to pass as a sane member of society, something they couldn't do because they were so visibly maimed as well as invisibly damaged. But how sane was I, really? I'd survived the insanity of war and still managed to retain some semblance of normality – didn't that make *me* the sociopath?

We arrived at his ward. It was a huge hall with patients in beds along the left, right and centre.

'He's in the centre row, over there,' said the nun, and then she was gone. I was alone with the madness.

I walked down the aisle scanning for my friend, but all I could see were patients weeping and wailing; others hit or cut themselves; and others still babbled away nonsensically to themselves. I wondered if they were closer to God. Closer to a God who was insane. Closer to the Creator of a world where sense was found in senseless slaughter. One grey-skinned patient picked obsessively at his scabs. I turned away in disgust and pity, and found Dolferl standing right in front of me, fully upright as if about to salute. I hadn't recognised him because he was clean-shaven. Well, almost: all that remained of his Kaiser Wilhelm moustache was a black rectangle under his nose. He was wearing a nightshirt with his Iron Cross pinned to it.

''Dolferl!' I laughed nervously.

'Is that you, Martin?' he asked.

'Yes, Dolferl, it is.'

'It's Adolf!' he snarled 'What's so funny?'

'Sorry.'

His stance combined with the nightshirt and Iron Cross made it hard not to laugh. Just then an inmate's guttural cry came from somewhere close by, startling me and reminding me where I was. And where Dolferl was. Christ, Dolferl, I thought; the homeless shelter, the trenches and now here. Why do you always end up in the most squalid places?

'What are you doing here?' he asked me. His voice had a strange hoarseness to it, a hoarseness I had observed in other gas victims too.

'Answer me! Why are you here?' he repeated.

'I wanted to see you.'

'Why?'

'Well, I suppose I was – '

'Curious?'

'Concerned.'

I couldn't get over the black square of hair under his nose. Why had he done that? 'Why did you shave off your moustache?' I asked.

'The Kaiser has fled,' he said. He patted and smoothed out what was left of his moustache. '*This* is Germany now.'

'All right,' I said, struggling to follow his logic. I looked into his eyes: they were pure and blue, as before. But they were also different. They had a disconcerting glint. Were they blind, or not? They unnerved me. I staggered backwards and gripped the iron frame of the neighbouring bed.

'Why did you laugh when you saw me?' he said, coming towards me. 'You think I look funny?' He grabbed me by the throat. So he *could* see – partially, anyway. 'Well, dear Martl, why aren't you laughing now?' He held my throat tightly and shook me. The last time we had come to blows was at Stumpergasse, when I had laughed at something he said: he had flown into a rage and thrown the first punch. But now he had learned how to kill. Now he was lethal.

'Dolferl,' I said, still in his grip, 'we don't have to fight.'

'You're a coward.' He laughed, letting me go.

I exhaled with relief. Slowly I turned around and took in the insanity that surrounded him. These people were the human debris of war. With his moustache, his medal and his nightshirt, Dolferl fitted perfectly into the demented menagerie.

'You can't see who I am, can you?' he asked cryptically.

I paused, choosing my words carefully. I didn't want to provoke him. 'Of course I can see who you are,' I said, eventually. 'The doctor says you'll recover your eyesight fully,' I added, hoping to redirect the conversation towards a more medical, factual situation. Something concrete.

Dolferl exploded with laughter. The black patch of hair under his nose danced above his yellow teeth. 'Everything has changed!' he exclaimed, arching his neck so that his Adam's apple protruded.

'What do you mean?'

'Everything.' He gestured towards the windows. 'The world has changed.'

'That's right. The war is over.'

'I have changed as well.'

'You mean . . . you're a different person now?'

'No. I *was* a different person then; now I am myself. And that's why they put me here.' He pointed at the others in the room.

'They put you here because – ' I stopped and took a step back. I'd thought I knew those eyes well, but it was as if someone else were looking at me. His eyes seemed almost illuminated, as if lit from within. He stared into me with that eerie look and said quietly: 'I've been given an order. By the Lord who created our people.'

I was at a loss. I didn't know what to say, so I said: 'When your eyesight is back to normal, I'm sure they'll – '

'I don't care what they will or won't do. I depend on no one.'

He radiated self-confidence. His eyes were full of purpose.

'Moving in?'

His question snapped me out of my thoughts. I realised that I was half-sitting on his neighbour's bed.

'Do you remember that part in *Die Meistersinger* where the choir sings "wake up"? "Wake up!" Wake up!" ' he sang, his hoarse voice flaying the air. 'Do you remember that?'

'I do.'

'How did you feel when you heard that just now?'

'I don't know. A little . . . uncomfortable I suppose.'

'Now imagine how the world will feel when our entire nation wakes up.' He laughed.

I felt a chill run down my spine.

'If we compare ourselves to the Almighty Will,' he continued, 'we realise what terribly weak creatures we are, do we not?'

'Yes,' I said.

'But there's something else too.'

'What's that?'

'That if we act according to that same Will, we become unimaginably strong.'

He stared straight into me, right into my heart and mind.[28]

28 See: Appendix 26, Hitler's Transformation.

Two days later, Dolferl was declared 'fully recovered' and released from the *Schützenhaus*. I had tried to talk sense into the doctors, but Dr Forster had been transferred and the Admissions Office wasn't interested in Dolferl's case. Only the extremely ill were treated. If you could walk, you walked – out of the hospital.

I had to find a train that would carry my unhinged friend and me to Munich. After hours of cajoling, haggling and waiting, we finally secured a spot on a Munich-bound train, squeezing into what had once been a cattle car. The journey home was a far cry from our glorious journey to the front four years before. There was straw on the floor and a pungent barnyard smell in the air. The odour was compounded by the putrid stench of the dozens of other soldiers who hadn't showered in weeks. There was no toilet and we had to defecate into a bucket in the corner. The wounded were moaning and hunger was eating into our stomachs. Our uniforms were rags. Many of us hadn't been issued winter coats; some didn't even have jackets, and were just wearing blankets over their shirts. The few times the train stopped and we had a chance to urinate outside, we were confronted by the harsh winter temperatures which chased us immediately back to the noxious warmth of the wagon, where we warmed each other with our body heat. Dolferl was sitting next to me, remarkably taciturn.

After hours of silence, I asked, 'How are you?'

'Remember combat?' was his answer.

'Yes,' I replied.

'Do you remember that intensity?'

I certainly did. I remembered the secure feeling within the confines of an invincible entity. I remembered attaining a new level of reality, a reality where I no longer perceived things as they really were; where I was past the point of distinguishing individual events; where all of my senses had merged; a reality with different laws and a different humanity; a reality where everything seemed possible. I remembered it all.

'Yes,' I said. 'I remember.'

'That's how I feel.'

'As if you're in combat?'

He nodded.

'But Dolferl, the war is over! Relax!'

'Why do I waste my time talking to a fool like you?' he snapped. 'Why am I always surrounded by incompetence?'

We sat through a few moments of charged silence. Then he turned to me, and there was that conviction, that light in his eyes again, that complete detachment from the reality around him.

'Don't you see that the door to paradise is wide open?'

I said nothing.

'There is a solution!'

'To what?'

He hadn't heard me. 'The German people don't know that I'm here yet. But they will, very soon.' He crossed his arms. 'My God!' he exclaimed, 'I have so much to do! I have only this one life, but enough to do for ten, maybe even a hundred!'

His eyes widened and shone even more brilliantly, the eyes of a Messiah called to elevate the world to perfection. What would happen to him once we arrived 'home'? Would he be sent to a mental asylum? I was dubious about any medical institutions in the midst of Germany's grand demise. Hopefully he would snap out of his deranged state, but what then? What would happen if he saw himself for who he really was: one of millions of soldiers returning from a war they had lost, a soldier with no family to turn to, and no friends? A soldier with no education, no job and no money, coming home to a shattered country?

After a twenty-nine-hour train ride, we arrived in Munich. Like us, the city was in a state of disarray. People were out of work, sick and starving. And now on top of this all these men returned from the war, and the only thing they had learned was how to fight: so fight they did. This time it was everyone against everyone else, in parliament as well as in the streets. The Bavarian King had absconded, leaving Munich in the hands of a red revolutionary chaos. The Socialists were fighting the Communists, who were clashing with the 'petty bourgeois'. The Conservatives battled it out against the Royalists, while the Nationalists were fighting amongst themselves and against everyone else.

At the train station in Munich there were no brass bands to greet us, just groups of soldiers wrapped in blankets, wandering up and down the platforms. They were walking to keep warm, waiting for trains that might never arrive. Fraught women searched the crowd for their loved ones. Their eyes darted from face to face among the mass of men, desperately seeking that someone they had known so well a lifetime ago. Once they found their returning soldier, the women could only hope that he would recognise them. The lucky ones stood staring at one another for endless moments, struggling to fathom how much the war and home fronts had turned them into strangers. We walked silently through the cacophony of names, cries and announcements. Dolferl's vision had improved: he could see what was going on around him: some soldiers sat and shivered on the wooden benches; others wandered in circles, numbing themselves to ignore their rumbling bellies and aching joints. No one had new clothes. Rags were stuffed inside sleeves as padding against the cold.

'The Swiss, Austrian and Italian borders are closed until further notice,' croaked the tannoy. 'All trains to and from these countries are cancelled.'

Leaving the station, we walked down Arnulfstraße, once a colourful, animated street. Now its neoclassical buildings were haunted by the ghosts of the past four years; sad and soot-stained, they only reinforced the depressed air of the city. It was a city of cripples. They were sitting on street corners, begging; blind soldiers, soldiers with one arm, one leg, no arms, no legs, migrants from one desperate moment to the next.

A man stood on a wooden crate, dressed as though he had stolen random garments from a clothesline. Above him red flags flapped angrily in the wintry gusts.

'The mighty have retreated to their velvet shelters,' he shouted, 'while we, the workers, the farmers and the soldiers are abandoned here, left with nothing but the ruins of a city they have destroyed! But from these ruins we will erect an empire of light, beauty and reason! Together we will create a communism of the spirit! Long live Kurt Eisner!'

'Damned traitors!' growled Dolferl, shivering.

'At last, we have shaken off the yoke of oppression!' shouted the speaker. 'Long live the Free State of Bavaria! Long Live the Revolutionary Workers' Council!'

Dolferl swayed unsteadily as waves of nausea overcame him. He grasped my arm, doubled over and threw up. Dolferl looked up at me, pale, wan and depleted. 'As you can see,' he said, his eyes flashing, 'mendacity makes me sick.' He pulled out some paper and wiped off any vomit that might have smeared his Iron Cross. In one of the few store windows that was not boarded up, he checked his appearance, patted his moustache and then straightened up.

Slowly, we made our way along the pavement. A group of children herded by nuns passed us by. They could have been orphans, I didn't know; but they definitely weren't peacetime children. They looked as desolate and exhausted as the adults. They, too, had internalised our national tragedy.

Dolferl gazed upon them. 'Look at them! Their souls have been torn from them! They have never experienced joy!' Dolferl slowly raised his eyes to the street lamps. 'I vow to give them back their childhood!'

And with that, any faint hope that Dolferl might have come to his senses during our long and silent train ride dissipated.

Further down the street a monk dipped a ladle into a pot, pouring soup into a metal bowl held by a one-armed soldier. Behind him, a one-legged soldier leaned on his crutches, holding his infantry-issue bowl. A grey line of people waited behind, trailing off into the grey dusk.

The street was only sporadically lit and we moved from darkness to light and back again. A heavy, middle-aged woman spotted Dolferl's medal. Her ruby lips rounded into an 'O'. 'Oh, they're my favourites! The ones with the medals!' she mocked, as we passed her in the light. Dolferl said nothing; he just stared into the void. The woman stepped back and from the corner of my eye I saw her features contort menacingly. She followed us into the dark, her high heels striking the pavement in sharp, pinging strides.

'I suppose you're proud of this shitty war,' she growled.

Ping. Ping. Ping.

'Well let me tell you something, Admiral, I'm not impressed!'

Dolferl and I quickened our steps. She followed suit.

'Not only did you inflict this hell on us, here you are parading around as if you'd won!'

We hurried on, leaving her behind.

'You can't blame her,' said Dolferl, 'these people don't know who's responsible for all this.'

I said nothing and thought of our opera that had dealt with a similar theme. Vienna seemed like our Atlantis, lost aeons ago.

The sorrow of Odeonsplatz was palpable as Dolferl and I made our way across the square. We didn't need to remind each other that this was where we'd been merrily roused to enlist, swept up by the sea that had carried us into war and which now had deposited us back on its shores, shells of our former selves. We both stood there, taking in the sombre Field Marshal's Hall at the end of the square. The sun had set behind the buildings, and the wind had picked up, cutting across our cheeks like invisible, icy razors. Dolferl's ears glowed pink and mine ached from the bitter cold.

Dolferl was looking at the sky. 'Why me? Why me of all people?'

'Why so serious?' I asked cheerily. 'We're back home. Everything will fall back into place again.'

He looked away, still deep in thought. 'How will I do it?'

'What?' I asked, trying to ground him by placing my hand on his shoulder. 'We'll pick up where we left off. You'll paint again.'

His eyes flew open: haven't you heard a single thing I've been saying? He brushed my hand off his shoulder. 'Paint?' he snapped, in disbelief. 'Are you blind? Can't you see what's happening all around us?'

'All I meant was that we all have to start anew!'

'Start anew?' He smirked. Again there was that glint in his eyes I'd first seen in Pasewalk. 'Start anew! That's it exactly.' He tilted his head back, looking straight up into the darkening sky. 'Well,' he continued, his tone much lighter, 'one day I will paint again.' He lowered his head and looked at me. 'I can see it already: I'll be retired and living in my villa in Linz on Mount Frein. I'll look out over the city and the Danube. I'll paint that beautiful town and then it will look exactly as I envisioned it in Vienna. But,' he said, raising his voice, 'before I can do that,' his hoarse voice grew louder, 'I have a job to do. And' – then he shouted – 'I will get that job done!'

His voice echoed around the desolate square.

' . . . *that job done* . . . '

His roar upset pigeons that had been pecking on the ground, hunting to find anything – any morsel that was edible.

' . . . *that job done* . . . ' echoed his words.

The startled pigeons flapped their wings and rose into the air. They circled the square three times: on their first pass, they flew no higher than the two blackened Bavarian lions that guarded the Field Marshal's Hall; on their second, they skimmed the top of the hall, and on the third they flew over the towers of the Theatiner Church and off into the dusk.

Dolferl had sunk further into his coat, staring straight ahead, hands in his side pockets. By the curb, a soldier was stroking the mane of a horse collapsed in the street and whispering into its ear. The horse was hitched to a wagon full of recruits with new uniforms and red armlets. They had never seen combat and had happily joined the Bavarian communist revolution.

'Pimps, layabouts and thieves,' hissed Dolferl. 'Our best human material is long gone.' He turned to the recruits on the other side of the street. 'Anyone know where the barracks of the List Regiment is?'

They just stared at us. None of them felt compelled to give him an answer.

'See?' he snarled. 'No respect for combat troops. Scumbags, laggards and cowards. They're only in it for food and lodging.'

I had to tell him. I hadn't said anything during our trip because I had feared his endless reproaches, but now the time had come: 'I won't be going to the barracks.'

He was visibly shaken. 'What?'

'Maybe I can stay with Francisca. If not, I'm not sure what I'll do. But I won't go back to the army.'

He was speechless: the notion that I would not want to continue being a soldier was unbelievable to him.

'Look,' I said, 'we've played at soldiers for long enough. And I think . . . '

You would have thought I'd struck him physically with my words: his body stiffened, his head tilted back and his eyes squinted. '*Played*? You think we've been *playing* at soldiers for the past four years? Right!' He struggled to regain his footing. 'Now it's serious!' He was trembling. 'Don't think you can treat me the way you treated your medal!'

I bit my lip. 'I didn't mean it like that,' I said.

'Then what did you mean?' he cried, red-faced. He was fit to burst. He had always been easily riled when I didn't pander to his fantasies, but now, after Pasewalk, he was more unstable than ever before.

The soldiers in the cart and even the horse looked over at us. Even in the frigid cold, I felt warm from the blush of embarrassment. Why hadn't I been a little more diplomatic?

I clutched Dolferl by the elbow to steady him. 'You're not well,' I said, softly. 'You have to rest. The doctor said – '

'Just shut up!' he screamed at me, shaking off my hand and rushing ahead.

'Dolferl, please!' I called, as I ran after him. 'I'm sorry!'

'Leave me alone!' he shouted. 'Go and seek your petty comforts!'

'Is this how we're to go our separate ways?' I shouted. 'After everything we've been through all these years?'

'I can do without the likes of you,' he retorted.

I knew he'd be able to eradicate any memory of me in an instant.

I stopped, and watched as Dolferl disappeared into the night.

The Four Seasons Hotel on Maximilianstraße – there it was, and therein she was: Francisca. The street, once one of the premiere boulevards in Europe, was now stripped of all splendour. The dark shop windows and doorways had a sinister air about them. The hotel, once inviting, was now forbidding. A stained crimson and gold flag hung limp and frayed above the hotel's main entrance. The banner's once golden letters proclaiming the name of the hotel had faded into a muted mustard yellow.

The dimly lit hotel entrance was a ghost of its previous incarnation. Inside, the lobby was musty and eerily silent. The potted palms were gone, probably killed off by the scarcity of heating fuel and the winter cold. A cleaning lady was sitting in one of the armchairs, resting her feet. There was no one behind the reception desk. Off to the side, the formerly elegant restaurant-cum-bar was closed. A man crossed in front of me with a top hat, cape and cane. I noticed he was wearing spats; I hadn't seen spats in years.

I walked up to the desk and rang the bell. A receptionist came out from behind the office door, her head lowered as if weighed down by her thoughts. Then she looked up, and we beheld each other. Memories flashed through my mind as she stood before me. We could only look, not speak, like the couples in the train station. Francisca looked unsure whether it was really me or a ghost – in war, you never know. She was standing in front of me – different, altered in the way dreams alter people. I smiled, and when I uttered her name – 'Francisca!' – she knew it was me.

I was immersed to my shoulders in the healing waters of my first decent bath in ages. The warmth soothed every ache in my body. Steam rose from the bathtub and ascended slowly to the ceiling, drifting through the crystal pendants of the chandelier. Luxurious white bath towels hung over the brass rack. Was this a taste of the peace to come? Across from me, Francisca leaned on the siding. Behind the rising steam, she looked like a Renoir. Her half-submerged breasts floated in the soapy water. Actually, it was my second bath that night. My first bath, alone, had been strictly for hygienic purposes. Years of wartime filth were embedded in my flesh. I was the colour of mud. I had burrowed into the earth and taken on its colour and texture, like some subterranean creature. I scrubbed myself almost raw to regain my skin's natural colour; in the process, the bath water had become so tainted that I'd had to refill the tub three times until it was clean enough for Francisca to get in.

Her face glided across the bath towards me as she came to kneel between my legs. I wrapped my arms around her and we kissed: gently at first, then I pulled her closer and our tongues met, connecting our hearts and our minds.

No longer a kiss imagined.

No longer a kiss desired.

A kiss lived.

Francisca struck a match, closed her eyes as if in prayer and inhaled; smoking black Turkish tobacco with a sprinkling of opium, a remnant from those nights in Vienna, giving us both the illusion that the war had never happened; that our lives had continued unperturbed.

She breathed deeply and passed it to me.

I inhaled and let the smoke settle in my lungs. As I did, I realised that I was experiencing the elusive 'something' which Dolferl had often mentioned during combat, and which Schopenhauer had written about: the 'present moment'. We were in each other's arms, talking quietly and laughing gently, her soft, white skin against my coarse, hirsute body, On the ledge of the bathtub lay the red velvet box that held our rings. Without a word, I flipped open the case. Francisca held out her left hand and extended her finger. I slipped the ring on.

'I do,' she said.

I cleared my throat as she slid the other ring on my finger. I coughed so much I could barely mouth the words 'I do'.

She kissed away my tears and smiled at me.

We were finally one.

The grey morning light drifted into the bedroom.

'Who controls Munich now?' I asked Francisca, as I stood at the window, looking out. Three storeys below, workers with red flags were denouncing the landlord/tenant system.

'What?' she answered from the bed, still half-asleep. With her red hair and bright skin, she looked like cherry ice cream on a porcelain dish.

'Are the communists still in power?' I asked.

She nodded. 'Eisner.'

'What kind of communist is he?'

'He's made Munich the capital of his "Independent Revolutionary People's Republic of Bavaria",' she said, distantly.

'What does that mean?'

Francisca shrugged: who knows? 'They call Bavaria a "Free State" now.'

'Are they Socialist Theorists or are they Soviets?'

'I don't know,' she said. 'Father says they take their orders from Moscow.' She paused. 'And he's not at all happy about that.' She stood up, naked, and stretched. 'I want to feel you against me again,' she purred, taking my hand and leading me back to bed.

By the time I woke up it was dark. Francisca had just come through the door. She took off her receptionist's jacket.

'What time is it?' I asked.

'Time to go to bed again,' she said, unbuttoning her blouse.

When you're starving life hardly seems worth the effort. No matter how much water you drink to dilute the acid in your gut, it never neutralises it completely. The pain in your stomach accompanies you like unending torture. I was rested but famished, and the hunger was twisting my belly and demoralising my mind.

'I'm going out,' I announced to Francisca, as she was dressing her jacket. Her eyebrows arched: what?

'I want to get us something delicious to eat.'

'Good luck,' she said, wearily. 'Believe me, there's nothing out there.'

'Why?' I asked, getting out of bed. Why, I groaned to myself, is life still impossible? 'Why? The war is over.'

'Granted,' she said, 'but peace has yet to come.' She looked at herself in the mirror, puffing out the shoulders and sleeves of her jacket.

'What the hell are you talking about?' I growled, instantly regretting my tone. I wasn't angry at her; I was irritable because I was hungry.

'Read the paper,' she snapped back.

She was hungry too.

'I'm sorry,' I said.

'For what?'

'For sounding so irritable. You know I love you.'

'I know you do,' she said. 'And I'm sorry I snapped. It's the naval blockade. The Brits are still blocking food, medicine . . . everything. Babies are dying, the sick – more than during the war.'

'But the war's over!'

'They won't lift the blockade unless we sign a peace treaty,' she sighed, 'a peace treaty on their terms.' I wasn't sure then if I hated the Allies more in this 'peacetime' than I had during the war.[29]

29 See: Appendix 27, The British Naval Blockade

As I entered the hotel lobby, I heard the angry voice of Erna, one of the hotel cleaners. She was screaming at Edgar, Francisca's father.

'How do you expect me to clean if I don't have anything to clean *with*? I need polish to do my job so I can get paid and keep myself alive. Alive, hah! For what?' She burst into tears. Times had been extremely hard during the war. But now they were worse. Even soap was now a treasured commodity from a bygone, prosperous era.

'I'm always starving,' I heard Erna cry, 'which is why I always have a headache.'

'Erna,' said Edgar, 'take the rest of the day off.'

'I can't,' she sobbed, 'I have to eat!'

I passed the hotel bar. If there had been any alcohol left, I would have opened a bottle to numb myself; instead, I went out on to the street on the hunt for food.

The grocery stores had all closed down. There were only a few street peddlers selling their produce: decaying potatoes, pork ears, a yellowed turnip, a small wedge of cheese, a tin of beans. I stopped and asked if I could pick up the tin and examine it.

The grey-haired woman behind the crate exhaled impatiently. 'If you must.'

I half-smiled: thank you.

The tin of beans must have been stolen from a dead Brit on the battlefield. On the label there was a picture of delicious red beans in a bowl. 'Wimple & Simms' was written in a cheery semicircle over the illustration. I turned the tin around and read: 'This product is packed with pride in Liverpool, England.'

The woman was staring at me with visible displeasure: either buy it or put it down.

'How much?' I asked.

'Twenty marks,' she said.

'Twenty marks!' I exclaimed.

'That's the going price,' she said.

'Let me think – ' I began to say, when a woman in a black embroidered opera coat suddenly snatched the tin from my hands. She had once been far richer than she was today, I could tell. Her eyes were level with mine. She smelled of mothballs.

'I beg your pardon!' I cried.

'Well, if you have to think about it, you're obviously not really interested in purchasing it.'

'That's not so,' I replied, snatching the tin back from her gloved hands. 'I was merely considering the price.'

She was shocked that I had grabbed it back.

'Young man!' she exclaimed, her eyes flashing angrily. 'I'm appalled at your uncouth behaviour!'

'My behaviour is no more uncouth than your own, madam,' I replied.

'I beg to differ,' she barked. 'I'm just a defenceless, elderly woman – '

'Please, madam. I was holding the tin; you took it from me.'

She shifted her umbrella, which had been dangling from the crook of her arm and presented it like a sword in a duel.

The woman behind the box gawked at us in perplexed amazement.

'I'm outraged at some people's comportment these days!' shrieked the opera-caped woman. I find your conduct loathsome.' She took a swipe at me with her umbrella. The metal tip darted right for my eye.

My wartime instinct resurfaced instantly. I blocked her strike with my left hand, and with the tin in my right fist, I punched the old woman in the jaw. She keeled over, with a scream: I ran. I ran through the grey, ghostly streets of Munich until my lungs ached. What had become of me? Assaulting old ladies for a tin of beans, stolen from a dead Brit?

Francisca was delighted with the beans we ate that evening. She was dying to know how I'd managed to get my hands on such a delicacy: I said I'd been lucky, and had got them for a bargain price. We went to bed that night with partly filled bellies, but I still didn't have the courage to tell her the truth.

A Different Kind of War

No one knows where He is. But we know He's coming. Soon.

February 1919, Munich
I wandered the starving streets of Munich in the morning. And as I walked, the city was still at war, fighting another kind of war. Peace was war now. I was about to turn the corner at Prannerstraße when a gunshot rang out. The hair on the back of my neck stood on end. My warrior instinct compelled me to the ground. I turned and saw a man in Bavarian Cavalry uniform standing a few metres from me, pointing his gun at a bald, bearded man heading towards the entrance of a building. He was clutching a bundle of papers in his hand and wore ovoid-framed lenses pinched to his nose. I recognised him from the papers. It was Kurt Eisner, Bavaria's Prime Minister, accompanied by two other men. Eisner considered himself an artist, not unlike the Dolferl of the past. He believed that political debate was an intellectual quest, rather than brokered power. He was a socialist dreamer, working on the creation of a self-styled utopia. He was an arguably accomplished poet, but an indisputably incompetent administrator. For all of his good intentions, he was unable to address the needs of a city wrought with desperation. Another shot rang out, and for an endless second Eisner billowed like a sheet in the wind, rocking back and forth on his heels, arms in the air, papers still in hand. Then the assassin fired another bullet, and Eisner fell forward. I turned to see someone jump on the assassin from behind, pinning him to the ground and snatching his gun.

I stood up, stunned. Was this the peace I'd fought so bitterly to attain?

'We know you're hoarding food and keeping it from the people!' yelled one of the 'social reformers' who swept into the hotel lobby wearing red armbands and spouting red rhetoric. They were young, brash and angry: idealistic Socialists on Monday, but vengeful Soviets by Friday. They were the new army policing the city since Eisner's death.

'Capitalist pigs!' jeered the sturdy young man as he approached the reception. He had a weathered complexion and carried his bloodied arm in a sling. His accusatory eyes were intent on rifling through every kitchen cabinet in search of a stash of caviar, champagne, maybe even chocolate truffles. Francisca stood her ground resolutely, prepared to tackle this gang of troublemakers. Edgar, her father, stood next to her. He was unusually quiet. These days, he was resigned to accepting situations he would never have tolerated before the war, including Francisca and I living together as husband and wife. Edgar had bigger problems to deal with. His livelihood was destroyed, and probably gone forever. He was a shadow of his former robust, opinionated self. The hotel windows were boarded up. Water was in short supply and the electricity was off most of the time. Edgar often wondered aloud if it could have been any worse if the Allies had descended on Munich themselves.

With his bloodied arm, the soldier pointed awkwardly to the lobby furniture: chairs, sofas and tables with ornate angels carved along the edges. 'Petit bourgeois trash,' he sneered. 'It reeks of decadence.'

'Actually, sir,' said Francisca politely yet firmly, 'it's all reproduction. Fake. The lot.'

'Real or not,' growled the revolutionary, 'it all burns the same.'

'Have some pity, I beg of you!' pleaded Francisca. 'We need this furniture for our clientele – '

'For what? To sit and talk, and plot against the people?' finished the communist.

'What is this?' cried Francisca. 'The sacking of Troy?'

'What the hell is a Troy?' barked the man.

'I was referring to Helen of Troy,' she explained wearily.

A tender-eyed young man with a red headband smiled. 'The face that launched a thousand ships,' he recited.

'The very same,' replied Francisca, glad of even momentary respite from the tension.

The man with the wounded arm exploded. 'Need I remind you that citing the work of a degenerate enemy of the people is considered treason?' He spat on the floor. 'Enough talk!'

Francisca flinched, then steadied herself. It was all too much. 'I never thought we would ever be invaded from within.'

'That's what revolution is all about!' said one of the men. 'Think of France!'

The new rulers were trying to fuse cultural and political liberation. They had transformed the *Frauenkirche*, Munich's cathedral, into a

'Temple of the Revolution'. A woman dressed as the 'Goddess of Reason' now ran the church. The government had declared war on the Pope, and all schools had been closed until the revolutionaries could decide what should be taught. A class struggle had been declared in which all enemies were threatened with death.

Francisca's father could take no more. 'This isn't liberation!' Edgar erupted. 'Can't you see you're being manipulated by the Jews?'

The government of the newly proclaimed 'Bavarian Soviet Republic' had been formed by two independent Jewish socialists and two Russian Jews. A few days ago, Béla Kun, a Hungarian Jew, had turned Hungary into a Soviet Republic. Now Hungary would be 'cleansed' like Russia, where hundreds of thousands had already died. With each passing day, Europe moved closer to the grand vision of my one-time drinking partner in Hamburg: one united continent of communist brothers. Communist leaders with surnames ending in 'stein' and the like horrified the nationalists, who saw their predictions coming true: Europe was soon to be held hostage by a sinister Jewish conspiracy.

'Come to the kitchen,' said Francisca quickly, desperate to divert attention from her father. 'Come and see for yourself how bare our cupboards are.'

The soldier with the bandaged arm pointed to the restaurant on the east side of the lobby. 'What about that?' he asked.

'Sir,' responded Francisca, gruffly, 'that place has been closed for nearly two years.'

What a sad, sick spectacle, to witness the revolution inviting itself into your house and stealing your furniture and food. They contemplated hauling away the huge industrial oven, but as luck would have it they didn't know how to disconnect it from the gas mains. Frustrated at finding our cabinets bare, they chose to tear the cupboards from the walls. We were told that the 'People's Wagon' would come by the next day to confiscate the refectory table and kitchen cabinets. The People's Wagon never came.

We sat by candlelight in the hotel kitchen and dined on sardines. The day before, I had bought a tin of sardines on the road and had stashed it in my army-issue backpack. The Soviet scavengers had been reluctant to loot a soldier's humble canvas bag, so the precious tin had been spared.

'It terrifies me,' said Edgar, and sighed. 'These animals are intent on destroying our life as we know it. If this ideology takes hold, soon we'll all be shot just for knowing the difference between a violin and a viola! For being enterprising and running our own business! Just for not being one of them, for not being a totalitarian barbarian. Is this the future of Europe? A communist hell?' Edgar's eyes were welling up. The communist success in Hungary had incited and agitated the revolution in Germany. Thousands of Berliners died every day in the streets as the communists took control. Communist mayoralties had now assumed power in most large German cities.

We dined, silently and slowly.

'You know what Bolshevism really is?' Edgar asked.

Francisca and I exchanged glances: it was going to be another of her father's tirades.

'Well?' he demanded. 'Do you or don't you?'

We bowed our heads evasively and continued to chew.

'Communism is the Jew's revenge on all Christians,' he declared. 'They're using this despicable economic theory to target our people, who've kept them in their place for centuries. It's their Spanish Inquisition! And isn't it ingenious how the Jews have even fooled Christians into helping them? You saw for yourself. I doubt there was a single Jew in that group!' Edgar shook his head. 'The Jews are the ones in power in all these red governments!' he said. 'In Munich, Budapest and Moscow!'

'But aren't these Jews intellectuals?' I interjected, 'Intellectuals who've broken away from the traditional Jewish community? Haven't they abandoned the Jewish religion?'

'How can anyone not see that Bolshevism is just Jewish dictatorship in disguise?' thundered Edgar. 'It starts with Karl Marx and it continues with Rosa Luxemburg, Liebknecht, Trotsky, Eisner, Kun, Toller, Levine – ' He stopped. 'Is there any more mustard?'

Francisca passed the jar to her father, but Edgar dropped his knife and covered his face with his hands. A low mournful wail emanated from behind his fingers. It was a cry in the dark seeking salvation, safety. It echoed through the empty kitchen.

He stopped. His fingers slipped away and exposed glistening eyes. 'I'm going to fight,' he announced. 'And I know I'm not alone! There are others like me. We're all going to fight!'

Francisca and I were walking cheerfully along Brienner Straße hand in hand on a Sunday afternoon, with no reason to be cheerful. Perhaps it was the weather: the stubborn sun had fought the grey winter clouds and its rays had finally won through, allowing dashes of light to dance across my face. I closed my eyes and let my face bask in the burgeoning warmth, imagining the green shoots of spring beginning to push their way through the soil. I felt Francisca's fingers throbbing with life and clasped her hand tightly with renewed vigour. I smiled at her. We had made it together through the war, a four-year winter. *All I know is that I love you.* We kissed passionately there on the street, in the crisp air of the new season. We kissed so our hearts could make a momentary home together. We kissed because nothing else mattered. We were cocooned in our joy, in the simple bliss of existence. Eventually we opened our eyes and smiled at each other: remember that time? Remember when you taught me to dance? Remember when we moved up and down like the painted horses on a carousel? Remember the first time we were alone together in a roomful of people? Without a word, Francisca clasped my hand and aimed it up at the sky. My other arm circled around her waist and without so much as a nod, we started to dance. Why? It didn't matter why. We did it because it was in the air, because of the promise of blossoming linden trees. We danced because we had given up on hopelessness and dire circumstance.

Edgar decided to put me to work and I was assigned the job I had held before the war: organising the hotel's cleaning staff. Not that there was much to do; the clientele of the luxurious hotel had dwindled during the war and now, with trigger-happy reformers spreading throughout Munich looting and plundering, there were no more guests checking in. The occasional wedding reception kept the hotel in business, together with the few organisations that met in the reception halls or private suites.[30]

One morning, Erna told me that she had found weapons in one of the private suites.

'What?' I asked, assuming I had misunderstood.

'Not just small guns – rifles!' she exclaimed, nodding her head.

'Which room?'

'Room Thirty-three.'

'Room Thirty-three,' I repeated, as I scanned the hotel register. Room 33 had been booked by a regular customer. According to the ledger, the client had paid in advance. He used the room at sporadic intervals.

Erna held the key up and shook it. 'See it for yourself, sir.'

I remembered seeing a group of men entering that room one Friday

30 See: Appendix 28, Four Seasons Hotel

night, all dressed in expensive business suits. Their behaviour and obvious wealth had been strikingly at odds with the prevailing scarcity. Who were these men? When I had asked Francisca, she had said she didn't know; all she knew was that they belonged to a study group that discussed Germanic antiquity. Apart from Room 33, the study group had rented five club-rooms, and another room as their office. When these men met in Room 33, they usually stayed there from eleven o'clock at night until two or three in the morning.

Erna and I walked down the hallway. Erna strode self-assuredly: she knew the hotel's every nook and cranny, having worked here for years.

'These characters are something else,' she remarked.

'What do you mean?'

'They've had a "Do Not Disturb" sign on the door for three weeks running,' she complained. 'I'm a professional. No one tells me not to clean a room for three weeks. I don't want mould growing on any walls I'm supposed to clean. No, sir! Not on my watch.'

Erna unlocked the door and I looked inside. It was deathly silent. The shutters had been closed, making the room dark and stuffy. The bed had been removed and a round table and several chairs placed in the centre.

'Look over here,' said Erna, ushering me over to the armoire.

She opened up the walnut doors and I peered into the darkness with silent awe. Leaning against the panel were five semi-automatic Bergmann MP18 rifles, 'trench sweepers' as we had called them in war. I stepped back. On the floor of the armoire there was an array of pistols; Luger 9mms and wooden-handled Mauser C96s.

'And that's not all,' said Erma, bending over and pulling out the wardrobe's bottom drawers. Boxes and boxes of bullets were arranged neatly in rows.

What were these men up to? I noticed a folded sheet of paper: a discarded leaflet. I opened it and flattened it out. It was an invitation to a public lecture by the study group, which called itself the Thule Society. The headline read: *Ancient Roots of Knowledge*. The leaflet was signed with the words *Sieg* and *Heil*. Underneath was the emblem of the Thule Society: a dagger across a shining swastika.

A voice woke me one morning that April. 'Miss Obermayer,' called the voice. Then there was rapping on the door. 'Miss Obermayer!' I knew then it was bad news. On the sixth 'Miss Obermayer', Francisca answered the door and I heard: 'A warrant has been issued for your arrest.'

'A what?'

'You are accused of complicity in a conspiracy against the Free State of Bavaria.'

'I need to speak to my father,' she said.

'Your father has already been detained.'

The plain-clothes officer and two uniformed guards with red armlets waited in the hall while Francisca dressed. She looked through her closet to find a garment suitable for a stay in jail.

'Why are they arresting you?' I stammered. 'It's totally incomprehensible!' But of course, that wasn't true. Nothing was incomprehensible in Munich these days.

Francisca was curiously calm, methodically going about her business. 'This one,' she said to herself as she took a flannel dress off a hanger. 'Here,' she whispered, as she passed me a business card. The name and address of a Dr Götz was printed on it. 'He'll get us a lawyer.'

She applied her lipstick with such nonchalance that I wasn't sure if she really grasped the gravity of her situation. She put on her camel-hair coat and glanced at herself in the mirror holding her overnight bag. Then she opened the door and presented herself to the police, asking them cordially: 'And which jail shall I be staying in?'

The 2nd Infantry Regiment was stationed in the barracks at Lothstraße. On my way to the barracks, a late afternoon fog rolled down the pavement and curled around the street corners. What was I to do? I desperately wanted to help Francisca and her father, but I had no idea how. What was the sense of getting a lawyer when there were no laws? All the communists knew was their rhetoric; they lacked practical knowledge of how to implement it. For all intents and purposes, the Munich variety of communism remained a social experiment. The only way to release Francisca and her father was to free them by force.

I climbed the steps of the barracks bypassing groups of soldiers and crossed the lobby to the front desk. There was something unsettling in all this: I was back at the home base of the regiment, with whom I had fought for four years, but there wasn't a single soldier that I recognised. My dead and maimed comrades had been replaced with fresh-faced cadets, but what was most disturbing was that they were all dressed, like our old adversaries on the Eastern Front: all wearing red armlets. It was as though the Soviets had won the war, not surrendered. I walked up to the cadet at the desk and didn't bother to salute. I didn't have to: I was a civilian now.

I asked for Dolferl, and the soldier sent me to a room on the first floor.

I knocked on the door.

'Come in!' responded a raspy voice.

The hoarseness from the gas attack had obviously stayed with Dolferl. I opened the door, and there he was, sitting next to a pile of gas masks.

'Oh, it's you,' he said matter-of-factly, looking up. Then he focused again on the mask he held in his hand. He unscrewed the mouthpiece, checked it, screwed it back on, labelled the mask and put it into a crate. He still had that odd little moustache.

'You're counting gas masks?' I asked.

'I'm not counting them, I'm checking them. No one knows better than I how important it is that they work properly.' He picked up another mask.

'Do you have any idea . . . ?' I stopped as my mind searched for the words to describe how awful things had become.

As usual, Dolferl anticipated what I wanted to say and answered: 'Isn't that exactly what I told you would happen?' He labelled the mask, put it away and picked up another.

'I don't understand you,' I said, 'you were the one who was always talking about fighting the communists. And now that they're wreaking havoc, you're sitting here counting gas masks?'

'*Checking*, Martl, *checking*.' Dolferl took up another mask in his hands.

'Dolferl! The communists are systematically destroying this city!'

'Well, here they've chased the officers away. Everyone is equal now and everything is decided by committee, soldiers' councils. I'm an elected representative.'

'You're *what*? Have you become one of them?'

Then I noticed his red armband and balked; it couldn't be true. Not Dolferl!

He grinned. 'Me? I'm no communist. I'm not even what they call a "Nationalist" around here.' He leaned his head back and closed his eyes. 'I'm not a follower of any group. I follow myself, no one else.' He opened his eyes and stared, that all-engulfing stare from Pasewalk.

I was disoriented and my stunned mind desperately tried to regain its bearings. To escape his gaze, I looked over at the mound of gas masks. 'They've arrested Francisca,' I heard myself say.

'And don't tell me, you want to raid the prison?' He laughed, hiding his teeth with his hand.

I shrugged. 'You have a better idea?'

'Sure!'

'Really?'

'Let's go to the opera! The *Magic Flute* is being performed tonight. It's only Mozart, but still – '

'*What?*' I cried.

'I can pay for us both. I'm on twenty marks a week now.'

'The communists are tearing this city apart, and you want to go to the opera?'

'My time hasn't come yet.' He was staring directly into me, and I felt that eerie Pasewalk presence in his eyes again 'So?' he persisted. 'Will you accompany me to the opera or not?'

I shook my head: no. Then I left.

The fog continued to slink through the town and there was an uneasy quiet on the boulevards that late afternoon A car or horse-and-buggy passed by every so often, or a truck laden with armed men flying red flags. But for some reason, there were almost no pedestrians – only some gloomy workmen with red armbands and rifles, guarding street corners. I looked at the business card Francisca had given me. Dr Götz. His office was in a prime location: Widenmayerstraße.

The office had the same feel as the address: old money, money that had made more money. I told the secretary that I was here on behalf of Francisca. She didn't know her, but when I mentioned her father, she told me to sit down and wait. It wasn't long before Dr Götz emerged through a door. He was wrapped in a black cape and wore a top hat, cane in hand. He was familiar but I didn't know where I knew him from. I introduced myself and he suggested to take a walk along the river.

'Isn't April mysterious?' he said, as we stepped outside the building. 'That moment before everything starts to bloom. You can't see anything and yet . . . it's all there. Veiled. Isn't it the most exciting time of the year?'

He was testing my patience: we had important matters to discuss. 'I'm sorry,' I said, 'but my fiancée and her father have been arrested.'

'I know,' he answered, and we continued to walk into the mist.

How could Dr Götz know of their arrest? I wondered, but I didn't ask. The grey fog had turned to blue and the few functioning gaslamps along the street were yellow orbs illuminating the darkness. Dr Götz's fine attire inspired begging palms to emerge from the mist towards him and when I noticed his spats, it slowly dawned on me where I had seen Dr Götz before: walking across the lobby in the hotel on a Friday night, going to Room 33. The room used by the Thule group. He was one of the men who had stored the weapons there; one of the men who made leaflets with shining swastikas. Dr Götz tipped his hat with his cane. 'Would you care for a bite to eat?' He must have sensed that I hadn't eaten all day.

I nodded.

'Good,' he said. 'A little warmth and some food and drink, and perhaps I can help you put your problems into perspective.'

The beer, potatoes and red cabbage gave me a renewed sense of wellbeing, not to mention renewed faith in the Munich restaurant business. The other eateries we had tried had all been closed. It was as if it were Good Friday and no one had told us.

'Aren't these Red economic ideas wonderful?' said Dr Götz, referring to the closed restaurants. He sipped his sherry. 'It's all part of the same plot. Now the Jews think they'll finally be able to achieve what their God commanded: world domination.'

'I know,' I said, hoping he would stop interrupting me as I savoured my food. No such luck.

'Did you ever wonder who's responsible for the mess we're in? And I don't mean this particular mess now. I mean in general; I mean life: the "human condition".' Dr Götz took another sip of his sherry, and smacked his lips at the dry taste. 'Did it ever occur to you that there must be something terribly wrong? All the suffering, all these terrible things that are happening. Every day, every hour, every second!'

I tried to block out what he was saying. All I wanted to do was enjoy my meal.

'Well, who created this mess? Who created the materialistic world we live in? And the suffering that comes with it? The God of the Jews! So who is this God, then? Is he not, in fact, the devil? But we are beings of light! And we're trapped in this material world. A world of darkness! We must free ourselves from it. Our fight is the struggle between light and darkness. It's a fight between the spiritual and the material.'

Dr Götz patted his lips with a napkin. 'Do you know how to fire a gun?' he asked, out of the blue.

'I do,' I replied.

'Well, that's all that matters. Not many of those commie Jews can do that. All they know is bookkeeping. Toller, the chairman of the latest government council, calls himself a great communist leader. What a joke!

I doubt he could lead a dog on a leash. Have you ever read any of his plays? He should be shot for those alone.'

I studied Dr Götz's expression. It seemed as artificial as a mask, as if its sole purpose was dissimulation.

'I hate those liberals!' he continued. 'And the conservatives aren't any better! They call themselves "democrats" but they just whine and whine, and nothing ever gets done. Nothing gets done because they don't know *how* to do anything!' Dr Götz's fist rapped on the table as if knocking on a door. 'I'll tell you who'll show the "democrats" how to deal with that Red scum.' He checked to make sure no one was listening, and then whispered: 'Our Free Corps!'

'Well,' I said, 'do you know any of these Free Corps people? Maybe they could help us to free Francisca and Edgar.'

'I'll make the proper introductions,' he said, taking another sip of his sherry.

Two days later, a message arrived at the hotel for me with a date, a time, a place. When the time came, I was there as arranged, in the back pew of the Theatiner Church. The marble silence of the church was a sanctuary from the desolate "peace" outside its walls and allowed me momentary respite from my fears for Francisca.

A man sat down beside me.

He was willowy and taut, his fingers extending like talons over the edge of the bench. His ears lay flat against his head. His face was bullet-scarred. He nudged me and got up. I followed, walking fifty feet behind. We crossed Marienplatz and entered a tavern, but he didn't go to a table or to the bar. Instead, he headed to the back as if to the bathroom, but opened a door and descended a flight of stairs. Two minutes later, I did the same. Surrounded by wooden kegs of beer, he introduced himself as 'B'. There was an implicit understanding that you never disclosed your real name to another operative.

I told him my name was 'M'.

He said I was to wait there for the leader, and then he left.

I sat on a stool for a torturous thirty minutes, my mind racing back and forth between the fear of what would take place and the exhilaration of soon having Francisca in my arms again. I was only too aware of the hideous irony that I might have to do gruesome things because of my love for her. My mind raced, searching for a civilised solution to my problem; but there was nothing civilised about this time and place. Here we were, I thought, living in this remarkable age of electricity, yet to achieve something truly important we had to revert to behaviour from the Stone Age.

The leader entered.

His name was 'R'.

He was a small man with perfect posture. He spoke quickly and economically. His face was featureless: eyes, a nose and a mouth, but nothing specific. He could easily blend into a crowd and be lost forever. The leader wanted to know about my war record.

I told 'R' I had been awarded the Bavarian Bravery Medal with Crossing Swords. I didn't tell him what I had done with it.

He asked me how many people I'd killed.

I asked him if he knew how many battles the List Regiment had fought; he didn't. I told him that after the thirtieth battle, I'd lost track.

'R' smiled. He asked if I had ever killed someone up close.

I said yes, recalling the incident in the rain with Dolferl but didn't divulge any details of that particular Christmas Eve. Yes, I had killed someone with my bare hands and yes, I remembered his life seeping from his body as I did it.

The leader said that they needed a good marksman.

I said that I wasn't bad. I asked 'R' if he could help me to free Francisca and her father.

He replied that they were planning to liberate Munich, and that part of the operation involved liberating the hostages that the Reds had taken. Would I be interested in helping them?

Absolutely, I said.

The leader likened the proposed operation to that of a surgeon and his scalpel. He just wanted to take out the key elements of the government, he said, without too much bloodshed.

'R' looked at me: we've all seen too much carnage.

I agreed.

He told me that they were planning their uprising for the first of May. His index finger pointed to his temple: it is all psychology. What better way to demoralise a communist than attack on their day of celebration? 'So,' he said, 'that's less than a week from now. I want to hit hard and fast.'

'R' wanted to know if I had kept any weapons.

I explained that I hadn't.

He said he'd make the necessary arrangements to have me armed. He gave me a note: another date, time and place.

I said I would be there.

We shook hands and left the tavern separately.

Out on the street, I couldn't escape my despair at the thought of bearing arms once more.

What was even more dispiriting was how quickly I acclimatised to my newly issued weapon. The pistol felt like an extension of my arm almost immediately. I remembered the early days of training for the Great War, when I'd had to adjust to carrying a weapon. This time around, the gun became part of me in a matter of minutes. All those pugnacious skills honed in the trenches quickly re-emerged; evidently they had never left me.

The slip of paper the leader had slipped me bore an address in Eching, on the northern outskirts of the city. It was an industrialist's estate that had once been the home of an eighteenth-century land baron, a small castle in the middle of a parcel of forested land. Because the location was so remote and isolated, the firing range there allowed the corps members to refine their shooting skills without drawing the attention of the outside world. Judging from the opulence of the estate, it was clear that the 'Oberland' Free Corps was amply funded by the owner of the manor. The privately financed Free Corps were the only troops that the government in Berlin could genuinely rely on. Most units of the disbanding regular army were of little use, infiltrated as they were by the Reds.

I estimated that there were about seventy men at this base, all war-hardened veterans, and I was told there were another three hundred and fifty Free Corps men situated at four other locations nearby. At the debriefing, we were told that the objective of our *coup d'état* was to join forces with loyal army units from Württemberg and Prussia outside the city. Together we would then launch an attack. Some of us were selected to assassinate Toller. The plan was to kill the egregious communist/poet at his Nymphenburg home where he wrote the plays so despised by Dr Götz.

The making of history is an elusive notion. When I had volunteered for the Bavarian Infantry that day in Munich all those years ago, I had deluded myself that I would be part of the historic tide of change. The same feeling had surfaced again during our last major advance in the war. For most of the rest of my time in the trenches, 'history' was an afterthought. What was foremost in my mind was the sickening drudgery of what I had put myself through. After the war my most lofty thought was to escape 'history': what I really wanted was to be home in my study, composing and playing music in my own private ivory tower where nothing of historical importance happened. All I wanted to be was content and insignificant. Yet here I was, in a dreary little truck, on the precipice of yet another historic event. I was being transported to the Munich terminal with a counterfeit red armband and my new comrades. It was early morning, still dark and I shivered in the cold. The truck rattled along as the wet green countryside gave way to Munich's brick cityscape. Half a mile away from the terminal, the truck broke down, forcing an unpleasant opportunity for contemplation upon me. I was on a reconnaissance mission: I was to walk the streets and assess the mood of the city. And I had another more specific goal to achieve: I had to find Dolferl and persuade him to convince our old regiment to join us in the fight. The battle plan called for 'the Whites' to circle the perimeter of the city and systematically converge on its centre. All this was supposed to happen four days hence. I hated sitting in this truck with a faked weapons-permit masquerading as a gun-toting communist, a communist set on making 'history'. I didn't want to spill any more blood. I glanced at the semi-automatic Mauser that lay by my side. Hopefully the Reds would lay down their arms peacefully, so the coup would be as painless as possible. All I wanted was to liberate Francisca and her father so that all three of us could be together again. We finally left the truck and marched the rest of the way to the central station. I waved goodbye to my 'comrades' as they drifted into the station, where they would board trains to rendezvous with regular army troops and other Free Corpsmen just outside the city.[31]

I headed towards Lothstraße, the home of my old regiment. As I walked up the steps into the building, a drunken infantryman stumbled out of the entrance, hoisting a bottle of beer and laughing, absorbed in some rambling soliloquy. Two equally merry and inebriated cohorts followed him, seemingly set on visiting Munich's infamous brothels. The dense blue smoke of Turkish tobacco greeted me as I entered the reception area of the building. Broken bottles lay strewn on the floor and stained walls framed drunken soldiers, oblivious to the filth.

I ascended the stairs to the second floor, hoping to find Dolferl in the

31 See: Appendix 30, Revolution in Munich

same room as last time. And indeed, there he was, still checking gas masks. He looked up at me as he tightened the screws around the goggles of a mask.

'What's this?' he called, pointing at my red armband.

'It allows me to carry a gun,' I said, 'just like you.'

'These things can never be too tight,' Dolferl said, twisting the brass knobs. 'I wouldn't want what happened to me to happen to anyone else . . . ' he muttered.

'Unless, of course, it's the enemy,' I said, thinking this would be an excellent introduction to my proposal.

'I'd love to see them all go blind,' he cackled, his cheeks reddening.

'Then why don't you loosen the screws?' I suggested. Here we were, after all, posing as communists. But there was a difference: I was carrying fake papers, while his were real. His red armlet was military issue while mine had been sewn together by the wife of some infuriated capitalist.

'I have orders,' he said.

'Orders from the enemy!' I said. 'Have you forgotten your rage when we attended the rally on Alexanderplatz?'

'I will deal with this enemy soon enough.'

'Dolferl!' I cried. 'The city is about to explode. On the way over, every person I passed was starving. Everyone was angry. Everyone has had enough!'

Dolferl rolled his eyes. 'Please, not another rumour about a coup.'

'But this one *is* going to happen. I'm part of it.' I paused.

'Well, good for you.'

'Surely you want to join us,' I said, light-hearted. I smiled, using one of the softening tactics he often employed.

'And when is this coup supposed to happen?' he asked.

'Four days' time,' I replied.

'May the third . . . '

'Exactly.' The plan to attack the bastards on their day of celebration had been changed.

'In the event of an attack, the regiment has decided to stay neutral,' said Dolferl.

'Neutral? You can't be serious!'

'If there is an attack I've planned a leisurely day of reading with plenty of pastries.' His lips curled cynically.

'I don't believe you!' I shouted. 'You swore you were going to fight for a new Germany!'

'And I will!' he said. 'But not under anybody else's command! Never again!' His chest swelled with determination. 'I've been fooled once. Now I'm going to fight my own fight!' The air around him seemed charged with energy. 'And I will fight to the end. There won't be a surrender. Ever!' The blind determination that I had witnessed at Pasewalk flooded the room. 'I will do what I have been called to do!' he cried.[32]

As if in reply to his outburst, a blast exploded somewhere outside. Dolferl and I ducked our heads. After the rattling of the windowpanes subsided, the distant crackle of snipers' shots could be heard.

'I'm leaving,' I said.

'Why? You'll be safer here.'

'I'm not thinking of myself,' I said. 'I'm thinking of – '

'Your girlfriend?' he sneered.

I watched my boots pounding down the stairs, Dolferl's laugh echoing in my ears as I raced to save Francisca.

Outside the barracks a group of people, some armed with butcher's hooks, others with pistols and knives were swarming around a pair of patrolling Red guards.

The soldiers stepped backwards, their guns poised. 'Don't come any closer or we'll shoot,' warned one of them.

Undeterred, the civilians moved a step nearer. Their resolve was tangible: death means nothing to us, you socialist scum!

'Stop where you are!' shouted the second guard. But the mob edged even closer. Then someone in the crowd shot at the guards: the smell of the gun mixed with the smell of warm blood. I felt sick; this was something I had hoped never to see again. Another bullet was fired: the two Reds lay dead on the pavement, leaving the insurgents to rejoice, cheering. I ripped off my armband before they turned in my direction. They looked at me, and I at them. I raised my pistol into the air in a victorious gesture.

'They're shooting hostages!' one of them screamed.

'Where?' I screamed back, instantly consumed by panic.

'Those Red animals are systematically murdering innocent people!'

'Where?' I sceamed in desperation.

'At Luitpold Secondary School!'

32 See: Appendix 31, Hitler during the Revolution

I imagined Francisca bound and blindfolded before a firing squad. 'We must stop them!' I howled.

'To the school!' yelled a squat, determined man, waving his rifle. 'Follow me to the school!' he screamed.

We raised our weapons in the air to show our unity. My counter-revolutionaries were about sixty feet away and walking towards me when a ripple of gun fire was heard from behind them. One by one their bodies flopped on to the cobblestoned street: behind them stood another line of men, all wearing red armbands. Before another shot was fired, I put my armband on, turned the corner and ran.

The church bell had begun tolling twelve when I came across a boy no older than ten. He was stunned by fear as he skirted about plumes of smoke and bloodied corpses, holding a red flag with the hammer and sickle insignia. He cried out for his parents and his wail conjured up the image of Francisca. What if I'm too late and she's dead?

A depressing silence followed the last of the twelve tolls. Out of the smoke I saw a group of people emerge. They were too obscured for me to see which side they were from, so I turned and skirted down an alleyway, where I saw three men and a girl standing against a wall. The girl had tied a red handkerchief around her neck to go with her armband. A hefty man wearing a black leather hat picked up a brick and launched it at her, striking her in the forehead with a dull crack. Her eyes rolled white and her tongue shot out as she slid to the ground. A man with a baker's apron applauded the strongman. Francisca could be suffering the same fate as this poor girl, I thought. My hands quivered and I could barely breathe thinking about it. The men started kicking and stamping on the girl. I nodded to them as I slipped my hand into my back pocket to push my armband further down.

I slipped alongside the city's buildings and down the streets, running a jagged diagonal across Munich: running and then stopping at the eruption of gunfire at nearly every other block. I had been so sure I would never again find myself in this situation after the armistice had been signed; yet here I was, virtually back in the trenches.

When I finally reached Kurfürstenplatz, long late-afternoon shadows flanked the boulevard. Red infantrymen were rummaging through a pile of dead bodies. As the soldiers looked up at me, I pulled the red armlet from my back pocket and waved it over my head. Yes, my comrades, I beamed silently, we're making world history. We're part of this global movement. They quickly lost interest in me and proceeded to rifle through the corpses. A bullet whisked by my ear from behind; I turned to find, of all people, the troops I had trained with in Eching. The revolt of the angry citizens had evidently triggered the invasion earlier than planned. I raised my gun. 'Charge!' I screamed, as I ran to a receded doorway. The twenty or so men from my unit poured on to the boulevard with angry determination. A regular army regiment from Württemberg followed. From the opposite direction, another unit of Free Corpsmen appeared. Bullets pierced the air as the Red scavengers fell over the dead from whom they had been pilfering. Then the Whites ran their greedy fingers over both sets of bodies.

Exhausted, I leaned against a door as my comrades from Eching bent over their kill. The sun was starting to inch towards the horizon: the day was slowly ending. Would the same be true of Francisca's life? Had we both survived the war, only for her to die in its lethal aftermath? I fought for my life every step of the way to the school. Street by street, the winners and losers of the revolt were reversed. Depending on who the current victor was, I either donned or discarded the armlet. But as my journey progressed through the smoke and peals of gunfire, I had to use my red disguise less and less. Two blocks from the school, I found that the Republikanische Schutztruppe was controlling the streets, much to my relief. Then, finally, the four-storey school building came into view. The sun was skimming the rooftops, slowly turning the clouds pink.

In the schoolyard, a dozen corpses lay strewn on the ground, blindfolded, their arms tied behind their backs. Snipers with submachine guns were perched in the attic windows on all four sides of the school. Every so often a barrage of bullets came spitting out from the top floor, making it impossible for the Republikanische Schutztruppe to storm the building.

I took cover around a corner facing the school. From where I was, it was impossible to identify the dead; I could only hope that Francisca wasn't among them. If she was still alive, she was in there somewhere, so close and yet impossible to reach. I clutched my pistol, and leaned against the wall: if only there was a way to take out the snipers! I cocked my gun, leapt out from the corner, and fired at the attic. The shots rang out as I ducked back for cover. I had no idea if my bullets had hit. A rumble rolled down the street from behind me. I turned to see an armoured car with a mortar on a field carriage. I strained to see which flag was blowing back and forth in the wind on the vehicle. I couldn't tell what it was in the fading light. But I could tell what it wasn't.

It wasn't red.

As the vehicle came closer, I could finally make out the markings on the flag: it was a black Prussian Eagle. The car stopped behind a wall and four soldiers emerged. They loaded the *Mienenwerfer* with a 30-pound shell, ratcheted the mortar up to about forty-five degrees and then quickly retreated back inside the vehicle. The car swung wide and swerved around the wall into plain sight of the school, giving the howitzer cannon a clear path to the building. Machine-gunfire from the school burst out in the direction of the cannon. One of the soldiers emerged again from the vehicle and crawled under the car. The barrage of bullets continued until there was a momentary lull. Immediately the soldier scrambled up from under the vehicle, quickly releasing the mortar's lever and sprinting away from the car. But he only made it a few steps before the machine-gunfire ripped across the yard again, bullets climbing the soldier's leg and up his spine, a shot for every vertebra. Instantly he fell to the ground. Meanwhile, the shell exploded out of the barrel of the mortar, making the carriage's wheels recoil backwards. The howling shell shot towards the edge of the school's roof, blowing it off the building with an enormous blast. The external wall buckled and collapsed, leaving a jagged flaming gap, exposing overturned school desks and blackboards. Red-armbanded men trailed out of the ruin with hands over their heads, but our sharp-shooters picked them off one by one. A blue pall of smoke settled over the schoolyard.

I ran to the blindfolded corpses and caught my breath: there was a red-haired woman amongst them: she was lying on her stomach, her arms bent at the elbows, hands tied behind her back. I looked closer. The face wasn't Francisca's. Thank God! But I recognised her; I'd seen her before. It was Countess von Westarp. She had manned the Thule Society's bureau in the hotel. I ran on towards the gaping hole in the building. The classrooms were burning, debris falling. I sprinted into the building and heard muffled screams through a door next to a staircase. I pulled the latch back and hauled the door open. The last of the daylight flooded down steps and into a cellar. Forty or so faces stared up at me, their eyes blinking, bewildered.

'It's alright!' I cried. 'You're safe!'

They stampeded up and out into the air, to the fading rays of sunshine.

'Martin!' Francisca was in my arms. My lips pressed against her ear. 'Marry me,' I whispered. 'Marry me!'

Her chest pressed against mine and we kissed as we had on that first day of spring.[33]

A week after the fighting, Edgar, Francisca and I strolled along the city streets. I noticed a brown and grey sparrow flitting between the branches of a linden tree, and then flying from one streetlight to the next. A week ago, that same bird would have been hopping from one corpse to another. Then, the rotting bodies of dead communists had been suspended from the street lights, and the stench of death mixed with the everyday smells of a city slowly returning to life. After the invasion there had been a spate of lynchings; the Whites had shot anyone suspected of being a Red sympathiser, and the bodies hung publicly as a reminder that the Whites were not only victorious, but vindictive as well. Overnight, Munich had changed from a utopian socialist experiment into a right-wing stronghold. The birds chirped happily despite the recent gory events, and perhaps we pedestrians took our cue from them. Passers-by were tense at first, but relaxed and smiled as we drew closer; smiled hesitantly, a smile that recalled the recent horror we'd all experienced.

As we neared Lenbachplatz, the *oom-pah-pah* of a brass band could be heard, and Francisca began to move in time to the music.

'It sounds like Munich has returned to its citizens again!' proclaimed Edgar. 'May it remain that way!' Then he had a sudden urge to find a piece of wood, a tree trunk, even a flagpole, to rap his knuckles against for luck. 'We need all the luck in the world to prevent this from ever happening again.' But there was not one scrap of wood to be found along the street, except for the splintered crates where pedlars had displayed their goods. The wood was so worn, dried and thin that it seemed to embody our dire past luck rather than the future good luck Edgar was after. 'We must stay vigilant,' said Edgar, 'this isn't over yet.'

We turned on to Lenbachplatz. In the centre of the square, an army band was playing a march. The regular army was in charge now, and Munich was effectively ruled by a military dictatorship – a benevolent dictatorship, we hoped.

'I just pray,' said Francisca, 'that the Whites aren't as bad as the Reds were.'

33 See: Appendix 32, Hostage Killings and anti-Semitism

'Hardly likely,' said Edgar, 'and if they are, they have good reason!'

'Edgar . . . ' I said, hesitantly. I remembered a question I had asked him before, but which he hadn't answered. 'Why did they arrest you?'

'Because they're pigs. Animals. Barbarians.'

'You weren't accused of anything in particular?'

'No.'

'And the lady?'

'Which lady?'

'The Countess von Westarp. She used to attend meetings held by that group.'

'What group? What are you talking about?' Edgar asked irritated.

'Those people with the swastika and the dagger as their emblem . . . what were they called?'

'The Thule Society,' said Edgar, evading eye contact.

'Why would the Reds arrest her? And kill her?'

'How should I know?' Edgar's voice was slightly higher than normal. He was still avoiding my gaze.

'It seems like the Reds were targeting that Thule Society . . . ' I persisted.

'Let it go, Martin! It's bad enough that I of all people should have been incarcerated.'

At my other side, Francisca was in her own world, swaying with the music. She genuinely didn't know why she'd been arrested. Edgar, I suspected, did. Recently the papers had published the photos of those who had been shot at the schoolyard. Apart from Countess von Westarp, I had recognised six more faces: they had all been regular guests at the hotel, and members of that obscure 'Thule' group. I suspected that Edgar was a member as well. Not only did he attend their public lectures, I had also caught sight of him slipping into a 'members only' meeting.

Francisca rose and balanced on her toes. 'I owe you so much,' she said. 'My life . . . everything!' She looked up at me as she had in the moments after the rescue. I thought back to her first night home at the hotel, when she had cried in my arms as she recalled the terror of hearing the gunshots in the schoolyard.

'Remember that letter I wrote to you about our baby?' she whispered. 'Our flower?'

'Of course I remember! You were wondering what features of yours and what of mine he would have.'

'Yes!' Her eyes glistened. 'You've survived, as have I. We're together.

There must be a reason.' She sighed. Her lips parted and I kissed her, oblivious to Edgar's presence.

'I think I know why the Reds arrested your father,' I said to Francisca that evening when we were alone in our room.

She looked at me questioningly.

'Do you remember that card you gave me? Dr Götz?'

'I do.'

'He's a member of the Thule Society.'

'Really?'

'It was Dr Götz who put me in contact with the unit that invaded the city.'

'Is that so,' said Francisca distantly, not listening to me. She slipped off her blouse.

'Those Thules are more than some group of eccentrics studying Germanic antiquity. They have an agenda. They have a secret political . . . '

Francisca had come up to me and unbuttoned my shirt. I wanted to tell her about the weapons in Room 33, but Francisca put her hand over my mouth and silenced me. And we kissed.

Even though the hotel was struggling to stay open, Francisca and I had never been happier. We held an ineffable understanding and compassion for one another. My life was hers as hers was mine, and together we were one beating heart and one loving mind.

But one piece of the puzzle was missing.

Dolferl.

It had been two months since I had last seen him. I didn't want to jeopardise the harmony between Francisca and me, but I felt a strange compulsion to meet with him. Perhaps it was mere curiosity or the need to assert my independence, but whatever the reason, I wanted to see him. One day, as I was running errands for the hotel, I dropped by Dolferl's barracks. He wasn't there, but I left him a note. Two days later a letter from him arrived at the hotel suggesting that we meet at the Schelling Saloon, a billiard hall near the University.

Dining tables were arranged around the billiard tables. A guest was chalking the tip of his cue as a handful of others stood and watched. Dolferl was sitting alone in a corner. I almost didn't recognise him: he wasn't wearing a uniform. For more than four years, I had never seen him in anything else. He was dressed in a traditional Bavarian jacket with a green collar, laced hiking boots and lederhosen. The military uniform had suited him perfectly; this folk attire seemed an ill-fitting costume. The billiard players hovered over the table while Dolferl sat in his own world. His moustache was a tight little rectangle that blackened the space between his upper lip and his nose. His hair was well groomed. He was eating apple strudel topped with a double portion of whipped cream, which he was spooning ravenously into his mouth. On the table lay a newspaper. *Are Jews Behind the Killing of the Cab Driver?* read the headline. Almost every crime in the city was now immediately associated with Jews. The fact that most communist leaders had Jewish backgrounds led even moderate Munich papers to denounce the Red Revolution as a sinister Jewish plot against the German people. Overnight, the most liberal city in Germany had become paranoid about the Jews.

Dolferl set the paper down on the table and looked up. He smiled. 'The city is waking up,' he said and patted the newspaper headline. 'Finally! Finally people are starting to understand.' Dolferl directed his gaze towards me. 'You're late,' he said.

'Sorry.' I sat down. 'I thought today was your day off.'

'I'm always on duty,' he said and shrugged. 'That's how it is in politics.' He took a mouthful of his strudel. 'It becomes your life. Like art.'

'You're in politics now?'

He smiled and looked directly at me with the eyes of a stranger. 'If one has realised the truth, that truth is valueless if the indomitable will to turn this realisation into action is lacking.'

'So . . . what are you doing?' I asked, wondering who he had quoted.

'I'm performing my first political task.'

'And what's that?'

'I'm an informant for an army investigation.' He wiped his mouth. 'We have to eliminate all those filthy traitors.' He sighed. 'Two dozen have already been executed. But you know what really infuriates me? Some of the worst offenders have been let off. And you know why? Because of their lawyers: crooks help crooks and the government pays for it.'

'Unlike the Russians, we live in a constitutional state.'

'Nonsense. Our justice system needs a radical overhaul. The guilt or innocence of a man must be determined by whether or not he is dangerous to the existence of the State. Nothing more.'

Dolferl scrutinised his plate. There was still some whipped cream. He looked around furtively – waste not, want not – lifted the plate up to his face and quickly licked off the remnants. Then he dabbed his mouth, nose and moustache with the napkin.

'It's almost flavourless,' he said, in a hoarse voice. 'The gas has made me lose my sense of taste. Now I need even more sugar than before.'

'But you look great,' I said, trying to redirect our conversation to a lighter subject as I pointed to his Bavarian operetta outfit.

'Thank you.' He looked at his watch. 'I have a class now.'

'Where?'

'At the university. Political science.'

'How come? You don't even have a school diploma!'

'Look at my curriculum.'

He handed a paper to me and I read: 'German History since the Reformation', 'Political History of the War', 'Socialism in Theory and Practice', 'Price Policies in the Economic System', 'Correlations Between Domestic and Foreign Policy' . . .

'I don't need a diploma,' he said. 'Everything happens as it should if you let Providence do its work.' His eyes widened, snaring me in his stare. 'All you must do is let Providence guide you.' I was powerless to resist the intensity of the moment. 'I've seen the light!' his eyes announced. 'I am the way and the destination.'[34]

It was all too much. I averted my gaze to the floor so I could collect my thoughts.

'The army sends you to university?' I whispered.

'They're training speakers, for the troops. The army is infected with the Red Gospel. We're going to change that: indoctrinate the troops with patriotism. We learn how to make an impression and how to emphasise appropriate points.' He stopped for a moment, pondering, then continued: 'The masses must be shaped, like a sculptor shapes clay into immortal form.' He looked up at the ceiling. 'I can see it,' he said. 'I can see that human clay become a beautiful work of art just like one of Myron's sculptures.'

July 1919, Munich

'Absolutely not,' declared Francisca, clutching the long list of friends and acquaintances she planned to invite to our wedding.

We had decided to marry the following year. Francisca wanted an elaborate, well-attended wedding; she had so many friends from her

34 See: Appendix 29, Hitler's Eyes

school days and colleagues from the theatre that her list of guests seemed endless. On my side, I had only my immediate family. Most of my comrades from the war were dead, and the whereabouts of those still alive were unknown. From my regiment I had only included Dolferl on my paltry list. I had to.

'Why can't I invite him?' I asked.

She scanned the darkened hotel ballroom and cringed at the thought of Dolferl attending our wedding reception.

'You have all your friends!' I said, as my hand gestured in exasperation towards the dance floor.

'That has nothing to do with it,' she growled. Her eyes narrowed, scrutinising me. 'You just don't get it, do you?'

'All I know is that I love you,' I began. 'And – '

'If that's the case, why can't you understand?' she said, turning away from me.

'Please! Don't you think your love is strong enough to withstand Dolferl for a few hours in a room filled with a hundred of your friends?'

Francisca shook her head vigorously: no, no, no. 'You're missing the point completely,' she said, getting up from the chair and crossing over to the centre of the dance floor.

'Oh, come on,' I said. 'I've been to see him, and he hardly – '

'You *what*?' she screamed.

'I saw him,' I replied, deliberately raising my voice. 'Just a few days ago.'

'That does it!' She flung her arms in the air. 'And you didn't even tell me? You're already keeping things from me! How will it be once we're married?' She retreated to the opposite end of the dance floor. 'I need to think!' she turned, wove her way through the maze of tables to the entrance, and slammed the door shut behind her.

Early the next morning, Francisca travelled to Herbert and Leopold's house on Lake Chiemsee. I had no idea when she might return.

'The runes are a means of communication. They're instruments, like a telegraph. Tools. To the Ancients, the runes were technical instruments for practical use . . . '

Forty of us were seated in five rows, eight chairs across. I was among members of the upper middle class: professors, government officials, factory owners and aristocrats. Some were Thule members; others, like myself, were guests.

The lecturer turned to the side, his patrician profile framed by a round black insignia of garland-entwined dagger and swastika that adorned the wall. 'Science is a belief system. It is based on the assumption that there is nothing more real than the physical, material stuff of the universe. And so also our laws of physics are merely part of that belief system. But there are other, alternative belief systems . . . '

The Thule Society, I had quickly learned, had been founded by Rudolf von Sebottendorff who had studied occultism in Turkey, where he had met Sufis, Islamic alchemists and dervishes. In Constantinople, he had founded another mystical lodge.

'There is another way to look at the universe,' the speaker continued. 'A way that is more advanced: the way of the Ancients. They created the runes. And the runes have not lost their power!'

I had asked Edgar if he could arrange for me to go to a Thule lecture. He had been reluctant, asking me why I was interested. I had lied, telling him of my long-standing interest in German prehistory. The real reason was that Francisca was still at Lake Chiemsee, and I craved some form of distraction. Edgar made the proper arrangements and I was invited as a guest. *The Holy Grail and the Runes* was the title of the lecture.

'The runes are a means of advancing your spiritual development. The runes lead us back to our historic past, but also show us the way to tomorrow. They are our past and our future!' The speaker bowed his head. 'Thank you,' he finished.

There was a moment of silence as we were all transported back from the mythic world of the runes to the reality of a five-star hotel in an impoverished, castrated Germany. There was a spattering of applause, which quickly increased as more of us were awakened by the sound, and eventually we were all clapping. Some lined up to thank the lecturer as others gravitated towards the side table where some simple pastries and coffee substitute were being served. Small groups of people were discussing the lecture. References were made to occult systems. Gnostic sources were quoted, along with Pythagoras and Hindu wisdoms. Amongst all of the spiritual chatter, I overheard snippets of other conversations.

'When will the rifles from Berne arrive?' I overheard a younger man asking.

'They'll strike in two groups,' said another.

'The swastika is the key that unlocks infinite power,' a woman whispered into another's ear.

I knew her. Leonie was a countess, married to a prosperous member of the Thule Society. He was part of the 'inner circle', the power base of the group.

More Thules started to arrive. They greeted one another with '*Heil!*' and answered with '*Sieg!*' raising their right arm and nodding ever so slightly.[35]

Countess Leonie winked at me. She was a flirt and was drawn to me, no doubt, because I was one of the younger men in the group. She was near Francisca's age so there was a curious pattern to all this. I was intrigued by her closely cropped black hair and jade green eyes, and liked her smoky, sexy laugh. I was curious, even though I was perfectly happy with Francisca. But it irked me that Francisca was the only woman I had ever known. Although I had wanted to marry her for a long time, the fact that it was finally happening made me apprehensive, so I played these harmless little games with myself. And the countess seemed to be playing along with me.

'Let's have our own little tête-à-tête,' Leonie suggested, 'while they have their secret little meeting.'

She was referring to the members' meeting after the lecture. It was a 'men only' council, as usual. I smiled: I was game.

As all non-members and all of the women were being politely asked to leave, Countess Leonie came up to me again. 'Let's go get a real drink,' she said, with feigned exhaustion.

We went to the bar opposite the hotel. It was the first bar in town that had reopened after the downfall of the Soviet government.

We took a seat. The countess smiled and said, 'They shouldn't do that.'

'What?'

'Exclude the women from their meetings,' she shook her head. 'They're only hindering themselves.' Her fingers massaged her pearl necklace. 'Female energy is so valuable.' She raised her glass of vermouth and we toasted. 'If they'd let the women take part,' Countess Leonie continued, 'they'd have made contact a long time ago.'

'Made contact?' I asked. 'With whom?'

Leonie looked at me. She crossed and then uncrossed her legs. 'Oh, what you don't know,' she said, teasingly.

'What do you mean?'

'There are so many ways to do it.' She winked.

35 See: Appendix 33, The Thule Society

'Ways?' I asked, wondering if Francisca had taught me everything I needed to know.

'Techniques . . . ' She winked again, and tilted her head: coquette. 'Spiritual techniques that the group uses,' she elaborated.

I was disappointed. Conniving trollop.

'Sebottendorff has taught them some very powerful skills: spiritual techniques you can only learn in practice.' The countess smiled: you actually thought you were going to bed me? She laughed.

Spiritual techniques, I mused, abandoning any other prospects involving the countess. My thoughts turned instead to the weapons in Room 33.

'Do these "techniques" include the use of weapons?'

'You mean the Thule fighting alliance?' Leonie laughed. 'That's part of the work. A necessity these days. But that's not what Thule is really about.'

'What *is* it about, then?'

'Knowledge.'

'Of?'

'The Armanen.'

'Excuse me?'

'You don't know Guido von List?'

'No.'

'But . . . aren't you Austrian?'

'Sure.'

'Guido von List is from Austria too. And you've never heard of him? Really?'

I said I hadn't, but I might have; had Dolferl mentioned him? I couldn't remember.

'I can't believe you've never heard of Guido von List,' she repeated.

'Should I have?'

'He's a prophet. Wondrous. Profound. Nothing less than life-changing. He sees things . . . '[36]

'What does he see?'

'An ancient prophecy whose time has come,' she said. 'Soon He will come and all will be revealed.'

'Who will come?'

36 See: Appendix 34, Guido von List

'He who has ultimate knowledge. Von List predicts that He will reveal the secret knowledge that the swastika represents.'

'And what does Thule have to do with this?'

Leonie looked to her right, then to her left. There was no one close enough to hear what she had to say, but even so she lowered her voice.

'This is strictly confidential. You must promise not to reveal it to anyone.'

'Of course.'

'Swear it.'

'I swear!'

She leaned towards me and whispered: 'Thule will bring about the emergence of the man with the ultimate knowledge. Just as von List has prophesied.'

'You really believe that?'

'Oh, yes!' Leonie said, and gazed into the distance. 'Now that Germany so painfully needs him. He is the essence of invincibility.'

'I don't doubt that that's their goal,' I responded, 'but how can they possibly succeed?'

Leonie's stare cut through me. My heart accelerated.

'Do you believe in a higher dimension?' she asked.

'Well, I used to believe in God . . . '

'I'm not asking about God. I'm asking if you believe there's something beyond the understanding of us humans.'

'Well, certainly,' I conceded.

'That's what I mean: the dimension beyond. It can be accessed by these ancient and powerful techniques.' Leonie cleared her throat to make her point. 'But those men' – she paused and looked at me. She spat 'men' as if she were saying 'bastards' – 'those men across the street refuse to acknowledge the female energy. Otherwise they would have made contact already!'

'With what?'

'With that . . . spark. They've used ancient techniques and have caused a rupture in the space–time continuum. Through that rupture, a spark from the higher dimension has come into being. Knowledge . . . ultimate knowledge . . . dormant for hundreds and thousands of years. But now it has been reborn.'

'Reborn? How?'

'It's alive. Alive in a man. *He* is the Chosen One.' Her eyes shone as she looked at me. 'I know you don't believe me,' she said. 'But mark my words: it will happen here. In Munich. Not just according to Sebottendorff. Astrology has predicted it too. And Nostradamus.'

'So where is this . . . "Chosen One" . . . now?'

'No one knows where *He* is. But we know *He's* coming. Soon.'[37]

37 See: Appendix 35, The Expected Saviour

A New Kind of Germany

Together we will build a nation that will last a thousand years.

My work as a hotel clerk continuously confirmed how far I was from the musical career I had held so dear in Vienna. The war and its aftermath had crushed not only my dreams, but everybody else's too. No one's life was turning out the way they had hoped, including Dolferl's, who no longer considered himself a visual artist. But somehow he had performed the miracle of alchemy: he had turned the shit of war into gold. He had re-invented himself and was actually inspired. I, on the other hand, was aimless, with an aching back from standing behind the reception desk for hours. I had become the person I had vowed never to become. I felt like a resounding failure. As I came out from behind the counter, I bumped into Dr Götz. Even though I routinely saw him when he attended the various Thule meetings, I barely recognised him: he wasn't wearing his usual top hat and cape. Instead, he was dressed in a modest brown wool suit.

'Any plans for tonight?' he asked, before continuing without waiting for my response: 'You're in for a treat.' The doctor and I swept out of the lobby and on to the street.

'Here,' he said, handing me a leaflet.

'See you there,' said Dr Götz, walking up to the curb. He was about to cross the street when I called out, 'Wait!'

The leaflet read: *Convention of the Deutsche Arbeiter Partei – DAP. Our Time Has Finally Come! 20:30 at Sterneckerbräu im Tal.* Dr Götz turned around with a reproving expression; there was an understanding within the Thule circle that open conversation was forbidden in public, whether among members or with guests.

'What?' Dr Götz asked, irritably, checking left and right to make sure no one was watching.

'What is this?' I asked, pointing to the leaflet.

Dr Götz whispered: 'We've founded a political party.'

'The Thule Society has?' I pretended to be surprised as I didn't want

Dr Götz to know I was aware of the group's subversive activities. 'I thought that now that the revolution has been quashed, the interests of the Thules were purely esoteric?'

'Think of the Freemasons. They're like us: a secret lodge. For them there was also a moment in history when the spiritual met with the material. This was when they initiated the creation of the United States. The only difference between the Freemasons and us is that they have the All- Seeing Eye and the pyramid as their logo, whereas we have the swastika and the dagger. Plus, the Freemasons are run by the Jews while we're purely Aryan.'

'What are you planning to do?'

'The same as the Freemasons – bring about the birth of a mighty empire; a German empire, of course.'

'How?'

'With the help of our party, the DAP. Tonight could be the night a new German realm is born. And who knows? Maybe *He* will reveal himself to us tonight.'

'Who?'

'The one. The one who will lead us. The one we've been waiting for.'

The Sterneckerbräu was a Bavarian restaurant with a small beer hall. The place wasn't particularly busy; in fact, it wasn't particularly anything. As I stepped into the main dining room, I got the impression that the place had an inferiority complex. It smelled of stale beer and cigars. The wood-panelled walls were decorated with paintings of red-nosed monks drinking pitchers of beer and ogling buxom waitresses. The distinctly poor ambience was probably the reason why the affluent members of the Thule Society had picked this venue as the meeting point for their political party. Here, their party could make contact with the largest section of German society: the workers.

A waitress approached me, and I told her I was there 'for the convention'. She led me out into a hallway. I turned a corner and walked towards an open door. An inscription above the doorway read: 'Veterans' Hall'. I entered the room, which was fashioned after a hunting lodge: several deer-antler lamps hung from the ceiling and sturdy wooden beams buttressed the walls. In the back, a Thule member was lecturing, but I could barely hear him as most of the three dozen or so men and women in the audience were talking amongst themselves, ignoring the speaker. I spotted Dr Götz in a corner. In his modest brown suit, he blended in perfectly with the labourers surrounding him. I tried to catch his eye but he looked through me as if he didn't know who I was.

I sat down alone at an empty table. The jumble of words interspersed the wisps of tobacco smoke that hung in the chamber. Through the grey mist, I tried to spot a familiar shape, but didn't recognise anyone apart from Götz. This little meeting was an interminable bore, but I had been invited by a man whose group kept the hotel in business and so I felt obliged to stick around, for a while at least. At the podium, the speaker was ending his speech. He reminded the audience that in a few minutes an open discussion would follow when I spotted a man I thought I recognised from behind. He wore a leather waistcoat and a fedora. He turned to the side and I caught my breath: it was Dolferl! What in the world was he doing here? I didn't want him to see me. I didn't want to get in trouble with Francisca again. But just as I was about to get up, the waitress came over to me. She was one of those Bavarian waitresses who had weathered many a rowdy crowd: blunt and brazen.

'A *Maas*?' she asked.

'Sure,' I said, still hoping I could escape without Dolferl noticing me.

The waitress walked away. As she passed Dolferl's table, he turned and suddenly I was staring him directly in the eye. He looked at me inquisitively. I got up and ambled over to him.

'What are you doing here?' he said, irked.

'I . . . I . . . ' I stammered. 'I got lost. I wanted a beer and then got lost in the hallway.'

He smiled towards the waitress, who rested my beer *Stein* on the table.

'Why are you here?' I asked him.

'Part of my job. They send me to check on political parties and groups. The *Reichswehr* must know what's going on. We don't want another Soviet regime,' he said. 'Judging from things, I don't think I need to stay any longer. These guys aren't Reds. They're just terribly boring.'

'Workers of the world!' A man with an unkempt grey beard had climbed up on to the podium. 'Come to order!' He waited until the noise in the room abated and continued. 'Everyone is invited to voice what they believe our party's focus should be. What exactly are our goals?' he asked. 'They must be defined!' He paused. 'How else will we achieve a peace in which we all can prosper again?'

'As usual,' sighed Dolferl, 'good faith and good intentions, but no idea of the battle that must be fought.'

'Yes, Professor Baumann,' said the speaker, gesturing to a gentleman sitting at one of the tables by the dais.

The professor stood up and approached the podium. He was wearing what looked like his best suit: a three-piece in grey that once must have given him an impressive presence. Now it sagged from his body like a windless sail. Clearly, the war and uneasy peace had ravaged his once imposing physique.

'Bavaria must finally be free again!' Baumann declared, at which some in the audience applauded. 'Bavaria must determine its future alone, without the rest, without Prussia.' Dolferl shook his head indignantly. 'Once we're independent,' declared the speaker, adjusting his monocle, 'we can talk to the Allies and revise the peace treaty.'

Dolferl glared out from under the rim of his hat. His eyes burned with rage; I could see his temples pulsating. 'Separatists,' he hissed. 'They must be stopped!'

' "Out of Germany and Independence"!' announced the speaker. 'That must be the party's motto!' Again, some hands clapped.

'Rubbish!' roared Dolferl's hoarse voice. He shot up from his chair, his shoulder barely missing the tray of a waitress. The steins on her tray rattled. A wave of uncertainty passed through the room. Dolferl turned to the waitress, took off his hat, and apologised with a nod. Then he turned back towards the podium and directed his glare like a weapon. The speaker adjusted his monocle: he would not be rebuffed. 'Out of Germany,' he repeated, 'for an Independent Bavaria!'

'That's exactly what our arch-enemy wants!' The words erupted from Dolferl like missiles launched towards the West. 'The French would love nothing more than a Germany fragmented into tiny, powerless shards!' He threw his hat on the chair.

'Bavaria has sacrificed enough victims for Prussia's mistakes,' retorted the speaker.

'What have you sacrificed, Herr Professor?' countered Dolferl. 'Where were *you* during the war? In your ivory tower?'

The professor turned red with embarrassment.

'Well, let me tell you where *I* was.' Dolferl's words rang out like shots from a machine gun. 'I was at Ypres three times! I fought forty-eight battles! I've been wounded twice, once in a gas attack! And *you* dare to lecture *me* about sacrifice?'

Dolferl's tirade had drawn the attention of his audience. All chatter had stopped. All eyes and minds were focused on him now. His hands folded pleadingly and his eyes looked heavenward. 'In this hour of despair, unity is what we need! Only united will we succeed!' Dolferl's right hand gripped his left and brought it close to his heart. He turned slowly so that everyone in the room had a clear view of him. 'We will not let ourselves be divided! Never!'

Never! reverberated off the walls.

'We will speak with one voice: with the voice of the strong. We will speak with the voice of those whose army has been defeated, not in battle, but by a mob of traitors at home!' His outstretched finger was aimed towards the heavens. His eyes flared. 'We would have won this war had we not been stabbed in the back by these Judases! Criminals like *you*, Herr Professor!'

'What right have you to accuse me!' retorted the professor.

'All traitors will be dealt with!' Dolferl pointed to the speaker. 'How much is the Jew paying you, Herr Professor?'

'How dare you! I won't allow – '

From some corners, people began to boo. 'Please,' pleaded the speaker as the booing continued to drown him out. 'We'll never become a proper party like this. We have to – '

'Enough!' shouted an elderly man. 'Enough whining!'

Dolferl pointed towards the professor as he turned to his audience. 'People like this traitor,' he said venomously, 'people like him have robbed us of our victory. They have done it once' – Dolferl's finger flew into the air – 'but they will never be able to do it again!' Then he exploded: '*Ever!*' He folded his arms over his chest and stood proud. 'We know now who these traitors are! They have shown us their faces. But that was their biggest mistake! Because now they can't deceive us any more!'

The atmosphere in the room was riotous by now. The professor retreated from the dais, grabbed his hat and scurried out.

'Once these traitors are dealt with,' Dolferl shouted after him, 'Germany will rise from its ashes!' His right arm soared up into the air again. 'Just like the phoenix!' His left hand was clenched over his chest. 'And finally, then, we will triumph! Over all of our enemies!'

Applause erupted in the smoke-filled room.

I looked around for Dr Götz, but he wasn't where I'd last seen him.

'Now let me ask you a question,' said Dolferl, walking to the head of the room. With his heavy boots, leather waistcoat, stiff white collar and odd little moustache, he didn't look very impressive; more like a waiter in a *Bahnhof* restaurant. Nonetheless, the room was rapt with attention. No words, no whispers, not even the slapping of beer mugs could be heard. When Dolferl had finally reached his position in front of the dais, he turned. He looked at his audience, still not speaking.

The silence was almost unbearable.

'Well,' he finally said, in a low voice, 'I was wondering about one thing: Versailles.' Like a lover, he whispered his question into the ears of the audience. 'Everybody seems to be talking about it these days. But what is it? Versailles . . . ' he repeated, with a snigger. 'The Treaty of Versailles. What is that?' He stopped. Again the crowd was hanging on his every word.

'Let me tell you what it is,' he whispered. 'The Treaty of Versailles is paper and ink. Who signed that piece of paper?' he said, much more loudly now. 'Anyone representing me? Or the two million left on the battlefield? Hardly! The ink on that paper doesn't concern us. It wasn't put on that paper by any of us. It was put on that paper by those very traitors!' Dolferl shouted. His hands gripped the lapels of his jacket and shook them. 'Traitors we are going to eliminate!'[38]

A toothless old man and two grey women stood up and applauded. 'Bravo! Bravo!'

Dolferl inhaled. 'They want us to believe that we are insignificant. They want us to believe that we are weak. They want us to believe that we lost this war. But how? Did the battles take place at Nuremberg, or Hanover, or Hagen? No! They were fought at Verdun, and at the Somme, and at Reims! For four years we occupied the enemy's lands! And now, all of a sudden, we lost the war? And we should pay war reparations? And lose our sovereignty? Not in the entire history of humankind has such a peace treaty been agreed!' He banged his fist on the lectern. 'Not a single enemy soldier stepped foot on German soil. Not one. And we lost the war?' repeated Dolferl. 'Do they really think we believe that?'

The crowd looked stunned.

'Two million were left on the battlefield. Two million have been cheated out of the victory they died for: two million who did not give their lives for the Germany of today! They gave their lives for a different Germany, a triumphant Germany. A Germany that brings freedom and justice to the world! *This* is what the two million want. They too have their rights, not just we, the survivors.' The words rolled from his mouth like an unfurling banner. 'There are millions of orphans, cripples, widows in our midst. They too have rights!' His head was eye-level with the

38 See: Appendix 36, Treaty of Versailles

audience, perspiration running down his forehead. 'Not one of them became a cripple, an orphan, or a widow for the Germany of today. We owe it to those millions to build a new Germany!' Dolferl's face was now drenched in sweat, his eyes wild. 'And I promise we will do that! Together, we will create a new Germany! A great Germany!' Dolferl took two steps forward, approaching the audience. Close. Confidential. 'We will create a great Germany,' he called, and then, louder: 'A great Germany.' Louder still: 'One holy empire of the German nation! In all its strength and glory! For the coming millennium! Together we will build a nation that will last a thousand years!'

He fell silent.

He stared at everyone in the room.

He had spoken.

He had given everyone back their self-respect. He had shown his scars. His wounds. He had let people feel them. He had shown them what had been taken from him, and from them all: their honour, their pride, their trust and their dignity. He had declared retaliation. He had sung his aria of victory, and respect, and redemption.

Dolferl stood proud.

I've shown you.

Now you show me.

A woman with the face of a bulldog rose. '*Deutschland, Deutschland . . .*' she began to sing. Her voice was strong and melodious, the voice of an avenging angel. Three women at another table got up and joined in. Two men joined in as well. More women's voices, and more men's. Some men stood up. More men and women followed. More and more people seated at the tables joined in. One after the other, everyone got to their feet. '*Deutschland, Deutschland, über alles*,' they chorused. The room erupted with the vigour of a crowd ten times its size. The crew from the kitchen had been drawn into the room; they and the waitress were singing too.

'*Wenn es stets zu Schutz und Trutze brüderlich zusammen hält . . .*' The room resounded with the anthem.

I looked around and glimpsed a rapturous Dr Götz. He was conferring with the Thule speaker and the man with the grey beard. Dolferl's impromptu performance had evidently made Dr Götz forget the rules regarding discretion in public. People were excitedly lining up at the podium to congratulate Dolferl. Dr Götz and his cohorts brushed by me, ecstatic. Their full attention was focused on Dolferl, who stood smiling behind the dais, basking in the enveloping glow of celebrity.

'They've sent me a membership card for their party,' said Dolferl, waving a white paper slip in the air. 'I didn't even ask for it.'

Fuelled by the stirring effect of Dolferl's speech, I had mustered up the courage and told Francisca that I was going to visit him. I asked her if it upset her in any way; at first she was taken aback, but she acquiesced because I had told her in advance. Upon leaving the hotel, a swell of relief washed over me. Since her return from Lake Chiemsee we hadn't spoken about Dolferl. Now for the first time the Dolferl issue had been dealt with candidly. Finally a normal balance had been restored in my relationship with Francisca. I might even be able to invite him to our wedding. In the barracks, I found Dolferl in his own private cubicle. It was as sparse as the little space he had inhabited in the men's shelter in Vienna: a bed, table, chair and sink; blank walls, three storeys above the street. The noise from all of the hoof and vehicle traffic below echoed deafeningly around it. I asked Dolferl how he was able to endure the cacophony.

'If you just allow it to merge with you,' he said, like a holy man on the banks of the Ganges, 'you no longer even hear it.'

He was sitting on his bed, feeding a mouse with bread.

'There you go, little one,' he cooed to his rodent pet. 'I know what hunger is. I can imagine the pleasure you're experiencing only too well.'

Imprinted on the paper he held in his hand were the black letters 'DAP'. Dolferl studied the card. 'They tell me they have big plans for me.' He laughed, covering his mouth with his hand. 'That pathetic little group has big plans for me!' He shook his head. 'As if I need them!'

He fanned himself with the card as the mouse disappeared into its hole.

'What I envision is beyond any political party! I envision a movement; a movement that will do away with all parties; a movement that will create a new state. A state whose purpose it is not just to provide "law and order". A state that will generate the new man! A man who is in tune with the laws of nature. A man in tune with Providence!' Dolferl waved the slip again. 'Should I sign this thing or not? Must I really put up with that menagerie of slow-witted fools?'

I didn't tell him who was nurturing and grooming this seemingly inconsequential party.

Dolferl settled back in his chair. 'What should I do? I can't waste time. I've been given a mission and the problems I am confronted with are gigantic. But how much time do I have? Both of my parents died young, and my health is deteriorating. I can feel it. The war has taken too much of a toll on me. And now I must fight an even bigger war!'

He looked around, worried and alarmed. 'My God! What shall I do?'

I fiddled with a bread roll Dolferl had offered me. 'Maybe you should ask your little friend,' I proposed. I motioned towards the mouse that was peeping out of its hole in the wall. I broke off two little pieces. 'If he takes this piece first,' I said, lifting up my right hand, 'then you join. But if he takes this piece first,' I said, twisting the snippet of bread in my left hand, 'you don't.'

Dolferl wasn't listening to me; he was lost in his worries. 'If I make the wrong decision, the consequences will be tremendous! It would wreck this nation for all time! And not only this nation: all mankind! What to do . . . I can't change my decision. Once I decide – that's it. For eternity!'

I leaned down to the hole where the mouse had retreated, and placed one piece to its right and the other to its left.

'All you have to do is wait. If he chooses the right first, you join. If he chooses the left, you don't.'

A whisker and a nostril poked out of the hole, sniffing. Then the head emerged from the darkness. Small paws groped out on the floorboards.

'What are you doing?' Dolferl protested.

'Right means you join. Left means you don't.'

The ears unfolded out of the hole. The little pink nose pulsated with fevered excitement. Then the mouse emerged fully and circled the morsel of bread on the left, sniffing and thinking. Then it rotated around the piece on the right. Thinking and sniffing. The mouse raised itself up on its hind legs, about to pick the chunk on the right. It crept closer, and then, for no apparent reason, was drawn to the left. To join or not to join.

'Don't bother me with such nonsense!' Dolferl snarled, and kicked the morsels away.

The mouse disappeared back into its hole.

Dolferl picked up a pen. 'I'm the one who makes the decisions.' He signed on the dotted line. Sealing the fate of humanity.

'I stand here before you as a soldier with a knife in his back!' Dolferl's eyes gazed out over the heads in the audience. It was a respectably large crowd; not as many as he had hoped for, but still big enough: big enough to mesmerise. Dolferl pointed his finger and motioned over his shoulder. 'The knife in my back came not from the battlefield, but from behind our lines! This saw-toothed blade was drawing blood as I battled on against the enemy in front of me. It is the ultimate betrayal. And who stuck this knife in our backs? Who? I'll tell you!' whispered Dolferl theatrically. He stepped closer to the platform's edge and bellowed: 'The Jew!'

His hands were fists, and his elbows bent as his arms crossed over his chest. Forty-five party members and associates were present, with another two hundred and fifty or so curious spectators in attendance at the Eberlbräukeller, an inn serving luke warm beer as the plaster crumbled off the walls. To get that many people to this particular place to listen to an unknown speaker was an impressive achievement in a city like Munich. Right-wing movements had mushroomed after the collapse of the Red revolution and fifteen interchangeable organisations were competing for followers.

'But at least now it is obvious! Now everyone knows that it's them! Them! All throughout history! For thousands of years! But I promise you: this time they will not get away with it! I will finish what Jesus started, but was unable to finish! This time, the ideals of Christ will become reality!'

An impromptu roar of approval met Dolferl's rants. This crowd was here in this particular dank and dim beer hall, and not elsewhere listening to some other radical with similar ideas, due to the efforts of the Thules. Some members had orchestrated a small but effective publicity campaign, and various advertisements had appeared in the Thule newspaper, the *Münchner Beobachter*. A sympathetic superior in the Reichswehr had boosted the operation by printing and distributing leaflets on Munich's thoroughfares. But there was one more ingredient, one that could not be measured empirically: myth. A myth conjured up by the Thule members. They had spread the word that the speaker was 'exceptional'.

And that he was.

There wasn't a doubt in my mind that Pasewalk had profoundly changed Dolferl. Whatever the experience he had undergone, it had made him markedly different from all of the other speakers. Since Pasewalk, he had been convinced that he had been assigned a mission, and the absolute religious certainty of his speeches resonated with the bestower of that mission: God.

'I don't need a secret lodge,' bellowed Dolferl at the members of Thule's inner circle. 'I don't need rituals and secret gatherings to make contact with Providence!' He slapped his flattened hand on his chest. 'Providence and I are one!'

I watched this folly unfold, sitting in a darkened corner of the Sterneckerbräu's backroom. When I had told Francisca that Dolferl was now lecturing for an insignificant right-wing party, my honesty had backfired immediately: Francisca had accused me of wanting to join the party. I reassured her that, as far as I was concerned, it was harmless entertainment, but she rebuked me by saying that though I might find this amusing now, I'd soon be caught up in fighting another civil war. I had called her silly, at which point she had turned and stormed out of the room. Fine, I'd thought; two can play at that game! So I had left, and come to this smoky backroom.

'Herr Hitler,' reprimanded an elder of Thule's inner circle, 'are you aware that without our assistance you wouldn't have been able to hold any of your speeches?'

'Who do you think attracted the hundreds of listeners at the Eberlbräukeller?' Dolferl retorted. 'You?'

'Do you realise,' interjected Alfred Harrer, the party's chairman, 'that without the initiative of the Thule Society, the DAP wouldn't even exist?'

'My dear sir,' answered Dolferl, leaning back in his seat, 'do you realise how Providence works? If an idea is meant to become a reality, one particular person is chosen to be its conveyor. And then Providence chooses those who will assist that conveyor. You have been chosen to provide the means, not to interfere with the message.'

Dolferl's delusion was perfectly compatible with the insanity of the Thule doctrines. I gazed at Dolferl and the committee with my mouth agape. There is no reasoning between lunatics!

'It fascinates and bewilders me, my dear sir,' continued Dolferl, with a sprinkling of sarcasm, 'why you just can't accept what is right in front of you.' He raised an eyebrow at their stunned silence.

Many Thule members had been present at Dolferl's public appearances, but there was strong disagreement between them as to who Dolferl was. The majority believed that Dolferl was 'The Drummer', a John the Baptist figure who would herald the coming of their German Messiah. Some thought he himself was that Messiah, while others insisted that he was a fraud.

'In your last speech, you said that you wanted to give the party a programme,' stated an elderly Thule member.

'Which I will do,' Dolferl said, 'certainly.'

'Well, all we are asking is that we be consulted. I have no doubt that we will approve your programme, but – '

'I don't need your approval!' shouted Dolferl, pounding the table. 'Do you really think I would put myself in a position where I depend on the vagaries of you spiritualists?'

'I will not allow for a party that doesn't conform to the ideas of its founders!' cried Harrer, the chairman.

Dolferl stood up in front of his chair and turned towards Harrer. 'Mr Chairman,' he said, 'can't you see that the founders have become absolutely irrelevant? I am here now!'

'All we want is to be involved in the discussion.'

'Discussion?' Dolferl glared at Harrer, his eyes ablaze like a torch searching for an escaped convict in the darkness. 'If Jesus were to return, do you think he would feel the need to negotiate with the Pope?'

The Thule members were stunned silent.

Harrer cleared his throat. 'Under such circumstances,' he said, 'I cannot continue to be the party chairman.'

Dolferl raised his eyebrows. 'Fine,' he said, 'then step down.' He smiled. 'My requests are these: first, any influence of a side-government or lodge over the party is to be excluded in writing; second, the party is to be renamed the NSDAP – *Nationalsozialistische Deutsche Arbeiter Partei*; third, I will be the one to make the final decision concerning the Thule symbol, the swastika.' He sat down and looked around the table. 'Otherwise, you leave me no choice but to leave the party.'[39]

The assembled Thules frantically deliberated on their predicament.

'Have I made myself clear?' asked Dolferl.

He had: his demands were met. Harrer stepped down. The Thule Society was now relegated to its new role: pay up and shut up.[40]

'Our party is only small. But a lone man once took a stand in Galilee, and today his teachings rule the entire world!' Dolferl stepped back on to the podium. It was February 1920, five months since his first appearance in public, and he was already addressing a crowd of more than two thousand listeners. Dolferl was on the verge of unleashing a lathered crescendo when a man's voice yelled: 'Go back to where you came from!'

There was a collective gasp at the interruption.

'Go back to Austria! Hatemonger!'

Dolferl scanned the crowd for the source of the dissenting voice. Immediately there was a commotion, caused by Dolferl's own private army, who were scattered in groups of seven or eight throughout the hall. They called themselves the Gymnastics and Sports Club. They were

39 See: Appendix 39, The Swastika
40 See: Appendix 37, Thule-DAP-NSDAP

wearing brown shirts and red armlets with a black swastika on a white circular background. They were a squad of thugs, mostly soldiers whom Dolferl knew from the barracks. He called them his 'wolves'.

I twisted around and saw a man who had been seized by brown-sleeved arms close to where I was standing. The man was about thirty, the same age as Dolferl and I. The staccato of kicking boots battering the curled-up man on the floor echoed around the meeting hall. A cap with a gleaming visor flew off the head of a ruffian as howls of agony pierced the din. The thugs knew their attack was sanctioned: Munich's chief of police, a man with Thule connections, would turn a blind eye.

'Stop,' said the leader of the wolfpack finally. The kicking ceased.

'Feeling better now?' The hooligan asked the man gasping on the floor.

'Yes . . . yes . . . yes . . . ' whispered the man, convulsed in pain.

The heavy-set leader raised his hand and blustered: 'Good!' He guffawed. 'Now watch this!' The ruffian then kicked the young man's head with his boot. Blood spewed up across the thug's jaw. He wiped it away with a laugh and then retreated with his Gymnastics and Sports Club into the crowd, leaving the unconscious heckler in a pool of blood.[41]

The crowd were unfazed by the incident as they returned their attention to Dolferl.

'And just as that man from Galilee took a stand, I am taking a stand! As will you! We are all going to take a stand,' shouted Dolferl. 'And together we will break the chains that have shackled us!'

'I don't understand this hold he has over you.' Francisca sat down on the bed and covered her face with her hands. We were both exhausted from our ongoing battle. 'I'm so sick of this,' she said.

I thought for a moment she was going to cry; but she didn't. Instead, her hands quickly fell away from her face and she stared at me. 'And to think that I wanted to tell you today that I . . . ' she stopped. Her fingers massaged her temples as if she could push our arguments from her head.

'What?' I asked. 'What did you want to tell me?'

'I'm pregnant.' She started to cry.

I could barely breathe. 'Francisca!' I exclaimed.

She didn't stop crying.

'That's wonderful! Now I know we'll never be separated!'

41 See: Appendix 40, The SA (Stormtroopers)

She looked up with adamant eyes. 'No!' she roared. 'Precisely the opposite! Now that I know I'm expecting our child, I will leave you if you go on that trip!'

Dolferl had invited me to join him and a few others on an excursion to the mountains. I had spontaneously agreed, knowing full well that it would mean another fight between Francisca and me.

She caught her breath. 'I would never go to a mountain with that madman again. Ever! And if you do, then you're too reckless to be a father.'

'But Francisca,' I said, 'we are going to a cottage. This trip will be entirely different from the one years ago.'

'I don't care. As far as I'm concerned, it's a choice you make now for the future. I don't want my child to grow up in the middle of a mob of' – she looked at me – *animals!*' she spat.

I took her hand but she pulled it away.

'Go.' She fixed her gaze on me. 'But don't expect me to be here when you return.'

I said nothing. I let the silence fester in the hotel room.

I wanted peace.

I had fought a war for peace.

All I wanted was peace.

I tried to catch her hand again but to no avail.

'Go with those pigs! Go to your little friend. Maybe some day in the future you'll realise for yourself what he is, in the final analysis: a sick charlatan.'

'I couldn't agree with you more,' I said.

Her eyebrows furrowed: what? 'Then I don't understand how you can still be his friend.'

Her skin was so soft. She was pregnant.

'You're right, Francisca, you're absolutely right. He's insane. Nobody knows that better than I do.' I looked into her eyes. 'Going on that trip, Francisca, means breaking away from him.'

'How's that?'

'I'll put a formal end to our friendship there,' I said.

'Why can't you tell him that here?'

'Because . . . ' I really couldn't say why. Dolferl and I had been through so much together and I felt I owed him the courtesy of making this parting of ways as civil and as heartfelt as possible. I was also vying for time, because I knew that thinking about severing ties with Dolferl and actually doing it were two entirely different things.

'It's because,' I said to Francisca finally, 'this is the way I plan to do it.'

She looked at me intently. 'This world is a dangerous place, but not because of people like Dolferl. Because of people like you who won't stand up to them.'

'Francisca,' I pleaded, 'when I come back from this trip, we'll start a new life together. We'll be a proper family then.'

I leaned forward to kiss her, but she turned her head away.

'I promise,' I said. 'I promise on the life of our child.'

I leaned forward again, and this time we kissed.

We drove to Berchtesgaden in two limousines. I was in the larger one with Dolferl, Hans Frank, Alfred Rosenberg and Dr Götz. Dietrich Eckart and Rudolf Hess followed in the second car.[42]

'A real Führer,' Dolferl said, 'is chosen to act differently than the leaders of the so-called "western democracies". He will not hide behind the shifting majorities of a parliament. We will do away with that nonsense. We will re-establish true and responsible leadership.'

The limousine sailed along the country road. The steep blue mountain peaks lay distant beyond the bonnet of the car.

Dietrich Eckart had chosen our destination. He had hoped Dolferl would be delighted; like everyone else, he strove to please him. Dietrich had said that the place in the mountains was 'remarkable'. It was close to the Untersberg, the 'wonder mountain' in which, according to an old myth, Kaiser Barbarossa was waiting for his return. Dolferl's appearance was interpreted by some Thule members to mean that the legend was becoming reality.

All participants in the excursion were somehow connected to the Thule Society, and all had prepared for this magical trip in their own idiosyncratic ways. Alfred Rosenberg, a firm believer in numerology, had told me that the fact that our group consisted of seven people was in itself significant. Rudolf Hess, himself no stranger to such thinking, had mentioned that Dolferl was the seventh member of the party's executive board. They all considered this an extremely positive omen, but not Dolferl. He didn't believe in numerology. He believed in only one thing: himself.

Dolferl rolled down the car window and let the air rush in. He inhaled

42 See: Appendix 41, Prominent Thule Members

and smiled: fresh, evergreen, mountain air. Oxygen and the promise of a crisp spring day.

'Strength lies not in the weight of numbers,' Dolferl said, 'but in energy alone. Even the smallest minority can achieve a mighty result if inspired by the most zealous, the most passionate will to act. World history has always been made by minorities – minorities led by an inspired leader.'

Dolferl had changed. There was a world of difference between this man and the one who had lectured in the trenches. I could feel the effect he had on the others. He had now spoken to thousands of people at once, and with every performance he had transformed more into the divine messenger he had envisioned himself to be at Pasewalk. His grand ideas no longer seemed as quixotic as they had before. On the contrary: the facts only confirmed what he had pictured. The membership of his party had exploded, and he was in negotiations to buy Thule's paper, the *Beobachter*.[43]

The limousine shifted gear as it ascended the foothills to the mountain. Through the side window, I glimpsed a grazing deer, so still and peaceful, I could almost count its spots.

'I don't care if they call us evil,' Dolferl continued. 'I actually think it would be quite alarming if the press applauded us. The more they hate us, the more we know that we are on the right track.'

I looked over at Dolferl's profile, and thought how he must relish it when his speeches caused bloody brawls. Dolferl was then at war again, a war that could be won. Easily. What were a few communist hecklers compared to what we had been through in the trenches? Whatever the situation, he was unfazed. Like his father, he happily brandished a horsewhip, and when the situation warranted it, he joined the mêlée enthusiastically. His 'wolves' were inspired by the boldness of their master; they wore the Kaiser's colonial army uniform of brown shirts and brown pants. The Treaty of Versailles had taken the colonies away; the uniforms had become obsolete and had been a bargain. Dolferl loved their decidedly imperial look. It was symbolic of the past, yet indicative of things to come. The limousine hit a pothole and I was jolted back into the discussion.

'Any leader of our hierarchy will have absolute authority downwards, and absolute responsibility upwards. So, ultimately, every leader will be responsible to the Führer. The Führer himself will also have absolute authority downwards and absolute responsibility upwards: to Providence

43 See: Appendix 42, Völkischer Beobachter

and Providence alone.' Dolferl turned to me. 'You have a question?' he asked, seeing my face.

'I was wondering . . . well . . . '

'Yes?' he said, impatiently.

'I was wondering if it isn't possible for everyone to have a connection with Providence. Why does Providence need a Führer to communicate?'

Hans Frank and Dr Götz looked at me as if I had affronted them. But Dolferl seemed indifferent.

'Think of Christ,' he said. 'He had the connection to God, not the disciples; he himself. Exclusively.'

'You're right,' Dr Götz said. 'The Christian religion is based on the Führer principle.'

'Of course it is,' Dolferl said. 'It's in tune with Nature. At least it was . . . in the beginning. Our movement is no different. We're in tune with the laws of nature as well. And therefore the Führer will do whatever it is that must be done. He cannot be bound by human concerns or laws or moral restrictions. He is infallible. Everything he says or does is history. Immediately.'

I leaned back in my seat. Dolferl had the Thule members just where he wanted them. They paid his bills and and opened doors for him to the upper classes. After a few *Abendgesellschaften*, social gatherings, Dolferl had become a society darling. As usual, he was pampered by older women. But unlike the Frau Zakreys of the past, these women were multi-millionaires.

'The Führer cannot make mistakes, like an ordinary person?' asked Hans Frank.

'No.'

'Why not?'

'Because what he does is what Providence wants of him. The Führer knows that and therefore he will never question his own decisions.'

'What ordinary people might consider the Führer's "mistakes" are only mistakes from their limited point of view,' explained Dr Götz. 'They're not mistakes seen from the divine perspective of the Führer.'

'That's correct,' said Dolferl.

'Even if his actions create suffering,' interjected Alfred.

'If a great figure walks,' said Dolferl, 'there will always be some innocent beings along the way who are crushed. That is simply the way of the world. The Führer cannot do anything about this. Even with all the power he has, he cannot change the way things happen.'

I couldn't believe I was listening to the same Dolferl I had known all these years. The absolute authority that permeated his words called Pasewalk to my mind again. What had happened to him there? My head began to spin as he talked about politics and art and proclaimed that to be a genius in politics you had to be an artist. My dizziness persisted until we finally arrived at the cottage, high up in the mountains.[44]

Dr Götz stayed in the shuttered cottage during the day. He complained that the sun was too bright and made him queasy and uncomfortable. He wanted to spend the day smoking cigarettes and leafing through *Natural Family Living* magazines that lay about the cottage. That was fine with me. The sight of Dr Götz in the full strength of the merciless noonday sun would have been frightening. Alfred, Rudolf, Dietrich, Hans, Dolferl and I went hiking. Dolferl was excited because he had never been to the summits that formed the jagged ridge around Berchtesgaden before. The pure mountain air fuelled our climb up the rugged twisting paths. Sheer granite walls and drops surrounded us on all sides. My calves ached as my perspiring body purged itself through rigorous exercise. Steadily we ascended the hillside as Dolferl delivered a continuous monologue, replete with hypothetical plans that envisioned a miraculously bright future for Germany.

'Faith is the mightiest facet our movement will create,' said Dolferl. 'A new faith. A new faith for the dispersed, seeking and straying masses.'

'A faith which will not fail them, or us, in this hour of confusion,' added Hans Frank.

'What we must win is the hearts and minds of the people of Munich,' added Rosenberg.

'Once you have Munich,' said Dietrich Eckart, 'you'll move on to Berlin.'

'And once we have Berlin,' responded Rosenberg, 'we have Europe.'

'And with Europe,' said Dolferl, looking out over the precipice, 'the world!'

'Imagine that world!' said Hans Frank.

'A world as pure as it is up here,' said Dolferl wistfully.

'With no Jews,' qualified Eckart. 'No Jews at all.'

'That would be too beautiful to be real,' said Frank. 'It will never happen.'

'Not necessarily,' replied Dolferl, inhaling the mountain air. He stood

44 See: Appendix 38, Hitler's Ideology

on the stony trail, determined and still. He was all that was righteous and good. He sat down on a rock and looked over the land in silence. The deep blue Königssee lake lay below the mountain ranges, cutting into the horizon. Just beyond those peaks lay Austria, the country and the past that Dolferl and I had left behind.

We all sat down in silence. I closed my eyes. I felt uneasy. It wasn't the air or the altitude. It was the promise I had made on the life of my child, my promise to Francisca. And now I was waiting for the right moment to tell Dolferl about my decision. Sitting between the silent men I tried to gauge their thoughts. What were they thinking? Did they really believe Dolferl was guided by God?

'Let's go,' Dolferl said eventually, getting up.

'Yes, my – what was it?' said Eckart. 'My what? My Führer!' Dietrich's eyes popped open with surprise at his own inspiration. 'My Führer!' he laughed, bowing exaggeratedly.

'Isn't it interesting that you should say that?' Rosenberg said, mysteriously. 'Adolf was talking about the Führer principle in our car on the way from Munich.'

'It only goes to show that we all share a deep connection with . . . our Führer,' said Rudolf Hess.

'I think it suits you, Adolf, I really do,' said Eckart.

'Fine,' said Dolferl, with a jovial smile. 'If you want to call me "Führer", so be it.'

'Spoken like the true Führer,' flattered Frank.

'Well, of course,' replied Dolferl, getting to his feet.

Dolferl was the first to reach a jagged ledge and leaned back against the mountain. Above us the blazing sun seared the earth with its rays. In the distance, indigo summits framed by colossal white clouds proclaimed the majesty of nature and the natural order of things. Dolferl peered down to the shadows of the clouds, shading pockets of the patchwork green lands. The wind picked up as if whispering to let us all know who and what we were witness to. Dolferl looked down at Rudolf, Hans, Dietrich, Alfred and me. He then turned and looked at a cave behind him. He clapped his hands and took two steps back, overwhelmed by a memory: 'I've dreamt this! I remember dreaming this! My God, I have seen all of this!' he exclaimed.

We said nothing.

'Do you remember, Martin, when I told you about my mountain

retreat? Remember I spoke of inviting you for a weekend, a decade in the future?' He stopped. 'Do you remember?'

'I do.'

'Remember I had designed the complex in my mind?'

'I remember.'

'I know! I know!' cried Dolferl, pointing around the bend in the path. 'Beyond that point, there'll be another cave. And I will build it there!'

Dolferl ran up the twisting trail and we followed behind him. Upon turning a corner on the path, in fact Dolferl found himself before a cavern.

'Come now,' said Eckart, 'you must have been here before.'

'Never physically,' said Dolferl, 'but I have been here in my vision!'

All three of us entered the cave. Dripping water and condensation coated the walls.

'Yes, yes,' sang Dolferl.

Yes, yes . . . came the echo.

'This is where I will build it!'

This, the cave echoed, *is where I will build it* . . .

Dolferl's arms were outstretched. We walked further into the pitch darkness.

'Look!' he proclaimed. He turned and looked back out of the mouth of the cave. Deep blue sky framed white-capped mountains and extended towards the white serrated horizon.

'This is where we'll spend our weekends' he said, as we exited the cave together. 'It will happen! It will! As it all will!'

'Yes, my Führer,' said Eckart.

This time Eckart said it differently. No laughter followed; it was solemn. Serious. Almost religious.

Dolferl noted the change in Eckart and nodded his head. Finally you are beginning to grasp who I am.

This was his Sermon on the Mount: the meek do not inherit the earth. Do not love your enemies: hate them. Destroy them. To believe me, you must believe in war, and in the guilt of all Jews. These things are self-evident. Follow your heart and become your hate. A man does not serve two masters. Man should serve only me. By serving me you are serving the Lord. Everything will fall into place. Our nation may be on the ground now, but this is transitory. All that is extraneous will change. All that is noble and pure will stay. And that change will be permanent. Unemployment will fade away. The current despair will fade. All that will cease to be. But all that is natural and true will stay. All that is real and unfading is on that mountain top.

Do you believe me or not?

Dolferl looked around at us. On that mountain top, in that sun, at that moment, I believed him, too.[45]

In the darkened room, Dr Götz, Dolferl, Frank, Eckart, Hess, Rosenberg and I were seated around the table. Dr Götz's pale face hung in the midst of a cloud of his cigarette smoke. Dr Götz said that after reading some magazines and after having smoked about twenty cigarettes, he had taken a nap. He had dreamt that he too was on the mountain top. He dreamt that Dolferl was talking about his visions. In Dr Götz's dream, Dolferl had said that he had dreamt about this mountain top and that he had seen it in his blindness. Dr Götz revealed all of this without a word from any of us. It was as if Dr Götz had been with us.

'So you believe now more than ever before?' enquired Eckart, looking directly at me.

'The party has big plans for Germany,' I said. 'And . . . now I can see that it may really happen.'

'It *will* happen,' said Eckart.

'But it won't be easy,' added Frank.

'We must only believe,' said Rosenberg, in a hoarse, smoky voice.

'With all our hearts,' added Hess.

'Are you willing to sacrifice all for our Führer?' questioned Eckart to my left. I glanced over to my right, where Dolferl was sitting with his eyes closed. He was both present and absent.

'Are you asking me?' I said, trying to evade answering.

'I'm asking all of us,' said Eckart, smoothly. 'Are we ready to sacrifice everything for our Führer?'

'Haven't my actions spoken louder than my words ever could?' said Hess.

'Oh, absolutely,' agreed Eckart, 'but this just makes it official. I'll ask every one of us now. And everyone must answer yes or no.'

I couldn't put it off any longer. I had hoped for a moment where Dolferl and I would be alone, but no such moment had materialised, so I had to speak. Now. I thought of Francisca and our child, and then said in a firm voice: 'Dolferl . . . '

45 See: Appendix 43, Obersalzberg

He opened his eyes, returning from wherever he had been; probably back on that mountain top, deep in the cavern, chiselling out the foundations for his mountain retreat.

'Call me by my real name.' His tone was biting. I had offended him in the worst possible way: I had reminded him of who he really was.

'Excuse me, Adolf,' I said, 'but I must tell you something.'

He didn't answer. He just looked at me in silence.

'It's not easy for me to tell you, but I can no longer be part of this.'

Dolferl's face was unchanged.

'Francisca is expecting. I'm going to be a father. You want me to be a fighter for the movement. I can't be with her and be with you at the same time.'

Dolferl just stared at me mutely.

'I don't know what else to say,' I continued. 'I suppose all that's left is for me to say goodbye.'

I had done it. I was waiting for his outburst. I was waiting for him to jump up and curse me, and accuse me of wasting his time, betraying our friendship, being a coward, having no character and no loyalty. But that didn't happen. Dolferl just sat there and looked at me. He didn't even stare. The others looked on in silence.

Then he spoke.

'Your words are just movements in the air. Waves. They don't matter. What matters is what I'm going to say to you now.' Dolferl leaned forward and pointed his index finger upwards. 'The masses are feminine. Their thoughts and actions are based on emotion. That's why music is of the utmost importance. I want you to compose a hymn for our movement; an anthem that will be played at our next gathering and from then on, whenever the party meets. You know my vision, and the hymn must fulfil it.'

Dolferl was dangling a golden carrot in front of me. We could be an unbeatable combination again: his magic; my music. I could hear the masses singing my song. I could see gold coins raining down from heaven, my life being made manifest just as Dolferl's was becoming true and real. The same might happen to me. My success would surely make Francisca happy. It had to, because it would provide a future for the baby.

Hans Frank leaned back in his seat. He smiled. See? See how the Führer makes things right? See how he provides?

That night, musical motifs circulated inside me as I was falling asleep. There was a beautiful brass melody heralding a triumphant new age in two/four time. My subconscious had started composing 'We are on the March', and the words came from nowhere. 'Oh, beloved Germany, beaten and bleeding, our borders receding, but in our hearts and our minds, we defeat our foes! We are on the march! We are on the march! For a beautiful tomorrow! Wipe away the tears, rejoice and destroy our fears! We are on the march! We are on the march! For a beautiful tomorrow!'

I woke up and searched for a pencil, hastily scribbling down what I had just heard. I hummed it. It was grand and self-assured and full of power. It was perfect. I knew that this was my moment. I knew then that the world was on the verge of opening up and offering itself to me. It wouldn't be long before the movement had spread throughout Germany. And who knows? Maybe the party would one day be everywhere in Europe; maybe even the world! And everyone would know my hymn. Everyone would hum it and sing it. Happily. I was going to make my mark as the creator of the movement's anthem! I was young and this was a once-in-a-lifetime opportunity to become more famous than I could ever have imagined. I thought about Francisca and how our dreams would become reality. How our future would be wonderful. Life had dealt me that hand and I was going to play it the way it was meant to be played.

I jerked awake. It was three in the morning. I was still in that house of visions. The light was on and the paper with my notes was on the bedside table. I was still dressed and I wondered if Dolferl was up. I grabbed the notes and went downstairs. I found Dolferl sitting alone in the living room, reading a biography of Frederick the Great. Without saying a word I went to the piano and sat down. I opened the lid and let my fingers stroll over the keys. Dolferl looked up.

'Can I play you something?' I asked.

He nodded – yes. He put the book on his lap, leaned his head on the rest of the chair and closed his eyes.

'Oh, beloved Germany, beaten-up and bleeding, our borders receding, but in our hearts and our minds, we defeat our foes!' My voice rang out across the living room and my hands pounded the keys in elated two/four time. The piano was slightly off-key, but I didn't care. 'This is where the percussion comes in,' I said, before I continued singing: 'We are on the march! We are on the march!' I ended with a triumphant flourish. My heart pounded in my chest. I lifted my hands away from the keys as I tilted my head and glanced over at Dolferl: what do you think?

He opened his eyes and raised his hands. At first his right hand softly patted his left and then with each successive slap, his pronouncement grew steadily louder and louder. His cheeks rose and a smile formed. 'Nothing less than remarkable!' he proclaimed. 'On my next rally you will play this hymn for our comrades!'

May 1920, Munich

I stood in front of our armoire mirror checking my brown shirt, brown jodhpurs and black riding boots one last time. I turned sideways to my left and focused on the red armband with the black swastika inside the white circle. Perfect. I was ready – ready to appear on the main stage, ready to conduct my anthem in public for the first time. My hands were clammy and my heart raced as I looked at my watch and thought of the thousands who were gathering just now. Dolferl's speech was to be rounded off with a rousing sing-along of 'We are on the March'. It had all been planned with great care. Flyers with the song's lyrics would be distributed amongst the crowd. Even my stealthy exit via the back door of the hotel had been planned in advance to keep Francisca unaware of what I was doing. We hadn't talked about Dolferl after that weekend trip and Francisca didn't know about my anthem. I smiled into the mirror, and my reflection smiled back at me. Tonight was the night I had been waiting for all my life: to think that my music would finally be heard outside my head! An ingenious composition of sounds, arranged to arouse moving patriotic sentiment. My anthem was a testament to my brilliance, not who I *really* was. That's it! I thought. That's how I'm going to explain this to Francisca tomorrow! How could she possibly say 'no' to all this? Suddenly the lock clicked and the door swung open. I turned and there she was.

'Jesus . . . ' gasped Francisca, staring at what I was wearing.

'W . . . what?' I stammered.

'This is a nightmare!' she cried. 'What in God's name are you doing?'

'I . . . I was going to explain everything to you . . . actually . . . my music will be played tonight in front of three thousand people!' I boasted. 'Three thousand people! My hymn is going to be famous.'

'Famous?' she shouted. 'Famous among sick fools! That does it! This is the end!'

'Think of it as a means to an end,' I pleaded, desperately.

'Never!'

'Can't you see I'm doing this for us?'

'What you were going to do for *us* was sever ties with that maniac,' she retorted. 'But – '

'I expected you to be a changed man after your weekend trip,' she bellowed. 'And I was right! Changed for the *worse*!'

'Francisca! This march will finance our new life as husband and wife, as mother and father. I'm the party's official musician! This is the opportunity of a lifetime!'

'You promised me you'd break your ties with him!'

'Yes, I did! But things have changed. And if you don't change with them – '

There was a knock on the door. I went over and cracked the door just wide enough to prevent whoever had knocked from seeing the distraught Francisca. Two men from the Gymnastics and Sports Club were standing outside. They were dressed like me: brown trousers, brown shirts and red armlets with black swastikas.

'I told you to wait outside!' I said, with a trembling voice.

The men shrugged. 'Please come! We're already late.'

I turned to Francisca. 'I must go.'

She looked squarely into my face. 'Frankly, Martin, you have proved a bitter disappointment.'

'Please . . . ' repeated the uniformed man, holding the door for me to follow.

I turned to Francisca. 'I want nothing more than to be a good husband and father.'

I slipped through the door and left.

'Such a thing as this . . . ' – Dolferl opened his arms gesturing towards the masses, 'such a thing as this is not borne from nothing, unless this birth is the result of a grand order . . . ' His impassioned voice rang through the huge hall across the expanse of reverent faces.

I sat on the podium waiting for the speech's crescendo. Dolferl was dressed as a 'man of the people': blue suit, white-collar shirt and subdued grey tie. His eyes gazed out over the heads below him while he performed his aria of retribution. On that stage he was more himself than he'd ever been before. On that stage, all of his hope and all of his hatred merged and he became his own work of art, his own ferocious art form. The audience stood entranced by the man in the spotlight.

Dolferl prepared to unleash his big finale: 'And this order was not given to us by some earthly superior. . . ' He was interrupted by a wave of ear-splitting cheers and applause. He tugged on his collar, loosening it as if to clear the way for the crowning glory of his address. And when the noise in the hall finally subsided he concluded: 'This order was not given to us by some earthly superior, this order was given to us by the God who created our people!' The audience erupted in rabid howls until Dolferl raised his arms, opened his palms and silenced the crowd. The noise subsided to isolated sprinklings of applause, and then to silence.

This was my cue.

I stood up in front of the band and looked down at my black polished boots to focus myself for a moment. Then I raised my arms. Behind me in the audience a voice screamed something I couldn't make out. The crowd hushed the voice with shouts of '*Ruhe!*' '*Zur Hölle mit ihr!*' '*Ruhe verdammt!*'

Dolferl stepped back from the dais, and nodded towards me: proceed. An opera soprano stepped up beside me. I elevated my arms to direct the musicians and the singer just as a cry for help sounded out from behind. For a moment I was disorientated. But then Dolferl impatiently gestured for me to begin. I swung my arms and the band set in. The soprano vibrated as the words 'Oh, beloved Germany' bellowed out of her.

It was happening! I was in flight. My art was victorious! If only Francisca could see how wrong she had been and how right I was.

'We are on the march!' the crowd whispered. The musicians played stronger as the opera singer put her hand to her ear and sang 'We are on the march!' Her other arm beckoned the people to answer. 'We are on the march!' they replied, a little louder. 'Again!' cried the soprano. 'We are on the march!' the crowd chanted.

I was on the march as well. Everything I had worked for in my life was beginning to blossom. I had truly arrived as an artist. The enthusiasm of strangers merging with my music! My melody becoming their collective consciousness! Thousands of people hypnotised by my art! Part of me inside all of them! This was the culminating moment of my life! This was how Dolferl had predicted it would be in that small, filthy room in Vienna. I was so unbearably happy I wanted to cry.

I looked to see the response of the men on the assigned chairs along the back of the podium. To my surprise, there were none of the euphoric looks I had expected. With grim faces, Hans Frank and Alfred Rosenberg were staring to somewhere behind me. I turned and, in the midst of the people, saw a woman being pummelled by brown-sleeved arms. Her red hair caught the footlights and I knew instantly who it was.

'We are on the march!' the crowd rumbled. 'We are on the march!'

For a moment Francisca's fragile body surfaced and then, just as suddenly, disappeared into the dark sea of people. More and more Brown Shirts ran to the spot.

'We are on the march!' hollered the crowd, answering the soprano. 'We are on the march for a beautiful tomorrow!'

I ran to the edge of the podium, peered out and saw the commotion swirl around Francisca. Brown–sleeved arms punched without pausing for even a moment. Brown-sleeved arms with red armlets like mine. I ran to the side of the stage, down the stairs and into the crowd. On the podium above me the singer blared out my song. 'We are on the march! We are on the march!'

I fought a path through the black labyrinth of torsos, arms and heads. I dodged opened mouths and mesmerised eyes and forged ahead into the unyielding swarm of bodies keeping me from Francisca.

The band blared the song's coda and the hall quaked with strident defiance. 'We are on the march!'

I battled closer to where Francisca was, but all I could see were foaming beer steins and gaping mouths howling and singing 'We are on the march!' I elbowed and pushed my way to where I could faintly hear the dull, fleshy thuds of a body being kicked by boots. Black polished boots like mine.

And there she was. Francisca lay on the floor soaked in blood, her lifeless eyes staring into the void.[46]

46 See: Appendix 44, The Psychotic Redeemer

Epilogue

The train compartment smelled of hot chocolate. The little boy sitting on the bench opposite me had been reprimanded sternly for dropping his cup by his irate grandmother. A spilled cup of chocolate was a terrible waste in these continuing hard times. I sat in my seat looking out at the platform bustling with travellers in the dusk. There weren't so many wearing rags as before; now most people were wearing clothes that were humble, but clean.

Perhaps things were getting better. Better for them – but not for me. The wrinkled man across from me complained of the candied smell and pulled down the window. Fresh evening air seeped into the car with wistful promise. It was spring again, and supposedly with it came the green hope of good things to come. I didn't see how. I was going home. Home to Linz. The train's whistle sounded and people hurried to their seats. A young couple entered, nodding and smiling before they sat down. Their pleasantries made no difference to me. I was lost, so lost. The train jerked backward and then forward as it slowly began to roll. The light overhead outlined my features in the reflection in the window. My face was projected on to Munich's moving walls and buildings as the train tore into the night, and into an uncertain future.

PART FOUR

APPENDICES

APPENDIX 1

Hitler's Opera

August Kubizek, Hitler's roommate in Vienna, notes in his memoirs, *Hitler mein Jugendfreund* (1955), that Hitler worked simultaneously on several plays and novels while they lived together. One day, Kubizek mentioned that he had learned in the Conservatory that the draft for a musical drama entitled *Wieland der Schmied* (Wieland the Smith) had been found in Richard Wagner's bequest. The young Hitler immediately set about researching the Wieland saga and came across the gory legend of King Nidur, who raped his daughter and killed his sons, later using their skulls as bowls.

Hitler was inspired to turn the legend of Nidur into an opera, which he would compose, while Kubizek would transcribe the composition to paper. Hitler tried to come up with a prelude to the opera and Kubizek noted down what his friend played on the piano. But Hitler did not just 'compose'; he also recorded the action in verse, devised the set and designed the costumes. For his opera, Hitler created three Valkyries who could float through the air, which worried the more practically-minded Kubizek. Hitler also experimented with the archaic musical instruments that had existed during the time of King Nidur. As Kubizek recorded in his memoirs forty years later, the 'overall impression of an event whipped forward by wild, unleashed passions' was still fresh in his mind. Kubizek states that Hitler worked as fervently on his opera as if 'an impatient opera director had set him a deadline that was far too tight'. Finding pen and ink too slow to work with, he used charcoal. He stayed awake through the night, ate nothing and barely drank. But whenever Kubizek reproduced what Hitler had 'composed', his friend was not happy with it. For many days and nights they worked on the prelude alone, but Hitler's aspirations were simply beyond his abilities.

Even though the results were pitiful, Kubizek marvelled at his friend's absolute commitment to 'the beauty, the nobility, the grandeur of the art'. Kubizek could not remember what became of their work, presuming that another obsession must have consumed Hitler, and he had probably abandoned it.

APPENDIX 2

Hitler and Books

On his time in Vienna, Hitler writes in *Mein Kampf*: 'I read a lot and I read thoroughly. All the time I had left besides work I spent studying.'[1] As much of what Hitler claimed in *Mein Kampf* has emerged as fabricated or simply untrue, this remark is disregarded by many biographers, or else relegated to the realm of legend; after all, Hitler was more famed for burning books than reading them. The general belief is that Hitler gained his insights primarily from newspapers and magazines. However, eyewitness statements and the results of recent historical research paint a different picture. 'There is no reason to doubt that when he was young, Hitler devoted himself to serious reading. World literature, non-fiction, the classics of philosophy.'[2]

Hitler did not just read books – he appears to have been utterly obsessed with them. According to August Kubizek, his roommate in Vienna, reading was a 'deadly serious business'[3] for Hitler. In Kubizek's words: 'That's the way it was with my friend, books, always more books. I can't imagine Adolf without books. At home he piled up books all around him. He always had to carry around the book he was reading at the time. Even when he wasn't reading at the moment, it had to be in his presence. When he went out, he always had at least one book under his arm. Sometimes taking books along became a problem. Then he would even refrain from going outside. Books were his everything.'[4] Kubizek also mentions the huge impression made by the library of the (Jewish) family Jehoda on Hitler. He says that Hitler visited the *Hofbibliothek* (court library) in Vienna so often that he 'asked him in all seriousness whether he planned to read every book in the library, for which Hitler shouted at me'.[5]

In Munich from 1912 to 1913, Hitler also seems to have read an extraordinary amount. His landlady, Frau Popp, was asked whether Hitler had ever brought women up to his room. She answered that she had never seen Hitler with a woman, though always with books. Her son also confirmed that Hitler continuously borrowed books from libraries. Hitler's roommate in Munich, Rudolf Häusler, complained that Hitler always read until three or four in the morning.[6] According to Kubizek, Hitler mainly studied textbooks and philosophical works. Works of fiction interested him less, although he did read classics such as Dante's *Divine Comedy*, Goethe's *Faust*, and *William Tell*. Hitler was particularly fond of Karl May's Wild West stories for boys. Albert Speer reports in his memoirs that during the Second World War, Hitler exhorted his generals to read Karl May to improve their weak powers of imagination. Before his execution in Nuremberg, Hans Frank, the General Governor in occupied Poland, recalled that Hitler mentioned having the works of Homer and Arthur Schopenhauer with him during the First World War.[7] Ernst Hanfstengel, a former supporter and eventual opponent of Hitler, had a close relationship with him after the First World War. He states: 'Hitler was neither uneducated nor socially awkward [...] My library came to experience his voracious appetite for books.'[8] When Thule member Dr Friedrich Krohn allowed Hitler to use his library, Hitler borrowed over 100 books from him between 1919 and 1921.[9] When Hitler ended up in prison in Landsberg as the result of his attempted coup in 1923, he used the time to read. 'Landsberg,' said Hitler to Hans Frank, 'was my college at the State's expense.' He is purported to have read every book he could lay his hands on there.[10]

After 1920, Hitler began to compile his own library, which grew rapidly within a few years.[11] In his 1925 tax declaration, Hitler claimed to have no property other than a writing desk and two cupboards containing books; in 1930, his spending on books had already reached 1,692 Deutschmarks – his largest deduction after expenditures on travel and transport.[12] In October 1934, Hitler took out fire insurance with *Gladbacher Feuerversicherung* for his six-bedroom apartment on Prinzregentenplatz in Munich. In this policy, Hitler estimated the value of his 6,000-tome library at 150,000 Deutschmarks.[13] Christa Schroeder, Hitler's long-time secretary, recalled: 'This passion for reading books and acquiring their wide-ranging contents let him expand his knowledge in almost all fields of literature and science. I was always amazed with his accuracy when giving a geographical description of an area or talking about art history or even discussing complicated technical subjects.'[14] As Chancellor of the Reich, Hitler not only had a library in Munich, but also another in the Imperial Chancery in Berlin. There, he collected books given to him on special occasions such as Christmas, his birthday and so on, and books he acquired himself. K. W. Krause, Hitler's valet, reported that 'Hitler possessed a library of several thousand volumes '[...] He acquired his knowledge from extensive reading [...] If a German book was published, it was presented to [Hitler] by me [the valet]. I had signed a contract with a large bookseller in Berlin to be supplied with every new book immediately [...] Hitler either returned the books presented to him the next morning, or had them incorporated into his library'[15]

Hitler owned a third library in the Berghof in Berchtesgaden. Photographs of his office on the Obersalzberg show multiple glazed bookcases.[16] Journalists who visited Hitler in the Berghof also reported seeing walls of books in his private chambers, though the number of books in the Berghof could not have exceeded a few hundred. That was not how it had been intended, however. Hitler's plans for the extension of the Berghof included a library of gigantic proportions, incorporating shelves for 61,000 volumes.[17]

Most of Hitler's books were looted during the last days of the war. The last 3,000 volumes were seized by the US Army after the war, and many of these also went missing. In January 1952, around 1,200 of the remaining copies were deposited at the Library of Congress in Washington. Another eighty books from Hitler's private library are part of the 'Rare Book Collection' in the John Hay Library at Brown University on Rhode Island, many of which carry the *Führer*'s bookplate: an eagle, a swastika, and oak branches between the words '*Ex Libris*' and 'Adolf Hitler'.[18]

APPENDIX 3

Arthur Schopenhauer

Since Hitler always strove to give the impression that his musings developed entirely from his own original thoughts, he did not disclose the intellectual sources that influenced him. Of the philosophers he studied, he seems to have read the works of Schopenhauer (1788–1860) most thoroughly. This contention is supported by observations from several contemporary witnesses, including Hans Frank, who remembered that Hitler had been carrying Arthur Schopenhauer's *Die Welt als Wille und Vorstellung* (The World as Will and Representation) with him during the First World War.[19] Hitler's secretary, Christa Schroeder, asserted that her boss could quote a full page of Schopenhauer from memory.[20] Hitler's interest in Schopenhauer is not surprising, as Schopenhauer was also the most important source of philosophical inspiration for Richard Wagner, whom Hitler worshipped passionately. In a letter to Franz Liszt in December 1854, Wagner describes Schopenhauer's philosophy as a *Himmelsgeschenk* (gift from God.)[21]

Schopenhauer's philosophy postulates that reality is divided in two, composed, simultaneously, of the animal and chaotic *Drang zum Leben – dem Willen* (impulse to live – the will) and the mental image with which the individual perceives reality, *Vorstellung* (representation). Humans are tied, both to *Wille*, which works through them, and to their *Vorstellung*, and are thus trapped in an existence full of suffering. A temporary alleviation from suffering is delivered through art, and music in particular.

For the vast majority of human beings, however, final salvation is achieved only through death. A chosen few alone are allowed to experience salvation within their lifetime: *grosse Einzelne* – mighty individuals or mystics – who are able to recognise their true selves. In becoming aware of his desires and transcending them, the mystic is no longer bound to them, just as he is no longer bound to representation. As the mystic transcends will and representation, he achieves Nirvana. (The artist reaches just one level beneath this.) To the *Vorstellung* (i.e. the thinking in concepts or ideas) Nirvana appears as *Nichts* (nothingness). The mystic, however, understands it as *Alles* (everything), an abundance which leads to the realisation that everything is connected to everything else.[22] Through the understanding of connectedness, the mystic knows that torturer and tortured, perpetrator and victim are opposite experiences within one and the same universal consciousness. This knowledge of the interrelatedness of all human beings leads the mystic to treat others with limitless compassion.

Compassion, according to Schopenhauer, is an emotion, of which all humans are capable. In experiencing compassion, each human being has an ethical compass to guide their conduct in relation to others. For Schopenhauer, this disposes of the need for moral rules and laws. In its final consequence, Schopenhauer's philosophy is concerned with overcoming suffering: those who have recognised that every individual is but a meaningless shadow of the true nature of the world lose interest in their own cravings and longings, which belong in the domain of the shadows. Racism and anti-Semitism clearly contradict Schopenhauer's understanding of the oneness of being. These ideas have no place in his philosophy. In an attempt to imply that Schopenhauer was an anti-Semite Hitler repeatedly quoted the philosopher, in *Mein Kampf* and elsewhere, as stating that 'the Jew' was 'the Master of lies'.[23] However philosophical research has so far been unable to provide evidence of such a statement in Schopenhauer's works.[24]

As a whole, Schopenhauer's philosophy has nothing in common with Hitler's ideology. But Hitler may have, as he did with other revered philosophers, borrowed certain parts of Schopenhauer's philosophy and assimilated them into his world view. It is possible that Hitler adopted the rejection of monotheistic religions from Schopenhauer, as well as the valuing of an ascetic lifestyle; Schopenhauer's attitude to death; his ideas about the function of art, in particular of music; the acknowledgement of the 'animal' in human nature . . . Hitler may have adopted some or all of these ideas. However, he ignored many of Schopenhauer's other important teachings, most importantly his ethic of compassion.

APPENDIX 4

Photographic Memory

Other than the 'suggestive power of persuasion' that Hitler suddenly began to exhibit after 1918, he did not have any special talents or traits that distinguished him, with one important exception: his phenomenal memory. This extraordinary capacity for recall had already been noticed by his friend Kubizek when they lived together in Vienna: 'The information he acquired in this way [by reading books] remained carefully filed away and registered in his memory. One search – and it was available again, and as accurately as if he had just read it.'[25] Henry Picker, who recorded *Hitlers Tischgespräche* (Hitler's Table Talks) 1974, in the Führer's headquarters, confirmed Kubizek's account: 'One trait of Hitler that always amazed everyone – even those not in his thrall – was his stupendous memory, which was able to retain even insignificant information precisely and recorded everything he had ever laid eyes on.'

Hitler's secretary, Christa Schroeder, was also aware of this trait in her boss: 'His memory was always in perfect order, a truly photographic memory which he knew to use to maximum benefit.'[26] Elsewhere, she says: 'I very often wondered how a human brain could retain so many things and facts.'[27] As Hitler had been interested in theatre architecture as a young man, he knew astonishing details about the composition of significant theatres. On visiting the Paris Opera following the French campaign in 1940, he commented that there was a box missing. The surprised head of management explained that the box in question had been removed during conversion works many years before.[28]

As Hitler read vast quantities of material extremely quickly, he amassed a huge volume of factual information over time, which his memory allowed him to access instantly. Naturally, this astonishing volume of knowledge made quite an impression on those around him.[29] According to his secretary, Christa Schroeder, Hitler reinforced the impression further by always making it appear as if 'everything he said was the result of his own contemplations, his own critical thought'.[30] She recalled that when she began to work for Hitler, he had presented a 'downright philosophical discourse[...] To my astonishment, I realised that this was simply the repetition of a page from Schopenhauer which I had read myself not long before.'[31] Hitler's memory also aided him in his speeches, most notably in the many exact figures which he quoted to impress his audience. Max Domarus, the editor of Hitler's speeches between 1932 and 1945, referred to this as Hitler's 'obsession with numbers'.[32]

The fact that Hitler used his remarkable memory consciously to impress those around him was documented by Manfred Koch-Hillebrecht in his book *Homo Hitler* (Munich 1999, p. 93 et seq.). The results of Koch-Hillebrecht's study are summarised below without further references. In a speech made to students in Allgäu in 1937, Hitler cited from memory the populations and sizes of the English empire (34 million km2 and 447 million people) and Russia (23 million km2 and 150 to 175 million people). The figures for France, the US, China, Belgium, Holland, Spain, Portugal, Brazil, Japan and Italy then followed. The Chief of Staff of the army, Halder, recalled a meeting in February 1941 at which Hitler quoted, again from memory, the annual Russian production of tanks for every year since the 1920s. Albert Speer, Hitler's architect and Minister of Armaments, also described the same phenomenon. He recorded that Hitler knew 'all weapons and types of munitions with their calibres, barrel lengths and firing ranges', as well as 'the stocks on-hand of the most important pieces of weaponry' and 'their monthly production'. Hitler's naval aide-de-camp, Karl-Jesko von Puttkammer, was also surprised by the detailed knowledge of his superior. 'He knew almost every ship of all important naval forces in the world and had exact details of their size, speed, armament and armour in his head. He also knew the power of the weapons, including the artillery, their range, penetrative force etc.'

Luftwaffe chief Göring confirmed von Puttkammer's assertion while a prisoner in Nuremberg: 'He knew the armament, armour, speed and draught of almost all important battleships in the world.' Those in the Führer's headquarters were well aware of the incredible power of Hitler's memory. Officers who had to report to him made very sure that the information they presented matched earlier reports exactly. Hitler immediately noticed any discrepancies. On 4 October 1941, Hitler received the new red armament catalogue of the Ordnance Office and used it as bedtime reading. The next morning, the army aide-de-camp Major Engel was amazed: 'Incredible that the Führer actually learned every single figure in that awful book full of numbers and could visualise them perfectly right before his eyes – even as far as the production of pistol ammunition.' Koch-Hillebrecht comes to the conclusion that Hitler was a 'savant', i.e. that he was able to memorise everything he observed as visual images. Savants can view a page, for example, from a telephone book for a few seconds, 'photograph' it internally and then read all of the numbers from the image stored in their memory. This ability occurs more frequently in children than adults, and is more common in men than in women. Autistics also often exhibit this savant-like ability.[33]

APPENDIX 5

Darwin–Schopenhauer

In *Young Hitler*, the Hitler character states that he regrets that Schopenhauer (1788–1860) knew nothing of Darwin's (1809–1882) findings. In fact, Hitler seems to have been of the opinion that Schopenhauer, had he been aware of Darwin, would have come to a different definition of the concept of *Wille* (the will – the force which moves everything). Hitler often used the concept of the will in a sense reminiscent of Schopenhauer.

The idea of the will appears along these lines, for example, in the Nazi propaganda film *Triumph of the Will*. The correlation with Schopenhauer is, however, purely superficial. The will of which Hitler speaks has a clear direction, as does the notion of evolution, which Charles Darwin described in his work *On the Origin of Species* (1859).[34] Darwin's theory is based on the realisation that the best adapted members of a species survive, so that they have a chance to propagate, which in turn leads to the developmental advancement of the species. By relating Schopenhauer's idea of the will to evolution, Hitler seems to have developed Schopenhauer further, with the help of Darwin – as if he had found a solution to the paradox of the inexplicable and inconceivable *Wille* as understood by Schopenhauer.

It is, however, exactly this understanding of the will as motivated by an objective that Schopenhauer rejected. According to his definition, the will is without direction, blind, chaotic and beyond any human conception. Consequently there can be no further development. Darwin's teaching of evolution is an idea born in that part of reality that Schopenhauer denotes as *Vorstellung* (representation). The *Kampf ums Dasein* (the struggle for existence), the *Überleben des Stärkeren* (the survival of the fittest) – for Schopenhauer, these things exist in order to be overcome. Anyone who, like Hitler, battles for power is acting in opposition to that which Schopenhauer sees as progress or advancement. In his battle, he remains shackled to *die Welt als Wille und Vorstellung*, and is unable to transcend it: for Schopenhauer, Hitler remains an existential failure.[35]

APPENDIX 6

Richard Wagner

'A fire was ignited from whose glowing heat the sword would be fashioned to restore freedom to the German *Siegfried* and bring back life to the German nation.'[36] What Hitler is exalting here in *Mein Kampf*, as though it were a Wagnerian tale of Germanic heroism, is in fact a rather profane affair: he is describing his proclamation of the NSDAP's party programme in the Hofbräuhaus in Munich. The heroic music of Richard Wagner (1813–1883) is said to have inspired Hitler as he wrote *Mein Kampf* during his incarceration in Landsberg. The prison authority allowed him to have a gramophone and Wagner records in his cell.

Hitler's reverence for Wagner is not just evident in *Mein Kampf*; the bombastic productions of the Nuremberg party congresses were also reminiscent of Richard Wagner's operas, so that there can be little doubt that the 'Master', as Hitler himself referred to him, had a great influence on the imagination of this civil servant's son from Braunau. In *Mein Kampf*, Wagner is lauded as a 'great reformer' and 'great fighter'. 'In one stroke, I was captivated,' wrote Hitler of the impact the opera *Lohengrin* had on him when he first saw it, aged twelve. 'From the moment Richard Wagner came into his life, he was obsessed by the genius of that man,' wrote Hitler's early roommate from Vienna, August Kubizek.[37]

The operatic world of Wagner is full of dramatics and displays of Germanic power. It is a world of heroes who die a hero's death, where the brave warrior is rewarded with victory by the gods, where treachery is punished by death, and valiant self-sacrifice earns the hero passage to Valhalla. In this Wagnerian world, Hitler felt at home. Good and evil, pure and impure confront each other here in eternal, irreconcilable enmity; gold becomes a curse, and blood seals the word of the truly pure who have attained eternal life. It is a world where parliamentarianism and majority rule have no place and where the people's leaders are obligated only to their calling. They are chosen ones, who rule with godlike powers and perform heroic deeds. The long-past, mythical epochs evoked by Wagner in his operas stirred Hitler's imagination and shaped his self-image. Hans Frank reported that Hitler once told him: 'I'm building my religion from *Parsifal* [. . .] One can only serve God in the guise of the hero.'[38]

August Kubizek describes the effect of Wagner's operas on his friend as 'like a rapture, an ecstasy [...] Listening to Wagner was not akin to what we would call "attending the theatre" for him, but the possibility of transporting himself to that extraordinary state he fell into on hearing Richard Wagner's music, that forgetting of oneself, that drifting off into a mystical dreamland which he needed to bear the immense tensions of his eruptive nature.'[39] Hitler's enthusiasm for Richard Wagner was not unusual. At the turn of the century, Wagner was considered the most important composer of his time. However, Hitler's incorporation of Wagner's operas into a racist world view was atypical of his contemporaries. Whether Richard Wagner actually wrote his operas from this perspective will never be definitively concluded, and the topic fuels a fervent academic debate to this day.

In addition to operas, Wagner also wrote compositions, essays and diaries. According to Kubizek, Hitler was familiar with all of these. 'He adopted the personality of Richard Wagner, yes, instilled him so completely in himself as if he had become part of his own being [. . . He read] his writings, letters, diaries, his self-portrayal, his confessions. He penetrated the life of this man more and more deeply.'[40] Motifs occur throughout Wagner's writings that can also be found in Hitler's worldview: an enthusiasm for revolution in which the boundaries between art, religion and politics are blurred; the desire for a society of nobles and equals without class differences; a fanatical rejection of materialism; hatred for decadent Western civilisation; a yearning for nature and the notion that the world must be destroyed for it to be saved.

In some respects, Wagner was probably also a personal role model for Hitler. Whether Hitler's vegetarianism was inspired by Wagner is disputed; but like Hitler, Wagner considered himself a genius who challenged the existing order and had no understanding of civic work for the purpose of earning a living. Wagner's longing for 'eternal fame' was shared by Hitler, and the determination with which Wagner pursued his philosophy without succumbing to intimidation in the form of persecution and rejection also served as an example to Hitler, according to Kubizek. Moreover, Wagner was a professed anti-Semite. He wrote the composition '*Das Judenthum in der Musik*' (Judaism in Music) 1850, to 'clarify the spontaneous abhorrence that the personality and nature of the Jews has for us, to vindicate this instinctive aversion'. At the end of the composition, Wagner states that if he wants to become a 'person', 'the Jew must 'stop being a Jew'; that is, give up his Jewish traditions, his culture and religion. Wagner's *Regenerationsschriften* (regeneration texts), which appeared shortly before his death, also include anti-Semitic passages. And in his letters, Wagner repeatedly mentions the Jews and compares them to the 'plague', 'rats', 'mice', 'warts', 'a swarm of flies' and 'trichinas'.[41] The spitefulness of Richard Wagner's anti-Semitism was no different to the Jew-baiting that prevailed in Vienna at the time the young Hitler lived there. As Hitler's anti-Semitism erupted during the last stage of the First World War, the anti-Semitic opinions of the 'Master' certainly confirmed his feelings. However, it is hardly likely that Hitler would not have become an anti-Semite had Wagner felt differently about this issue, and so it seems somewhat simplistic to blame Hitler's anti-Semitism on that of his hero.

Hitler's life appears similar to a sequence of scenes that could have originated from the mind of Richard Wagner. One recurring motif which plays a pivotal role in Wagner's operas is the impossibility of experiencing the 'true love' in this world. For Wagner, the 'great love' is only possible through renunciation or death. As if enacting Wagner's philosophy, Hitler married Eva Braun only to meet death with her shortly thereafter. While the Third Reich was collapsing all around him in a violent, bloody *Götterdämmerung*, Hitler insisted on perfect staging to the very end: the marriage service, which was held at night in his bunker in Berlin, was to be performed with all bureaucratic formalities. Messengers were sent out to find a licensed registrar in the embattled, burning city in the middle of the night. It took a while, but eventually a district head official in a *Volkssturm* uniform stood before Hitler and his bride. By a grotesque coincidence, the man's name was Wagner.[42]

APPENDIX 7

Gustav Mahler

From 1897 to 1907, Gustav Mahler held the most important post in Europe's operatic scene as the first bandmaster and director of the Vienna Court Opera. Birgitte Hamann examined the young Hitler's attitude towards the Jewish opera director in detail in her book Hitler's Vienna *(Hitlers Wien*, 1996). The results of this research are summarised below. Gustav Mahler conducted the unabridged operas of Wagner, and, together with the stage designer Alfred Roller, uncompromisingly transformed the Vienna Opera into a 'temple of music and theatre', although he was not without his critics, who vilified him for his

'Jewishness', despite his conversion to Catholicism. When this racial hostility was further compounded by personal tensions with singers and musicians, as well as criticism of his financial conduct and his frequent absences, Mahler finally quit his post, exhausted. 'I'm leaving because I can't deal with that rabble any more,' Mahler wrote when he left Vienna.[43]

When Hitler came to Vienna in 1908, Gustav Mahler had already resigned. However, even after Mahler's departure, no fewer than twenty-one productions by Mahler/Roller remained on the Vienna Court Opera programme, and so the heated discussions about Mahler's productions continued unabated. Two factions stood in irreconcilable opposition to one another: one demanded that Wagner be conducted unabridged as Mahler and Roller had staged it, while the other, including the anti-Semites, called for massive edits and conceptual changes. The disagreements even came to blows: in June 1908, anti-Semites and Mahler opponents brawled with Mahler supporters in the gallery of the Court Opera. Hitler's Viennese roommate, August Kubizek, reports that Hitler clearly supported Mahler. According to Kubizek, he 'greatly admired' the Jewish opera director.[44] Even in the memoirs Kubizek wrote on behalf of the NSDAP, he wrote of Mahler: ' . . . Who may have been a Jew, but was still highly regarded by Adolf Hitler because Gustav Mahler had taken the musical dramas of Richard Wagner and produced an utterly brilliant version of these for that time'.[45] Those who, like the young Hitler, spoke up for Mahler, were viewed by the anti-Semitic camp as sympathisers with the 'hook-nosed Mahlerians' and 'Hebrews', and were reviled as 'Jewish lackeys'. This may be seen as further evidence that, while living in Vienna, Hitler's anti-Semitism was either negligible or non-existent.[46]

APPENDIX 8

Anti-Semitism in Vienna

As with other ethnic and religious minorities, Jews were excluded, subjugated and persecuted in Europe for centuries. 'Religious anti-Semites' accused the Jews of having nailed the Son of God to the cross, and the devil was often depicted with Jewish facial features. Less widespread was the 'spiritual anti-Semitism' asserted by mystics and supporters of Gnosis. This was based on the notion that the god of the Jews had created the material world, but the world of matter was a prison of light in Gnostic thinking. Therefore the creator of 'this world' was in fact the devil, so spiritual anti-Semites attacked Jews as devil-worshippers.

Whatever the religious pretext on which denunciation of the Jews was based, the trigger for their persecution and suppression was usually economic in nature. At times of financial crisis, people sought to lay blame for the prevailing despair on the weakest members of society – the minorities – and in Europe this usually meant the Jews. At other times of tension – during periods of revolution and war – violent clashes often arose in which Jews were the victims. In quieter eras, the employment options of the 'diabolical Jews' were often limited to work as merchants and moneylenders, provoking the resentment of non-Jewish traders and causing Jews to be decried as profiteers and cut-throats.

In the eighteenth century, the restrictions placed on the Jewish population of Europe were gradually lifted, and towards the middle of the nineteenth century they became equal citizens in Germany and Austria. Those among them who were willing to give up Jewish traditions and ways of life became fully integrated into civil society and made important contributions to culture and the sciences, finding their political homeland with the social democrats and in the liberal movement, which championed the protection of minorities. The assimilation process encouraged understanding on a human level, and the centuries-old prejudices were slowly forgotten. The dissemination of anti-Semitism in German-speaking countries was limited to a handful of outsiders – while financial times remained prosperous. Towards the end of the nineteenth century, however, the 'Gründer Depression' struck, eclipsing all previous economic crises. Primarily small- and medium-sized merchants were forced to close, and entire classes of society were affected by the rapid deterioration of the economy. In the search for 'culprits', the old anti-Jewish prejudices were revived. As the spear-head of liberalism, the Jews were also blamed for debasement of morals by religious and conservative circles. Everything politically and culturally distasteful to the conservatives was alleged to be of Jewish origin: socialism, communism, rationalism, and all liberal Western traditions in general. What differentiated the Jews from the Germans was no longer a matter of religion; people now believed they could discern a fundamental difference in *being*. The national character of Germans was 'noble' – i.e. patriotic, idealistic and altruistic– while the national character of Jews was 'corrupt' – i.e. unpatriotic, materialistic and entirely self-serving. Doctors, lawyers and businessmen suddenly saw themselves surrounded by Jewish competitors, and in nationalist (*völkisch*) circles, a new form of anti-Semitism emerged: 'racial anti-Semitism'.

'Racial anti-Semites', which later came to include Hitler, claimed that the low morals of the Jews were the result of the poor quality of their racial characteristics: their blood, as it were. The great threat from Jews was therefore that they debased the racial purity of the peoples with whom they mixed. Racial anti-Semites such as Wilhelm Marr (1819–1904), Eugen Dühring (1833–1921), Theodor Fritsch (1853–1933) and Houston Stewart Chamberlain (1855–1927) warned, in their writings, of the danger presented by Jewish blood to the Aryan master race. Racial anti-Semitism allowed old prejudices to re-emerge in a contemporary, seemingly 'scientific' guise. Racial anti-Semitism was also more radical than its religious and spiritual counterparts, as according to its theory the act of christening was no longer sufficient for salvation. To protect the blood of one's own race from contamination by Jewish blood, Jews had to be ghettoised or expelled from the country – measures which were fervently debated in *völkisch* circles at the end of the nineteenth century.

During the years that the young Hitler spent in Vienna, the 'Jewish question' was discussed more vehemently there than anywhere else in German-speaking Europe. This was because there were many more Jews living in Vienna than in any other German city. In the mid-nineteenth century, Vienna had only around 6,000 Jewish inhabitants; by 1910, this number had risen to 175,000. The city had been inundated with Eastern European Jews in particular, who stood out from the locals: unlike the long-established, assimilated Viennese Jews, the Eastern European Jews wore sidelocks, black hats and kaftans; and spoke Yiddish, Russian or Polish. Jewish harassment was commonplace in Vienna. 'In this city at the turn of the century, radical anti-Semites demanded punishment of sexual relations between Jews and non-Jews as sodomy, and the monitoring of Jews during Easter to prevent ritual child murder.'[47] The slogan 'Don't buy from Jews' spread quickly, to the disadvantage of Jewish businesses and stores as well as Jewish pedlars. The pan-German *Annual for German Women and Girls* stated: 'Every German who buys his Christmas presents from Jews dishonours himself and disgraces his own traditions.'[48]

To counter the anti-Semitic fervour, the Jewish community in Vienna attempted to rapidly assimilate their tattered Eastern counterparts. They supported them with financial aid, inconspicuous clothing and German lessons for the children. But the generosity of Viennese Jews merely attracted even more impoverished Jewish immigrants from the east.[49]

Although the long-established 'German Jews' strove to distinguish themselves from 'Eastern Jews', and there was even talk of 'anti-Semitic Judaism', this was meaningless to racial anti-Semites. They considered all Jews to be dangerous, regardless of how socially adapted and 'conscious of German culture' they were.

The religious anti-Semites, such as the conservative Viennese mayor Lueger, also turned public opinion against the Jews. 'Down with the terrorism of Judaism', the mayor's party demanded, while the *Deutsche Volksblatt* wrote: 'Who leads social democracy? The Jews Adler and Ellenbogen! Who helps them in public? The entire Jewish press! And who provides the money? Jewish high finance!'[50] At an election meeting, Mayor Lueger is quoted alluding to pogroms in Russia, saying: 'We in Vienna are anti-Semites, but we are not cut out for murder and manslaughter. But if the Jews should threaten our Fatherland, neither shall we know any pity.'[51] Rumours were also circulating of a global Jewish conspiracy while Hitler lived in Vienna. According to the regional newspaper *Brigittenauer Bezirksnachrichten*, in 1912, 300 international businesspeople 'of the Jewish tribe' had convened. These '300 kings of our time' were alleged to be the true rulers of the world, who were reducing the old monarchs to mere figureheads. The German nation was being destroyed and 'denationalised'. The formation of an 'international banking alliance based in Washington' was supposedly planned, and would soon 'publicly dictate its world laws'. High finance would 'take up the succession of the empires and kingdoms, and with a much greater authority, as their authority will extend not over a country, but the globe.' The article ends with the words: 'The Jew turns the wheel of history with a sneer.'[52]

As the 'Jewish problem' was massively debated in public by the various anti-Semitic factions, everyone who lived in Vienna at the turn of the century was familiar with the arguments of the anti-Semites, regardless of where each stood individually on the issue. In the *völkisch* camp, with which the young Hitler felt an affinity, the anti-Semites were represented in particularly large numbers. Hitler must have known the precise details of the arguments of Viennese anti-Semites, even though he himself may not have been manifestly anti-Semitic at that time.[53]

APPENDIX 9

Hitler and Jews in Vienna

There is not a single anti-Semitic remark in the novel during Hitler's period in Vienna, despite the infamous hatred of Jews that consumed him later in life. His will, which he composed at 4 a.m. on 29 April 1945 in his bunker in Berlin, shortly before committing suicide, ends with an instruction to maintain 'ruthless resistance against the world poisoner of all nations, international Judaism'. Millions of Jews paid for Hitler's racist insanity with their lives; yet, apparently, this man was not an anti-Semite during his time in Vienna. Could this be true? As unbelievable as this may seem, and as difficult as it is to reconcile with our understanding of Hitler, it really does seem to have been the case. All of the findings of the historical research into his life in Vienna certainly support this contention.[54]

Hitler also appears to have had no discernible anti-Semitic leanings during his time in Linz. While there, he felt an unprofessed love for a girl whose surname he must have known. It occurred to Franz Jetzinger in 1956 'that Stefanie's surname sounded typically Jewish [Isak]; she wrote to me: "Because of my name, I was often taken for a Jew". Adolf could not possibly have known that she was not, but he still wanted to marry her; his hatred of Jews cannot have been very intense at that time.'[55] None of the contemporary witnesses from Vienna considered reliable by historical researchers could recall any anti-Jewish comments from Hitler. They all reported that he had not shared the prevailing anti-Semitic mood in the city. In fact, he is said to have admired the Jews for their resistance to persecution, praised Heine's lyrics and the music of Mendelssohn and Offenbach, and taken the view that the Jews were the first civilised nation, having abandoned polytheism in favour of a belief in one god. He also reportedly held Christians rather than Jews responsible for profiteering, and regarded the common anti-Semitic allegation of ritual Jewish killings as nonsense.[56]

While residing at the men's hostel, Hitler was strongly critical of 'the Jesuits' and 'the Reds' in discussions, but never mentioned the Jews, according to contemporary witness Karl Honisch.[57] Neither could Rudolf Häusler, the men's hostel resident with whom Hitler went to Munich in 1913, remember Hitler expressing any anti-Semitic statements when later asked about this by his daughter.[58] Another contradiction of the adamant anti-Semitism for which Hitler was later known is the fact that he presented Dr Bloch, the Jewish doctor who treated his mother, with one of his paintings while he was in Vienna. Hitler also wrote Dr Bloch several postcards from Vienna and expressed his deep gratitude to him.[59] In exile in America, Bloch later said that he believed Hitler harboured no anti-Semitic feelings at that time. Hitler's fervently positive opinion of the Jewish conductor Gustav Mahler is discussed separately in Appendix 7. His conspicuously large number of Jewish friends and Jewish business partners during his time in the men's hostel are detailed in Appendix 18. Reports from contemporary Viennese witnesses on Hitler's attitudes towards the Jews also concur with statements from Hitler's war comrades. Evidently he also did not appear to be anti-Semitic as a soldier during the First World War.[60]

Hitler's own portrayal of his feelings towards Jews during his time in Vienna differs considerably from the findings of historians.[61] In *Mein Kampf*, Hitler claims that while in Vienna, he changed 'from a weak cosmopolitan into a fanatical anti-Semite'.[62] However, *Mein Kampf* is not an autobiography in the normal sense. The book was written purely for propaganda purposes. In it, Hitler declares his political views and illustrates them with a convenient account of his life story. By merging his life and his ideology into one, he sought to provide evidence that it was his destiny to become Führer. Had he acknowledged that he only became an anti-Semite towards the end of the First World War (the general opinion held among historical researchers), his leadership abilities could have been called into question. Anti-Semitism spread throughout the nationalist (*völkisch*) movement in Germany towards the end of the First World War and became politically 'fashionable' in certain circles. For the image of a Führer steadfastly leading his people, it was much more convenient for Hitler to have been ahead of the crowd as a young man in this important aspect of his world view. However, in *Mein Kampf* Hitler admitted to 'worryingly depressive thoughts' and an 'inner spiritual struggle' relating to the 'Jewish question'. He may have admitted this because he was only too aware of the truth behind his supposedly 'unshakeable stance' towards the 'international poisoner of nations' in his Vienna days. By admitting an initially ambivalent attitude himself, he neutralised in advance any unflattering revelations from contemporary witnesses who could contradict his claims.

But how could Hitler not have been anti-Semitic in Vienna? This is particularly remarkable in view of the fact that Jewish harassment was rife at the time, and anti-Semitism was not preached only in the *völkisch* community.[63] The two politicians admired by the young Hitler, Schönerer and Lueger, were both professed anti-Semites, and anti-Semitism often figured prominently in publications by the different popular race theorists.[64] Also, the many hateful anti-Semitic passages in Richard Wagner's writings which Hitler had studied intensively in Vienna cannot be disregarded. And the *völkisch* seer Guido von List, so crucial to Hitler's career later on, was no friend of the Jews either. In his biography of Hitler (1998), Ian Kershaw suggests two possible hypotheses for Hitler's stance. Firstly, his anti-Semitism could have been so slight originally that it had been unremarkable to contemporary witnesses against a background of general Jewish discrimination. Alternatively, Hitler may have deliberately concealed his anti-Semitism because he needed the help of various Jewish residents of the men's hostel to sell his paintings. One further possibility is raised in this novel, suggesting that Hitler studied the anti-Semitic arguments of the *völkisch* circles thoroughly in Vienna, but felt at the time that the struggle against the 'Slavic Peril' took precedence over the conflict with the Jews. This was the position of the Viennese Deutschradikale Party of Karl Hermann Wolf.[65] Whatever the reason for Hitler's restraint in Vienna and during the Great War, there was no evidence of it in Munich in 1919. From the very start, Hitler's speeches were characterised by a fanatical anti-Semitism.

APPENDIX 10
Friedrich Nietzsche

It can be assumed that Hitler, being an avid reader, was familiar with the writings of Nietzsche, at least in passing, although there is no indication that he was a particular admirer of the philosopher. This is understandable given that Hitler valued clear, systematic structure, which is absent from the writings of Nietzsche, who did not leave behind a structured philosophical body of work, but rather poetic aphorisms whose interpretation depends greatly on the prior knowledge of the reader. There are certainly terms in Nietzsche's writings that must have appealed to Hitler, such as the concept of 'Jewish–Christian slave morality'. But through the filter of Hitler's world view, Nietzsche's intended meaning is often twisted and inverted.

Nietzsche's philosophy stands in stark contrast to Hitler's *Weltanschauung*. Not only does Nietzsche's anti-rationalism contradict Hitler's rational and pseudo-rational analysis of the world, Nietzsche also repeatedly indicated that he viewed himself as a European, a 'world citizen', and not a German. Nietzsche had nothing in common with the xenophobia of the German Nationalists. Consequently, in 1884, he called the first verse of the German national anthem, which contains the line '*Deutschland über alles*' ('Germany above all'), the 'most idiotic slogan in the world'.[66] Neither could the individualist Nietzsche muster any enthusiasm for a 'strong state'. Quite the opposite: he felt the state had robbed the individual of the last remnants of his freedom.

Philosophical research has long proven that Nietzsche was no anti-Semite, and in fact despised anti-Semites deeply. Not only did Nietzsche repeatedly characterise himself as an 'anti-anti-Semite', he also demanded explicit confirmation that those around him felt the same. 'He parted ways with his anti-Semitic publisher, and his sister's marriage to the anti-Semite Förster led to an open family feud [. . .] In a letter to Overbeck, he credits Kaiser Wilhelm highly for ridding himself of the anti-Semitic advisers to the crown on his accession to the throne.'[67] 'The Jews have spirit,' Nietzsche said.[68] And elsewhere, he writes: Unpleasant, even dangerous traits are found in every nation, everyman; it is cruel to demand that the Jew should make an exception [. . .] Nevertheless, I would like to know how much we, on balance, must forgive a nation that, not without the culpability of us all, has had the most pitiful history of all peoples, and to whom we owe the most noble man (Christ), the purest sage (Spinoza), the most powerful book and the most effective moral law in the world.'[69] And even as he was on the verge of losing his sanity, Nietzsche wrote with a trembling hand: 'I want all anti-Semites to be shot.'[70]

The fact that the general public still believes that Nietzsche helped greatly to pave the way for National Socialism is due in large part to his coining of the phrase *Übermensch* ('super-man').[71] Both the Nazis and their opponents equated the term *Übermensch* with the Aryan racial ideal of National Socialism. However, this interpretation has nothing in common with Nietzsche's intended meaning of the word. Nietzsche's *Übermensch* describes someone who has overcome 'this world', who is no longer imprisoned in it, and who is therefore 'beyond good and evil' – someone of 'formidable goodness', says Nietzsche in *Also sprach Zarathustra*. Nietzsche's *Übermensch* is most accurately compared to Buddha, and there's evidence to suggest that Nietzsche saw Buddhism as one potential way of becoming an *Übermensch*, a state of existence that could only be attained through love.

Everything in Nietzsche's philosophy indicates that he could not have meant the *Übermensch* to represent a biologically bred superior being, as propounded by the racist philosophers Gobienau or Chamberlain. In fact, Nietzsche's writings contain various confirmations that he categorically rejected racism and everything relating to it. 'Shun anybody involved in the race-swindle', was one of his countless notes on the subject.[72] In addition to the *Übermensch* concept, there are a number of other terms in Nietzsche's writings, such as the 'will to power', that can easily be misunderstood as fascist without the appropriate explanation. Nietzsche's sister, Elisabeth Förster-Nietzsche, also caused great damage to her brother's reputation. As the administrator of her brother's estate, she contributed greatly to Nietzsche's philosophy being reinterpreted through the lens of National Socialism in the Third Reich. To adapt Nietzsche's texts to the Nazi ideology, Elisabeth Förster-Nietzsche altered some of her brother's writings and even went as far as forgery.[73]

APPENDIX 11
Hans Goldzier

During the time Hitler lived in Vienna, the self-taught, independent Viennese scholar Hans Goldzier (pseudonym Th. Newest) published eight small volumes entitled *Einige Weltprobleme* (Some World Problems, 1908). The records of Otto Wagener indicate that Hitler studied Goldzier's writings in detail.[74] The Jewish-sounding name 'Goldzier', printed beside the pseudonym on the title page of *Einige Weltprobleme*, does not seem to have troubled Hitler. This perhaps confirms his indifferent attitude to Judaism during the Vienna years.

In his writings, Goldzier espoused eccentric pseudo-scientific theories and idiosyncratic philosophical opinions. Amongst others, he described Newton's laws of gravity as an 'error'; he alleged that the moon is made of iron; that the cradle of humanity was located at today's North Pole; and that it is damaging to kiss children, as this deprives them of vital energy. Volume 6 of *Weltprobleme* contains Goldzier's design for a new morality: 'The individual or societal way of life, which preserves and improves the species, is good. Everything else is bad.'[75] Goldzier asserted that, should it prevail, this new morality, based on 'natural laws', would result in a fundamental change in the lives of peoples. 'With this kind of morality, which has its foundations in natural law and forces the necessary recognition due to its self-evident nature, an unprecedented metamorphosis in the lives of all civilised races could occur.'[76]

It is possible that Hitler took on Goldzier's idea of a morality grounded in biology, or at least found impetus for his own thoughts. In conversation with Wagener, Hitler explained the necessity to 'remove' 'worthless life' (people with disabilities) using Goldzier's theory. However, 'biological morality' was not the only of Goldzier's theories which Hitler found 'impressive', underscoring his sympathy for *Wahrheitsforscher* (researchers of truth) as opposed to *Katheder Wissenschaft* (academic science). Hitler also subsequently developed an enthusiasm for Hans Hörbiger's *Welteislehre* (World Ice Theory), in which Hörbiger explained the formation of the planets as the result of the penetration of an ancient sun of massive proportions by a planet of ice. The *Hohlwelttheorie* (Hollow Earth Theory), which suggests that the earth is hollow and that the universe exists in the interior of this 'earth' rather than the outside, is also said to have interested Hitler.

After his failures in school and rejection by the Vienna Art Academy, Hitler saw himself as an unappreciated genius and remained open to the ideas of outsiders and eccentrics for the rest of his life.[77] 'If I find a scientist who is searching for an alternative path, I will support him in opposing the exact sciences, which in any case reject all that is new', said Hitler in 1942.[78]

APPENDIX 12

Racism in 1900

When Hitler lived in Vienna racist theories were popular in Viennese middle-class circles. This was due to the high proportion of immigrants: Czechs, Slovaks, Poles, Ruthenians, Slovenians, Serbs, Croats, Romanians and Hungarians comprised more than fifty per cent of the city's population.[79] However, there is evidence that Hitler did not develop his racist mindset in Vienna, but in fact had already exhibited a similar outlook in Linz, where he seems to have been influenced by his nationalistic history teacher, Dr Leopold Pötsch: 'The "defensive battle" against the advance of the Slavic peoples' had been a 'central theme' amongst students, according to a former schoolmate.[80]

The racist attitude of the Viennese was not a fringe mentality: it was shared by many leading scientists, physicians, professors and social thinkers in the Western Hemisphere. While Hitler was pursuing his 'private studies' in Vienna, ideas about a reorganisation of society along racial lines were being incorporated into the thinking of the middle classes, not only in Austria and Germany, but all over Europe and in the US. The militant guardians of public opinion proposed the 'fight for existence in the life of the nation' as both necessary and healing. Contempt for the 'lesser' races was combined with the notion that the ultimate goal was the overall improvement of the human race. Racial theories, which took as their objective the improvement of the racial quality of the nation, increasingly became the object of scientific research. For many, the idea of a racial superiority which purported to have its foundation in science and biology had more persuasive power than the humanitarian proposal of individual human rights. With the help of 'science', the demand for equal social and political opportunities was negated and racist authors proclaimed that the most important task for mankind was to take control of the higher development of the species.

The authoritative mastermind of these racial theories was the French diplomat and historian Arthur de Gobineau (1816–1882). In his racial hierarchy, the white (Aryan) race was supreme. The 'progressive mixing of races' was seen as the main reason for 'cultural degeneration'. Like other racists who came after him, Gobineau was neither especially nor exclusively anti-Semitic. However, he did count the Semites amongst the inferior races. The psychologist Francis Galton (1822–1911), a half-cousin of Darwin, combined Gobineau's ideas with Darwin's insights into evolution and claimed that the suppression or eradication of 'weaker' races by 'stronger' ones was in the service of mankind. Galton, often regarded as the father of Social Darwinism, devised plans to improve the British race through selective breeding and called for the painless 'elimination' of people with disabilities and terminal illnesses. According to Galton, the reproduction of those displaying particularly 'positive' racial characteristics was to be encouraged. In German-speaking countries, the most influential racial theorist was the English biologist Houston Stewart Chamberlain (1855–1927). In his book *The Foundations of the Nineteenth Century* in 1899, Chamberlain advocated racial breeding in humans. 'Do the so-called "noble" animal breeds arise out of promiscuity and chance? No, they arise through sexual selection and through the strict upholding of a breed's purity [...] Crossing obliterates character.'[81]

Chamberlain's work popularised the theory of Social Darwinism in wide circles both in Germany and Austria and gave anti-Semitism a pseudoscientific legitimacy. The German Kaiser Wilhelm II was so taken by Chamberlain's book that he made it compulsory reading for school-teachers. By 1934, twenty-four editions of the book had been published.[82] But although racist ideas were advocated by world-renowned scientists like Ernst Haeckel (who influenced Sigmund Freud), such theories initially had no practical consequences in Europe.[83] This was different in the US. State measures to exterminate Native Americans were welcomed enthusiastically by European racists, as was discrimination against people of African origin. Woodrow Wilson, Teddy Roosevelt and Franklin D. Roosevelt were just a few of the many prominent members of the eugenics movement, which considered the blond-haired, blue-eyed Nordic type to be the pinnacle of the human development. The goal of the eugenicists was the selective breeding of North Americans.[84] The plan was to identify so-called 'defective' family trees and disable the reproductive capacity of those deemed weak and inferior – the 'unfit'.

Eugenics research, race theory and race science became part of the curriculum of universities such as Stanford, Yale, Harvard and Princeton. Racist studies were financed by the Carnegie Institution, the Rockefeller Foundation, the Harriman railroad fortune and other corporate philanthropies and led to a national policy of forced sterilisation and segregation, as well as marriage restrictions, enacted in twenty-seven US states. Ultimately, eugenics practitioners forcibly sterilised some 60,000 Americans, barred marriage for thousands, and segregated thousands in 'colonies'. In 1911 a Carnegie-supported 'Preliminary Report of the Committee of the Eugenic Section of the American Breeder's Association' explored eighteen solutions on 'the Best Practical Means for Cutting Off the Defective Germ-Plasm in the Human Population'. Point eight was euthanasia.[85] From the perspective of the European Social Darwinists, the US appeared progressive and future-oriented. Hitler writes appreciatively in *Mein Kampf*: 'The Teuton of the American continent, who has remained racially clean and pure, has risen to rule it.'[86]

APPENDIX 13

Hitler and Sex

At the turn of the century, young Viennese men usually had their first sexual experiences with prostitutes. Whether this was also true of the young Hitler is not known. His friend and roommate August Kubizek tells of a trip the two took to Siebensterngasse one night, an area frequented by prostitutes. According to Kubizek, the visit was Hitler's idea. Hitler reportedly observed the prostitutes and clients with interest, and then damned the 'harlots' arts of seduction'. Kubizek also mentions a couple of nights when Hitler did not return home, but otherwise he knew of nothing that might suggest that his friend had paid a visit to a prostitute; nor does Kubizek make any mention of Hitler having a girlfriend. At any rate, it would have been difficult to receive a 'female acquaintance' in their lodgings due to the generally strict rules for subtenants in that era.

Young Hitler's quixotic love for Stefanie is Kubizek's only indication of any interest his friend had in the opposite sex. During his time in the Viennese men's hostel, Hitler evidently had no female relationships. No contemporary witnesses recall seeing Hitler in female company. Paying for prostitutes was an impossibility during that time due to his dire financial situation. When Hitler moved to Munich, his finances were still scant, as a result of which he also would have been unable to pay for sex there. Neither does Hitler appear to have had any girlfriends in Munich or during the war. According to witnesses, he did not accompany his comrades when they went in search of women in the occupied towns and cities. There is also no evidence of Hitler having female acquaintances during the revolutionary upheaval in Munich.

It generally seemed to have been mature women who felt drawn to Hitler. Frau Zakreys, his landlady in Vienna, was as affectionate to the young Hitler as Frau Popp, from whom Hitler rented a room in Munich before the First World War. As a young party leader, Hitler received a lot of backing from older, maternal women. Primarily the wives of influential businessmen, they supported the aspiring politician wherever they could. Hitler's Viennese *Schmäh*, saccharine Austrian charm, came in very helpful. However, these relationships with older women were definitely non-sexual in nature. It is entirely possible that Hitler was still a virgin when he became friends with Geli Raubal, 'Mizzi' Reiter and Eva Braun in the 1920s. These women were all considerably younger than him – Hitler was thirty-seven and 'Mizzi' Reiter just sixteen when they met for the first time in Berchtesgaden. His niece, Geli Raubal, who shared his Munich apartment with him, was nineteen years his junior, and twenty-three years separated him and Eva Braun. Hitler shared this preference for women who were either much younger or much older than him with his father, whose first wife Anna had been fourteen years his senior, while Klara, Hitler's mother, was twenty-three years younger. 'There is nothing more beautiful than cultivating a young thing,' Hitler said later in the Führer's headquarters. 'A girl of eighteen, twenty is as malleable as wax. It must be possible for a man to leave his mark on every girl. That is all women want.'[87] Hitler's appreciation of a certain type of 'femininity' is substantiated by another statement he made on a separate occasion: 'I can sit beside young women who leave me completely cold, who I don't even sense, who even irritate me in fact [. . .] And then with a girl like little Hofmann or Geli, around them I become happy and jovial, and if I listen to their silly banter for an hour – or if they just sit near me – then all tiredness and apathy disappears.'[88]

Historians disagree as to whether there was sexual contact between Hitler and these 'girls'. Even his closest confidants had differing opinions about this. Ernst 'Puzzi' Hanfstaengel later said that Hitler was such an egomaniac that he would have been unable to stir up even the 'scrap of consideration' for another person that was required during sex. Hitler's architect, Albert Speer, felt differently. He said that Hitler had indeed used Eva Braun to 'regulate his hormone balance'.[89] Hitler's long-time secretary, Christa Schroeder, also wondered about the sex life of her boss: 'Hitler loved the company of beautiful women without a doubt, and was inspired by them. He needed eroticism, but not sex [. . .]. Hitler loved to have beautiful women around him, but a certain shyness, even fear, of making a fool of himself held him back from having affairs with women [...]. If you want to call it abnormal, this shyness that held him back from affairs with beautiful women for fear of illness or fear of compromising himself, then he was abnormal.[90]

'Christa Schroeder believed that Hitler did not even have sex with Eva Braun. She suspected that this relationship was just a 'cover', to feign a non-existent 'sexual masculinity' to those around him.[91] But if this 'sexual masculinity' was not real, what was? Was Hitler a sexual deviant, as some authors suspect? They report of manic masturbatory behaviour, excretory perversions and sadomasochism. However, these theories are pure speculation, as is the suspicion that Hitler was homosexual. After 1920, he was under very close surveillance by his political enemies, and a sexual relationship with a man would almost certainly have been uncovered – although latent homosexuality cannot be ruled out. After all, Hitler surrounded himself with tall, blond, fit aides-de-camp, and spent most of his life in male company.[92] Several researchers have wondered whether Hitler might have been impotent. Suggested causes include a syphilis infection, an allegedly missing testicle or a penis injury during his youth. However, there is no convincing proof supporting these allegations. From all that we do know about Hitler, what does seem certain is that his libido must have been rather underdeveloped. This was an advantage in his political career that should not be underestimated. Dietrich Eckart, eventual mentor of Hitler, is reputed to have said of the long-awaited Führer: 'He must be a bachelor. Then we get the women.'[93]

Hitler's publicly displayed abstinence was unlikely to have been any great sacrifice considering his suspected low sex drive. Perhaps the ecstasy of the masses gave him the satisfaction he lacked in the sexual arena. Perhaps, then, his oft-repeated declaration that he could not marry because he was 'married to Germany' was meant more literally than was generally assumed. In his book *Hitlers Liste* (Hitler's List, 2003), Anton Joachimsthaler reconstructs the Führer's friendships in detail, using gift lists and other source material. This book is probably the most detailed investigation of Hitler's sex life to date. In summary, Joachimsthaler quotes the words of Ulrich Schlie: 'In the years of the German dictatorship, the private life of the Führer was hermetically shielded from the prying eyes of his ordinary citizens. Yet again, the principle proved true that the less you know, the greater the curiosity and the more virulent the speculation. When the curtain rose slowly over the private affairs of Adolf Hitler after the war, the disappointment was great. The spectacle failed to materialise. The secret was that there was no secret.'[94]

APPENDIX 14

Hitler's Disappearance

For narrative reasons, the loss of contact between Hitler and his friend is described differently in the novel to how it actually occurred. Since the novel otherwise depicts the events of Hitler's life in correct chronological order, the actual sequence of events is briefly outlined below.

August Kubizek, Hitler's friend and roommate in the Stumpergasse in Vienna, travelled to Linz in July 1908 to complete his military service, after which he intended to return to their shared apartment in Vienna. While Kubizek was in Linz, the friends remained in contact through letters and postcards. Hitler's last letter to Kubizek is dated 17 August 1908; several postcards also arrived after this date. None of Hitler's messages hinted that he had decided to move out of their shared room. On 20 November 1908, Kubizek returned to Vienna. To his surprise, the landlady Frau Zakreys explained to him that Hitler had moved out without leaving any message. Hitler had disappeared without a trace for no known reason, and it took several weeks for August Kubizek to come to terms with the sudden loss of his roommate. After that Kubizek only encountered his long-lost friend once more, on 12 March 1938 in Linz, when the Reichskanzler (chancellor) Adolf Hitler was on a state visit to the recently annexed Austria.[95]

After the young Hitler had left Stumpergasse, he rented a room for several months, and then lived on the streets and in homeless shelters. In February 1910 he moved to the men's hostel in Meldemannstraße, where, the Jewish Joseph Neumann took Kubizek's place as friend and confidant. When Hitler left the hostel in May 1913, he was accompanied by Rudolf Häusler, with whom he moved into a shared room in Munich. During the First World War he made friends with Ernst Schmidt, who accompanied him after the war for his first two months in Munich. In order to tell Hitler's story from a consistent perspective, Hitler's four friends have been amalgamated into one character in the novel.

APPENDIX 15

The Hitler Family

Hitler's ancestors on both his father's and mother's sides came from the Waldviertel, a poor, backward region of the Austro-Hungarian Empire. Hitler's forebears were from Döllersheim and Strones. His father, Alois, was born in Strones, as was his paternal grandmother, Maria Anna Schicklgruber, making it an area of great significance in the Hitler family history.

Following the annexation of Austria, the post office of the city of Döllersheim included the proud inscription 'Home Town of the Führer' on its postmarks. To residents' surprise, however, the postmark was promptly banned by the authorities. A surprise also awaited the inhabitants of Strones, where Hitler's father and grandmother had been born: a few months after the *Anschluss*, they were evicted from their homes. The same fate befell the residents of Klein-Motten, where Hitler's grandmother had died. And the inhabitants of Döllersheim, who had already renamed their church square Adolf Hitler Platz, were also forced to evacuate their town. A total of 2,002 people were resettled and 419 buildings completely levelled, because the Führer had decided to turn Strones, Döllersheim and the surrounding area into Western Europe's largest troop drill ground. The army took the evacuated towns under fire, and artillery grenades reduced the birthplaces of Hitler's ancestors to rubble. The graveyard where Hitler's grandmother was buried disappeared beneath the debris of the Döllersheim church.[96]

Some researchers have assumed that Hitler's actions were an expression of his hatred for his father. Contemporary witnesses reported that Alois Hitler, a customs official, had been a 'brutal, choleric type'. He was characterised as a 'petulant know-all and miser', and seemed to have had few friends, if any. At night, Alois Hitler often came home drunk and beat either his wife or one of the children. He reportedly beat his son Adolf with a hippopotamus-hide whip, similar to the one later carried by the young party leader. According to Adolf's sister Paula: 'He got his beating every night.'[97] In *Mein Kampf*, Hitler describes his father as a 'dutiful state official', and mentions tensions because his father had insisted he become a civil servant, while the young Hitler was determined to succeed as an artist. As Chancellor of the Reich, Hitler told his inner circle: 'I did not love my father, and feared him all the more. He was irascible and quick to strike a blow.'[98]

There is no doubt that Adolf Hitler had sufficient reason to harbour negative feelings towards his father. However, there could be one other reason for the destruction of his ancestors' home towns: his father's uncertain parentage. When Hitler's father, Alois, was born in Strones in 1837, his mother, Maria Anna Schicklgruber, refused to divulge the name of the child's father, and Alois was given his mother's name. Then, at the age of thirty-nine, Alois Schicklgruber changed his name to 'Hitler'. Before a notary, Alois revealed the man whom his mother had married five years after his birth to be his father: the travelling miller's assistant Johann Georg Hiedler. By the time Alois changed his name, his mother had been dead for twenty-nine years, and the alleged father had been dead for nineteen years. Why Alois suddenly decided to change his name and why the notary recorded 'Hitler' and not 'Hiedler', remains a mystery. The questionable lineage of his father must have been very awkward for the racial purist Adolf Hitler. After all, he and his party placed the utmost importance on clear evidence of lineage. Only those who could prove their descent from 'Aryan parents and grandparents' beyond doubt were allowed to become civil servants in the Third Reich. In fact, Hitler's family tree made the headlines both at home and abroad from 1932 onwards. *Hitler's Jewishness Confirmed by Notary*, proclaimed the *Wiener Extrablatt* in July 1933, while the Austrian *Abendblatt* reported: *Sensational Tracks of the Jew Hitler in Vienna*.[99] Hitler's opponents gleefully quoted Jewish-sounding names in his family tree, and after the war it was said of Hitler's father that he was not the son of Hiedler, but of a Jewish merchant named Frankenberger. It was even rumoured that Hitler's grandfather had been a member of the Rothschild family. All of these rumours were investigated thoroughly by historical researchers and have been refuted.

However, Hitler's uncertainty about his lineage could explain the destruction of Strones and its environs, and also the fact that after the Austrian *Anschluss*, the German Secret Police immediately searched for all documents relating to Hitler's ancestors and family. But it should not be forgotten that Hitler had always tried to eliminate the traces of his past, not just the details of his parentage.[100] Hitler biographer Joachim Fest came to the conclusion that 'to veil and transfigure his true person was one of the main endeavours of his life. Few other figures in history have stylised themselves so forcibly and concealed their true selves with such seemingly pedantic consistency.'[101] Some inhabitants of Hitler's ancestral birthplace came to experience his efforts to transfigure his true self in full. Those who happened to share the same surname as him were forced to call themselves 'Hietler'. The official Oberdonau directory of 1942 lists just one Hitler, namely 'Adolf Hitler, Chancellor of the Reich'. Five other names had been changed to Hietler.[102]

When Adolf Hitler was born in Braunau am Inn in 1889 as the fourth child of Klara Hitler, he was the first of Klara's children to survive, the three others having died shortly after birth. One reason for the poor health of her offspring (another brother of Adolf's born after him also died) may have been the close relationship between Klara and Alois: the much younger Klara was the half-niece of her husband. Seven years after the birth of Adolf, his sister Paula was born. Alois had brought two children from a previous marriage to the family: Alois and Angela. The Hitlers moved several times, and their family life was far from harmonious. Adolf's half-brother, Alois, was just fourteen years old when he left home forever following a terrible fight with his father. After that, Adolf had to endure even more of his father's beatings. Whereas the young Adolf was abused by Alois, he was spoiled by his mother. Klara Hitler could not refuse her only surviving son anything he wanted, and as a result Adolf was besotted with his mother. This did not change after he became Chancellor of the Reich. His butler, Karl Krause, recalled: 'He had a photo of his mother on his nightstand, it was on his writing desk, in the library, and in the study.'[103]

When Alois Hitler died in 1903, the family lived in Linz. Adolf was fourteen years old, and for the first time something akin to peace reigned in the family. But soon Adolf's academic performance deteriorated and his mother was eventually forced to take him out of school. In 1907 Klara Hitler underwent an operation for breast cancer. Contemporary witnesses confirm that Adolf was particularly self-sacrificing in taking care of his mother. When she died later that same year, three days before Christmas, the young Hitler was overcome with profound anguish. The Jewish physician Dr Bloch, who treated Hitler's mother until her death, recalled later in exile in America that 'he had never in his career seen anyone as filled with grief as Adolf Hitler'.[104] While Hitler went to Vienna, fought in the First World War and then started his political career, his sister Paula lived reclusively, first in Linz, then Vienna. After 1908, she heard nothing from her brother. The aspiring party leader then contacted his sister in 1921, after which they maintained sporadic communication by letter and telephone. They met in 1936 at the Winter Olympics in Garmisch. At this encounter, Hitler arranged for his sister to take the name 'Wolf' in order not to draw any unnecessary attention to herself. He arranged for her to receive a modest pension of 250 Deutschmarks a month initially, and later 500 Deutschmarks. Every Christmas, she received 3,000 Deutschmarks from him. Contact between the two remained limited to a few letters and telephone calls.

In 1945, Paula was taken to Berchtesgaden by the SS at Hitler's instruction, where she was later arrested and detained by US troops. She was soon released, as she had not been a party member nor otherwise politically active, and lived in Berchtesgaden from then on, supported by state welfare. In interviews, she indicated that she did not attribute any personal responsibility to her brother, as he 'was merely assigned a role on the chessboard of the Lord'.[105] In 1957, Paula, who was again using the name Hitler, initiated a legal challenge to the Bavarian State over her brother's inheritance. She did not live to see the end of the legal dispute, dying on 1 June 1960 in Berchtesgaden, where she was laid to rest.

Hitler's half-sister Angela married while Adolf lived in Vienna, and was then named Raubal. Her daughter, Geli, lived with Hitler in Munich at the end of the 1920s. Opinions differ as to the nature of the relationship between the two. Some researchers suspect that Hitler was sexually involved with his much younger half-niece, just like his father, whose half-niece was Hitler's mother. When Geli committed suicide in 1931, Hitler moved her mother into his residence in Berchtesgaden, Wachenfeld House. Angela managed the household for him until she was forced to leave after an argument with Hitler's mistress Eva Braun in 1936. Angela Raubal died in Dresden in 1949. The only Hitler whose ancestral line still exists today is Adolf's half-brother, Alois. After leaving the family home at fourteen, he worked in gastronomy in various countries, including England and Ireland, where he married the Irishwoman Bridget Dowling in 1910. During the Nazi era he ran a wine bar in Berlin. Word quickly spread of the possibility of drinking with the brother of the ascetic Führer, and the bar was a commercial success. Patrick Hitler, son of Alois, tried to blackmail his famous uncle with revelations about the family's history but was unsuccessful. He then toured the US giving interviews on the theme of 'why I hate my uncle'. Patrick Hitler became a marine, called himself 'Hiller' at first, then 'Stewart-Houston', married and died in the US in 1987 at the age of seventy-six. His three sons live in the rural community of Patchogue on Long Island. According to the author David Gardner, who visited them in 1998, they have never married or had children.[106] The historian John Toland reports that one of Patrick Hitler's sons was named Alex Adolph. According to Toland, he has again taken the surname Hitler and currently lives under the name Adolph Hitler in Patchogue, Long Island, USA.[107]

APPENDIX 16

Hitler in the Men's Hostel

When the nineteen-year-old Hitler left the room which he had shared with August Kubizek in Stumpergasse on 18 November 1908, he registered his new address with the police as Felberstraße 22, *Tür* 16 (door 16) that same day. Nothing is known about the kind of accommodation it was; it must have been very simple, however, as Hitler cannot have had much of the money left that he had brought from Linz. Hitler lived in Felberstraße for nine months and then registered his address as Sechshauser Straße 58, *Tür* 21 on 20 August 1909. After three weeks he gave notice of his departure from that address, without filing a new registration.

The year 1909, and particularly the winter, must have been a very difficult time for the young Hitler. He evidently tried to keep his head above water with odd jobs, but does not seem to have been very successful. The urban vagrant Reinhold Hanisch later reported to have encountered Hitler during winter in the homeless shelter in Meidling.[108] Hundreds of homeless people stood in long queues in front of the Meidling hostel every evening. As not all of those waiting could be admitted, many people spent the night starving and freezing on the road in front of it, in order to have a chance at least to gain entry the next evening. Again and again it happened that the sick or the vulnerable froze or starved to death in front of the gates of the home.[109]

Hitler visited free soup kitchens for the poor at this time, notably the soup kitchen in the hospital of the Sisters of Mercy, where a relative of his former landlady, Frau Zakreys, observed 'how he stood in line for the monastery soup; ' his clothing had become very worn and I felt sorry for him as he had been so well dressed in the past'.[110] Reinhold Hanisch reported that Hitler seemed 'sad' the first time he encountered him in the homeless shelter. He had been exhausted, starved and footsore, and his blue patterned suit had taken on a purple tint due to the rain and the disinfection process in the hostel.[111] Hitler teamed up with the experienced vagabond Hanisch, and together they attempted to make some money from odd jobs, which was not easy due to the number of people searching for work. When Hanisch discovered that Hitler could paint, he made him a deal: Hitler would paint postcards and Hanisch would attempt to sell them in guest houses. The proceeds would be split between them. So Hitler began to paint postcards in cheap coffee houses, and Hanisch actually managed to sell them. The proceeds allowed them to escape homelessness. On 9 February 1910, Hitler and Hanisch moved into two simple, yet clean and warm single cabins in a men's hostel in the workers' district of Brigittenau. Hitler lived there for the next three years. When Hitler and Hanisch had a falling out, two Jewish inmates from the men's hostel, Joseph Neumann and Siegfried Löffner took over Hanisch's role and sold Hitler's postcards and watercolours.

On 24 May 1913, Hitler left the men's hostel to move to Munich with his hostel friend Rudolf Häusler.[112] Until the summer of 1914, the two lived in Munich, first in a shared room and then separately. During that time Häusler took on the role of salesman and sold Hitler's paintings. When the First World War broke out, the two friends went their separate ways. Häusler travelled back to Vienna to register with the Austrian Army, whilst Hitler registered as a volunteer with a Bavarian regiment.

APPENDIX 17

Hitler and the Occult

As Hitler was pursuing his private studies in Vienna, the 'occult sciences', as esotericism was also known in the nineteenth century, were flourishing. In the wake of the success of works by the Russian-British mystic Helena Petrovna Blavatsky (1831–1891), a flood of publications appeared on the subject of magic and mysticism, and esoteric books became bestsellers. In the German-speaking region of Austria-Hungary, Ariosophy was very popular among esoterics. The Ariosophic groups were influenced by the racist philosophy of the occultist Guido von List (1848–1919), and were often closely linked with societies with a German nationalist, *völkisch* and political bent.[113] As a result of the intersection of esotericism and *völkisch* ideology, Ariosophic mystics and occultists were often mentioned in German nationalist newspapers.[114] The young German nationalist-minded Hitler would certainly have been exposed to such ideas in Vienna.[115] The many books Hitler read whilst in Vienna would almost certainly have included esoteric works, particularly the papers of Guido von List.[116]

After the war, Hitler maintained close, amicable links with various members of the esoteric-Ariosophic Thule Society, particularly Dietrich Eckart, Rudolf Hess and Alfred Rosenberg. Dietrich Eckart, whom Hitler described as his 'polar star', worked on Hindu writings, studied the mystic Angelus Silesius, and called himself an 'expert in magic'; Rudolf Hess, the eventual Deputy Führer, devoted himself extensively to astrology; and Alfred Rosenberg, the Nazi philosopher who became the minister for the occupied areas of the Soviet Union in the Second World War, was influenced by Ariosophic and Hindu ideas. In addition to these former Thule members, there were other men in Hitler's immediate environment who shared a penchant for esotericism: Professor Karl Haushofer, for example, who was a crucial contributor to the formation of the alliance between Germany and Japan, was an authority in the field of Asiatic mysticism. He has been linked with Eastern secret societies by various authors, and committed suicide by hara-kiri in 1946. SS leader Heinrich Himmler engaged passionately in esotericism and based his organisation of the SS leadership on the model of occult societies. He planned to breed a racially pure elite of Aryan *Übermenschen* at his *Ordensburgen* schools, and familiarise them with occult teachings. Himmler also founded the Ahnenerbe e.V., a research society that financed the exploration of secret esoteric wisdom not just in Germany, but also in occupied France, Tibet and India.[117]

The large number of esoterically minded comrades in Hitler's immediate vicinity is striking. But does this make him an occultist too? Timothy W. Ryback has traced the 'intellectual footsteps' left by Hitler when reading books in the form of notes, underscores, exclamation marks and so on. Ryback examined the 1,280 books owned by Hitler and currently stored in the Library of Congress in Washington, and in the John Hay Library at Brown University on Rhode Island.[118] Ryback estimates that these represent less than ten per cent of the books Hitler owned, most of his library having been lost in the post-war chaos.[119] The books preserved in both collections are mostly presentation copies from the authors and gifts given to Hitler on birthdays and at Christmas by comrades-in-arms, functionaries, admirers and political freeloaders. He probably never even opened many of the books, while others had clearly been read, bearing margin notes and underscores in Hitler's handwriting.

Ryback ascertained that a relatively high number of the books (around 145 out of 1,280) are on religious and esoteric subjects.[120] From Western occultism to Christian works and Eastern mysticism, everything is represented – the teachings of Jesus can be found in Hitler's library, as can the predictions of Nostradamus. One book with an especially high number of margin notes and underscores is *Magie: Geschichte, Theorie und Praxis* (Magic: History, Theory and Practice) by Ernst Schertl, published in 1923. One of the sentences most clearly marked in this book reads: 'He who carries no demonic seed within himself will never bear a new world.'

Also of note in this context are the eight volumes by the philosopher Johann Gottlieb Fichte (1762–1814), which contain a dedication by the controversial director Leni Riefenstahl dated 20 June 1933 (To my dear Führer in deepest adoration). Ryback reports that there is one section in the Fichte books which is particularly highlighted. The sentences are underlined, with a mark in the margin as well as an exclamation point. In the paragraph, Fichte describes the Holy Trinity in the following way: he defines the Father as 'a natural universal force'; the Son as the 'physical embodiment of this force'; and the Holy Ghost as an expression of the 'light of reason'. Fichte's definition of the Trinity resembles Hitler's theories, in *Mein Kampf*, where 'natural laws' are equated with divine commandments. Elsewhere, Fichte asks: 'Where did Jesus derive the power that has held his followers for all eternity?' Hitler underscored the answer with an especially thick line: 'Through his absolute identification with God.' The following section is also clearly highlighted by Hitler: 'God and I are One. Expressed simply in two identical sentences – His life is mine; my life is His. My work is His work, and His work my work.' Hitler paraphrased these words in a speech on 27 June 1937: 'As weak as the individual is in his entire being and actions in the end compared with almighty Providence and its will, so immeasurably strong is he at the moment when he acts in the spirit of this Providence!'[121] *My work is His, and His work is mine.*

'If Hitler *was* as deeply engaged with spiritual issues as his books and their marginalia suggest, then what was the purpose of this pursuit?' asks Ryback. Hitler's identification with Christ, which continually resurfaces in many of his public and private statements, is certainly confirmed by Ryback's research, as is his interest in spiritual and religious matters, which punctuated conversations within his inner circle.[122] However, Hitler believed himself to be superior to occultists. In the inner circle, Hitler scoffed at 'Himmler's Germanic traditional and herbal wisdoms' according to contemporary witnesses.[123] Hitler's public statements also highlight his deprecatory attitude towards 'mystically inclined investigators of kingdom come', particularly his 'cultural speech' of 1938, which is reproduced in Appendix 38. Hitler certainly did not consider himself a mystic or occultist, but rather a 'man-god', and the herald of a new doctrine of redemption.[124]

APPENDIX 18

Hitler's Jewish Friends

Despite painstaking investigation, historical researchers have been unable to find a personal reason for Hitler's hatred of the Jews. Hitler was not refused admission to art school by a Jewish professor, nor was he infected with syphilis by a Jewish prostitute – these myths have been definitively discounted through meticulous research. Even Hitler himself did not cite a negative personal experience with Jews.

In *Mein Kampf*, only an encounter with a 'figure in a long caftan with black hair' is mentioned, which reputedly led Hitler to address the arguments of anti-Semites for the first time. Analysis of the accounts of contemporary witnesses indicates that Hitler not only had no negative experiences with Jews in Vienna, but in fact had a remarkable number of Jewish friends and business associates. At the time Hitler resided in Vienna, around eight to ten per cent of the city's population were Jews. This was also the approximate ratio of Jewish residents in the men's hostel Hitler lived in. However, the proportion of Jews among Hitler's associates was far higher than this percentage. In fact, it almost seems as if the young Hitler preferred to spend his time with Jews. Historian Brigitte Hamann examined these connections in her book Hitler's Vienna *(Hitlers Wien*, 1996) in more detail; the results of her investigations are summarised below.

Hitler sold his paintings almost exclusively to Jewish dealers: Morgenstern, Landsberger and Altenberg. The master glazier Samuel Morgenstern was his most consistent buyer. The art dealer Peter Jahn, who later searched for Hitler's artwork on behalf of the NSDAP, attested to the extremely good relationship between Hitler and Morgenstern. Morgenstern introduced the young painter to private clients, including the Jewish lawyer Dr Joseph Feingold, who also became a patron. Not only could Altenberg not remember Hitler making any anti-Semitic statements, he in fact asserts that Hitler seems to have preferred Jewish dealers. Hitler's men's hostel friend Hanisch recalled that Hitler had often said that 'you can do business with the Jews because they're the only ones prepared to take a risk'.[125] Hansich's statement is confirmed by an anonymous resident at the hostel in the spring of 1912: 'Hitler got on extremely well with Jews, and once said they were a clever people who stick together better than the Germans.'[126]

Hitler's best friend during his time at the men's hostel was a Jewish copper polisher named Joseph Neumann, with whom Hitler once disappeared for a week. Another Jewish resident, Siegfried Löffner, took Hitler's side when he felt conned by another (non-Jewish) resident, and reported the incident to the police. Hitler also maintained a friendly relationship with the one-eyed Jewish locksmith Simon Robinson, which led Robinson to support Hitler using money from his disability allowance. Rudolf Redlich from Moravia was another Jewish friend of Hitler. While Hitler was still living with August Kubizek, his roommate took him along to a family music evening held by an affluent Jewish family called the Jahodas. Afterwards, Hitler had only positive comments to make about his hosts and absolutely nothing critical to say. The Jewish general practitioner from Linz, Dr Bloch, who treated Hitler's mother, received hand-painted postcards from Hitler for years on which Hitler expressed his gratitude. As the status of Jews deteriorated dramatically under the Nazi campaign of terror, Dr Bloch managed to get a petition through to Imperial Chancellor Hitler. Hitler responded immediately and prevented the doctor and his wife from being taken to a collection camp. In 1940, Dr Bloch and his wife emigrated to the USA. As his medical degree was not recognised there, Dr Bloch was no longer able to work as a doctor, and he died penniless and far from home in the Bronx in New York in 1945.[127]

Samuel Morgenstern was less 'fortunate'. The reliable art buyer and patron of the homeless Hitler wrote to the Imperial Chancellery in 1939 to ask for help. 'On 10 November, my business was closed as a result of legal measures and my trading license simultaneously withdrawn, thereby leaving me entirely without means [...] I am sixty-four years old, my wife is sixty, we have been dependent on public generosity for many months and intend to emigrate to find jobs abroad [...] My humblest request to Your Excellency is to have it decreed that the Property Trading Office grant a small remuneration to me in foreign currency for my unencumbered property in District 21, which by official estimate is worth R.M.4,000.00, in return for ceding said property to the State, so that I may produce the required landing funds and live modestly with my wife until we obtain jobs.'[128] The letter did not reach Hitler. Morgenstern and his wife were taken to a collection camp and deported to the ghetto of Litzmannstadt (Lodz) in 1941. Together with 160,000 local Jews, 20,000 Jews from Germany and 5,000 Roma gypsies from Burgenland the Morgensterns were packed in unbearably cramped conditions. In 1943, Samuel Morgenstern died of exhaustion. His wife was deported to Auschwitz extermination camp in 1944. Two years later she was declared dead at the request of her brother.[129]

APPENDIX 19

Political Role Models

Hitler always maintained a determined silence about the mentors who had influenced him. This makes all the more conspicuous the detailed passages in *Mein Kampf* about two politicians he encountered as a young man in Vienna, and whom, by his own account, he regarded highly: Georg von Schönerer and Dr Karl Lueger. In the political arena the two party leaders were enemies, and Hitler's analysis of their qualities and mistakes demonstrates his ability to identify strengths even in his political opponents – strengths he could then use in his own politics.

Ideologically, the young Hitler clearly sided with Schönerer and his *Alldeutsche Partei* (Pan-German Party). Schönerer's rejection of democracy, parliamentarianism, pacifism and social democracy was later incorporated by Hitler into his *Weltanschauung*, as was Schönerer's opinion of art, rejecting the *Wiener Moderne* as 'international' and 'Jewish'. As an MP, Schönerer fought against the influx of Russian Jews. But even assimilated Viennese Jews whose mother tongue was German and who regarded themselves as German were rejected by Schönerer, who was a vehement exponent of racial anti-Semitism, previously unknown in Austria, which Hitler also advocated after the First World War. However, Schönerer did not only agitate against Jews: he campaigned against all non-German nationalities in the monarchy. It was therefore only natural that

Schönerer's Pan-Germans were anti-Habsburg and championed the annexation of the German parts of the Habsburg empire to Germany. The young Hitler learned a great deal from the politics and ideology of the Schönerians, and years later his NSDAP also adopted the Führer cult from the Pan-German Party. 'The Pan-Germans swore faithful allegiance to their "Führer", sang Schönerer songs [...] composed poems to him *ad gloriam* [...] page-long congratulations appeared each year in the *Alldeutsches Tagblatt* under the heading: "Heil to the Führer!" '[130] The political views of the 'Führer' Schönerer were dogmatic truths for the Pan-Germans. These were never contested within the party, and neither were any majority decisions taken. The Führer commanded; the party followed.

When Hitler came to Vienna, however, Schönerer was politically finished and his party inconsequential, with only three parliamentary seats. Hitler attributed Schönerer's failure to the fact that he had focused too much on the bourgeoisie and neglected the working classes. Hitler also felt that Schönerer had failed because of his fight against the Catholic Church: Schönerer advocated a 'national Christianity', and equated the Catholic Church with anti-Teutonic Roman missionaries. Not only was Schönerer thereby creating another 'fragmenting' enemy in addition to the Habsburgs, the socialists, the Jews and the Slavs, this was an enemy against whom victory was not possible in the prevailing situation. 'The policy of the Pan-German movement in deciding to carry through a difficult fight against the Catholic Church,' wrote Hitler, 'can be explained only by attributing it to an inadequate understanding of the spiritual character of the people.'[131]

Schönerer's failure in his battle against the Catholic Church certainly taught Hitler a great deal: he never publicly declared the Christian Churches his opponents, and remained a member of the Catholic Church all of his life.[132] Another aspect that may have accelerated the downfall of the Pan-Germans is not mentioned by Hitler: their sectarian Teutonic cult. The Schönerians had their symbols and identifying marks: the cornflower, the runes, the 'Heil' greeting and the German battle songs. They celebrated Sonnwendfest, Julfest and Ostarafest [...] Before marriage, the Aryan lineage and 'biological health' of the partner had to be verified. Children were given Germanic names and were raised according to 'old German customs' [...] Women did not wear make-up and wore homely hairstyles and clothing [...] The Schönerians adhered to eating rules and were largely vegetarian. They strengthened their bodies with physical education and gymnastics, in the open air wherever possible [...] Schönerer [did away with] the Christian calendar and introduced a new calendar [...] by which the year 1888ad became 2001an. The Roman month names were also changed to old German: Hartung, Hornung, Lenzmond [...][133] The Teutonic cult of the Schönerians is somewhat reminiscent of the ideals and activities of the Nazis. As far as cultish-sectarian elements within the Nazi movement were concerned, however, Hitler always called for moderation and restrained sectarian zealots such as Himmler and Rosenberg.[134] The reason for Hitler's restraint might be related to the example of Schönerer, whose sectarianism met with a lack of understanding and rejection among the majority of the Viennese.

While Schönerer's power was waning when Hitler came to Vienna, his adversary, the leader of the Christsoziale Partei, Dr Karl Lueger, achieved one success after another. The conservative Lueger had acted very astutely by highlighting his social activities, Hitler judged. Lueger also loved to stage large assemblies like a people's tribune. In his speeches, he adapted to the mental level of his audience, simplifying the difficult, attacking the enemies of his listeners, intensifying their antipathies and delighting in raging against religious and national minorities. This recipe for success, with which Lueger rose to the office of Mayor and 'Lord of Vienna', was later adopted by Hitler. He writes: 'For one must never judge the speech of a statesman to his nation by the impression which it leaves on the mind of a university professor but by the effect it produces on the people. This is the sole criterion of the orator's genius.'[135]

However, Lueger was faithfully loyal to the Habsburgs, which Hitler disliked, and was not a racial anti-Semite, opposing the Jews for religious reasons and demanding their 're-Catholicisation'. However, his anti-Semitism was verbally caustic and allowed him, as it later did Hitler, to unite different groups of voters behind one unifying enemy. Everything his voters rejected, Lueger blamed on the Jews: liberalism, capitalism, the stock market, the press, intellectuals, modern art, women's emancipation, and so on. Hitler stressed that Lueger had correctly assessed the psychology of the masses: 'The art of leadership, as displayed by all truly great popular leaders in all ages, consists primarily in consolidating the attention of the people against a single adversary and ensuring that nothing will fragment that attention.'[136]

Hitler may also have learned a thing or two from Lueger's talent for self-staging. 'He loved public appearances as "Handsome Karl", with the golden mayoral chain, surrounded by a horde of attendants and municipal officials, particularly ministers in regalia and acolytes who swung the stoup at all large opening ceremonies.'[137] Hitler expressly praised the Christsoziale Party's handling of the Church, and wrote: 'They avoided all conflict with a religious institution and so secured the support of the powerful organisation represented by the Church.'[138] It is remarkable that Hitler, despite his admiration for Schönerer and Lueger, apparently did not succumb to their anti-Semitism during his time in Vienna.[139]

The reason why the young Hitler was not an anti-Semite is mentioned in Appendix 19. Hitler may have been influenced by a third Viennese politician, Karl Hermann Wolf, who urged Germans to unite against external threats, irrespective of their religion. Although Hitler does not mention Wolf in *Mein Kampf*, he did receive him at the party congress of 1937.[141] By the time Hitler came to Vienna, Wolf had turned his back on Schönerer's party and founded his own, the Deutschradikale Partei. Wolf's main political goal was 'Slav resistance' and he warned against allowing anti-Semitism to supersede resistance against the Czechs. He advocated the principle that 'in a "threatened land", all Germans must hold together, be they Jews or Christians'.[142] Wolf was honoured with a ceremonial NSDAP funeral on his death in 1941. Schönerer and Lueger did not live to see the rise of their 'pupil'. Lueger was buried in Vienna in 1910 with great pageantry, while Schönerer died a lonely man in the Waldviertel in 1921.

APPENDIX 20

German Superiority

Because Germany did not exist as a nation until 1871, an inferiority complex had emerged in the nineteenth century which intellectual circles attempted to offset by claiming that Germans were spiritually and morally superior to all other people. The slogan '*Am deutschen Wesen soll die Welt genesen*' (the German spirit shall heal the world) was coined, the argument being that to make the world a better place, Germans would have to ensure that German culture and values prevailed.[143]

Peoples in the east and south of Europe were thought to be too 'primitive' to change the world for the better. Americans, it was claimed, were the descendants of proletarian emigrants and slaves, and would never be able to achieve the intellectual and moral standard that would allow them to contribute to the higher goals of humanity. The Germans also felt superior to the countries of Western Europe, particularly the English.

Although the British ruled over a global empire, culturally England was deemed to be of merely incidental significance. The Germans considered themselves the pioneers of an impending world culture that contrasted with the materialistic and decadent British 'civilisation'. German intellectuals raved that in the new world culture inspired by Germany, the human spirit would truly reign at last, and its capabilities could then finally be fully exploited. German philosophers and intellectuals did not tire of affirming their belief in Germany's superiority. They asserted that the country's compulsion to command the world through wars and conquests was justified by the superiority of German culture. The fact that Germany had long lagged behind other Western nations economically was seen as an advantage: this had spared Germans the fate of decadence and the cultural downfall that German intellectuals perceived to have befallen France and England. In 1914, however, Germany's economy made dramatic advances. Germany's electrical and chemical industries had already overtaken the British equivalents in volume, and Germany was well on the way to producing more steel than England.

German intellectual circles considered the looming threat of the First World War anything but a disadvantage. The war was perceived as a purging of European cultures that were poisoned and contaminated. There was absolutely no doubt that Germany would win the war because it was taken as given that the nation with the more significant culture would be the victor. In the eyes of the Germans, the First World War was a 'just war', a 'war of cultures [...] at the heart of which lay the mission of German culture to inaugurate a new age in European civilisation'.[144] German metaphysics battled against British imperialism and French irrationality. Intellectual circles were mobilised and Germany's cultural sphere became an essential part of the war effort. Literature in particular was utilised for the war and served 'as part of a broader cultural mobilisation'.[145] To the German population, the First World War was portrayed as a war between 'merchants' and 'heroes', where the British were greedy merchants out for purely material gain, while the German heroes defended the idealistic values of German culture. When the English referred to 'culture', it was said they meant 'convenience'; they confused 'truth' with 'facts'; 'good' with 'useful'; 'love' with 'solidarity'; and 'human nature' with 'the English'.

APPENDIX 21

Hitler and Animals

Hitler had only been at the front for a few short months when a white terrier strayed into his trench. The dog had probably belonged to an English officer. Hitler captured the 'deserter' and it was not long until the terrier had accepted his new master. Hitler named him Fuchsl (Little Fox), and from then on the dog was his constant companion. Three years later, in the August of 1917, Hitler was stationed near Colmar. There, a stranger rummaged through his rucksack and stole his art materials. Fuchsl disappeared too, and Hitler never saw him again.[146] In later years, Hitler owned several dogs and the Nazi propaganda machine eagerly disseminated photos of the Führer with his dogs to demonstrate his fondness for animals. In fact, Hitler does seem to have had an affection for animals, dogs in particular. Opinion is divided as to whether one can attribute his vegetarianism to this love of animals. However, his preference for vegetarian food did lead to his experimenting with a vegetarian diet for his German shepherds.

After Hitler had come to power in 1933, one of his first acts as a legislator was to put slaughter animals under state protection. An appropriate law set out what measures were to be taken to avoid 'unnecessary agitation and pain' for animals during slaughter. It was only after this measure that Hitler ordered the abolition of the unions.[147] In 1933, the Nazis also passed a decree prohibiting animal vivisection. In a radio address, Hermann Göring explained that anyone acting in breach of this decree would face deportation to a concentration camp.[148] In the same year, a *Reichstierschutzgesetz* (Reich Animal Protection Law) was passed, which granted animals in Germany more rights than in any other country in the world. On 3 July 1934, at the same time as Hitler had 150 political opponents murdered during the *Nacht der langen Messer* (Night of the Long Knives), new rulings were passed which prohibited hunting on horseback with dogs. The official Nazi biography by Erich Gritzbach cites the words of the Hunting Master of the Reich (Reichsjägermeister) Hermann Göring: 'Whoever tortures animals violates the instincts of the German people.'[149]

That the Nazis protected helpless animals but mercilessly murdered helpless children and the disabled seems initially contradictory. We only recognise it as consistent when we observe Hitler's intellectual world. Animals were to be protected as part of 'eternal nature', just as this eternal nature was to be protected from 'degenerate' and 'unnatural' life. According to Hitler's world view, people with disabilities, Jews, Sinti and Roma stood in the way of the 'natural' evolution of humanity and were therefore to be 'removed'. Hitler's German shepherd, Blondi, given to him by his secretary Martin Bormann as a present, accompanied him even in his last days in the bunker in Berlin. On 29 April 1944, after his marriage to Eva Braun, Hitler tested the effectiveness of his potassium cyanide capsules on his dog. They worked.[150]

APPENDIX 22
Hitler's War Record

Hitler once said: 'Without the army none of us would be here; we have all come from this school at one time.'[151] The experiences of the First World War made an indelible mark on Adolf Hitler and his generation. Machine guns, tanks, aeroplanes and modern artillery made it possible to commit industrial mass murder on a hitherto inconceivable scale. Whitney Harris, right hand of the US chief prosecutor at the Nuremberg trials, said in an interview: 'I am absolutely convinced that Adolf Hitler was just a name representing the total worldwide collapse of ethics in the twentieth century. It began in 1914 with the First World War, when everyone killed everyone and there were no longer any moral standards. Revenge was the order of the day, every excuse justified.'[152]

Hitler, who was in close contact with the command staff as a dispatch runner, learned to view the First World War from the perspective of a captain who must be prepared to use his own soldiers 'as cannon fodder' for the sake of strategic success. As an infantryman, Hitler found himself in situations where troops fought 'man to man', and he had to learn to overcome the instinctual aversion to killing. The gruesome experiences at the front also confirmed his social-Darwinist world view that 'life is a continual savage battle'.[153] Like a minority of soldiers in all armies throughout time, Hitler experienced combat as a significant personal enrichment. He described it as 'a great formative event', a 'monumental impression', 'overwhelming', and said in 1941: 'I am immeasurably lucky to have experienced the war in this way.'[154] The ever-present risk of death made all differences and divisions between the individual soldiers disappear and they became 'one large community'. Hitler must have experienced this with marked intensity as he had neither a homeland nor a family to speak of. He despised the Austro-Hungarian 'racial mix'; his parents were no longer alive, and he had lost contact with his sister, Paula, and half-sister, Angela, years before. His few acquaintances from Munich sent him letters and packages initially, but from mid-1915 onwards these communications also dwindled. His regiment became everything to him: friends, family and home.

That his regiment was all he had was probably the main reason why this peculiar Viennese artist, who had previously lived according to whim, transformed into a model soldier. The indolent late riser learned to discipline himself and carry out commands reliably. And he came to believe that Providence was on his side. Hitler's regiment, the RIR 16, or 'List' Regiment, fought in almost every great battle in the First World War. When the RIR 16 was first deployed, it consisted of 3,600 men. Four years later, by November 1918, including soldiers who had replaced fallen comrades, 3,754 troops from the regiment had been killed. Only a handful of those who had travelled to the front in 1914 were still alive. Hitler's survival was not due to particular prudence on his part. In fact, he volunteered to become a dispatch runner, one of the most dangerous assignments in the regiment. While his comrades were at least partially protected from enemy artillery fire in the trenches, as a runner between the front line and the command post he was completely exposed to grenades, missiles and machine-gunfire. Several dispatch runners were often sent on the same mission as it was likely that only one of them would make it through alive. Hitler was always among the survivors.

The claim that Hitler's decision to become a dispatch runner was a cowardly evasion of service in the trenches, as his political opponents would later allege, is not borne out by the facts. His superior, the regiment's aide-decamp Friedrich Wiedemann, described Hitler as 'courageous', 'reliable' and 'daring'.[155] His regimental commander, Friedrich Petz, spoke of Hitler's 'personal verve', his 'unrestrained bravery', his 'iron composure' and his 'coolness' in a letter from 1922.[156] This was confirmed by Lieutenant Colonel von Tubeuf, also in 1922.[157] During the NSDAP's fight for power in the 1920s, Hitler repeatedly demonstrated his 'unrestrained bravery' and 'coolness'. His first supporters and fellow campaigners admired him as a leader who could not only talk tough, but was also willing to get stuck in himself whenever chaos and brawls broke out in beer cellars and at rallies. Hitler was wounded twice at the front (in October 1916 and October 1918) and decorated several times. He received the Iron Cross 2nd Class (2 December 1914); the Military Service Cross 3rd Class (17 September 1917); the Regimental Diploma for Outstanding

Bravery before the Enemy (9 June 1918); the Medal for the Wounded in Black with Swords (18 May 1918); the Service Medal 3rd Class (25 August 1918); and the Iron Cross 1st Class (22 July 1918).

The Iron Cross 1st Class was an exceptional honour. Of the 11 million German soldiers who fought in the First World War, only 163,000 received this medal, almost all of whom were officers.[158] Hitler was one of very few corporals to be awarded the Iron Cross 1st Class. This high distinction was the first extraordinary success in Hitler's hitherto unremarkable life. The proposal for decoration came from the deputy regimental commander of RIR 16, Baron von Godin, and read: 'Hitler has been with the regiment since deployment and has proven himself brilliantly in all battles in which he fought. As a dispatch runner, he demonstrated exemplary coolness and verve in both static and mobile warfare and was always willing to carry messages voluntarily in the most difficult situations at great risk to his life [...] I deem Hitler to be completely deserving of decoration with the Iron Cross 1st Class.'[159] Hitler himself never mentioned the circumstances behind this honour. He may have wanted to avoid acknowledging that he owed this important award to the recommendation of a Jew, of all people: Lieutenant Hugo Gutmann. During the Nazi era, it was reported that Hitler had received the medal for single-handedly capturing twelve Frenchmen. Other reports spoke of twenty and more captives. However, no evidence of this has been found. It is now generally assumed that Hitler was awarded the Iron Cross 1st Class for delivering a message under heavy artillery fire and thereby saving German positions from bombardment.

The fact that Corporal Hitler was not promoted for four years despite his bravery was attributed to a 'lack of leadership qualities' by his superior, Wiedemann: ' At the time, Hitler really was not officer material in the opinion of the military [...] His attitude was lax, and his response when asked a question anything but militarily concise. He usually held his head tilted to the left. None of this matters during a war. But a man must ultimately be somehow suited to the role of officer if he is to be justifiably promoted to Lance Sergeant. We in the regimental staff did once actually consider promoting him to Lance Sergeant purely to decorate him. However, we decided against this in the end, not least because Hitler himself did not want to be put forward for promotion.'

Another superior, Max Amann, testified the same in Nuremberg in 1947. On approaching Hitler to congratulate him on his promotion, Hitler stared at him in horror and said: 'I would ask you not to do that, I have more authority without stripes than with stripes.'[160] The fact that he was 'just' a common soldier served Hitler well later in his political career. As a soldier at the front, he could speak with the authority of a man who had risked his life for Germany. In the eyes of the public, however, he also distinguished himself positively from the career officers who were seen as the architects of Germany's defeat. His decoration with the Iron Cross 1st Class as a mere common soldier further improved his standing. Even after the First World War, Hitler never truly ceased to be a soldier at heart. When he left the army on 31 March 1920, he was already forming his private army, the SA, together with Ernst Röhm. No sooner had he come to power than he began steering resolutely towards the Second World War, as if obsessed. Some psychologists speculate that the traumatic but positively experienced key events of the First World War motivated Hitler subconsciously, and that he acted under the influence of a 'repetition compulsion'.[161]

APPENDIX 23

The Jewish Conspiracy

As the spectre of defeat loomed in the First World War, German nationalists, who had been the most vociferous in calling for war, began to search for a scapegoat. And they soon found one: the Jews. It did not matter that Jews made up only around one per cent of the population in Germany, had a falling birth rate and would in all likelihood have disappeared from Germany by the end of the twentieth century.[162] The theory of Jewish guilt rapidly gained support, particularly in German nationalist circles, but was also helped by the fact that Emperor Wilhelm II and the chief strategist of the German Army, General Ludendorff, were convinced that the downfall of Germany was the result of a Jewish conspiracy.[163]

Already present among certain groups of nationalists, support for anti-Semitism began to increase. Heinrich Class, chairman of the Altdeutscher Verband, said at the time, 'I will not shy away from any means and in this regard [referring to the *Judenpolitik* (Jewish policy)] keep to the quote from Heinrich von Kleist, coined in reference to the French: Strike them dead, the Last Judgement will not ask you for your reasons!'[164] Such radical anti-Semitism was initially limited to a few fanatics in nationalist circles. However, rapidly spreading theories of a global Jewish conspiracy ensured it gained support amongst the general population. These theories depicted socialism and communism as Jewish fabrications designed to undermine the ruling order and give the Jews power over naïve, helpless populations. It was claimed that capitalism served the same purpose and helped Jewish bankers and Jewish stock-market speculators to rule the financial world.

The theory of a great Jewish conspiracy made it possible to explain away a wealth of political events: capitalism and Marxism were actually secret allies, devoted to establishing a Jewish world order. This conspiracy theory captured the imagination of broad sections of the population throughout Europe. It was an extension of older conspiracy theories based on the stereotype of the 'ever-wandering Jew'. The great upheavals of the new century and the insecurity these engendered gave new life to old fears of the Jews, particularly in a Germany gripped by crises. In the last years of the war, many publications on the subject of the Jewish conspiracy appeared in Germany. 'Die Rede des Rabbi' (The words of the Rabbi), f or example, appeared in the right-wing magazine *Deutsche Erneuerung* (German Renewal) in January 1918. In this piece, it was claimed that the war had been started by the Jews to plunge Germany into chaos, allowing them to take control of the country. Other similar publications included *Judas Schuldbuch, eine deutsche Abrechnung* (Judas's Debt Register, a German Account) by Wilhelm Meister and *Weltfreimaurerei, Weltrevolution, Weltrepublik, eine Untersuchung über Ursprung und Endziele des Weltkrieges* (World Freemasonry, World Revolution, World Republic, an examination of the origin and ultimate goals of the World War) by Dr F. Wichtl. Within a year, these two publications alone achieved a circulation of over 50,000.[165]

Many of the conspiracy theories originated in Russia, where they had been concocted and circulated by the Tsarists during the Russian Civil War. Between 1917 and 1918, these theories were brought to Western Europe by Russian refugees in hectographical form. The most famous of these defamatory documents is entitled *Die Protokolle der Weisen von Zion* (The Protocols of the Learned Elders of Zion).[166] *The Protocols* detailed a supposed secret meeting on the fringe of the first Zionistic Congress in Basle in 1897. At twenty-four meetings, an anonymous Jewish leader outlines plans for Jewish world domination, which includes the following quote: 'God has granted to us, His Chosen People, the gift of dispersion, and from this, which appears to all eyes to be our weakness, has come forth all our strength, which has now brought us to the threshold of sovereignty over all the world.'[167] *The Protocols* gave the impression that Jews, living in many countries around the world, were members of a highly organised secret movement, and had been pursuing an imperialistic plot for centuries. It was claimed that their goal was to eliminate all national borders and bring down all non-Jewish governments to replace them with a Jewish world government. The Jews also allegedly intended to abolish all religions other than Judaism. According to *The Protocols*, this was the Jews' mission as the chosen people. At the end of the struggle, it was said that a king from the house of David would rule over the world. To achieve this great mission, it was claimed that an invisible secret Jewish world government supported every effort to undermine non-Jewish institutions. All wars were said to have been started as a result of Jewish plots purely to damage non-Jewish states and strengthen the global power of the Jews.[168]

It is highly probable that Hitler came across publications proclaiming a global Jewish conspiracy while he was on leave from the front line in Berlin in 1917 and 1918. Copies of a German translation of *The Protocols of the Learned Elders of Zion* had been in circulation in Germany since 1918, and it is feasible that Hitler read it while on home leave in Berlin. However, it is more likely that he learned of *The Protocols* in 1919/20 from Thule Society members Dietrich Eckart and Alfred Rosenberg.[169] What is certain is that *The Protocols* made a big impression on him. In *Mein Kampf*, Hitler writes that they 'uncover the character and the actions of the Jews in their inner connections and their ultimate goals with a horrific certainty'.[170] The first printed translation of *The Protocols* was published by Gottfried zur Beeks in Germany in 1919. An English and a Polish translation also appeared that year, followed by American and French editions in 1920.[171] Henry Ford promoted the book in the US, and by the start of the 1920s several hundred thousand copies were in global circulation. 'It [*The Protocols*] became the book of the hour. A respectable British newspaper, the *Morning Post*, devoted a series of articles to it. Even *The Times* demanded an investigation to determine what truth there was in the protocols.'[172]

In 1921, the English journalist Philip Graves discovered that passages from *The Protocols* and a 1864 political satire by Maurice Joly, *Dialogue aux enfers entre Macchiavel et Montesquieu*, matched word for word. Further investigation revealed that *The Protocols* had been forged by the Russian Secret Service between 1894 and 1899. *The Protocols* were also exposed as a forgery in several trials.[173] Even Joseph Goebbels had no doubt that *The Protocols* had been fabricated. 'I believe in the intrinsic but not in the factual truth of *The Protocols*,' he said in 1924.[174]

APPENDIX 24

The Beginning of Hitler's anti-Semitism

In *Mein Kampf* Hitler claims he had already become a 'fanatical Anti-Semite' in Vienna. However, according to historical research, this claim does not correspond to the known facts.[175] And not only in Vienna: there is no indication that Hitler did anything to identify him as an anti-Semite during his time as a soldier. Shortly after the war, however, in Munich, he had suddenly transformed into a radical anti-Semite, who was intimately familiar with the pertinent arguments of the time. Hitler's first documented attack on the Jews dates from 25 August 1919, nine months after the end of the war.[176]

That Hitler made no conspicuous anti-Semitic comments until sometime around the end of the war is not unusual. Not everyone who counted themselves part of the *völkisch-national* (ethnic nationalist) camp were automatically anti-Semites.[177] And even the anti-Semites among the German Nationalists had fallen silent because Emperor Wilhelm II had announced on the eve of the First World War that he no longer knew any parties; he only knew Germans. However, as defeat became a foregone conclusion, the old prejudices and phobias resurfaced with even more vigour. The Jews were now defamed as war profiteers, shirkers and defeatists, and provided the nationalist camp with the necessary scapegoat. The disastrous result of the First World War must have shaken Hitler to the core, as he strongly believed in German superiority. The global Jewish conspiracy theories which were disseminated by German nationalist circles provided a welcome explanation.[178] Doubtless, Dietrich Eckart and other members of the Thule Society encouraged Hitler in his anti-Semitism after the war. Fundamentally, though, he knew all there was to know on this topic. Anyone who sympathised with German nationalistic circles in Vienna would have been familiar with the arguments of the anti-Semites.[179]

APPENDIX 25

Hitler at Pasewalk

Hitler often said that 'a secret known by two people is no longer a secret', according to his secretary, Christa Schroeder. In fact, Hitler concealed many things – particularly anything relating to his private life – under a veil of secrecy. Thanks to painstaking historical research, today almost all of these secrets have been revealed. However, the 'secret of Pasewalk' was unknown for a long time because no one suspected a secret behind Hitler's stay at the hospital there. The records that could have illuminated this obscure time in Hitler's life have disappeared; they were removed by the Nazis. It is only in recent years that several authors have added to the fragmented findings of historical research or reinterpreted existing data, making a broader public aware of this important moment in Hitler's life.[180] The circumstantial evidence that has emerged all points to the same conclusion: the poisonous gas exposure and its psychological consequences represent *the* decisive turning point in Hitler's life. After suffering a gas attack in Werwick on 14 October 1918, Hitler and other injured comrades were taken to Bavarian Field Hospital No. 53 in Qudenaarde, near Brussels. This hospital specialised in war wounds and was fully capable of treating soldiers who had been exposed to gas. All of the injured soldiers from Werwick were given further treatment in Qudenaarde – all, that is, except one: Hitler. He was put on a train and transported around 1,000 kilometres back to Germany, to a small town near the Polish border called Pasewalk. But why?

Why was Hitler separated from his comrades, when all of the soldiers in that group had suffered the same injuries and required the same treatment? Why the huge expense of a journey taking at least five days, at a time when thousands of more seriously wounded men would have needed transport home? The explanation is contained in an edict from the German War Office dated 29 January 1917. According to this, the military doctors were not permitted to treat soldiers diagnosed as 'war neurotics' together with other wounded men; the 'war neurotics' had to be transferred immediately to special institutions.[181] Soldiers who had been unable to cope mentally with their experiences on the front line were considered a serious threat by the military leaders. It was feared that this 'war neurosis' could spread like an epidemic, and that the combat morale of all of the wounded men could be jeopardised if these patients were not immediately removed. War neurotics were also suspected of faking psychotic behaviour in order to avoid serving on the front line. To make obedient soldiers of them again, they were subjected to electric shock treatment and punished in other ways.

Special psychiatric hospitals were therefore set up in remote rural areas. In the hospital at Pasewalk, the war neurotics were allegedly housed in the so-called '*Schützenhaus*'. This building had served as a shooting range and variety theatre before the war, and had been requisitioned by the army.[182]

Whether war neurotics were actually treated in the *Schützenhaus* cannot be determined for certain; the records relating to the role of this ward within the hospital at Pasewalk have vanished. But the fact that the *Schützenhaus* was staffed with the neurologist Dr Kroner and the highly qualified captain in the medical marine corps and professor of psychiatry Dr Forster, strongly suggests that the *Schützenhaus* must have been a specialist psychiatric ward.[183] Like the internal documents from Pasewalk Hospital, Hitler's medical files have also disappeared. There is no documentation of the type of treatment he underwent or his diagnosis. However, the circumstances of his transfer to Pasewalk indicate with great likelihood that he was categorised as a war neurotic by the doctors in Qudenaarde. The US Secret Service (Intelligence Division of the Office of Naval Operations) came to the same conclusion. The OSS created a psychological profile of Hitler under reference number N 31963 during the Second World War. When it was developing this profile, the neurologist Dr Karl Kroner was questioned by American agents in Reykjavik in March 1943 about Hitler's treatment. (Hitler was at Pasewalk from 21 October until 19 November 1918; Dr Kroner worked at Pasewalk during this period. Because of his Jewish ancestry, he emigrated to Finland after Hitler seized power.) Kroner stated that he had not treated Hitler personally, but had been present when Hitler was examined on admission, and recalled that Hitler's subsequent treatment had been administered by Dr Edmund Forster. According to Kroner, Forster had diagnosed Hitler as a 'psychopath with hysterical symptoms'.[184] This diagnosis was confirmed by Balduin Forster, Edmund Forster's son. In an interview with Hitler researcher R. Binion, Forster confirmed that his father had mentioned having referred to Hitler as 'hysterical' at Pasewalk.[185]

It is not hard to imagine what the publication of Forster's diagnosis would have meant for the career of the aspiring politician. Had it become known in Germany in the 1920s that Hitler was a former psychiatric patient, he would surely have been seen in a different light, and the course of world history may well have taken a different path.[186] In *Mein Kampf*, Hitler describes his injury resulting from his gas poisoning as a form of 'blindness'. Significantly, in this context, this diagnosis is missing from Hitler's war muster roll, according to which he was suffering from 'gas poisoning'.[187] Kroner's statement to the US Secret Service was the first definite indication that there was much more to Hitler's stay at Pasewalk than recuperation from an eye injury. The records of the US Secret Service were not made available to the public until 1973. They had been kept under lock and key until then for thirty years, with other secret service files. When Dr Kroner's statement was finally made public, historians barely acknowledged it. For one thing, by the 1970s the prevailing opinion was that there was nothing fundamentally new to be discovered about Hitler's life. In addition, sources of information regarding Hitler's convalescence at Pasewalk were still scarce: Hitler's medical files were nowhere to be found, and there was no other additional material to support Kroner's claim. The Pasewalk episode therefore continued to receive scant consideration in the following years, as is demonstrated by its absence from Ian Kershaw's detailed 1998 biography of Hitler.[188] Kershaw does not even indicate the possibility that Hitler might have undergone psychiatric treatment at Pasewalk. As in *Mein Kampf*, Kershaw's book only mentions an eye injury as the reason for Hitler's stay at Pasewalk.

The fact that this very episode, which could be the key to understanding the personality and history of Hitler, remained so unresolved motivated the authors D. Lewis and B. Horstmann to undertake further research. In their books, *The Man Who Invented Hitler* and *Hitler in Pasewalk*, they list a great deal of circumstantial evidence, all indicating that Hitler did actually undergo psychiatric treatment at Pasewalk. They also list documents that lead to the conclusion that there was an obvious attempt on the part of Hitler and the Nazi authorities to cover up the Pasewalk episode. This circumstantial evidence is particularly impressive. Had Hitler really only been treated for an eye injury, there would have been no reason to eliminate all tracks leading back to his stay at the hospital there.

The key witness to the events, Dr Forster, was head of the university psychiatric clinic in Greifswald after the war. It is not difficult to imagine his feelings as he followed the political progress of his former patient. He must have known how dangerous the knowledge in his possession was. But what was he to do? Were he to reveal his knowledge and bring a halt to Hitler's rise to power, he would doubtless have put his life in danger: the Nazis were not known for dealing with their opponents in a restrained manner. Furthermore, Forster was subject to the physician's obligation to maintain patient confidentiality. If he had made Hitler's treatment at Pasewalk public, it would have meant the end of his career. He therefore had no option but to remain silent and watch Hitler as he made huge advances towards absolute power.

However, although Hitler had many supporters in the 1920s, he also had many opponents. One of these opponents, General Kurt von Schleicher, must have learned of Hitler's encounter with psychiatry at

Pasewalk. It is not known how the Pasewalk episode came to the attention of von Schleicher, but B. Horstmann's research indicates that it was discussed in von Schleicher's family. The general was evidently aware that he would be putting himself at great risk if he tried to get his hands on Hitler's medical records. Nevertheless, in 1932, von Schleicher commissioned a close friend, the Secret Service officer Ferdinand von Bredow, to confiscate the records of Hitler's treatment at Pasewalk. Until that time, the file had been stored in an army archive, the Krankenbuchlager Berlin. Hitler's medical file actually disappeared shortly thereafter from the Berlin archive, but a few months after the file was seized, Hitler became Chancellor of the Reich. In June 1934, General Kurt von Schleicher and Colonel Ferdinand von Bredow were shot dead by the SS.[189]

Max Amann, head of the Imperial Press Office of the Nazis (and Hitler's superior in the First World War) stated during the Nuremberg trials that Hitler's Pasewalk records had been stolen from von Schleicher's or von Bredow's home by the SS after they had been murdered. Amann claimed that after the death of the Imperial Protector of Bohemia and Moravia, Reinhard Heydrich, the Pasewalk file was found in his writing desk. His successor, Ernst Kaltenbrunner, allegedly took it, and it was never seen again.[190] The whereabouts of the records are unknown to this day. However, apart from the medical file, there was also the key witness to the events: Dr Forster. Shortly after Hitler came to power on 30 April 1933, an investigation was launched against the psychiatrist by the secret police, the Gestapo. On 1 September 1933, Forster was suspended from service at the clinic in Greifswald.[191] On 11 September 1933, after an interrogation by the Gestapo, Dr Forster was found dead in his bathroom by his wife. He had shot himself. Mrs Forster told police that her husband did not possess the type of gun used in his suicide. The police were unable to determine the source of the weapon.[192]

APPENDIX 26
Hitler's Transformation

Contemporary witnesses who came to know Hitler before the end of the First World War had nothing extraordinary to report about him. He was described as an introverted armchair scholar and practical joker, with no exceptional traits or any extraordinary talents. And he was no gifted orator; quite the opposite, in fact. Rudolf Häusler, with whom Hitler shared a room in Munich before the war, complained of his long-winded and monotonous monologues.

Although a mediocre artist by trade, Hitler considered himself a creative genius. But even this gross overestimation of his abilities was not particularly exceptional. This delusion of personal greatness has been common among actual and would-be artists throughout time. Hitler was characterised by a certain intransigence in his thinking, but he was intelligent and would certainly have been able to study at university had he not left school early and put paid to an academic career. According to Viennese acquaintances, he had a tendency to be vindictive, was narrow-minded and irascible – negative traits certainly, but hardly unusual. Neither was Hitler alone in being unfortunate enough to have been abused by an authoritarian father in childhood. The fact that Hitler was prejudiced, particularly against people of other races and nations, was also nothing remarkable. Such prejudices were as commonplace in Vienna at the turn of the century as they are today around the world. Hitler adored his mother, loved animals and nature, was fond of children and spent much of his time in Vienna contemplating how to improve the lot of the lower classes. He had interests in architecture and eccentric theories on the origins of the world; he idolised 'Germanness', was a bookworm and opera fan, and had a sweet tooth. He worshipped women from a distance, avoiding closer contact with the opposite sex. The only special quality that set him apart was his photographic memory, which enabled him to learn entire pages of text off by heart.

This was the person named 'Man of the Year' by *Time* magazine in 1939.[193] The British Prime Minister, Neville Chamberlain, said of Hitler: 'It is impossible not to be impressed by the power of this man.'[194] And after a visit to Berchtesgaden, Lloyd George, the British Prime Minister during the First World War, described Hitler as 'a born leader, a magnetic, dynamic personality with a single-minded purpose'.[195] In five long years in Vienna Hitler had not managed to make a single influential friend who could have saved him from the homeless shelter; but after the end of the war, he became a popular, key figure among Munich's social elite within a few months. Events at which he spoke soon became so overcrowded that even the largest halls in Munich, with room for over 2,000 people, were no longer big enough, and he was forced to switch to a circus arena. The captivating magnetism he emanated at these rallies is well documented. There are also countless testimonies from his supporters describing Hitler's hypnotic power over them. The following is a typical account, from Kurt Lüdecke, a former supporter of Hitler, who was later sent to a concentration camp: 'My critical faculties were momentarily disabled [...] I had an experience that can only be compared to a religious conversion.'[196]

Hitler's tendency to deliver endless monologues was well known to his war comrades; but no one could recall Hitler being able to instil anything resembling enthusiasm with his long-winded speeches. Nor had anyone observed the 'hypnotic power' for which he was so famed after the war. And no army companion ever reported Hitler believing he had a special 'mission', let alone a calling to save the German people. In fact, although Lance Corporal Hitler repeatedly risked his life during the war, he never received a promotion. 'Back then, the opinion in the military was that Hitler was not senior rank material,' said his superior officer, Fritz Wiedemann, in an assessment.[197] His army comrades described Hitler as an unprepossessing lateral thinker, eccentric, zealous, obedient and modest.[198] Max Amann, one of Hitler's military superiors, was asked during the Nuremberg Trials whether the eventual Führer had stood out as an orator during the war. Amann replied in the negative. 'But after the war, in 1919/20, I didn't know him any more. An unknown fire burned within him.'[199] Fritz Wiedemann reported a similar impression at a regimental meeting in the early 1920s: 'I could see instantly that he had become a different man.'[200] There is no doubt that Hitler's astonishing power over his audience was first discernible immediately after the end of the First World War.[201] Before then, no one had noticed it. But what suddenly caused Hitler to become 'a different man'? What event turned this ordinary person into the despot whose impact on the twentieth century is unparalleled?

Hitler's dramatic personality change can be pinpointed precisely to the days immediately following his exposure to poisonous gas in Werwick, Belgium. As outlined in Appendix 25, a trail of circumstantial evidence suggests that after the gas attack he underwent psychiatric treatment in a hospital near the Polish border. From their investigations, D. Lewis and B. Horstmann have suggested that Dr Forster may have treated Hitler under hypnosis, and that he had thereby unintentionally awoken the Führer in him. Forster was indeed a hypnotherapist, and hypnosis was not an unusual method of treatment at that time, particularly for war neurotics. However, it seems unlikely that hypnosis could provoke such a profound and permanent change in a person's being, as was the case with Hitler. But it essentially makes no difference whether Hitler's psychological metamorphosis was triggered through treatment by hypnosis, a severe shock on the front line, the effect of the poisonous gas (most probably mustard gas), a near-death experience (NDE) or a combination of these factors.[202] What matters is that Hitler underwent a radical internal change in the period immediately following his gas poisoning. The fact that this experience was judged differently by the doctor and the patient is only natural. While the treating doctor diagnosed a 'hysterical psychosis' in Hitler, the patient believed he had received a divine mission.

Karl H. von Wiegand, chief correspondent for Hearst International News Service in central Europe during the 1920s and 1930s, said in an interview with the US edition of *Cosmopolitan* magazine in 1939: 'In simple words he [Hitler] once related to me how his divine mandate came to him. It was just at the close of the war, in November 1918, as he lay in Pasewalk Hospital, blinded from a gas attack on the front. "And as I lay there it came over me that I would liberate the German people and make Germany great." '[203] Ernst Hanfstengel, a close confidant of Hitler from the days after the First World War, and subsequent adviser to President Roosevelt, similarly records: 'Hitler made it known early that while in the infirmary in Pasewalk he received a command from another world above to save his unhappy country. This vocation reached Hitler in the form of a supernatural vision.'[204] In an article on the aspiring politician for *The Nation* in 1923, Ludwell Denny reported: 'During the war he was wounded, or through fright or shock became blind. In the hospital he was subject to ecstatic visions of a victorious Germany, and in one of these seizures his eyesight was restored.'[205] On 9 January 1923, the *Münchner Post* wrote of Hitler: 'He lay in a military hospital. It is said he was stricken by a kind of blindness. And he was freed from this blindness by an inner ecstasy which showed him the way to free the pan-German people from the materialistic enslavement by Marxism and capitalism. He, Hitler, sees it as his duty to free his people. The whole will of this man is determined by the belief in his Messianic mission.'[206] In an early biography from 1935, Rudolf Olden quoted from Hitler's cross-examination in the district attorney's preliminary investigation into his trial for high treason in 1924: 'He heard voices, and the voices called upon him to become Germany's saviour.'[207]

However, Hitler then changed his statement in the main proceedings. Suddenly 'visions' and 'voices' were no longer mentioned. Now Hitler stated only that he had decided to become a politician after learning of the revolution while at Pasewalk.[208] Hitler describes his experiences at Pasewalk in *Mein Kampf*, the book he wrote in prison in 1924, six years after his treatment, in a similarly detached manner. According to this, he was cured at Pasewalk Hospital from blindness induced by the gas poisoning. The passage culminates in the words: 'I, for my part, decided to go into politics.'[209] As unemotional as that sentence may sound, it does provide subtle information about how crucial the experience at Pasewalk must have been to Hitler. Without the decision to become a politician, he could never have become what he considered himself to be: the saviour of Germany. But why is the divine mission so often discussed in early years no longer mentioned in either Hitler's court testimony or *Mein Kampf*? Why did he suddenly omit all references to divine powers when describing the events in Pasewalk?

The answer is found in an editorial published in the *Frankfurter Zeitung* on 27 January 1923: '[...] that Hitler had been wounded in the war during the time of the revolution, suffering a type of blindness that had triggered an inner ecstasy in him which instructed him to become the liberator of his people. It is a remarkable case of war neurosis. These people doubtless experience their obsession intensely, as the delusion eliminates any complexity, and that alone makes a huge impression in the spineless times we live in. These people are certainly not lacking in activity, but rather in the sense and value of the goals by which their will is guided – which is why they are so dangerous in their obsession to the nation as a whole. This is the stuff of which the Leader of National Socialism is made.'[210] As he sat in remand, it must have dawned on Hitler that offering his opponents such valid and devastating arguments on a plate was extremely unwise. The last thing he would have wanted was for his opponents to suspect what he needed to conceal from the public at all costs: that he had indeed been diagnosed a war neurotic at Pasewalk. It is hardly surprising therefore, that Hitler addressed the events at Pasewalk with pointed detachment in *Mein Kampf*. In the years that followed, there is no evidence that Hitler referred to his episode at Pasewalk as a paranormal experience again. In fact, there is no indication that he even mentioned the moment when he 'decided to go into politics' ever again. This, of course, does not mean he himself was not still convinced that what had happened at Pasewalk was of vital significance; to comprehend Hitler's development, it is essential to understand his own interpretation of his experience at Pasewalk. And with all that we know about him, his interpretation is clear. Rudolf Olden describes this in his 1935 biography as follows: 'But that the belief in a calling propels him forward, leads him through the thorn bush of difficulties, supports and maintains him in defeat, is demonstrated irrefutably by his career.'[211]

An analysis of Hitler's personality before and after Pasewalk shows that neither his character nor his convictions had changed. His racism, his anti-Semitism (probably unleashed in the last year of the war), his opposition to democracy and international organisations and his exaggerated love of 'Germanness' – all this had been present *before* Pasewalk, as had his violent temper, vindictiveness, tendency towards arrogance, delusion of genius and the certainty he acquired during the war that divine Providence was on his side. The difference between 'before' and 'after' is not, therefore, that he thought differently or that his character had changed. Hitler was the same, average person after his experience at Pasewalk as he had been before. But there was one crucial difference: what had previously been assumption had now become absolute certainty to him. Before, he had 'believed' himself to be a genius; now he 'knew' it. Previously, he had 'believed' that divine Providence protected him; now he was utterly convinced of it. His political convictions had also now become 'absolute truths'.

This unshakeable certitude gave Hitler something he had previously lacked, and served as the Archimedean pivot from which he could lift the world off its hinges. He could build on it and develop his teaching. But this certainty also gave him something else: the ability to represent his views with a fanaticism never before seen, and his character traits would now be unleashed with the same vehemence. The energy that suddenly flowed from his own unwavering conviction was reinforced by the validation of his supporters. As the enthusiasm of his supporters grew, Hitler's absolute belief in his mission was further strengthened. In the end, millions believed in him and placed the entire power of a modern Western state at the feet of a coarse, contrived commoner: Adolf Hitler. Neither his political views nor his character were primary reasons for Hitler's transformation into the very personification of evil: rather, it was the abundance of power he suddenly came to possess. Fuelled by this unlimited authority, the dark side of his views and his character quickly spiralled out of control. Only with this power could he have imposed his will to the extremes of Auschwitz and Stalingrad.

Although Hitler was careful not to draw public attention to the events at Pasewalk, he could not prevent his first supporters from remembering his early accounts. The myth of the 'awakening of the Führer' lived on, and Pasewalk became a pilgrimage site for Hitler's followers during Nazi rule. However, in an attempt to eliminate the last traces of Hitler's stay at Pasewalk, the hospital was razed to the ground by the Nazis in 1934. An oratory and a meeting hall were built, and a procession area created. A bronze bust of Hitler was erected in the main hall. And above it, in hammered bronze, was the phrase: 'I, for my part, decided to go into politics.'[212] When Hitler came to Pasewalk on 25 October 1932 on the campaign trail, many of his supporters must have been very excited about what he might say at this historic site. And his speech was indeed remarkable. The *Pasewalker Zeitung* reported: 'Unfortunately, he did not utter a syllable about the fact that he had once been cured of serious gas poisoning in Pasewalk.'[213]

APPENDIX 27

The British Naval Blockade

At the beginning of the First World War, England continued to adhere to existing international agreements. However, this was to change after 1915. In violation of the martial maritime law in force at the time, England blockaded the entire North Sea. Widespread minefields were planted and England refused to consider the safety of the neutral merchant shipping trade. In 1916 all utility goods were declared contraband, and from 1917 onwards the English Navy took to seizing neutral trading vessels. Even protests by the US government against this flouting of international law did nothing to dissuade the English government from its policy.

The *Hungerblockade* (hunger blockade) had devastating consequences for the civilian populations of Germany and Austria. In the *Kohlrüben-winter* (turnip winter) of 1916–17, the supply difficulties reached their peak. Thereafter, until 1919, Germany remained in a continuous supply crisis. The author Stefan Zweig reported that starving people would break into railway cars in train stations to rummage for food. Women and children from the cities stole potatoes from farmers' fields and the owners of cats and dogs did not leave their pets to roam the streets, for fear they would end up on someone's dinner table.[214] From 1917 onwards, the first symptoms of starvation began to appear. 'Oedemas, [...] tuberculosis and alterations of children's bones caused by rickets were observed in all larger towns and industrial regions [...] Aside from schoolchildren and adolescents, the elderly and those with chronic illnesses suffered most from the lack of food.'[215] 730,000 civilians succumbed to the hunger blockade.[216] 'A committee of American women travelling through Germany by order of Herbert Hoover, chief of war relief and later president, reported in July 1919, "If the conditions continue which we have seen in Germany, a generation will grow up in Central Europe which will be physically and psychologically disabled, so that it will become a danger for the whole of the world." '[217]

From the British perspective, the blockade was a success. The British Foreign Minister, David Lloyd George, in retrospect declared it to be 'the deciding factor in the victory of the Allies'.[218] In fact, the hunger blockade did lead to an increasing ill will towards the war amongst the German population. In many cities it came to disturbances and *Brotkrawalle* (bread riots). However, the hunger blockade also had another effect: it became a powerful propaganda tool for Hitler. Above all, the fact that the breach of international law continued after the ceasefire of 11 November 1918 and remained in place until the signing of the Treaty of Versailles infuriated the people and fuelled resentment against the politics of the British. It was not difficult for Hitler to convince his listeners that a treaty signed under such extortive conditions held little value. As the hunger blockade had claimed victims in so many German families, it did not fade from memory, particularly in the cities, for a long time. The Nazi propaganda machine continued to exploit these memories during the Third Reich; during the Second World War there were constant reminders of the 'brutality of the Allies' and the hunger blockade.[219]

APPENDIX 28

Four Seasons Hotel

Around the turn of the century, the Hotel Vier Jahreszeiten (Four Seasons Hotel) in Munich was the premier place to stay. It offered Wilhelmian pomp and a dignified atmosphere of luxury so successfully it attracted guests such as the press baron Joseph Pulitzer, Henry Ford and the King of Siam. In 1914, only weeks before their assassination triggered the First World War, the Austrian heir of the throne Franz Ferdinand and his wife Sophie von Hohenberg stayed in the hotel. At the time the Thule Society made the Four Seasons their home the hotel was owned by the brothers Max and Adolf Obermayer.[220]

From August 1918,the Obermayers rented rooms with seating for up to 300 people to this lodge for the purpose of giving public lectures. The Thule Society also rented smaller 'club rooms' for their secret meetings and their office. Their emblem was mounted in the rooms taken up by the society: a swastika with a sword. During the communist rule between November 1918 and May 1919, the Thule Society invited other right-wing groups to conspiratorial meetings in the hotel, with the goal of overthrowing the communist government. The Red Guards became aware of their activities, and found weapons and fake identification papers during a search of the hotel. Several Thule members were arrested, among them the secretary of the society, Heila von Westarp. The execution of those arrested by the Red Guard provided welcome propaganda ammunition for right-wing agitators in the period following the revolution.[221]

APPENDIX 29

Hitler's Eyes

Albert Speer, Hitler's national architect and Minister for Armaments, recalls: 'It was in the spring of 1931 in connection with the so called *Stennes Putsch*, a kind of revolt in the Berlin SA. After Hitler had removed Stennes, he ordered all the members of the SA and the connected associations to a roll call in the *Sportpalast* [palace of sports]. Surprisingly Hitler did not make a speech, but performed an impressive ritual. He stepped out into the rows of uniforms. Complete silence fell. Then he began to pace down columns. One could only hear his footsteps. It lasted hours. Finally he arrived in my row. His eyes were focussed rigidly on those assembled; he seemed to want to obligate each man through his gaze. When he came to me I had the impression that a pair of wide open eyes took possession of me for an immeasurable time.'

The hypnotic power of Hitler's eyes is the object of countless reports. The Hitler biographer R. Binion quotes 'from a very large number of people, who have by their own admission, fallen under the spell of Hitler's eyes: Karl Dönitz, Joachim v. Ribbentrop, Ernst Kaltenbrunner, Johann Ludwig Graf von Schwerin-Krosigk, Constantin Hierl, Paul von Hindenburg, Franz von Papen, Werner von Blomberg, Hjalmar Schacht, Hans Frank, Kurt Lüdecke, Ernst Hanfstengel . . . '[222] What is striking is that the 'compelling power' of his blue eyes only emerged after 1918. Neither contemporary witnesses in Vienna, nor his comrades from the First World War, retained any particular memory of his eyes.[223]

APPENDIX 30

Revolution in Munich

By September 1918, the leaders of the German Army had to accept the fact that the war had been lost. General Erich Ludendorff called for a ceasefire; the Allies demanded the abdication of the Kaiser and there was uproar amongst the population of Germany. Hunger, social misery and the countless victims of war had turned the people against the government. When on 29 October 1918 navy sailors in Kiel and Wilhelmshaven mutinied, the uprising turned into a revolution, and within days revolutionary workers' and farmers' councils came to power in all of the large German towns.

In Munich, a group of radical artists and intellectuals joined forces with the leaders of the anti-clerical Bavarian Farmers' Association and groups of disillusioned soldiers. On 7 November 1918, the revolutionaries marched to the residence of the Bavarian king, who fled Munich with his wife and three daughters in a rented cab dressed in civilian clothes. In other parts of Germany also, the collapse of the monarchy was unstoppable. State princes abdicated one after the other, as did Kaiser Wilhelm II. On 9 November, the Social Democrats and the communists declared the Republic in Berlin. In Munich, the journalist/philosopher/pacifist/socialist Kurt Eisner declared Bavaria a *Freistaat* (free state) two days earlier and had formed a left-wing, revolutionary government.

Only a few weeks later, there was a split within the revolutionary movement in Munich and elsewhere. Two anti-monarchist factions stood in increasingly irreconcilable opposition to one another: on one side were the socialists and conservatives, who demanded a parliamentary democracy; and on the other side the communists, anarchists and bolshevists, who wanted to enforce a system of workers' and farmers' councils. In Berlin, street battles erupted between the hostile revolutionaries. The situation was aggravated by privately financed *Freikorps* (voluntary corps) units, some of which fought their own personal battle (against any type of republic), whilst other units joined forces with the parliamentary faction. Parts of the official army fought on both sides simultaneously. The novelist Oscar Maria Graf (1894–1967), who lived in Munich at the time, relates: 'There was open war in Berlin. Gruesome news reports arrived: cannons thundered on the roads, flame-throwers were in action, machine guns roared.'[224] The chaotic battles between *Freikorps*, communists, Army, social democrats and conservatives cost thousands of lives all over Germany.

In Munich, the situation became increasingly tense, but had not yet deteriorated to fighting in the street. In long debates, advocates of the parliamentary system asserted themselves, and on 12 January 1919 parliamentary elections were held in Bavaria. The main losers of the election were the ruling revolutionaries. Of the 190 seats in the *Landtag*, Eisner's party only received three mandates. As Eisner was on his way to announce his resignation, he was shot dead by a right-wing radical. Now the revolution had a martyr. Eisner suddenly appeared as the spearhead of a socialist paradise and received a triumphal burial attended by 100,000 people and twenty bands. His death also resulted in an act of retaliation in the *Landtag*, which left three members of parliament dead. All of a sudden, the previously bloodless Munich revolution had taken a violent turn.

At the end of March, when it became known that Béla Kun had come to power in Hungary with a bolshevist revolutionary government, the left-wing radicals were given new impetus and the communist writer Ernst Toller, the poet and anarchist Erich Mühsam and the philosopher and anarchist Gustav Landauer declared the Räterepublik Bayern (Bavarian Soviet Republic). The elected government fled to Bamberg, while the three artist-politicians wanted to forge 'brotherly connections' with Russia and Hungary and rejected any collaboration with the parliamentary system in Berlin. The revolutionaries intended to realise a 'society without coercion', in which the 'free development of the individual' was the highest legally protected interest. Landauer declared that: 'Everyone works according to what they feel is right; the relationship of subordination is abolished, the legal way of thinking has ended herewith.'[225] One radical decree followed another, most of which could not be enforced due to the lack of 'state powers', which contradicted the self-conception of the anarchists. Hence, chaos reigned in all areas of daily life. An attempted putsch by the Republikanische Schutzwehr (Republican Defence Force), who were loyal to the government in Bamberg, was violently suppressed by the Red Army, and seventeen people lost their lives.

During the fighting, a further revolution took place and a second soviet government was declared under the leadership of Eugene Leviné and Max Levien, who aspired to copy the bolshevist rule in Russia. The new rulers immediately expanded the Red Army until its membership reached 20,000. This reinforcement was urgently required, as the Bavarian government in Bamberg had requested troops from Berlin, who had begun marching on Munich together with *Freikorps* units. After initial successes, the Red Army was soon made acutely aware of its inferiority. On 2 May, the *Weissen* (Whites) conquered the city after heavy fighting, which left between 600 and 1,000 dead. In the following weeks, over 2,000 supporters of the revolution were executed or given long prison sentences. Crimes perpetrated by rightwing supporters, on the other hand, generally did not reach court, or if so, resulted in mild sentences. The state concessions regarding rightwing violence turned Munich into a haven for radical right-wing groups and finally into the *Hauptstadt der Bewegung* ' Capital of the Nazi Movement' under Hitler in the 1920s.[226]

APPENDIX 31

Hitler during the Revolution

When Hitler was discharged from the military hospital in Pasewalk on 19 November 1918, the First World War had already come to an end. Hitler travelled by train to Munich, where revolution had broken out and the left-wing revolutionary Kurt Eisner had seized power.[227]

On 21 November, Hitler registered with the 2nd Infantry Regiment, which was billeted in a school. Here, too, the atmosphere was charged with revolution. Soldiers and officers had joined forces and *Soldatenräte* (soldiers' councils) had taken command. Hitler and his fellow soldiers would have had the opportunity to join a right-wing volunteer corps, such as the Republikanische Schutztruppe (Republican Defence Force), which led a putsch against the Munich revolutionaries on 14 April, but he remained with the army, subordinate to the left-wing revolutionary commanders. However, by all accounts he was no longer the inconspicuous soldier, invisible to most. For the first time, the previously self-conscious, inhibited Hitler stood out amongst the nameless to be voted *Vertrauensmann* (confidant) of the regiment in mid-February. Two months later he was voted onto the *Batallionsrat* (battalion council) by his comrades. There are no clear and undisputed findings as to his own political position at the time, but his decision to stay in the army suggests he must, at least, have remained neutral in relation to the left-wing revolutionary government.[228]

As one revolutionary government supplanted the other, the Munich garrison took no side. There was very little to do in the barracks. Hitler was assigned to check gas masks and was stationed on watch at Munich central train station for three weeks. When the Munich garrison was incorporated into the Red Army in April, all soldiers were obliged to wear a red armband – an obligation which Hitler cannot have avoided.[229]

Hitler's career as a member of the Rote Garde (Red Guard) did not last long, however. On 1 and 2 May, loyal government troops and right-wing *Freikorps* occupied the city and toppled the communists. Hitler's regiment, which had not engaged in the fighting, was disarmed, the soldiers' councils were dissolved and the right-wing military took control of army and city. Inquiries were established to examine the behaviour of soldiers during the revolution, in order to clear the army of any left-wing revolutionary elements. Hitler was appointed to one of these inquiries.[230]

Under the leadership of the nationalistic anti-Semite Karl Mayr, the *Nachrichtenabteilung 1b* (News Division 1b) endeavoured to stabilise the political situation in Bavaria and within the army. Mayr assembled a group of officers and soldiers to be fast-tracked to become 'trained anti-bolshevist propaganda officers'. Hitler also belonged to this group, further evidence that he was no longer the slightly odd, silent introvert that his comrades had encountered during the four years he spent at the front. After completing public speaking courses, the *Aufklärer* (educators) were to counter left-wing revolutionary ideas amongst the troops with their own propaganda. The courses lasted five days and were held at Munich University. They contained German history, philosophical, economic, as well as domestic and foreign political themes.[231]

In August 1919 Hitler gave his first public address to soldiers recently released from war captivity.[232] On this occasion he attracted attention as an 'outstanding and passionate' speaker, according to several eye-witness reports. On 12 September 1919, on Mayr's orders, Hitler visited a meeting of the DAP or *Deutsche Arbeiter Partei* (German Workers' Party) in order to gather information about its activities. During the ensuing discussion, Hitler made a spontaneous speech which enraptured the audience and launched his political career.[233]

APPENDIX 32

Hostage Killings and anti-Semitism

Before the First World War, Munich had a reputation as a liberal and cosmopolitan city. The author Oscar Maria Graf (1894–1967) described the mood there as follows: 'Christians preached in assemblies, nudist supporters made their demonstrations, individualists and biblical researchers, people heralding the onset of the thousand-year Reich, and codgers espousing polygamy, peculiar Darwinists and race theorists, Theosophists and spiritists were up to harmless mischief.'[234]

For those with extreme right-wing and anti-Semitic sensibilities, Munich was a tough place to be. This is illustrated in the letters of Karl Mathes, who attempted to found a branch of the Germanenorden (Teutonic Order) on behalf of *völkisch anti-Semit*e Theodor Fritsch in Munich in 1913 and who complained repeatedly of the difficult conditions in the liberal city.[235] Few could ever have imagined before the First World War that just a couple of years later, Munich of all places would become the centre of right-wing extremism, and eventually the capital city of Hitler's movement. The city's first shift to the right occurred during the war when the British naval blockade caused immense suffering amongst the civilian population, generating sympathy for right-wing politics. The Treaty of Versailles, which was generally perceived as a humiliation, further strengthened the position of the right wing, as did the chaotic communist governments that came to power after November 1918.

After the revolution was crushed, Munich became a centre for those opposed to the democratic Weimar Republic: members of extreme right-wing free corps; unemployed soldiers; officers mourning the demise of the monarchy; radical right-wing students; influential members of secret societies; anti-Bolshevik refugees from Russia; adventurers; mercenaries; and careerists.[236] Various local, national and international events resulted in increasingly radical right-wing and anti-Semitic sentiments spreading throughout Munich. The right-wing agitators used the Munich Soviet Republic, communist Hungary and communist Russia as evidence that socialism and communism were a front for a single force: international Judaism.

Jews were in fact disproportionately represented among the revolutionaries of the left-wing movements in Europe because after the fall of the old aristocratic political orders, revolutionary movements gave intellectual Jews the opportunity to hold leading positions in politics for the first time.[237] Those on the right were not interested in hearing that the Jewish revolutionaries were intellectuals who had broken with the traditional Jewish community and abandoned the Jewish religion; also, the fact that the actions of Jewish revolutionaries were directed equally against the Christian and Jewish bourgeoisie was deemed irrelevant. Oscar Maria Graf reports that the first anti-Semitic pamphlets appeared in Munich in January 1919. '[The leaflets] were usually seen in small milk or grocers' shops, or posted secretly on walls.'[238]

As proof that 'the Jews' would stop at no brutality, right-wing agitators in Munich cited an event that was to play a dominant role in their propaganda: the hostage shootings in Luitpold Gymnasium (grammar school). Shortly before the counter-revolutionary White troops took the city, seven captured Thule Society members (including one female, the secretary of the society), two White combatants and the Munich art professor Ernst Berger were executed one by one in the schoolyard. Right-wing propaganda revelled in exploiting this gruesome act of the Reds. It was reported that the victims had been dismembered (which the police denied) and that the act had been brutal revenge by the Jews against the German population. In reality, the command to shoot had been given by the *non*- Jewish commander of the Red Guards, Rudolf Egelhofer. The right-wing propaganda also ignored the fact that one of those executed was a Jew (Professor Berger).

For those on the right, the murder of the hostages was proof of the brutality of the Jews and the danger they presented. Long after the end of the revolution, reports of the hostage murders persisted in the Munich newspapers and even *The Times* in London reported the incident under the headline 'Shooting of Hostages. Munich Savagery'.[239] Hitler recognised the propagandist value of the hostage murders and marked its anniversary for years. Every 30 April and on All Saints' Day, the Nazis held vigils at the graves of the murdered Thule members and in the yard of the 'blood school'.[240]

APPENDIX 33

The Thule Society

'When I first knew Adolf Hitler in Munich, in 1921 and 1922, he was in touch with a circle that believed firmly in the portents of the stars,' remembered prominent American journalist Karl H. von Wiegand in an interview with *Cosmopolitan* magazine in 1939.[241]

The 'circle' mentioned here by the chief correspondent from Hearst International News Service was a society listed in the Munich Register of Associations as a harmless study group that researched early German history. Members were affluent, influential people from Munich society: professors, noblemen, manufacturers, senior officials, businesspeople. Before Hitler came into contact with the Thule Society in 1919, the group had already been organising public talks on various Celtic and Teutonic cultural topics for some time. However, the public was not aware of what took place at the secret meetings, to which only Thule members were invited. In reality, the Thule Society was much more than an innocent study group: it was a secret brotherhood. The emblem of the Thule Society was the swastika (facing anti-clockwise like the Nazi symbol) and a dagger. The name Thule referred to the old Ultima Thule, the Land of the North, the mythological homeland of the Teutons. Like Atlantis, legend had it that Thule was a vanished civilisation. The members of the Thule Society believed that the lost civilisation of the Teutons had possessed psychic abilities that were far beyond the technical achievements of the twentieth century. They hoped to rediscover the secrets of this legendary civilisation through occult practices.

There were 'Teutonic' secret societies of this kind in Austria and Germany from the mid-nineteenth century. The spiritual concepts of these factions can be grouped under the term 'Ariosophy', coined by the Austrian seer Guido von List.[242] These Ariosophic groups were independent of each other organisationally, although many of them were more or less closely linked through personal friendships and mutual members. The notions of the Ariosophes referred to Hindu, Gnostic and hermetic ideas. Magical practises from early and medieval Teutonic times played an important part and the different groups were influenced variously by the Pythagorists, the Neoplatonics, the British mystic Madame Blavatsky, the Rosicrucians, Jakob Böhme, Paracelsus and others. As different as the mystic/magical concepts of the individual groups were, they were linked by their belief in the racist philosophy of Guido von List, which asserted the superiority of the Aryans. In their organisational structure, rituals and terminology, the Ariosophic groups resembled the Freemasons, whom they nevertheless rejected due to their supposed 'infiltration by Jews'. As with the Freemasons, there were different levels of initiation in the Ariosophes. The members were gradually introduced to the practises of ritual magic. In these rituals, light, colours, rhythms, symbols or aromas were used to focus mental powers and channel them in a specific direction. The Ariosophes believed this would enable them to bring about changes on the material plane.[243]

The Thule Society was the Bavarian branch of the Ariosophic Germanenorden (Teutonic Order), an association of occultists formed in Leipzig in 1912 by the esoteric and anti-Semite Theodor Fritsch.[244] In 1916, after a meeting with Fritsch, Baron Rudolf von Sebottendorff assumed leadership of the Bavarian arm, calling it the Thule Society.[245] Sebottendorff was an adventurer and occultist, born in Hoyerswerda, Saxony, in 1875 under the name Ernst Rudolf Glauer. In his autobiography *Der Talisman des Rosenkreuzers* (The Talisman of the Rosicrucian),

Sebottenorff discusses his life, which N. Goodrick-Clarke has researched in more detail.[246] Glauer-Sebottendorff had worked on ships, travelling to New York, Sydney, Cairo and Constantinople. He eventually settled in Turkey and there first became involved with occultism. He established contact with the Mevlevi sect of the Whirling Dervishes and was acquainted with the teaching of the Sufis. In his studies, Glauer-Sebottendorff came to the conclusion that Islamic mysticism had Aryan roots. This opinion linked him with Guido von List. The forefather of Ariosophy proclaimed that not just Islam but *all* religious systems were derived from one single original religion, the religion of the Aryans. In 1910, Glauer-Sebottendorff founded a mystic lodge in Constantinople. One year later, he was adopted by Baron Heinrich von Sebottendorff, and so became a baron himself. He returned to Germany in 1913 and married the daughter of a prosperous Berlin businessman. Three years later, he assumed leadership of the Thule Society in Munich.

Women were scarcely represented in the Thule Society, the higher levels of initiation being reserved exclusively for men. Those wishing to join had to complete a questionnaire and submit a photograph, which was examined for purity of race. The following 'blood declaration' also had to be filed: 'The undersigned assures to the best of his knowledge and conscience that no Jewish or coloured blood flows through his veins or those of this wife and that there are no family members of coloured race among his forefathers.'[247] Unlike most other Ariosophic groups, the Thule Society was not content merely with influencing material circumstances through visualisations and ritual magic: the group was also politically active. When the Bavarian King was deposed and the communists took power in November 1918, the opulent meeting place of the Thule Society, the luxury Four Seasons Hotel, became a centre of counter-revolutionary activities.[248] The Thule Society also set up a fighting division that took an active part in the power struggle during the revolution in Munich.[249] In April 1919, it enlisted volunteers, who were smuggled by train in their hundreds to Eichstätt to participate in the attack against the communist regime from there.[250] After the overthrow of the communist government in May 1919, the Thule Society shifted its political activities to the field of propaganda. In October 1918, when German defeat in the First World War was imminent, the Thule Society established a Political Workers' Union, from which the DAP (Deutsche Arbeiter Partei, German Workers' Party) arose. Individual Thule members then appeared as speakers in the DAP. As depicted in this novel, Hitler came across the small, insignificant party during a lecture in September 1919. Soon afterwards, he became the fifty-fifth member of the party. Hitler must have quickly realised who was behind the DAP, because he promptly demanded an end to the influence of the Thule Society over the party. Two months after Hitler joined, he set down points of order that stated: 'Excludes all forms of dictation [for the party committee] by a superior or lateral government, whether it be a circle or lodge, once and for all'.[251]

This put an end to the Thule Society's influence over the DAP. Thule party chairman Karl Harrer resigned. However, some Thule members maintained close contact with Hitler after the separation of the Thule Society and DAP, most notably the eventual Deputy Führer, Rudolf Hess, and the subsequent editor-in-chief of the most important Nazi paper, the *Völkischer Beobachter* (Nationalist Observer), Dietrich Eckart. It is known that Eckart soon came to see Hitler as the long-awaited 'saviour'.[252] Rudolf Hess also seems to have been mesmerised by Hitler. Most Thules saw Hitler as the 'drummer', the herald, the prophet of who was to come. Some, like Rudolf Hess, might have seen him from the very beginning as being 'the one'. But certainly there were also other opinions of Hitler in the Thule Society. It is very likely that the ex-DAP chairman Harrer was not the only one to reject the monopolisation of the party by Hitler. It seems reasonable to assume that Hitler would have been the cause of disagreements and divisions within the Thule Society.

At any rate, after Hitler joined the DAP, the Thule Society fell quiet. It was not involved in the power struggles between the different radical right-wing groups and splinter groups in Munich at the start of the 1920s. It is not proven that Hitler ever set foot in the meeting rooms of the Thule Society in the Four Seasons Hotel. Johannes Hering's notes on meetings of the Thule Society between 1920 and 1923 mention the presence of several Nazi leaders but never Hitler himself.[253] Hitler certainly knew how to use his contacts with influential Thule members to his advantage. Their patronage and financial support was of decisive importance during the initial period of his rise. Dietrich Eckart put Hitler in contact with affluent Munich residents, and Thule sympathiser Wilhelm Frick, adviser of Munich's Chief of Police, guarded his party protectively.

Driven by Hitler's relentless propaganda, the DAP (which Hitler renamed the NSDAP) rapidly developed into a mass movement. The National Socialist movement no longer had anything in common with the conspiratorial gatherings of the Thule members. The dignified atmosphere of the Four Seasons with talks on the early Teutonic age and magic initiation rituals as outlined by Guido von List was in stark contrast to the party meetings in beer cellars, where drunkenness, raucousness and often brawls were commonplace. The mass deployments of the SA (Stormtroopers) were also a world apart from the rarefied atmosphere of the luxury hotel. It is hardly surprising that the number of Thule members who joined the NSDAP was relatively low. However, some of those who did join the party later took up important positions.[254]

After 1926, there were no further signs of life from the Thule Society, but it reappeared with the triumph of the Nazis in 1933. Sebottendorff, who had lived abroad since 1919, re-emerged in Munich and published a book entitled *Bevor Hitler kam* (Before Hitler Came). He also published a magazine, the *Thule Bote* (Thule Herald), and organised Thule meetings at the Four Seasons Hotel again. However, the rebirth of the Thule Society was short-lived. When the second edition of Sebottendorff's book was about to appear in 1934, it was seized by the Nazis and the author was imprisoned. His fate had been sealed when he claimed that Hitler owed his initial successes to the Thule Society. Hitler, who never mentioned the Thule Society in *Mein Kampf* or elsewhere, knew that it could only harm him politically if it were to emerge that such a close link existed between an obscure society of spiritualists and the start of his movement. There are contradictory accounts of Sebottendorff's eventual fate. N. Goodrick-Clarke reports that Sebottendorff travelled through Switzerland to Turkey, where he committed suicide in 1945 after Germany's defeat. Reginald H. Phelps quotes Sebottendorff's publisher, H. G. Grassinger, who claims that Sebottendorff was killed by the Nazis. The Thule Society continued to exist officially until 1937 and then quietly disbanded.

The Thule Society is significant to the Nazi movement not just because Hitler assumed control of the DAP from it. Sebottendorff, the Grand-master of the Thule Society, was also the owner of the Eher publishing house, which Hitler bought in 1920. He turned the newspaper produced there into the *Völkischer Beobachter* (Nationalist Observer), which quickly became the most important weapon in the Nazi propaganda arsenal.[255] Additionally, evidence suggests that Hitler also appropriated the Thule Society's emblem, the swastika, as well as the '*Sieg Heil*' form of greeting.[256]

Hitler took the party, his first supporters, the newspaper, the gestures and the swastika from the Thule Society and used these external aspects as a 'suit of armour' (in the words of Sebottendorff).The Grand Master of the Thule brotherhood is not exaggerating when he claims that it was this 'suit of armour' that helped Hitler to gain power in a period of time that would otherwise seem unnaturally short. The many links between Hitler and the Thule Society have been proven incontrovertibly by historical research. The counter-revolutionary activities of the Thule members during the revolutionary period in Munich have been examined and documented in detail. Conversely, the occult background of this secret society – the rituals and esoteric teachings of the Ariosophes – is barely acknowledged in serious historical texts and is often not even mentioned. There are, however, countless non-scientific books that deal mainly with the occult aspect of the Thule Society. As the correlation between the Thule Society and the beginnings of the Nazi movement is not disputed, the fact that the Thule Society was also an occult lodge opens up a virtually endless realm of possible speculation. Some 'Nazi occult' authors come to the conclusion that the roots of National Socialism can be found in the occult philosophies of the Thule Society. However, this is not strictly accurate. The extent to which certain aspects of Guido von List's world view may have been incorporated into Nazi ideology is discussed in more detail in Appendix 34, Guido von List.

Historical science may never have addressed the theories of Nazi occult authors seriously, but the flood of Nazi occult publications has created its own reality over time. In the world of these theories, National Socialism becomes a movement controlled by higher powers. Some authors claim that Hitler was used by the Thule members for their purposes. Hidden Masters of the Thule Society allegedly manipulated Hitler using telepathy and turned him into a medium. Other authors claim that Hitler was instructed in magical practices by the Thule Society. However, there is not the slightest evidence of the secret command group that was supposed to have controlled Hitler, or of Hitler's occult leanings.[257] .What can be said with great certainty on the basis of historically proven fact is that Hitler exploited the Thules, and not vice versa. He maintained the necessary contact as long as it was advantageous to him. Once he no longer needed the Thule Society, he ignored it and denied it. However, that does not mean that the mystic notions of the Thules did not play a significant part in Hitler's rise. On the contrary: what would have become of Hitler if he had not come across this society? What would have become of his delusions if certain members of this group of influential people had not validated them? This in turn could only happen because the spiritual beliefs of the Thules led them to expect a messianic figure, a saviour, referred to as '*der Starke von Oben*' (literally: the Strong One from above).

The myth that immediately formed around Hitler and was instrumental in his meteoric rise to power has its origin in the beliefs of the faithful disciples of Thule.[258]

APPENDIX 34

Guido von List

The millennia-old swastika symbol was popularised in esoteric circles throughout Austria and Germany by the Austrian writer Guido von List (1848–1919). List called the swastika *Hakenkreuz* (literally 'hook cross'), a term later used by the Nazis. However,[259] List's significance in the story of Hitler is not limited to his role as the 'Father of the Swastika'. Through his writings, List prepared the ground for the belief in a pan-German world Reich, a racially pure utopia, and most importantly, a German saviour, the 'Strong One from Above', who would make this utopia a reality.[260] The views of this *völkisch* occultist influenced Hitler's early devotees, and very probably also Hitler himself. In Hitlers Wien (Hitler's Vienna, 1996) Brigitte Hamann stated that 'during Hitler's period in Vienna, List's main works appeared in rapid succession. They were covered so extensively in the pan-German newspapers [which Hitler read] readers could inform themselves thoroughly without ever having to buy one of his books.'[261] There are also indications in the memoirs of Hitler's friend Kubizek that young Hitler not only studied von List's works in the papers, but owned at least one of Guido von List's books personally.[262]

List was born in 1848. At the age of fourteen, he had a vision in a church. This experience shaped the rest of his life, as he subsequently became involved with the Ario-Germanen, a passion that stayed with him until his death. The Ario-Germanen, a term List coined, are the blond, blue-eyed Aryans whom List also called 'people of light' or '*homo europaeus*'.[263] He believed that these were the genetically preordained rulers of the world. As a sign of his Aryan 'racial nobility', middle-class List gave himself the surname prefix 'von' and began to perform eccentric 'research': he described the religion and society of the prehistoric Aryan culture on the basis of intuitive insight. The findings of archaeological research were acknowledged by List only if they confirmed what he had 'intuitively observed'.[264]

The fact that the Viennese Academy of Sciences refused to recognise List's 'research' did not prevent his supporters from revering him as a prophet. Throughout Austria (and later also in Germany), groups emerged that were devoted to the 'Wisdom of the Aryans' or Ariosophy – another term coined by List. In 1907, List's supporters (which included wealthy industrialists and Lueger, the Mayor of Vienna) established the Guido von List Society, which published List's writings. List claimed that he had rediscovered the old knowledge of the Armanen, who had been priests, judges and teachers in ancient Ario-German times. He believed that this rediscovery was a sign that a new phase in the development of mankind was at hand, and wrote: 'But it is set down in the original law of nature, of becoming, transforming and passing into new existence, that [...] the Ario-Germanic Armanen-ship will be reborn – even if in another form – awakening from apparent death and in a renewed brilliant existence as a mentor of deliverance to show future ages the paths to sun redemption.'[265] List prophesied that the coming of a redeemer, who would proclaim the 'ancient wisdom in new vestments', was imminent, and wrote: 'But although Armanen-ship as the body or the form of its teaching, died away, the spirit, the Armanen doctrine, lived on eternally, outside reality, improving, deepening, and is now pressing with fortified strength for another rebirth and is currently creating a new body, that is, a new physical form, which is the very same *Starke von Oben* of whom *Völuspa* sings and says: 'And he comes to the ring of the chieftains the *Starke von Oben* to settle the dispute. He decides all with simple conclusions. That which he builds will last eternally.'[266]

The Völuspa Prophecy to which List refers is part of the old Nordic Edda myth. Like John in Christianity, List saw himself as the herald of a new era, a new religion and a (German) saviour. The fact that the expectation of a 'German messiah' was part of the creed of the Ariosophic Thule Society in Munich, and consequently helped Hitler at the beginning of his career, is explained in more detail in Appendix 35, The Expected Saviour.[267] The Völuspa Prophecy of the 'Strong One from Above' who was to come to 'settle the dispute' was repeatedly referenced in List's books. When Hitler appeared, the prophecy suddenly seemed to make sense. Hitler did in fact settle the differences between quarrelling right-wing groups and parties, and united them under his leadership. The voices that had been calling for the separation of the Catholic south from the Protestant north of Germany had also been silenced, and Hitler had managed to gain both separatists and communists for his party. When elected Chancellor of the Reich in 1933, he presented himself as the man who had 'settled differences' and who had succeeded in unifying a Germany at risk of disintegration. His religious affiliation, which meant nothing to him personally, had an important symbolic power in this respect. Hitler, the Catholic, governed the Reich from Protestant Berlin. He appeared to be above not just political parties, but religious faiths. For the occultists within the Nazi movement and in the party elite (Himmler, Rosenberg, Hess), his ascension to power must have been the final proof that Hitler truly was the prophesied redeemer.

As the reawakening of Aryan culture was imminent, according to List, the past he 'sensed' was of the utmost importance for the future of *homo europaeus*. List claimed that the culture of the old Ario-Germanen had been far more advanced than the culture of twentieth-century *homo europaeus*. He claimed the former, advanced civilisation had declined because the Ario-Germanen had mixed with 'foreign races and mixed races' that had immigrated to Europe from Asia and Africa. As a result, the Aryan intellect had been 'more or less depreciated [...] in the ratios of blood mixing'.[268] At the same time, the Aryans' genetic legacy had improved the quality of foreign races and enabled them to found cultures.

During the age of their advanced civilisation, said List, the Ario-Germanen had ensured that their own blood remained pure. Everything had been subordinated to this 'holy' purpose, including religion.[269] However, knowledge of the importance of maintaining racial purity had supposedly been lost over time. List was convinced that the predicted dawn of Wodanism in a 'contemporary form' would result in the Aryan mixed races that had developed in Europe being bred back into the original 'noble race'.[270] He writes: 'The half-blood Ario-German, whose perception is clouded by his bastardised blood, requires guidance by an Ario- Germanic racial law – German law – that will rise again, because it must rise again!'[271] Contempt for the 'foreign nation' (the Jews) can also be inferred from List's writings, although List's anti-Semitism was quite restrained compared with prevailing sentiment in Vienna at the time.[272]

List founded a secret society which he called Armanenschaft in 1907. With the aid of the secret Armanen knowledge, Armanenschaft was to be the spearhead in the race war to establish a new spiritual Germany. The symbol used by Armanenschaft members for identification was the swastika. In 1911, List created the High Armanen Order (HAO), which had similar aims to Armanenschaft. List's secret societies had links with the Ordo Novi Templi of Lanz von Liebenfels, the Artamanen; the Bayreuth Ring and other *völkisch* groups and lodges in the German Reich such as the Deutsch-Nationale Handlungsgehilfenverband, the Reichshammerbund, the Germanenorden and the Thule Society.[273]

In 1932, one year before Hitler came to power, Lanz von Liebenfels, an Ariosophe and member of the Guido von List Society, boasted that Hitler was 'one of our disciples'.[274] As many of Guido von List's views also occur in National Socialism, one might assume that the roots of Hitler's world view can be found in the occult setting of the Ariosophes; in other words, that National Socialism represents the political realisation of Guido von List's race mysticism. This would be an oversimplification, however. As stated above, the young Hitler would undoubtedly have encountered List's ideas in Vienna. Later, as Führer, he shared List's vision of a 'worldly religiousness', a religiousness that 'paid homage' to 'realism'.[275] However, it is highly unlikely that Hitler was enthusiastic about the esoteric and old- Germanic speculations of the Ariosophes. The revival of the ancient Germanic cult was just as alien to Hitler as the aversion to modernity and technology prevalent in Ariosophic circles. In fact, Hitler scoffed at '*völkisch* travelling scholars' who 'daydream about old-Germanic heroism, of grey antiquity, stone axes, spear and shield' in *Mein Kampf*.[276] But this does not preclude the possibility that the eclectically minded Hitler incorporated various set pieces from List's ideas into his world view, thereby basing it on a pseudo-rational foundation. List's concept of the degeneration of the prehistoric Aryans through the mixing of races is found in *Mein Kampf*, as is the claim that only Aryans are able to found cultures.[277] List's visions of a 'race state' and 'race laws', the emphasis on equal training of physical and mental abilities in the young and the importance of marriage as a means to breed the 'highest quality offspring possible'[278] also reappear in National Socialism.[279] The division of a future Aryan state into '*Gaue*', as proposed by List, was carried out by the Nazis, and the farming industry was officially named Reichsnährstand in the Third Reich, a term coined by List for agriculture. The Marshal, who according to List was 'directly beneath the king'[280] in Wodanism, became Reichsmarschall Göring under the Nazis, a previously non-existent position in Germany.

List's ideas seem to have shaped Hitler's self-image as well. At public rallies, Hitler repeatedly referred to himself as a 'tool of destiny' and also said in his speeches that he attributed his power to the fact that he acted 'in the spirit of Providence', and therefore embodied 'Divine will'.[281] List characterises the Armanen, the leaders of the Ario-Germanen, in much the same way. He writes that the Armane who knows and embodies the universal knowledge 'ascends in it', so that the Armane 'risking his own human life, his own material advantages, draws his followers with him rapturously, not veering left or right, charging straight towards his goal of the Sun.'[282] The following passage from List also exhibits striking similarities with Hitler's self-image: 'The feeling of inwardness, the awareness of carrying his God with all of His traits enclosed within him, created that elevated self-confidence in the strength of one's own spirit, which grants miraculous power, miraculous power that lives within all people strong of spirit who believe utterly without doubt in this force.'[283] According to List, the Armane comes to the realisation 'of his own immortality through oneness with God'[284] which is the key to absolute, godlike power: 'The more man is aware of his godliness, the more he gains power in equal measure over everything and raises himself up ever more to God himself.'[285] Compare this to Hitler's declaration on 27 June 1937: 'As weak as the individual is in his entire being and actions compared with almighty Providence and its will, so immeasurably strong is he at the moment when he acts in the spirit of this Providence! Then that power flows down upon him that has distinguished all great phenomena in the world.'[286]

A note written in a book from Hitler's library currently stored in the Library of Congress in Washington suggests that the correlation between List's and Hitler's world views could be more than coincidental. The book, by the Indian philosopher Rabindranath Tagore, contains the following handwritten dedication from 1921: 'To Mr Adolf Hitler, my dear Armanen brother, B. Steininger'.[287]

APPENDIX 35

The Expected Saviour

'The ravens may still circle the Untersberg, where the Armanen spirit awaits its rebirth, but the signs are amassing that tell us the time is nigh when the gateway must open for the coming of the Reborn One, for the 'Strong One from Above', who will come to end the dispute with simple conclusions, to give the renewed Armanen law to all peoples for the emergent new era. So we stand before the morning *Götterdämmerung* of the Aryan spirit, so as the mists rise, so will the *Waberlohe* rise up, which gives birth to the new sun.'[288]

These words, which conclude Guido von List's book *Die Armanenschaft der Ario-Germanen* (The Armanen-ship of the Ario-Germanic People)[289] convey the mood of certain esoteric circles in Germany and Austria at the start of the twentieth century. Wistfully, the Ariosophes, inspired by

Austrian Guido von List, awaited 'His' coming.[290] The Ariosophes were not alone; supporters of the politically oriented Pan-German Movement also longed for the arrival of a 'liberator figure'.[291] The publisher Julius F. Lehmann, who published racist and nationalistic texts, was particularly active in the local Munich branch of the Pan-German Society. Even before the First World War, Lehmann had hoped that Germany would produce a 'new Luther', someone with the qualities it would take to lead a battle 'in which the foundations will be shaken, a battle that would force the entire nation, in fact the entire world, to take a stand on the ultimate issues'.[292]

Guido von List's Ariosophes envisaged the prophesied German Messiah as a man with superhuman qualities. List, who was revered by his followers as a prophet, said that: 'There have been and will be men-gods – that is, highly developed egoities of the genus *homo sapiens* – throughout time. It is they who bring about progress, leading the masses to higher goals, excitedly and excitingly [...] They were – and still are today – in possession of that extraordinary divine instrument of power that lies dormant in less developed people, merely awaiting development.'[293] List foretold that the German Redeemer, whose appearance was imminent, would reign as a man-god and establish a new world order in which a Pan-Germanic Reich would rule the world. This worldwide change would be preceded by a radical spiritual transformation in German-speaking countries. 'A spiritual revolution – or "scientific", if you will – is drawing near, to be followed soon by a moral transformation in Ario-Germanic people which will answer the social question just as the sociologists want, but by entirely different means than the socialists would ever dream of using.'[294]

Though Ariosophes were too few in number to play any significant role in society, the different Ariosophic groups included leading officials and members of the upper classes.[295] Consequently, List's doctrine was passed on primarily in circles that were socially influential. After the defeat in the First World War and the outbreak of communist revolutions throughout Germany, the yearning for a saviour figure gripped larger sections of the German population. The power vacuum left behind after the flight of the German Emperor and the petty squabbling between the party-leaders in the Reichstag stirred up hopes for a strong man who would finally bring order. The national conservatives were searching for a 'new Bismarck', while those in Protestant circles conjured up the 'new Luther'. The German nationalists, for their part, watched with great interest the emergence of the cult of *Il Duce* in Italy.

The Ariosophes, who had been hoping for the appearance of the German Messiah since before the war, expected him to arrive at any moment. The coming of the saviour now, in the darkest hour, was consistent with the Ariosophes' Hindu-inspired philosophy of continual becoming and passing. They believed that the downfall of the old always contained the new. So it was that the 'old' prophet, List, died the same year that the 'new' redeemer, Hitler, entered the public spotlight with his speech at the Sterneckerbräu. Shortly before his death, List declared that defeat in the war was a necessary purification that would be followed by the final salvation of the German people.[296] The coming redeemer was also a central theme pursued by the Thule Society, inspired by the credo of Guido von List. Referring to the Thule Society as a 'circle that believed firmly in the portents of the stars', the chief correspondent of Hearst's International News Service Karl H. von Wiegand said in an interview in 1939: 'There was much whispering about the coming of another Charlemagne and a new Reich.'[297] Thule member and publicist Dietrich Eckart expressed his anticipation in a poem he wrote in the summer of 1919, months before he met Hitler for the first time. In the poem, Eckart refers to 'the Great One', 'the Nameless One', 'Whom all can sense but no one saw'.[298] A leaflet written by Fritz von Trützschler, another Thule member, contains the following sentence: 'No one knows today who this man is and when he will come. But if the field is worked, he will appear. That is our belief!'[299]

Lance Corporal Hitler returned to Munich and into this widespread anticipation. If it is true that Hitler had not been cured of the psychological effects of his poisonous gas exposure, he was not in a 'normal' state at that time.[300] Neither was the country to which he returned 'normal'. After the collapse of the monarchy and the revolutionary upheaval, society was in turmoil. This was the ideal setting for a fictitious figure who initially existed purely in Hitler's mind to take actual form. And conditions were also ideal for projecting the attributes of a fictitious figure onto a man of flesh and blood. Hitler's fiction struck a chord with the distorted sense of reality of the German people, who were clutching at illusions since reality offered no security.[301] Whatever it was that had happened to Hitler in Pasewalk, after this experience he 'knew' that he had a divine mission to fulfil.[302] The 'exceptional' aura that Hitler radiated after his stay at the infirmary was first noted by members of the Thule Society. On meeting Hitler for the first time, Dietrich Eckart is said to have seen in him the 'coming man of Germany'.[303] While the account of Eckart's enthusiasm may have been subsequently exaggerated, excitable young Thule member Rudolf Hess (and eventual deputy of the Führer) does indeed seem to have immediately viewed Hitler as the awaited saviour. He is reported to have exited 'beaming' from one of Hitler's speeches and called out: 'Only the man, the man! He is all!'[304] Ilse Hess's description of the effects of her husband's first encounter with Hitler is reminiscent of a religious conversion: 'He was like a new man, alive, beaming, no longer defeated and depressed. Something completely new, something shocking must have happened to him.'[305]

However, the overwhelming majority of Hitler's early supporters did not think that he could be the Great One they were all hoping for. They took Hitler to be a herald of he who was to come. The term 'drummer' was bandied about and Hitler, who does not appear to have been clear about the nature of his mission himself, willingly assumed this role. 'I wanted to be the drummer at that time not out of modesty, but because I feel that this is the ultimate goal,' he said during his trial for treason on 27 March 1924.[306] Whether drummer or saviour, the aura of being the Extraordinary One surrounded Hitler from the beginning. This aura is hugely important because it made Hitler and his party prominent among the fifty active political parties in Munich. The myth that surrounded Hitler from the very beginning allowed his party to attract more attention within just a few months than the fifteen other parties in Munich that all represented nationalistic interests. On 12 September 1919, Hitler spoke publicly for the first time in the Sterneckerbräu as part of a discussion group, to an audience of forty-three. One month later, he spoke at the Hofbräu cellar on Wienerplatz in Munich. He was still completely unknown, as was his party, the DAP. However, 131 people turned up that night. And when he spoke at the Eberlbräu cellar one month later, 300 people came to hear him. Three months later, he announced his party's agenda before an audience of 2,000.

Neither an advertising campaign financed by generous followers nor Hitler's talent for oration can explain the huge increase in attendance.[307] As demonstrated by the careers of countless politicians around the globe, speaking talent alone does not automatically attract the attention of the public. As in all professions, starting up is the hardest stage in politics. A politician, even the most talented, needs years and often decades of hard work to achieve any kind of public profile. Not so for Hitler: his party's membership grew from fifty-five to over 20,000 within three years.[308] This is despite the fact that what Hitler had to say was neither original nor new. Nationalist agitators had been peddling the same mix of prejudices, phobias and the prospect of salvation since before the war. But even if there is truth in the hypothesis that Hitler owed his first ever successes largely to the word generated by the Thules and the myth that formed around him, it still does not explain his meteoric rise. If the myth was all there was, Hitler's career would never have emerged from the beer cellars of Munich. Like a flash in the pan, the moment would quickly have passed. But Hitler was able to flesh out the myth. He did not disappoint his audience. It was not *what* he said that stirred up a frenzy; it was *how* he said it that mattered. The public sensed that Hitler really was something extraordinary, nothing like the leaders of other parties, who came across as mere mortals, weak and unsure, while he seemed to follow his path with unswerving certainty. Hitler could convey the feeling that he was absolutely sure of himself and had no doubt that he would achieve a 'great, shining, common goal'.[309]

His rapidly increasing number of supporters strengthened Hitler's 'unshakeable belief' that he was special, and the energetic interaction between Hitler and his first supporters led to a rapidly growing party. He 'received baskets of adoring letters, in nationalistic circles people spoke of Hitler as the German Mussolini, he was compared with Napoleon'.[310] Now more and more of his followers saw him as the expected Redeemer.[311] Hitler's speeches reflect the development of his self-image in the early 1920s, from drummer to pioneering forerunner to heroic leader. It may well be that certain ideas of Guido von List which Hitler picked up in Vienna had an influence on his world view and the path he pursued.[312] However, it seems implausible that Hitler took advantage of the moment to mimic the Redeemer or his herald simply because he knew of the prophecies of Guido von List. When Hitler arrived in Munich, there was nothing to suggest that he was preordained to a special role. He had neither money, nor notable qualifications, nor connections.[313] He was a nobody in a sea of nameless war veterans. Where would this lance corporal from Braunau suddenly get the idea to pose as Germany's Redeemer or his herald without any inner impetus? And would Dietrich Eckart and others really have fallen for such a pantomime – even if they were yearning for a messiah?

However, List's ideas could have contributed to Hitler imbuing his experience at Pasewalk with a certain meaning. It is feasible that Hitler, who had to come to terms with his 'supernatural' experience, found an explanation for it in List. There was also a moment in List's life when he was temporarily blinded, which was hugely important for him. List claimed that the secret of the runes were 'revealed' to him in his blind state. Hitler may also have believed himself to be 'exceptional' in the same way as the Armanen, mentioned repeatedly by List in his books.[314] According to List, Armanen are those people who 'recognise their destiny and its irrefutable necessity and insert it into the fate of the universe, and therefore are allowed to swell to that horrific greatness, in that they have overcome everything ignoble in the consciousness of their divinity and seem to have become "destiny itself" '.[315]

This vision of List's is strikingly similar to the self-image of the eventual Führer. He too believed himself to be called by destiny and made every conceivable effort to grow to an 'horrific greatness'. In the consciousness of his 'divinity', he also believed he had overcome everything 'ignoble' within him and had become 'destiny itself'. For Hitler's career to succeed, three prerequisites had to be fulfilled: 1) a nation longing for a new beginning after defeat in a war, famine, revolutionary turmoil, national humiliation and economic chaos; 2) a man convinced of his 'mission' beyond all doubt; and 3) a group of believers who were awaiting just such a man.

The doctrines of the Thule Society confirmed Hitler's self image. All at once, not only did he know that he was exceptional, these others evidently 'knew' it too. All at once, not only Hitler believed he was the Chosen One with a divine mission, but the world around him began to share his vision of himself.[316] It was at this moment that the second most decisive turning point in Hitler's career after his experience in Pasewalk occurred. Because Guido von List had prepared the ground and Hitler found a small circle of believers in Munich, he was able to carry out what he believed was his 'divine mission'.

APPENDIX 36

The Treaty of Versailles

On 18 January 1919, the representatives of the victorious powers of the First World War convened in the Hall of Mirrors at Versailles to negotiate the terms of a peace treaty. The date and location had been chosen deliberately: 18 January was the birthday of the German Reich, which had been founded on that day in 1871, also in the Hall of Mirrors at Versailles. Naturally, the humiliation was immediately understood as such in Germany. That the negotiations excluded a German delegation was also viewed as an indignity.

Despite these negative portents, broad sections of the German population believed in a fair peace, a 'peace without losers', as US President Wilson had promised. However, as the terms of the treaty were revealed in Germany, there was immense disillusionment. Nobody had expected such draconian demands. In 440 articles, the treaty stipulated what was expected of Germany to the most minute detail. Germany was to cede all of its colonies to the Allies and lose 13% of its territory, where 10% of the German population lived. 75% of German iron ores, 68% of its zinc deposits and 26% of German bituminous coal would in future become the property of the Allies. Germany was to surrender almost its entire merchant fleet to the Allies, in addition to 5,000 locomotives, 136,000 cars and 130,000 agricultural vehicles. All private German assets in the Allies' territory were declared forfeited. In addition to all this, Germany was to surrender 50,000 horses and 135,000 dairy and beef cattle at a time when England was maintaining its naval blockade in breach of international law, and the German population was starving.[317] The union desired by the majority of German and Austrian parliamentarians was prohibited by the treaty, and instead of including the new democratic Germany in the community of democratic nations, the allied victors humiliated the country by denying it membership of the newly established League of Nations. It is hardly surprising that the majority of Germans felt like the pariahs of the post-war order.[318] The fact that the treaty blamed Germany entirely for the First World War inspired particular resentment. The alleged sole responsibility of Germany justified the demand for reparation payments, in addition to insistences on military disarmament.

As the treaty only obliged Germany to disarm, not stipulating the disarmament of the other nations, the Germans feared that they would have to live in financial and military slavery to the victorious powers for generations. The reparation payments were not just to compensate for damages incurred through the war; they were also to finance the military expenses of the Allies. As the Allies did not want to conclusively specify the amount of the reparations, the Germans were to sign a blank cheque which would burden future generations. When the German government attempted to make counter-proposals, they were wiped from the table and a bare ultimatum issued: either the German government signed, or the country would be occupied by Allied troops.

In Germany, a storm of outrage erupted. There could be no talk of a 'negotiated peace', and almost all parties described the Treaty of Versailles as a dictate that must not be signed. The government withdrew as it did not want to take responsibility for agreeing to the treaty. Eventually, however, it became clear that there was no alternative. The politically splintered country would hardly have been able to present serious resistance to occupation by the Allies. On 28 June 1919, Germany signed the treaty. But this did not do anything to change its widespread rejection. The Treaty of Versailles also further exacerbated the unstable political situation of the young German republic. The commanding generals of the First World War, Ludendorff and Hindenburg, had started the *Dolchstoßlegende* (Stab-in-the-back Legend), which claimed that the war had been lost because of the revolution in Germany. The revolutionaries, it was alleged, had stabbed 'the undefeated army' in the back. In fact, the reality was quite the reverse: the war had not been lost because revolution had broken out; revolution had broken out because the war had been lost. But only a small number of Germans really knew how hopeless the military situation had been. For most Germans it was simply incomprehensible how a war could be lost at a time when millions of German soldiers were in enemy territory. On the surface, the slogans of the nationalistic speakers that the 'November criminals' had forced the militarily superior Germany into a fatal ceasefire seemed to make sense.

The Treaty of Versailles poisoned the political mood, and economic hardships were no longer blamed on the war, but on Versailles and the government that had signed the treaty. Broad sections of the German population felt that they had been lured into a 'shameful peace' with false promises and were prepared for revenge whenever the opportunity arose. Accordingly, the writer Bertolt Brecht called the Treaty of Versailles a 'ceasefire in a thirty-year European war'. Others called the treaty a 'starting shot for the coming war'. The Machiavellian wisdom that one must never humiliate an opponent whom one cannot fully defeat had been disregarded by the victors of 1918.

APPENDIX 37

Thule–DAP–NSDAP

The *Nationalsozialistische Deutsche Arbeiter Partei* (National Socialist German Workers' Party) or NSDAP came into existence a world away from the rough hordes of the Nazi movement: in the club rooms of the exclusive Four Seasons Hotel in Munich. Here, in October 1918, the members of the occult Thule brotherhood decided that the time was ripe to gain political influence among the proletariat. Karl Harrer was chosen to establish links with the working classes.[319]

Harrer, who was a sports reporter with the conservative *Münchner-Augsburger Abendzeitung* newspaper, went on to found a political workers' group with the metal worker Anton Drexler. Shortly after the group was founded, revolution broke out.[320] During the months-long rule of the communists in Munich, Harrer and other Thule members convened with Drexler and his work colleagues for weekly secret meetings. The main speaker was Harrer. In his speeches, he discussed topics such as: 'Could we have won the war?', 'How it came to war' and 'Germany's greatest adversary: the Jews!'.[321] In January 1919, Harrer and Drexler founded the Deutsche Arbeiter Partei (DAP: German Workers' Party) together with two dozen locomotive construction workers in the Fürstenfelder Hof restaurant. After communist rule came to a bloody end in May 1919, the DAP began to make public appearances and organise addresses and assemblies in the smoky back rooms of small bars. Speakers included the Thule members Alfred Rosenberg, Gottfried Feder and Dietrich Eckart.[322] However, the elitist members of the Thule Society were not interested in joining the political party they had created. The Thules saw the DAP as a means for gaining influence over the masses which would then allow them to control things clandestinely.

On 12 September 1919, the DAP held an assembly in the Sterneckerbräu in the centre of Munich. There were forty-four attendees, including Adolf Hitler, who had been ordered to attend by his superior at the Reichswehr, which was covertly gathering information on the political activities in the city. After Feder's address, there was a general discussion which Hitler used to give his own speech, making a huge impression on those present. A few days later, Hitler received a message stating that he had been accepted into the DAP as a party member. On 16 September, Hitler confirmed his membership, and just a month later gave his first party speech in the Hofbräukeller at Wienerplatz before an audience of 131 people. It was the first large public appearance of the DAP. Another month later, Hitler gave a speech in the Eberlbräukeller, in front of an audience of 300. On February 1920, just a few months after Hitler's first public appearance, the party celebrated its first mass assembly before 2,000 attendees in the festival hall of the Hofbräuhaus.[323] From that moment on, Hitler and his party were taken seriously in political circles in Munich. But how was it possible that a tiny, unknown party with a completely unknown orator was able to mobilise an ever-increasing audience within just a few months, and then convene a large-scale event in Munich's most tradition-steeped place of assembly, the Hofbräuhaus?[324]

The propaganda circulated by the Thule Society was certainly helpful. Some, though by no means all Thule members, were convinced that Hitler was the herald of the German messiah, or possibly even the messiah himself they were all awaiting. But apart from word-of-mouth, another factor was required to facilitate Hitler's first successes: steady material support. Someone had to pay for the posters and leaflets advertising the events; the hiring of the halls had to be financed; and the other costs incurred through organising such assemblies had to be funded. Neither the penniless Hitler nor the party chairman Drexler could do this. To this day, those who provided the vital financial injections have not been definitively identified. On this matter, Joachim Fest writes in his biography of Hitler (1973): 'The National Socialists themselves have fuelled the most outrageous hypotheses through the hysterical secrecy with which they sought to obscure the matter of their funding. The documents on the numerous libel actions settled during the Weimar years because of never-ending accusations were hidden or destroyed after 1933, and from the early days it was a general rule not to store any evidence of material contributions [...]'[325]

Hitler's superior at the Reichswehr, the nationalist Karl Mayr, probably supported the party to a limited extent, but there must have been other sources of finance. The supposition that Hitler was supported by individual Thule members seems plausible, as they were sufficiently affluent to provide sponsorship. The 'hysterical secrecy' regarding the party's funding also suggests the Thules, whose operations were generally furtive. However, Hitler did not permit the Thules to exert any influence over 'his' party.[326] Immediately after the motion was drafted, Thule member Karl Harrer resigned from the board of the party. It was now led by Drexler, whom Hitler could easily influence. After Harrer's resignation, Hitler drew up a party programme with Drexler and renamed the party the National Sozialistische Deutsche Arbeiter Partei (NSDAP). Following the rally in the Hofbräuhaus on 24 February 1920, the ascent of Hitler and the NSDAP was rapid. The number of members rose sharply, from fifty-five when Hitler joined to 20,000 members three years later, at the end of 1922.[327]

APPENDIX 38

Hitler's Ideology

When Martin Bormann, Hitler's powerful private secretary, was asked by his son what National Socialism was, he retorted: 'National Socialism is the will of the Führer! End of subject!' Of the historians and political scientists who have addressed Hitler's ideological notions in depth, many would agree with Bormann. They see National Socialism purely as a construct that allowed Hitler to make absolutes of ideas he had collected through reading and declare them as a political programme. It is also often argued that the term 'National Socialism' is misleading, and what it actually refers to is 'Hitlerism'. Whatever National Socialism was, it had been 'thought out to the end' when Hitler came to Munich after the First World War. When he set down his ideas six years later in *Mein Kampf*, they had certainly been influenced by Dietrich Eckart and others, but nothing new had been added to what Hitler had voiced in his first speeches. Even during Nazi rule, there was no consolidation or elaboration of the ideology. The only programmatic work of the Nazi movement, *Der Mythos des 20. Jahrhunderts* (The Myth of the Twentieth Century) 1930, written by the Nazi 'philosopher' Alfred Rosenberg, was not endorsed by Hitler. He called the content of the book 'Rosenberg's private opinion'.

In *Mein Kampf*, Hitler writes on the subject of ideology that 'wherever [people] have reached a superior level of existence, it was not the result of following the ideas of crazy visionaries but by acknowledging and rigorously observing the inexorable laws of Nature.'[328] A brainchild of 1900s Western thought, Hitler believed in the absolute truth of science. To Auguste Comte and other influential thinkers of the time, science was eternally true: not just in certain controlled circumstances, not just provisionally, but true always and absolutely. Comte had insisted that human history revealed scientific laws; Karl Marx claimed to have discovered these laws, as did the various racist theorists who based their views on their interpretation of Darwin's scientific model of natural selection.[329] Hitler describes the 'inexorable laws of Nature' as follows:

'Every crossing between two breeds which are not quite equal results in a product which holds an intermediate place between the levels of the two parents. This means that the offspring will indeed be superior to the parent which stands in the biologically lower order of being, but not so high as the higher parent. For this reason it must eventually succumb in any struggle against the higher species. Such mating contradicts the will of Nature towards the selective improvements of life in general. The favourable preliminary to this improvement is not to mate individuals of higher and lower orders of being but rather to allow the complete triumph of the higher order. The stronger must dominate and not mate with the weaker, which would signify the sacrifice of its own higher nature. Only the born weakling can look upon this principle as cruel, and if he does so it is merely because he is of a feebler nature and narrower mind; for if such a law did not direct the process of evolution, then the higher development of organic life would not be conceivable at all.[330]

Hitler adopts the view of H. S. Chamberlain and other racist philosophers here, who claimed that the mixing of 'higher' and 'lower' races impeded the higher development of humanity. Preventing the mixing of races and thereby taking the evolution of man into one's own hands was the aim and focus of Hitler's 'teaching'. This is also substantiated by the following passage from *Mein Kampf*:

'Everything on this earth can be made into something better. Every defeat may be made the foundation of a future victory. Every lost war may be the cause of a later resurgence. Every visitation of distress can give a new impetus to human energy. And out of every oppression those forces can develop which bring about a re-birth of the national soul – provided always that the racial blood is kept pure. But the loss of racial purity will wreck inner happiness forever. It degrades men for all time to come. And the physical and moral consequences can never be wiped out. If this unique problem is studied and compared with the other problems of life, one can easily see how unimportant they are by comparison. They are all finite; but the problem of the maintenance or loss of the blood purity will last as long as man himself exists.'[331]

It was only natural that world domination was deemed to fall to a state that had recognised this 'eternal truth': 'A state that dedicates itself to maintaining its best racial elements in the age of race poisoning must one day become master of the world.'[332] However: 'Should man attempt to rebel against the iron logic of nature, he will come into conflict with the very principles to which he himself owes his existence as man. His actions against nature must therefore lead to his own defeat.'[333] Consequently, for Hitler, there was only one alternative. Either a state arose that operated a 'biological policy' and assisted 'eternal nature' in advancing evolution with the help of race laws; or humanity would perish in the not-too-distant future in the 'general mash of races'. So Hitler was fighting his fight not just for Germany, but, so he believed, in the interest of all mankind.[334] 'Race maintenance' was one half of the 'granite foundation' on which Hitler planned to erect his 'Germanic state of a German nation'. The other half was the 'aristocratic principle of nature', the 'inexorable law that it is the strongest and the best who must triumph and that they have the right to endure'. This was adopted from H. S. Chamberlain and other Social Darwinists who had applied Darwin's conclusions about plants and animals to human individuals and nations.[335]

These two 'laws of nature', the right of the stronger and race maintenance, are the root of all of Hitler's other notions, including his anti-Semitism and the land reclamation in the East, where colonies of racially pure Aryans were to be established. Hitler also attributed his rejection of Western democracies to the right of the stronger. To him, the system of parliamentary democracy was a perverse degeneration. It contravened 'the aristocratic principle of nature', as the 'parliamentary principle of vesting legislative power in the decision of the majority rejects the authority of the individual and puts a numerical quota of anonymous heads in its place'.[336] Instead of Western democracy, Hitler proclaimed 'Germanic Democracy', where 'the Führer-legislator' is directly elected by the people. Thereafter, the Führer no longer needs to have his decisions approved by a parliament or similar body. He pursues 'divine Providence' alone, as no human authority is above him, and then employs strong Führer personalities. These in turn employ Führers, and so on. A pyramid of Führers is created, and nobody is elected from below any more by a pack of 'weaklings' who 'hang around in committees and parliaments', each Führer being appointed instead from above. They can each then exercise authority downwards without having to take 'voter interests' into account. 'Incorruptibly' and 'freely', they can serve 'the supreme'. As the Führer-legislator is guided by Providence, the commands the lower Führers receive from above are ultimately divine in nature. This eliminates the need to speculate about the content of these commands. Anyone who does not carry out the instructions of his Führer or criticises them is opposing the Führer-legislator at the top of the pyramid and therefore, ultimately, God. In this way, the 'right of the stronger' becomes Hitler's 'Führer Principle'.[337]

In a similar rational and seemingly logical and therefore compelling way, Hitler attributed all of his political ideas, right up to his day-to-day policies, to the two aforementioned 'inexorable laws of nature'. He even believed he could predict the outcome of a future war with Russia in this manner. In *Mein Kampf*, he writes that a conflict with Russia would pass off victoriously as Russia was on the brink of collapse. The old Germanic ruling class had been replaced by a new Jewish leadership. But as the lowest race morally, he alleged, the Jews were not capable of organising and maintaining a state. Therefore 'the end of Jewish rule in Russia will be the end of Russia as a state. We are predestined by fate to be witnesses of a test of power that will be the most violent confirmation of the rightness of the *völkisch* race theory.'[338] The war against Russia did not, however, produce the result predicted by the 'law of nature', and Hitler's race theory was buried beneath a monumental pile of rubble.

The fact that Hitler's 'teaching' had millions of supporters was certainly due in part to his logical-sounding, congruously structured arguments. The main reason for the success of Hitler's *Weltanschauung*, however, was the charisma of the man himself. This charisma in turn had its origin in Hitler's absolute faith, which was beyond all doubt.[339] Despite his seemingly rational world view based on 'laws of nature', Hitler was no atheist. The anti-Semites regarded atheism as a typically Jewish attitude. Atheism, they claimed, was the natural consequence of the Jewish inability to sense 'higher', 'metaphysical' perceptions. With great reverence, Hitler refers to the 'Creator', 'divine Providence', 'the will of the Lord', and so on in his speeches. And he claimed not just to believe in the divine, but to 'know' the 'divine will'.[340] Accordingly, he writes in *Mein Kampf*: 'Nations that make mongrels of their people, or allow their people to be turned into mongrels, sin against the Will of Eternal Providence.'[341] Consequently, 'God' was always present in National Socialism, as evidenced by the words 'God with us' inscribed on the belt buckles of Hitler's soldiers. The Führer had come to shake the world awake and remind it of the Lord's intent: the higher development of man. 'He who dares to place his hand on the highest likeness of the Lord [the Aryans], commits an outrage against the benevolent creator of this miracle and contributes to the expulsion from paradise,' he explains in *Mein Kampf*.[342]

Hitler promoted his 'race religion' with great skill. Just as the Catholic Church had intentionally erected its cloisters and churches on pagan places of worship to reap the power of the pagan faith, Hitler exploited the power inherent in the Christian faith for his own doctrine by appropriating terminology from Christianity, but linking it with the values of National Socialism. He did this repeatedly in his speeches, using terms such as 'faith', 'will of the Lord', 'divine commandments', and so on. Repeatedly making it very clear to his inner circle that he did not have

Christian ideas in mind, Hitler was visibly concerned with giving the impression that his 'teaching' was a purely politically secular matter that had nothing to do with religion.[343] He proclaimed in *Mein Kampf* that 'political parties have no right to meddle in religious questions',[344] and went on to express similar sentiments in many of his speeches. Only astute observers would realise that this was someone posing as a purely secular leader, who in fact was heralding his own religious doctrine of racial redemption.

Hitler was extremely careful not to provoke any unwanted attention from the Christian churches. Although he criticised them for their 'indifference at the profanation and destruction of a noble and unique creature [the Aryan]',[345] he never directly opposed them. He was a clever enough politician to know that he could ill afford a clash with the churches while creating a national movement or while waging war.[346] But after a victorious conclusion to the war, co-existence with the churches would have ended, and Hitler would have been able to pursue his real goal: the establishment of his new doctrine of redemption. He had stressed many times within his inner circle that the 'actual construction of Germany' would only begin after the war.[347] Hitler was certainly megalomaniacal, but in no way naive. He did not believe that the millennium of the impending Hitler era could be based upon an external political order. His Thousand-Year Reich that was to take over from the millenniums of Christianity was to be founded on his doctrine of redemption. In this teaching, divine will was congruent with Darwin's theory of evolution (or rather, with Hitler's understanding of it).[348] By proclaiming his theory of evolution as quasi-religious dogma, Hitler believed he had overcome the agonising contradiction between faith and science.

The precise character of this doctrine of redemption, blessed by the Lord and the science of nature in equal measure, this 'religion of evolution', has never been experienced by mankind in its final form – fortunately. Hitler was probably not quite sure of its character himself. What was clear was that which he rejected: an atheistic-materialistic world view on the one hand, which he negated as Jewish; but also the new pagan-mystic world view with which people such as Himmler and Rosenberg toyed. Hitler scoffed at obsessions such as these, both in *Mein Kampf* and privately.[349] A more traditional form of 'positive Christianity' was also unfeasible to Hitler. He did not consider himself a Christian reformer.[350]

Hitler repeatedly stated that his teaching had nothing to do with the values of Christianity nor with new pagan-*völkisch* notions. Nowhere is this expressed more clearly than in his Cultural Speech from 1938, an abridged version of which is reproduced here: 'National Socialism is a cool doctrine of reality based on the keenest scientific knowledge and its mental form. By having opened and opening the heart of our people for this doctrine, we do not wish to fill it with a mysticism that is outside the purpose and goal of our teaching [...] National Socialism is not a cultish movement, but a *völkisch*-political doctrine developed from purely racist insights. Its meaning relates not to a mystic cult, but to the maintenance and guidance of the blood-chosen people – so we have not places of worship, but assembly and marching squares. We have not cult groves, but sport arenas and playing fields [...] Mystically inclined occult investigators must therefore not be allowed to worm their way into the movement [...] There is no mysterious intuitiveness at the top of our agenda, but clear recognition and, therefore, open confession. By placing the maintenance and continued preservation of a being created by God at the centre of this recognition and this confession, we serve to protect divine work and so fulfil divine will, not in the mysterious twilight of a new place of worship, but before the open countenance of the Lord [...] Our cult is concerned solely with maintaining the natural and therefore also the divinely intended. Our humility is to bow unconditionally before divine laws of existence being revealed to us mortals and respect them.'

This speech makes especially clear Hitler's aims: the creation of an exclusively secularist, earthly 'religiousness' to be expressed in rituals that had been (and were to be) created by the Nazis. This was exactly what Guido von List had in mind when he wrote that the religion of Wodanism 'knew how to find the apolar direction between spiritualism and materialism by paying homage to the known reality, "realism" '.[351] In Hitler's racially pure Aryan state of the future, Aryans were to 'pay homage' to a reality acknowledged as divine. Even though Hitler never proclaimed a utopian vision, the direction for his nation's future progress was clear: over the course of the millennium, the state founded by Hitler would grow into Guido von List's perfect nation of men-gods.

Many historians have rightly indicated that Hitler figures atypically among the most important men in history. There is no doubt that as a commander, he valued human life as little as Caesar or Napoleon, and that he has shaped world history in a similar way – but somehow he does not sit well among the other giants of the past. What sets him apart from other war-hungry tyrants is the mission he believed he had been called to fulfil, the mission to enforce the 'brazen natural law' of evolution. But as his perception of evolution was based on a pseudo-scientific racist philosophy, Hitler considered it his 'holy obligation' to slay the disabled, Sinti and Roma gypsies and Jews. The religious sense of mission that led him to commit mass murder is more reminiscent of a cult leader than a state leader, a cult leader such as Jim Jones, who, along with his followers, committed suicide in Guyana in 1978; or the sect leader Shoko Asahara, who attacked the Tokyo underground with poison gas in 1995; or Marshall Applewhite, who committed suicide with the followers of his Heaven's Gate UFO sect in California in 1997. However, as Hitler was not the leader of a small cult, but in fact ruled a powerful industrialised nation, his actions caused human suffering on a gigantic scale. This will ensure that humanity does not forget him so quickly. 'My life shall not end in the mere form of death. It will, on the contrary, begin then,' Hitler once said.[352] His prophecy will probably be fulfilled – but not the way he imagined it.

APPENDIX 39

The Swastika

In 1935, two years after taking power, the National Socialists declared the swastika to be the national emblem of the German Reich. The swastika flag simultaneously became the sole national flag. Whether on stamps, belt buckles, lampions or ceiling frescos, the swastika became ubiquitous in the daily life of the German people after 1933. How this symbol came to be used by the Nazi Party is a much-discussed topic which has led to wide-ranging speculations.

Hitler first encountered the swastika at the age of six. He attended elementary school at the cloister of Lambach in Austria, where the symbol can still be found at various locations to this day, being part of the crest of a former abbot. According to the monks, who were questioned on the matter by the author, the emblem is not in fact an image of the swastika, but a representation of crossed carpentry nails symbolising the abbot's profession. Some researchers have claimed that Hitler chose the swastika as the party symbol because it was familiar to him from his childhood. This is definitely one of the least likely theories.

The swastika is one of the world's oldest ideograms. The word 'swastika' is Sanskrit, meaning 'it is good', in the sense of 'so be it'.[353] The oldest occurrences of this symbol were discovered in the Valley of Euphrates and Tigris and in the Indus Valley. Some of them are over

3,000 years old. Swastikas were used in the cultures of the Tibetans, the Chinese, the Indians, the Japanese and the Native Americans. In northern Europe, swastikas were used by the Celts. They are found on stones from around 1000bc, often together with other cross structures. In its long history, the swastika has taken many forms: standing straight or at an angle, with straight or curved arms, the ends facing clockwise to the right, or in the opposite direction. There are many different opinions on the meaning of the swastika. Some authors claim that the anti-clockwise swastika (the Nazi emblem) symbolises misfortune and destruction, while the clockwise version represents happiness and abundance, but this theory ignores the positive connotations of the anti-clockwise swastika in many cultures. Both versions occur in different contexts and can often only be understood in relation to each other.

The many different contextual meanings that swastikas can have make it impossible to ascribe an exclusively positive or negative meaning to either of the two variants. The swastika was used in many places in German folk art. In Scandinavia and the Baltic States, the symbol was linked with the god of thunder and called either '*Hamarsmark*' (hammer sign) or '*Thorshamar*' (Thor's hammer). Among the Indogermans, the swastika is believed to have symbolised the sun. This interpretation was also adopted by the Nazis, who saw the swastika as a 'light sign'. In the course of Christianisation, the swastika disappeared from Europe as a symbol and was virtually unknown in Germany until the middle of the nineteenth century. It was reintroduced in German-speaking countries under the name '*Hakenkreuz*' (literally 'hook cross') by the Austrian mystic and founder of Ariosophy Guido von List (1848–1919). In his book *The Secret of the Runes*, List described the swastika as the symbol of the 'ultimate knowledge of the abiogenesis of the universe'.[354] List included the swastika in his rune alphabet, although it is not part of the scientifically confirmed rune sequences: the swastika was only found *beside* runes on inscriptions. List gives no information in his book on how he came to include the swastika in his rune alphabet. Some researchers have assumed that List copied the swastika from the Russian/British mystic H. P. Blavatsky (1831–1891).[355] As the swastika is used in both Hinduism and Buddhism, Blavatsky included it in the seal of her theosophical movement.

At the end of the century, the swastika was initially used as a secret sign of identification among the followers of different Ariosophical groups. Soon thereafter, the swastika came to be used openly as a crest by large German nationalist associations.[356] The swastika was the official symbol of the German Gymnasts Federation, the Wandervogel movement and some Freikorps units after the First World War.[357] Both the clockwise and anti-clockwise swastikas were used by German nationalist organisations, with no stipulation of a preferred version. The swastika (together with a dagger) was also the insignia of the Thule Society, a secret lodge based on the Ariosophical teachings of Guido von List. The Thule Society gave rise to the DAP (Deutsche Arbeiter Partei, German Workers' Party), which became the NSDAP under Hitler.[358] In May 1919, four months before Hitler first came into contact with the DAP, the dentist Friedrich Krohn composed a manifesto for the party entitled: 'Is the swastika suitable as a symbol for National Socialist parties?'[359] Krohn was a member of both the DAP and the Thule Society.[360] In an interview after the war, he indicated that he had proposed a party symbol of a swastika with curved arms (like that of the Thule Society) but facing clockwise as opposed to anti-clockwise (the direction of the Thule Society swastika).[361] It was black on a white background in a red circle. According to Krohn, Hitler adopted the colouring but changed both the direction of the swastika and the curved arms.

Hitler's swastika was anti-clockwise (like the Thule insignia) and had straight arms. At the founding meeting of the Starnberg NSDAP in May 1920, the party symbol as modified by Hitler made its first public appearance.[362] Hitler's description of this event in *Mein Kampf* confirms Krohn's account, but differs in a few details.[363] Additionally, Hitler makes no mention of the Thule Society. However, as the Thules used the swastika as their insignia, there is no reason to assume that Thule member Krohn's creation had been inspired from elsewhere. Ultimately, the trail of the swastika as a Nazi symbol therefore leads to the Thule Society and consequently to Guido von List.

APPENDIX 40

The SA (Stormtroopers)

The Gymnastics and Sports Club of the (NS)DAP took over event security at public assemblies of the party in 1919–20. The troop, which initially consisted mainly of soldiers known personally to Hitler, dealt with troublemakers in a very brutal manner. As the Munich police tolerated the violence of 'patriotic' groups, however, these attacks usually went unpunished.

At the end of 1921, Hitler renamed the Gymnastics and Sports Club the *Sturmabteilung*, SA (Storm Department). Its membership grew rapidly under its leader, Ernst Röhm, who had joined the DAP shortly after Hitler in 1919. Röhm had suffered serious facial injuries as an officer in the First World War, which had permanently disfigured him. In post-revolutionary Munich, he moved between the War Office and various freecorps organisations. This gave the 'Machine-Gun King', as he was known, access to arms depots that were kept secret due to Allied restrictions. When a demonstration took place against the Weimar government in Munich on 16 August 1922, the SA appeared publicly for the first time with a formation of 800 men and its own flag.[364] Afterwards, the number of members rose rapidly and the SA became the indispensable backbone of the power structure in the Nazi movement.

By September 1930, the number of SA members had grown to over 100,000 men. Hitler now commanded the largest private army in the world. When Hitler legally came to power in 1933, the SA hordes, numbering over 4 million men by then, demanded their 'German revolution' and acted against its political opponents with extreme brutality, often arbitrarily and without orders. 100,000 men and women, mainly communists, but also other opponents and Jews, were imprisoned in makeshift SA camps, some being brutally tortured. Around 500 to 600 prisoners died as a result. In public, the SA also operated with increasing tyranny after Hitler's accession to power, and their arrogance and incendiary behaviour even provoked the rage of Nazi supporters. Complaints came from all sides: commerce, administration and industry protested in the Chancellery of the Reich against the increasingly intolerable abuses by the SA. Hitler called on his people to exhibit moderation, but this had little effect. At the same time, SA chief Ernst Röhm threatened to ensure that the German revolution did not lose momentum, declaring his intention to form a powerful people's militia, alarming the leaders of the army, who wanted to avoid coming under Röhm's control at all costs.

The tensions between Röhm and the heads of the Reichswehr (army) intensified, and Hitler had to decide who had the upper hand in this dispute: his party's army, or the army of the state which he controlled. Hitler opted for the Reichswehr, and obligated Röhm to limit the power of the SA.[365] Although Röhm did accede to this demand, there was now talk in the SA and behind Hitler's back of a 'second, actual' revolution. The 'jumping jack' (Hitler) was to disappear and make way for the 'real Führer'. Conservative political circles in turn aligned themselves against the Nazis with the leaders of the Reichswehr.

Hitler was now threatened on two sides: a potential coup by the Reichswehr together with the Conservatives, and a potential coup by the SA. He had to act – or perish. Hitler chose action. With a gun in his hand, at 7 a.m. one morning he stormed into the hotel room where Ernst Röhm was sleeping and placed him under arrest. Subsequently, murder squads using the codeword '*Kolibri*' were sent out throughout the Reich, executing leading SA members and also using the opportunity to kill a few other political opponents. Röhm was shot in prison.[366] Hitler legalised the murders afterwards using a 'self-defence law'. This was not difficult as the suppression of the SA was received with great relief on all sides. At Göring's command, all police documentation of the 'Night of the Long Knives' was destroyed, as a result of which the exact number of victims remains unknown. According to estimates, between 150 and 200 people fell victim to Hitler's murderous order.

The SA was cleansed in the months that followed. Disciplinary procedures were initiated, many SA members were expelled from the organisation and the power shifted to the SS (*Schutzstaffel*, Protection Squad), a much more disciplined unit which had originally been formed to safeguard Hitler personally. The SA now became Hitler's lapdog, only biting when its master instructed, such as on *Kristallnacht* (Night of the Broken Glass) in 1938, when the SA destroyed Jewish homes and businesses and set fire to synagogues. Otherwise the SA was now little more than it had been stipulated to be at its inception: a gymnastics and sports club.

APPENDIX 41

Prominent Thule Members

As the primary characteristic of a secret society is secrecy, it is not surprising that the historical sciences have little concrete information about the occult aspects of the Thule Society – their rituals, initiations and so on. The possibility for speculation, on the other hand, is endless, which has resulted in the publication of many fantastical theories.[367]

There is also a great deal of speculation about the identities of the leading Thule Society members. From Hermann Göring to Joseph Goebbels, almost all of the big names of the Nazi party are declared Thule members in one book or other. (Göring and Goebbels were definitely not Thule members.) All knowledge about the identities of the Thules is based either on the testimony of the members themselves or on the list of members which Thule master Rudolf von Sebottendorff published in his book *Bevor Hitler kam* (Before Hitler Came) in 1933.[368] How accurate and complete Sebottendorff's list is remains open to debate, and there are good reasons to doubt its accuracy.[369]

Current historical research has accepted as fact that the individuals named in the novel – Rudolf Hess, Hans Frank, Alfred Rosenberg and Dietrich Eckart – were members of the Thule Society. All three later occupied leading positions within the Nazi movement. Dietrich Eckart was made editor-in- chief of the Nazi propaganda newspaper *Völkischer Beobachter* (*The People's Observer*); Hans Frank became General Governor in occupied Poland; Alfred Rosenberg rose to the position of Party Ideologist and was made Reichsminister (Minister of the Reich) of the occupied Eastern Territories; Rudolf Hess had the steepest career trajectory and became the Führer's deputy.[370]

APPENDIX 42

Völkischer Beobachter

The *Völkischer Beobachter* newspaper was the most important propaganda tool of the Nazi party, with a circulation of 1.7 million in 1942. The Munich-based Eher publishing house, which published the *Völkischer Beobachter*, also issued many other Nazi texts, including *Mein Kampf*. When Max Amann, who managed the Eher Verlag business, was questioned during the Nuremberg Trials, it emerged that both he and Hitler had been made multimillionaires by the wild success of the publishing firm.[371] However, Hitler's goal, when he bought the publishing house in 1920, was not financial success. His aim had been to unite the many small nationalist parties, organisations and groups in one single party, the NSDAP, thus creating a powerful national movement. To achieve this, he required a platform from which he could convince those on the right of his vision. The *Völkischer Beobachter* provided the ideal prerequisites for this: the newspaper was known in right-wing circles and established as a 'brand'; it characterised itself as 'standing above the [right-wing] parties' and regularly published columns 'from the movement' and 'from *völkisch* parties'. It belonged to Rudolf von Sebottendorff, the Grand Master of the Thule Society.

Exactly why Sebottendorff decided to sell the publishing firm is not known. Some authors suspect that he was in financial difficulties, while others believe he had lost interest in the company. It is also possible that

Sebottendorff had intentionally sought to ensure the NSDAP obtained possession of his paper. After all, the NSDAP had emerged from the DAP, a creation of Sebottendorff's Thule Society. In December 1920, the publishing house was sold to Anton Drexler, the chairman of the NSDAP. One year later, in November 1921, Hitler acquired all shares in the company, making him the sole owner of the firm.[372]

APPENDIX 43

Obersalzberg

The area around Berchtesgaden, a village in the Bavarian Alps, is said to be among the most beautiful places in Germany. Long before Hitler came here, the poet Ludwig Gangkofer wrote: 'Lord, let those whom you love fall in this land.'

Hitler first came to Berchtesgaden at the start of 1923 to visit Dietrich Eckart, who was in hiding there in the Moritz guesthouse. Eckart was wanted by the police for insulting the President of the Reich, Friedrich Ebert, in the *Völkischer Beobachter*. Hitler also stayed in the Moritz guesthouse, which was situated on the side of Obersalzberg Mountain, with a magnificent view of the Untersberg massif. The Untersberg had always been the subject of myths and legends. It is said to be hollow, with palaces, churches, cloisters, gold mines and silver deposits inside. This underground world is supposedly inhabited by giants and dwarves, and at night the sound of battles can be heard from within. When the giants rise to its summit at the witching hour, it is as if the mountain is surrounded by flames. But the greatest secret harboured by the 'magic mountain' is that of Emperor Barbarossa, who was once transported to its inner depths.[373] Ravens circle the peak of the mountain at the Emperor's command, with orders to tell him when the time has come to reappear in the world. The dwarves would then accompany the Emperor in full battle dress. Guido von List, the father of Ariosophy, believed – probably correctly – that the myth of the Emperor had heathen roots. According to List, the ravens indicated that Wotan had originally lived in the Untersberg. In a prophecy in 1911, List linked the long-awaited German Redeemer with the Untersberg: 'Its gate must open for the emergence of the Reincarnated, for the "Strong One from Above".'[374] As Hitler repeatedly returned to Berchtesgaden after his first visit, it was rumoured in esoteric circles that the time had come when the old prophecies would come true.

Hitler retreated to Berchtesgaden to finish his work on *Mein Kampf* and moved into Wachenfels House on the Obersalzberg in 1928, which he initially rented and later bought. He could easily afford the purchase price as he earned abundant royalties from *Mein Kampf*. After coming to power in 1933, the Obersalzberg became a site of pilgrimage for Hitler supporters from all over Germany. On some days, up to 5,000 visitors came. In 1936, Hitler converted Wachenfels House into the Berghof. After its renovation, the Berghof contained around thirty rooms. In addition to living rooms and bedrooms for Hitler and his guests, there were rooms for staff and security personnel, as well as conference rooms and lounges. At the Berghof, Hitler received ambassadors, presidents and kings, and held staff meetings.

In 1939, the NSDAP presented Hitler with a small house at the peak of the 1,834 metre-high Kehlstein Mountain as a fiftieth birthday gift. At the edge of an escarpment with a drop of 150 metres, a road was built that is still the steepest mountain road in Germany today. The road runs for 1,700 metres and leads to a 130-metre-long tunnel. At the end of this tunnel, there is a brass lift fitted with lead crystal glass. It travels silently through the mountain and directly up into the Kehlstein house, even today. In addition to Hitler's private grounds, there was a party area on the Obersalzberg with hotels for the guard details; a theatre and residential quarters for employees. Party secretary Martin Bormann built a house for himself here, as did Hitler's architect Albert Speer and the head of the Luftwaffe, Hermann Göring. During the Second World War, an enormous system of underground bunkers and passageways was excavated within the Obersalzberg. When Berlin was surrounded by the Russians in 1945, discussions were held on moving the Führer's headquarters to Berchtesgaden. However, Hitler decided against this, and remained in Berlin. On 16 July 1944, Hitler visited the Obersalzberg for the last time.[375]

APPENDIX 44

The Psychotic Redeemer

In the spring of 1943, the precursor to the CIA, the US Office of Strategic Services (OSS), commissioned the Boston psychoanalyst Walter Langer to draw a psychological profile of Adolf Hitler. Using reports from contemporary witnesses, agents and other sources, Langer and his team were to analyse Hitler's personality. Langer also developed scenarios anticipating the Führer's future behaviour and foretold his final days with astonishing accuracy. In the event of defeat, he predicted, Hitler would fight to the bitter end and eventually take his own life.[376]

Since Langer's analysis, countless psychologists, physicians and psychohistorians have attempted to explain the Hitler phenomenon. Some physicians base their approach on the hypothesis that Hitler had inherited a genetic handicap.[377] Other researchers have ascribed Hitler's behaviour to various pathological causes, such as: Somatisation Disorder; Antisocial Personality Disorder; Borderline Personality Disorder; Post-Traumatic Stress Disorder (PTSD); childhood trauma; combat trauma; and post-hypnotic trauma. Hitler has been classified as a shame-avoidant personality, and some researchers believe he exhibited symptoms of advanced syphilis infection and other untreated ailments. Some studies ascribe his behaviour to suicidogenic tendencies; others to early signs of Parkinson's disease; others still to the interaction of various other factors. Indeed, researchers agree on only one thing: that Adolf Hitler was not 'normal'. They share this view with Hitler, who did not consider himself normal, either. After his stay at Pasewalk, he frequently asserted that he was on a divine mission. An identification with Jesus Christ also emerged in the years after 1918. At a Christmas celebration in 1926, seven years after Pasewalk, he stated that he wanted to 'make the ideals [of] Christ a reality. The work that Christ had begun, but had been unable to finish, [Hitler] would complete'.[378] In another speech, he said that he should be crucified if he did not fulfil his obligations.[379] The more successful he became, the more he was convinced that he was an instrument of destiny. 'There is a higher calling,' he said, 'and we are all nothing more than its tools.'[380] Among these 'tools', he viewed himself as The Chosen One, acting in complete harmony with the divine law that controls everything. 'As sure-footed as a sleepwalker, I walk the path that Providence calls me to walk,' he said in a speech in 1936.[381] And he assured his followers: 'But if this Almightiness blesses an endeavour as it has blessed ours, then men can never destroy it.'[382] Even an event as secular as a political election was assigned a religious character by Hitler: he portrayed the German parliamentary elections as a 'judgement of God', spoke of 'holy signs' and a 'divine election', and referred to polling day as the 'pilgrimage of the nation'. Hitler also repeatedly emphasized the vital importance of his faith: 'Only faith could move these mountains. Once my faith in the German people made me start this colossal battle. And in their faith in me first thousands, then hundreds of thousands, and finally millions have followed.'[383] In a speech in 1936 Hitler said: 'If resolve and faith come together so fervently, even

Heaven cannot withhold its consent.'[384] And on another occasion he said: 'This order (to create the Nazi movement) was not given to us by some earthly superior, this order was given to us by the God who created our people!' From the start, Hitler's rallies were more akin to a 'religious revival movement than a normal political event'.[385]

The US Secret Service report, which so accurately predicted Hitler's behaviour, concluded that his evocation of the divine was not mere cynical public pageantry. Those compiling the report were surprised to find that the available information led to only one conclusion: Hitler truly believed what he was saying. He appeared to be genuinely consumed by a profound belief in a supreme force – a force that manifested itself in him. Over and over again, he invoked the 'almighty', 'destiny', 'fate' or the 'divine law', and was always quick to compare himself with Jesus Christ; in a speech in 1921, he said: 'We [the NSDAP] may be small, but one man once also stood up in Galilee, and today his teaching rules the entire world.'[386] And in 1936, he said: 'If we come together here, then the miracle of this reunion fulfils us all. Not all of you can see me, and I cannot see all of you. But I sense you and you sense me! [...] So you come [...] to [...] experience the feeling for once: now we are together, we with him and he with us, and we are now Germany!'[387] In 1937, he called out to the crowd: 'This is the wonder of our time, that you have found me, [he was interrupted by long applause] that you have found me among so many millions! And that I have found you, that is Germany's fortune!'[388] Statements such as these punctuate Hitler's speeches like red flags, and it often appears as if a religious rather than a political leader is speaking. 'People of Germany,' he proclaimed in 1936, 'I have taught you faith, now put your faith in me!'[389]

In fact, Hitler's conviction did transfer to his followers, who believed as fanatically in him as he himself did in the power that guided him. A poem by Baldur von Schirach, the leader of Hitler Youth, ends with the words: 'The pure faith you gave us, pulses destined to move through our lives. My Führer, you alone are path and goal.'[390] A rapidly increasing number of people came to believe in Hitler's self-image, assisted by the Nazi propaganda machine. It was insinuated that the Führer had overcome all things 'ignoble'. He had no weaknesses. In public, Hitler was never seen wearing glasses, and as he genuinely did not drink alcohol, smoke or eat meat, he appeared to be above all human cravings. The Führer's girlfriend, Eva Braun, was not known to the German public until after their deaths. People saw Hitler, with his utterly unshakeable self-belief, as 'the helper, the rescuer, the saviour in the hour of their greatest need'.[391] In their eyes, Hitler was not the usual politician: he was a being sent by God.[392]

Shortly after Hitler was released from prison in Landsberg in 1925, V. Corswant, the eventual Gauleiter (Nazi district leader) of Pomerania, wrote: 'Now we will see whether he is guided by God or not. If so, he will succeed, even though almost everyone appears to speak against him today.'[393] And two days before Christmas in 1926, the party paper, the *Völkischer Beobachter*, wrote: 'The rising star in the Christmas night points to the redeemer [...] the new redeemer, the saviour of the German people from infamy and distress – our Führer Adolf Hitler.'[394] Joachim Fest quotes the words of a Thüringen church council: 'Christ is come to us through Adolf Hitler.'[395] These statements were not the exception; they were the official creed, as it were. The head of the Deutsche Arbeitsfront (the umbrella association of employees and employers), Robert Ley, said in a speech: 'We believe National Socialism to be the only sanctifying faith for our people [...] And we believe that our Lord has sent us Adolf Hitler.'[396] The Reich Minister for Church Affairs, Hans Kerrl, declared: 'A new authority over that which Christ and Christianity truly represent is arisen – Adolf Hitler. Adolf Hitler is the true Holy Spirit.'[397]

The more support Hitler won, the more he embodied the divine Messiah – which in turn reinforced the people's belief in him. This reciprocal validation, which had started off between a few supporters and their idol, was increasingly enacted between a man and his nation. The more fanatically the masses believed in Hitler, the more they reinforced his belief in himself, no matter what. When a series of almost unbelievable political successes followed shortly after he came to power, the momentum became unstoppable. An avalanche of quasi-religious fanaticism was triggered, and the Führer immediately accepted the religious adoration spontaneously lavished on him by the masses. Hitler viewed his successes as a visible sign from a higher dimension that he was on the right path. Every danger that he overcame, every assassination attempt he survived was additional proof. Every decision he made seemed to be of divine origin. Public events, particularly the Nuremberg party rallies, became holy rituals. In a show befitting his image, he appeared to descend from a higher plane to his people, as if a heavenly messenger. 'I believe my life is the greatest novel in the history of the world!' he wrote to Alda Klein, an acquaintance from Munich, in 1934.[398] William Teeling told of an enormous photo of Hitler at the Nuremburg party rally in 1937, under which it read: 'In the beginning was the word.'[399]

Every Hitler Youth leader, every German official and every German soldier had to swear an oath to the man through whom 'higher powers work towards our destiny: Adolf Hitler'. Millions and millions of people, an entire nation, were swearing allegiance to this figure who seemed to be the word of God made man.[400] Doubting himself had by now become absolutely impossible. 'Divine Providence has willed it that I carry through the fulfilment of the German task,' he said.[401] And the writer Auguste Supper responded with the poem: 'Blinded, but ready, we now look into the red dawn of Germany's greatest era. Blessed be the saviour who has brought about the new dawn! In his coming we are experiencing God.'[402] The paper *Das Schwarze Korps* (Black Corps) wrote: 'When you see our Führer, it is like a dream; you forget everything around you; it is as if God is approaching you.'[403]

The rapture of the masses was unrestrained at this point, as was Hitler's belief that he was the Chosen One. 'I do not need you to confirm my historical greatness to me,' he rebuked his inferiors.[404] Hitler now made his decisions as if intoxicated. From matters of law to the redevelopment of entire cities – he considered himself the highest authority in all areas and wanted the last word in every decision. And he got what he wanted. The *Concise Dictionary of German Jurisprudence* from 1937 states: 'That which the Führer indicates of social norms as proper, or conversely as immoral, and therefore as right or wrong, is so, without the need for a formal law.'[405] And thus, the man with no secondary school qualifications became the highest judge in the land; the postcard painter became the premier expert in the fine arts; and the lance corporal from the First World War became the supreme strategic planner of the entire German Army.

Those in Hitler's immediate vicinity acted as if bewitched by him. SS Chief Heinrich Himmler wrote that in Hitler, one 'of the greatest luminous figures has found its incarnation. Goethe was such a figure in the artistic field, Bismarck in the political sector, the Führer is such in all areas, political, cultural and military'.[406] It is no wonder that Hitler came to believe: 'I cannot be mistaken. What I do and say is historical.'[407] The feeling of omnipotence and the belief in his own infallibility increasingly affected Hitler's judgement. He became a prisoner of his own mental creation – a creation he was unable to abandon, even at the very end. In July 1944, he said: 'I believe that he who boldly fights in this world in accordance with the natural laws that a God has created and who never capitulates, I believe that he will not be abandoned by the lawmaker, but will finally receive the blessing of Providence.'[408] Many of his closest confidants also remained trapped by the collective delusion to the very end. On 31 December 1944, four months before the end of the Third Reich, Reichs minister Joseph Goebbels wrote:

'If the world really knew what he [Hitler] has to say and give to it, and how far his love extends beyond his own people to all mankind, then they would bid farewell to their false gods in this hour and pay homage to him. He is the greatest of the personalities making history today; he stands far ahead of them all in the foresight of things. He towers over them, not just in genius and political instinct, but also in knowledge, character and willpower [...] He is truth itself. One only needs to be near him to physically sense how much power he exudes, how strong he is and how much strength he can impart to others. He exudes an uninterrupted stream of faith and his steadfast will extends towards greatness. There is no one in his extended circle who is not touched by it.'

And in the last edition of *Das Reich* magazine (16-1945), the journalist Herbert Hahn wrote of Hitler: 'His confidence and belief in his mission [are] as strong as ever. In the fateful present, even his daily companions and colleagues amazedly and assuredly sense the unparalleled solitary greatness of the man who is proving stronger than the greatest misfortune.' And indeed Hitler seems to have genuinely believed to the very end that he would be saved by Providence. During the last weeks of the war many high ranking officers came to his bunker with the intention of pointing out the hopelessness of the continuing war effort. When they returned to their troops most of them were 'proselytised'. Hitler's unshakeable belief in the final victory had convinced these experienced military experts that despite the devastating situation at the front the war would not be lost.[409]

The enemy troops had surrounded Berlin almost entirely and Russian tanks were just a few kilometres from Hitler's bunker when President Roosevelt died on 12 April 1945. Hitler was convinced that fate would now miraculously turn in his favour. 'At the moment when fate has taken the greatest war criminal of all time from this earth,' he said, 'the turning point in this war is decided.'[410] And on 20April, ten days before his death, Hitler said in a telegram to Mussolini: 'In resolute defiance of death, the German people and all those of the same spirit will bring this attack to a halt [...]'[411] It was only on hearing the machine-gunfire of the Russian Army from his bunker that Hitler's confidence in a divine miracle crumbled. Suddenly, the man-god who had evolved beyond everything 'ignoble' displayed human sentiment: he wanted to marry. After the wedding, which was performed with all proper formalities, there was a short feast, after which Hitler dictated his will. His failure must have been clear even to him by then, but he was unable to escape his delusion. Even up until his farewell to his closest colleagues and the shot with which he ended his life, he sought to lay the blame for his downfall elsewhere – on his fellow combatants who had 'betrayed' him; and on his people, who had 'proven the weaker'; but not on himself. The Führer seemingly had no doubt in the righteousness of his actions, even to the bitter end.

Psychopathological analysis seems like a natural option for explaining the Hitler phenomenon. Of the approaches mentioned at the start of this paragraph, some are certainly more convincing than others. But even if physicians, psychologists and psycho-historians could agree on a conclusive diagnosis, one problem would still remain: Hitler did not suffer his delusion in a psychiatric institute, but in fact managed to create a cultural reality that – for a while, at least – determined the day-to-day life of a large Western industrialised nation. This extends far beyond the understanding of what is generally meant by the term 'insane'.

All of the information revealed about Hitler in the years after his death is consistent with the assessment of psychoanalyst Walter Langer, who investigated Hitler's psychology on behalf of the US Government and came to the conclusion that Hitler genuinely was gripped by a 'profound belief'. And in fact Hitler's faith did 'move mountains', as has the faith of the founders of religions. In the eyes of his followers Hitler even performed 'miracles' at the start of his government, both political and economic. For many Hitler was a redeemer figure, similar to Buddha. And as with Hitler at Pasewalk, there was a moment in Buddha's life that triggered a profound inner transformation. Afterwards, Buddha too was 'a different person' and exuded a persuasive power that influenced many people and created a new cultural reality. The Apostle Paulus, founder of the Christian religion, experienced a similar moment of sudden inner change as did many Christian and non-Christian saints. But there the similarities end: religious founders such as Buddha and Paulus instructed their followers to strive for compassion and love. These values were alien to Hitler. Today we know the horrific results of his transformation. Hitler certainly did not undergo the same inner experience as Buddha or Paulus. But what exactly *did* he experience? Despite their far-reaching consequences, these kinds of transformations have so far not been the subject of intensive scientific study.

Most historians to date have shied away from these questions by deeming Hitler's experience at Pasewalk insignificant. One popular argument is that Hitler did not in fact undergo any defining experience after his injury, and merely *claimed* to have had a supernatural encounter in order to foment the myth of the Führer. However, this approach can explain neither Hitler's sudden personality change after WWI nor his meteoric rise and the researchers are ultimately compelled to acknowledge that: 'Adolf Hitler [...] is an existential research problem for both historians and depth psychologists alike'.[412]

The Hitler phenomenon cannot be comprehended rationally if only 'rational' explanations are permitted. Without the 'irrational' experience at Pasewalk, Hitler's story cannot be understood. And another irrational factor is of crucial importance in comprehending Hitler's career: the Thule Society and their philosophy. Hitler could continue to misinterpret his experience as a divine mission only because a small group of people validated his obsessive belief. As long as the two factors of the Thule Society and Pasewalk are disregarded, Hitler remains a mystery. Things do not become rationally comprehensible by denying irrationality. After all, irrationality is a fundamental driving force that must not be underestimated – and nowhere more so than in history.

Notes to the Appendices

1 A. Hitler, *Mein Kampf*, Munich 1936, p. 21
2 P. Gassert, D. S. Mattern, *The Hitler Library*, Westport 2001, p. 1
3 A. Kubizek, *Hitler mein Jugendfreund*, Wien 1953, p. 225
4 A. Kubizek, ibid., p. 244ff
5 A. Kubizek, ibid., p. 225
6 B. Hamann, *Hitler's Wien*, Munich 1996, p. 567
7 H. Frank, *Im Angesicht des Galgens*, Munich 1953, p. 46
8 E. Hanfstaengl, *Zwischen Weissem und Braunem Haus*, Munich 1970, p. 44
9 R. G. L. Waite, *Psychopathic God*, New York 1977, p. 56
10 H. Frank, *Im Angesicht des Galgens*, Munich 1953, p. 46–47, summarised in: I. Kershaw, *Hitler 1889–1936*, from the English translated by: J. P. Krause and J. W. Rademacher, Stuttgart 1998, p. 298
11 E. Hanfstaengel, op. cit., p. 52ff
12 O. J. Hale, 'Adolf Hitler Taxpayer', in: *The American Historical Review* 60 (1955) S. 830–842
13 T. W. Ryback, *The Atlantic Monthly*, May 2003
14 C. Schroeder, *Er war mein Chef*, Munich 1985, p. 75
15 K. W. Krause, *Zehn Jahre Kammerdiener bei Hitler*, Hamburg 1950, p. 48ff
16 See photograph in F. Schaffing, E. Baumann, 'Hitler Hoffman', *Der Obersalzberg*, Munich 1985, p. 105
17 Bavarian Capital Archive Munich, Charts and Maps, Obersalzberg, Haus Wachenfeld, 5456
18 P. Gassert, D. S. Mattern, op. cit., p. 1ff
19 H. Frank, op. cit., p. 46
20 C. Schröder, op. cit., p. 77
21 *Briefwechsel zwischen Wagner und Liszt*, vol. 2, Leipzig 1887, p. 45
22 Ref. A. Schopenhauer, *Die Welt als Wille und Vorstellung*, vol. 1, p. 508 in: *Werk-und Studienausgabe in elf Bänden*, Züricher Ausgabe, Zurich 1977
23 A. Hitler, op. cit., p. 335
24 W. Weimer, *Der Philosoph und der Diktator*, Schopenhauer Jahrbuch, Würzburg 2003, S. 163,
25 A. Kubizek, op. cit., p. 226
26 A. Zoller, *Hitler privat*, Düsseldorf 1949, p. 40
27 C. Schröder, op. cit., p. 76
28 M. Koch-Hillebrecht, *Homo Hitler*, Munich 1999, p. 90ff

29 Rochus Misch, Hitler's bodyguard, also mentions Hilter's 'photographic memory'. R. Misch, *Der letzte Zeuge*, München 2008, pp. 143, 163
30 A. Zoller, op. cit., p. 41
31 C. Schröder, op. cit., p. 77
32 M. Domarus (ed.), *Hitler – Reden und Proklamationen*, Würzburg 1962, p. 10
33 The American doctor Benjamin Rush first described the inexplicable abilities of savants in 1789. Despite intensive research, no scientific explanation for the phenomenon has yet been found.
34 The full title of Darwins book reveals its potential for controversy: 'On the Origin of Species by Means of Natural Selection or the Preservation of Favoured Races in the Struggle for Life.'
35 See also: Appendix 3, Arthur Schopenhauer
36 A. Hitler, op. cit., p. 406
37 A. Kubizek, op. cit., p. 83
38 H. Frank, op. cit., p. 213
39 A. Kubizek, op. cit., p. 195
40 A. Kubizek, op. cit., pp. 83, 84
41 See: M. Gregor-Dellin, D. Mack (eds.), *Cosima Wagner, Diaries II*, Munich 1977; see letters pp. 235, 293, 454, 460, 599, 888
42 M. Domarus (ed.), op. cit., p. 2234
43 See: G. Scheit, W. Svoboda, *Feindbild Gustav Mahler*, Vienna 2002, p. 9
44 A. Kubizeck, op. cit., p. 192
45 A. Kubizeck, 1st version of memoirs, *Linz OÖLA, Materialien Jetzinger*, p. 24, quoted from: B. Hamann, op. cit., p. 95
46 See: Appendix 10, Hitler and Jews in Vienna
47 J. S. Jones, *Hitlers Weg begann in Wien*, from the English translated by: Sylvia Eisenburger, Berlin 1990, p. 129m, quoted from: Ian Kershaw, op. cit., p. 102
48 K. Ivo (ed.), *Annual for German Women and Girls*, Vienna 1904, p. 78, quoted from: B. Hamann, op. cit., p. 476
49 See: B. Hamann, op. cit., p. 483ff
50 *Deutsches Volksblatt*, 06. 12. 1905, p. 1, quoted from: B. Hamann, *Hitlers* op. cit., p. 489
51 *Deutsches Volksblatt*, 06. 12. 1905, p. 6, quoted from: B. Hamann, op. cit., p. 490
52 See: B. Hamann, op. cit., p. 494
54 See: A. Joachimsthaler, 'Hitler's Will' in *Hitlers Ende*, Munich 1995, p. 192
55 F. Jetzinger, Hitlers Jugend, Phantasien, Lügen – und die Wahrheit, Vienna 1956, p. 145
56 Summary of the report by R. Hanisch, 'I Was Hitler's Buddy', part I–III *New Republic*, 5/12/19 April 1939, pp. 239–242, 270–272, 297–300, quoted from: I. Kershaw, op. cit., p. 101
57 Contemporary witness Karl Honisch, quoted from: I. Kershaw, op. cit., p. 100
58 B. Hamann, op. cit., p. 498
59 See: I. Kershaw, op. cit., p. 100

60 See: A. Joachimsthaler, *Hitlers Weg begann in München 1913–1923*, Munich 2000, pp. 97, 171
61 See: A. Joachimsthaler, *Hitlers Weg begann in München 1913–1923*, Munich 2000, pp. 97, 171
62 A. Hitler, op. cit., p. 69
63 See: Appendix 8, anti-Semitism in Vienna
64 See: Appendices 12, Racism in Vienna 1900; 19, Hitler's Political Role Models
65 Wolf, like other racists, believed that 'all Germans in a "threatened land" must stick together, whether Jewish or Christian'. Wolf's political stance is described in more detail in Appendix 19, Hitler's Political Role Models. Brigitte Hamann mentions that Wolf was received by Hitler at the Nuremburg Party Rally in 1937. According to a report in the *Neue Wiener Tagblatt*, Hitler acknowledged Wolf's mindset in 'appreciative words' B. Hamann, op. cit., pp. 385, 386
66 Quoted from: C. C. Malzahn, '*Die blödsinnigste Parole der Welt*', Spiegel Online, *Kultur*, *Literatur*, 24. 06. 2006
67 R. M. Lonsbach, op. cit., p. 53
68 Quoted from: R. M. Lonsbach, op. cit., p. 42
69 Quoted from: R. M. Lonsbach, op. cit., p. 47
70 Quoted from: R. M. Lonsbach, op. cit., p. 55
71 See also: B. H. F. Taureck, *Nietzsche und der Faschismus*, Leipzig 2000
72 R. M. Lonsbach, op. cit., p. 89
73 See also: C. Diethe, *Nietzsches Schwester*, Hamburg 2001
74 See: O. Wagener (ed. H. A. Turner), Hitler aus nächster Nähe, Aufzeichnungen eines Vertrauten 1929–1932 (Hitler Up Close, Observations of a Confidant, 1929–1932), Berlin 1978
75 Th. Newest (Hans Goldzier), '*Des Lebens Zweck und Urquell*', *Einige Weltprobleme*, bd. 6, Vienna 1908, p. 192
76 Th. Newest (Hans Goldzier), ibid.
77 See also: Appendix17, Hitler and the Occult
78 H. Heims (ed. W. Jochmann), *Adolf Hitler, Monologe im Führerhauptquartier 1941–1944, Aufzeichnung vom 20/21. 02. 1942*, Hamburg 1980, p. 285
79 W. A. Jenks, *Vienna and the Young Hitler*, New York 1960, pp. 38–39, quoted from: I. Kershaw, op. cit., p. 64
80 B. Hamann, op. cit., p. 29
82 Ref: H. G. Zmarzlik, Der Sozialdarwinismus in Deutschland, Vierteljahreshefte für Zeitgeschichte, Munich 1963, p. 259
83 D. Gasman, *The Scientific Origins of National Socialism*, London, 2007, p. 34
84 Ref: D. Kevles, *In the Name of Eugenics*, New York 1985
85 E. Black, *The Horrifying American Roots of Nazi Eugenics*, San Francisco Cronicle 11.24.03, see also: E. Black, *War Against The Weak: Eugenics and America's Campaign to Create A Master Race*, New York 2004
86 Ref: A. Hitler, op. cit., p. 314
87 H. Heims, op. cit., p. 230, quoted from: A. Joachimsthaler, *Hitlers Liste*, Munich 2003, p. 24

88 O. Wagener, *Hitler aus nächster Nähe, Aufzeichnungen eines Vertrauten 1929–1932*, Frankfurt 1978, p. 102 quoted from: A. Joachimsthaler, op. cit., p. 32
89 See: J. Fest, *Die unbeantworteten Fragen*, Hamburg 2005, p. 60
90 C. Schroeder, op. cit., p. 153, quoted from: A. Joachimsthaler, op. cit., p. 33
91 See: C. Schroeder, ibid., p. 153, quoted from: A. Joachimsthaler, ibid., p. 34
92 'Hitler had an absolute physical aversion to "same-sex love". It was high-grade decadence to him. He felt that to permit it meant the beginning of the end of a nation.' Quoted from: H. Picker (ed.), *Hitlers Tischgespräche im Führerhauptquartier*, Wiesbaden 1983, p. 235
93 K. Heiden, *Adolf Hitler, Zeitalter der Verantwortungslosigkeit*, Zurich 1936, p. 76, quoted from: A. Joachimsthaler, op. cit., p. 24
94 A. Joachimsthaler, ibid., p. 10
95 See: A. Kubizek, op. cit., p. 253ff
96 H. Slapnicka, *Hitler und Oberösterreich*, Grünbach 1998, p. 25ff
97 CIC interrogation of Paula Hitler on th 26th of May 1945 in Berchtesgaden. Microfilm DJ13, University of Philadelphia, Library, quoted from: A. Joachimsthaler, op. cit., p. 41
98 Comments from Hitler to Christine Schroeder and Johanna Wolf, quoted from: A. Joachimsthaler, ibid., p. 41
99 See: B. Hamann, op. cit., p. 70
100 H. Slapnicka, op. cit., p. 102ff
101 J. C. Fest, *Hitler, eine Biographie*, Frankfurt 1973, p. 29
102 H. Slapnicka, op. cit., p. 25
103 Interview with Hitler's butler, Karl Krause, MPR Munich 1998, quoted from: A. Joachimsthaler, op. cit., p. 45
104 Interview with Dr E. Bloch by J. D. Ratcliff in *Collier's Magazine* dated the 15th of March 1941, quoted from: A. Joachimsthaler, ibid., p. 44
105 W. Zdral, *Die Hitlers*, Frankfurt 2005, p. 224
106 See: 'The Rise and Fall of Hitler's Irish Nephew', *Evening Herald*, p. 28, Dublin, 17. 08. 2006
107 See: W. Zdral, op. cit., p. 100ff
108 See: B. Hamann, op. cit., p. 225
109 See: B. Hamann, op. cit., p. 222
110 See: F. Jetzinger, op. cit., p. 263, cited from : B. Hamann, op. cit., p. 213
111 See: B. Hamann, op. cit., p. 225
112 See: B. Hamann, ibid., p. 227ff
113 See: Appendix 34, Guido von List
114 See: B. Hamann, loc. cit. See also: Appendix 34 Guido von List
115 See: B. Hamann, op. cit., p. 285ff
116 See: B. Hamann, loc. cit. See also: Appendix 34, Guido von List
117 See: V. and V. Trimondi, *Hitler, Buddha, Krishna*, Vienna 2002
118 'Sometimes writing in the margins of a page is recognizably in Hitler's jagged cursive hand. For the most part, though, the marginalia are restricted

to simple markings whose common "authorship" is suggested by an intense vertical line in the margin and double or triple underlining in the text, always in pencil; I found such markings repeatedly both in the Library of Congress collection and in a cache of eighty Hitler books at Brown University. Hitler's handwritten speeches, preserved in the Federal German Archives, show an identical pattern of markings.' Quoted from: T. W. Ryback, *The Atlantic Monthly*, May 2003

119 See: Appendix 2, Hitler and Books

120 Ryback reports that around 130 titles in the Library of Congress collection and over a dozen in the John Hay Library have occult, spiritual or religious content

121 M. Domarus (ed.), op. cit., speech on 27. 6. 1937, p. 704

122 See: H. Picker (ed.), op. cit.

123 R. Spitzy, *So haben wir das Reich verspielt*, Munich 1986, p. 131 quoted from: B. Hamann, op. cit., p. 319

124 See also: Appendix 34, Guido von List

125 There were in fact unsold paintings by the young Hitler in the offices of Morgenstern and Altenberg which the NDSAP found twenty-five years later. B. Hamann, *Hitlers Wien*, Munich 1996, p. 500

126 Anonymous, 'My friend Hitler' p. 11, in: 'The story of *Mein Kampf*', Vienna Library Bulletin, 6 (1952), No. 5/6 pp. 31–32, S. Aronson, *Reinhard Heydrich und die Frühgeschichte von Gestapo und SD*, Stuttgart 1971, quoted from: I. Kershaw, op. cit., p. 100

127 See: B. Hamann, op. cit., p. 500

128 B. Hamann, ibid., p. 509

129 See: B. Hamann, ibid., p. 512

130 B. Hamann, op. cit., p. 337

131 A. Hitler, op. cit., p. 118

132 See: Appendix 38, Hitler's Ideology

133 B. Hamann, op. cit., p. 350

134 See: Appendix 38, Hitler's Ideology

135 A. Hitler, op. cit., p. 534

136 A. Hitler, op. cit., p. 129

137 B. Hamann, *Hitlers* op. cit., pp. 396, 397

138 A. Hitler, op. cit., p. 130

139 See: Appendix 9, Hitler and Jews in Vienna

140 Note missed from sequence.

141 See: B. Hamann, op. cit., p. 376ff

142 B. Hamann, ibid., p. 385

143 This phrase is taken from the '*Rachelied der Deutschen*' ('*Revenge Song of the Germans*', 1813) by Ernst Moritz Arndt

144 W. G. Natter, *Literature at War 1914–1940: Representing the 'Time of Greatness' in Germany*, New Haven and London 1999, p. 123

145 W. G. Natter, op. cit., p. 9

146 Ref. J. Toland, *Adolf Hitler*, New York 1976, p. 71ff

147 Ref. Reichsministerium des Inneren (HRG), Reichsgesetzblatt Jahrgang 1933 Teil I, Berlin 1933, pp. 203, 212

148 H. Göring, *Rundfunkrede* vom 28 August 1933

149 Ref. *Daily Telegraph*, London, 16. 06. 2006

150 C. Cross, *Adolf Hitler*, London 1974, p. 405

151 Quoted from J. C. Fest, op. cit., p. 101. On another occasion, Hitler declared that 'the war had transformed him'. See also: H. Picker (ed.), op. cit., p. 323

152 W. Harris, interview with Spiegel Online 16. 11. 2005

153 H. Heims (ed. W. Jochmann), *Adolf Hitler, Monologe im Führerhauptquartier 1941–1944, Aufzeichnung vom 25/26. 09. 1941*, Hamburg 1980, p. 71

154 W. Jochmann (ed.), loc. cit.

155 'Nobody who knows him [Hitler] well would deny his courage. He has proven himself in the field as a daring, especially reliable dispatch runner who truly has earned the Iron Cross I and was nominated for it several times. He was the model for the unknown soldier who did his duty calmly and quietly.' Quoted from: Wiedemann Papers, Institute of Contemporary History, Munich, MA 149, quoted from: A. Joachimsthaler, *Hitlers Weg begann in München 1913–1923*, Munich 2000, p. 154

156 'Hitler was an extremely diligent, eager, conscientious and dutiful soldier [. . .] The personal verve and unrestrained bravery with which he has faced all perils in dangerous situations and in battle deserve special mention. His iron composure and coolness never deserted him. When the situation was most dangerous, he volunteered for service runs to the front line and performed these with complete success.' Testimony from Friedrich Petz in February 1922, NSDAP Main Archive, HIMC, File 47, Reel 2, quoted from: A. Joachimsthaler, op. cit., p. 159

157 'Tirelessly ready and willing to serve, there was no reason and no situation where he would not always have volunteered for the most difficult, troublesome and dangerous missions, always ready to sacrifice his peace and life for others and his Fatherland.' Testimony from Lieutenant Colonel A. D. von Tubeuf on 20. 03. 1922, NSDAP Main Archive, HIMC, File 47, Reel 2, quoted from: A. Joachimsthaler, op. cit., p. 168

158 A. A. Purves, The Medals, Decorations & Orders of the Great War 1914–1918, London 1975, p. 112

159 Proposal of the Deputy Regimental Commander of RIR 16, Baron von Godin, to award the Iron Cross 1st Class to Hitler dated 31. 07. 1918, NSDAP Main Archive, HIMC, File 47, Reel 2, quoted from: A. Joachimsthaler, op. cit., p. 168

160 Deposition by Max Amann at Nuremberg on 05. 11. 1947, Max Amann *Spruchkammerakt*, Special Records Office, *Bayr. Hauptstaatsarchiv*, Munich, quoted from: A. Joachimsthaler, op. cit., p. 158

161 See also: T. L. Dorpat, *Wounded Monster*, New York 2002, p. 107

162 See: N. Cohn, *Warrant for Genocide*, London 1967, p. 173

163 See: N. Cohn, *Die Protokolle der Weisen von Zion*, Cologne 1969, p. 75

164 H. Berding, *Moderner Antisemitismus in Deutschland*, Frankfurt 1988, p. 178

165 N. Cohn, *Warrant for Genocide*, London 1967 p. 126ff

166 See also: V. Losemann, *Rassenideologien und antisemitische Publizistik in Deutschland im 19. und 20. Jahrhundert*, Düsseldorf 1984

167 A. Rosenberg, *Die Protokolle der Weisen von Zion und die jüdische Weltpolitik*, Munich 1923, p. 86

168 For more information, see: G. zur Beek (ed.), *Protokolle der Weisen von Zion*, Berlin 1924

169 See: W. Horn, *Führerideologie der NSDAP 1919–1933*, Düsseldorf 1972

170 A. Hitler, op. Cit., p. 337: '*mit geradezu grauenerregender Sicherheit das Wesen und die Tätigkeit des Judenvolkes aufdecken*'

171 See: U. Fleischhauer, *Die echten Protokolle der Weisen von Zion*, Erfurt 1935, pp. 9, 12

172 K. Heiden, *Der Führer*, Boston 1944, p. 20

173 For further information, see: N. Cohn, *Die Protokolle der Weisen von Zion*, Cologne 1969

174 See: P. Kennicott,'Protocols of Zion: The Life of a Fraud & Its True Believers', *Washington Post*, p. C01, 22 4. 2006

175 Ref. : Appendices 9, Hitler and Jews in Vienna; 18, Hitler's Jewish Friends; and 7, Gustav Mahler

176 Ref.: A. Joachimsthaler, op. cit., p. 244

177 See: S. Breuer, *Die Völkischen in Deutschland, pp. 25-35*, Darmstadt 2008

178 Ref. : Appendix 23, The Jewish Conspiracy

179 Ref. : Appendix 8, anti-Semitism in Vienna

180 For more information, see: D. Lewis, *The Man Who Invented Hitler*, London 2003; M. Koch-Hillebrand, *Hitler, Ein Sohn des Krieges*, Munich 2003; B. Horstmann, *Hitler in Pasewalk*, Düsseldorf 2004

181 War Office, '*Grundsätze für die Behandlung und Beurteilung der sog., Kriegsneurotiker*', Berlin 29. 01. 1917, UA Thübingen, 308–89, in P. Lerner, *Hysterical Men*, Cornell University, New York 2003, p. 54. See also: P. Riedesser, A. Verderber, *Maschinengewehre hinter der Front – Zur Geschichte der deutschen Militärpsychiatrie*, Frankfurt 1996, p. 27ff

182 By the time Hitler arrived, the *Schützenhaus* was under the command of Dr Wilhelm Schröder. See: D. Lewis, op. cit., London 2003, p. 17

183 See: B. Horstmann, op. cit., p. 64

184 See: B. Horstmann, op. cit., p. 26ff

185 R. Binion, *Hitler Among the Germans*, New York 1976, p. 10

186 'Where the German public was concerned, hysterical disorders reflected a "weakness of the will" caused by either an "inferior nervous system" or a "degenerate brain".' D. Lewis, op. cit.„ London 2003, p. 242. Quoted from: P. Horn (1915) cited in J. Brunner, *Psychiatry, Psychoanalysis and Politics*, p. 354

187 See: E. Deuerlein, *Hitlers Eintritt in die Politik und die Reichswehr*, *Vierteljahreshefte für Zeitgeschichte*, Stuttgart 1959, p. 181

188 I. Kershaw, op. cit., p. 136ff

189 B. Horstmann, op. cit., p. 15ff

190 See: S. J. Hegner, *Die Reichskanzlei 1933–45*, Frankfurt 1966, p. 182f., quoted from: B. Horstmann, ibid., p. 21

191 See: Forster, Univ. file, Bl 63, quoted from B. Horstmann, ibid., p. 168

192 See: B. Horstmann, ibid., p. 169. See also: D. Lewis, op. cit., p. 286

193 See: *Time* magazine, 2 January 1939, Vol. XXXIII No. 1

194 Neville Chamberlain in a secret meeting of the English cabinet, quoted from: P. W. Fabry, *Mutmaßungen über Hitler*, Düsseldorf 1969, p. 1

195 Lloyd George, who had recently met Hitler at Berchtesgaden, described him in these glowing terms in a *Daily Express* article written at the request of Lord Beaverbrook. Cited in: 'Hitler's Olympians', *Observer Magazine*, 29 September 1968, quoted from: D. Lewis, op. cit., p. 3

196 Quoted from: P. W. Fabry, *Mutmaßungen über Hitler*, Düsseldorf 1969, p. 22

197 F. Wiedemann, op. cit., p. 26

198 See also: A. Joachimsthaler, *Hitler in München*, Munich 1989

199 Cross-examination of Max Amann in Nuremberg on 05. 11. 1947, Max Amann, *Spruchkammerakt*, Special Records Office, *Bayr. Hauptstaatsarchiv*, Munich, Bd1, sheet 27, quoted from: B. Horstmann, op. cit., p. 52

200 F. Wiedemann, op. cit., p. 54

201 In September 1919, before Hitler's first public appearance, his superior officer, Captain Karl Mayr, addressed him as 'The very honourable Mr Hitler'– 'certainly no ordinary form of address from [an important general staff officer] to a lance corporal' E. Deuerlein, *Hitlers Eintritt in die Politik and die Reichswehr*, *Vierteljahreshefte für Zeitgeschichte*, Stuttgart 1959, pp. 184–5

202 'Mustard gas is a fluid, relatively stable warfare agent [. . .] According to recent studies, even miniscule quantities that may not cause any acute symptoms produce toxic reactions.' G. Hesse, *Hitler wie ihn immer noch keiner kennt*, Berlin 2004, p. 30

203 K. H. von Wiegand, *Cosmopolitan*, New York, April 1939, 28–29, p. 152 quoted from: R. Binion, op. cit.

204 Hyde Park 'Adolf Hitler', (3, XII, 42) 40 quoted from: R. Binion, ibid., p. 137

205 L. Denny, 'France and the German Counterrevolution', *The Nation*, CXVI 1923, p. 295 quoted from: R. Binion, loc. cit.

206 Quoted from: D. Lewis, op. cit., p. 255

207 R. Olden, *Hitler*, Amsterdam 1936, p. 62. The whereabouts of the records from the preliminary investigation are no longer known

208 E. Jäckel and A. Kuhn (Hg), *Hitler, Sämtliche Aufzeichnungen 1905–1924*, Stuttgart 1980, p. 1064, quoted from: I. Kershaw, op. cit., p. 136ff

209 A. Hitler, op. cit., p. 225

210 *Frankfurter Zeitung* dated 27. 01. 1923, quoted from: P. W. Fabry, op. cit., p. 24

211 R. Olden, op. cit., quoted from: B. Horstmann, op. cit., p. 143

212 See: B. Horstmann, op. cit., p. 204

213 C. H. Hartmann, K. A. Lankheit (eds.), *Hitler Reden, Schriften, Anordnungen*, Band V/2, Dok. 36, München 1998, p. 109

214 Ref: M. Koch-Hildebrand, *Hitler Sohn des Krieges*, Munich 2003, p. 28

215 A. Roerkohl, *Hungerblockade und Heimatfront*, Stuttgart 1991, p. 321ff

216 Ref: M. Koch-Hildebrand, op. cit., p. 28

217 Max Warburg, *Aus meinen Aufzeicheungen*, (*From My Notes*), ed. by Eric Warburg, New York 1952, pp. 57ff., 80ff. See also: *Münchner Post* (*Social Democratic Daily*), Nr. 263 from 11/19/19, Article: '*Die Hungerblockade und ihre Folgen*'

218 D. L. George, *The Great Crusade*, New York 1918, p. 16, quoted from: A. Roehrkohl, op. cit., p. 15

219 H. Schadewaldt, *Hungerblockade über Kontinentaleurou*, Munich 1941. See also: A. C. Bell, *Die Englische Hungerblockade im Weltkrieg 1914–1915*, introduced by V. Böhmert, Essen 1943

220 The name used in the novel is "Obermayer", not "Walterspiel". The testimony of a close family member of Max Obermayer in Munich, known to the author, suggests that in contradiction to the findings of historical research in 1918/1919 the hotel was owned by the brothers Adolf and Max Obermayer. An article by the *Süddeutsche Zeitung* from July 25th 2008 by Astrid Becker *Sisi und die Wellenbadschaukel* seems to confirm this statement.

221 Ref: D. Rose, *Die Thule Gesellschaft*, Tübingen 1994. See also: Appendices 30, Revolution in Munich; 32, Hostage Killings and Antisemitism

222 R. Binion, *Dass ihr mich gefunden habt . . .*, New York 1976, Stuttgart 1978, p. 159ff

223 Ref: B. Hamann, op. cit., p. 576

224 H. Kapfer, C. L. Reichert, *Umsturz in München*, Munich 1988, p. 84

225 F. Willing, *Die Hitlerbewegung*, Hamburg 1962, p. 25

226 See: Appendices 30, Revolution in Munich; 32, Hostage Killings and anti-Semitism

227 See: Appendix 30, Revolution in Munich

228 The majority of the information about Hitler during the time of revolution in Munich was taken from: A. Joachimsthaler, op. cit., p. 177ff

229 See: Appendix 30, Revolution in Munich

230 Ref. A. Joachimsthaler, op. cit., p. 219

231 See: A. Joachimsthaler, ibid., p. 224

232 Hitler held his first speeches between the 19. 8. 1919 and the 25. 8. 1919 in Camp Lechfeld

233 See: Appendix 37, Thule–DAP–NSDAP

234 H. Kapfer, C. L. Reichert, *Umsturz in München*, Munich 1988, p. 134. See also: D. C. Large, *Hitlers München*, Munich 1998

235 Matthes to Rüttinger, 12. 12. 1912, and 19. 10. 1913. See also: Rüttinger to Matthes, 21 and 24. 11. 1913, Main Archive, Koblenz, No. 885, quoted from: R. Phelps, 'Before Hitler Came', *Journal of Modern History*, 1963, p. 245

236 See also: H. Wilhelm, *Dichter, Denker, Fememörder*, Berlin 1989, p. 98

237 N. Cohn, *Warrant for Genocide*, London 1967, p. 122

238 Quoted from: H. Kapfer, C. L. Reichert, op. cit., p. 84

239 *The Times*, London, quoted from P. Orzechowski, *Schwarze Magie-Braune Macht*, Zurich 1990, p. 22

240 H. Gilbhart, *Die Thule Gesellschaft*, Munich 1994, p. 141

241 Karl H. von Wiegand, 'Hitler Foresees His End', *Cosmopolitan*, New York, April 1939, p. 152 quoted from: R. Binion, op. cit.

242 See: Appendix 34, Guido von List

243 This information is contained, for example, in: N. Goodrick-Clarke, *The Occult Roots of Nazism*, New York 1985, p. 17ff. See also: D. Rose, op. cit., p. 19ff

244 See also: P. G. J. Pulzer, *Die Entstehung des politischen Antisemitismus in Deutschland und Österreich 1867–1914*, Gütersloh, 1966. Pulzer described Fritsch (1852–1934) as the 'most important anti-Semite before Hitler'. Fritsch's *Handbuch der Judenfrage* was reissued dozens of times

245 R. Sebottendorff, *Bevor Hitler kam*, Munich 1933, pp. 53, 62. According to Rudolf von Sebottendorff, the Thule Society had 250 members in Munich and 1,500 throughout Bavaria in November 1918

246 N. Goodrick-Clarke, op. cit., p. 135ff

247 R. Sebottendorff, op. cit., p. 42

248 The Thule Society also invited other nationalistic groups to conspiratorial meetings at the Four Seasons. These included the Alldeutschen (All-Germans); Rohmeder's Schulverein (School Association); and the Hammerbund (Hammer League). See also: R. Sebottendorff, op. cit., p. 62

249 The Thule Battle League had a branch on the outskirts of Munich in Eching and maintained contact with the legal Bavarian government in Bamberg. Members of the League carried out acts of sabotage against Munich's Red Army and planned to kidnap the communist state leader, Kurt Eisner. It appears that there was also a connection between the Thule Society and Eisner's murderer, Count Arco-Valley. See also: H. J. Kuron, *Freikorps and Bund Oberland* (Dissertation, Erlangen. n. d. [1960]), pp. 16–19; R. Sebottendorff, op. cit., pp. 106–13; D. Rose, op. cit., pp. 39, 43; H. Gilbhart, op. cit., p. 92

250 See also: H. Gilbhart, op. cit.; D. Rose, op. cit. On the 19th of April 1919, Sebottendortff was authorized by Bamberg to set up a freecorps. Consequently he opened a recruitment office in the Hotel Deutscher Kaiser in Nuremberg (R. Sebottendorff, op. cit., pp. 125–34.) Sebottendorff's account is confirmed by the Nuremberg Thule member Franz Müller ('*Erfahrungen eines alten Vorkämpfers*', HA Koblenz No. 1249, see: R. Phelps, 'Before Hitler Came', *Journal of Modern History*, 1963, p. 259.) Sebottendorff's 'Oberland' freecorps then took part in the conquest of Munich. The freecorps fought along the Ruhr in 1920 and against Poland in Oberschlesien in 1921. The successor, Bund Oberland, played an important part in Hitler's coup in 1923

251 Draft of standing orders for the DAP from December 1919, BA Koblenz NS2627 quoted from: A. Joachimsthaler, op. cit., Munich 2000, p. 265

252 See: Appendix 35, The Expected Saviour

253 Johannes Hering, '*Beiträge zur Geschichte der Thulegesellschaft*', manuscript from 21 June 1939, HA Koblenz, NS 26/865, quoted from: N. Goodrick-Clarke, op. cit., p. 201

254 See: Appedix 41, Prominent Thule Members

255 See: Appendix 42, Völkischer Beobachter

256 See: Appendix 39, The Swastika. See also: F. Willing, op. cit., p. 87: 'The "heil" greeting gradually appeared in the Munich National Socialist Party in 1920. It was already in use before World War I by the Austrian nationalist movement, which had adopted it from the nationalist associations of the *Altreich* [old empire].' H. Bühmann, '*Der Hitlerkult*', in K. Heller, J. Plamper (eds.), *Personenkulte im Stalinismus*; Göttingen 2004, p. 123: 'The "Heil" greeting evidently comes from the *Turner* [gymnast] movement, and was therefore part of traditional German usage.'

257 See: Appendix 17, Hitler and the Occult

258 See: Appendix 35, The Expected Saviour

259 See: Appendix 39, The Swastika

260 See: Appendix 35, The Expected Saviour

261 B. Hamann, op. cit., p. 294

262 See: B. Hamann, ibid., p. 299

263 See: Guido von List, *Urgrund*, Berlin, undated, p. 3

264 'The intuitive perception of the organic being of the universe and therefore the laws of nature forms the unshakeable foundation for the Aryan doctrine of redemption or "*Wihinei*",' quoted from: Guido von List, *Das Geheimnis der Runen*, Vienna 1907, p. 17

265 Guido von List, *Die Armanenschaft der Ario-Germanen*, Vol. I, Berlin 1922 (3rd edition), p. 46

266 Guido von List, ibid., p. 47

267 Ariosophes founded the Reichshammerbund and the Germanenordenr. The Ariosophic Germanenorden is directly linked with the Thule Society in Munich. In his book *Bevor Hitler kam*, Rudolf von Sebottendorff, the Grandmaster of the Thule Society, names Guido von List and his disciple Lanz von Liebenfels as sources of his lodge, in addition to the Ariosophes Baron Wittgenberg and Theodor Fritsch. See: R. Sebottendorff, op. cit., p. 31–33

268 Guido von List, *Die Armanenschaft der Ario-Germanen*, vol. I, Berlin 1922, p. 4ff

269 Guido von List, *Das Geheimnis der Runen*, Vienna 1907, p. 54. 'The high significance of this custom [of the Ario-Germanen] lay in the aim of systematically breeding a "noble race" which would then remain racially pure through strict sexual laws,' quoted from: Guido von List, *Die Armanenschaft der Ario-Germanen*, vol. I, Berlin 1922 (3rd edition), p. 31

270 See: Guido von List, *Das Geheimnis der Runen*, Vienna 1907, p. 53; Guido von List, *Der Übergang vom Wuotanismus zum Christentum*, Leipzig 1911, p. 31

271 Guido von List, *Die Armanenschaft der Ario-Germanen*, vol. I, Berlin 1922, p. 86

272 Some authors assume that List copied parts of the doctrine of the English-Russian mystic H. P. Blavatsky. Jews had already been described by H. P. Blavatsky as 'misguided', and she had referred to the Jewish religion as 'decadent'. See: H. P. Blavatsky: *Die Geheimlehre*, 4 volumes, reprinted from the 1899 edition, Den Haag O. J., vol. II, p. 491ff

273 See: B. Hamann, op. cit., p. 294

274 Lanz an Frater Aemilius, Brief, datiert 22. 2. 1932 in Wilfried Daim, *Der Mann, der Hitler die Ideen gab*, München 1958, p. 12

275 See: Appendix 38, Hitler's Ideology

276 A. Hitler, op. cit., p. 396

277 A. Hitler, ibid., p. 323

278 See: Guido von List, *Das Geheimnis der Runen*, Vienna 1907, p. 20

279 Racism, which was at the core of both List's and Hitler's world views, was not exclusive to Ariosophic circles in the late nineteenth and early twentieth centuries. Hitler could also have been inspired by the race ideologies of Gobineau and Chamberlain or other Social Darwinists. See: Appendix 12, Racism in Vienna 1900

280 Guido von List, *Die Armanenschaft der Ario-Germanen*, vol. I, Berlin 1922, p. 33

281 See also: Appendices 44, The Psychotic Redeemer; 17, Hitler and the Occult

282 Guido von List, *Die Armanenschaft der Ario-Germanen*, vol. I, Berlin 1922 (3rd edition), pp. 15, 16. According to List, the Armanen alone possessed the 'secret of power'. The Armanen, who had been forced underground by Christianization, had passed down the 'secret of power' to the present day through secret brotherhoods. This 'original knowledge' or 'universal knowledge' of the Armanen had been retained in the secret societies of the Templers, Johanniter Order, Rosicrucians and Freemasons. (See: Guido von List, *Die Armanenschaft der Ario-Germanen*, vol. I, Berlin 1922, (3rd edition), pp. 53, 68, 77.) According to List, even the Jewish cabbala was nothing more than 'Wudonistic-Armanic traditions in Hebrew vestments'. (See: Guido von List, *Die Armanenschaft der Ario-Germanen*, vol. I, Berlin 1922, (3rd edition), p. 77ff.) However, with a few exceptions, those instructed in the various secret doctrines were no longer aware of the true meaning of their knowledge.

283 Guido von List, *Das Geheimnis der Runen*, Vienna 1907, p. 12

284 Guido von List, *Die Armanenschaft der Ario-Germanen*, vol. I, Berlin 1922 (3rd edition), pp. 16, 17

285 Guido von List, ibid., p. 94

286 M. Domarus (ed.), op. cit., speech on 27. 6. 1937, p. 704

287 R. H. Phelps '*Die Hitler Bibliothek*', in: *Deutsche Rundschau* 80, July 1954, p. 925. According to N. Goodrick-Clarke, Dr Babette Steiniger was an early member of the NSDAP. See also: N. Goodrick-Clarke, op. cit., p. 199

288 Guido von List, *Die Armanenschaft der Ario-Germanen*, vol. I, Berlin 1922, p. 70. '*Waberlohe*' is a word from German mythology describing a ring of fire that can only be penetrated by a hero

289 The Northern Europeans – the Germans, British, Dutch, Danes, Swedes, Norwegians and so on – were, according to List, the descendants of the 'Ario-Germanen'. See: Guido von List, *Der Übergang vom Wuotanismus zum Christentum*, Leipzig 1911, p. 106

290 The coming of the Saviour, *Der Starke von Oben*, is foretold in the Völuspa Prophecy, the first part of the old Nordic poem Edda: 'And it comes to the ring of the chieftains, *der Starke von Oben* to end the battle. He decides all with simple conclusions. That which he builds will last eternally.' Quoted from: Guido von List, *Die Armanenschaft der Ario-Germanen*, vol. I, Berlin 1922, p. 47

291 The members of the All-German Movement envisaged the merging of Austria with the German Empire. There was also talk of a pan-Germanic utopia, where Austrians, the English, the Dutch, Danes, Swedes, Norwegians and so on would live under German rule. List and other Ariosophes sympathized with this movement, which first appeared in Austria and spread into the German Empire towards the end of the nineteenth century

292 D. C. Large, op. cit., p. 28

293 Guido von List, *Der Übergang vom Wuotanismus zum Christentum*, Leipzig 1911, p. 101

294 Guido von List, *Die Armanenschaft der Ario-Germanen*, vol. I, Berlin 1922 (4th edition), p. 89

295 See: Appendix 34, Guido von List

296 N. Goodrick-Clarke, op. cit., p. 47

297 Karl H. von Wiegand, 'Hitler foresees his end', *Cosmopolitan*, New York, April 1939, p. 152

298 '*Doch hält die Wacht, die treue Wacht, ein Großer. Der Tonjer nicht, ein anderer ist uns nah. Vertraut und fremd zugleich, ein Namensloser, den jeder fühlt und doch noch niemand sah . . .* ' ('Yet a Great One holds watch, the loyal watch. Not the Tronjer, but another is near us. Trusted yet alien, a Nameless One, who all can sense but no one saw . . . ') H. Wilhelm, *Dichter Denker Fememörder*, Berlin 1989, p. 104. M. Plewnia reports that this poem was first made public on the 2nd of December 1919. M. Plewnia, *Auf dem Weg zu Hitler*, Bremen 1970, p. 82

299 M. Plewnia, ibid., p. 63, quoted from F. Willing, op. cit., p. 48f

300 See: Appendix 26, Hitler's Transformation

301 Hitler, in a speech in 1922: 'That is the greatest thing that our movement shall achieve: to find a new solid faith for these broad searching and misguided masses that does not forsake them in this time of confusion. A faith on which they will swear and build so that they at last may find a place again somewhere that gives their heart peace. And we will achieve this!' Quoted from: A. V. von Koerber, *Adolf Hitler, Sein Leben, Seine Reden*, Munich 1923, p. 34

302 See: Appendix 26, Hitler's Transformation

303 M. Plewnia, op. cit., p. 67

304 R. Binion, op. cit., p. 123ff. Hess explained: 'You once hearkened to a man's voice and it beat on your hearts, it awakened you, and you followed this voice'

305 Ilse Hess, *Gefangener des Friedens, neue Briefe aus Spandau*, Leoni 1955, p. 5. In his book, *Das Gesicht des 3. Reiches* (*The Face of the Third Reich*, 1963), Joachim Fest reports that Hess entered a competition organized by the University of Munich shortly after he first met Hitler. The question was, 'What type of person must the man be who will lead Germany back to greatness?' In his essay, Hess described how he experienced Hitler, and won the competition

306 E. Boepple (ed.), *Adolf Hitlers Reden*, Munich 1934, p. 118, quoted from: W. C. Langer, *Das Adolf Hitler Psychogramm*, transferred from English by F. Bruckner, Zürich 1972, p. 48

307 Hitler's name wasn't even mentioned on the poster that advertised the event on the 24th of February 1920 in the Hofbräuhaus. See: A. Joachimsthaler, op. cit., p. 270

308 See: A. Joachimsthaler, ibid., pp. 271, 295, 307

309 H. Frank, op. cit., p. 40

310 I. Kershaw, op. cit., p. 175

311 'In December 1922, Hitler was described in the *Völkischer Beobachter* as a special leader for the first time, *the Führer* Germany was awaiting.' Quoted from: I. Kershaw, op. cit., p. 233. The racist Houston Stewart Chamberlain, son-in-law of Richard Wagner, who was highly regarded by Hitler, was also convinced of Hitler's 'exceptional quality' after meeting him in 1923. 'That Germany gives birth to a Hitler in the hour of its greatest need, that proves there is life in it,' he wrote. Quoted from: J. C. Fest, op. cit., p. 259

312 See: Appendix 34, Guido von List

313 When Hitler came to Munich from Pasewalk, his 'assets' amounted to RM15. 30. See extract from Hitler's bank statement in: A. Joachimsthaler, op. cit., p. 185

314 'So it must be acknowledged as consistent that the psychological influence of Armanen-ship [. . .] actually still asserts its influence [. . .] today, indeed, it prepares and determines the development of the future under its ever-increasing influence in a decisive way.' G. List, *Die Armanenschaft der Ario-Germanen*, vol. I, Berlin 1922, p. 9

315 G. List, ibid., p. 69. Hitler may have obtained further affirmation from the fact that List claimed remnants of the pure Ario-Teutonic race had settled in outlying areas, in 'Old Sachsenland, in the Elbe marshes, in lower Austria, in the valleys of the Krems, the Kamp and the Isper.' The Kamp flows through the area of woodland from where all of Hitler's ancestors came. See: G. List, *Die Armanenschaft der Ario-Germanen*, vol. II, Wien 1911, p. 179

316 'I believe,' said Hitler in a speech, 'that it was also God's will to send a boy from here [Austria] into the Reich, to allow him to grow up, to install him as the leader of the nation.' Quoted from: M. Domarus (ed.), op. cit., speech made on 09. 04. 1938, p. 849

317 See: Appendix 27, The British Naval Blockade
318 See also: G. Krumeich (ed.), *Versailles 1919: Ziele, Wirkung, Wahrnehmnug*, Essen 2001
319 R. Sebottendorff, op. cit., p. 73
320 See: Appendix 30, Revolution in Munich
321 H., A. Koblenz No. 76, quoted from: R. Phelps, 'Before Hitler Came', *Journal of Modern History*, 1963, p. 255. See also: D. Rose, op. cit., p. 96
322 See: F. Willing, op. cit., p. 62ff
323 See: A. Joachimsthaler, op. cit., p. 263ff
324 See also: Appendix 35, The Expected Saviour
325 J. C. Fest, op. cit., p. 240
326 Draft motion for the DAP dated December 1919, BA Koblenz NS 26 27, in: A. Joachimsthaler, op. cit., p. 265
327 See: A. Joachimsthaler, ibid., pp. 271, 295, 307
328 A. Hitler, op. cit., p. 316
329 See: J. Appleby, L. Hunt, M. Jacob, *Telling the truth about history*, New York 1994
330 A. Hitler, ibid., p. 419
331 A. Hitler, ibid., p. 360
332 A. Hitler, op. cit., p. 782
333 A. Hitler, ibid.,, p. 314
334 Henry Picker noted the following statement from Hitler: 'I am striving for a state in which each individual knows: he lives and dies to preserve his kind.' H. Picker (ed.), op. cit., on 13. 12. 41, p. 81
335 See also: Appendix 12, Racism in Vienna 1900
336 A. Hitler, op. cit., p. 87
337 See also: A. Hitler, op. cit., pp. 378, 379, 501
338 A. Hitler, ibid., p. 743
339 See: Appendix 44, The Psychotic Redeemer
340 See: Appendix 44, The Psychotic Redeemer
341 A. Hitler, op. cit., p. 360
342 A. Hitler, op. cit., pp. 421, 422
343 See also: H. Picker (ed.), op. cit.
344 A. Hitler, op. cit., p. 127
345 A. Hitler, ibid., p. 630
346 As early as 1928, he wrote in a letter: 'At a time when a few years may be decisive for the life and future of our people generally, the National Socialist movement [. . .] is being weakened internally by its amalgamation with religious problems.' Quoted from: B. Dusik, K. A. Lankheit (eds.), *Hitler-Reden, Schriften, Anordnungen*, Munich 1994, letter dated 25 . 7. 1928, p. 24
347 See also: H. Picker (ed.), op. cit.
348 352A See: Daniel Gasman, *Haeckel's Monism and the Birth of Fashist Ideology*, New York 1998

349 A. Hitler, op. cit., p. 394ff. See also: R. Spitzy, op. cit., p. 131 quoted from: B. Hamann, op. cit., p. 319

350 See also: A. Hitler, op. cit., p. 127

351 Guido von List, *Urgrund*, Berlin, undated, p. 12. See also: Appendix 34, Guido von List

352 J. P. Huss, op. cit., p. 210, quoted from: W. C. Langer, *Das Adolf Hitler Psychogramm*, translated from English by Ferdinand Bruckner, Zurich 1972, p. 52. According to Huss, Hitler made this statement as he inspected the Dome des Invalides promptly after taking Paris in 1940 and closely examining Napoleon's tomb

353 See: E. Neumann, *Herrschafts-und Sexualsymbolik*, Stuttgart 1980, p. 7

354 In his book *Das Geheimnis der Runen*, Guido von List introduces the swastika as a 'secret' eighteenth rune. List's swastika faces anti-clockwise (like the Nazi symbol). According to List, the swastika, the secret eighteenth rune, is concealed by the *known* eighteenth rune so that its secret ('the triple sacrosanct secret of eternal birth, eternal life and eternal recurrence') can remain hidden. Guido von List, *Das Geheimnis der Runen*, Vienna 1907, p. 21. According to List, the swastika is also included in different knights' coats of arms as a hidden symbol (e. g. two swastika facing each other in the Maltese and St John's crosses) and in city crests (e. g. the crest of the City of Pyrmont). Guido von List, *Das Geheimnis der Runen*, Vienna 1907, p. 41. '[The swastika] symbolizes the God who reigns over the universe and the individual as Creator and Preserver.' Guido von List, *Das Geheimnis der Runen*, Vienna 1907, p. 44. See also: Appendix 34, Guido von List

355 See: S. Heller, *The Swastika*, New York 2000, p. 8

356 U. Degreif, *Woher hatte Hitler die Swastika, Zeitschrift für Kulturaustausch*, Stuttgart 1991, p. 310

357 See: B. Hamann, op. cit., p. 298

358 See: Appendix 33, The Thule Society

359 See: Appendix 37, Thule–DAP–NSDAP

360 See: F. Willing, op. cit., p. 84

361 See: F. Willing, loc. cit.

362 See: F. Willing, loc. cit. According to verbal and written statements from Friedrich Krohn, Josef Fuess, Karolina Ghar and Erna Hanfstengel, the Starnberg flag was sewn by Mrs Fuess, Ms Schüßler and Ms Jenny Haug. DAP member and goldsmith Josef Fuess designed the party emblem using the flag as a template

363 See: A. Hilter, op. cit., p. 136ff

364 See also: I. Kershaw, op. cit., p. 221ff

365 R. Moorhouse, Killing Hilter, p. 83, New York, 2006

366 See also: I. Kershaw, op. cit., p. 636ff

367 See: Appendix 33, The Thule Society

368 The second edition of the book *Bevor Hitler kam* was confiscated by the Gestapo. See also: Appendix 33, The Thule Society

369 H. Gilbhart, op. cit. See also: D. Rose, op. cit.

370 Dietrich Eckhart is only listed as a 'guest' in Sebottendorff's list. However, many authors count him as one of the main leaders within the Thule Society. The following men, who later made their careers within the Nazi Party, were certainly members: Hans Frank (Governor-General of occupied Poland from 1939); Karl Fiehler (Lord Mayor of Munich from 1933); Hans Bunge (leader of the Leibstandarte Adolf Hitler – Adolf Hitler's Bodyguard Regiment); Heinrich Jost (head of the SS Geheimdienst – Secret Service). In the case of the following people membership is contested: Gottfried Feder (State Secretary of the Ministry of Economics from 1933–1934); Dr Rudolf Buttmann (chairman of the bavarian NSDAP); Franz Gürtner (NS Minister for Justice); Wilhelm Frick (NS Minister of the Interior); Julius Streicher (Editor of *Der Stürmer* – inflammatory Nazi newspaper *The Stormer*); Ernst Pöhner (President of the Munich Police Force in the 1920s), amongst others. SS leader Heinrich Himmler, who has been aligned with the Thule Society by several authors, was not a member. Nevertheless, Himmler's father is supposed to have been a member of Guido von List's Hoher Armanen Orden (High Armanen Order). Ref: H. Wilhelm, *Dichter, Denker, Femenmörder*, Berlin 1989, p. 45 and P. Orzechowski, *Schwarze Magie – Braune Macht*, Zürich 1990, p. 20. See also: R. Sebottendorff, op. cit.; D. Rose, op. cit., p. 79

371 At the time of surrender, Hitler's account at the Eher Verlag still held 7 million Reichsmarks that he had not withdrawn. See: Max Amann, *Spruchkammerakt*, Nuremberg 30. 10. 47, Special Records Office S, Munich, quoted from: A. Joachimsthaler, op. cit., p. 148. See also: W. C. Schwarzmüller, *Hitlers Geld*, Wiesbaden, 2001, p. 183

372 See also: W. Zdral, op. cit.; D. Rose, op. cit., p. 104ff; N. Goodrich-Clarke, op. cit., p. 147

373 In other versions of the Untersberg legend, it is Karl the Great who lives within the mountain

374 Guido von List, *Die Armanenschaft der Ario-Germanen*, vol. I, Berlin 1922, p. 70

375 For more information, see: J. Neul, *Adolf Hitler und der Obersalzberg*, Rosenheim 1997; F. M. Beierl, *Hitlers Berg*, Berchtesgaden 2004

376 The report remained classified until 1972 and was published that same year: W. Langer, *The Mind of Adolf Hitler*, New York 1972. A German version appeared in Zurich in 1972 under the title *Das Adolf Hitler Psychogramm*, translated from English by Ferdinand Bruckner

377 After the war, American troops managed to secure documents from the Munich headquarters of the NSDAP that had been compiled by the Gestapo at the start of 1944, the turning point of the war, outlining a high number of mental illnesses in Hitler's extended family. The fact that Hitler's second cousin, Aloisia V., a schizophrenic undergoing treatment in Vienna, was murdered in a gas chamber was not discovered until sixty years later. See: Facts, Zurich, 8. 2005

378 E. Deuerlein, *Der Aufstieg der NSDAP*, Düsseldorf 1968, p. 266

379 M. Domarus (ed.), op. cit., speech made on 24. 02. 1933, p. 214

380 M. Domarus (ed.), ibid., speech made on 09. 04. 1938, p. 849

381 M. Domarus (ed.), ibid., speech made in Munich on 14. 03. 1936, p. 606

382 M. Domarus (ed.), ibid., speech made in Regensburg on 06. 06. 1937, p. 700

383 M. Domarus (ed.), ibid., speech made on 25. 03. 1938, p. 836

384 M. Domarus (ed.), ibid., speech made on 06. 10. 1936, p. 651

385 W. Carr, *Adolf Hitler, Persönlichkeit und politisches Handeln*, Stuttgart 1980, p. 17, quoted from: I. Kershaw, op. cit., p. 196

386 E. Jäckel (ed.), *Hitler, Sämtliche Aufzeichnungen 1905–1924*, speech made on 21. 04. 1921, Stuttgart 1980, p. 366. At another point, Hitler says: 'When I came to Berlin a few weeks ago [. . .] the Jewish materialism disgusted me so thoroughly, that I was almost beside myself. I imagined myself almost like Jesus Christ when He came to His Father's temple and found it taken by the money-changers. I can well imagine how He felt when He seized a whip and scourged them out.' Information from Ernst Hanfstaengel, quoted from: W. C. Langer, *Das Adolf Hitler Psychogramm*, translated from English by Ferdinand Bruckner, Zurich 1972, p. 49

387 M. Domarus (ed.), op. cit., speech made on 11. 9. 1936, p. 641

388 M. Domarus (ed.), ibid., speech made on 13. 9. 1936, p. 64

389 M. Domarus, ibid., speech made on 20. 03. 1936, p. 609

390 H. Bühmann, op. cit., p. 122: 'We often heard your voice and listened silently and folded our hands, as each word entered our souls. We all know that one day, we will be free of distress and oppression. What is one year in the passing of an era? What is a law that tries to impede us – the pure faith you gave us, pulses destined to move through our lives. My Führer, you alone are path and goal.'

391 Quote from a Hamburg teacher who spoke of images of 'gripping faith' after an electoral rally attended by 120,000 people in April 1932, quoted from: J. C. Fest, op. cit., p. 458

392 The similarities between Hitler's appearances and Guido von List's account of his Armanen priests is striking. See: Appendix 34, Guido von List

393 H. Bühmann, op. cit., p. 121

394 *Völkischer Beobachter*, 23. 12. 1926, quoted from: J. C. Fest, op. cit., p. 354

395 Quoted from: J. C. Fest, ibid., p. 610

396 F. W. Doucet, *Im Banne des Mythos. Die Psychologie des Dritten Reiches*, Esslingen 1979, p. 68

397 Emily D. Lorrimer, *What Hitler Wants*, London 1939, p. 6, quoted from: W. C. Langer, *Das Adolf Hitler Psychogramm*, translated from English by Ferdinand Bruckner, Zurich 1972, p. 71

398 See: A. Joachimsthaler, op. cit., p. 299

399 W. Teeling, *Know Thy Enemy!* London 1939, p. 2, quoted from: W. C. Langer, *Das Adolf Hitler Psychogramm*, translated from English by Ferdinand Bruckner, Zurich 1972, p. 71

400 As Hitler drew freely on distinctly Christian religious language only few people acknowledged the need to choose between the cross and the swastika during the Third Reich, even within the Church

401 J. P. Huss, *The Foe We Face*, New York 1942, p. 281, quoted from: W. C. Langer, *Das Adolf Hitler Psychogramm*, translated from English by Ferdinand Bruckner, Zurich 1972, p. 46: 'No power on earth can shake the German Reich now, Divine Providence has willed it that I carry through the fulfilment of the Germanic task.'

402 '*Nun schauen wir, geblendet, doch bereit, ins Morgenrot von Deutschlands größter Zeit. Der Retter, der ihr Bann brach, sei gesegnet! In seinem Kommen ist uns Gott begegnet.*' Quoted from: K. H. Bühner (ed.), *Dem Führer, Gedichte für Adolf Hitler*, Stuttgart 1939

403 *Das Schwarze Korps*, on 30. 01. 1941, Sequel 5

404 H. Rauschning, *Gespräche mit Hitler*, Zurich 1940, p. 161

405 Quoted from: F. W. Doucet, op. cit., p. 72ff

406 Quoted from: F. Kersten, *Totenkopf und Treue, Heinrich Himmler ohne Uniform*, Hamburg 1952, p. 34

407 O. Strasser, *Hitler and I*, Buenos Aires 1940, p. 67, quoted from: W. C. Langer, *Das Adolf Hitler Psychogramm*, translated from English by Ferdinand Bruckner, Zurich 1972, p. 42

408 M. Domarus (ed.), op. cit., speech made on 05. 07. 1944, p. 2117

409 See: B. F. von Loringhoven, *Mit Hitler im Bunker* Berlin 2006

410 Hitler said this on the 16th of April 1945 in his order of the day to soldiers on the Eastern Front. See: *Schramm*, vol. IV/8 p. 1589ff, quoted from: A. Joachimsthaler, *Hitler's Ende*, Munich 1995, p. 134

411 M. Domarus (ed.), op. cit., p. 2226

412 T. Kornbichler, op. cit., p. 139

Bibliography

Appleby, A. J., Hunt, L., Jacob, M., *Telling the truth about history*, New York 1994

Aronson, S., *Reinhard Heydrich und die Frühgeschichte von Gestapo und SD*, Stuttgart 1971

zur Beek, G. (ed.), *Protokolle der Weisen von Zion*, Berlin 1924

Beierl, F. M., *Geschichte des Kehlsteins*, Berchtesgaden 1994

Beierl, F. M., *Hitlers Berg*, Berchtesgaden 2004

Bell, A.C., *Die Englische Hungerblockade im Weltkrieg 1914–1915* introduced by V. Böhmert, Essen 1943

Berding, H., *Moderner Antisemitismus in Deutschland*, Frankfurt 1988

Binion, R., "*… daß ihr mich gefunden habt*", from the English translated by Abel, J. and Dengler, A., Stuttgart 1978

Binion, R., *Hitler among the Germans*, New York 1976

de Boor, W., *Hitler-Mensch-Übermensch-Untermensch*, Frankfurt 1985

Black, E., *War against the Weak: Eugenics and America's campaign to create a master race, New York, 2004*

Breuer, S., *Die Völkischen in Deutschland*, Darmstadt 2006

Bühner, K. H. (ed.), *Dem Führer, Gedichte für Adolf Hitler*, Stuttgart 1939

Chamberlain, H. S., *Die Grundlagen des 19. Jahrhunderts*, München 1912

Charlier, J. M., de Launay, J, *Eva Hitler, geb. Braun*, Paris 1978

Cohn, N., *Die Protokolle der Weisen von Zion*, Köln 1969

Cohn, N., *Warrant for Genocide*, London 1967

Conradi, P., *Hitler's Piano Player*, New York 2004

Cross, C., *Adolf Hitler*, London 1974

Daim, W., *Der Mann, der Hitler die Ideen gab*, München 1958

Darwin, C., *The Origin of Species, New York 1995*

Dean, S. R., (ed.) *Psychiatry and Mysticism*, Chicago 1997

Degreif, U., *Woher hatte Hitler die Swastika, Zeitschrift für Kulturaustausch*, Stuttgart 1991

Deuerlein, E., *Hitlers Eintritt in die Politik und die Reichswehr, Vierteljahreshefte für Zeitgeschichte*, Stuttgart 1959

Deuerlein, E., *Der Aufstieg der NSDAP*, Düsseldorf 1968
Diethe, C., *Nietzsches Schwester*, Hamburg 2001
Domarus, M. (ed.), *Hitler – Reden und Proklamationen*, Würzburg 1962
Dorpat, T. L., *Wounded Monster*, New York 2002
Doucet, F. W., *Im Banne des Mythos. Die Psychologie des Dritten Reiches*, Esslingen 1979
Dusik, B. and Lankheit, K. A. (eds.), *Hitler-Reden, Schriften, Anordnungen*, München 1994
Fabry, P. W., *Mutmaßungen über Hitler*, Düsseldorf 1969
Fest, J., *Die unbeantworteten Fragen*, Hamburg 2005
Fest, J. C., *Hitler, eine Biographie*, Frankfurt 1973
Fleischhauer, U., *Die echten Protokolle der Weisen von Zion*, Erfurt 1935
Frank, H., *Im Angesicht des Galgens*, München 1953
Freund, R., *Braune Magie*, Wien 1995
Gasman, D., *The Scientific Origins of National Socialism*, London, 2007
Gasman D., *Haeckel's Monism and the Birth of Fascist Ideology*, New York 1998
Gassert, P. and Mattern, D. S., *The Hitler Library*, Westport 2001
George, D. L., *The Great Crusade*, New York 1918
Gilbert, M., *Kristallnacht*, London 2006
Gilbhart, H., *Die Thule Gesellschaft*, München 1994
Goebbels, J., *Vom Kaiserhof zur Reichskanzlei*, Berlin 1942
Goodrick-Clarke, N., *The Occult Roots of Nazism*, New York 1985
Grabner-Haider, A., *Hitlers mythische Religion*, Wien 2008
Gregor-Dellin, M. and Mack D. (eds.), *Cosima Wagner, Tagebücher II*, München 1977
Haeckel, E., *Die Welträthsel*, Bonn 1903
Hamann, B., *Hitlers Wien*, München 1996
Hamann, B., *Hitlers Edeljude*, München 2008
Hanfstaengl, E., *Zwischen Weissem und Braunem Haus*, München 1970
Hartmann, C. H. and Lankheit, K. A. (eds.), *Hitler Reden, Schriften,Anordnungen*, Band V/2, München 1998
Hawkins, P., *Dr. Bucke Revisited*, London 2004
Hegner, S. J., *Die Reichskanzlei*, Frankfurt 1966
Heiden, K., *Adolf Hitler, Zeitalter der Verantwortungslosigkeit*, Zürich 1936
Heiden, K., *Der Führer*, Boston 1944
Heims, H. (ed. W. Jochmann), *Adolf Hitler, Monologe im Führerhauptquartier 1941–1944*, Hamburg 1980
Heller, K. and Plamper, J. (eds.), *Personenkulte im Stalinismus*, Göttingen 2004

Heller, S., *The Swastika*, New York 2000
Hesse, G., *Hitler wie ihn immer noch keiner kennt*, Berlin 2004
Hist. Museum, Wien (ed.), *Judentum in Wien*, Wien 1987
Hitler, A., *Mein Kampf*, München 1936
Horn, W., *Führerideologie der NSDAP 1919–1933*, Düsseldorf 1972
Horstmann, B., *Hitler in Pasewalk*, Düsseldorf 2004
Huss, J. P., *The Foe We Face*, New York 1942
Ivo, K. (ed.), *Annual for German Women and Girls*, Wien 1904
Jäckel, E. and Kuhn, A. (eds.), *Hitler, Sämtliche Aufzeichnungen 1905–1924*, Stuttgart 1980
James, W., *The varieties of religious experience*, New York 1994
Jenks, W. A., *Vienna and the Young Hitler*, New York 1960
Jetzinger, F., *Hitlers Jugend, Phantasien, Lügen – und die Wahrheit*, Wien 1956
Jetzinger, F., *Hitler's Youth*, foreword to the English translation, London 1958
Joachimsthaler, A., *Hitler in München 1908-1920*, Frankfurt 1992
Joachimsthaler, A., *Hitlers Liste*, München 2003
Joachimsthaler, A., *Hitlers Weg begann in München 1913–1923*, München 2000
Joachimsthaler, A., *Hitlers Ende*, München 1995
Jones, J. S., *Hitlers Weg begann in Wien*, from the English translated by Sylvia Eisenburger, Berlin 1990
Kapfer, H. and Reichert, C. L., *Umsturz in München*, München 1988
Kershaw, I., *Hitler 1889–1936*, from the English translated by J. P. Krause and J. W. Rademacher, Stuttgart 1998
Kersten, F., *Totenkopf und Treue, Heinrich Himmler ohne Uniform*, Hamburg 1952
Kevles, D., *In the Name of Eugenics*, New York 1985
Koch-Hillebrecht, M., *Hitler, Ein Sohn des Krieges*, München 2003
Koch-Hillebrecht, M., *Homo Hitler*, München 1999
von Koerber, A. V., *Adolf Hitler, Sein Leben, Seine Reden*, München 1923
Kornbichler, T., *Adolf-Hitler Psychogramme*, Frankfurt 1994
Krause, K. W., *Zehn Jahre Kammerdiener bei Hitler*, Hamburg 1950
Krumeich, G. (ed.), *Versailles 1919: Ziele, Wirkung, Wahrnehmung*, Essen 2001
Kubizek, A., *Hitler mein Jugendfreund*, Wien 1953
Kulturamt Stadt Wien (ed.), *Wien um 1900*, Wien 1964
Langer, W. C., *Das Adolf Hitler Psychogramm*, from the English translated by F. Bruckner, Zürich 1972

Large, D. C., *Hitlers München*, München 1998

Laski, M., *Ecstasy in Secular and Religious Experiences*, New York 1961

Lerner, P., *Hysterical Men*, Cornell University, New York 2003

Levenda, P., *Unholy Alliance*, New York 1995

Lewis, D., *The Man Who Invented Hitler*, London 2003

von List, G., *Der Unbesiegbare*, 1898

von List, G., *Das Geheimnis der Runen*, Wien 1907

von List, G., *Der Übergang vom Wuotanismus zum Christentum*, Leipzig 1911

von List, G., *Die Armanenschaft der Ario-Germanen*, Vol. I, Berlin 1922

von List, G., *Die Rita der Ario-Germanen*, Wien 1908

von List G., *Die Religion der Ario-Germanen*, Leipzig 1910

von List G., *Die Ursprache der Ario-Germanen*, Leipzig 1914

Loringhoven, B.F., Mit Hitler im Bunker, Berlin 2006

Lorrimer, Emily D., *What Hitler Wants*, London 1939

Losemann, V., *Rassenideologien und antisemitische Publizistik in Deutschland im 19. und 20. Jahrhundert*, Düsseldorf 1984

Miller, A., *Am Anfang war Erziehung*, from the English translated by Suhrkamp, Frankfurt 1980

Misch, R., Der letzte Zeuge, München 2008

Moorhouse,R., *Killing Hitler*, New York 2006

Natter, W. G., *Literature at War 1914–1940: Representing the 'Time of Greatness' in Germany*, New Haven and London 1999

Neul, J., *Adolf Hitler und der Obersalzberg*, Rosenheim 1997

Neumann, E., Herrschafts- und Sexualsymbolik, Stuttgart 1980

Newberg, A., *Why God won't go away*, New York 2001

Newest, Th., *Einige Weltprobleme Vortrag 1–8*, Wien 1908

Olden, R., *Hitler*, Amsterdam 1936

Orzechowski, P., *Schwarze Magie-Braune Macht*, Zürich 1990

Picker, H. (ed.), *Hitlers Tischgespräche im Führerhauptquartier*, Wiesbaden 1983

Pilgrim, V. E., *Muttersöhne*, Düsseldorf 1986

Purves, A. A., *The Medals, Decorations & Orders of the Great War 1914–1918*, London 1975

Rauschning, H., *Gespräche mit Hitler*, Zürich 1940

Reichelt, W., *Das braune Evangelium*, Wuppertal 1990

Richardi, H.-G., *Hitler und seine Hintermänner*, München 1991

Riedesser, P., Verderber, A., *Maschinengewehre hinter der Front – Zur Geschichte der deutschen Militärpsychiatrie*, Frankfurt 1996

Röder,Th, Kubillus, V., *Die Männer hinter Hitler*, Malters 1994
Roerkohl, A., *Hungerblockade und Heimatfront*, Stuttgart 1991
Rose, D., *Die Thule Gesellschaft*, Tübingen 1994
Rosenberg, A., *Die Protokolle der Weisen von Zion und die jüdische Weltpolitik*, München 1923
Schaake, E., *Hitlers Frauen*, München 2000
Schadewaldt, H. *Hungerblockade über Kontinentaleuropa*, München 1941
Scheit, G., Svoboda, W., *Feindbild Gustav Mahler*, Wien 2002
Schopenhauer, A., *Die Welt als Wille und Vorstellung, Werk-und Studienausgabe in elf Bänden*, Züricher Ausgabe, Zürich 1977
Schroeder, C., *Er war mein Chef*, München 1985
Schwarz, B., *Geniewahn: Hitler und die Kunst*, Wien 2009
Schwarzmüller, W. C., *Hitlers Geld*, Wiesbaden 2001
Slapnicka, H., *Hitler und Oberösterreich*, Grünbach 1998
Stout, M., *Der Soziopath von nebenan*, from the English translated by Petersen, K., Wien 2006
Speer, A., *Erinnerungen*, München 1969
Spitzy, R., *So haben wir das Reich verspielt*, München 1986
Strasser, O., *Hitler and I*, Buenos Aires 1940
Taureck, B. H. F., *Nietzsche und der Faschismus*, Leipzig 2000
Teeling, W., *Know Thy Enemy!* London 1939
Trimondi, V. and V., *Hitler, Buddha, Krishna*, Wien 2002
Wagener, O. (ed. H. A. Turner), *Hitler aus nächster Nähe, Aufzeichnungen eines Vertrauten 1929–1932*, Berlin 1978
Waite, R. G. L., *The Psychopathic God Adolf Hitler*, New York 1977
Warburg, M. (ed. Warburg, E.), *Aus meinen Aufzeichnungen*, New York 1952
Weikart, R. *From Darwin to Hitler*, New York 2004
Whiteside, A. G., *Georg Ritter von Schönerer*, Graz 1981
Wiedemann, F., *Der Mann, der Feldherr werden wollte*, Dortmund 1964
Wilhelm, H., *Dichter, Denker, Fememörder*, Berlin 1989
Willing, F., *Die Hitlerbewegung*, Hamburg 1962
Zdral, W., *Die Hitlers*, Frankfurt 2005
Zmarzlik, H. G., *Der Sozialdarwinismus in Deutschland, Vierteljahreshefte für Zeitgeschichte*, München 1963
Zoller, A., *Hitler privat*, Düsseldorf 1949